THE CRY OF MERLIN

JJ SHEFA & PATRICIA O'DONOVAN

ISBN 9781634438469

Printed by Village Books in Bellingham WA.

A Note to Our Readers:

This story first found the authors in 1985. We have decided to let it remain in that time. That is why characters don't text, consult GPS, or take selfies in the English countryside. It is also why Gwen is able to transfer a plane ticket to her name with an ease that no longer exists, even for a travel agent. We hope that any other seeming anachronisms that may appear are not bothersome, and will be resolved by this note.

Also, we want to mention the use of the terms Romani, Romanai, Romany, Gypsy, and Traveller. Two of the characters in this story are of Romani heritage. The names by which people identify themselves are of course very important, and sometimes confusing. We have consulted many sources to learn how best to represent this. Understanding the usage of these terms is one of the threads of this story. As you read, please know that all the terms are used as correctly as possible within the context, and always with respect and value.

Acknowledgements

The authors give their heartfelt thanks to Leesann, who has championed this
book for many years.

We are also grateful to Brendan S. Clark, Publishing Director at Village
Books, for his patience, encouragement, and help, also to Becky Roser, for
her generous belief, to Alison, for heroic typing and persistence,
And to Kira, for computer wizardry and sparkling support.

We also thank Rod Burton, for his excellent help with the cover design,
William, for wanting to see this finished, and Judy, Trene, and Teresa, for
steadfast friendship and help in many ways.

And our gratitude always to William van Duyn.

This Book
is
For Everyone.

CHAPTER ONE

It was eleven at night, in the forest beyond Far Tauverly. Suddenly, out of the dark woods, came a single bell-like cry; a sweet, clear, wild cry that held within it a quality of infinite longing. The cry rang through the night just once. The whole forest grew still in its wake.

In the village of Far Tauverly, a spring rain fell gently on the budding trees and the dark streets. A visitor walking along those streets might well have been struck by how quiet they were. Through a window here and there could be glimpsed a housewife, wearily finishing the day's washing up at her kitchen sink, or a man dozing in an armchair by the flickering light of a telly. For the most part, though, the windows were dark, and the shades were drawn.

Only the Greenstone Arms afforded a note of real cheer. The light from the pub's diamond-paned windows spilled, ruddy and bright, onto the damp pavement outside.

Drawing closer, a visitor would have noticed the welcoming glow of firelight gleaming on oaken beams and polished copper pots. Through the thick, wavy old glass could be seen ten regulars, each clearly seated in his or her usual spot. A game of darts was in progress, and two old women in the corner had their heads together, obviously sucking the very marrow from a bit of gossip. Other regulars sat in amiable silence near the fire. Behind the bar a middle-aged woman in a faded flowered dress, her figure generous of hip and bosom, her face rich in kindness and humor, poured out hefty measures of amber-colored ale.

The pub exerted a strong appeal, especially since, through a crack in one of the windows, came the scent of beef pie. And yet, even with a hand on the door, a visitor might well have hesitated. The group inside seemed as private as a family relaxing in their living room. Though they were not all related by blood, long years of association had interwoven these people, like tree roots interlaced beneath the earth.

Yes, to enter The Greenstone Arms by day was easy, was charming; but to penetrate its privacy late on a rainy night was quite a different matter. And so, with a bit of a sigh, a visitor would probably have turned away from the pub, and walked on.

The main street of Far Tauverly led past the bakery, the greengrocer's, the tiny post office, a few houses, and the Norman tower of St.

Aethelrood's Church, hard by the fifteenth-century vicarage. Beyond this point, the road curved into dense forest on either side.

That dark curve of the road gave any visitor an acute sense of leaving the human world behind. Beyond that curve, you stepped into the ancient realm of the woods. There the wind sang to itself in its own language; the branches of beech and oak swayed in time to its music. On this particular night, the inhabitants of Far Tauverly may have been for the most part soon to head for their homes and beds, but the forest was wide awake, full of the thousand rustlings and the urgent business of spring.

The rain stopped; a new moon peered through the scuttling clouds. By its small light, a visitor could have continued along the wood-bordered road for nearly a mile, before being confronted by a gate; an iron gate, over twelve feet high and ten feet wide. Its graceful bars and scrollwork dated from Regency times. The stone pillars on either side of the ironwork were far older. On top of each of the pillars was carved a lion rampant. For twelve centuries, these lions had faced each other. Compared to the strength of their locked gaze, the iron scrollwork, a mere hundred and seventy years old, seemed like a newcomer on the scene.

Beyond the lions and the iron bars lay the grounds of a great estate. By the faint moonlight, the silhouette of a distant manor house could just be discerned. One window was alight there.

Once again, the strange cry rang out. A visitor, standing alone in the darkness by the lion gate, might well have been shaken by its plea. And in the distant manor house, the one person still awake who had been gazing thoughtfully at the squalor of papers on his desk, heard the cry, sat bolt upright, and exclaimed:

"What the devil was that?" But of course, there was no reply.

***

At the same time, evening was approaching in Denver. Gwendolyn Fields, auburn hair, gray eyes, sat at her desk in the Mercury Travel Agency. She stared out onto the street, past a life-size painting of the Greek God Mercury on the plate glass window. In addition to his usual winged cap and sandals, this Mercury carried a suitcase in one hand, and a plane ticket in the other. Despite the luggage, he was leaping eagerly toward an unknown destination. Staring down her upcoming thirty-fourth birthday, and nearly two years at a job she had taken only to recover from years of teaching

6

elementary school, Gwen often regarded the winged one's invitation as unanswered.

"Gwen! You'd better get moving on that Jensen itinerary! They want it first thing tomorrow morning!"

Trish, the manager of Mercury Travel, stepped between Gwen and the window. She blew impatiently on her long nails to dry the fuchsia-colored polish she had just applied. "Will you have it on time?"

"Sure!" Gwen sighed, looking back at her desk. With her two coworkers both out on vacation, Gwen decided the best way to avoid Trish was to bury herself in the task at hand.

Gwen found her notes on the Jensen's trip to Europe, and began to type them dutifully into the computer. She had just reached "Arrive Brussels Airport" when the door of Mercury Travel was flung open and a gravelly voice announced, "Sugar, it's me!"

"Mrs. Gordon," Gwen exclaimed. "Come in!"

Gwen was pleased to see Elyse Gordon, a wealthy, Texas-born widow who was one of her best clients. After a lifetime of hardship, Mrs. Gordon had come into what she called "a Swiss vault full of moolah." She was determined to spend a good portion of that money on "seein' the world." To that end, she frequently appeared at the agency with one of the romantic novels she was addicted to reading.

Mrs. Gordon's favorite novelist was Henrietta Amberly, known as the "Grand Dame of Romance." Amberly was an author Gwen never thought she would read, but had secretly come to enjoy. Having majored in literature in college and written her master's thesis on the figure of Puck in *A Midsummer Night's Dream*, Gwen had at first been surprised by how much she enjoyed Henrietta Amberly.

The novels had become part of her endearment for Mrs. Gordon. Now, whenever Mrs. Gordon appeared, tossed another lurid-covered Amberly romance set in Monte Carlo or Bermuda onto her desk and said, "Send me there, Sweetness," Gwen looked forward to reading the book. "And make me look like the heroine while you're at it!" Mrs. Gordon would add with a twinkle in her eye.

Gwen enjoyed transporting Mrs. Gordon to the locales of her fancy. In the last three years, she'd planned trips for her to places as varied as Atlanta, Egypt, Paris, and even India. She wondered what new horizon was beckoning to Mrs. Gordon now.

Mrs. Gordon headed toward Gwen's desk, definitely making an entrance. She wore her customary outfit of a mink coat over a track suit; today's sweats were hot pink. Her bunion-covered feet were squashed into high-heeled gold sandals. As usual, her blue-tinted hair was carefully rolled around tiny rollers, and covered by a bright, flowered scarf. Gwen realized that in the two years she had known her, she had never seen Mrs. Gordon's hair *out* of rollers.

Satisfied that she had attracted the attention of the entire office, Mrs. Gordon settled into her favorite chair. "Sugar," she began excitedly, "This is gonna be the best trip yet!" She leaned closer, and Gwen caught a whiff of Eau de Joie, mingled with scotch. "Avalon, Sugar!" Mrs. Gordon whispered conspiratorially. "Camelot!"

She plunked a paperback trilogy about King Arthur down onto the desk. Gwen was pleased to note that it was yet another work by Henrietta Amberly. *She surely is prolific,* Gwen thought.

"It's all in here," Mrs. Gordon said, thumping the books, "All the names and places! And in case that's not enough, I brought you some more." She added several modern travel guides to England to the pile. Her wise old eyes sparkled with anticipation.

"There it is," she said. "I'm on the trail of King Arthur! Book me a tour to another time, darlin'! I want to meet the Once and Future King himself! I want - "

Mrs. Gordon's enthusiasm was interrupted by loud barking from the street. She peered past the painted Mercury at her stretch limo, parked outside.

"Just look at those damned dogs," she exclaimed. "They're going to ravage Lucius!"

Gwen followed her gaze and saw Mrs. Gordon's two Dobermans and three golden retrievers frolicking inside the car, barking frantically and slobbering on Lucius, the long-suffering chauffeur.

Mrs. Gordon darted to the door, yanked it open and bellowed, "Down, Beaumont! Down, Fletcher! Down, Cassock!" The barking increased happily at the sound of her voice. Mrs. Gordon turned back to Gwen.

"Guess I gotta go. Just remember; I want a trip to Camelot! Don't worry what it costs, I want to see every place those books mention! Call me when you got it figured out, Sugar! You're the miracle worker!" She dashed out the door.

Gwen spent the next few hours working on the Jensen itinerary and tidying up her desk. She had the office to herself now. Trish had left at six. Trish had again surprised her by offering to stay late and help Gwen finish.

She stretched and walked over to the water cooler for a drink. *I'll be reading a new Henrietta tonight*, she thought happily. She caught a glimpse of her own reflection in the mirror over the water cooler.

"I could be one of those Amberly heroines," she mused. She tossed back her head, thrust out her lower lip and murmured, "She was a humble governess, but the blood of a royal line burned in her veins." This was a line from *The Princess of Paris*, by Henrietta Amberly. The effect was not successful, and Gwen burst into laughter. Her delicate features did not match the rather sultry looks of the heroines who graced the covers of an Amberly novel. She turned her face this way and that, and decided that her looks needed something dramatic.

Maybe I should dye my hair ash blonde, she mused, *or dark red . . . or bright red . . . or why not emerald green?* She laughed at the thought. *I could never carry that off*, she thought. *I'm far too plain.*

Most people would not have agreed with Gwen's assessment of herself. She had fine, pale skin with a splash of golden freckles on her straight, neat nose. Her dark auburn hair was pulled back in a French braid that drew attention to her long, slender neck. Her features were gentle. Yet in her hazel eyes there was something unruly, a spark of unspoken fire that made her eyes seem sometimes light brown, almost golden, at other times grey-green. Those changeable eyes beneath dark brows were the only intensity in an otherwise quiet face.

"Too plain," Gwen said again with a sigh. She turned away from the mirror, and decided it was time to pack up and go home. She began to put the books Mrs. Gordon had left on her desk into her briefcase. One fell to the floor: *The Shell Guide to the West Country*, she read as she bent to pick it up. Her eye was caught by a picture on the page it had fallen open to: a photograph of a large iron gate, with a wooded landscape just beyond it. She put the guidebook with the others, and was reaching for her raincoat. Suddenly, with extraordinary vividness, she saw the gate again, but this time in her mind's eye. It was flanked by two stone pillars. There were lions on those pillars and beyond them, a forest of oak and beech. It was a spring night. She could hear the rustling of the forest, feel the bite of cool rain on her face, and smell the scent of damp earth and new green shoots poking

9

through it. And there was something else, a sound, a ringing note, as if someone had plucked one string on a harp, and it was echoing, echoing . . .

Just as mysteriously and suddenly as it appeared, the image was gone. Now she heard the hum of traffic outside, and the sound of the janitor vacuuming the office next door, but no distant music.

"How very strange," she said aloud.

***

It was one-thirty in the morning in Far Tauverly. Only two people were still awake. One was the occupant of the lighted room at the manor house. The other was Logan Knowelles, the local postman. Several hours earlier, he had fallen asleep over his third pint at the Greenstone Arms. Rather than disturb him, Mrs. Hodges, the innkeeper, had slipped a pillow under his head and covered him with a quilt.

"Let the lad sleep," she'd said fondly at closing time.

Logan, at sixty, was ten years older than Mrs. Hodges, and scarcely a lad. But after raising eight children, the innkeeper had come to view the world as one large unruly family, all in need of help. She understood, by that time in her life, that there were those who had the lifetime job of being a parent to the human mob, and she was one of them. So, she had pulled the quilt up over Logan with the same tenderness she would have shown one of her own grandchildren, turned off the lights, and locked the door of the common room behind her. In the corner booth, Logan slept on, snoring soundly.

Now he woke with a start. For a moment, he wondered where he was; then he quickly recognized the pub. It wasn't the first time he'd dozed off there.

Logan sat up, and looked around the dark room. He had the strong sense he wasn't alone there. Someone, or something, was there with him. Not a person, but a presence of some kind, perhaps a ghost. This did not frighten Logan at all. The room felt safe and peaceful. He heard the steady drumming of rain outside, and that made the warmth of the pub even cozier.

He had been dreaming, he realized, but he could not quite remember of what. Colors came to him; yellow, gold. There had been banners, and a great crowd of people in costumes from long ago—and music. Yes, there had been distant music in the dream, of which he could remember only one, clear note. A phrase came into his mind as well: "And at last they came to Joyous

Garde." Joyous Garde had been the name of Lancelot's Castle, or so the old stories said.

The bells of St. Aethelrood's struck two. He had only been asleep for three hours, Logan realized, yet he felt refreshed and clear. He wrapped the quilt around himself like a cloak and sat quietly in the darkness, watching, listening.

Once again, he had the strong sense that he was not alone. Something was there with him. Whatever it was, it filled the room with peace and sweetness; and it seemed to Logan that life, for all its troubles, was still a shining, glorious thing, with great meaning hidden within it, like a treasure to be found. He felt that he, Logan Knowelles, for all his silver hair, was still young and bold enough to seize it. This keen joy lasted only for an instant, but the instant was as clear as one note plucked upon a harp.

"How strange," Logan whispered to himself in the darkness. "How wonderful!"

CHAPTER TWO

Filipo Alejandro de las Reynas strode into the offices of Mercury Travel. In respect to Mercury's namesake, he wore a green satin baseball cap, trimmed with silver wings.

"Hey, everybody," he called out, "The world's another day older and so are you! What are you gonna do about it?"

No one answered this question, but everyone looked up. People always did when Filipo came into a room. Although he was only of medium height and build, people always thought of him as being a big man; he seemed to fill up any space he stepped into. Perhaps this was because he exuded so much concentrated life. In his early fifties, Filipo had lived hard. It showed in the lines of his tanned, weather-beaten face, and in his flattened, lion-like nose that had clearly been broken more than once. His iron gray hair curled fiercely around his strong face. There was a sense of the bull or the bighorn sheep about Filipo's head and shoulders; he looked ready to charge at life, with brown eyes that sparkled with liveliness and curiosity as he surveyed the room.

"Hey, *Carissima*," Filipo called to Gwen, "Time for lunch!" There's a new Thai restaurant on Speer Boulevard, and I'm taking you there, now!"

"Terrific!" Gwen replied. "But it's only eleven, and I don't go to lunch until – "

"No problem," Filipo interrupted confidently. "I bet *Doña* Patrish will let you go a little early. She's probably glad for some alone time in the office."

"Well," said Trish, "I suppose it's all right..."

"I'll get my coat," said Gwen quickly, hoping to be out the door before Trish changed her mind.

"So, *Doña* Trish, *ca va?*" Filipo asked. "I think you're working too hard! You're looking at that computer too much! Does it look back at you yet? Certainly, eyes as beautiful as yours were never meant to gaze at computers all day! Am I right, *Doña* T?"

Before Trish could reply, Gwen returned. Filipo offered her his arm. Then he announced to the office, which he was accustomed to being a bit more populated, and perhaps to the world at large, "*Mesdames et Monsieur*, I will leave you with some words of wisdom from the *Rubiyat* of Omar Khayyam:

'Since nobody has a lien on tomorrow,
Gladden the sad heart now,
Drink wine in the moonlight, my dear,
Because the moon will revolve a long time,
And not find us.' "

Trish looked perplexed. People often did after one of Filipo's incantations. He bowed, and with a final "*Au revoir, ma cherie!*" escorted Gwen out the door.

A few minutes later, having survived her friend's driving once again, Gwen relaxed gratefully in the charming restaurant. The soft pink walls and gentle lighting were a welcome relief from the glare and jangle of downtown Denver. Once again, Filipo had found a quiet gem. He turned and said something to the waiter in a language Gwen suspected was Thai. Filipo's ability to pick up languages never ceased to amaze her.

"They just stick to me like lint," he explained. "A word here, a phrase there, and hey; pretty soon you can talk to someone in their own tongue—a courtesy."

The result was that in addition to his native Basque, Filipo was fluent in several other languages. His conversation was a perpetual adventure, for if he couldn't find the word he wanted in English, he'd borrow one from French or Spanish or Italian. Yet somehow, he always made himself clear.

"Can I recommend the lemon grass soup?" he suggested now. "It's excellent. And let's have the mushroom curry. And then you can tell me all about this King Arthur trip that's got you so enchanted."

"It does have me enchanted," Gwen admitted, "and I've really enjoyed the time I've spent planning it. I'm almost sorry that Mrs. Gordon is picking up her tickets today. Now there's nothing left to plan! But I know she'll have a wonderful time. I've got her booked to spend the first two nights in a little village in Somerset. Far Tauverly, it's called. It's not a famous Arthur site, but the countryside nearby was mentioned in one of those Henrietta Amberly romances she loves. And it does lay claim to having a Merlin's Oak, and a Merlin's Spring."

"Merlin's Oak? What's that?"

"The legends say Merlin never really died. He was just put under a spell by his own student, Nimue. Some stories say she has him held in a magic spell inside a tree. Others say a cave, or a hillside, or a spring. You'd be amazed at how many Merlin's Hills, and Oaks, and Wells there are scattered all over England! Far Tauverly isn't even one of the famous ones, but it seems like such a lovely place for Mrs. Gordon to recover from jet lag, and get her bearings."

"A curious legend, about Merlin," Filipo remarked. "I have heard scraps of it before, but I had not realized how widespread it is."

"Yes; it's strange, you know. Arthur isn't supposed to be dead either; 'not dead, but sleeping, to reawaken at the hour of England's greatest need.' That's what the stories say. So, there are hundreds of Arthur's hills and mounds as well, each claiming to be the spot where he and his knights lie concealed in their magic sleep."

Gwen hesitated then added, "You know this trip is different from any other I've planned." "How so?"

"Well, every time I've worked on it, funny things have happened."

"What sort of funny things?"

"For instance, I saw this photograph in one of the guidebooks. It was of a gate to some old estate; a lion gate. But when I tried to find the photograph again, I just couldn't. It just wasn't there."

"You sure you didn't just overlook it?"

"No," Gwen insisted. "I looked through every page in every book, and it just wasn't there. It's as if it had vanished. Yet I know I saw it! And I've even dreamt about that lion gate. And —" Gwen hesitated.

"And?" Filipo prompted, his curiosity clearly piqued.

"Once there was even a figure, a man, on the other side of the gate in my dream. It was misty. I couldn't quite make out his features, but he called something out to me. Then the dream faded and I woke up feeling that there's something very important I'm supposed to remember, or do...but I can't quite remember what it is." Filipo looked enthralled.

"And, there's something else," she continued. "In that dream, I heard this sound. It was like a harp, like someone playing one note on a harp; like a voice, or the call of a bird." Gwen struggled to find the right expression. "It wasn't quite like anything I've ever heard."

"*Le Cri de Merlin*," Filipo said softly, yet intensely.

"What?"

"'The Cry of Merlin.' It's another fascinating legend about your friend, the wizard," Filipo explained. "I haven't heard it in years, but what you say today has brought it to mind. In Brittany, the people talk of a sad, mysterious cry. They sometimes hear it in the woods. No one can ever find its source, but whoever has heard it, even once, is haunted by it for the rest of their lives. 'Merlin's Cry,' they call it."

"Hmm," Gwen said, "there's something else. That first night, when I saw the photo in the guidebook, I could have sworn that I heard that cry, just for an instant; and I wasn't asleep, just standing beside my desk at work. I know that sounds crazy, but it was so real."

"It doesn't sound crazy at all," Filipo reassured her.

"I wonder if Mrs. Gordon will hear it when she's over there."

Filipo smiled. "I hope she does. She'd be thrilled." He had heard many stories about Mrs. Gordon. Although he had never met her, he had developed a great fondness for her. Sensing his friend's need not to say too much about this mysterious cry, Filipo asked about Mrs. Gordon's latest adventures.

"You won't believe what she did on the last trip, the one to Egypt," Gwen continued. "To begin with, she bribed a guard to let her stay all night in the Great Pyramid."

"And did she commune with the spirits of the Pharaohs?" Filipo asked hopefully.

"She claims she did, actually. But she also got arrested! The night watchman found her. So then, of course, she needed to be bailed out."

"This sounds too good to miss," Filipo said appreciatively. "Tell me all."

***

It was five in the evening in Yorkshire. At a campsite, far out on the moors, a Romani named Annie Lee sniffed the wind. She could smell damp earth, the salt of the distant sea, and the rowan wood of her own campfire. All that was as it should be. But there was something else on the wind, something not right.

She closed her eyes, and sniffed again. She looked like a wise old hound testing the breeze.

Distress, she thought. *Something is in great distress.* The Clydesdale horse tethered nearby whinnied, and pawed the earth, as if it shared her concern.

"It's all right, Chieftain," Annie Lee said to the horse. "We will find out what this is soon enough."

She gave herself a little shake, went to the campfire, and poured a mug of fresh-brewed coffee. She held to the Romani belief that coffee should be "as black as night, as sweet as love and as strong as sin," and she made hers accordingly. Easing her old bones down onto a boulder, she sipped the fierce brew, and awaited developments.

Had some hiker still been out as evening came upon the windswept landscape, they might have glanced at Annie Lee's campsite, and smiled. Her ornate green and gold wagon and the trail of wood smoke curling up from her fire lent the perfect touch of quaintness to the wild scene. As for Annie herself, she was the kind of old woman people refer to as odd, but harmless.

Her appearance was indeed eccentric. She wore a faded calico skirt, a brown, much-mended man's sweater several sizes too big for her delicate frame, gray wool socks, and Wellington boots. Over all this, she had draped a fringed shawl of peach-colored silk, fastened at one shoulder with a baby's nappy pin. Strands of her wispy white hair escaped from beneath the blue bandanna tied around her head, and fluttered in the rising wind.

She looked like the kind of ragged old dear who might tell your fortune for a pound. However, those who approached her to have their palms read ("Oh, come on, George, it'll be fun! She looks a proper Gypsy, doesn't she? What harm can there be in it? It's all for a lark, isn't it, pet?") were in for a surprise. Before the stranger even had a chance to offer their hand, Annie Lee would look at them shrewdly with her bright, cornflower blue eyes, and say, "Your palms are wet with sweat, and there's a great worry due to cross your life line in about two years time." Whilst they were wondering how she'd figured that out from ten feet away, Annie Lee would begin to sniff the air. Suddenly her visitor would feel as if all the scents of deodorant, toothpaste, and cologne had been stripped away from them, and that what remained smelled none too good. Annie Lee, on the other hand, smelled lovely. Like mint, and new-mown grass. Everything about her, from her white, wrinkled skin to her mismatched clothes seemed fresh-scrubbed and sun-dried. Not what they had expected in a Gypsy, somehow.

"Your Grandmother died of diabetes," Annie Lee might suddenly announce, "and you're due to get it too, if you don't mend your ways. You eat too many sweets.. Wait right there!"

With that, Annie Lee would dart into her wagon, rummage around, and emerge a moment later with a packet of herbs in her hand.

"This will help you change your habits. Take it as a strong tea, three times a day. Should last you about two weeks; after that it's up to you. You are worth the effort, you know. Good-bye and good luck." Then she would turn briskly away, expecting no payment, on to the next task at hand.

Her ability to diagnose and her knowledge of herbs were remarkable enough, but Annie Lee had another gift, as well. "The Calling" was how she described it, to those few she spoke of it to at all.

She would never forget the first time she had felt The Calling. She had been about five years old. She was fishing with her brothers, in a little stream in Kent. Suddenly, she felt as if someone was tugging at her. The feeling was as real as if someone had been next to her, pulling on her sleeve. But there was no one there. She had been so surprised she'd dropped her fishing pole into the water.

"Clumsy girl," her brother had snarled at her in Romani. "Stupid donkey!"

Ordinarily, such comments would have started a tumbling, scratching fight between them. But on that day, Annie Lee had looked at her brother distantly, as if his insults were no more to her than the chattering of a sparrow. Without a word, she had headed toward the signal that had called to her from the northeast, as clearly and persistently as if someone was calling her name, over and over. She didn't even swerve a few feet in her path to cross the stream on a fallen log; she just waded across like an otter, clambered up the other bank, and went on, straight as an arrow through brambles and over fences, until she came to the source of the signal: a fox, with its leg caught in a trap. She never wondered, until afterwards, how she had found it, or how she had known to pick some broad, fuzzy-looking leaves that grew nearby, and wrap them around the fox's leg.

"You did the right thing," her Grandfather told her when she brought the wounded creature to him. "That leaf staunches blood."

Fascinated, Annie Lee had watched as her Grandfather gave the fox a concoction of herbs to make it sleepy. Then he set the tiny bones, and sewed the wound closed with neat, swift stitches.

"A clean break," he had said. "It was very lucky that you got there before he began to struggle with the trap. The Angel of Foxes must have put you in the right place at the right time."

She helped care for the fox until one day, with a flick of its tail and a last, foxy grin it had bounded into the forest and disappeared, into its own world again. From that time on, Annie Lee's life was never the same. Morning, noon, and night she questioned everyone about herbs and cures. She went with her mother to gather burdock and comfrey; from her Aunt she learned how to dry mint and chamomile. Her Grandfather showed her how to douse for water, and taught her the right time of the year and month to pick each different herb.

At the same time, something remarkable happened to Annie Lee's sense of smell. She simply woke up one morning, and found that everything smelled ten times stronger than it ever had before. Her Grandmother's feet smelled like old onions; mint on the roadside smelled as if it was being crushed right beneath her nostrils.

"It's like I've gotten glasses for my nose," she told her mother. "Remember when Aunt Gita finally got spectacles, and she couldn't believe that she could really see all the leaves on the trees? Well, it's like that for my nose. It's the same smells that were always there, but more so."

"That's very weird," her mother had said, "but perhaps it's a gift."

As time passed, Annie Lee began to discover meanings in smells. Certain diseases had certain smells. So did diseases of the heart and soul. Greed had a combined sour/sweet smell, like fallen apples left on the ground; fear smelled acrid; laziness was musty, like a room too long unaired. Over time, Annie Lee learned which herbs and flowers helped to counteract which smells.

Through it all, The Calling continued. Sometimes it came every day for a month. Other times it went quiet for an entire season. But it always returned. Over the years, The Calling had pulled Annie Lee to the sides of young mothers in labor, wounded soldiers, fevered cows, or an elm tree infested with beetles. Sometimes the life in distress was that of a child, just coming into the world. Other times, it was an old, old life, getting ready to leave. Sometimes the pain was of the body, sometimes of the mind. Often Annie Lee could offer a cure, other times only the comfort of companionship. She did not know why The Calling brought her to some lives in need, and not to others. She only knew that when It called, she answered. This made her life very simple.

She had not been surprised, therefore, on that April afternoon, when The Calling came again. She had been searching for early violets when the familiar signal of distress had tugged at her, coming this time from the left.

She hurried back toward her campfire. The signal came again; so strong that she fell to her knees, retching with dizziness and nausea.

"Well, I never felt anything like that before," she said to Chieftain a few minutes later when she had recovered herself a bit.

Next, The Calling began to shift directions, like the wind before a storm. It seemed to come from everywhere at once. Then it vanished, leaving Annie Lee shaken. That was when she decided to sip her coffee, and send out a signal of her own.

I am here. I am willing, she thought. *Please tell me where to go.*

She thought this over and over, like someone sending out an SOS. Then she waited. Slowly, somewhere over the edge of the horizon, a reply began to gather. Then, without warning, it crashed down upon her like a mighty wave of grief, pain, and fear that left her gasping for breath. In all her seventy years, Annie Lee had never felt so great a cry for help.

The signal settled down to a steady pulsing that tugged at her from the South and West. Not only was It stronger than any she had ever felt, but she had the sense It was coming from farther away than ever before; perhaps several days journey away.

Shaken, but with a determined step, Annie Lee put out the campfire, and began to pack up her gear.

The Clydesdale whinnied enquiringly. "Yes, Chieftain," the old woman replied, "We are going on a journey. And I am afraid. I don't know what is calling yet. I only know that we must go to meet it to the South and West, in Somerset, I think, in Somerset."

Her cornflower blue eyes were worried. Chieftain was not worried at all. He tossed his noble head, so that his beautiful brown and white coat gleamed, and his white mane streamed in the wind. He rolled his lustrous eyes with the pleasure of one who is young, and bold, and born for danger.

Annie Lee sighed. "You're supposed to be a farm horse," she muttered.

Chieftain snorted at the mere thought. His owner smiled. She had, after all, chosen him for precisely that fire in his eyes. She could scarcely blame him now for being true to that very spirit.

As for Chieftain, his mighty hooves danced impatiently upon the earth, as if to say, "To Somerset! To Somerset! Onward we go, to meet great things in Somerset!"

***

At that same moment, in Bangkok, a butler polished a tabletop, before setting a vase of flowers down upon it.

The tabletop was made of black lacquer, of so smooth and even a gloss that it resembled black ice. It was a very long tabletop. Its black depths reflected the arched windows of the room it sat in.

The windows overlooked a harbor. Forty stories below the noise of that unhappy city filled the narrow streets. None of that disturbance reached the penthouse that the black lacquer table sat in. The sounds of the city could not penetrate the custom-made, tinted glass in the windows. Smells and heat were filtered out by a special ventilation system that kept each room at the perfect temperature and humidity to protect the artwork housed within it. That artwork was considerable: fifteenth-century Italian tapestries, Egyptian sculptures, Rembrandts. The cream of every time and place filled the quiet rooms. Each work was displayed to best reveal its particular beauty. Whoever had assembled this collection had a keen eye for the genuine. Indeed, the curators of several great museums would have been shocked to learn how many treasures were actually here, while the world's finest forgeries were in their care.

In one corner of the room stood a small, exquisitely carved China closet, lit by a dim light. Inside were several bejeweled cups, at least a half dozen silver crosses inlaid with gleaming gems, an ancient gold candlestick, and an Egyptian eye of Horus. Though perfectly displayed, the objects looked even more out of place then the great works of art, having been torn from churches, temples, and pyramids where for centuries they had lived. Not everyone was impressed by the penthouse and its contents, however.

"A mortuary for art," the Swiss maid, Helga, often muttered. "Not good; this place is not good."

Perhaps the butler agreed with her, perhaps not. "Keeps himself to himself," the other servants said of him. If indeed he felt that the place was "not good," he certainly realized, like the rest of them, that the pay was very, very good. And he had certain pressing debts to pay off, as well as other obligations that money alone could not absolve, so he appreciated the immunity his employer offered him. Not even the fiercest members of the Indonesian Mafia would touch someone who worked for his particular master. Neither would most police forces. That was good on both counts for the butler, who currently called himself Luan Tey. At twenty-four, he was already wanted in seven countries.

Now his white-gloved hands set the vase down on the black lacquer table so carefully that the flowers, white orchids, did not even tremble.

It was two a.m. in Bangkok. Far from being asleep, Luan Tey was on duty, and in impeccable uniform. His employer, who kept unusual hours, was up, and that meant everyone was up.

Luan Tey bowed silently, and left the room. His feet made no noise on the pale gray carpeting. He seemed scarcely to part the air as he moved through it. His golden face was a polished mask, as if his thoughts were miles away. Nonetheless, as soon as he was out of the room, he paused behind the door to listen. His employer had called an emergency meeting with one of his top aides, and Luan Tey wanted to know why. Usually, he found it more prudent not to know the details of his master's business. On this occasion, though, he had an instinct that events were brewing which would involve him. He felt it best to be prepared.

The aide spoke first: "Sir, as I told you over the phone, the work in Zaire has been halted. An earthquake. It is uncertain when mining can resume."

There was a pause. Then a second voice spoke. It was deeper, slower than the first. "Well," it said, "that is unfortunate."

The voice betrayed no alarm; not even annoyance. It was a cultivated voice, an affable voice. It spoke an easy, cultured English, but beneath that were flavors of other origins. What countries exactly had blended to form the voice would be hard to define. Like the black lacquer tabletop, it had a hard, dark polish, difficult to penetrate.

"Well," the voice continued, pleasantly, affably, "here is what we'll do. We'll get in touch with that fool in England."

"The one in Somerset, Sir?" the aide asked nervously.

"Exactly. The one in Somerset."

"Right away, Sir."

Luan Tey glided silently away from the door, having heard enough. He wondered what kind of place Somerset might be, for his instinct told him he would be seeing it soon enough.

***

Gwen and Filipo had just finished their coconut ices. The waiter set before them two cups of spicy Thai coffee laced with cream. Filipo opened the tin of Three Castles tobacco he carried everywhere, and deftly rolled a cigarette. Instantly, a waiter approached.

21

"Don't worry," Filipo reassured him. "I'm not going to light it. This is as close to smoking as I allow myself these days." With great deliberation, he began rolling a second cigarette. Gwen sensed that the conversation was about to take a different turn.

"I guess you put in some late nights, planning that trip for Mrs. Gordon," said Filipo, smiling.

"Yes," Gwen answered cautiously, knowing Filipo was leading up to something, in his own, inimitable manner.

"And I guess it's lucky you had that free time," Filipo mused. He picked up one of the cigarettes and held it with obvious enjoyment. Gwen knew that had he not been trying to kick the habit and had the restaurant allowed, he would have smoked a half dozen already. "Of course, you could have been out dancing with some wonderful man."

"Oh, Filipo!" Gwen exclaimed, torn between exasperation and affection. For the moment, exasperation won out. "We don't need to go into all that again," she added, realizing with chagrin that her words had taken on the stuffy tone she so disliked in herself.

"Hey, very good!" Filipo said. "Just a touch of Grace Kelly in *North by Northwest*, right? Puts you in your place, with devastating grace. Personally, I prefer your young Lauren Bacall. That sense of adventure she has in *To Have and Have Not!*"

Gwen sighed. One of Filipo's annoying yet endearing arts was his way of describing people's behavior in terms of movie roles, usually from the 1940s and '50s. His comparisons were invariably right on the mark, making them hard to ignore.

He now dropped his bantering tone and looked at her with an expression of kindness and concern on his rough-hewn face.

"Look, babe, I don't mean to interfere. I'm your friend, and I'm worried about you. It's been over two years since you broke up with . . . What was that asshole's name?"

"His name was David—and he wasn't an asshole!"

"Whatever," Filipo said lightly. "He's history now. The point is it wasn't an easy time for you. But it's time for you to start going out again."

"I go out with you all the time," Gwen protested.

"Sure, sure," said Filipo, "but I don't count. You need to meet a man. You need a *family*."

"I have a family," Gwen said, a little too quickly. "We exchange Christmas cards. And besides, you're like family."

"Yes, we're friends and have been from the moment we met. We will always be friends, *Carissima*. But I'm talking about a man to fall in love with, maybe even to marry. God knows, I like the ladies, but for whatever reason, it's not romance between you and me."

"I'm not looking for a man to marry," Gwen said firmly.

Filipo raised his eyebrows in a quizzical you-could-have-fooled-me manner, but all he said was "Listen, love's at the heart of life. In my experience, if you want Life, you gotta pray for it, seize it, coax it, fight it, make love to it, just about anything except wait for Life to show up on your doorstep like the morning paper. If you want to exist, okay, just keep on breathing for a few decades. But if you want to live, well, that's something else again. Then you gotta throw your heart into loving someone, something, and have the rest of you leap in afterwards."

Filipo paused to sip his coffee. He looked across at Gwen questioningly, as if trying to gauge her reaction. "I'm afraid I've stuck my nose in your business and my foot in my mouth," he said ruefully. "I need a chiropractor for my conversations. Forgive me, it's just that I care about you."

"Oh, Filipo, it's okay," Gwen interrupted, "truly it is. I'm glad that you care enough to be honest with me. I know there's truth in what you're saying. Maybe it's time, finally, to think about dating again. But there's not exactly a line of applicants waiting at the door. It's not like I'm one of those Henrietta Amberly heroines, choosing between fascinating suitors. I'm not exactly Guinevere, caught between Lancelot and Arthur," she laughed. "I guess Mrs. Gordon's trip is really on my mind."

Filipo nodded. "You know something? I think this trip isn't for Mrs. Gordon; I think it's for you." Their eyes met for a moment, then Gwen looked up, startled.

"Oh, my God! What time is it?" Gwen exclaimed. "Mrs. Gordon's going to be at the Agency to pick up her tickets in"- she glanced at her watch - "seventeen minutes. Trish is at lunch by now. I've got to be there, or she'll miss her plane!"

"No problem," replied Filipo, instantly at her service. "I'll get you there in a jiffy."

A mere twelve minutes later, they came to a screeching halt in front of Mercury Travel. Noticing Gwen's startled face, Filipo shrugged and said, "I can't help it, Miss G, I learned to drive in Rome."

"That was a red light back there!"

"True, but we cleared the approaching bus with a magnificent margin, no? Listen, I'm the safest driver you'll ever meet, you know why? Because I know that everyone else on the road is a lunatic, so I drive with the great defensiveness. But I can't see obeying rules when they aren't, at that moment, needed. Hey, tell me this: In all the times you've ridden with me, has anyone ever gotten hurt? Have I ever even gotten a ticket?"

"No," Gwen admitted, "but I can't imagine why not."

"It's all in the timing," Filipo said grandly. "Once you hit your right speed for driving, you can't really stop for every little thing. It's more important to aim for your destination and maintain your momentum. Now, reach into the back seat and grab one of those signs."

Filipo kept a wide selection of notices in his back seat; that said everything from "Press" to "Delivery," and an enigmatic "Official Business," which he had lettered himself.

"Better take the one that says 'Clergy,'" he told Gwen. "I've been too preachy today." He propped the sign in the car window and escorted Gwen to the office door.

"Sorry I gotta hurry," he said, kissing her lightly on the cheek, "but a student's gonna show up at my place at one-thirty. Mostly he plays the guitar like he's chopping potatoes. Then, every once in a while, he hits a passage from Rodriguez and, Santa Maria, it's like the full moon slips through the strings and into your soul! Maybe the boy has a drop of Basque blood in his veins, although his name is Cohen. Fingering needs work, though. Now that little girl, Sarah— remember, I told you about her? Ah, fingering as *delicata* as raindrops on a rose, but hesitant strumming."

There was nothing like the subject of his guitar students to bring out the Pyrenees poet in Filipo. Gwen was just about to remind him that they were both in a hurry, when some sixth sense made Filipo glance over his shoulder, just in time to see a meter maid headed right toward his double-parked car.

"Ah! Time to regain the momentum!" he cried. With a parting "Adios!" he leapt back into his car and turned the wrong way down an alley, moments before the meter maid walked past.

A note was taped to Gwen's computer screen. Deciphering Trish's scrawl, she read: "Gwen, Mrs. Gordon called. She canceled the whole trip! A grandchild arrived a month early, and she's flown to Michigan to help out. She thanked you for all your trouble. She'll call soon. P.S. I didn't cancel her tickets yet, figured you could do that."

"Oh damn!" exclaimed Gwen. She was surprised by how disappointed she felt.

All that planning, gone to waste, she thought. *It wasn't just a trip, it was art!*

She remembered what Filipo said at lunch: "I don't think this trip is for Mrs. Gordon, I think it's for you."

Maybe he was right, Gwen thought. *I wish I could go.*

And so you can, a little voice at the back of her mind said, a voice that reminded her of Carlotta, the spunky heroine of Henrietta's *Coy on the Caribbean.* Carlotta, she remembered, had been a fiery young girl whose impulsive nature got her into no end of trouble; yet it did, eventually, find her a wonderful man.

"Just change all the reservations from Mrs. Gordon's name to your own. With a first class ticket, it's easy to do. You've got the computer right there. Just do it."

"I could never afford it …." Gwen told herself aloud.

"*Au contraire,*" the Carlotta in her mind replied cheerfully. "You've got next to nothing on your credit card, and with your limit, we'll just make it."

Gwen realized her passport was certainly valid, waiting for her, in her top dresser drawer.

"Almost as if it was meant to be," Carlotta mused dreamily. "You and me on the open road. Destiny. Kismet."

"There's no time," Gwen reasoned. "The flight leaves in three hours." Now she sounded to herself more like Jennifer, the prim governess of one of her favorites—*Captured in Cardiff.*

"Just enough time," Carlotta continued. "Leave work now. Twenty minutes at the bank, home by three. Throw some clothes into a suitcase, call Filipo, catch a cab to the airport, you'll be there well before four-thirty."

Gwen brought Mrs. Gordon's itinerary up on her computer. She looked at all the wonderful destinations: Salisbury, Tintagel, Glastonbury. . . . With her hands on the keys, she hesitated.

I could do it, she thought. *Just take out 'Gordon' and type in 'Fields.' Just like that. Just to see what it looks like...*

She typed her name into one space and now read: "Gwendolyn Fields, arrive Heathrow, April 17th, 8:30 a.m."

It looked fine, she decided.

***

Two and a half hours later, Gwen was running full tilt through Denver International Airport. It wasn't until the plane was over Nebraska and the stewardess was serving drinks that the reality of what she'd done began to hit her.

Well, Trish knows by now, she realized. She'd left a note on her desk that read: "Dear Trish. Destiny called, had to answer. See you in three weeks, if still have job. Yours, Gwen." At least her two coworkers would be back tomorrow from their vacations.

She had stopped on the way to the airport to call Filipo. He must have been teaching in his basement studio, because his answering machine had come on:

"*Buenos Dias, Shalom, Salaams,* and *Guten Tag!* You have reached—me! And if you don't know who that is, then hey, you've got the wrong number anyway! But that's okay, if you say something interesting. But first, before that infernal beep, I play for you a poignant passage from medieval Spain, an old dance called an *Estampe.* So, hey, get comfy, and here we go!" The tune began furiously. Gwen waited for the beep, and then called out breathlessly.

"Filipo, this is fantastic! I'm taking the trip. Mrs. Gordon canceled, and I'm going! I'm going to England! Back in three weeks, could you please water the plants? You know where the key is. Thank you so much. I'll call you from England somewhere! The cab's here—gotta go!"

Now, at last, she found herself high amid the clouds.

"Something to drink?" the stewardess asked.

"Champagne, definitely," she ordered.

She took out her itinerary and looked at it, smiling widely. The next morning, she would arrive in London, where a rental car would be waiting for her.

And by this time tomorrow, she mused happily, *I'll be in . . . let's see . . . that's right . . . in Far Tauverly, in Somerset!*

CHAPTER THREE

Logan Knowelles contemplated stopping at the Greenstone Arms for a pint of celebration. He was halfway through his postal route. It was only one-thirty. The sun was bright. That alone was cause enough for festivity. Why not have a pint?

Just then, Mrs. Grimsby called, "Oy, Logan! Do you have a letter from my sister in Bristol? I wrote her over a week ago. I was sure she'd be answering by now!"

"Right you are, there's a note right here," Logan replied. To himself he added, *Best leave that pint til later. But perhaps Charlotte Grimsby will offer me some of her famous hard cider.*

Adjusting his postman's cap, he headed across the street. His walk was unmistakable: springy and birdlike. In spite of his silver-white hair, no one at first glance would have taken him for sixty. He moved almost as a child would, from point of interest to point of interest, pausing to gaze at a newly bloomed flower or an unfamiliar car. In his own odd way, he was quite dapper. He had the short, compact grace of a jockey or a dancer. His clothing was old but impeccably tidy. He favored woolen plaid shirts, corduroy trousers, and tweed jackets that had been cleaned and worn to a perfect softness. Even when off duty, he wore his postman's cap at a jaunty angle. Unless the weather was very warm, he was sure to have a camel's hair wool scarf wrapped around his throat and tossed over one shoulder.

Logan's face was as distinctive as the rest of his appearance. It was a gaunt, hollowed face that spoke of a long and difficult life, which his bantering manner denied. A tragic-comical face, really. The first feature people noticed was Logan's nose. Long and narrow, it seemed to have been made for ferreting out secrets and had long ago earned him the name "Cyrano." As if the nose wasn't startling enough, Logan's large ears stuck out from his head like the handles on a jug and seemed to be permanently cupped forward by invisible hands, as if their owner didn't want to miss a single word of the world's story. There was dignity, however, in Logan's deep-set eyes. They were dark blue; their gaze was clear, grave, and searching. They often seemed sad, even when the rest of Logan's remarkable face was smiling. The eyes were sparkling cheerfully now, though.

Logan reached into his postman's bag with an air of mystery. He looked from the bag to Mrs. Grimsby's broad, freckled face.

"Well, there is something here for you," he said, pulling out a slim, blue envelope, "but I'll never be believing it's from your sister. It's yet another missive from one of your countless admirers."

"Now, Logan Knowelles," said Mrs. Grimsby, flattered yet ruffled. "You know very well I've been happily married to my Tom these thirty years!"

"Age cannot wither, nor custom stale, thy infinite variety," Logan replied soulfully.

"A fat lot you know about my 'infinite variety,'" said Mrs. Grimsby, grabbing for her sister's letter.

"No! No!" cried Logan. "It's from 'him,' my rival in your affections! Only Coleridge could express my feelings: 'I die! I weaken! I faint! I fall!' I've always wondered why he wrote that in backwards order," Logan mused. "He stays pretty active for a man who declares himself dead in the first words. Nonetheless, it does express my delicate state. Unrequited love threatens the very fiber of one's being, it—"

"What will it take to revive you then?" interrupted Mrs. Grimsby, having heard many variations on this theme from her poetic postman. Logan gave her a calculating glance out of the corner of his eye.

"Only a glass of your famous hard cider, made by your own white hands, will stave off my certain heartbreak and untimely death." Logan glanced at the sky for further inspiration: "Ah, yes, when the winds of spring again do blow, the daffodils shall bloom as golden as they do now, but their beauty shall not find me here again to—"

"Talking to yourself again, Logan?"

Startled, Logan looked around and realized that Charlotte Grimsby had disappeared into her house, to get the cider, he hoped. Now, her next-door neighbor, Florence Selby, was leaning against the fence, regarding him with gentle amusement. Florence was as thin as Mrs. Grimsby was broad, and her hair, which she assured everyone was "still red by nature," clashed terribly with her lavender print dress.

"If the mountain won't come to Mohammed," she sighed, with only a trace of irritation.

"It looked to be midsummer before you made it to my house, so I thought I'd just come to get my mail. And also, Logan dear, I wonder if you'd be so good as to deliver these peach preserves to the Vicar. Now, where's me mail?"

28

"Ah, better you hadn't asked," sighed Logan, stuffing the preserves into his commodious bag. "It's a bill from Marks and Sparks, in Taverton. Charge overdrawn again?"

Fortunately, at this moment, Mrs. Grimsby reappeared with a stoneware pitcher of hard cider, three glasses, and a large platter of bread and cheese.

"Ah!" exclaimed Logan, "How unexpected! The Bright Ones in the Land of the Ever Young couldn't be better served! Ladies, let us break bread together! I've worked up enough of a thirst to drain the pitcher at a single draught, as Culculain did with the Horn of—"

"Since when did it ever take you much to work up a thirst?" chided Mrs. Grimsby. "I swear Logan, you should have been one of those bards of old, the way you do go on. Now stop nattering a moment, and have a bite."

"Precisely," Logan agreed.

For a few minutes, the only sounds were of contented munching, punctuated by the occasional swallow of cider, as the three neighbors leaned against the fence, enjoying their impromptu lunch.

As Logan reluctantly drained the last of the cider, a car turned into the street, commanding the attention of all three. It was a silver Jaguar. It glided through the spring sunlight like a blade: elegant, swift, imperial.

"There goes that Swindon," commented Mrs. Selby, pointedly raising an eyebrow.

"Heard tell he had the paint specially mixed for that car. Ordinary paint wouldn't do," Mrs. Grimsby said with a sniff.

"Must have cost a pretty penny. Not that he has to worry about money. Not like some folk, who have to do without just to pay the utility bill," Mrs. Selby put in.

"Aye, it is expensive," Logan agreed, "but you have to admit, it's as smooth as glass. Of course, as Homer tells us in the Odyssey, 'Beware the smooth, it oft times lies; the rough is honest, and lovely to discerning eyes.'"

"Well, I don't know about your Homer, but that Swindon's a smooth one, that's for sure. Whole family is. New money, they are. And they didn't come by it honestly, either."

"Not like the Grenistons," Mrs. Grimsby said, a note of pride in her voice.

"Ah well, the Grenistons," Logan proclaimed, "they're of the land."

"Blood will tell," Mrs. Selby added, sounding the final note.

Logan hesitated, then said, "Well, ladies, there is truth in what you say. And yet, any person's story is like an iceberg. You only see the tip of it from outside. Let us not be too precipitous in our judgments, even of young Swindon."

Mrs. Grimsby's face softened slightly. "Ah, well, I suppose you're right."

"Hmmpf!" said Mrs. Selby. "Where there's smoke, there's fire! I heard just the other day that Swindon started action to foreclose the Walmsleys. And Bob Walmsley being out of work these two years—and six kids to bring up!"

"Seven," corrected Logan, unheard.

"Foreclosure! Oh, you don't say," sniffed Mrs. Grimsby, leaning further across the fence.

"Yes, indeed," Mrs. Selby replied. "I heard it from Jim Stilton, you see."

The two of them looked settled in for an extended gossip. Unnoticed, Logan walked back across the street to finish his route. Just as he passed the Greenstone Arms, a car pulled up. He noted the rental sticker in the rear window and the spatters of mud on the side.

Someone's driven a long way, he thought, curiosity piqued. Not that many travelers came to Far Tauverly, even in the height of the tourist season, which had not started yet. The arrival of a new visitor was always something of an event, and if it was a paying guest, a welcome addition to the town's pocketbook.

A slender young woman got out of the car. Spotting the sign of the Greenstone Arms, she pulled a suitcase out of the car and headed toward the inn. As she reached the door, she turned, as if she felt Logan's gaze upon her. For a moment, their eyes met. He had a brief impression of delicate features, pale skin, auburn hair piled loosely on her head like a crown, a blouse of royal blue silk. The stranger favored him with a quick, soft smile, then disappeared into the inn.

Logan realized he'd been holding his breath. "Oh, bright Rhiannon, fairest lady of The Five Worlds," he intoned, "Thou hast brushed my gray world with sunlight, and scattered jewels before my path!"

"Oy, she's a looker, all right," a cheery voice said nearby. Logan saw the eldest of the Walmsley children standing at his side. It was Osgood, who, at eleven, already considered himself a connoisseur of the feminine race.

30

"She is a vision of loveliness," Logan corrected gently.

"Yeah, like I said, she's pretty," Osgood replied, missing the poetic distinction. "But I've got some postal business to transact with you." The boy pulled several grubby letters out of his pocket. He carefully scraped a bit of licorice off of one and began reading the names on the envelopes in a stately voice, like a herald announcing arrivals at court:

"From the Independent Kingdom of Green Stone Forest. To the Queen of England, regarding the welfare of her subjects and the problems of the present school system."

"Message received," said Logan gravely, taking the first letter.

Osgood continued, "From the Independent Kingdom of Green Stone Forest. To Robin Hood, concerning an exchange of tactics."

"Received."

"And the last one for today: From the Independent Kingdom of Green Stone Forest, to Mahatma Gandhi, concerning India's desperate situation."

"Mahatma Gandhi? Are you sure?" Logan asked gently, not yet taking the letter.

"Absolutely," said Osgood. "We saw him in a movie on the telly last night. He's in a lot of trouble, and we'd like to help." Reluctantly, Logan stuffed that letter as well into his bag.

"We know we owe you for postage on the last letters," Osgood continued, "and we were wondering if you might accept this apple and these rare rocks, found by our royal geologist, as payment."

With equally regal authority, Logan replied, "Her Majesty's Postal Service is able to exchange the recognized coinage of any realm. And here, by the way, is a letter for you."

Osgood seized the envelope, and read aloud: "Sir R. R. R. Greniston, Lord of Greniston Manor, Conservative Member of Parliament, Knight of the Bath and Fellow of Cambridge. To: The Independent Kingdom of Green Stone Forest. Concerning: Personal matters of the utmost importance and urgent diplomacy."

Osgood beamed. "Look, Logan," he said, "sealing wax! And it has his family crest on it. In gold. Lord Greniston's a right 'un! He always answers!"

"Well, now that matters of state are completed for the moment," Logan said, "I've got two questions to put to you. First, was it you who put treacle in the Vicar's mailbox?"

Osgood looked suddenly blank. Logan tried to sound stern as he continued: "Because you know, those mailboxes are Her Majesty's property! You can't go putting treacle into the property of one of your fellow monarchs."

"Certainly not," Osgood agreed.

"Yes, well, if you should just happen to discover who the culprit is, perhaps you'd let them know that they're breaking the laws of England?"

"Absolutely, Sir," said Osgood with a smart salute. "The Independent Kingdom of Green Stone recognizes the existence of England and its laws."

"Very generous of you, I'm sure," Logan murmured, trying to hide a smile. "Now, as for the second question, I was wondering if you'd be good enough to complete my route again? Here's the letters; only five left. And these peach preserves go to the Vicar, from Mrs. Selby. Try not to drop them. As for payment . . . ," Logan rummaged in the depths of his bag. His fingers closed upon a foil-wrapped package.

"Aha!" he said, "This looks promising!" He realized it was the date muffins Mrs. Owens had asked him to deliver to the Watkin's house two days ago. "Oh well, too late now; gone a bit stale for sure," Logan mused. He handed the package to Osgood, along with a fifty pence piece.

"Muffins!" Osgood exclaimed joyfully, ripping open the foil. "And cash! All right!"

After devouring one of the muffins in record time, Osgood lifted his grubby fingers to his mouth and gave a shrill whistle. In response to this signal, there was a rustling in a nearby lilac bush. Logan caught sight of a head of tousled red hair which could have belonged to any one of the young Walmsleys.

"I'll just deliver these provisions to my sentinel and then finish your route," Osgood said.

"Fair enough. Give my regards to the Kingdom," Logan called after him.

As he walked toward the inn, Logan mused about the Walmsley children, as he often did. On the one hand, he was charmed by the imaginary kingdom they had created—what he knew of it, that is; for the children kept their secrets carefully guarded. He knew they considered the woods and fields around Far Tauverly to be theirs and that they declared themselves to be an Independent Monarchy, with Osgood as King and the others as members of a High Council, although Amy and Rutherford, both being under three, were not as active in decision making as the other five. He also knew that the children had deigned, by letter, to establish diplomatic relations with several of the world's great governments. He often caught glimpses of the Walmsleys, absorbed in their own mysterious business, in unlikely places. Once he had even thought he had glimpsed them near the forest bordering Greniston Manor. It had been by moonlight, so he had never been quite certain if he had glimpsed their forms darting for cover in the trees or if he had really heard a snatch of silvery laughter.

It's awfully late for those kids to be out here, he had thought at the time. *And Lord Greniston wouldn't like it if he knew they were on his land.*

When he had questioned the children about it the next day, they all staunchly claimed to have been tucked in their beds.

Whatever they were up to, all the fantasy in the world couldn't cover the grim facts of their lives: a drunken father, out of work for two years and more; an overworked mother; never quite enough food on the table; enormous freedom to run wild; and now, the new trouble of the foreclosure. Logan was disturbed, but not surprised, that the children seemed to be unable to distinguish between fact and fantasy. They sent letters to every great figure that caught their interest, not only to people of the present day but to Gandhi and Sherlock Holmes and the crew of the Starship Enterprise as well. Once they had even written to Alexander the Great and then, every day for a month, asked if he had answered yet. It was as if everything they read about or saw on television was real to them. Logan was at once charmed and disturbed by this. At first, he had thought their flood of letters to be but a passing fancy. Now, over a year after the business had begun, he was torn between telling the children some hard facts, which he knew would bring more grimness into their already grim lives, or going to the opposite extreme and answering some of their more impossible missives himself. He rather fancied penning a note from King Alfred the Great, or the Admiral in Chief of the Romulon Fleet.

Who's to say, he mused now, *what's real and what's true? Haven't I comforted myself with daydreams often enough? And yet, perhaps this has gone too far. . . .*

By this time, Logan had reached the door of The Greenstone Arms. He decided to put his worries to one side and have that pint.

That lovely lady who arrived a few minutes ago is in there, he realized. *Perhaps she's downstairs right now.* Adjusting his cap to its jauntiest angle, Logan entered the pub.

***

Gwen was happy to discover that the room she'd booked for Mrs. Gordon at the Greenstone Arms was every bit as clean and cozy as the brochure she'd seen back in Denver had promised. The room's gabled windows looked out over a small garden behind the inn. The shadow of a cherry tree's branches made a delicate tracery on the white walls. There was a window box full of daffodils, and the afternoon sunlight, filtered through their bright yellow petals, was a glorious sight.

"I hope everything is satisfactory," said Mrs. Hodges, comfortably, as if she knew that it could hardly be found otherwise.

Gwen's gaze took in the brass bed with its cheerful coverlet of red and white, the maple dresser, the soft blue armchair nestled snugly by the windows, the polished oak floor, and the clean, ivory throw rugs. The room smelled of lemon oil and lavender. Through the closed door beside the wardrobe was a private bath—a luxury, indeed, in an English inn. After the plane ride and the long drive from Heathrow, Gwen was looking forward to a shower.

"The room is beautiful," she said sincerely. "And it's so quiet," she added, realizing that instead of the distant hum of Denver traffic to which she had long been accustomed, what she heard was birdsong.

Mrs. Hodges laughed. "I suppose it is that, after the bustle of America. Now, my dear, I've saved some of the lunch special for you. So why don't you freshen up, and come down and have a bite? My shepherd's pie and a pint of ale will make you feel right at home, I guarantee it! Oh, and by the way, the gas heater's on the north wall there. You get an hour for a shilling, and it does get cool in the evenings, so you'll be needing it. And the hot water's on from six a.m. 'til nine, and then from four to nine in the evening, so you'll want to plan your baths accordingly. Well, I'll just let you freshen up, shall I? See you in a few minutes, dear."

Gwen was a little disappointed that her anticipated shower would have to be postponed, but she knew it was standard practice in most English inns to turn the hot water on for only a few hours a day. Mrs. Hodges' four hours in the evening was unusually generous, as was the rate on the little heater. She decided to simply wash her face and freshen up.

She was delighted to discover a deep tub with claw feet in the bathroom. On a bamboo stand beside it was a basket full of soaps and oils. Gwen decided that a long soak in a tub full of Caswell and Massey's Apricot Bubble Bath would be worth waiting for. She splashed her face with bracingly cold water, tidied her hair, and hurried happily downstairs.

The lower level of the inn seemed dark after the sunny bedroom. Gwen paused at the foot of the stairs to get her bearings. She realized that the hum of conversation she'd heard coming down the steps had stopped. The customers in the pub, all of whom were men, she noted, had fallen silent and were unabashedly staring at her. Feeling a little awkward, Gwen made her way to a table by the window. The men remained silent and continued to stare at her in a way that Gwen found surprisingly rude. It didn't make her feel unsafe, exactly, just very much an outsider. As if sensing her discomfort, Mrs. Hodges poked her head out of the kitchen, and exclaimed, "Oy, you, Bill Saxton, and you, Rafe Fergus; what're you gawkin' at? Keep your eyes to yourselves or get out of my establishment, thank you very much! And the same goes for the rest of you! Don't pay any mind to them, Miss Fields, they don't mean any harm. Just have the manners of baboons, they do. I'll be right out with your lunch."

"Sorry, Mabel," one of the men called to Mrs. Hodges. One or two of the others nodded rather sheepishly in Gwen's direction, and gradually, the hum of conversation resumed.

"You mustn't mind our stares," a light, pleasant voice said at her shoulder. "It's just that we so rarely see a beautiful stranger here, I fear we've quite forgotten how to welcome them."

Gwen looked up and found herself gazing at the bluest, friendliest eyes and the most extraordinary nose she had ever seen. She thought she had rarely seen a face of so much character. She had the sense the man's greeting hadn't been just a glib compliment; he'd actually wanted to offer her a warmer welcome than that gauntlet of appraising stares, and she was grateful to him for that.

"Please, won't you join me?" she asked.

The dark blue eyes looked hopeful, but the man hesitated.

"Really," Gwen assured him, "I'd like the company."

Reassured, the man sat down across from her.

"Gwen Fields, American tourist," she said, offering him her hand.

"Logan Knowelles," he replied. "Local Postman."

"Postman and all around do-little," laughed one of the men at the bar. He spoke just loudly enough for his voice to carry, but Gwen pretended not to hear him.

"Aye," another man chimed in, "Logan'll tell anyone a bit of gossip in exchange for a free pint."

"Or two," someone else added. General laughter followed, but it was not friendly laughter that included Logan. Gwen got the impression that being a bit odd, he was the usual target of jokes, which he probably pretended not to mind. In her company, however, it was a different matter. He stared awkwardly at the tabletop, his usually pale cheeks flushed with embarrassment.

Gwen looked over said, "Excuse me, were you speaking to us?" A startled silence fell over the room.

"Because if you were, you'll need to speak up so that we can all hear you clearly. If what you have to say is worth saying, that is."

Gwen realized that she was using exactly the words and tone she'd often used to address rude students with in the past, when she had worked as a substitute teacher. The technique worked in this situation as well.

After a few moments of awkward silence, one of the men said gruffly, "Best be gettin' on, lads."

"Aye," the others agreed. One by one, they put their money on the counter and left without another glance in Gwen's direction.

I've done it again, Gwen thought. *I've rushed headlong into someone else's business. I hope I didn't embarrass him. Maybe I should have left it to Logan to defend himself.*

"By Heaven, that was bold," Logan said appreciatively. "Do realize, though, that in a matter of seconds, you've made four enemies - and one staunch friend," he added warmly.

Any worries Gwen might have had that her impulsive defense of him had embarrassed Logan vanished when she saw the look of charmed amusement on his face. "You said you are American," he added, "and now I believe it. Yanks rush in where angels fear to tread!"

"American with an Irish Granny," Gwen replied. "Even worse."

They both laughed. Now that they had the pub to themselves, Gwen felt quite at ease with Logan. Mrs. Hodges emerged from the kitchen bearing a crockery plate piled high with steaming shepherd's pie. In the other hand, she carried a pint of amber-colored ale.

"There you go, luv," she said to Gwen, "tackle that! And mind you finish every bite. You look like you could use it! I'll just be in the kitchen if you need anything."

"This is enormous," Gwen whispered as soon as Mrs. Hodges was out of earshot. "Logan, please share this with me."

"Oh, I couldn't," he said, eyeing the pie, and especially the ale, with a loving glance. Although he had just snacked well on Mrs. Grimsby's cheese and bread, Logan was keenly aware that his own larder at home was nearly empty.

"Of course you could," urged Gwen. "You heard her. She wants me to finish every bite, and I can't hurt her feelings! Here, I'll take the fork, you take the spoon. You're facing the kitchen, so just keep an eye out in case she comes back, and dig in!"

"Well, when you put it that way," said Logan, already reaching for the mug of ale.

In a remarkably short time, most of the shepherd's pie and all of the ale had vanished.

"Delicious," sighed Gwen, leaning back into her chair.

"Ummm," agreed Logan contentedly.

For a few minutes, the two sat together like old friends, sharing a companionable bit of peace. Gwen realized that she had been traveling, by cab, plane, and car, for over twenty-four hours. What a relief it was at last to be still!

"I can't believe I'm actually here in England," she exclaimed. "I've dreamt about coming here for years, but this is the first time I've ever actually been out of the United States."

"Ah," said Logan, lifting the regrettably empty ale mug. "Well, here's to all your travels to come!"

"Have you traveled much?" Gwen asked.

"Oh, aye, once upon a time. In Her Majesty's Service in my youth. The Royal Navy. That was years ago. Stationed in Grenada, Malta, Alexandria, and enough other hot, foreign places to last me a lifetime. No offense to those who love to travel, of course," he added hastily.

"None taken," Gwen assured him with a smile.

"I guess I'm a local lad," Logan said. "I get nervous if I stray more than ten miles from this place."

"So you were born in Far Tauverly?"

37

"Oh, aye, I should say so. Right over at Kestrel Farm. My Mother was Welsh, but my Dad and his family have come from this land for over three hundred years."

"Three hundred years!" exclaimed Gwen, "What a long time!"

Logan laughed. "Why, that makes me but a newcomer here! There's many a family in this town can trace their lineage back five hundred years and more. Why, this very inn we're sitting in was built in 1140."

"Eleven forty," Gwen said reverently.

"Parts of it are from then. Of course, it was remodeled, so to speak, in Tudor times. But you can still see some of the original stones over there by the fireplace. Indeed, there was probably some sort of inn or shelter here for longer than anyone knows, for there's a spring nearby, and the road that runs through Far Tauverly was a path even before Roman times. Aye, many a traveler has surely sat here and rested his bones before moving on, just as you and I are now."

As Logan spoke, Gwen's gaze traveled over the ancient stones and the smoke-blackened beams of the inn. The past seemed very close now; Gwen could easily imagine an Elizabethan Lord, or a Norman Lady, a Roman soldier, or even earlier travelers sitting at similar wooden tables by the same stone fireplace. And before that, perhaps, around a campfire by the roadside.

The sun had gone behind the clouds, she realized, and a light spring rain was spattering the diamond-shaped windowpanes. Glancing out, she saw the trees beyond the houses across the way swaying against the cloudy sky. The sudden darkness increased the intimacy of the scene.

As if he, too, felt the spell of the past, Logan closed his eyes and sang:

"O, Western Wynde,
   When wilt Thou blow,
   That the smalle rain
   May rain down,
   And I in my lover's arms, again . . . "

His face changed as he sang. A dignity came over his gaunt features. Gwen thought he would have looked quite at home in the robes of some bard of long ago. As he sang the ancient lay, Gwen felt that she could hear within it the longings and sorrows of all the lovers that ever had lived since time began. She felt tears spring to her eyes, not the cheap, easy tears a sentimental movie might evoke, but tears from somewhere very deep—tears for the old, old mingled sorrow and richness of life itself.

This man is an artist, and he doesn't even know it, Gwen realized, with respect.

When the song was finished, neither spoke. Gwen felt it would be an insult to compliment Logan. It seemed the greatest honor she could pay him would be to wish not to break the rich silence the music had caused. They sat together in the darkness of the rainy afternoon, all three of them: Gwen, Logan, and the presence of the past.

Then Mrs. Hodges came bustling in. "Oy, you two," she exclaimed, "no need to be sitting in the dark!"

She turned on a light that cast a cheerful rosy glow over the room. "Now, then," she said to Gwen, "how'd you do with that pie? My goodness, you almost finished it! I don't know where you put it, a delicate thing like you! Mind you, I'm glad you enjoyed it! And the ale's gone, too!"

Mrs. Hodges cast a shrewd glance at Logan. "Well, I dare say you'd like some coffee now, with some real Somerset cream—every bit as good as Devonshire, you know—and you two could do me a real favor, and finish the last of the raspberry trifle. I've already got apple tarts on the menu for tonight, you see. And perhaps it would be well to light the fire a bit early. It's gotten right chill in here since that rain started. Logan, would you tend to it? There's a luv."

"Sure thing," he responded cheerfully.

He was back to his usual self, Gwen realized, whistling a jig as he fussed with logs and newspaper. In no time at all, he had a merry fire started. He came back to the table, dusting the grime off his hands, just as Mrs. Hodges returned with two dishes of raspberry trifle and two cups of fresh, hot coffee. Logan dug into the dessert with gusto.

"I suppose," Gwen said, "that living here all your life, you know a lot about the local legends and folklore." His mouth too full for speech, Logan merely nodded enthusiastically.

"Well, then, do you know where Merlin's Oak is? And Merlin's Spring?"

Logan's eyes lit up. Wiping his mouth on a napkin, he said, "Absolutely! I could take you there, if you like! Of course, it's on Lord Greniston's land, but he wouldn't mind if you came with me. I'm . . . er, his groundskeeper, his steward, actually. Unofficially, of course. So there would be no problem with my escorting you."

"Great," said Gwen. "I'm going to be here for two more days. Why don't we go tomorrow?"

"First thing!" said Logan brightly.

"Now, here's another question for you," Gwen continued. "Is there anywhere around Far Tauverly a gate . . . a kind of special gate, wrought iron, with two stone lions on either side?"

"Why, that would be the Greniston Gate," Logan said. "It's the main entrance to Greniston Manor. But how did you know?"

"I saw a photo of it in a book," Gwen explained, "and it caught my interest."

"A photograph?" Logan sounded surprised. "That's odd. Lord Greniston's a very private man. He doesn't allow any tourists or photographers anywhere near his home."

"But it was in a guide to Somerset," said Gwen.

Logan shrugged. "Someone must have taken it without permission. They better hope Lord Greniston never finds out! But yes, the gate is there right enough. You simply go down the main street of Far Tauverly, which is just about the only street of Far Tauverly, past the church. Then there's forest on either side. That's all Greniston land. And if you follow the road for about half a mile, you'll come to the gate. We could go there, tomorrow, too, if you like."

"Wonderful!" said Gwen.

"Are you interested in English history?" Logan asked.

"Some of it," Gwen replied. "Especially King Arthur." Briefly, she explained to Logan how she came to be on her journey at all.

"But that's wonderful!" Logan exclaimed, his eyes sparkling. "Why, you've had an adventure already! Do you realize how many people have longed to do just what you did? Ah, the appeal of it: to walk out on a drab job, and not look back! Everyone dreams of it, but you had the courage to do it!"

"I'm not sure courage is the word," Gwen began.

"Certainly it is," Logan said. "I wonder if your co-workers have realized you aren't coming back from lunch yet."

Gwen laughed. "Actually, I left a note."

"And came half a world, in pursuit of King Arthur! Well, if it's Arthur you're after, there's a great deal of lore in these parts. There's the Oak and the Spring, which you know about, but there's also the Tauverly Chalice. . . ."

"What chalice?" Gwen asked, intrigued.

"Why, the famous one," said Logan. He seemed surprised she hadn't heard of it. "It was found a few years ago on the Greniston land. It was in all the papers. Archeologists and scholars were debating whether it was the Holy Grail or not."

"What happened to it?"

"Oh, it's right here in Far Tauverly," Logan said proudly. "They wanted to take it to the British Museum, but Lord Greniston wouldn't hear of it, and fortunately, he has influence. So it's right here at our very own Historical Society which is run by the Pennington sisters; you must meet them. No, the furor over the chalice died down after the first few months, but, of course, it is irreplaceable to us. Especially since it bears out the prophecy."

"What prophecy?" Gwen asked, highly intrigued by this time.

"Ah. The Greniston Prophecy. You see, there have been Grenistons on this land for as long as anyone knows. Evidently, they were here in the days of Arthur, because the legend says that Arthur himself swore the Lord Greniston of that time to a great gease to be upon him and all his descendants."

"A geese?" asked Gwen, looking truly confused.

Logan laughed. "Not the birds. It's an old word for a sacred promise. It's all about some jewels that the Greniston family is to hold in trust for Arthur, until he returns to claim them. One of the jewels is called *The Green Stone*. Some people say that's where the Grenistons got their name: Greniston, Green Stone . . . it could be. Perhaps the original green stone was an emerald. Legend has it that it was supposed to be set into the chalice. But when the chalice was found, one setting was empty. Whatever stone had been there had long before been pried off."

"And do the Grenistons have it? And the other jewels?"

Logan shook his head. "No one knows for sure. They claim not. But local opinion holds that the jewels are hidden somewhere in Greniston manor or on the land and that the family themselves may no longer know where."

"Well, they'd better find them," said Gwen. "What if Arthur comes back and claims his treasure?"

Logan laughed. "They'll have some warning. Evidently, certain signs will herald the fact that Arthur is about to reappear in England's greatest hour of need, as the old tales say. In fact, one of the Grenistons, a Lord Peter Greniston, who lived in the 1500s, wrote it all down in a kind of poem. It's a very mysterious poem, a kind of riddle. No one has ever been able to figure out exactly what it means."

"I bet we could figure it out," Gwen said impulsively.

"Do you really think so?" Logan was clearly bemused at the idea. Everyone in Far Tauverly had always dismissed the prophecy as rigmarole. It had never occurred to him that it could actually be deciphered.

"Sure," said Gwen confidently. "Look, that Lord Peter, whoever he was, wrote the poem so that people would remember what the Grenistons promised King Arthur. He didn't write it to make them forget. So the clues to understanding it must be here, in this place. And we can find them. Why not?"

Logan looked appreciatively at Gwen. The firelight caught the red-gold highlights of her auburn hair. He noticed that her eyes, which at first he'd thought were gray, were flecked with gold and sea green as well. It was beautiful to see her: her pale skin flushed delicately with excitement, her fine features animated. By this time in his life, Logan was a shrewd judge of character. He saw intelligence, kindness, and courage in Gwen's face as well as a gentle beauty that he suspected younger men often overlooked.

Now Logan Knowelles, you old fool, he thought to himself. *Don't be falling in love with a lass half your age!* He sighed. Well, romance might be out of the question, but he felt sure that he and this lady were destined to be friends. *Lady,* he thought, *yes, that is the word for her. Not some false word for an artificial, hoi-de-toi-dee pain in the rump, but 'lady' as it might have been used in the Middle Ages, when the poets wrote of gentle knights and ladies faire. Lady Gwen. Gwendolyn Fields,* he mused. *Gwen, in old Welsh, meant white and shining. Gwenevere had meant white wave, or white phantom—something beautiful that vanished, like the foam on a crest of the sea. But white fields have a beauty that would last, that could be counted on. The Shining Lady of the Fields. Yes, that suits her. . . .*

"Logan?"

He realized he hadn't heard a word Gwen had said for the last few minutes.

"What were you thinking?" she asked. "So many expressions played over your face."

Embarrassed, Logan said quickly, "Oh, I was just thinking that you American girls are very spirited and bold. Ready to take on a challenge at the drop of a hat! But in a very ladylike way, of course," he added quickly.

Gwen laughed. "No one's ever called me ladylike before. Schoolmarm, maybe! I did some teaching before I became a travel agent. And I don't know about bold, although it has a nice ring to it. Impulsive, I think. But I can tell you this: I do feel amazingly lighthearted, as if great things are just around the corner!"

"Well," cried Logan, lifting his coffee cup in a toast, "Here's to feeling lighthearted and bold!"

"Lighthearted and bold!" echoed Gwen. "And to mysteries," she added.

"To mysteries!" Logan responded. "And here's to King Arthur and his story, which has brought us together to meet this happy day!"

"To Arthur!" cried Gwen.

"To Arthur!" Logan agreed.

For an instant, he had a fleeting impression of other voices crying, "To Arthur! To Arthur!" as if on that very spot, long ago, lords and ladies had gathered and pledged their fealty with those same words. Swords raised, glinting by firelight; garlands, and bright banners; and the voices ringing out: "To Arthur! To Arthur!"

Then the moment passed, and he was gazing into Gwen's friendly eyes, and Mrs. Hodges was saying, "Are you two still here? Now Logan, you've kept Miss Fields gabbing long enough. Besides, I've got to set up for supper soon. And she's had a long day and needs to rest."

"How rude of me," Logan exclaimed. "Miss Fields, excuse me, I didn't even think. . . ."

"Nonsense," said Gwen firmly. "I enjoyed every minute of it. And please, call me Gwen. I think I am ready for some sleep now, but I am counting on our plans for tomorrow."

"I'll pick you up here at nine," Logan said. "By the way," he added in a whisper, "don't mention our little excursion to anyone. If they knew I was taking you to see the Greniston land, well, then they'd all be wanting tours, and it would never do."

"Mum's the word," said Gwen.

A few minutes later, she started to run a bath for herself only to discover that the water was ice cold. Evidently, it took the water heater a little while to get going. She decided, instead, to go for a short walk.

The rain had stopped, but the pavement was still damp. No one seemed about. From the smells of cooking that emerged from the brick houses she passed, Gwen deduced that the motto of Far Tauverly was "Early to bed and early to rise," for it was not yet five. By now, her steps had led her past a butcher's, a greengrocer's, and a tiny laundrette, all closed. Next, she came to a sign that read "Far Tauverly Historical Society," with an arrow that pointed down a drive which disappeared into some trees. She walked on and saw the tower of St. Aethelrood's some distance ahead. The road curved on beyond it, into dense woods.

That must be the Greniston land, Gwen thought. *I'll just walk on a little further.*

As she walked along the road, Gwen thought she saw a movement in the trees on her left. No, perhaps it was only the breeze. More clouds were gathering, and a few raindrops spattered lightly down. Gwen shivered a little and walked on.

Suddenly, a small figure darted out from the trees and stood in the road, smiling at her. It was a little girl with long, tangled red hair and an elfin, mischievous face. She wore a faded blue shirt, many sizes too big for her, with a bright scarf as a belt. With her tanned, bramble-scratched legs and the twigs caught in her hair, the girl looked almost like a sprite from the fairy realms. She stood in Gwen's path as if she were the gatekeeper to the forest itself.

"Hello," said Gwen with a smile.

The girl smiled, too, but did not speak.

"My name's Gwen. What's yours?"

The child's gray eyes sparkled, but still she did not answer.

"Is this the way to Greniston Manor?"

The girl nodded but did not budge from the center of the road. Just then, a strange whistle broke the silence. Five notes, slow and deliberate. As if in response to a signal, the girl scampered down the road, gesturing for Gwen to follow her. More than ever, she looked like an elfin creature out of a fairy tale.

The road led deeper and deeper into the forest. Gwen had the sense of being watched from the trees. She wouldn't have been at all surprised to see Robin Hood and his Merry Men suddenly leap down onto the path.

The little girl stopped and pointed down the road. Gwen could just discern a pair of tall, iron gates. The girl pointed to them, making it clear that Gwen was to go on alone.

Gwen gazed into the child's clear, gray eyes. They seemed to sparkle with so much that was unspoken. Gwen remembered that in many myths the hero or heroine was helped by a guide, often an animal, old person, or child. Always, the hero had offered something in return for their help. Gwen felt that she, too, should offer this strange girl some payment. She reached into her purse, and her fingers closed upon a cameo brooch.

Oh dear, she thought. She had just bought the antique brooch a few days before, and it had set her back a few lunches. Against its background of Wedgewood blue were two figures, a man playing a harp and a lady listening. It was set in silver filigree.

For a moment, Gwen thought of giving the girl something cheaper, perhaps a lipstick. But it seemed to her that the gift of the brooch, like everything else that had happened to her lately, was fated.

Fair is fair, Gwen thought, as if abiding by the rules of some magical game. *It s what my fingers touched first.* She handed the brooch to the girl.

The child's face lit up with joy. Clearly, she had no way of knowing the brooch's monetary value, but just as clearly, she appreciated it merely for its beauty. She pinned it carefully onto her ragged shirt, looked at it with great satisfaction, and then, with a last smile for Gwen, darted off into the forest with a peel of bright, silvery laughter.

Gwen waited for a few moments, but the girl did not reappear. It began to rain in earnest. Gwen thought about turning back, but seeing the gates so close, she decided at least to take a look at them.

The sky seemed to have grown darker very quickly. As she approached the gates, Gwen had the strange feeling that she was walking into the landscape of her dream. There was the same half-light, the same drumming of rain and sighing of wind. And there were the ancient stone lions, just as she'd so often seen them, and the ornate iron gates. She peered through the bars at the dirt road that curved and disappeared into the trees beyond.

Without even thinking, Gwen raised her hand to open the gate, like someone who had done it many times. Suddenly she caught her breath. There was the figure, the figure from her dream. A man was coming down the path.

When he saw her, he stopped. Now she could see his face, as she hadn't been able to in the dream. It was a dark, rough-hewn face with a high forehead, hawk-like nose, stubborn chin, unkempt black hair, and shining dark eyes. Looking at him, Gwen had an impression of great intelligence and of power, held in reserve. His broad-shouldered form seemed to loom at her from the misty path with a kind of menace. Suddenly, the man spoke.

"Lady!" he cried in a booming voice, "What dost thou at the gate?" The lady did not reply, but for an instant, she returned his gaze. They seemed to look at each other for a long time with the same bold, penetrating look. And then, without speaking, she turned and disappeared into the gathering darkness.

CHAPTER FOUR

"How mysterious!" said Logan happily. "How romantic!" He and Gwen were strolling down the main street of Far Tauverly as Logan delivered the last of his mail. In the cheerful morning sunlight, the whole encounter seemed like a dream.

"That was him all right," Logan was saying. "No doubt about it. Lord Greniston himself! Excuse me," he added, "I just must pop into the greengrocer's here."

"I'll wait outside," Gwen replied. She settled comfortably onto a bench. She could hear Logan conversing with the shopkeeper and some customers: "Oh yes, the Cubbage's baby is doing well. Saw it myself just this morning. No, another girl. Lisette, they named it . . . that would be for his aunt, on the father's side, the one that went to Bristol and started a beauty parlor. . . . Yes, that's right. . . . Oh, and by the way, Mrs. Muckleridge, as long as you're here, here's a letter from your friend in Portsmouth, and the Vicar says to tell you the Lady's Guild meeting is postponed until Friday. He has to go into Porlock on Thursday. No, his teeth, you know. Yes, yes, it is a shame. . . . Deliver a message to the bakery? Absolutely, Miss Watson. Yes, three dozen. . . . Quite right, I'll make sure Tom gets it in person. . . . You say he's been seeing the Potter girl? Oh, really? Dance at the Grange Hall? Well, well, well. . . . Now, you know . . . "

On and on the voices went, the woman's a soft murmur and Logan's a high, cheerful chirping. *No wonder it takes him the whole morning to deliver ten letters,* Gwen thought, amused. She didn't mind. She felt quite content to sit on the bench and watch the life of the village. Across the way, Mrs. Hodges was scrubbing the windows of the Greenstone Inn. Somewhere out of sight, she heard the sound of a push mower, lazily crossing a lawn, while someone whistled a wandering tune. An Irish setter ambled across the street, intent upon its business. Three wrens disputed possession of a breadcrumb, and that was the most dramatic thing happening.

How clean and bright the colors are, Gwen thought, remembering the brown grime that covered her windows in Denver. Here, in the mild April sunlight, the daffodils and snowdrops gleamed like jewels.

"Lovely, isn't it?"

Gwen looked up, startled, at the man who had stopped by the bench. He looked down at her, smiling. The first impression she had was one

48

of fairness. Everything about him was light and smooth. He had the kind of effortless good looks it is hard not to stare at: feathery flaxen hair, brushed back from an elegant face. Only his lashes were dark, and that served the better to highlight his light, gray eyes. He wore a suit of the same pale gray as his eyes. Everything about him, from his long, thin hands to his silk tie, spoke of elegance. Yet his smile was easy, charming, even a bit shy. Somehow, before Gwen had even realized it was happening, he sat down on the bench beside her. Quite close, really. She noticed that he smelt, ever so faintly, of some expensive cologne. For some reason, her mind went back to the evening before, and the dark, rugged face of Lord Greniston, and she found herself comparing the two. She decided that she felt safer with this fair man, yet she found herself suddenly shy in his presence. She was acutely conscious of his gaze upon her.

"You must be Miss Fields," he said. "Mrs. Hodges told me we had an American visitor. Please allow me to introduce myself. I'm Geoffrey Swindon. I didn't mean to impose upon you, striking up a conversation like this, but I couldn't resist. It's so rare that we get a fresh face here."

Gwen looked up to smile at him then, and was startled by the intensity of his gaze. He was staring right at her, his gray eyes frank and level in their admiration. There was something quite wistful in their honesty. He made no effort to look away or speak but just sat there quietly, his head tilted to one side, resting on his thin, elegant hand as he stared at her.

Gwen felt herself blushing and was relieved to see Logan coming out of the greengrocer's at last. Did she imagine it, or did he take a step backwards when he saw Swindon sitting beside her?

"Logan," she said, "I've just run into Geoffrey Swindon - ."

"We've met," Logan said tersely. It was the first time Gwen had heard any trace of coldness in his voice.

"Logan and I have known each other for years," explained Swindon. "Indeed, I can't remember this town without him. Where would we be, without our bard?" The words were said kindly, but Logan ignored them.

"What brings you to town, Geoffrey?" he asked coolly.

"Business, business," sighed Swindon.

"Oh," said Logan, "the Walmsley property?"

For a moment, Swindon looked startled. Then he said smoothly, "No, another property. I'm here to meet the realtors who want to look at it. They'll be staying at Swindon house, you know."

"That's probably best," said Logan. "I doubt that Mrs. Hodges would have them."

"Oh, Logan," Swindon said impatiently. He turned to Gwen, saying, "I'm afraid, Miss Fields, that you've stumbled onto one of our local feuds. Some of us would like to see the land hereabouts developed so that all can share in its wealth. While others," Swindon raised his hands helplessly, "would not."

"Fortunately, that decision isn't up to you," muttered Logan. "Lord Greniston will never give you permission to set one foot on his land."

"We'll see," said Swindon. Although his voice was reasonable, there was an edge to it. "Lord Greniston," he added, for Gwen's benefit, "is our local squire. He claims that the land in question is his; it's on my estate, actually, they border one another. But Lord Greniston gets these ideas of his own. He's something of a recluse, so you probably won't get a glimpse of him while you're here, but – "

"On the contrary," interrupted Gwen, "we've met."

Swindon was frankly amazed. "You've met Greniston?"

"Yes, last night, when I was taking a walk through the woods. He was quite charming, actually," she added. Logan's jaw dropped. Actually, when Gwen remembered him, she wasn't sure that the word "charming" was the one that most applied, but she suddenly wanted to defend the rough-hewn Lord Greniston.

"Well, yes, he can be very charming," Swindon agreed. "When he's having one of his good spells, there's no one more delightful to be around. That's what makes the other times so hard to witness." He shook his head. "What a pity," he added, evidently to himself. "What a waste. But then, Miss Fields, forgive me. You surely didn't come all the way to Far Tauverly to hear about our sorrows! Will you allow me to redeem myself by giving you a tour of the countryside? Please say yes; humor me. I'll pick you up here at, say, eleven tomorrow? We can stop somewhere for lunch on our rambles. That's my car, across the square, the gray one." Swindon waved in an offhand manner toward the silver Jaguar parked outside the inn. "So we're agreed," he continued, before Gwen had a chance to respond. "I'll pick you up at eleven tomorrow."

"Why, yes," Gwen heard herself saying. "I would like that very much."

"Splendid!" Swindon said. For a moment, he looked genuinely delighted; then his attention shifted to his car. Perhaps he was late for an appointment.

Gwen felt an odd misgiving. *I really don t know anything about him. But 1 m sure it will be all right.* The itinerary she had planned for Mrs. Gordon had her leaving the next morning at six, but she had already been assured by Mrs. Hodges that her room would be available for several weeks, should she choose to extend her stay. It looked like she was going to, at least by a day.

She noticed, looking over Swindon's shoulder, a movement near his car. Just for an instant, an elfin face, framed by long, unruly red hair, peered over the hood, then disappeared. Gwen recognized the little girl she had met the night before on the road through the woods. She noticed that Logan saw her too. Unseen by Swindon, Logan caught Gwen's eye and raised a finger to his lips. As the church bell tolled half-past nine, a black limousine appeared at the far end of the street.

"Ah, that must be the realtors," said Swindon. "Right on time. Well, good-bye Logan. Miss Fields, until tomorrow!" They watched Swindon walk up to the limousine.

Gwen's attention was drawn back to Swindon's car. She heard a strange snuffling sound, which was quickly covered by what sounded like one boy, then others, doing a loud and spirited imitation of an Indian war cry. The far door of Swindon's car opened.

"Logan, what is going on over there?" she asked.

"Wait a minute," Logan whispered, a gleam in his eye.

By this time, two well-dressed men had emerged from the limo and were following Swindon to his car. Gwen thought that they looked more like her idea of Scotland Yard: quiet, watchful, and too deliberately nondescript. At the same time, Gwen noticed the red-haired girl and three boys darting into the nearby bushes.

Smiling, Swindon opened the door on the passenger side. But suddenly, he yelled and leapt back, bumping into the realtors. Out of the car tumbled a mother pig and a brood of piglets. The air was instantly filled with squealing as the animals ran frantically in circles around the men's feet.

From the bushes came the sound of children's voices. The red-haired girl and three ragged-looking boys peered around the bushes. Swindon tried to continue smiling, but his face was flushed with embarrassment, or perhaps anger.

"Swindon's a swine!" the boys chanted, "Swindon's a swine!"

Swindon spun around and lunged toward the sound, only to trip over a pig. By the time he caught his balance, the children, shrieking with laughter, had disappeared down an alley.

Logan, a smile of satisfaction on his face, moved on. Gwen, too, found herself smiling inspite of herself. "You knew they were up to something," she said. "Why didn't you say anything?"

Logan shrugged. "Why did you say Lord Greniston was charming, when you told me that he looked a bit dark and startling?"

"I'm not sure," Gwen admitted. Logan walked on, humming a little tune, and slipped two letters through a brass mail slot.

"You don't like Swindon, do you?" Gwen asked.

"Nope," said Logan, shortly.

"He seems quite nice to me," she protested.

"Hmmm," said Logan.

"Well, what have you got against him?" she asked, genuinely curious.

Logan murmured, "'Beware of the smooth and polished; it deceives the searching eye. The Gods love trouble, and in the rough does virtue lie.'"

"So, you think Swindon's smooth," Gwen mused.

Logan snorted. "Don't think, know! Why, just look at those 'realtors!' Since when do realtors arrive in fancy limousines? And they just didn't look right."

Inspite of her wish to give Geoff Swindon the benefit of the doubt, Gwen had to admit that she agreed with Logan.

"Mark my words," Logan continued, "No good will come of it."

After this pronouncement, Gwen glanced at Logan and noticed his mouth was set in a prim line. Not wanting to put a damper on their day together, Gwen decided to change the subject.

"I'm glad we've got such a glorious morning for our outing," she said. "I can't wait to get started."

Logan brightened immediately. "Yes, it's a rare day in April when the sunshine lasts! And we could get an even earlier start if you could help me with the mail. If you wouldn't mind that is?"

"Of course not!" said Gwen. "But would it be allowed?"

Logan laughed. "As Her Majesty's sole postal representative in this village, I do hereby proclaim thy gracious assistance absolutely allowable."

"Well, when you put it that way . . . "

"Wonderful! Here's three letters for you, and all easy to find. I'll take the rest and meet you back here in half an hour. Here's one for Florence Shelby; that's her house right there. Another for the Asterbys; they're on the far side of her. And the last is for Lettice Pennington, one of the Pennington sisters that run the museum. You might want to stop in and see the chalice while you're there. And, of course, they have Lord Peter's prophecy, and framed very nicely, too."

"Then I shall certainly start with the museum," said Gwen, "for I must consider the clues in this mystery we plan to solve. Remember: 'Lighthearted and Bold!'"

Logan looked quite pleased that she had remembered their pact. "Lighthearted and bold!" he replied. "And a bit light-footed as well, would come in handy just now. I'll meet you back here as soon as can be," he added in a whisper, "and we'll be on our way to the mound!"

"Far Tauverly Historical Society—This Way," the hand painted sign proclaimed. Gwen followed the arrow pointing down a tree-lined drive. Half-hidden by a tangle of beeches, apple trees, and rhododendrons was an elegant, if run-down, Georgian house. Its stone walls were covered with ivy. The drapery of rippling green and the surrounding froth of budding branches gave the house the quality of an elderly lady who does her best to soften the ravages of age with artful layers of scarves and lace. Gwen felt an instant liking for the old place. Most of it seemed to be in use as a private home, but one wing had a smartly painted red door and a sign that said, "Hours: Monday, Wednesday, Thursday, 9-3. Please knock firmly."

Gwen headed for that door, cautiously picking her way along a path of crumbling bricks that obviously was not used very often.

"It's Miss Fields!" Wyatt Walmsley sputtered excitedly. "She is heading twoad the museum wight now!" He was peering through the kitchen windows of the Georgian House, reporting Gwen's movements to his siblings and to the elderly Pennington sisters, Lettice and Althea.

The Walmsley children had come rushing into the sisters' kitchen only moments before, obviously fresh from some escapade. "I'd rather not know what you've all been up to," Althea had said. "You'd better just sit

53

down and have some scones." Now, the arrival of both the children and an American tourist in one morning was proving almost too much for Lettice.

"Oh dear," she sighed, "I'm sure she wants to see the chalice, too! It's too much, first that man yesterday, now this. All this sudden interest in it!"

"Now, now, Lettie," her sister replied, "it's nice that people are finally taking an interest in our local heritage."

"But most of them aren't local people," Lettice complained, in a quavering voice. "Realtors from London, and scientists—or so they said—and some very strange types indeed! I'm sure that little man yesterday was something very foreign; his skin was quite golden! And now this American girl. Woman. Whatever she is."

"Miss Fields is all right," Osgood said staunchly. "She is Logan's friend."

"Wogan says she is a 'Damsel of Honor Most Fair, the Wady of the Shining Fields,'" Wyatt exclaimed. Unlike his brothers and sisters, who were all redheaded, seven-year-old Wyatt had hair as pale and finely curled as the fluff on a dandelion. When he was excited, as he was now, his hair seemed to stand out from his head even more than usual. "Wogan says she is superwative," he added.

"Logan, Logan!" Rutherford Walmsley chanted happily. He was only two. He sat on his sister Claire's lap, feeding scones to the Pennington sisters' calico cat, Banshee.

"She hath weached the museum door," Wyatt reported, peering eagerly through the lace curtains.

"You really shouldn't be spying on her dear," Lettice said gently. "It's not polite."

"It's not spying," Osborne, Osgood's twin, pointed out. "It's observing. After all, we are the true guardians of the chalice. It was found in our kingdom. All visitors to it concern us."

"Yes!" Wyatt chimed in enthusiastically. "We are the 'Watchers and Pwotectors of the Independent Kingdom of Gweenstone!' We – "

His sister Claire looked up from beneath her tangle of long red hair. She did not speak but ever so slightly shook her head, as if in gentle warning. Wyatt instantly fell silent.

"I'm sure I don't know what you children are talking about half the time," Althea Pennington sighed. "Not that it isn't always pleasant to see you, of course. But surely you are late to school already?"

Osgood shrugged. "Charles is there," he said, implying that even one Walmsley representative was more than the school deserved—or perhaps could handle.

"Nevertheless, I think you really should go, too, my dears. So hurry up then, and finish your scones. We'll see you later, perhaps."

"Yes," Lettice agreed. "We're having buttered toast at tea-time." In the distance could be heard a firm, persistent knocking.

"It's Miss Fields," reported Wyatt, still at his post at the window. "She ith still knocking. The Damsel doth not abandon the siege."

"Oh dear," exclaimed Lettice, truly rattled now. "Has she been out there all this time? I'd rather hoped she'd just slip away. Now I suppose we really must let her in, and there's the table to clear, and I did so want to watch the gardening program at ten! 'How to Set in Your Begonias for Perfect Results,' it's to be this time. The Vicar told me about it, although, of course, begonias are not his main passion."

"Don't worry, Lettice," said Althea soothingly. "I'll deal with Miss Fields, and I'll clear the table later. You just get the children off to school, and go watch your program."

Gwen was just about to walk away, when the bright red door opened at last. She found herself eye to eye with a prim, sharp-eyed old lady, who smelled fiercely of lavender water and Pears soap.

"Yes?" the old lady asked crisply.

"I'm sorry to bother you, but Logan Knowelles asked me to deliver your mail."

"Oh he did, did he?" the old lady sniffed. "He seems to have more helpers than a fox has fleas! Not that that's your problem," she added, softening a little. "I'm sure it's very nice of you to be willing to help. Ah, I see Lettice's horticulture magazine has come. She will be pleased. Well, thank you very much." Althea seemed about to close the door.

"There's one other thing," Gwen said quickly. "I wonder if I might come in to see the chalice."

Althea sighed, but she opened the door wider and nodded.

"This way dear," she said, as she led Gwen into a large, dimly lit room. Gwen reflected that everything about this Miss Pennington seemed ready to crackle, from her well-starched white blouse to her faded but clean taffeta apron. Even her iron-gray hair grew in tiny, crimped waves, and it seemed that if she had loosened it from the tiny, tight bun she wore it in and drawn a comb through it, sparks would surely have flown and snapped.

"It's in this case here," Althea said. "I'll just go turn on the lights."

A moment later, an ancient overhead fixture flickered into uncertain life. Gwen found herself standing amidst the most unusual collection of old things imaginable. In one corner stood a dusty suit of armor, missing one glove. In another was a jumbled shape marked "Hand loom, 1593." There were glass cases filled with arrowheads, flints, and bits of old embroidery. Along one wall was a collection of pressed flowers. The label read, "Flowers of France and Belgium. Gathered by Lt. Jonathan Asterby, 5ᵗʰ Company, Her Majesty's Lancers. Died in action at Flanders Field, aged 24. Kindly donated by his brother, Wilfred Asterby, of Far Tauverly."

Poor Jonathan, Gwen thought. *His flowers made it home, but he did not.* She wondered what he had been like, that young man of many springs ago, who had wished to preserve forever the passing beauties of eglantine, violet, trefoil, and love-in-a-mist.

She felt that she could have happily spent hours exploring the museum's contents, but she was keenly aware of Althea in the background, polite but definitely waiting for her to be finished. She turned her attention to the chalice.

At first, it seemed a disappointment. It was about the size of a small cereal bowl, with a squat, sturdy neck. The metal it was made of did not look like silver nor even pewter. It was a dull, battered gray that looked durable, if nothing else. This chalice seemed more like something to hold a horse's oats than to be the mystic grail of legend. Gwen almost turned away after just a cursory glance.

Then some trick of the light caught her eye. Now, the inside of the chalice seemed to suddenly gleam like candle flame. The radiant metal it was made of shone, now white-silver, now white-gold. Around the inner edge of the cup was a thick, filigreed border, in a design of interlacing vines and Celtic knots. Gwen saw that within the floral design were worked tiny glimpses of life: three hunters pursuing a stag, a maiden playing a flute, a farmer at his plow, a King riding forth on his horse, a peasant sleeping beneath a willow tree, and a child leaning over a stream. All of life seemed portrayed there. The images were so small and so finely wrought in silver and gold that it was hard to believe that human hands had made them. Here and there, amidst the interlacing design, were set tiny gems of every color—pink, apple green, deep blue, amber-orange, yellow-gold, sea-green, crystal-clear amethyst—all as tiny and gleaming as chips of colored snowflakes. There was one setting, larger than the others, that was empty; perhaps that was where the emerald needed to be replaced.

"This is amazing," Gwen said. Althea smiled, evidently well accustomed to the effect the chalice had on newcomers.

"Take a step forward," she suggested. Gwen stepped forward. The sunshine from the windows poured into the chalice like a wine. The pale metal within it gleamed as though the cup were filled to overflowing with light itself. The tiny figures around the border now seemed to float upon a surface of light, and the tiny gems danced like colored raindrops.

"Who would have thought . . . "

"That something so plain could hold such beauty within it? Who indeed," said Althea quietly.

"And this came from right here in Far Tauverly?" Gwen marveled.

"Yes. From Arthur's Mound, on the Greniston land."

"Logan told me there is a prophecy, a sort of poem about the Grenistons."

"Ah. That would be Lord Peter's poem. Over here," said Althea. She led Gwen to the south wall, where a framed piece of parchment occupied the place of honor, next to an oil painting of a rakish young man in a Cavalier's outfit.

"That is Lord Peter Greniston," Althea said. She spoke fondly, as if the young man in the portrait was a favorite nephew of hers, instead of someone who had been dead and buried for several hundred years.

Gwen decided that the picture looked a little bit like the Lord Greniston she had glimpsed the night before. This man was finer boned, though, and his long, curling hair was chestnut, not black. His dark eyes sparkled with life, as if he had just heard someone make a jest, or a challenge, and his smiling lips were open, as if he was about to reply. He wore a blue hat with a magnificent white plume and a cape of emerald green trimmed with gold and silver brocade. His right hand rested fondly on the head of a spaniel, while his left held high a wine glass full of burgundy, in an eternal toast.

"Light-hearted and bold," Gwen murmured, remembering her own toast with Logan.

"Well, he was both those things," said Althea. "And very brave as well. He fought to uphold Bonny Prince Charley, of course. The Grenistons were all Cavaliers."

Gwen leaned forward to read the poem:

"When the ftranger findf; no, wait. Those are Ss, aren't they that look like Fs?"

"It's hard to decipher the old script, if you're not used to it," said Althea. "Let me help." In a clear, firm voice, she began to read:

"'LORD PETER'S PROPHECY
  When the stranger comes to the lion's gate
  And woods with Merlin's cry resound
  When Knobbly Hill doth tremble and shake
  Then must the treasure swiftly be found
  A throne, a crown, a speaking sword
  A golden lady, a silver lord
  Twelve true jewels to shine and meet
  Where gold springs from the ground

  Then Arthur from ancient sleep shall wake
  Deep in the greenstone mound
  And rise to battle for England's sake
  Summoned by a grail found
  Encircled by gold
  This is the time-
  Light set free for all mankind

  Yet, if no jewels be gathered there
  This have I seen in waking dream:
  Brightest light turns darkest night
  Nor leaf, nor creature, nor human face
  In this nor any other place –
  World's despair.'"

"No one's ever quite been able to make out what it all means," Althea added when she finished.

Gwen studied Lord Peter's face. "Yet he doesn't look like the kind of young man who would want to mislead people," she mused.

"Certainly not. He took his stand and made it known, whatever the cost. The Grenistons have always been like that."

"So he wanted his poem to be understood. By those who wanted to try."

"I suppose he did," Althea acknowledged. "I never thought about it that way, but it makes sense. We have some copies of the poem in modern script," she added, "if you would like to take one." Althea picked up a piece of paper from a pile near the chalice.

"Yes, I would, very much," said Gwen. Althea gave her a copy, and then moved toward the door. Somewhere in the far distance, Gwen heard a television: a sprightly bit of theme music, and then a man's voice saying, "Of all the annuals which can grace your borders or beds, begonias love moisture the most." She sensed that it was time for her to leave. She gave a last, backward glance at the dashing young Lord Peter. His bright, glad eyes gazed at her across the centuries. A ray of sunlight danced upon his wineglass and made it gleam, crystal and ruby.

Lighthearted and bold, she thought with a smile.

***

"Once upon a time there was a King. And one day it came into his mind to go a-hunting. Off to the wild he did ride, with hunters and hounds all at his side. There they saw a pure white stag, with antlers full five-foot span. 'Give chase!' the King did cry. And so they did, and so they did, unto a man. Over hill and dale the swift stag ran. So far and so fast did it run that one by one the hunters dropped away; even the hounds gave up the chase, and stood panting as they swayed. Then only the King rode on. Onward the white stag led him, onward. Into a deep forest, it did bound, and the King rode in right after it. The stag's hooves upon the earth did make no sound; it scarcely seemed to touch the ground. Onward the King rode, into the green wood's heart. And there, for all his skill and all his art, he lost sight of the pure white stag. All alone he found himself to be encircled by the forest's living tapestry; the watching shadows, and the looming trees. On he rode, and lost was he. He began to hear, far-off, a strange and lovely music, such as fairy-folk do make. Then the King was sore afraid, knowing his own mistake. Into the fairy realms had he wandered, and they are hard to please. Even as he wondered if they would find him, he saw tiny lights flicker amongst the trees.

'Here I am no royalty,' he thought, 'only a mortal man.' And from that telling moment, his adventures all began. . . ."

Logan paused in his tale. He and Gwen had reached the stone wall that marked the border to the Greniston land. They stood upon the sun-dappled road and looked at the interlacing branches that rose, enticingly, above the barrier.

"This is a good place to enter," Logan said. "More private than marching through the main gates. I thought it might be more fun, you see, to keep our outing to ourselves."

"Whatever you say," said Gwen. "You be the white stag and lead me into the magic realms. I do but follow, in your spell."

"Right, then!" Agile enough, despite his silver hair, Logan scrambled onto the wall and reached back to help Gwen.

"Just put your foot on that fallen branch there, it's steady. That's right. Then hop down onto this patch of moss, and there you are."

A moment later, Gwen found herself in another world. This was forest as she had never seen it: a forest that for hundreds, perhaps thousands of years, had been left to itself. Some of the trees were enormous—oaks whose trunks were ten feet around and whose mighty branches formed cathedral vaults, pierced by shafts of soft, golden light. In other places, the light was filtered through a moving, stirring froth of budding leaves, so that the air itself seemed green and gold. Far below, on the forest floor, was a living tapestry of bush and vine and wildflower, a miniature forest within the forest, which seemed to hold within itself world upon world, more intricate than the finest lace imaginable. And upon it all lay the touch of a profound stillness.

"This way," said Logan, whose voice had naturally shifted to a whisper. "There's a path over here."

The trail Logan had found led them deeper and deeper into the Greniston land. Sometimes the dense trees gave way to clearings where they could glimpse the high, blue vault of the spring sky. Then the path led on, and a few minutes later, they would find themselves in a pine grove, listening to the sighing of the wind through the fresh green needles. Once, they came upon a hidden meadow, through which a willow-lined stream meandered. Climbing a small hill, they saw Greniston Manor in the distance, surrounded by open lawns. They gazed at it in silence, then turned away, back into the woods.

Now and again, they came upon some touch of humans in the forest. Gwen saw the remnants of stone paths and, once, a small pavilion covered by old vines that she was sure would bear roses in a few weeks time. Yet everywhere, the forest was in the process of recovering its own. Whoever Lord Greniston was, he certainly preferred to be surrounded by wilderness, Gwen realized. The only life they saw was that of the woods. They heard the piercing sweetness of a lark's song in the distance, glimpsed a rabbit scuttle into its burrow. All about them the forest went on about its vast, various, wordless business, as it had for thousands of years.

And yet, Gwen felt the woods were not unaware of their passing. Every step of the way, she had the sense of being watched. And she had the strange feeling that somewhere, far-off in the forest's heart, something long asleep now stirred, wakened by their footfalls. Oddest of all, perhaps, she had the sense that this was not the first time she and Logan had found their way through these woods, although she knew it had to be.

I have been here before, she thought. *The woods were younger then, yet I remember.*

The sunlight sparkled on a beech tree, a squirrel chattered. She stopped to look around, delighted at a glimpse of flame-blue bluebells in the distance.

"This is like being in the heart of a jewel," she said, gazing up to where a tracery of branches met high overhead. The green of the leaves shone like glittering emeralds.

"Aye, that it is," said Logan, softly.

Just then, a low whistle broke the quiet. It sounded quite near-by and to the left.

"What was that?" Gwen exclaimed.

For a moment, Logan looked startled, too. Then he smiled. "Must be elves." Gwen could not quite tell if he was joking or not.

"There's a little clearing up here I thought would be a perfect place to take a rest."

"And it's high time for our picnic," he added.

"Maybe it is elves watching us," Gwen said, following him. "If ever there was a place where magic could be true, it would be these woods."

Logan looked back at her. He cocked his head to one side like a bright, curious bird, and said,

"Ah well, truth to tell is easy to say,

61

But truth may lead us far on a day,
For who's to say what's not, what's so,
Save those who on truth's search do go?"

Gwen laughed, delighted at the spontaneous rhyme. She didn't think she would be able to answer in kind, but to her surprise words seemed to spring to her lips of their own accord:
"You speak in riddles, gentle guide,
Yet I seek wisdom at your side.
If you would make your meaning plain,
Then pray thee, speak thy rhymes again."

Logan plucked a long blade of grass, and waved it in time to his words as he replied:

"To see some magic is thy wish –
Well, little rhymes may catch big fish.
Now you may find this jester's wit
Is but the babbling of a twit.
That may be as that may be,
But here's a truth for you to see:
The place that lies most far away
Is the one we live in everyday;
No magic is so rare to find
As that which lies most close to mind."

Gwen gazed at Logan's smiling face, and for an instant she had again the sense that they had been in this place together before; that she had known him a long, long time; and that the rhyming was an old, old game between them, laid aside for a little while, and now effortlessly resumed. She felt great warmth for him as she said:

"Wisest of fools, my jester true,
Ever I learn much from you.
Now, old friend, let's be on our way,
To find adventure on this spring—"

62

Suddenly she stopped.

"Did you hear that?" she whispered.

"Hear what?" said Logan, rather nervously.

"It sounded like horse's hooves and the jingle of a bridle. Just beyond those trees."

They waited, holding their breath, but no further sound broke the quiet.

"Must have been those elves," Logan said with a relieved grin. "Maybe they're hungry, and want us to give them some picnic crumbs. Come on, the clearing's just ahead."

After the huge breakfast she had at the inn, Gwen would never have believed she could be so hungry for lunch, but the fresh air and the hike had whetted her appetite. The makeshift feast of kippers, oranges, cheese, and crackers that Logan spread out looked princely to her. She added a Cadbury's Fruit and Nut bar as her contribution, and they fell to. For several minutes, the only sounds were of contented munching. Only after they had finished their repast, being careful to leave several choice morsels for elves and magpies, and sat leaning against a fallen tree, passing back and forth a bottle of Whitby's Ale that Logan had magically produced from his knapsack, did Gwen ask, "What's Knobby Hill?"

"Knobby Hill? Oh, just a hill hereabouts," replied Logan dreamily, "Where did you hear about it?"

"It's in Lord Peter's prophecy," Gwen explained.

"Ah, so you did get inside the museum."

"Yes, indeed. What's more, Miss Pennington gave me a copy of the poem. I brought it with." Gwen fished the poem out of her pocket. As she did so, something bright and golden fell upon the grass.

"What's this?" asked Logan. He leaned forward, and picked the object up. "A button," he said. "Looks old-fashioned. And not just brass, either, by the look of it. Where'd you get it?"

"Nowhere," said Gwen, puzzled. "I mean, it wasn't in my pocket before."

"It's got a daffodil on it, engraved in the gold," Logan said. He frowned. "Funny, but I'm sure I've seen this somewhere before, though I can't think where." He handed it back to Gwen. "Perhaps you picked it up in the museum somehow."

"Yes," she said doubtfully, putting it back in her pocket. "Well, anyway, now for the poem." She began to read:

"When the stranger comes to the lion's gate
And woods with Merlin's cry resound
When Knobbly Hill doth tremble and shake
Then must the treasure swiftly be found
A throne, a crown, a speaking sword
A golden lady, a silver lord
Twelve true jewels to shine and meet
Where gold springs from the ground
Then Arthur from ancient sleep shall wake
Deep in the greenstone mound . . . "

Gwen looked up. "Wait a minute, Logan, I just realized something! This prophecy, it's happening now."

"What do you mean?"

"Well, I'm a stranger, and I found the Lion's Gate."

"True," said Logan, reluctantly playing the devil's advocate. "But many visitors have come to that gate in the last four hundred years. And I haven't heard anything about Knobby Hill trembling. Nor has Merlin's cry been heard."

"But it has," said Gwen. "I've heard it."

Logan sat bolt upright now. "What do you mean?"

As briefly as she could, Gwen explained the haunting cry she had heard when she began to plan her trip, the cry that Filipo had suggested might be the cry of Merlin. When she finished, Logan looked very thoughtful.

"Strange, passing strange," he murmured.

"Do you believe in . . . ," Gwen paused, not quite sure how to put her question.

"In prophecies and legends?" Logan finished for her. "Indeed, I do. Mind you," he added rather wistfully, "nothing too supernatural has ever happened to me. Just a sense of things out of the corner of me eye sometimes and the presence of the past. But I believe all kinds of things are possible. And it's odd, you know, these last few nights . . . "

"What?" Gwen prompted.

"I've had strange dreams," Logan said. "Not bad ones at all, but strange. When I wake up, I can't quite remember them. But I have the oddest sense of . . ."

"Of having been in another time?"

Logan looked at her. "Exactly."

"And when you wake up, do you feel there's something very important that you are supposed to do, only you can't quite remember what it is?" Logan nodded.

"Those are just the kind of dreams I've been having, ever since I started to plan this trip," Gwen said.

The two friends looked at each other. It had grown very still in the forest, and the sun had gone behind the clouds. Gwen shivered.

"We'd best be on our way, if we want to see the mounds before it rains," Logan said, getting up.

"Do you still want to keep our pact to figure out the prophecy, now that it seems to have gotten a bit more real?" Gwen asked, half-jokingly.

Logan met her gaze. His dark blue eyes were serious. "Absolutely," he said quietly. "More than ever."

They walked on a few steps. To their right, Gwen heard the same strange, low whistle she had heard when they first entered the woods.

"I heard it, too," Logan whispered.

They stopped in their tracks and listened. The whistle did not repeat itself, but through the branches of an apple tree, they glimpsed two figures approaching, some distance away.

"It wasn't them who whistled," Gwen whispered. "It came from somewhere much closer. But look, it's those two realtors; the ones that Swindon met this morning!"

"Realtors, my foot," sniffed Logan. "If they were proper realtors, they'd have come through the main gate. But they're sneaking around like, like trespassers!"

"And they're on their own," Gwen pointed out. "If they had made an appointment, surely Lord Greniston would have let you know, since you're his Steward."

"Ah, yes, of course," Logan replied. "But I'm sure Lord Greniston doesn't know they're here. Swindon probably told his usual lie and said this was his land."

"Oh no," Gwen gasped. "This can't be the land he wants to develop! Not this forest!"

"Indeed it is," Logan said. Then he raised a warning finger to his lips. The two men were quite close now.

"The most concentrated deposits should be beneath the stream that lies to the east of the larger mound," one of them said. "It's got to be right around here somewhere."

"Deposits," Gwen whispered. "That sounds like mining . . . "

Again, Logan raised his finger to his lips.

"It looks an isolated spot," the other man was saying. "It should be easy enough to arrange a time to take some samples."

"Samples! This is outrageous," muttered Logan. "I'm going to get them out of here! Order them off the property!" He started to push through the branches by which he and Gwen were screened. Then he paused. "I've got a better idea," he said. "I'll get them out of here and find out what they're up to! Do you think you could find your way back to the village alone?" Gwen looked doubtfully at the dense woods behind them.

"Not that way," Logan said. "We're quite close to the gates now. All you have to do is cross Arthur's Mound, which lies ahead. Go on through the oak grove, and you'll come to the main drive. Just turn right on that, go about half a mile, and you'll find yourself at the lion's gate, and then there's the road to Far Tauverly."

"That sounds simple enough."

Logan beamed. "I'm sorry to interrupt our expedition like this, but this is important. We need to find out what these louts are up to!"

"Oh, absolutely," Gwen agreed. "All part of the same mystery."

"Right. Well, here's my plan. You stay hidden here. They look like rough characters, and I don't even want them to know you're here. So wait 'til I've lured them away, and then, very slowly, start back. We can meet tonight at the inn, and I'll let you know what I've found out. But later, so they don't connect you with this place in any way."

Gwen smiled at the intrigue, which seemed so natural to Logan's mind. "You must have been a spy in another lifetime," she whispered.

"Perhaps I was. Now, just remember, stay out of sight 'til we're well away."

With that, Logan plunged out of the underbrush, yelling, "Oy, you two! Poaching is illegal, you know!"

"We're not poaching," the first man said.

Logan laughed. "That's what they all say! Let me see what's in that rucksack! Pheasant, I don't doubt!"

"This is ridiculous!" The other man protested. "We're realtors, from an agency in Bristol! We've come to look over this land."

"Realtors! Hah! In a pig's tiny eye, you're realtors! Trespassers, that's what you are! Trespassers on the Greniston land, and I am the Steward of that land, and I'm telling you to get off it!"

At the mention of the name "Greniston," the two men exchanged a look. The first one spoke in a more conciliatory tone. "Perhaps we inadvertently strayed over a boundary," he said smoothly, "but we meant no harm. Surely, you'll allow us to complete our little survey. We need to look over patterns of water drainage, you understand, and things like that don't recognize man-made boundaries."

"Fine with me," snapped Logan. "I shall just walk back to the house and let the dogs out. You can debate the issue with Lord Greniston's pack of attack-trained wolfhounds."

Wolfhounds? Gwen thought nervously from her hiding place. She sincerely hoped the dogs were an invention on Logan's part.

"I've half a mind to call the police," Logan added. "Let them sort you out."

A quick look passed between the two men. *They definitely don't want the police called in,* Gwen realized.

"It's clear there's been a misunderstanding and that we are in error," the second man said graciously. "We really do apologize. If you can show us the quickest way out of here, we'll be on our way."

"I'll do better than that," said Logan sharply. "I'll bloody well escort you all the way back to the village. I want to be sure you lot are well out of here. And so would you want to be, if you knew what's good for you. Clouding over, it is, and twilight will come early. The Greniston Mounds are no place to be after nightfall," he added darkly.

The men looked amused rather than intimidated. They exchanged a glance that seemed to say, "Better humor the old fellow."

"Lead the way," the first one said.

"Of course," Logan continued in an aggrieved tone as he led them through the trees, "as long as I'm going all the way to town, I'll probably stop at the inn and have a pint. Must do something to make this bloody inconvenient trip worth my while."

He spoke the words with such heavy significance that the men could scarcely ignore it.

"Then you must let the pint be on us," one of them said. "And a bite of early supper, too."

"Well . . . ," Logan hesitated as long as he could. "I suppose that's only fair."

Their voices faded as they disappeared into the forest. True to Logan's instructions, Gwen remained in her hiding place for several minutes, even though a light rain had begun to fall, and the sky was growing darker by the moment. Now she understood what Shakespeare had meant by "the uncertain glory of an April day."

She knew that Logan's intent was to loosen the men's tongues with ale and find out what they were up to—and get a free pint or two in the bargain! She had to agree with his suspicion that they weren't realtors, but she also suspected it would take more than a pint of local brew to make them drop their guard. Still, Logan seemed pretty sharp himself, and he might well ferret out a clue or two.

By now, the drizzle of rain had turned into a definite shower, and a cold one at that. A keen little wind circled the woods. Gwen's damp scarf felt plastered against her cheek, and the raincoat that had felt almost too bulky earlier now felt surprisingly flimsy.

Time to go, she decided. *I'm sure I've waited long enough.*

She clambered out of the underbrush and back to the trail that led to the mounds. It wasn't a path here but really more of a faint trace that wandered between the trees. She had to concentrate to follow it and to avoid slipping on the patches of mud and dead leaves. Perhaps that was why she didn't realize how close she was getting to the mounds, until she was almost on top of them.

It was the stillness that alerted her. One moment she was trudging down the track, her wet shoes scrunching and squeaking at every step. The next moment, she stopped, as if someone had gently cautioned "Shhh," but there was no one there.

Looking up, she saw that she was at the very edge of the clearing where the larger mound lay. The clearing was oval, about sixty feet long and forty feet wide. It was surrounded by tall oak trees. Very old, those trees must have been, to have grown so high. Their rain-blackened trunks were twisted and shaped by countless seasons. High above, their branches met in a delicate tracery of twigs and new leaves that made a tent over the mound, softening the drumming of the rain.

Gwen stepped through the ring of trees, into the clearing. The ground was covered with a carpet of last year's leaves, worn to a shade of soft, gleaming russet, almost purple in places.

As if they had been stained with wine, Gwen thought. At the center of the clearing was the mound itself, a swelling of earth perhaps thirty feet long and ten feet wide. The wine-colored leaves lay upon it like a royal mantle.

All around the clearing, just at the edge of the trees, was a ring of daffodils. They had been planted deliberately, Gwen realized, although that might have been long ago, for they had gone a bit wild now, straggling here and there into the clearing or out into the rich tangle of surrounding forest. Originally, though, she realized, they must have been planted to trace not the oval outline of the clearing but the shape of a circle within it.

That s strange, Gwen thought, *that someone would do that in so wild a spot.*

She moved to the center of the clearing, cautiously stepping onto the mound itself. At the far end of the mound, there grew a solitary oak that stood apart from those that ringed it. The tree's great, heavy branches hung to the ground in many places, as if weighed down by the weight of centuries. Old, old, older than old the tree seemed. Gwen had read that oaks could live to be five hundred years old or more, and looking at this one, she believed it. Yet from its ancient branches sprung a froth of tender green leaves as fresh as spring itself. They looked like a new garland on an old wise man's head.

"Merlin's Oak," Gwen whispered.

As if in reply, a small, sweet breeze stirred for a moment around the glen. Then the stillness returned. In the quiet, Gwen heard a faint trickling of water.

There must be a spring nearby, she realized. *Of course, it s Merlin s Spring. Logan mentioned it.*

The quiet and the sense of being protected by the great circle of trees was peaceful and comforting. *I shall call this The Chapel of the Wood*, Gwen thought.

Despite her damp hair and chilled feet, there was something so lovely about the place that Gwen felt reluctant to leave it. The quiet was not just an absence of noise but a presence in itself—the presence of something very old and faithful.

Perhaps it is Arthur, she thought. *Perhaps this really is his mound, and he lies beneath it, not dead, but merely sleeping, to reawaken at England's hour of greatest need, just as the old stories say.* Even if it wasn't literally true, the mystery of the story seemed totally real in this most special place.

Appealing as the thought was, the early darkness Logan had predicted was beginning to gather between the trees. If she waited much longer, she realized, she might not be able to find her way out of the forest.

Logan said to head straight across the clearing, through the oaks, and the drive would be right there, she reminded herself.

She headed through the trees in what she thought was the right direction and soon found herself stopped by an impenetrable tangle of holly bushes. She returned to the mound.

Perhaps I've gotten turned around somehow, she thought. *But no. Merlin's Oak was to the right when I came, and there it is. . . . Perhaps the path is further this way. . . .*

She headed into the woods again, and again found herself stopped, this time by a hedge of wild rose vines. Once again, she returned to the mound.

"Now, this is very strange," she said aloud. She was beginning to feel like the king in Logan's story, who pursued the white stag into the woods and found himself lost in the fairy realms.

And I never did find out what happened to him, Gwen realized. *Logan didn't finish the story.*

"Not that I'm scared," she added, speaking aloud again, as if to reassure herself that she, at least, was real enough. "But this feels so strange, as if the place itself is keeping me here. Elves, if you are there, would you tell me if that's true? What does the place want of me? That's what I'd like to know!"

"And what I'd like to know," a deep voice boomed, "is what the devil you are doing on my land again?"

CHAPTER FIVE

Gwen spun around, and found herself face to face with the Lord of Greniston manor. From the scowl on his face, he looked to be in no pleasant mood.

"Oh dear," Gwen blurted out, "it's you again."

"'Dear' was not the word I had in mind," Lord Greniston replied. "Tell me, is trespassing a profession with you, or just a holiday passion?"

"I'm not trespassing," Gwen replied, trying to muster some dignity. "Logan, your Steward, brought me here."

"Logan, my . . . *Steward?*" Lord Greniston asked, incredulous, yet seeming to savor the moment.

"Yes. I assumed he had cleared my visit with you. He said there was no problem."

"I see," muttered Greniston. "And just where is my loyal Steward now?"

He sounded quite sarcastic, which Gwen found annoying. "Being loyal," she snapped. "He went to make sure that those realtors left your land."

"Realtors?" Greniston thundered. "What realtors?" He looked furious now, and fully ready to strangle her in his rage, in lieu of a better target. *He must be well over six feet tall*, Gwen realized. *He's lean, but he's strong.* She wondered how Glorietta, from *Rapacious in Ravenna* would react in a similar situation.

"I said what realtors?" Greniston bellowed.

"You needn't yell at me," Gwen said icily. "As for what realtors, why the ones that Swindon sent, of course. Unless the place is normally so swarming with them that you don't know which . . . "

"Swindon!" Lord Greniston clenched his hands in fury. "He couldn't!"

"Oh, but he did," Gwen said sweetly. "You don't know much about what goes on around here, do you?" she added.

Greniston glowered at her and ran his fingers through his untidy black hair. He seemed to have gone for a stroll in the rain without cap or umbrella, although he had at least tossed a much-weathered raincoat over his shoulders.

"You're all wet," Gwen remarked, implying that there were those who hadn't the sense to come in out of the rain.

"So are you," Greniston replied. "Your hair is all plastered to your forehead and your mascara stuff is all dribbling down your face."

"Oh no!" exclaimed Gwen, lifting a damp sleeve to her eyes.

"Never understood why women wear that stuff," Greniston remarked. "It's made of shoe black or something. And of course, they test the foul mixture on poor little rabbits and things. Imagine preening one's vanity at the expense of torturing one's fellow creatures."

"I only use brands they don't test on animals," Gwen said haughtily.

"Oh gawd, how *American*!" Greniston exclaimed scornfully. "Blithely slaughtering the rain forests and then getting all sentimental about a few laboratories full of monkeys. Disgusting creatures, monkeys, full of ticks and – "

"A moment ago, you said it was rabbits, and you called them poor innocent creatures, or some such banality - "

"That was purely for the sake of argument," Greniston retaliated. "I am no animal lover. Why, if I saw a baby seal right now, I'd probably kick it."

Gwen was fairly sure he had said this just to annoy her, but nonetheless she was revolted by it. She could not imagine his ancestor, Lord Peter, saying such a thing, even in jest.

"You," she said icily, "are the coarsest man I have ever met; ungracious, unkind, and unfit to bear the name of Greniston!" To her surprise, Greniston did not respond with a further volley of his own. Instead, his dark face seemed suddenly to shut down.

"I've no time for this," he said abruptly. "You can't stay here. You'll catch your death of cold. Follow me to the house. Robert can drive you back to wherever it is you come from."

He turned and started to trudge away, clearly expecting her to trail after him like a guilty child.

"No, thank you!" Gwen exclaimed. "Just show me the path, and I'll see myself out."

"Too much bother," Greniston called over his shoulder.

Gwen never really knew how what came next happened. One moment, she was looking down at the cold, clammy mud by her feet. The next moment, she had scooped up a healthy handful of that mud, and yelled, "Greniston!"

He turned around. Her aim was true. For a moment, Gwen thought a headlong sprint into the trees might be her best course of action. Then, to her relief and surprise, Greniston began to laugh. It was wonderful, deep laughter that seemed to surge up from some rich, generous source within him.

"*Touché*," he said at last, wiping the mud from his eyes. "I'm sure I quite deserved that. Please forgive me for being such a boor, Miss—or should I say Ms. . . . ?"

"Fields. *Miss* Gwendolyn Fields." Gwen blushed, realizing that she had deliberately used "Miss" to let him know she wasn't married. *Why do I care what he knows about me?* she thought, a bit irritated with herself.

"Miss Fields. Now, Miss Fields, would you do me the honor of accepting the hospitality of Greniston Manor? It has been famous in its day. Kings have dined well there. Admirals and even film stars have stayed the night. So what do you say to a hot bath, a change of clothes, and an impromptu feast of whatever Mrs. Fitzpatrick can find in the larder? After which, Robert will drive you to the inn, where I assume you're staying. Doesn't that sound better than pneumonia? It's up to you, of course."

"Well. . . ." The invitation did sound welcome. And Lord Greniston seemed to have become quite amiable. What had Geoffrey Swindon said? "There's no one more charming—when he's having one of his good spells."

Even if he s a raving lunatic, it ought to be safe enough with Robert and Mrs. Fitzpatrick there, whoever they are, Gwen reasoned. In any good Henrietta Amberly novel, she knew that Mrs. Fitzpatrick would turn out to be Lord Greniston's ravishing mistress, half Irish, half Japanese, an exotic beauty he had rescued from white slavers. And Robert would be his nefarious younger brother, handsome in a sleeker, urbane way. "He was raised in Paris," Lord Greniston would explain to her, later.

While these thoughts passed through her mind, Greniston tilted his head to one side and seemed truly to look at her for the first time. "'She dwelt among untrodden ways,'" he mused, "A maiden fair, with something rare about her face, her way, her auburn hair. I came upon her in a wild place. . . . She was speaking to the wind. . . . She turned to greet me face to face. . . . Her company I did entreat. . . . She balked . . . while frostbite overtook my feet."

Gwen burst out laughing. "All right," she said, "I accept."

73

Greniston beamed. He took her hand in his firm grasp and said, "It's reassuring to know that you are flesh and blood, Miss Fields, and not a mere phantom of the air. Now come along, and we'll get some brandy into you to warm those chilled white fingers."

An hour later, Gwen found herself gazing at Greniston across a long, rosewood dining table. At the far end of the table, on the other side of silver candlesticks, flowers, and several yards of white damask tablecloth, the Lord of the manor sat dunking his roll in his soup.

"Ought to be a good spread tonight," he said, with his mouth full. "Sometimes I forget to eat for a couple of days, so Mrs. Fitzpatrick likes to fill me up when she gets the chance. By the way, speaking of that venerable lady, she seems to have done the miraculous and found you something lovely to wear around here. You look enchanting in that dress . . . gown. Whatever it is."

Gwen smiled. "It belonged to your Great Aunt Jennet," she explained. "I hope that's all right." She had been nervous about wearing the delicate Victorian dress. With its high lace collar and long full skirt of pale pink muslin, it surely belonged in a museum, not facing the perils of a five-course meal.

"Meant to be worn," Greniston exclaimed. He gestured dangerously, a full wine glass in his hand.

"That's what Mrs. Fitzpatrick said," Gwen acknowledged. (Mrs. Fitzpatrick had turned out to be an eminently respectable Irish housekeeper of at least seventy.) "Besides, there was nothing else that looked like it might fit. I'm a bit taller than Mrs. Fitzpatrick."

Greniston chuckled. "I should say so; although just about as slender. Anyway, don't let Mrs. Fitz's white-haired frailty fool you. She's a tiger when she wants to be. Like Helena, in *Midsummer Night's Dream*: 'Though she be but little, she is fierce!' And she's done wonderfully well by you tonight. Yes, it definitely suits you, that old-fashioned gown, and your hair up like that."

"You clean up rather well yourself," Gwen said lightly. It was the first time she had a chance to get a clear look at Greniston, having seen him before only at twilight. She had to admit that she was impressed by what she saw. He was every bit as tall, lean, and broad shouldered as she had thought. With his dark hair combed back—he actually seemed to have washed it—she had a chance to study his face. Yes, she could definitely see the resemblance to his ancestor Lord Peter. The same strong chin, hawkish nose, and high cheekbones. It was in the eyes, though, that she saw the greatest resemblance. *This* Lord Greniston's brows were darker, and his eyes were brown, not gray. But the same intelligent fire gazed out of them. The current Lord's gaze was more troubled though, clouded by worry and a trace of something darker.

But then, he is older than Lord Peter in that portrait, Gwen realized. She guessed this Lord Greniston's age to be between thirty-eight and forty-three. Yet she did not think it was just a few more years of experience that made his gaze seem heavier than that of his ancestors.

Something's troubling him, Gwen realized. Yes, beneath his bantering manner, she was sure there was an unspoken pain. Lord Greniston peered around the vase of arythium lilies at her.

"How's the weather down at your end?"

"Everything is very nice." Gwen said politely.

"What's that?" Greniston leaned forward. "Can't hear you! This is ridiculous! I'm coming down there, although I may have to take a bus!"

He grabbed his soup bowl, sloshing beef bouillon onto the white tablecloth. The elderly manservant who stood nearby, waiting to bring in the next course, sighed.

"Cheer up, Bosley," Greniston said as he walked by. "I'm not such a bad barbarian to work for. Just the Genghis Khan of table manners!" He plunked down next to Gwen and said, in a confiding tone, "You know, I almost never eat like this myself." He gestured toward the huge, walnut-paneled room. "Bit off-putting, wouldn't you say? All the portraits of generations gone by, grimly watching you chew."

Gwen giggled. *Perhaps I've had enough wine,* she realized.

"Still," Greniston continued, "If I don't make an appearance once in a while, the servants get nervous. Usually I have them leave the food on a tray outside my study door. I'm much too busy working to stop for meals."

"And what work do you do?" Gwen asked with real interest.

"Oh, this and that, this and that," Greniston said quickly. "Tell me about yourself."

"I'm a travel agent," Gwen said. She paused. *God,* she thought, *it sounds so drab.* "At least, I was a travel agent. I've probably lost my job."

"Oh," said Greniston, his mouth full of salad vinaigrette, "how's that?"

Gwen found herself telling him the practical side of her recent adventures, but she did not mention the cry of Merlin or her strange dreams.

75

"So," Greniston mused when she had finished, "you might say you owe it all to that author your Mrs. Gordon is so fond of—what's her name?"

"Henrietta Amberly."

"Ah, yes, I've heard of her. Old bag calls herself 'The Grand Dame of Romance' or some such rot. Can't write worth beans of course. If you had a hundred monkeys with a hundred typewriters locked in a room, how long would it take them to come up with the complete works of Henrietta Amberly? About five minutes, I should guess."

"You've read her works, then," Gwen said, "having formed so scornful a judgment of them."

Greniston guffawed; that was the only word for it. "Wouldn't waste my time reading that slop!"

"Then how do you know it is slop?" Gwen asked.

"My dear girl," said Greniston, "one has only to walk past any news stand or train kiosk to be assaulted by her latest travesty. Actually, it's probably always the same book; she just changes the names and places. All the heroines on those lurid covers look the same."

"I'll grant you the covers are awful," said Gwen, "but I think Henrietta Amberly is a cut above the rest when it comes to romance fiction."

"Done a comparative study, have you?"

"Only for Mrs. Gordon. My master's thesis was on Shakespeare."

Greniston raised an eyebrow. "I see," he said. "On those little known plays, 'The Romances' no doubt?"

For the second time that day, Gwen felt that the only way to respond to this man was to throw something at him. She eyed the salad bowl longingly, but the presence of Bosley restrained her.

"I'm sorry, Miss Fields," Greniston said meekly, offering her a lily he had fished out of the vase on the table. It was exquisite, its white petals flecked with crimson, and it was dripping onto her dinner roll.

Gwen softened. "All right," she said, taking the flower and putting it into her water glass."

"So the lady is interested in Shakespeare," Greniston mused. "And King Arthur. And she has the courage to act upon a moment's spur, . . . drawn to forests. . . . Yet it's strange that, of all places, you should come to Far Tauverly. Most people on the trail of Arthur never even find out about this place."

Gwen felt she didn't want to mention the photograph in the guidebook and risk sending Greniston into another flash of real temper. "Are you interested in Arthur?" she asked.

"Do you play the piano?" Greniston replied, with a devastating smile.

"Well, yes, but what . . . ?"

"Terrific!" beamed her companion, bounding out of his chair. "I'll be right back!" With that, he dashed out of the room.

Bosley approached, undaunted, it seemed, by Greniston's erratic behavior. He took away the soup bowls and placed a plate of broiled salmon before Gwen.

"Next course, Miss," he murmured.

As Gwen lifted the first bite of fish to her lips, Greniston came running back into the room.

"Grab the plates, Bosley," he cried, "We're moving to the music room!"

"You'll love this room," Greniston continued, grabbing her by the hand and fairly dragging her out of the dining room and down the hall. "It's one of my favorite spots!"

A few minutes later, after a rather breakneck journey down stone corridors that she barely glimpsed, Gwen found herself thrust cheerfully forward, into a turret room.

"This is charming," she exclaimed. Tall stained-glass windows with lancet tops filled the curved walls. Although large enough to have a black baby grand squeezed into it, the room gave a feeling of intimacy. In one corner, she saw a pile of brightly colored cushions and what looked like remnants of a child's playroom. Gwen noticed a stuffed clown doll, an intricate model ship, and a miniature tea set of rose and white porcelain.

"My sister Julia and I spent a lot of time in here as children," Greniston explained. "It's where we hid when we were evading the governess. Or rather, governesses. We went through several before I was sent away to school. Julia used to hold tea parties under the piano. 'For the fairies,' she said. I was sometimes allowed to attend. The only other guests were that clown there and Rupert, our St. Bernard. He was strictly forbidden inside, but, of course, we always found ways to smuggle him in."

Greniston looked up and realized that Bosley was standing in the doorway, patiently holding the plates of salmon. "Oh, Bosley," he exclaimed penitently, "I am truly sorry. How rude of me. Just put those plates any old where."

"Very good, Sir," murmured Bosley, carefully placing the dishes on a window seat.

"Now then," Greniston said to Gwen, "have a seat at the piano. Here's what I want you to play." He placed a tattered piece of parchment before her.

"This looks ancient," Gwen said. "Is it an original manuscript?"

"Either that or a very early copy," Greniston replied. "Don't let me put you off," he added. "Just play, play."

Gwen suddenly felt very shy. She had never considered herself a fine pianist, and she had not played at all for several months.

"I hope you're not expecting too much," she warned.

"Don't worry," her host said, his mouth full of salmon. "Can't play a note myself, admire anyone who can. Can't even sing; tone deaf, they tell me. But I love to listen. Just got hold of this, and I must hear it. Fortunate you turned up," he added in a pleased voice.

Tentatively at first, Gwen began to pick out the melody. It had the feeling of a very old dance, spirited but not too fast. There was a truly haunting lilt to the melody. Out of the corner of her eye, she caught a glimpse of Lord Greniston. He was half-pacing, half-dancing around the room, occasionally giving a little skip, as he waved time with a forkful of salmon. As she grew more certain in her playing, he began to hum along, loudly and off-key. Once she realized that he was off in another world with the music, Gwen relaxed and began to enjoy herself. She saw at the top of the page the name of the music: "Lady Carey's Dompe." She vaguely remembered from a long-ago music appreciation class that a dompe was a kind of Elizabethan dance. She wondered who Lady Carey had been and if she had written the music or simply inspired it.

"That's it!" Greniston suddenly exclaimed.

"That's what?" asked Gwen, caught by the music and not wanting to miss a beat.

"No time to explain," Lord Greniston cried, heading for the door. "Must get back to work!" He was halfway out the door before he seemed to remember her presence. "It's been fine meeting you," he said. "Stay as long as you like. Finish your meal, play the piano, whatever you wish. Robert will drive you back whenever you're ready."

With that, he turned and was gone. Gwen heard him muttering to himself, "Of course! She's dancing! Now I see! She's dancing!" as he disappeared down the hall.

For a moment, Gwen simply stared after him. Then she burst out laughing, in appreciation of his sheer unpredictability. Just then, Bosley appeared in the doorway, holding a wine bottle and two fresh glasses.

"He's gone," Gwen said.

"Very good, Miss," Bosley replied, sounding not in the least surprised. "Would you care for some more wine?"

In spite of Lord Greniston's absence, Bosley continued to serve her elaborate meal. After the salmon, he brought in fruit and cheese, then an exquisite orange liqueur, followed sometime later by chocolate biscuits on a Wedgwood plate and a demitasse of the best coffee Gwen had had in England.

She quite enjoyed her solitary meal. When she was finished, she picked up a slim book from the side table.

"'Wholly Writ,'" by Leo Hawker," she read aloud. "It looks like a play."

She got as far as Act I, Scene I, and found her thoughts drifting back to Lord Greniston. She remembered the look on his face as he'd dashed from the room. Perhaps he was just stark, raving mad, but she had recognized the look in his eyes; it was the pleased amazement of an idea dawning, and that was irresistible to her.

Filipo would like Lord Greniston, she decided.

Just then, a young man appeared in the doorway. He had on a chauffeur's uniform and held a set of keys in his hand. Gwen thought he must be the "Robert" whom Greniston had mentioned earlier. He looked no more like a character out of a Henrietta Amberly novel than Mrs. Fitzpatrick had. The words "local lad" were written all over him.

"Bosley said you might be needing a ride, Miss."

"That's very kind," Gwen said. Actually, she felt reluctant to leave Greniston Manor, but she realized it must be getting rather late. She hoped Logan wouldn't be too worried.

"Yes, I suppose I must be going," she acknowledged, "but first I must return this dress to Mrs. Fitzpatrick."

"Oh no, Miss," Robert said. "You're to keep it, please. Lord Greniston's expressed orders. Your other things are in here," he added, holding up a valise. "All dried and ironed."

"But I couldn't accept this dress," Gwen protested. "It's a treasure."

"Lord Greniston's wishes, Miss," Robert repeated. "I wouldn't cross him, Miss, if I was you. Might set off one of his moods. Besides, it ain't like he's goin' to wear it, is it Miss?" The words were said very respectfully but accompanied by such an impudent grin that Gwen had to smile.

"I rather think not," she agreed. "By the way, are you Robert?"

"The one and only," he answered cheerfully.

On the way back to the inn, Robert kept up a steady stream of banter about Greniston, Mrs. Fitzpatrick, and life at the manor. That is, until Gwen asked, "Just what sort of work does Lord Greniston do?"

"I'm sure I wouldn't know, Miss," Robert said politely but firmly.

Well, well, well, thought Gwen, *and you wouldn't tell me if you did. There's loyalty beneath that impudence.* She liked Robert for that. "Okay," she ventured. "But perhaps you'll tell me what his first name is?"

Robert shook his head. "Sorry, I can't."

"Why not?"

"Because I don't know it, Miss."

"What?"

"Lord Greniston won't tell anyone his first name. It starts with the letter R, but he won't reveal anything else. Won't even tell Mrs. Fitz, and she's been with the family since before the flood, so to speak."

"Won't tell anyone," Gwen mused. "Why not?"

Robert caught her eye in the rear view mirror. His face was solemn, but there was a twinkle in his eye.

"Because he hates it, Miss."

"Does he now?" Gwen smiled. The thought of being able to address Greniston casually by his loathed first name the next time he grew impossible was an appealing one. Better even than mud or handfuls of salad vinaigrette. "I shall have to find it out," she murmured.

"Very good, Miss," Robert replied with a grin.

When she reached the inn, Gwen found that Logan was already sound asleep in the corner booth. He looked so peaceful that it seemed a shame to wake him, so she wrote a note inviting him to breakfast the next morning and slipped it under his sleeve. Then she headed up the steep stairs to her room, realizing that she would quite welcome a good slumber herself.

It was as she was brushing her hair that she noticed something small and shining on the dresser. Looking more closely, she saw that it was the gold button she and Logan had examined earlier.

That's funny, she thought. *I could have sworn I left that in my raincoat pocket. Oh well.*

She inched her way into the chilly bed—American central heating had its advantages, she was beginning to understand—and hoped that she would warm up soon. Still, the bed was clean and soft and smelled of lavender. She turned off the lamp and soon was drifting toward sleep, except for the thought of a little gold button that seemed to roll merrily into her mind.

"It doesn't add up, Watson," said a little voice in her mind (which now seemed to have acquired the accent of Sherlock Holmes). "She never took the first button out of her raincoat. And for that matter, how did the first button come to be in her pocket? It seems scarcely the sort of trick Althea Pennington would play. Yes, mark my words, old friend, there's more here than meets the eye."

After a few minutes of trying unsuccessfully to ignore this, Gwen switched back on the light, scampered across the cold wood floor, and reached into her raincoat pocket. Her fingers closed around something small, hard, and shiny. She pulled it out, and there, in her hand, was a gold button, with a filigreed design of a lion rampant holding a daffodil like an upraised sword. Just like the button that twinkled happily at her from the dresser top.

It was difficult to feel afraid from such jaunty objects; nonetheless, Gwen did wonder what was going on.

"Someone's trying to tell us something, Watson," she said aloud. "Who is it? And what do they want?"

There was, of course, no reply. Only the sound of the night wind in the branches of the apple tree outside her window and a playful spattering of rain against the glass.

CHAPTER SIX

"Amazing," Logan said as he spread a plentiful helping of Mrs. Hodges homemade strawberry preserves onto his toast. "Do you know, you're probably the first person to have been invited to the manor in, oh, at least five years."

"Not really?"

"Oh yes! Lord Greniston is amiable enough when he comes into town, but he's fiercely private about his home life; almost reclusive, some would say."

"He didn't seem at all like that last night," Gwen replied, sipping her tea and wishing it was a cup of the excellent coffee she had last night at the manor. Mrs. Hodges was a wizard in the kitchen, but strong morning brew was not among her accomplishments. Gwen realized, when she thought about it, that most of the great lives she so admired, from Shakespeare to King Arthur himself, had accomplished all they did without ever tasting a single drop of java. She wondered how they had coped.

"You must have hit it off," said Logan.

"I wouldn't say that, exactly," said Gwen, remembering the handful of mud she had flung. "And sometimes he was rather odd, but very nice, all the same. Very generous, and fun, actually, in an unusual sort of way."

Logan chewed on this information, along with a mouthful of sausage. He and Gwen were sitting at what had already become *their* table at the Greenstone Arms. The meal Mrs. Hodges had provided was, as always, of gourmet quality, but Logan noticed that Gwen, who seemed a girl of good appetite usually, wasn't eating. He wondered if it was a first symptom of love-sickness. Ever one to assist Cupid's arrows, Logan felt that Lord Greniston could find no finer gem than Gwen and that Greniston just might do for her, too, if he minded his Ps and Qs. "Of course, it's early days yet," he mused, "but if they did fall in love and get married, then she would stay right here in Far Tauverly. . . ."

"But tell me about your adventures," Gwen was saying. "How did it go with the realtors? Did you get any information out of them?"

Logan shook his head. "Got nothing out of 'em except two pints and a beef pie. They stuck to their story that they work for a firm in Bristol and have been engaged by Swindon to look over the property with an eye to development."

"Oh, Swindon," sighed Gwen, "I wish I'd never agreed to go out with him. How can he even think of building anything on that land, of all places? It would be like putting a parking lot in the middle of Chartres Cathedral, only worse, somehow."

"Condos for Bristol commuters and weekend homes for the trendy London crowd, that's what he's got in mind, if not something worse," Logan murmured darkly.

"Maybe I could cancel," Gwen said. "He's not coming 'til eleven. I could get a headache."

"Good idea."

Gwen thought about it, then shook her head. "I've always hated standing people up, and canceling at the last minute is just one step away from that. No, I'll go; I gave my word."

She had scarcely admitted to herself that part of the reason she wanted to avoid the date was that she half-hoped to run into Lord Greniston. The thought would have come as no surprise to Logan, who couldn't help noticing how often her gaze wandered to the window, as if she was looking for someone who just might be passing by. Logan smiled to himself. To his mind, events were progressing well. However, given the fact that it was only eight thirty in the morning, he thought Greniston's appearance unlikely just yet.

"Have some sausage," he suggested. "It's excellent."

Absentmindedly, Gwen put some food on her plate, and then forgot to eat it. Logan watched, fascinated, as she poured herself another cup of tea and then, instead of putting sugar in, dreamily reached for the salt. She never noticed until she took a sip, and then she burst out laughing.

"I don't know where my mind is this morning," she exclaimed.

But I do, Logan thought happily. Gwen's gaze had already returned to the window.

"Wednesday today," Logan remarked, as if making idle conversation. "Mrs. Peevey will be sending four dozen homemade scones to her grandson in the Navy. Stationed off the coast of Scotland, he is, in the North Sea. Bloody cold, I'm sure. He and the other lads must truly appreciate the treats she sends. Puts currants in 'em, and candied orange peel. Up before dawn, she is, so she can send 'em off every Wednesday, first thing. Faithful as clockwork. Something else happens every Wednesday. What is it? Oh, yes, Lord Greniston comes in to pick up his mail. Unless he's up to London, but

83

he hasn't been recently. Never makes an appearance 'til late afternoon, though. Shows up at the post office about four. Knows I'll be back from my route then, you see. And then, like as not, he'll drop in here, for a quiet pint. Often does, on Wednesdays."

Gwen made some rapid mental calculations. Swindon was picking her up at eleven. He had mentioned lunch and a drive in the country. She could easily contrive to be back before four without offending him.

"Pass the toast, please," she said brightly. "I suddenly feel quite wide awake."

***

Some twenty-five miles away, in Bath, Luan Tey was also eating breakfast. He sat on a park bench, munching a roll and sipping tea out of a Styrofoam cup. He had been sent on an errand to the bank and had decided to take a few minutes for himself on the way back. He found the luxurious townhouse his employer had rented oppressive and welcomed any opportunity to escape from it, however briefly.

Now he gazed across the green expanse of park at a group of children trying to fly a kite. Their shrieks of laughter and happy voices seemed to him to come from another universe.

"Take off your shoes!" an imperious old voice ordered.

Luan Tey turned and met the gaze of a fierce old lady. She was bent over almost double and leaned unsteadily on a cane. Her head trembled on her frail neck like a white flower on a weak stem. Her teeth were bad, and she smelled of medicines and mustiness. Yet there was still a fire in her clouded eyes that suggested that, even now, she was not used to being disobeyed.

She tapped her cane against his feet. "Young man, I said take off your shoes—and your socks!"

Luan Tey set down his tea and took off his expensive Italian shoes and his navy blue silk socks. His employer liked even the servants to wear the best, the very best.

"Hmmpff," the old woman said, scrutinizing his slender, gold-skinned feet, "You're a terrible man."

She said it without surprise or judgment. For his part, Luan Tey agreed with her. He had long ago come to the understanding that in the right circumstance, most people can be driven to do just about anything. He certainly knew this to be true of himself. As far as he was concerned, what the world calls goodness was no more than a tissue paper mask on a demon's

84

face. The question with most people was not whether they were evil or not, but simply what circumstance it might take for their evil to emerge. Lucky were the ones whom life never tested, who could fall asleep each night and call themselves "good." But for those who had met their demon, there was no return to innocence, ever. Only the repetition of evil and living out the prison sentence of one's days. He knew, for this was his life.

"You can tell everything from a person's feet," the old woman continued. "If you know how to read the evidence. Every crease, every bump, reveals the character. I was a podiatrist to the Prince of Wales, you know. That's seventy years ago. I'm ninety-seven now. I've massaged Winston Churchill's feet and his flibbertigibbet mother's, too. Oh yes, I have seen feet. They can paint their faces and dye their hair, but feet don't lie."

She poked again at Luan Tey's feet with her cane and eyed his instep. "You've murdered," she remarked dispassionately. "And worse."

Luan Tey nodded.

The old woman nodded, gazing at a nearby cluster of tulips. She stood there so long, swaying slightly, that Luan Tey thought perhaps she had forgotten him entirely. He reached for his socks. Then she turned back and said brightly, "Do you know why this park is round? It's from Roman times. Used to train their horses to pull chariots here. This is where they taught them to go around the curves. Around and around."

She leaned very close to Luan Tey, as if to confide something to him. As she did so, she staggered and caught her balance by putting her hand on his shoulder. Luan Tey was surprised by the weight of that hand, as heavy as the hand of death itself. Her face was like a death's head, too, leering so close to his that he got a strong whiff of her rotten teeth. He found it strange that he, who had so often been death's agent, should find its face so shocking.

"I'm too old," the old woman cackled, still resting her hand on his shoulder. "Everyone in my family wishes I'd die, and so do I. But I'll never let 'em have the satisfaction of knowing that."

She steadied herself and continued. "There's a ghost in this park, you know. I know, I live up there." She gestured toward one of the Regency row houses that backed onto the park. "I hear him, at night. I can't sleep. My arthritis. So I sit at the kitchen table and do my crosswords. Not very interesting anymore, when you've done as many as I have, but it's something. The Abbey bells toll out one, two, three in the morning. Then he comes, the ghost of the Roman charioteer. He drives his horses around and around the park. I can't see him, but I can hear the horses' hooves and the jingle of their bridles. Oh, yes. And sometimes I hear another sound, a wild cry of despair, like he's crying out for help. Poor devil! Condemned to repeat the same pattern forever and ever! Around and around, and never able to break free! Poor devil! But then, we're all poor devils here, aren't we? You know, you do."

"Oh, Gramma, there you are!"

A teenage girl in blue jeans and a T-shirt came running up to them. She grabbed the old woman's arm and began to lead her away.

"I hope she hasn't bothered you," the girl said to Luan Tey over her shoulder. Her glance took in his bare feet. "Oh dear, I guess she already has. She's always running away from the flat and telling people about their feet. Mum says she should charge for it, because it's as good as having your tea leaves read, really."

"Susan! Stop chattering! You mustn't interrupt my consultations!" the old woman said, feistily.

"Oh, Gramma Lil, please don't be difficult. Do come along home now. Mum's furious, and besides, it's almost time for your program. You know, your quiz show."

The old woman turned suddenly helpless. Whether her confusion was real or simply a ploy to soften the girl's annoyance, Luan Tey could not tell.

"My quiz show," she said querulously. "Yes, I do love my show. Whatever you think is best, dear, whatever you think is best. Where are we, anyway? Why have you brought me out here?"

"It's all right, Gramma, just come along with me."

The old woman hobbled along for a few steps, leaning on the girl's arm. Then she stopped and looked at Luan Tey quite shrewdly again.

"Play the pools, young man?" she asked.

Luan Tey shook his head.

"Oh you should, you should. It's up to a million pounds now. Doesn't hurt to have a go. There's always a chance, you know. Always a chance, no matter how great the odds."

With that, the old woman turned away and allowed herself to be led back to the row houses. The girl talked to her soothingly about the custard that had been made for her as a special treat.

Luan Tey took a thoughtful sip of his now ice-cold tea. An omen, the old woman was an omen. Good or bad, he was not sure, but he would have preferred no omens at all in his life. Yet, ever since he had first overheard his employer discussing this business in Somerset, his life had been full of small warnings. The cup, for instance, the one Miller had sent him to that village to look at. It was strange. Actually, he had liked it far more than most of the old art his boss collected. The cup had a power to it. But he did not for a moment believe that his employer had simply sent him to look over its setting with an eye to stealing it, or as Miller put it, "acquiring the piece by any means possible." No, there was something else going on. And then there was Miller's comment: "On Friday, I will have a special little job for you."

A special little job. That usually meant something more skilled than theft. Poison in a diplomat's sherry, a bomb in the right cafe at the right time, brakes in a competitor's car that inexplicably failed at the precise moment he rounded a mountain curve. Luan Tey had a talent for special little jobs. Yet somehow he dreaded this one. What horror could his employer wish to unleash in that quiet little village? Well, he had said Friday, and this was Wednesday. He would find out soon enough, he supposed. But he did not like it, not at all.

***

"We're almost there," said Swindon. "I do hope you enjoy this place as much as I do. You know," he added, "you're the first person I've ever invited here. I always come alone. It is . . . oh, I don't know, a sort of sanctuary, I suppose."

Gwen smiled uncomfortably, reminded yet again of everything Swindon had done to let her know that her company was very special to him. He had met her at the inn with a bouquet of pale pink roses surrounded by a froth of green ferns; he had brought along a shawl of cashmere wool, "in case you get chilly in the car." He had even purchased an entire collection of CDs on her behalf.

"I didn't know what kind of music you'd like," he explained. "My own taste runs pretty exclusively to Bach. So I picked up a variety in Bristol yesterday. I do hope there's something there that suits your fancy."

Gwen looked over the box of discs. It contained everything from Chopin Etudes to Billy Joel and Broadway musicals. Evidently, Swindon had tried to account for every kind of American taste. She imagined him standing in the music store in his pale gray suit, his fine, pale hands holding a disc of "The Supreme's Greatest Hits" as if it was an object from another planet, asking in his elegant voice, "And this, would a young American lady like this one?" She was touched and embarrassed that he had gone to so much trouble and felt guiltier than ever that she had almost canceled their date. As if to atone, she selected a disc of a Vivaldi concerto and put it on.

"So you are fond of classical music, then?" Swindon said eagerly. He sounded almost like a lonely child, who had at last discovered someone who enjoyed the same games he did.

"Among other kinds," Gwen replied.

"You know, every summer, there is a marvelous music festival in Bath. The very best performers. This summer's program will include the Bach Fugue in A minor. We could go there for an afternoon performance, have a light supper at Popinjay's, and go to the theater afterwards."

"I don't think I'll be here long enough for that," said Gwen gently. "Summer's months away, and I'm only staying in this area for a few more days. Thank you, though."

As easily as Swindon had made the invitation, he retreated from it. "Of course," he said. Then, lightly, effortlessly, he turned the conversation to the wildflowers by the wayside, *like a perfect gentleman*, Gwen thought. For a moment, she compared Swindon's smooth manners to Greniston's abrupt ways. Swindon had, beyond a shadow of a doubt, the kind of polish and poise referred to as "good breeding." Just at the point when she felt embarrassed by her own lack of conversation, he exclaimed, "What a pleasure it is to be with someone who doesn't babble on just for the sake of filling the air with words. Your quietness is a real refreshment, if you don't mind my saying so." And he looked at her with an appraising intent that made her feel she was somehow a rare find.

For most of the drive, though, Swindon chattered lightly on, filling a silence that could have been awkward with a running commentary on everything from the flora and fauna to the history of the countryside, about which he seemed endlessly knowledgeable. As he spoke, Gwen found herself intrigued by how handsome was Swindon's appearance. Everything about him, from the way his flaxen hair feathered lightly about his face to the slender fineness of his aristocratic features, set him apart from anyone else she had ever dated. She imagined how Filipo would assess Swindon's appearance: "The charm of Fred Astaire, and the looks of Leslie Howard. Yes siree, Babe, it's Ashley Wilkes gone continental!" She smiled and wondered what her friend would have said about Greniston.

Swindon drove on, languidly, one hand on the wheel, the other tapping time to Vivaldi on the leather dash. The silver Jaguar seemed almost to guide itself along the road. Never before had Gwen realized how accurate the phrase "the engine purred" could be, but that was exactly what this motor did. Like Swindon, the car's progress seemed effortless, smooth, polished.

"There it is," Swindon said happily. "There's our destination."

He pointed toward the crest of a hill. Nestled among lime trees stood an elegant stone house. There was, in its Regency architecture, a note of flawless restraint; it had the perfect symmetry of design that makes no demands upon the eye, that soothes and calms.

The Jaguar glided up the long, snowdrop lined drive and came to an effortless halt at the entrance. A uniformed man was there to meet them, obviously anticipating their arrival. In an instant, he was opening Swindon's door.

"Good afternoon, Mr. Swindon."

"Afternoon, Saunders," Swindon replied, with what seemed like the perfect blend of warmth and decorum. Swindon himself hurried to Gwen's side of the car and opened the door for her. Taking her arm delicately, yet protectively, he led her toward the house. Above the door hung a wooden sign upon which was elegantly painted a leaping white hare and, in pursuit, a pack of eager hounds. Above them, in beautiful script, was the name "The Hare and Hounds."

"Come this way," said Swindon, ushering her into the foyer. A maitre d', who looked exactly as maitre d's in old movies looked, greeted them. He was tall and portly and looked as though he moved through the high seas of restaurant life as calmly as a luxury liner moves through choppy waters. He wore a black tuxedo, had an immaculate white napkin draped over one arm, and bowed, ever so slightly, as they approached.

"Mr. Swindon, a pleasure, Sir," he murmured.

Swindon must come here a lot, Gwen thought. *Everyone knows his name.*

"Yes, well, hello, Fortenoy," said Swindon. "I have a guest today. I believe I'd asked for that table by the terrace window."

"Very good, Sir," said the maitre d'. "Right this way, Sir."

"He quite intimidates me," whispered Swindon as they followed the waiter across the dining room. "He's a bit like an undertaker, or an Oxford Don."

Gwen smiled—and wished she hadn't. It bothered her, somehow, to be making fun of the man quite literally behind his back. She could not imagine Lord Greniston doing so; if he had something rude to say, he blurted it out to your face and grinned, hoping you'd snap back.

Again, she felt a twinge of guilt. *I shouldn t be comparing Swindon to Greniston*, she thought, *especially not while l m his guest*. Annoyed with herself, she made a point of saying, as they sat down, "This is a wonderful place." The maitre d' looked faintly shocked, managing to convey, by his silence, that open praise was not a done thing in that setting. Swindon, however, looked unabashedly pleased.

"I'm so glad if you like it," he beamed. "It's a very special place to me. Will you have some champagne?"

Almost before Gwen could say, "Yes, please," the champagne appeared, magically being poured into the exquisite glass that yet another waiter had set before her.

"Now," said Swindon, "what else will you have?"

Gwen looked over the menu he handed her. It was in French, which did not dismay her. She could read what most of the gourmet dishes were; she simply had never tasted any of them.

"Why don't you order?" she suggested.

Swindon smiled and murmured something to the waiter, who replied with the inevitable "Very good, Sir," and glided away.

Sipping her champagne, Gwen relaxed a little and admired her surroundings. Through the windows to her right, she saw the wide expanse of the Bristol valley: gleaming deep green hills beneath a sky of pale, new-washed blue, flecked with feathery clouds. To her left was the dining room: fawn gray walls, mauve carpeting as thick as moss, comfortably stuffy paintings of hunt scenes and still lives, and a sea of tables covered in gleaming white clothes, with one pink rose in a silver vase on every one. It was elegant, expensive, and, she realized, totally deserted.

"It's odd that we're the only ones here," she remarked. "This seems like such a nice place."

Swindon grinned, his cool features suddenly boyish. "I reserved it," he said.

"Oh, yes, the table is the nicest one," Gwen assured him.

Swindon laughed. "No, the restaurant. I reserved it, for us."

"You what?" was Gwen's response, a surprised exclamation she was sure the maitre d' would have attributed to her uncouth American temperament.

Swindon laughed again, seemingly delighted by her amazement.

"It wasn't that hard," he said. "I own the place."

"You own this restaurant? But . . . but . . . good heavens," said Gwen, at a loss for words.

Swindon smiled, his face looking natural and friendly now, his happiness contagious. He placed his thin, chiseled hands over hers and said, "You don't know what a rare pleasure it is for me to spend time with someone like you. It's as if I see my old English world afresh through your eyes." He finished speaking but did not take his hands away.

"It's very kind of you to say that," Gwen faltered, "but you scarcely know me."

"Oh, I can tell what you're like, Gwen," he replied, gazing steadily into her eyes.

Fortunately for Gwen's composure, the waiter arrived with their soup. Beef bouillon, she saw, suddenly reminded of Greniston dunking his roll into his bowl. She smiled fondly at the thought.

"Penny for your thoughts," Swindon said gently.

"Oh, oh, I was just thinking that you are a generous man," Gwen lied, "and that I'm not sure I belong here. To tell you the truth, Geoff, I'm not at all used to wealth."

Swindon smiled. "Perhaps it's an acquired taste. Most people seem addicted to it. Funny thing, money. Personally, I've always agreed with what one of your American writers, Emerson, said about it: 'Money, in its causes and effects, can be as beautiful as roses.' It all depends on what you do with it, doesn't it? I'd like to use mine wisely. I have plans—plans for Far Tauverly, for instance. It may be picturesque, but some of the people live in a very demoralizing poverty. I'd like to help them," Swindon continued, "but in a way that lets them keep their self-respect. These people don't need charity, they need jobs." His voice lost its smoothness for a moment, and Gwen heard in it a new note of earnestness, and of frustration.

"I have such plans," her companion went on. "And they could work, I know they could, and benefit everyone, but," Swindon suddenly stopped himself. "Forgive me, Gwen, for bringing up such a dreary subject. The welfare of Far Tauverly is a bit of an obsession with me, I suppose. But you are here on holiday, to enjoy yourself, not to hear my tales of woe. Let's talk of something pleasant, please—like you, for instance."

"No," insisted Gwen, "I want to know what the problem in Far Tauverly is. I really do."

"Well," Swindon continued reluctantly, "You heard some of it from Logan the other day, I'm sure, though I don't know what version of the story he's got hold of. I'd like to develop some land that has been in my family for generations. Nothing intrusive, something elegant—a first-rate resort hotel with a good restaurant, a bit like this one, perhaps. Nothing that would harm the setting. . . ."

"But there are no authentic buildings on that land." Gwen mentioned.

Swindon smiled. "Neither is this one authentic," he said. "It's entirely a modern reproduction."

"Not really," said Gwen. She felt amazed, yet oddly cheated, as if they were dining on a movie set instead of at the real thing.

"Oh, yes," said Swindon. "So it can be done, you see. And even a hotel would bring a great many jobs to a small place like Far Tauverly. It wouldn't take much to turn things around there. But there are . . . obstacles."

"Lord Greniston?"

"Yes," said Swindon frankly. "He isn't too concerned with the welfare of the place. But you mustn't judge him too harshly," Swindon added quickly. "He isn't well, really."

"What do you mean?"

"Oh, don't misunderstand; he's fit as a fiddle physically. The Grenistons always are. But mentally . . . well, he's brilliant, of course, and that's what makes it all the more tragic." He looked up at Gwen as if determining whether to go on.

"You see, he and I were boyhood friends. Well, perhaps not friends, exactly; he is seven years older than me. But I worshipped him, and he, in his kindness, spent a great deal of time with me. Neither of us had any brothers, you see, and the estates border each other. No one could have been more warm, more kindly. But then he went away to college and to a stint in the military, and then he did a stint in the foreign service—embassy work. When he finally came back, after his parents were both killed in a train accident, he seemed a changed man. Unpredictable, reclusive. He barricades himself in that estate like a medieval king under siege. I've tried in vain to renew our old friendship, but he won't even see me. And, of course, this dispute over the land makes it all the worse. But the needs of Far Tauverly aren't going to go away, just because two old friends have fallen out."

Gwen toyed with her food thoughtfully. She still could not bear the thought of someone building anything in the mysterious woods, whoever they belonged to. Yet she was getting quite a different picture of Swindon's motives than she had before. He certainly didn't seem to have in mind the tract housing Logan had described, let alone anything more sinister. And then there was Lord Greniston. In spite of his erratic behavior, she found it hard to believe that he was actually mentally unbalanced. *And yet*, she realized, *I scarcely know him.*

"I've troubled you," Swindon said, "and that was exactly what I didn't want to do. We really must change the topic now, I insist. I'll tell you what, let's have our coffee and dessert in the lounge area, and I'll teach you how to play darts. I bet you've never played a good, solid game of English darts, have you?"

"I've never played any kind of darts at all," Gwen said.

"Well, come along then, it's high time you learned, young lady!" He led her to a smaller room, much cozier than the dining area. Long sofas, covered in dusty rose velvet, were placed along the oak paneled walls. A fire crackled merrily in a huge, black marble fireplace. And on the walls, in addition to a dart board, were more paintings of hunting scenes.

"Do people around here really go hunting a lot?" Gwen asked.

"That they do," Swindon replied. "Fox hunt most weekends. Would you like to go to one?"

"Oh no," exclaimed Gwen. "I think they're horrible! I mean," she paused, uncertain as to whether she had offended him or not.

Swindon smiled. "I'm not a great one for the hunt myself," he said. "But they do serve a purpose, you know. Foxes ravage the farmers' chickens, and they, after all, are living creatures, too."

Gwen had to admit that this was true, yet she couldn't help thinking there must be a more humane way to control the fox population than pursuing them over hill and dale with a pack of baying hounds. Oscar Wilde's description of a fox hunt came to mind: "the unspeakable in pursuit of the inedible." She felt that Greniston would appreciate the phrase.

"Watch this," said Swindon. He picked up one of the darts and nonchalantly hit a bull's eye. And then another.

Gwen could not help noticing that he had taken off his suit jacket and rolled up the sleeves of his white silk shirt. For so slender a man, he gave a surprising impression of strength.

"You try," he said, plucking out the darts and handing one to Gwen. His hand brushed hers ever so lightly as he did so, and Gwen felt aware of his touch with amazing clarity.

Gingerly, she flung the dart. It made it, barely, onto the board. She was very glad it hadn't pierced one of the paintings on the wall.

"Close, close," Swindon said encouragingly. "But you aren't throwing quite right. It's not just from the wrist, you see, but from the whole arm. Here, let me show you."

He came up behind her, so close that she could smell the marvelous, expensive scent he wore and just feel his taut body brushing against hers. "Now then," he said, taking her arm lightly in his, "swing from the elbow, like this, you see?" He guided her arm through the movement, not once but several times. Then he stepped back. "Now you try."

She did, and the dart, to her delight, zoomed into the next-to-inner circle of the target.

"Bravo! Well done!" cried Swindon. To Gwen's regret, he did not step closer to her but moved away and picked up his coffee cup.

"A toast," he said, "to your great future as a dart player! But we can't toast with this, we must have some brandy!"

Over Gwen's protests, Swindon ordered two snifters of brandy and then two more. Soon they were laughing together, and keeping score of the dart game or even finishing it became so impossible a task that they both collapsed, giggling, onto the nearest sofa. And when they did, it seemed like the most natural thing in the world for Swindon to put his arm around her.

"Ah, Gwen" he said, "I can't remember when I've had a nicer time, really. You're a very special woman, you know."

Gwen started to speak, but before she could say a word Swindon laughingly interrupted, "I know, I know, you're going to say I barely know you. But believe me, I'm a shrewd judge of character, when I'm interested. And I am," he added, "interested."

***

In the East End of London, a young man named Davey Lee was truly enjoying his cigarette. Three days out of the lock-up, and the simplest things hadn't lost their savor yet. A cup of tea. Sleeping in, if he felt like it. Not to mention chatting up the girls down at the Crown and Scepter. He hadn't lost his touch in that regard, he'd been glad to see; they still gathered round his soulful, black-haired good looks like bees to clover. And rightly so, he felt; he knew how to treat a girl.

Yes, he thought, *life is good, life is grand.* He took another slow, luxurious drag on the cigarette and watched his friend Ned set down to work. Ned was in the antiques business, so to speak. He could take a modern-day bit of lumber and, in a matter of weeks, turn it into the loveliest Queen Anne dresser or Tudor sideboard you ever did see. Right now, he was beating a bureau with a bit of chain wrapped in an old sock to give it just the right nicked-up look.

"Beautiful," breathed Davey. "I do like to see an artist at work."

"Ta," acknowledged Ned. "I'll be doin' wormholes next, if you want to watch." In the back of the warehouse, a phone rang.

"See who it is, would ya mate?"

"Right-o," Davey replied.

A few minutes later he returned, looking amused. "You're never gonna believe this, Ned."

"Try me."

"My Grandmother, Annie Lee . . . "

"That daft old bird that does the healings?" Ned interrupted.

"The same."

"She ain't dead, is she? I know you was fond of 'er."

Davey Lee shook his head. "No, not dead. But she's gone and got herself arrested. She's in some town in Avon. Hamble-on-the-Beck. And she wants me to come and bail her out! She's been callin' all around to find me; the cops let her make extra calls."

Ned threw back his head and laughed. "What's the old girl in for, train robberies and bigamy?"

"Obstructin' traffic on the M5. I thought she had the sense to keep that caravan and horse of hers on the side roads. But she caused a huge jam-up right on the highway. Then she resisted arrest."

Ned shook his head. "That's the trouble with your Gran, no experience in crime. No finesse, really."

"Too true," replied Davey with a sigh. "Well, I guess I better catch a train down there and spring her. God knows, she's done the same for me enough times. Never thought I'd see the day when the tables was turned."

"Ah, well, savor the moment lad, savor the moment. You fixed well enough for cash?"

Davey nodded. He had not been idle since his release from prison. Only the day before, he had relieved a cash register in a Mayfair Haberdashery of some of its excess. The idea of bailing his Gran out with stolen funds was very appealing. *Handing over hot notes to a copper*, he mused. *It has a certain poetic justice.*

"I'd best be on my way," he told Ned. "Annie doesn't like to be stuck inside of anywhere for very long, let alone inside a jail cell."

***

As Davey Lee set out to help his Grandmother, the Lord of Greniston Manor was having some legal problems of his own.

"A deed to the Greniston woods," he thundered. "What the devil is this rubbish?" He hurled the letter from his solicitor halfway across the room.

"Swindon doesn't have a leg to stand on," he snarled. "That's been Greniston land for centuries!"

There was no one to hear his fury except the bust of Shakespeare, which sat on a shelf above Greniston's cluttered desk. Greniston now found himself addressing that bust, as he so often did.

"Bloody ridiculous of me to get upset," he said. "Steadworthy'll handle it; he always does. It's just annoying of that young fool to show such bloody cheek! Starting a tempest in a tea-pot, just when my work was finally going well again."

Greniston tugged off his necktie and tossed it, with practiced grace, so that it landed lightly around the bard's neck. Slumping into his favorite armchair, Greniston fell into a bit of a reverie.

"It definitely was useful having that Miss Fields around last night," he remarked to Shakespeare. "Plays the piano quite nicely, once she gets going. Wonder how long she's going to be in Far Tauverly." He stared dreamily out the window at the broad expanse of lawn he had led Gwen across just the evening before.

"She really should see the mounds in the sunlight," he mused, "rather than in a twilight downpour. You know, Will, I think I'll just take a little stroll into the village. Pick up the mail. Hold down the fort, old boy."

***

The silver Jaguar glided up before the Greniston Arms.

"I'll walk you to the door," said Swindon.

"Oh, you needn't do that," protested Gwen.

"But I insist," he replied.

It was just then, as they were walking up the sidewalk to the door of the inn, that a familiar figure came striding down the street.

"Greniston!" exclaimed Swindon warmly. He headed toward the other man, his hand outstretched.

"How dare you!" muttered Greniston through clenched teeth.

He glowered at Swindon. Then his gaze fell upon Gwen. He seemed aghast to see her there, clearly in Swindon's company.

"Good afternoon, Miss Fields," Greniston said in the iciest tones imaginable. "I trust you are well?"

"Don't worry, Greniston," Swindon said heartily before Gwen could reply, "I'm taking good care of her. In fact, she was kind enough to be my guest for lunch today."

"Indeed," said Lord Greniston in an arctic voice. "Well then, I see my presence is not needed here, and I'll intrude no further."

"Lord Greniston," Gwen began.

"The devil take you!" snarled Greniston. Without a backward glance, he strode away.

Swindon looked sympathetically at Gwen. "I told you so," his expression seemed to say. "He's in one of his moods now." He took her arm and led her gently to the door of the inn.

"Miss Fields—Gwen," he said, "I don't know how long you're planning to stay in Far Tauverly, but I sincerely hope it will be long enough for you to be my guest again. I have enjoyed today more than I know how to say."

He kissed her lightly on the cheek, and then he was gone, and the silver Jaguar was gliding away, down the street.

By the time she reached her room, Gwen was fuming.

"How could Lord Greniston be so rude?" she muttered. "And he was so kind just last night."

"What was it Swindon had said?" she wondered. "'There's no one more charming, until his moods are upon him.'"

Gwen still found it hard to believe that Greniston was actually mentally ill. Yet even Logan had called him almost a recluse. And she was beginning to wonder just how keen her own perceptions were. Swindon was certainly different than she'd thought him to be.

I don't know why I'm so concerned about either of them, she thought irritably. *I'll leave here in a day or two, and that will be the end of it anyway. Let them settle their own feud. Come to think of it, maybe I just should just leave today and drive on to Salisbury. Logan would be disappointed, though.*

She definitely looked forward to spending more time with Logan. And there was their pact to consider: "Light-hearted and bold." Perhaps they wouldn't discover the meaning of the Greniston prophecy, but she didn't want to leave without trying. Although, right now, the mysterious cry that had haunted her seemed little more than a dream.

I won't decide anything right now, Gwen thought. *What I need is a bath and a nap.* And for once, she realized, the hot water was actually on when she needed it.

Later, as she was gratefully dozing off, warmed by the little gas heater in the corner and her fluffy blue velour robe, she heard a small deliberate sound, like a coin falling on the throw rug beside the bed.

How odd, she thought dreamily. She looked over the edge of the bed. Something bright gleamed inside of one of her slippers. She reached for it. Her fingers closed around a small, golden button. A *third*, golden button.

"This is not possible," Gwen said aloud. "This button was not in my slipper just minutes ago. I know, because the slipper was on my foot. The door is locked, and no one but me has been in this room since I locked it. It is not possible for this to be here."

Possible or not, the button gleamed jauntily in her hand. She bit it. It was not a dream.

Outside, in the garden below, a man began to sing a wordless tune.

"Da-dee dum dee da dum," he sang, very sweetly, in a full, rich baritone. There was something familiar about the tune.

It's the melody Lord Greniston had me play last night, Gwen realized. Yet she knew it was not Lord Greniston singing now, for he could not carry a tune in a bucket. This voice was melodious and true.

"Da-dee dum dee da dum," the voice sang cheerfully, as if the melody was not ancient but the latest hit song that all toes were tapping to.

Gwen jumped out of bed and rushed to the window. There was no one in the garden below. Yet, very distinctly, she heard a man laugh, a joyful, daring laugh.

Perhaps I ought to be scared, she thought. But instead, she found that she was relieved to discover that the mysteries of Far Tauverly had not ended.

I must definitely stay on a few days more, she decided. When she turned away from the window, she, too, was humming the ancient melody.

CHAPTER SEVEN

A green day, a gray day, a day so still you felt that you could hear the very leaves breathe. The sky was a solid vault of pale gray, the sky not of an all-day rain, but of an all-day mist.

A great quiet lay upon the grounds of Greniston Manor. On the park-like lawns the air was so still that the hanging branches of the willows did not even stir in it. The reflections of the trees on the ornamental pond did not so much as waver. Even a solitary duck, floating on the surface of that pond, seemed scarcely to move.

The life of the wild wood was quiet as well. From time to time, a robin sang out the liquid notes of its rain-song. Here and there, a leaf rustled, or a bird flew from one tree top to another. But every blue forget-me-not, every angled, rambling vine, every noble tree and blade of grass gleaming a dark, rich green in the mist seemed caught within a magic net of quiet, like a forest under an enchantment.

Upon King Arthur's Mound, the fallen leaves glowed silver and garnet. Round about it, the daffodils leaned this way and that, their trumpets turned pensively downward in the moist air. The bark of Merlin's Oak glistened with mist, and the ancient tree wore its crown of new leaves, as if still grateful, after so many centuries, to feel the benediction of yet another tender spring.

Here, at Arthur's Mound, was the heart of the heart of stillness. Here the silence was profound. It was as if the many lives of the forest were not sleeping but were waiting, watching, gathering in their many strengths for whatever might happen next.

Stillness lay upon Far Tauverly as well. The slate roofs of the homes shone silver in the mist. The usual morning sounds were subdued. Gwen woke early, feeling much refreshed. When she went downstairs, Mrs. Hodges served her orange juice without the usual update on the latest village news. Her smile was warm, though, and she said "I'm glad you've decided to stay on a bit, dear. It's a pleasure to have you."

The quiet mood suited Gwen, who felt she had much to think about.

Perhaps I'll use the rental car and go for a drive today, she thought.

When she stepped outside, she saw Logan sitting on a bench.

"Good morning," she called softly.

He smiled and waved for her to join him. She could tell that he was glad to see her, but the hush of the day seemed to have affected him as well.

"How are you?" Gwen asked.

Logan sighed ruefully. "Ah well, it's one of those days when everyone and their cousin has decided to write letters. And I feel like they're all in my mailbag." He sighed again. He looked so forlorn that Gwen decided she could easily take a drive some other day.

"Perhaps I could help you deliver them," she suggested. "I enjoyed doing it last time."

"You did?" Logan asked, with a glint of hope in his eye.

"Oh, absolutely. And it would suit my mood to a T. The perfect excuse to walk about and think one's own thoughts."

"I often feel that way about delivering mail myself," Logan said appreciatively. He did not add that he could well understand if she had much to think over. Like half of Far Tauverly, he had witnessed yesterday's encounter between Swindon and Greniston, but he felt it kinder not to mention it. He said "Well, if you're sure, . . . but it isn't right, you know, asking you to share my work, and not being able to pay you for it. Wait! I know! I've got a capital idea! I can make supper for you! That is, if you're willing to come?"

"Why, certainly," said Gwen. "But don't feel that you have to, I'm glad to help."

"Oh no, I must; I want to," said Logan. "Dinner will be served at, shall we say, half past seven, at the post office? I've a back room there, where I often stay when the trek back to my house seems too far; it's a bit outside the village, you see. I guess you could call the room at the post office my 'flat in town,'" he added with a chuckle. "I've got a little hot plate there, and it's amazing what you can concoct with two burners and a little ingenuity. I promise it won't be nasty burned beans or anything like that," he added hastily.

"I know it will be delicious. I shall look forward to it immensely," Gwen said firmly. Logan beamed. His gaiety at the prospect of entertaining was infectious, and Gwen felt her spirits lifted, too.

"Well, then," Logan said, "Now I feel a little better about handing these to you." He offered her several letters. "These are all on Milsom Road and easy to find. Until tonight, then?"

101

With a smile and a tip of his postman's cap, Logan shouldered his leather bag, which Gwen realized did look quite heavy for a man of his age, and started happily on his way. She looked through her envelopes and saw that she was to visit Florence Grimsby, the greengrocer's; a Col. G. B. Prithwell, retired; the Rev. Sterling, Vicar of Far Tauverly; and last, but surely not least, the Walmsleys.

This, she thought with a smile, *should be interesting.*

***

Annie Lee's day was starting in quite a different fashion. "Bail is set at fifty pounds," the magistrate intoned.

"No problem, glad to do it, Guv," Davey Lee said, handing over several wrinkled notes. He couldn't help grinning every time he glanced at his Grandmother, sitting stiffly in the docket beside a policewoman. Pretty young thing, that police woman. Tendrils of blonde hair curled from beneath her cap and trailed down her slender neck. Davey Lee tried to imagine her out of uniform. Out of any uniform. She must have felt his gaze upon her, because she turned to look at him. Davey winked. The policewoman looked away, her cute little nose in the air. *Oh well*, Davey thought, *plenty more where that came from. Thank God. Yes, thank God for the inexhaustible supply of women in the world. God love em, every one. Skinny ones, plump ones, pert ones, shy ones, blondes, brunettes, or red heads; Bantu beauties, Hindu lasses in their saris and bangles, or London matrons with perfect lipstick and blue tinted hair.*

God, Davey Lee reasoned, loved them all. And if it was good enough for God, then shouldn't he, Davey Lee, follow suit? It wasn't that he wanted to bed them all. Deeper than lust, which he quite enjoyed, was the fact that he loved the feminine. He loved the fact that women existed at all. The hardest part about being in jail for him was being deprived of the sight and company of women. What joy it was now to be back among them. Even the old char woman in the hallway outside the courtroom, with her frizzed hair half-hidden by a faded scarf and a cigarette drooping from her red-smudged lips, had looked like a Venus to him. He had never met a woman who didn't have a beautiful possibility in her. Why, even old Gran over there had shown a neat ankle in her day, and there was still a rare loveliness about her rosy cheeks and blue eyes. Who knows, the old girl might surprise them all and marry a fifth time. You never knew when she had a beau up her sleeve.

"Mr. Lee!"

102

Davey looked up, realizing he'd gotten so distracted by his favorite topic that he hadn't heard a word the magistrate was saying.

"Sorry, Guv. You was sayin', Guv?"

(Davey was not certain why he found himself speaking with a Cockney accent. Perhaps because he had just been spending time in the East End. Accents and mannerisms sometimes just came over him out of nowhere. On this occasion, the Guv business seemed to be going over well with the Judge, so Davey decided to stick with it.)

"The prisoner is released to your recognizance, to return here for trial in ten days time. I want to impress upon you, Mr. Lee, that creating a public disturbance, obstructing traffic on Her Majesty's thoroughfare, and resisting arrest are not charges to be taken lightly."

"No, Guv. Sir. Your Honor," said Davey, as piously as he could manage.

"Well, you seem an upright young man, and I'm impressed that you would come so willingly and so quickly all the way from London to assist your grandmother, at some cost to yourself, I might add."

"I was glad to do it, Sir," said Davey, managing, in spite of his dark, curly hair and roguish good looks, to radiate the innocence of a choirboy.

"I had considered placing your grandmother in a public nursing home for her own safety as well as that of the driving public's. However, since you are here, and seemed prepared to take responsibility for her . . . "

"Oh, right-o. I mean, certainly, your Honor."

"Well, then, we will see you both in ten days time. That will be all."

"Excuse me, your Honor, but what about the horse and wagon?"

"Those will remain in the custody of this court until the trial."

Uh-oh, thought Davey, *not good*. However, he nodded respectfully to the magistrate and got his Grandmother out of the courtroom as quickly as he could.

The old girl was in bad shape. He'd expected that. No Romani person likes public buildings, be they hospitals or courtrooms. Jails were the worst of all. His own sensitivities to such things had gotten a bit dulled in the twelve years he'd spent on his own in London, ever since he was fifteen. Annie Lee, though, was still fussy about such things. She had been locked up for over a day, now, which he was sure was the longest amount of time she'd been confined in all her life.

"I've got to get clean," she said, as soon as they got outside.

"You didn't pick up any lice in there, did you?"

"No. No, it's just the place."

Davey understood. It was not the contact with non-Romani people that made his Gran feel defiled. She was not bothered by that. It was simply having been forced to stay in a place that felt "not good" to her. He saw her eyeing the public fountain that sat in a dismal little park at the center of town and realized he'd better act quickly or she'd be headed for it and adding indecent exposure to her list of misdemeanors. Not that he had ever been able to understand what was indecent about exposing the naked human form. *If it's good enough for God, who made it*, he always reasoned, *shouldn't it be good enough for the rest of us?*

"There's some running water," Annie said, veering toward the fountain. Davey put his arm around her, and steered her in another direction.

"Come on, Gran," he said, "I've got a better idea."

The snooty clerk at The Rose and Swan wasn't too happy about renting them a room, but when Davey pulled out his wallet, still fat with pound notes, the man had silently handed him a key.

Annie Lee didn't like the hotel bathtub as well as she would have liked a forest stream, but even she seemed to realize she couldn't be too choosy just then. Davey Lee left her soaking in a hot tub, having given him instructions to wash her clothing right away.

"Sure, Gran," he had said. But one look at her faded skirt and old brown sweater convinced him otherwise. For one thing, she would have wanted him to wash the clothes in the old Romani way, using separate buckets for things worn above the waist and those worn below, and he just didn't want to bother with it. For another, he could see it was high time the old girl had some new duds.

Tweeverton didn't offer much in the way of fashion. He couldn't see Annie in the sensible house dresses or pants suits on offer from the local Marks and Sparks. Then his eye lit upon a little boutique called Michelle's. Worth a try.

He was a bit taken aback to be greeted by a bald young woman dressed all in black. He knew it was currently fashionable, in some circles, for girls to shave their heads. He found it startling. But after the first shock, he decided that a bald head could be rather fetching, in its way.

"Shopping for your girlfriend, luv?" she'd asked him.

"Naw, for me Gran."

"Never!" laughed the girl.

So he told her the whole story. She got right into the spirit of it. They settled on a long, full, blue satin skirt the girl said was meant for evening wear, but which Davey thought would do nicely for everyday. He also got a white silk blouse with lace at the collar and cuffs, a deep green velvet vest, and several long scarves in shades of orange, rose, and lime. When it came to colors, Davey felt the more and the brighter, the better. After all, God had made the rainbow, and if it was good enough for the Big G, shouldn't it be good enough for the rest of us? To complete the outfit, he chose red leather boots, white silk stockings, a complete set of shocking pink underwear, and a small gold chain, for his Father had always told him "every true Romani must always have about them a bit of silk and a bit of gold."

When the girl told him the price, he gave a low whistle, but he didn't really mind. Life was too short to be stingy. Besides, hadn't God been generous with him? No one ever came up to him with a price tag for his next breath of air; no angel had ever showed up to charge him for the pleasure of a sunset. So why should he, Davey Lee, be mean about some clothes? He was glad, though, that his intuition had led him to that cash register in Mayfair. The funds were definitely coming in handy.

A few minutes later, he bounded up to their room at The Rose and Swan with one arm full of pleasantly rustling packages, the other holding a bag full of hot fish and chips, and the phone number of the boutique clerk in his pocket.

Annie Lee was sitting naked on the bed, with only a clean sheet wrapped partially around her like a toga. Davey Lee knew she wouldn't eat until she had put on clean clothes, so he put the fish and chips on one side.

"Dear Granma," he said in Romani, "I beg you to accept these clothes in honor of all the times you have helped me. You have given me food when I was hungry, shelter when I was cold, comfort when I was alone. Please accept these small gifts in return."

Gravely, Annie Lee accepted the packages. She examined the clothes in silence, taking her time, not the least embarrassed by her own partial nakedness. *She is like that, she is like no one else,* Davey thought.

Not for the first time, Davey felt profoundly grateful for his Gran's eccentricity, if that was even the right word for it. Only with her did he not feel a secret whisper of loneliness deep in his soul.

Davey was by nature a very sociable person. That and his gift of mimicry allowed him to fit into many situations. When he was in London, he spoke like a Cockney. In Shropshire, he had the accent and manners of a farm lad. Once, in Oxford, he had even succeeded in stealing a Don's robes, and impersonating a visiting professor of Egyptology. A cluster of young students had invited him to the dining hall, and he had entertained them well with stories of his latest dig in the Valley of the Kings, and Emilia, his beautiful assistant from Lichtenstein. He had sustained this enjoyable new identity through roast chicken, peas, and delicious dinner rolls with fresh butter. But when the raspberry trifle was being served, he noticed some professors across the room scrutinizing him in a none-too-friendly manner. At that point, he had bid a fond farewell to his young companions, sprinted out of the dining hall, and across the campus, shedding academic robes as he ran.

He had felt right at home being Dr. Ahmed Merriweather, Anglo-Egyptian archeologist. He felt right at home in most situations, he realized, and yet not quite anywhere. Not even with his Romani family.

"You need to honor your Romani heritage. You are Romani, never forget that." Davey had heard this all his life. Yet he was not quite sure what it meant.

He had relatives who couldn't abide the word "Gypsy." They saw it as an insult, and insisted on being referred to as "Romani," which harkened back to long ago origins in India. Others cheerfully referred to themselves as "Gypsies," or even "Romani Gypsies." Then there was the use of the term "Travellers." Not so much an ethnic term, as a description of a way of life, those who travelled from place to place, be it by horse drawn barrel wagon, or by motor homes. "Travellers" could include Irish Gypsies, and Tinkers, those not of Romani blood. Yet Romani could be considered "Travellers" in their life style.

To make matters more complicated, many Romanai no longer wandered, but led settled lives, sent their children to school, went to university, and did well in the *gadjo,* non-Gypsy world, yet considered themselves proudly Romani, a credit to their heritage.

"You give us a bad name," Davey's father had told him every time he got in trouble with the law. "Don't let down the honor of the Romani. Stop acting like a stereotype."

Davey understood. It was a stereotype that all Romani were thieves. He felt, though, that his own struggles with the law had nothing to do with his background. He had simply been born with a gift for theft, a genius for improvisation and mimicry, and a need to sort out his own morality that he kept avoiding, but knew he had to face sooner or later. None of this, as far as he could see, had to do with him being Romani. It was just part of the struggle and joy of him being ... himself. Whatever that truly was.

His relatives never saw it that way, though. Those who resented the *gadjo* world applauded his skill at crime. Those who lived educated, achieving lives were distressed by it. And those who lived traditionally saw his behavior only in terms of how it reflected on being Romani. It was like living in a photograph taken through a colored lens. Everything was tinted a shade of Romani. Davey valued being Romani. If the Romani language and customs and music were lost, if no one any longer traveled the by ways and secret places of the world with caravans and Clydesdales, it would be a terrible thing. So clearly, being Romani meant something to him; it was a deep part of him. But sometimes he didn't want it to be *all* of him.

Thank God for Gran, he thought. *Somehow she understands all this, without needing to say a word about it.* Like him, she was Romani, but she was also something else.

Just as he thought of his Gran, he heard her voice.

"Davey," she said gently, "Davey."

She was standing by him, tugging softly at his sleeve. Embarrassed, Davey realized he had slipped into another one of his reveries. "Out to lunch again," was what his family called it. But his Gran referred to his dreaminess as "mind journeys," and was never bothered by him being momentarily "away."

"Sorry, Gran," Davey said.

His Grandmother just smiled, and held up the clothes he had given her.

"I'm going to go put these glad rags on," she said, with a twinkle in her eye.

She went into the bathroom and closed the door, as if the act of dressing was somehow more private than that of being semi- naked in a sheet. Through the door, Davey heard her humming to herself, which was a good sign. When she emerged, he whistled in appreciation.

"You look smashing!" he exclaimed.

The blue satin skirt, white blouse, and green vest fit her perfectly. She had wrapped the rose-colored scarf around her head and wore the gold chain not around her neck but wrapped around her slender waist. The red leather boots caught the light as she stepped into the room.

She saw herself in the full-length mirror and smiled. Then she began to twirl and dance around the room like a young girl in her first party dress. Davey Lee relaxed. The clothes were a hit.

Annie Lee came up to him, took his face in her pale hands, and said in Romani, "Thank you, my dear, for helping me so generously in my time of need." She kissed him on the forehead, and Davey Lee was struck, as he always was, by how good she smelled. It wasn't just the scent of soap from her bath or the posh, violet smell of the new clothes; it was her own smell, the smell of rain and meadow sweet. Her hands upon his face felt dry and warm as sunshine.

"I was glad to do it, Gran," he said, switching back to the English he was actually more comfortable speaking. "Now, let's eat! I'm starved!"

He had been afraid she wouldn't touch the food,she was very particular about what she called "the energy of whoever cooked it." Fast food did not usually pass muster with her. But somehow, the act of his bringing it made the meal acceptable. From the speed with which she polished off her share of fish and chips and washed it down with Guinness, he figured she hadn't eaten a bite since they put her in the lock-up. Hadn't considered it kosher, so to speak.

"Now, we must do something about Chieftain," she said.

"Well, Gran, it's only for a few days. I'm sure we can work out a way for you to visit him."

"No, no, no," said Annie. "We have to *spring* him. Like you *sprung* me. He can't stay with strangers for a week. Besides, we have to leave, now, today!"

"Now, Gran," said Davey, "What's this all about?"

A few minutes later, he was almost wishing he hadn't asked.

"So you got your Calling," he said, "and you're trying to go to it. But how can it be so far away and keep on for so long?"

"I don't know," said Annie. "But the more I head South and West, the stronger it becomes. I think we're very close now, less than twenty miles. And I must get there! That's why I was on the M5, you see. I thought it would save some time. I never counted on there being so many cars. A real inconvenience, all those cars."

"Too true," acknowledged Davey sympathetically.

"So you see," his Grandmother concluded, "why I have to leave tonight."

"But if you leave, you'll be in more trouble with the law. Just stick around 'til the hearing. I'll pay whatever fine they wallop you with, and you can be on your way."

"No time," said Annie. "That judge and his laws don't matter a flea's fart in the wind to me, Davey. I must answer the Calling, now. *That* matters. I don't know what is going on, but I must respond to it, now."

Davey sighed. "The trouble with you, Gran, is you're weird."

Annie Lee laughed. "I know. Even other Gypsies think I'm strange." She shrugged.

Davey sipped his second Guinness, and looked at her. She sat there now, on the edge of the bed, with her frail old hands calmly folded in her lap and a look of peaceful determination in her blue, blue eyes. Any other old bird would have been dithering and weeping by now, but Annie was serenity itself. He knew that if he didn't agree to help her, she would slip out the door as soon as he wasn't looking. She'd try to get Chieftain by herself and be arrested again before the night was done. He couldn't let that happen. Besides, upon reflection, he felt it might not be a bad idea for him to disappear for awhile, considering that cash register in Mayfair. Vanish, like a snowflake on a hot stone. And what better place to do it than the countryside in spring, as only the Romani knew it? Yes, he could do with a bit of a ramble.

"Okay," he said, "I'll help you."

"Thank you, Davey," she said sweetly, looking not at all surprised.

"But there's terms. I am not signing on as your student, to learn about those weeds and things. We've talked about that before. I know how bad you want an apprentice, but it ain't me; it's not my look out. So that's clear, right?"

"Of course, Davey."

"Right. I'm just coming along for a week or two to help with this Calling thing. Actually, if we do it right, we might figure that out and still have you back here in time for your court date."

"Yes, dear," Annie said meekly.

109

"I suppose you're determined to bring Chieftain with? We couldn't just rent a car or something?"

Annie Lee shook her head. "He is part of this, somehow. Besides, the wagon has all my herbs, and I may need them."

"Well, then, you're right, we'll need to spring him as soon as possible. All the same, we'd better lay low 'til nighttime."

Annie Lee looked down at her lap and smiled.

"Whatever you say, dear."

***

Two more houses to go, thought Gwen. In the last three hours she had seen snapshots of Mrs. Grimsby's niece's latest baby, heard more about turnips than she had ever dreamed possible from the greengrocer, and taken tea with Col. G. B. Prithwell, lately retired from the RAF, who had been stationed for many years in the Canary Islands and whose knowledge of the lesser-known customs of that place was, she soon discovered, considerable.

The Walmsleys next, she decided. She was curious to see the home of the red-haired children who seemed to be the terror of Far Tauverly. She feared the letter she bore would be unwelcome, though. It was addressed to "Robert Walmsley, 38 Milsom Road." The return address said "Aldington Collection Services." Gwen rather hoped that no one would be home, and she could slip the letter quietly through the slot. Such encounters seemed to be a rarity in this place, though. People opened their doors before she was halfway up the walk, curious to chat with a new face.

Gwen did not have to look at the number on the gatepost to know she had found the right house; it was unlike any other in Far Tauverly. All the houses were built of red brick or gray stone, and in that regard, this one was no exception, being of the gray stone variety. And like the other houses, it had a slate-tiled roof and a narrow chimney. There the resemblance ended. The other houses in the village were almost fiercely tidy, with their front lawns well-mowed or planted with well-groomed rose bushes, soon to flower. This house, however, seemed not so much to sit upon the land as to sprawl all over it, as if it had not been built, but rather come about by some kind of collision of elements or a drunken fairy's enchantment. Its door tilted one way and its windows another, and the ancient roof sagged in the middle. The curtains at the windows were half off the rods, with just a bit of lace or flowered chintz hanging there; more as if to pay lip service to the idea of a curtain than to do the actual work of a curtain.

As for the garden, it was a wonder of confusion. Between the low stone fence near the street and the house grew a knee-high field of weeds and grass and wildflowers, Sweet William and hyacinth, all intertwined as if some giddy child had simply tossed handfuls of seeds to the wind, and this was the result. In one corner of the lawn, if so it could be called, grew a venerable willow tree. A rather labyrinthine tree house peered from amid its branches. Strung between the tree and the house were several lengths of rope, which seemed to be serving as clothes lines, if indeed the articles hanging there could be called clothing. By their sunbleached appearance, they seemed to be in permanent residence upon the lines, like tattered banners, flapping sadly in the wind.

Through this jungle of a lawn prowled several cats and a Golden Retriever. Gwen put her hand on the gate, and the retriever growled. Then, having a change of heart, it came forward, snuffled at her hand in a slobbering fashion, and wagged its tail.

Gwen could not find anything that resembled a mailbox anywhere.

I suppose I shall have to knock on the door, she thought, reluctantly.

As she stepped down the path toward the house, the dog leaned lovingly against her right leg as though glued there, while two of the cats kept weaving around her feet, purring loudly.

The path was littered with toys of every description. Lego sets, tricycles, buckets, balls, dismembered dolls, and stuffed rabbits and bears all lay where their small owners had dropped them, and all were in a bedraggled state, as if their lives were even harder than that of most toys.

Gwen reached the front steps. The door, which had once been painted blue, was ajar. Inside, she glimpsed a dim jumble of furniture and toys that made the lawn seem neat. From somewhere in the back of the house, she heard the sound of a television.

Someone's home, she thought, with mixed feelings. She saw that the faded blue door boasted a brass knocker shaped like a lion's head. Someone, it was true, had inked a pair of black mustachios on the lion's proud face. Gwen reached up for the brass ring the lion held in his teeth, and the entire knocker came off in her hand.

Oh dear, she thought. Inside the house, a baby began to cry. Not a lusty demand for food, but a thin little splinter of protest, weak as watered gruel.

Gwen looked at the unhappy letter in her hand and thought about reaching through the half-open door and just leaving it amidst the debris on the nearest table. Just at that moment, though, a man appeared in the doorway.

"What do you want then?" he demanded fiercely. "I'm telling you, if you're from that damned collection agency, you're not welcome here. And if you're from the school, I don't know where the kids are. Why can't you keep track of them? That's your job, isn't it?"

The man was large, unshaven, and balding, but with enough red hair left to leave no doubt of his identity. He was dressed in faded, wrinkled clothes that looked like he'd slept in them for the last several days.

"Mr. Walmsley?" Gwen asked.

"What of it if I am? Which I ain't sayin' I am."

"Logan, the postman, asked me to deliver this to you. I'm helping him with his rounds today. I couldn't find your mail box, so I, er, knocked."

She handed Mr. Walmsley the letter, along with the brass door knocker. He tossed the latter aside. He glowered at the letter. Then, reading the return address, he cursed.

"Damn them, damn them, damn them!" he cried. "Where do they think the money's supposed to come from?"

He seized a lamp from a nearby table and hurled it against the wall.

Gwen felt the time might be ripe to take her leave, but catching sight of her frightened face, the man struggled to get a grip on himself.

"My God, I'm sorry, luv," he said ruefully. "I disgust myself sometimes, and that's a fact." He looked at her for the first time. "New here, aren't you?"

"Just visiting,"

"And how'd you meet Logan then? Ah, well, never mind, everyone with ears and the price of a pint meets Logan soon enough."

The man ventured a smile, and Gwen saw the remnants of rugged good looks on his weary face. *He's not that old,* she realized, *only in his thirties.*

The man smoothed his shirt, as if noticing for the first time how wrinkled it was. "I'm sorry," he repeated, "I must have given you a real fright. I'm not myself these days. Please let me make it up to you by offering a cuppa. My wife's about the place somewhere, and I'm sure she'd like to meet you."

Gwen had no wish to stay in that sad place a moment longer, but the man's eyes held such an appeal to be allowed to restore a shred of his dignity that she could not refuse it.

"That would be very nice," she replied. The man seemed relieved.

"Come in, come in," he said, ushering her through the chaotic living room toward the kitchen in the back.

"Marianne!" he called, "We've a guest!"

The kitchen was just as chaotic as the rest of the house but more cheerfully so. Its windows overlooked the back lawn, and Gwen could tell that on a sunny day the room would be bright and warm. The sink was full of dishes, and so were the countertops, yet there was an air of activity about the room that made it seem brighter than the rest of the house. A red oilcloth, somewhat smeared with jam, covered the table. On it sat a small, black and white television and several empty beer bottles. A ginger cat lay resting in the dish rack, and a black and white one snoozed on top of the refrigerator. Every bit of wall space was covered with bright children's drawings.

"Have a seat," said the man, pulling out a rickety chair. "I'll just see where the Missus is."

A woman appeared in the doorway, cradling a baby in her arms. Everything about her seemed as faded and worn as the laundry that hung on the line outside. Her hair was a mousy brown, and even her blue eyes were faded, as though washed by too many tears, yet there was a gentleness, a mildness about her that was soothing. If she was surprised to see a stranger there in her kitchen, she did not show it but merely smiled faintly and put the kettle on.

"Marianne, this is—what did you say your name was?"

"Gwen Fields."

"Right. This is Gwen Fields, and she's visiting here, God knows why. Logan asked her to deliver the mail, so I thought it might be nice if we offered her some tea."

Marianne's thin hands were already placing cups and saucers on the table. She smiled shyly at Gwen but said nothing.

"Where are you from then, Miss Fields?" asked Mr. Walmsley.

"America. Denver."

"Denver! That's the Wild West, isn't it? Cowboys and ranches and all that?"

113

Gwen smiled. "Not quite, I'm afraid. More like office buildings and concrete."

"Hmmm," said the man. "Plenty of jobs there then, right? Not like here. Here, damn it, if a man gets laid off one job, it seems like he can never find another. Go on the dole, they say, but by God, I'm telling you, it eats away at you, it really does; all your self-respect is gone."

"Bob," his wife said, quietly. Her voice was singularly sweet and seemed to recall the man to the best of himself with a single word.

"Sorry, Miss Fields," Mr. Walmsley said, a bit shamefaced. "I'm not fit company lately, that I'm not."

"It's all right," Gwen said, hoping he believed her.

Marianne placed before them a plate of thinly sliced bread, spread with whitish margarine. Then she poured three cups of tea and rather shyly sat down, taking the baby back into her arms, where it began to wriggle and coo.

Gwen glanced around the kitchen, hoping to find a topic of conversation that would not set off Mr. Walmsley's depression and might bring his wife out of her shyness a little. Wherever she looked, she saw pictures by children: bright paintings in tempera, penciled scrawls, crayon sketches. Many degrees of skill were evident, but all shared a common undaunted approach. One in particular caught her eye: a painting of two lions, looking very much like the lions on the Greniston gate. Between them gleamed what seemed to be a large emerald.

"Osgood did that one," Mr. Walmsley said, following her gaze. "Got a rare talent, he has."

"It looks like they all do," Gwen said appreciatively. "How many children do you have?"

"Seven," said Mr. Walmsley, "including the youngest, here."

A frown returned to his face. "Seven kids," he muttered, "and where's the money to feed them supposed to come from?"

For a moment, Mr. Walmsley stared moodily into the distance. Then, with a muttered "Excuse me," he grabbed a bottle of beer from the counter and charged out the door.

"You must excuse Bob, Miss Fields," Anne Walmsley said, in her sweet, gentle voice. "He doesn't half worry about the kids, and it's been hard on him, being laid off and all. He's a good man, though, I wouldn't want you to think otherwise."

"Of course not," said Gwen.

"I'll walk you out."

They stood for a moment at the door, looking at one another. Gwen gazed with respect at the other woman's drawn face and weary but uncomplaining smile. Anne Walmsley examined every detail of Gwen's appearance as well, from her pink earrings to her flowered silk blouse. There was no envy in her gaze, only a wistful wonder, as if she had forgotten such nice things existed. When their eyes met again, a look of feminine sympathy passed between them.

"It was nice to meet you," Gwen said honestly.

"Nice to meet you, too. But I'd better be getting back now." Rather reluctantly, Mrs. Walmsley closed the faded blue door.

One more letter, Gwen thought, feeling she had seen a bit more of life in Far Tauverly than she had bargained for. *The Vicar. That should be nice and uneventful.*

Gwen crossed the churchyard of St. Aethelrood's, heading toward the vicarage next door. She was struck by the great number of yew trees that dotted the grounds. They were ornamental yews, the kind that people trim into decorative shapes or even into birds and animals. These yews had obviously been carefully formed into something, but just what she could not quite tell. The one nearest her looked like three lumpy masses of green. There was, however, a small label at its roots, which she bent over to read.

"The Three Wisemen approaching Bethlehem," it said.

She stepped back and considered the bushes again but was unable to tell whether the wise men were on camels or approaching on foot.

She wandered about the lawn, pondering other groups of bushes. She gazed in perplexity at "Christ on the Road to Emmaus, The Woman at the Well," and a Nativity Scene in which lumps that might be sheep mingled with angels or possibly shepherds. She was about to move on to "Moses in the Desert," when a cheery voice called out, "How nice to see someone enjoying the Yew Garden! Hello, my dear. You must be Miss Fields! I've already heard about your arrival from the baker, Mrs. Hodges, Mrs. Grimsby, and three of the Walmsley children! Welcome to Far Tauverly. I'm Reverend Sterling, the Vicar here. Although I suppose you gathered that already, the collar does rather give me away."

There was something about the Vicar that made it impossible not to smile. Perhaps it was because he himself seemed to be forever beaming. He was a round, pink-faced man, whose bald head was as shiny as a polished Easter egg. A few wisps of sandy hair curled wistfully about his ears, and his brows were shaggy, like a terrier's. His bright blue eyes gazed out from behind steel-rimmed spectacles. It was the spectacles, perhaps, that gave him the look of a schoolboy. He looked like he was dressed as a vicar for a part in some school fete and had wandered away from the rehearsal.

Because he was near-sighted, the Vicar stood disconcertingly close to people and stared at them, his head tilted to one side. He did so now, following right beside Gwen, ushering her through the garden.

"Now this," he said, gesturing toward another bunch of yews, "is the arrival of Joseph of Arimathea at Glastonbury Tor. Not exactly a Biblical topic, but definitely part of our religious lore."

"It's amazing," said Gwen, feeling that the word was an accurate reaction. "Do you actually trim all these yourself?"

"Oh, absolutely, absolutely. I do all the garden work myself. But I say, won't you come in and have a spot of tea? What a pity my wife is away from home just now, but perhaps you'll meet her if you stay on for a few days. Yes, come this way, please. Mind the herbaceous border, yes, right this way."

Still chattering, the Vicar led Gwen into the house. She soon realized that his conversation was constant, like the burbling of a stream, and rarely called for response. She could relax and almost think her own thoughts, surrounded by the flow of words like a stone in the current. She wondered if the Vicar's wife was a quiet woman, perhaps even a touch deaf. Certainly, she was a good housekeeper, for the parlor the Vicar led Gwen into was immaculate. The lace curtains gleamed white, like cascades of snowflakes against the sparkling windows; the furniture smelled of lemon oil; the wood floors shone as if newly polished. It was a fussy room but a kindly one as well. Gwen sank gratefully into a peach-colored armchair.

"I do think," the Vicar was saying, "that the festivity of the occasion merits, perhaps, a drop of sherry—don't you, my dear? I am sure Alice would not object, if she were here. Yes, I do think sherry is quite in order, though it is not yet two. But then, why not risk censure? I doubt if the Almighty is overly concerned if we occasionally have a drop before supper. Besides, I have somewhere—where is that tin?—oh, here it is—on the sideboard, fancy that!—some excellent sherry biscuits, the very thing, you see. Yes, now. Here you are."

Gwen sipped the amber-colored liquid and leaned back into the armchair. Her host seemed to be describing, in some detail, a rare species of lily he had just read about. It would have been easy to slip into a doze, and Gwen wondered if Mrs. Sterling sometimes did. She sat up just in time to hear the Vicar say, "And so, while gardening is my summer passion, the miniatures fill my winters. So, come along, and I'll show you my latest project."

She followed him to his study. In the center of the room was a large table, on which rested what Gwen at first thought was a model train track. On closer inspection, she saw that it was actually a model of Far Tauverly and the surrounding countryside. The detail was amazing. There was a tiny Greenstone Arms, complete down to its painted sign and the flowers in the window boxes. She recognized, in the garden behind it, the apple tree that she saw from the room of her window. And there was the museum, and the bakery, the post office—it was complete in every detail. Even the forest beyond the village was there and a miniature Greniston Manor.

"This is marvelous," exclaimed Gwen.

The Vicar beamed. "I've been working on it for twelve years, now. I want it to be accurate in every detail. You can see here, on the North side of the church, I'm trying to capture the exact reds and blues of the thirteenth-century windows. Hard to match, though . . . "

Gwen's gaze wandered across the road from the church, to the Walmsleys' house. She saw that in spite of his wish to be accurate, the Vicar had upgraded its appearance. Its lawn was mowed, planted with hyacinths, and the only toy in sight was a tidy swing set. Gone was the tree house in the willow, and the wildflowers and the clothesline.

Noticing her interest, the Vicar said, "I took the liberty of tidying up the Walmsleys' a bit. They are, umm, a good but unruly family."

"I believe they have fallen on hard times," said Gwen. "Mr. Walmsley is out of work."

The Vicar blinked. "Oh? Yes, I have heard about that. And of course, it's very hard to keep a place neat with five children running about . . . "

"Seven," interrupted Gwen, "They have seven children."

The Vicar looked surprised. "Oh really? I'm embarrassed to admit I lose track of those children. They rather run together like a pack of young hounds. Good children, but lively. Now, over here, you see, is the McFaulton Garden, which is what I'm working on. You will note the rambling clematis vine. I've managed to get just the right shade of purple for the petals. . . ."

Gwen felt a twinge of irritation with this man who knew more about every garden in town than he did about the family across the street. Then she thought of how often Filipo always reminded her, "You have to take people as they are, Gwen. The whole cloth." Perhaps the Vicar was nearsighted toward one family in his parish. On the other hand, he cared for his garden down to the last yew leaf, and that was worth something too, surely. *Don't judge people so impulsively*, Gwen told herself, *like you always do.*

"And over here," the Vicar was happily saying, "are the famous, dare I say, world famous? Well, perhaps not quite, and just as well. But certainly, I may venture to say the famous, at least locally, in our little world, mounds. The larger one, of course, is Arthur's Mound. And there, of course, is Merlin's Oak. If you look closely, you can see the Oak itself, and hard by to the West, some beeches. Quite a challenge, the bark of those beeches was. . . . ."

"And those golden flowers in a circle around the mound, those would be the daffodils?"

"Yes. They were the main reason I chose to portray Far Tauverly at just this time of year, so that the daffodils might be in bloom on the mound. If you look closely," he added, handing her a magnifying glass, "you can see that each flower—there are three hundred and thirty seven of them, by the way—is exact. Six petals, center trumpet, three-part stamen."

"Amazing," said Gwen. "You know," she added, "I seem to be seeing a lot of daffodils lately." She reached into her pocket and pulled out one of the golden buttons.

"I . . . um . . . found this the other day, and I've been showing it to everyone, but no one knows whose it is. I think it must be an antique and possibly valuable."

Rev. Sterling took the magnifying glass and carefully scrutinized the button. "Oh my," he said appreciatively, "that is unusual! And such fine and delicate workmanship, too. A lion, holding a daffodil. . . . Now, I have seen that somewhere before, . . . not on a button, but I've seen that emblem. A very odd symbol, though very appealing, of course. But where? Ah yes, of course! Lord Peter's shield!"

"Lord Peter Greniston? The one whose portrait is at the museum?"

"Yes," said the Vicar. "So glad you've had the chance to see some of our antiquities, by the way. Far Tauverly has quite a fascinating history. There has been a village on this sight since at least six hundred AD, if not earlier, you know, and while digging in this very garden, I myself have found flints which seem to date from - "

"But about Lord Peter's shield," Gwen urged, gently trying to lead the Vicar back to the point.

"Ah, yes, how silly of me! It's in *The Yellow Portrait*. Not the one at the museum. *The Yellow Portrait* hangs at Greniston Manor. Lord Peter's journals are there, too."

"Really?" said Gwen.

"Oh yes, fascinating reading, too. He was quite a student of local history, you know. Very intrigued by King Arthur and the mounds."

"I read his prophecy."

"Ah, that's just the beginning. Evidently, his journals are full of his thoughts on the subject. I, of course, was scanning them to find the plans of the Greniston herb gardens; they were quite extensive in Lord Peter's day. A master gardener he was, among many other things. Quite the 'man for all seasons,' as they say. Even had yew hedges—ahead of his time, in so many ways. Yes, I enjoyed my glance at those journals very much. Lord Greniston kindly allowed me to read them a few years ago. I couldn't take them away from the manor, of course, but I was invited to come every afternoon and sit there in the portrait gallery and, under the very gaze of Lord Peter himself, read the journals at the very table where they perhaps were written. Marvelous experience. And Lord Greniston very kindly had tea sent up to me. A very fine tea, every single day. Three kinds of cheese, and Mrs. Fitzpatrick's Irish soda bread."

"Do you suppose Lord Greniston would let me look at those journals?" Gwen ventured to ask.

"Why, my dear, I'm sure he would. What a pity he's gone away."

"Gone away?" To her own surprise, Gwen's heart skipped a beat.

"Yes. I ran into Robert at the greengrocer's, and he told me that Lord Greniston went up to London this morning."

"Will he be back soon, do you think?" Gwen felt instantly embarrassed at how intent she sounded, but the Vicar didn't seem to notice.

The Vicar shook his head. "Hard to say, hard to say with Lord Greniston and his little jaunts. Sometimes he's gone for a few hours, sometimes several weeks. Staff never know what to expect."

"I see," said Gwen. She was startled by how disappointed she felt. It wasn't as if she could look forward to seeing Greniston again, not after their wretched encounter on the street the day before. Yet the thought of not seeing him again was even worse.

"Yes," the Vicar was saying, "Lord Peter's shield is the only place I've seen a lion with a daffodil. Never seen a button like this before, though," he added, rather regretfully handing it back to Gwen. "Very lovely. Such detail, and so small." From the wistful tone in the Vicar's voice, Gwen realized that perhaps the old question of how many angels can fit on the head of a pin was a real and appealing one to him.

"Thank you for all your help," she said. "I think I must be going now."

"Ah. Well, before you go, I don't suppose you'd like to sign my petition, would you?"

"Your petition?"

"Yes. It's for Amnesty International. Trying to exert pressure on the Turkish government to release a political prisoner there; a very brave young woman named Hazemi. Now, where is it?"

Rather dismayed, the Vicar eyed his desk, which, Gwen was relieved to see, was the one oasis of messiness in that house. She was glad, somehow, that the Vicar's sense of tidiness wasn't perfect after all. Evidently, his wife wisely dusted around the clutter of papers and books on the old, roll-top desk.

"Must be here somewhere. . . ."

As the Vicar searched, Gwen thought he would have seemed more likely to be circulating a petition about tulip planting in the Tweeverton Parks rather than the freeing of political prisoners.

"Ah! Now, here's one about food to Somalia! Why not sign this one while I continue my little quest, here. Here's a pen. And here's another about grain to Yugoslavia; that one calls for a donation, actually. Perhaps you'd care to? Every penny helps. . . ."

"You seem to be involved in a great many causes," Gwen remarked.

"It's all just one cause, really," the Vicar replied. "We mustn't lose sight of the big picture, you know."

More surprised than ever, Gwen remembered something else Filipo often said, "People are always more than they seem to be." And here was the Vicar, whose idea of heaven might be a miniature cosmos that could fit into a thimble, urging her to keep a big picture. Perhaps he didn't know every need of his own fellow villagers, yet he saw the world as one big village. Yes, Filipo was right: people were always more than they seemed to be.

"Now this is last Sunday's sermon. Some little thoughts of mine on Christ at Emmaus. But where that other petition is, I can't think. Alice would know. Thank goodness she is due back on Saturday. The 8:32 train to Tweeverton; I'm to pick her up at the station of course. Or was it the 9:32? Ah! Here is a catalogue of crocus blooms. Some very nice ones, too. Must show it to Lettice Pennington—we share a horticultural passion—if I may use so daring a phrase without risking your censure, my dear. But where . . . ?"

"I'll tell you what," said Gwen, "I'll stop by tomorrow or the next day and read the petition. That way, you can have plenty of time to find it."

"Ah! Quite the best plan," said Reverend Sterling, looking relieved.

***

The bells of St. Aethelrood were tolling three o'clock as Gwen crossed the vicarage lawn. The mist was thicker, now. She made her way among the uncertain shapes of sculpted yews, passing between "The Return of the Prodigal Son" and "Ruth Amid the Alien Corn." She thought she saw a movement to her left, as if someone had quickly darted into the bushes. At first she thought it was one of the Walmsley children, but the figure had seemed too tall for that of a child.

"Hello?" Gwen called out. There was no reply. Her own voice sounded odd to her, cushioned by the mist, somehow.

She walked on toward Milsom road. She had the strangest certainty that she was being watched.

"Hello?" she called out again.

Once again, only silence answered her. Yet it was a silence that seemed to listen. Someone was there, watching her, she was sure of it.

Then, to her right, only a few feet away in the mist, it seemed, a man began to sing. He had a pleasant baritone voice. The melody he sang was becoming familiar to Gwen, although she had not realized it had words to it.

"J'attends ma belle toujours,

121

Ah, c'est ne pas heureux;
Elle ne me dit rien,
Ah, Dieu, qu'elle me reviens . . . "

The words brought a haunting quality to the spirited dance Gwen had played just the evening before last. The voice was cheerful enough; quite a cultivated voice, but with something odd in the way it accented the French.

"Hello?" Gwen called out again.

"Chere dame, m'ecoute, j'espere.
Que vous m'aide, je suis vers."

Gwen translated the words: "Dear Lady, hear me. I hope that you will help me, for I am true."

Now the mysterious singer merely hummed the melody, sweetly and truly, with a note of great longing in the sound. Although still unseen, the voice seemed so close at hand that Gwen's spine tingled.

"Where are you? *Who* are you?" she called.

The voice simply faded away. Gwen looked in every direction, but there was no one there—only the trees and the yew sculptures and the gathering mist. The world now seemed very quiet.

Whatever happens with Swindon or Greniston, Gwen thought, *I'm not leaving Far Tauverly until I find out what all this is about.*

CHAPTER EIGHT

Logan Knowelles fussed happily with his "frying pan stew." It was one of his specialties, and involved the slow simmering of chicken, scallions, mushrooms, peas, basil, dill, and a secret broth, until these ingredients reached a moment of perfect harmony, which, unless his nose deceived him, was fast approaching.

Perfect. He turned the hot plate burner down very low, so that the stew would be ready to serve, not the moment Gwen arrived, but about twenty minutes later.

Next, he turned his attention to the dessert course. On the counter that was supposed to be used for sorting mail sat four dishes of chocolate pudding. Logan had made the pudding from an instant mix. The box had been damaged, and the grocer had given it to him for practically nothing. Now, using a penknife, half a bar of Cadbury's chocolate left over from the picnic with Gwen, and a few fresh mint leaves from Lettice Pennington's garden, Logan sculpted chocolate roses to decorate the puddings. Now that these were complete and cooling nicely, it left a burner free for the kettle. For the rest, there was a loaf of bread, which scarcely seemed day-old, sliced cucumber, olives, and the piccalilli relish Mrs. Grimsby had kindly contributed to the feast.

"You must have some garnish on the side to make it a proper company dinner," she told him. She had also kindly lent him plates and cups from her second best blue willow china, when Logan, in a panic, had discovered he did not have enough matching dishes to serve two people. He thought that the dishes looked quite nice on the makeshift dining table he'd contrived from his desk. With a sheet as a tablecloth, hanging almost to the floor, you could hardly tell it was a desk at all. He had put Gwen's chair at the knee well, so that she would have more room. He himself would sit sideways along the back, dining "side-saddle."

A bouquet of daffodils and grape hyacinths in an old pickle jar that looked just like a vase, if you didn't scrutinize the rim, and some candles in wine bottles completed the decor. Mabel Hodges had given him the empty bottles, or at least she would have if she had been there at the moment he passed the inn's trash cans. As for the candles, they were a contribution from Her Majesty, Queen Elizabeth. They were white household candles, the kind to be used if the power blacks out. They came with the official postal emergency kit, along with a packet of band aids and a bottle of mercurochrome. Technically, they were government property; however, Logan reasoned that if Queen Elizabeth had met Gwen, she would certainly want to be entertaining her at Buckingham Palace and therefore would not begrudge the loan of a few candles, did she but know about the situation.

They added quite a continental touch, Logan felt. The candles glowed, the china sparkled, the air smelled delicious, and a beautiful young lady was coming to dinner. On any other day, Logan's happiness would have been complete. On this day, though, a fluttering panic kept rising near his heart. It was those envelopes, those cursed envelopes. They had arrived in the morning mail bag, he'd seen them right away. One from the tax department, the other from the Postal Service itself. Both addressed to Logan Knowelles. Two stern-looking government envelopes. He had received many such envelopes in recent months. He always stuffed them hastily into some drawer or cubbyhole, muttering, "I'll look at it tomorrow." After enough tomorrows, he would come across one of the envelopes again, and murmur, "Oh dear! Look at that postmark! Oh well, it must be quite obsolete by now." Then he would toss the letter away, unopened, feeling that somehow, by the sheer process of passing time, its contents had been dealt with.

Such envelopes had been coming more and more often lately, however. One of them this morning had displayed a strident yellow sticker that commanded: "URGENT! GOVERNMENT BUSINESS. RESPOND AT ONCE." The other simply had the return address of the National Bureau of Taxes, enough to strike terror into any heart. Logan had quickly stuffed both envelopes into a drawer, but he knew they were there. All day, they had seemed to clamor at him through the wood. He looked at the drawer now. In spite of the candlelight, the flowers, and the guest on the way, he knew that The Letters were in there, waiting.

"You can't avoid it forever, old lad," he told himself. For Logan, this was quite an admission. He was a master of the art of sweeping unpleasantness under the carpet. This time, however, it was more like trying to sweep a mountain under a doormat.

He sighed. It wasn't just The Envelopes that were bothering him. It was Gwen. After their picnic at the mound, he had wondered if he should avoid her altogether. Not because he didn't enjoy her company but because he enjoyed it too much. His feeling toward her were tinged with romance, though not particularly with sex, with which Logan had never been comfortable, even in his marriage. He felt toward Gwen as a knight or jester in some old tale might have felt toward a great lady: he wished to be useful to her in some noble way. She also brought out a protectiveness in him, long unused. He was sixty, she was thirty-two. She could have been his daughter, he realized.

For a moment, he wondered if Katherine, his wife, dead these twenty years, would have liked Gwen as a daughter. It was still a sorrow, still an ache, indigestible as a stone in the gullet, that they had had no children. Certainly, they both had wanted them.

He allowed himself now to think of Katherine, as he rarely did anymore. He had met her while he was in the Navy, stationed in Borneo at the time, having just been sent there from Malta. Three days after arriving, he had been injured, not in any combat, but in a jeep accident, while delivering supplies to the officer's mess. The three-part break in his leg had kept him in traction for several weeks. Katherine had been a day nurse in his ward. How he had looked forward to seeing her arrive each morning to thrust open the curtains to let the sunshine in. She signaled the end to each night of pain and sweat and sleeplessness. She was sunshine, clean sheets, and all that was good. Her uniform was always crisply starched and sweet smelling, her dark brown hair, pulled back into the regulation braid, always gleamed. Her cheeks were red and dimpled, her eyes were brown and bright. She was a strapping Yorkshire lass, but from the city, Logan learned. Her father owned a fabric shop in Leeds. She seemed to enjoy seeing Logan each day, just as he looked forward to seeing her.

"Oh, Logan Knowelles, how you do go on!" she always giggled, when he told her the latest gossip about Dr. Madison and the night nurse.

"As I live and breathe, it's true. Three a.m., and they're slipping into the linen closet for a cuddle. I rang for my pain pill five times, but they had other fish to fry."

She liked it even better when he told her about his family home, Kestrel Farm. "It lies hard by a village called Far Tauverly, in Somerset. Some folks call it a lonely place, but I think 'tis the most beautiful one in the world. High on a hillside, overlooking the Avon Valley. It's only a simple stone farmhouse, mind you, but there are beech trees planted nearby, and in the spring, the smell of lilacs from the back yard fair knocks you over. Then, in June, the roses come, pink on the trellis near the house, white and yellow bushes on the south wall that gets good sun, and all along the fences, dark red ramblers. My Mum planted them all, being a great one for roses."

"It sounds a grand place," Katherine had said wistfully. Her family's house in Leeds had a garden the size of a postage stamp, and all that grew in it were some straggling daisies, their petals always gray with dust from the factories.

"Your family must love it very much," she said, after one especially loving description by Logan.

"Well, they did do. They were all killed in the war. Coming home from Sunday service, in the wagon. An air raid. Hit them on the open stretch just past Knobbly Hill. No time to run for cover, they were all killed instantly, even Hawthorne, the horse. But I was at home, you see, in bed with a cold. I've never known whether to be sad or glad about that."

Nurse Katherine had looked very sympathetic, obviously imagining that boy, who was one minute a member of a happy, rambunctious family of twelve and the next, alone in the world. She could understand why, the day he'd turned eighteen, he had enlisted. Not only to fight, but to atone for having survived while his family had not.

"But Kestrel Farm is mine, free and clear," Logan had continued. "It waits for peas and oats to be planted again and for a crop of children to fill its rooms," he added shyly, embarrassed to say much more.

He didn't need to, Katherine got his meaning quite well. When his discharge came, ten months later, they were married by a Navy chaplain. Two very young people, embarking on the journey called marriage. Their brief honeymoon on Malta had not been a wild success, but Logan had told himself, "It's natural for a young couple to be awkward about . . . things. It'll all take care of itself once we're back on the farm."

As long as he lived, he would never forget the look of shock on Katherine's face when they had first stepped into the front hall of Kestrel farm. She looked as if he had promised her a palace and brought her to a bombsite. Slowly, not even taking off her coat and hat, she had walked from room to room. She hadn't said a word. She hadn't needed to. For the first time, Logan understood what the farm was bound to be for her: a cold place, a poor place, with faded, mildewed wallpaper and shabby furniture and the ghosts of the past in every corner.

Perhaps he had described it too glowingly, in that hospital bed in Borneo. Perhaps he himself had remembered it through the happy filter of childhood's eye rather than how it was now. Then, too, the words, as he spoke them, had taken on a life of their own; perhaps, in truth, the view had never been quite so majestic as he described it, nor the roses quite so red, even at the height of June. And Katherine, as a city girl, was not prepared for the harsh isolation of farm life, which Logan had never thought to mention, having always known and liked it. Hard though the shock was, Katherine rose to the situation majestically. After those first few minutes of silence, she had never complained once, but had fallen to scrubbing and sewing and weeding until the old place had looked almost cheerful again.

Logan worked with a will, too. But he was never as good at the farming as Katherine was with the housework. He hadn't been trained to it; he had always been a tag-along younger brother who might end up helping out or doing some work in town, so what he knew of farming he had picked up around the edges. He made enough, just enough, to support them, and he hated the work. If they weren't in debt, they were always only a few pounds away from it. Logan couldn't understand why this bothered his wife so much. But then, she was the kind of woman who was always nudging a man somehow: "You promised to weed the beans three days ago; change your shirt, the Vicar's wife's coming to tea, the least you could do is help with the washing up once in a while, but there you are, with your nose in another book. . . ." There was no end to it with her somehow. She didn't even like to see him head out the door on a Saturday with his fishing gear.

"It would be different if you caught something," she sniffed, "but off you go to doze in the sun, and me with three loads of laundry to do."

The unspoken thought between them both was that children would help. Children would inspire him to work harder. Children would soften her hard edges. They tried. Logan was inclined to a method of prayer and hope; Katherine took the scientific approach. Consulting her charts and temperature readings like some court astrologer calculating the most favorable moment for an audience, she would announce briskly at dinner, "Tonight's the best night of the month." Her forthright manner did nothing to ease Logan's natural shyness. Neither did his own rare, furtive trips to Tweeverton to consult the sex manuals on the bottom shelf, back wall, near-the-eye-of-the-clerk-so-the-kids-don't-look-at-'em of Hartley's Book Shop. He found the graphic ink drawings of couples entangled in the most unnecessary-seeming positions embarrassing and the cheery, explicit texts to be an awful mixture of the clinical and the coyly smarmy. He didn't want all this complication; he just needed help to find some natural confidence. A visit to a first-class prostitute might have done him a world of good, but such a thought was out of the question to Logan, who took his marriage vows seriously. The books, however, offered no help at all, and in the end, he always put them back on the shelf hastily, made miserable by the clerk's knowing smirks and the fear that someone who knew him might walk in at any moment. Not for the world would he have dreamed of buying such a manual, let alone showing it to Katherine, who would have laughed. "Just like you, Logan," she would have said, "looking in a book for everything."

Still, in their joyless, loyal way, he and Katherine had kept on trying, until they had finally decided, in their late thirties, that children were a bygone hope. They had retired, with unspoken relief, to their separate bedrooms. By that time, they had achieved the kind of armed truce that Logan imagined many couples arrived at. It was clear to them, and probably to everyone who knew them, that they were making the best of a bad job. That was what you did in his day. Terrible between them was the unspoken blame: if you had been more of a man, you would have given me children; if you had been more of a woman you would have drawn them out of me; you've used up my youth and prettiness for milking a cow and counting out pennies like they were gems, and it's lonely, lonely, on this awful farm; you've nagged my manhood away with your pickiness. Logan knew these to be venomous feelings, but most people's thoughts, he had come to believe, were a mixture of stinkweed and lilies, if you looked close enough. To their credit, he and Katherine had tried hard not to wound each other with their disappointments, and only in their worst fights had they done scarring damage to each other. And they had had their good times, too. He couldn't say there had been no good times: playing Scrabble at the kitchen table on winter nights, the occasional trip to the sea-side at Weston Super Mare, the peach pies Katherine made because she knew he especially liked them, the time he had bought her that hat in Bristol—a ridiculous blue feathered thing that had cost a whole month's grocery money, but he had been glad to get it, because, when she put it on, she looked so young and pleased and hopeful, like she had when he first met her. No, he couldn't say they hadn't had their good times. Besides, there was between them something else: a steadiness, as real and quiet as bread or as earth beneath one's feet. And that was worth something, surely?

When Katherine had died, quite horribly, of cancer, in Tweeverton Hospital, he had been devastated. Oddly enough, in those last few weeks, they had regained some of the warmth that had first brought them together. This time, though, he was the nurse, and she the patient. He had brought her flowers, candies, magazines and had stayed by her bed from morning until the nurses kicked him out at night.

"We seem to get along best in hospitals," he had joked.

"Perhaps we should have lived in one," she joked back.

He had pleaded with her not to die, yet he hadn't really wanted her to continue in such pain. In the end, she had slipped away, with a minimum of fuss, at eight p.m. on a Wednesday evening in November; considerately after supper and before lights out, like the tidy soul she had always been.

As soon as possible after her death, Logan had got the postman's job and had more or less moved to Far Tauverly. That had been twenty years ago, and in all that time, he had been back to Kestrel Farm only two or three times each year, just to check on things. He couldn't bear the thought of living there, yet he couldn't bear to sell it. So there it sat on its hillside, collecting back taxes to itself the way a dog gathers brambles.

Logan sighed. It had been a long time since he had thought so much of Katherine, God rest her soul. Would children have made so great a difference? And if they had had them, would any of their daughters have turned out like Gwen?

He could imagine no young lady he would have been prouder to be kin to. Yet, in all his delicate mingling of feelings toward her—courtly lover, daughter that never was, long-lost sister—the strongest was simply that of friend. Logan had not had many friends in his lean life. Oh, everyone knew him, and he knew everyone, very well indeed. He never opened sealed mail, but he considered return addresses and postcards fair game. After all, if people didn't want their private business known, they shouldn't splash it all over the back of a view of Brighton's beach, should they? No, there wasn't much Logan didn't know about the ins and outs of Far Tauverly. Yet, sometimes, that very knowing made him feel the most lonesome of all, for he was always the observer, looking into the windows of other people's lives.

Gwen was the first person in a long time who had seemed to want to know about him. Everyone else turned to Logan to get the latest bit of gossip or to buy, for the price of a pint, a scrap of some old tale to ease their boredom. But Gwen actually seemed interested in Logan. She didn't find him just a quaint figure of fun but, instead, an equal companion. At first, he couldn't believe his good fortune. Then caution had set in. After all, she was leaving soon. Perhaps tomorrow or, at best, in a few days. Why open long-sealed doors, only to have to close them again? He had his ways to get through the lonely times—a pint here, a chat there—it got him by. Why risk disturbing his delicate balance for a few days of friendship? And yet, he knew he would. Gwen brought Life into his existence. And Life, in Logan's opinion, though bittersweet, was always worth it.

Someone knocked on the post office door. Seven-thirty. She was right on time. Logan hurried to the door and opened it wide.

"Come in!" he cried gladly. "Come in, come in, come in!"

***

On Knobbly Hill, two sentinels of the Independent Kingdom of Greniston exchanged a look of alarm.

"The ground," Osgood whispered, "it's shaking."

"Yes," said Charles.

In the stillness of the evening air, on that quiet, misty day, the two boys could feel the earth trembling, right up through the soles of their feet. It was a very faint trembling, but it had never been there before. Granted, they had not been to the Hill in several weeks. It was, properly speaking, only a province of their domain, being outside of the Greniston land, on the Eastern edge of the village. Most of the time, Knobbly Hill was mainly frequented by young lovers seeking a bit of privacy. Still, remnants of a mosaic, half-covered by wild myrtle and nettles, gave evidence of the fact that there had once been a Roman villa there, although the Walmsley children preferred to think of it as "Arthur's Fort." They patrolled it, rarely but faithfully, to make sure all was well.

"It's in the prophecy," Osborne said. "'And Knobbly Hill doth tremble and shake. . . .'"

"I know," replied Charles. "But you know what? I think it's just from the cars down there. On the highway."

The two boys gazed down at the M5, cutting its way across the plain some two miles away. They could see, in the shadows of sunset, the lights of commuter's cars heading home from Bristol to the outlying villages. It was true that the ground beneath their feet was shaking in the exact way that distant traffic might make it vibrate.

"I think there's just more cars there than ever before," said Charles, ever the one to seek a reasonable answer. "I don't think it's magic, just cars."

"All the same, it's in the prophecy. Maybe the cars are part of the magic, or are a bad magic. It says that Arthur will return when we need him the most, after all. Arthur Rex, King of all Briton, and Solemn Trust of the Shining Mound, may soon be returning. High Council must be called!"

Charles nodded, and the two sentinels hurried off about their urgent business.

***

An hour later, on a farm outside of Hamble-on-the-Beck, Annie and Davey Lee were engaged in urgent activities of their own.

"He's going for it," Davey whispered.

He and his grandmother watched from behind a row of forsythia bushes, as the watchdog gulped down the hunk of meat they had tossed him. At first, Davey had feared that Annie would be unwilling to drug the beast, being so uncommonly dotty about animals as she was, but perhaps even she found it hard to like so unpleasant-looking a boxer-pit bull mix.

"Just enough to make him sleep for a few minutes," she had agreed, picking the needed leaves from her store of herbs. They had sprinkled the leaves into a lump of ground beef and tossed it in the direction of the cur, praying that he was hungry. Now, but a few slobbering gulps later, the dog was staggering toward an inviting pile of hay. Ten more seconds, and he was fast asleep, a cherubic looking smile on his ugly mug.

Well, thought Davey, *let's keep our fingers crossed.* Finding out the farm where the coppers had billeted Chieftain and settling the dog were easy matters. Now for the real artistry. He left Annie Lee generously oiling the wheels of her caravan, which the duffers had left right in the yard. Davey approached the stables. He slipped into the dark brown peace of the building as easily as a knife passing through butter. He paused as soon as he was inside, letting his eyes grow accustomed to the dark, and gently, oh so gently, letting the latch fall back behind him.

Old, familiar smells rose to greet him: hay, manure, leather, and the wonderful, homey smell of horses themselves. Like many Romani babies, Davey had been partly nursed on mare's milk, nestling in a pile of straw beside a newborn foal. He had known the touch and smell and ways of horses ever since he could remember.

131

"Be easy, my darlin's," he whispered to them now, in Romani. "Be easy, be safe, and above all, be quiet." Chieftain neighed hopefully, recognizing his scent.

"Hush, my brave one, my champion, my treasure. Your freedom is only moments away, but you must be quiet now." As if he understood, Chieftain grew still.

Davey glided across the stable to the stall where Chieftain was tethered. He could feel the other horses with their great, liquid eyes watching him in the darkness. How he loved them, the valiant arch of their necks, their gleaming manes, and the sweet, steady strength of their breath.

"I wish I could set you all free for a nighttime gallop across the fields, my lovelies," he whispered, "but I dare not risk it. Another time, perhaps."

Stealthily, he wrapped the pieces of felt he had brought with him around Chieftain's great hooves. Next, he muzzled him gently. Then slowly, ever so slowly, he opened the stall, and led the mighty creature out. His steps made not a sound.

Outside, Annie had finished oiling the caravan's wheels. Now she was tying down anything that might make the slightest noise. Together they hitched Chieftain to the traces, moving as slowly and quietly as figures in a dream.

Normally Davey would not have attempted a venture like this one until after midnight, when everyone was sleeping. But his Gran had been so restless to be on her way that he had reluctantly agreed to start earlier. The farmer and his family were still awake. Davey and Annie waited, then, until the detective show they were watching in the farmhouse reached a particularly noisy chase sequence, then they drove as silently as they could down the long drive toward the road.

Once they were well away from the farm, they stopped so that Davey could light the caravan's kerosene side lamps. The moon would be full in another five nights, he reckoned, but this night was misty and overcast. On the dark country roads, they needed the light.

"Turn here," Annie said, as they came to a side road about half an hour later. "We're very close." As near as Davey could figure out, consulting his map by the light of a match, they were getting close to a village called Far Tauverly.

The stillness of the night, the pockets of mist, the silent movement of Chieftain's muffled hooves thrilled Davey Lee's blood. Ah, this was the life! A woman, a horse, the road stretching before one, and the delicious sense of not knowing what would happen next! In the darkness, Davey Lee smiled. He was in his element, now. Birds lived in the air, fish lived in the sea, but he lived in the Great Unknown, that was his element.

"This is it," Annie whispered. "Find a way into these woods, and we'll look for a place to camp. Whatever is Calling, these woods are Its source."

***

"Logan, it's a masterpiece," said Gwen, savoring the last of the frying pan stew. Logan beamed.

"Everything," she continued, "the flowers, the candlelight, it's wonderful."

She would have added that he himself, as well as the room, looked handsomely turned out, but she felt that that would embarrass him. He wore a dark blue velvet jacket that had surely seen better days but had clearly been brushed and aired for the occasion. His silver hair gleamed, and she detected about him the distinct odor of Old Spice.

She was glad she had dressed up for the occasion herself. After much deliberation, she had chosen to wear her powder blue dancing dress. Its high neck and long sleeves were modest enough, but it fit snugly until just below the hips, then in billowed out into a full, filmy skirt. The hem and cuffs were trimmed with ice-blue sequins and feathers—fake feathers, Gwen had taken care to make sure; she didn't want anyone killing birds on her behalf.

"Hey, Ginger Rogers in *Down to Rio*," Filipo had exclaimed the first time he saw the dress. That had made Gwen worried that the dress might be a bit much for most of the Denver nightspots she could afford to frequent. She had brought it with her to England in the hope that perhaps in London she might have a chance to wear it; it appealed to the Henrietta Amberly side of her imagination. "'I thought you were but a mousy little missionary,' the Count breathed in Evangeline's ear, 'until I saw you in that dress. It clings to your form like mist to a slender birch. It enflames me!'" At least, that was the effect a similar dress had had in *Lost in London*. She didn't intend to enflame the passions of Logan, but she thought he might appreciate its old-fashioned sexiness. To complete the rather '30s look, she had styled her hair in a sleek chignon and wore pearl earrings as her only jewelry. She knew that the open-toed silver high heels that went with the dress would make her obviously

133

taller than Logan, but she felt certain that he was man enough to handle that with ease.

"M'Lady, you look fit to be dancing at the Ritz!" Logan had exclaimed when he saw her.

"I'm going somewhere far more important," Gwen had said. "I'm dining with you."

Then, from under the white lace shawl she had draped over her shoulder, she drew out a bottle of Sauvignon and two wine glasses. It was the best vintage The Greenstone Arms had to offer.

"Mrs. Hodges said we could borrow the glasses until tomorrow," she explained.

Bless you, Mabel, thought Logan, who had experienced a momentary panic about how to serve the wine, his borrowed dishes being pressed into service down to the last saucer.

The dinner had begun merrily enough, with toasts and jokes and news exchanged, yet beneath the revelry, Gwen felt that Logan was troubled about something.

He hasn't seemed himself all day, Gwen thought. *I wonder what's wrong.* She didn't find out until after he cleared away the stew plates.

"So, Logan," she had said, munching a cucumber slice, "what is this 'other place' where you sometimes live, your country home? You were very mysterious about it. Have you got a mistress and fifteen illegitimate children stashed there?"

To her horror, Logan buried his face in his hands and sobbed.

"Oh dear," exclaimed Gwen, "what's wrong?" She hurried over to him and put her arm around his shoulders.

How thin he feels, she thought, as he continued to weep.

"It's all right," she said. "Whatever the trouble is, I'll help you. We're friends, remember? But please, tell me what's wrong."

Logan continued to sob so heartily that she amended her soothing murmurs to "Just have a good cry, if that's what you need."

At last Logan pulled himself together enough to ask for a handkerchief. Gwen found him one and then rose and looked at his bookshelves, to give him time to collect himself.

The office was as tiny and tidy as a ship's cabin, and the main feature of it that struck the eye was the hundreds of books stored on every possible shelf and windowsill. Gwen glanced at some of the titles: *The Complete Works* of *Shakespeare*, *Little Dorritt* and *Great Expectations*, *Out of Africa*, *Kim*, *Pride and Prejudice*, *A Story Like the Wind*. In her quick scan, she noticed, besides the novels, many autobiographies and collections of journals and letters. She saw *Seven Pillars of Wisdom*, by T. E. Lawrence; *The Meditations of Marcus Aurelius*; and the collected letters of Joseph Conrad, Virginia Wolf, and many others. *Well, of course*, Gwen thought with a smile. *Being a postman, he would want to read their mail.*

What she saw most of were volumes of poetry, legends, and folklore. She saw works by Yeats, Auden, Rilke, Mansfield, and Hopkins, as well as Medieval Welsh poets like Daffd Ap Gilliam, Taliesin, and Amergin. There was a copy of *The Little Golden Book of Fairy Tales*, which, from its crayon-scrawled inscription, seemed to be a birthday present from the Walmsley clan, and weightier tomes like *Myths and Legends of the Celtic Race*, the *Mahabaratta*, and *Shinto Tales*. There were collections of stories from every time and place—from Bali to the Blackfeet Indians, from Peru to Penzance—and shelves full of teaching stories from Rabbis, mullahs, wandering sadhus, sages, saints, and shamans.

These books are his friends, Gwen realized. She could well imagine the many winter nights Logan had spent perusing them. What impressed her even more than the fact of how lovingly the books were gathered on the shelves was the certainty that much of the wisdom they contained was now gathered in Logan, whose memory, she knew, was keen.

He knows hundreds of these stories, she thought, *I'm sure of it. He's a Living Treasure.* She had seen, a few months before, a television program about "The Living Treasures of Japan," human beings who had attained so great a skill in some art or craft that the government recognized them as part of the living wealth of the country. Glimpsing the richness that lived in Logan, Gwen felt that he was at once overworked and underused. Even though he made light of the work of his mail route, she knew that carrying the hefty leather pouch could not have been easy for him. On the other hand, he clearly could be telling greater stories than the scraps of gossip most people asked him for.

There's got to be a way to help him, Gwen mused. She didn't have the answer yet, but she put the matter on the back burners of her mind, to simmer there, while she turned her attention to the immediate need of finding out what was troubling her friend so much. From the sounds of it, Logan had finished blowing his nose.

135

"My Grandmother always used to say, 'a trouble shared is lighter by half,'" Gwen began. "If you'd be willing to tell me what's wrong, I'd be willing to listen. Maybe I can help."

Logan laughed gently. "It's very kind of you, but I doubt if you can, unless you've got influence with the tax department. You see, it's my farm, Kestrel Farm. I owe thousands of pounds of back taxes on it."

"Oh dear," said Gwen.

"Oh yes," replied Logan with a rueful smile. "I send them what I can from my salary, but that's just a drop in the bucket. The debt's been mounting for years. And lately, the tax people have been sending a lot of letters. Another came this morning."

"What did it say?" asked Gwen.

"I didn't open it. I was too afraid."

Logan looked so embarrassed that Gwen quickly said, "Of course not. I would have done the same thing," although she knew she wouldn't have.

"I know what they want, though," Logan sighed. "They want their money. I don't have it. It's pretty simple, really. Let's have some pudding," he suggested. "This subject could use some sweetening up." He rose, brought the chocolate puddings to the table, and put the kettle on.

"Is there any way you could get a bank loan or something?" Gwen asked.

Logan shook his head. "I've tried. But the place is old and run down, and I'm not a good credit risk. The only thing left is to sell it. I might just make enough to pay the taxes. But God, I don't want to do that!"

"It might be for the best, though," Gwen said gently. "Especially if you don't spend much time there anyway. Perhaps some young family could buy it and farm the land."

"Ah, if only they would, I'd be glad to sell!" Logan exclaimed. "But all the young folk, they don't want to farm anymore. They're all moving to the cities, looking for work. No, I'm afraid that only someone like Swindon would buy it." A note of bitterness crept into Logan's voice. "He would tear down the farmhouse and build a shopping mall or a trendy restaurant. I can't let that happen. The land around Far Tauverly has been my friend at times when no one else has. I can't see it be covered in concrete, I just can't!"

"I can understand that," said Gwen sympathetically.

"Besides," continued Logan, "the farm is all I have, really, for my old age."

He paused, once more blinking back tears, and Gwen sensed that they were nearing the meat of the matter.

"You see," Logan said, "that's the rest of it. The other letter, the one from the postal department—I'm afraid they're writing to suggest an early retirement. I'm almost sixty-one, it's bound to happen soon anyway. And lately, there's been talk of doing away with the post office in Far Tauverly altogether. Just have a truck come up every day from Tweeverton. What a shame that would be! You wouldn't get some young bloke from out of town knowing everyone's name, or passing Florence's peach preserves onto the Vicar. All anonymous it would become. Of course, it's bound to happen if Swindon has his way and builds commuter condos. The route would be too much for one man on foot, for sure."

Gwen felt it wiser not to mention that Swindon did not seem to have condos in mind. She got the drift of what Logan was saying and could not dispute the threat of it for his way of life. By that time, the kettle was whistling shrilly; she got up and made them both some coffee. Logan had everything neatly laid out on the counter: cups, filters, spoons, a small amount of French roast—obviously purchased especially for the occasion, because he'd heard her laments about English coffee—and a half pint of cream.

He doesn't eat this well most of the time, Gwen realized. She wondered just what Logan did eat usually, since he was forever sending money to the tax people and spending a good deal of the balance on books.

No wonder he's always hinting for a pint and a bite at the inn, she thought. *He's really hungry*. She resolved then and there to treat Logan to several sumptuous repasts in the next few days.

Logan sipped the coffee with obvious enjoyment, stirring in several spoonfuls of sugar until it was as sweet as melted ice-cream.

"This is grand," he said.

Watching him, Gwen thought of how many cups of coffee she'd purchased at expensive cafes and gulped without real appreciation, tossing the styrofoam cup into the trash as she hurried on her way. Then she looked at Logan's frugal world, where everything possible was savored and reused with care. The comparison left her thoughtful.

After several sips of coffee, Logan seemed fortified to reapproach the subject of The Looming Letters.

"If they do want me to retire . . . when they want me to retire . . . I don't know what I'll do. You see, I've always counted on having the farm to return to, if I had to. But if the farm goes, and then I lose this job . . . , well, of course I'll lose this place."

He looked fondly at the tiny office that had clearly been his sanctuary for so many years.

"I'm actually not supposed to live here at all," he revealed. "But I've always felt I could justify the cot as an emergency precaution, in case the weather was too bad to get back to the farm or a customer became faint, you know, . . . and if an inspector should happen to come, perhaps he won't notice the books. . . ."

Gwen thought that sounded as likely as not noticing the magnificent nose on Logan's face but decided not to say so.

"There'd be a pension," Logan mused on. "I might be able to rent a room in town and live nicely, if I learned to be more careful than I am now. . . ." Gwen could scarcely imagine what "more careful" might be.

"The problem is," Logan went on, "if anything went wrong, if I got ill, I'd be at the government's mercy. I've nothing put by and no kin left. They would pack me off to a charity home in Bristol. I don't know if you've seen those places, but they aren't very nice. Huge grim buildings, with ten beds in a ward, and you're just a number and a name on forms. And you're a charity case, so if they want to test new drugs on you, you have to say yes, that's what I hear. I don't want to end up that way, among strangers in a strange place. I made up my mind long ago that if I had to die lonely, I'd die lonely at Kestrel farm, with the wind and the beeches for company; I'd leave from the very spot I came in at, like so many others in my family have. It seems natural, somehow, to die in the place where you were born—it's like your particular gateway, so to speak. But I think that's not to be, and I must face what must be faced."

Gwen looked at Logan with admiration, feeling that he was very brave to consider his own death so unflinchingly. At the same time, she thought it wasn't good for him to dwell on it quite so much, so she said warmly, "Logan Knowelles, don't be talking about death! You're good for another twenty or thirty years yet!"

Logan brightened. "Do you think so?"

"Yes indeed! If you take care of yourself. Which I doubt that you do. For instance, do you take vitamins?" Logan shook his head.

"Well, first thing tomorrow, I'm getting you a huge bottle of them—and you're going to take them."

For a moment, his delicate Gwen sounded just like Katherine often had. Logan chuckled to himself. Perhaps every woman had a touch of the army sergeant about her: "She Who Must Be Obeyed." He found he didn't mind the bossiness as much as he had twenty years ago. It was a luxury to have someone care at all.

"Yes, Sergeant Major," he said, with a twinkle in his eye.

"Right," Gwen continued crisply, undeterred. "And another thing, we're going to look at what's in those letters. Now, tonight." Logan balked.

"It's best to know what you're up against," Gwen said gently. "Truly it is. I'll read them and let you know what they say. That way it won't be so bad."

Logan sighed and fished the crumpled envelopes out of the drawer where he had stuffed them. Gwen opened the one from the Post Office, with its strident yellow sticker, first.

"I told you that you were bold," Logan said, admiringly. She looked the letter over, then burst out laughing.

"What does it say?" Logan asked anxiously.

"It's a survey," Gwen replied. "It's not about retirement at all. Listen to this: 'Dear Mr. Knowelles, Although our office has written to you several times, you have consistently failed to complete and return the AG3457 Survey Form, concerning the usage and flow of postal office supplies in your local department. This form has been sent to every postmaster, as part of an all-Britain effort for more efficient postal service. We regret to say that you are one of the few government employees who have consistently failed to respond to our repeated requests. Please do your part, by completing form AG3457 (once again enclosed) and RETURNING IT AS SOON AS POSSIBLE'." Logan sank back in his chair, practically fainting with relief.

"A survey!" he exclaimed, "it's just a bloody survey!"

"Yes, and you should hear it," Gwen continued. "Three pages of questions like (and I quote): 'Would you consider the usage of pencils in your office to be (please circle one): A) insufficient, less than three a month, B) moderate, (5-10 a month) or C) Excessive, (over 10 a month.) Note: if answer is A or C, please use back of page to explain why'."

By the time Gwen had reached question 47, "Please describe the flow and usage patterns of paper clips in your facility; i.e., are they recycled, and if so what proportion are not recycled and why," she and Logan were both giddy with laughter.

It's done him a world of good to have a good cry, and then a good laugh, Gwen thought.

"Now for the other letter," she said.

"I was afraid you'd remember that," Logan murmured. She opened the letter from the tax bureau. It took her a while to penetrate the legal-sounding language, but when she did so, her face grew sober.

"It's bad, isn't it?" fretted Logan.

"Well, it is, I'm afraid," Gwen said gently. She could think of no other way to soften the blow; it seemed best to just spit it out. "They want a first payment of £9,000 and thirty-seven pence by the fifteenth of next month, or the case goes to court. And they want the remaining 17,000 before the end of the year."

Logan's face went dead white. Gwen looked at him with concern.

"I'm all right, M'lady," he assured her. "It's just the shock of hearing the exact figure, like that. It makes it inescapable, somehow."

"The fifteenth of May, that's almost five weeks away," Gwen calculated. "Don't give up yet. There's still time. If you can't get a bank loan, perhaps you can borrow the money from someone in Far Tauverly."

Logan shook his head. "There are generous people in Far Tauverly but no wealthy ones. And I couldn't ask for charity from families that already have trouble putting food on the tables! It wouldn't be right!"

There was a sudden fire in Logan's eyes that made Gwen feel she had best tread carefully here.

"Of course not, of course not," she assured him. "But there are some people with money. Like Lord Greniston, for instance."

Logan looked shocked. "I wouldn't dream of asking Lord Greniston for help," he said.

You wouldn't, but I might, Gwen thought. She felt that whatever misunderstanding had happened between her and Greniston, it could not matter once she made Logan's situation clear. And if that failed, there was Swindon himself, whom she felt Logan tended to misjudge. *Logan may feel too proud to ask for their help,* Gwen thought, *but I'm a stranger here, and I don't mind what they think of me, as long as they hear me out.* She decided, however, to mention none of this to Logan until she had some happy news for him. And even then, it would take tact and possibly some white lies to make it acceptable.

"I shall have to sell the farm," Logan said. He sounded quite calm now. "Swindon has already made me an offer. I shall have to sell to him and try not to think of what he'll use the land for. Perhaps I'll have enough left over for a little holiday to the Isle of Man, or to Wales. Yes, Wales. I've always wanted to see the place my mother's people came from. I'm not over fond of travel, but I'd like to see some places nearby."

Gwen was glad that Logan seemed relieved to be facing the facts, yet she did not want him to give up before he had to.

"Promise me one thing," she said.

"M'Lady, you've helped me so much tonight I can deny you nothing. Ask me what you will."

"Promise me that you won't even try to sell the farm for at least two weeks. I want to think about this; there may still be a way to keep it. Don't worry," she added, seeing the look of concern on his face, "I promise I won't go blabbing your private worries all over the village. Truly."

After all, she reasoned to herself, *Lord Greniston is not the whole village.*

"But let's give it a few more days," she said to Logan. "Something may turn up."

Logan laughed. "Now you sound like me: 'Something may turn up.' But yes, if you wish, I won't approach Swindon for two weeks. You have my word on it. And now I have a request. You've helped me very much tonight. You don't know what it means, to talk things through with . . . a friend." He paused, savoring the word. "I don't know how to thank you. But reality has never been a strong point with me, and I've had about as much of it as I can handle tonight. What do you say we leave my troubles behind for the nonce, and spend the rest of the evening in a merrier mode?"

"Agreed!" said Gwen. "And I've got something to help with that." Out of her silver evening bag, she pulled her second contribution to their feast, a small bottle of Drambuie.

Logan's eyes lit up. "Perhaps if I washed the coffee cups. . . ." A few minutes later, they were each happily ensconced in a chair, with a cup of the potent liquor. Logan lit the small gas fire, and they wrapped themselves in blankets from his cot, to ward off the evening chill.

"Let's talk about your holiday," said Logan. "What part of our sceptered isle are you bound for next?"

"Far Tauverly," Gwen replied.

"You mean you haven't tired of the gem of Somerset yet?" Logan asked. He tried to make the question light, but Gwen could hear within it the strain of desperate hopefulness that said, without words, "Please stay."

"Actually, I'm going to spend my whole vacation here," she said. "I spoke with Mrs. Hodges about it today, just before I came here. She said my room at the inn is available for the remaining two and a half weeks. With the rental car, I can easily drive to the other places I want to see and usually be back here to spend the night. Actually, I was wondering if you'd be willing to come with me sometimes, perhaps to Stonehenge and Tintagel. If you were free for a whole weekend, we could even go together to Cornwall, or to Wales, to see your mother's village. Only if you'd like to, of course. It would be much more fun for me to have the company. And you must let me treat," she added, searching her mind for a believable lie, "because, you see, I can write it all off to my expense account at work. This is sort of a research trip for future tours, so you could earn your way by helping me evaluate some inns and things. Only if you'd like to, of course."

Logan looked dazed by the vistas of possibilities opening before him.

"Like to?" he replied, "Why, to accompany you on your quest would be the greatest honor, the greatest joy that . . . "

"Does that mean 'yes'?"

"Absolutely."

"Great," said Gwen, with a happy smile. Logan, too, was smiling broadly. "I was afraid you were leaving tomorrow," he said.

"I thought about it," Gwen admitted. "I got all confused about Swindon and Greniston. Part of me just wanted to run away from both of them and have a nice, uncluttered trip."

"I'm afraid I didn't help matters," Logan acknowledged, "snarling on about Swindon. He's not all bad, actually. But I would hate to see you get serious about him. I just think you can do better. He doesn't hold a candle to, oh, Lord Greniston, for instance." Gwen smiled at this attempt at subtlety. "But I know it's none of my business if you go on a date with Geoff Swindon, and I'm sorry I was an ass about it." Logan paused, struggling to remain magnanimous and detached. Then curiosity got the best of him and he burst out with, "But how was the date?"

"He treated me very handsomely and was quite the gentleman all the while. As for the rest, I guess you witnessed our encounter with Greniston in front of the inn?" Logan nodded.

"Well," Gwen sighed, "that's the last I've heard from either of them. However, I'm not staying on in Far Tauverly because of either of those gentlemen. No, it's because of three other men that I'm still here."

"Three other men?" asked Logan, bewildered. The population of eligible men in Far Tauverly was scant, to say the least.

"Yes," Gwen continued, "and one of them you know quite well." Logan looked baffled.

"He's my friend, Logan Knowelles," she explained. Logan blushed beet-red, so Gwen hurried on.

"And the second man, well, he's a real mystery."

"But who is it?" Logan asked, his long nose fairly quivering with curiosity.

"Oh, you probably know him better than anyone else in Far Tauverly does."

"I can't think who you mean. . . ."

"A man of middle years, of extraordinary valor, handsome in a rugged sort of way. . . ."

"But not Lord Greniston? And he's from around here?"

"Definitely a local lad," Gwen replied. "However," she added, "I never said he was single, you know." Logan looked shocked.

"Yes, he's a married man. Though not happily married, if you believe the local gossip. Been married for oh, almost 1300 years. Surely you know him. His name is Arthur . . . Arthur . . ."

"Pendragon!" Logan finished with a grin.

"Right!" said Gwen. "The mystery of King Arthur brought me here, and I've decided I'm not going to abandon that quest just because Greniston looks at me cross-eyed and Swindon gets me rattled."

"Bravo!" said Logan.

"Besides, you and I have a pact, to solve the mystery. And I propose we work on that this very night."

"But wait," said Logan, "who is the third man?"

Gwen's face grew more serious. "Don't laugh," she said. "I honestly think he might be a ghost. It all began with that gold button that was in my

143

pocket, the one with the lion holding the daffodil. Someone keeps leaving them in my path, and either that someone is a true Houdini at appearing and disappearing, or . . . "

"Or a Visitor From Beyond the Veil," said Logan, with relish. "Please, tell me every detail."

***

In a tree house a quarter of a mile away, desperate matters indeed were being discussed.

"High Council of the Independent Kingdom of Greniston is hereby convened!" Osgood intoned.

"Shhh!" Charles warned him, "Mum will hear you!"

"She can't hear us out here," Osgood scoffed, reverting to less than kingly tones.

Charles glanced nervously through the branches of the willow tree, toward their bedroom window. He knew that their bedclothes had been carefully shaped to look like sleeping forms, but he didn't know if they would fool an expert like their mother.

"Couldn't we hold High Council inside?" he asked. "They'll be furious if they catch us out here so late."

"By rights we should be at the Shining Mound," Osgood replied haughtily. "At the very least, we must meet here, in Willowgard, Outpost Most Royal and Hallowed."

Charles sighed. He supposed he should leave well enough alone. It had taken almost an hour to get Osgood to agree to settle for the tree house. Only the fact that the baby, Amanda, had the colic, and was likely to keep Mum and Dad awake all night had dissuaded him from ordering them all to creep out to the mound, one by one. This was safer by far, though he still hoped they didn't get caught, not with Dad in the foul mood he'd been in the last few days.

Osgood began to speak, and even Charles forgot his worries in the thrill of the adventure that lay before them.

"The High Council here is met, to discuss Matters of the Utmost State," Osgood began. "For the Prophecy of Arthur begins to happen. A Stranger has seen the Lion's gate - "

"That's Miss Fields!" Wyatt interrupted excitedly. "Miss Fields hath cometh to the wion's gate!"

Claire smiled but put her finger to her lips.

"Merlin's Cry has been heard. . . ."

The children grew solemn at the memory of the mysterious sounds they themselves had heard in the forest, only two days before.

"And now, Knobbly Hill doth tremble and shake. . . ."

"Right beneath our feet," Osborne put in excitedly. "The ground shook! We could feel it!" Charles nodded confirmation of this fact, whatever the reason for it had been.

"And so it must be," Osgood intoned, "that soon, very soon, the rest of the Prophecy will come true. King Arthur, Arthur Pendragon, King of the Britains, the Once and Future King, will return."

As one voice, the children sighed, a sigh of wonder and of longing about to be fulfilled.

"King Arthur Himself will rise at last from the Shining Mound and rule fair England once more," said Osgood, awed by his own words.

"King Arthur," the others whispered.

"We will stand fast," Osgood said.

"Standfast," his siblings echoed.

"We will guard the kingdom."

"Guard the Kingdom."

"We will be ready to serve."

"Ready to serve."

"By the Greenstone, we swear."

"By the Greenstone, we swear," they all concluded, except Rutherford, who, being only two, was fast asleep in Claire's arms.

For a moment, the spell of the chanting held them silent. Then Osgood said crisply, "Right. Now, we must go on full alert. Enemies have been sited at the mound."

"Who is that?" interrupted Wyatt, in a loud whisper.

"The realtors," Osborne hissed back.

"Oh." Wyatt nodded. Osgood silenced them both with a glare.

"Therefore, full guard on the mound, starting tomorrow morning. Osborne and Charles, you take the first shift. Wyatt, do you stand guard at the museum, to protect the chalice. Too many people have been looking at it lately, that's what Althea and Lettice said. Claire and I will go to school, taking a note, which I shall forge, saying that everyone else has the flu. Then I can get ill at lunch, and leave early, and be back to relieve Osborne and Charles. Claire, act sicker and sicker all day. That way, they won't be surprised if none of us are there the next morning." The others nodded. It was a good plan.

"What about Wutherford?" Wyatt asked.

Osgood considered his youngest brother, whose rosy lips were parted in a drooling snore.

"He can guard the house," Osgood decided eagerly, "along with Amanda."

A shrill watery cry pierced the night.

"Speaking of Mandy, she's awake again," Charles reported, peering through the branches. "A light went on. Dad's up."

"High Council is hereby ended for the moment," said Osgood hurriedly, "but all to stay on alert, 'gainst Arthur's certain return."

***

Saint Aethelrood's bell tolled twelve midnight. Logan Knowelles stood on the road to the Greniston land.

It had been eleven-thirty when he escorted Gwen back to the inn. Her good company and the tales of Arthur she had pulled from his memory had left him wide awake, so he had decided to walk on for a while. As the road curved out of the woods, he noticed a small curl of wood smoke rising from the forest. He sniffed the air. Rowan wood, it was. Gypsies, most likely. Well, the Grenistons had never minded a few of the Romani folk on their land. He walked on.

How still the night is, he thought. He stopped, to enjoy the quiet. Quiet it was and misty, and still, and deep. He had felt this exact same quality of stillness before . . . but where? Then he remembered. It was the same hush, that waiting moment, that fills the theater when the audience and the players are assembled on the other side of the curtain, the lights go down, and the play is about to begin.

CHAPTER NINE

The next morning, Wyatt Walmsley, Chalice Sentinel Most Faithful of the Independent Kingdom of Greenstone, sat contentedly underneath a table in the Far Tauverly Historical Society. It had been an easy matter to gain entry into the Pennington sister's kitchen and through their house into the museum. For the first few minutes, Wyatt had simply enjoyed being alone in the quiet room, filled with so many fascinating things. There was even a mummy's hand, which a turn-of-the-century Far Tauverlyite had brought back from a tour of duty in Egypt. Wyatt was strongly tempted to open the glass case and touch the hand, still half-wrapped in linen strips.

Fortunately, the sound of Lettice trimming the hedges just outside the north window reminded him of Osgood's stern command: "Don't go roaming around in there, knocking things over. Find a hiding place, and stay in it. At the first sign of foul play, report back to me on the double."

At first, Wyatt considered hiding inside the full suit of armor, minus a thumb, that had always so enchanted him. However, upon reflection, even he had to admit that it looked too tall and too difficult to get into without making a real racket. Then his eyes lit upon the table. It held a collection of needlework done by the ladies of Far Tauverly from the 1400s to the present. The table itself was covered with a beaded Victorian cloth that reached to the floor. Wyatt crawled beneath the table with ease. The faded gold cloth formed a tent all around him. If he peered through one of the threadbare patches, he had a fine view of the case that held the chalice.

Pleased with this retreat, Wyatt unpacked the provisions he'd brought in his school bag: cheese and chutney sandwiches, McVitey's chocolate wafers, an orange, and a stack of his favorite Super Heroes Comic Books. He began to read *The Masked Avenger and the Agents of Darkness*.

Perhaps he dozed. Suddenly, though, the Chalice Sentinel Most Faithful sat bolt upright. He was not alone in the museum. His first thought was that perhaps Althea had come in to dust. But he did not hear her firm, sharp footsteps on the wooden floor, nor the scratchy rustle of her clothing. Whoever was there was moving very slowly and softly, like a cautious shadow.

Wyatt put his eye to the threadbare patch. A man was crawling in one of the windows! He was a skinny little man. His hair was black, and his skin was a lovely tanny-gold color, like the wood of the dresser his Mum called "bird's eye maple." The man slipped lightly to the floor and moved quickly to the case that held the chalice. He took a knife out of his pocket. Wyatt noticed he was wearing tight, black gloves. Fascinated, he watched the man jimmy open the lock of the case and oh-so-quietly lift the lid. He took out the chalice, wrapped it in a piece of soft-looking cloth, and slipped it into an overnight bag. Then he did a strange thing: from under his jacket, he took out another chalice, which seemed to look just like the first. This he put back into the case, which he closed with great care. Then, silently, lightly, he slipped back out of the window, taking the overnight bag and the real chalice with him.

Wyatt sprang into action. Grabbing his knapsack, he ran to the door of the museum and let himself out. Fortunately, neither of the Pennington sisters was in sight. The foreign man was just moving toward the fence, crawling behind a row of elms. Wyatt paused. "At the first sign of foul play, report back to me." That was Osgood's command. But Osgood and Claire were still at school, and Osborne and Charles had been ordered to stay at the mound. If he didn't follow the thief now, the chalice might be lost forever.

Wyatt hesitated no longer. His path was clear. Now he was Super Hero Wyatt, Agent Extraordinaire. When the thief slipped over the fence and headed northwest along the stream beyond it, Wyatt was right behind him.

***

"Is there any reply to the note from Mr. Swindon, Miss?"

The maid waited in the doorway, clearly hoping for a hint about what was going on between the American tourist and the local "catch."

"He isn't waiting down there for an answer, is he?" Gwen asked worriedly.

"No, Miss. He dropped the note off and asked me to give it to you. Along with the flowers, Miss." She nodded toward the bouquet of red roses and white lilies that she had just put on Gwen's dresser. She thought the bouquet was stunning, but she didn't much fancy the vase it had come in— all heavy and modern-looking, glass, not very pretty at all. But the flowers more than made up for it.

"Well then, I'll look at the note and call him later," Gwen said. "Thank you, Mary."

She wasn't sure if she should tip the maid but suspected, rightly, that Swindon had already done so, lavishly.

"Because if you were wanting to send an answer, Miss," said Mary, lingering in the doorway, "wouldn't be no trouble at all for me to run it over to 'im," she added, clearly hoping for an opportunity to glimpse the inside of Swindon House and Swindon himself, no doubt.

"That's okay," Gwen said kindly. "I'll call him later." With a sigh and a last look at the bouquet, Mary departed.

Relieved, Gwen returned to bed and pulled the covers up to her chin. The room seemed freezing; she didn't think that she'd ever get used to the absence of central heating. Nine o'clock tolled the bells of St. Aethelrood's.

"Too early to be sending billet doux," muttered Gwen. The combination of Drambuie and wine from the night before had given her a strong inclination to sleep in. Perhaps until noon. She opened the expensive, ivory bond envelope.

"Dear Gwen," the note began, "I apologize for such short notice, but I wonder if you would do me the honor of accompanying me to the theater tonight? There are several good plays on in Bristol right now, and it's not a far drive at all. If you care to look over the enclosed theater notices, you could choose the play that most appeals to you, and let me know." The note went on to give a number where she could reach him, but only for the next hour.

I don t think I ll go, Gwen thought. The invitation was flattering, and she was not averse to seeing Swindon again, but she sensed that his interest was serious and moving too swiftly for her. She picked up the phone by her bed to call him and decline. It rang as soon as she touched it, causing her to jump and bang her head on the bedpost.

"Hello?" she said shakily.

It was Swindon. "Miss Fields? Gwen? I hope I didn't wake you. . . ."

"Oh, no. Thank you for the flowers, and the invitation. I was just about to call you, tho - "

"Yes, that's what I'm calling about, actually. It turns out that I have to leave my office here at home early, and I didn't want to miss your call. So I just thought I'd ring you up, and see which play you want to see tonight."

"Well, actually, Geoff - "

"Perhaps you haven't had a chance to look the choices over. I'll tell you what's playing. There's *Henry V*, a revival of *The Mousetrap*, the Bristol Rep production of *Wholly Writ*, - "

"Did you say '*Wholly Writ*'?" asked Gwen. She'd heard that name somewhere before. *That's the play I started to read at Greniston's,* she realized, *in the music room.*

"Yes, it's by Leo Hawker. The critics say it's a brilliant interpretation. That play is very, very special to me. If that's your choice, it suits me admirably."

"Well, now, you see - "

"I'm terribly sorry," Swindon interrupted, "this is awfully rude of me, but there's a transatlantic call on the other line, and I must get it. I'll pick you up at six, if that's all right. I look forward to tonight immensely."

He hung up before she could get another word in. Exasperated, Gwen called back. The line was busy for the next twenty minutes, then there was no answer.

"Damn it," she muttered. Once again, she found herself committed to a date with Swindon to which she had never, exactly, said yes.

***

In London, at that same hour, a very different encounter was beginning.

"Well, so how have you been, all these months?" Lord Greniston asked kindly.

Deirdre O'Connell, the internationally famous Deirdre O'Connell, commonly referred to as Ireland's greatest living actress, recently nominated for an Oscar for her role as Parnell's mistress in *The Long Sorrow*, favored him with a searching glance from her dark blue eyes.

"Well enough. And you?"

"Oh, excellent, actually."

"Which is why you called me, out of the blue, after an absence of over a year, to meet you here?"

"You chose the place, Deirdre," Greniston replied. "I'd never suggest this dump."

Deirdre smiled. "I never could understand why you didn't like this place. I think it's charming."

Lord Greniston sighed, half exasperated, half amused. "As usual, we've been here three minutes, and we're already sparring."

"Some things never change," Deirdre replied sweetly.

Greniston glowered down at the tiny white demitasse cup on the table before him. "I wish there was some brandy in here—if any could fit. Do

150

the meals come in the same proportions? That ought to suit your perpetual diet."

"It's espresso," Deirdre said patiently. "It's supposed to be small. Which you know perfectly well."

"Oh, espresso!" bellowed Greniston. He adopted the most simpering of Oxford accents and turned to address the fortunately nearly empty restaurant. "Espresso! Of course! And I thought it was the oil change from my car! Silly old me! And such a cunning little cup, and a spoon to stir it with. We are being sophisticated, aren't we, Deirdre?"

His companion saw that, as he so often did, Greniston was treading a fine line between a humor that, though outrageous, meant no one harm and a wit that was laced with blackness. She decided to take his comments as good hearted, for both their sakes.

"You still are the most impossible man," she said lightly.

"Some things never change," Greniston replied, in perfect imitation of her own voice. He paused, his expression suddenly serious. "Like your beauty," he added. "That never changes."

Deirdre did not blush or smile at the compliment. She met his gaze gravely, as if measuring his sincerity. That frankness had been part of what had first attracted Greniston to her—that and her stunning loveliness. Hers was an elegant beauty, of smooth white skin and waist length blue-black hair. Her striking features, high forehead, high cheekbones, and startling dark blue eyes rimmed by long black lashes could be seen and admired all the way to the back row. Up close they were, though lovely, almost too intense at times. Her figure, too, was almost too perfect for everyday life. She was tall and, thanks to a relentless regime of diet and exercise, slim yet, as Greniston had always put it, "expressive" where needed. Her voice, too, had been so molded for the stage that even in her moments of greatest sorrow or anger, her tone had a practiced richness and beauty. And all the while, beneath the cultivated appearances, her real thoughts were often as hidden as an Irish landscape in mist, but, as Greniston well knew, when she did put her cards on the table, she could be devastatingly honest. Today, she seemed to have favored the enigmatic approach. The white dress she wore, though elegant, was high-necked and severe, as if she wanted to reveal as little of herself to him as possible. Yet he glimpsed, beneath the collar, a strand of pearls he had given her, when things were much different between them.

"Beauty might not change," she said softly now, "but relationships do. It's over, Gren."

Lord Greniston smiled ruefully. "You always did have a way of cutting right to the core, dear."

"What else matters?"

Deirdre leaned forward and gazed at him, concern and kindness in her eyes. "You're writing again, aren't you?" she asked. "Is that why you wanted to meet, after so long? To get some of the inspiration you said I used to give you? You've hit a dull spot and need to be renewed. That's it!"

"No!" protested Greniston, rather too swiftly. "That most certainly is not *it*! Just wanted to see you. Came up to town, gave you a call, perfectly natural."

Greniston paused and gave a grimace of disgust at his own words. "No, that isn't true at all," he admitted. "Things are so confused, and I wanted to talk to you, precisely because of that very way of getting to the core you have, uncomfortable though it may be."

"You're in love!" Deirdre exclaimed suddenly, her intuition alerted.

Greniston choked on the espresso he had finally, reluctantly, agreed to sip.

"Don't be absurd!" he sputtered, "I haven't seen a woman in months! Unless you count Mrs. Fitzpatrick . . . and that Miss Fields, who keeps trespassing on my land."

"Miss Fields," said Deirdre, "so that's her name."

"It is not!" protested Greniston. "I mean, that is her name, but she is not my amour, if that's what you're hinting at. You notice I haven't had the poor taste to ask about your latest romances. Of course, why bother? One has only to pick up a cheap tabloid to read about your escapades: 'Film star caught in love triangle with Fergie's secret paramour,' I believe that was the latest."

He's never going to forgive me for breaking it off between us, Deirdre realized sadly, *even though he wanted out as well.* Aloud, she said, "Why Gren, how sweet of you to notice." Her voice was like honey over ground glass, and she instantly regretted the words. *Why is it always so easy for us to wound each other?* she wondered. "Actually," she added in a lighter tone, "the paper was wrong, for once. I've been far too busy with work for love. We're rehearsing for *Lear* at the National. Cordelia. I turned down the Abbess part in the

Bristol *Wholly Writ*. Too painful. But Nancy Lockridge is playing it beautifully I hear. Have you been to see the new production?"

"You know I don't go to performances of my own plays," Greniston growled.

"Oh, really? That's odd. I'm sure I was escorted to several performances of Leo Hawker's plays by a gentleman who strongly resembled you."

"Yes, yes, but I wasn't there to see the plays. I merely had to confirm that they weren't making a complete botch of them."

"Touchy, touchy," murmured Deirdre. "But then, all playwrights are that way."

"I am not a playwright!" seethed Greniston. "I just happen to write sometimes!" Before Deirdre could think of a suitable retort, the waitress appeared and put a plate down before each of them.

"What's this?" asked Greniston, deflected from his bad mood by genuine surprise.

"It's your raisin flan," said Deirdre. "You just ordered it five minutes ago."

"You're absolutely right," he agreed. "But I have to talk to you, and I can't in here. Everything is too little here. Feel like if I breathe, I'll knock something over. Tiny tables, tiny portions, tiny little spoons in tiny little cups . . . "

"All right, all right," said Deirdre, "we'll go. But we have to bring the flan. You can't just leave good food sitting on a plate."

Greniston sighed. "I keep forgetting that Dublin childhood of yours. Waste not, want not. You always were one for sending the crumbs off to starving brats in Pango-Pango, or somewhere like that. I mean, what good would this flan be by the time it got to them? A solid lump of hardened goo, bring their little innards to a grinding halt - "

Deirdre fixed him with a look of disgust that would have been clear in the third balcony. Greniston found himself clumsily wrapping the pieces of flan in a napkin. He reached into his pocket, pulled out two ten pound notes, and left hemt on the table with a friendly "Keep the change" to the waitress.

"Impossible," muttered Deirdre as they left. But she said it fondly.

It had been raining, and the damp streets of London glistened. By unspoken agreement, Greniston and Deirdre turned toward the river.

"God, it feels good to breathe fresh air again, after that stuffy little place," exclaimed Greniston.

Deirdre sensed that there was no challenge intended in the comment, so she made no retort. They walked on for a few blocks in silence. When they came in sight of the gray river, flowing beneath a gray sky, Deirdre spoke.

"Well, what's really on your mind, Gren?" she asked.

"It's all a-tangle," said Greniston, absentmindedly taking the flan out of his pocket and starting to crumble it into pieces for the gulls.

"Hey," said Deirdre teasingly, "that's me dessert, mate!"

Lord Greniston glanced down, as if wondering where the pastry in his hands had come from. "Did you want some?" he asked.

Deirdre laughed, and shook her head. "Still the same absentminded genius," she said. "I'll never forget the time you forgot where your car was parked, and you took taxis for three weeks before the police found it for you."

"I was working on a play," protested Greniston. "That doesn't count! No one is normal at a time like that!" Then, seeing the grin on Deirdre's face, he relaxed and laughed as well. "I'm glad we can still do something besides fence with each other," he said.

"Me too. Now, what's this tangle you're in?"

"Oh, Swindon's on the warpath again. But this time, his tactics have sunk to a new low. Imagine asking out that innocent Miss Fields, just to get my goat."

Hmm, Miss Fields again, thought Deirdre with a smile.

"I'm tired of these petty games," Greniston sighed. "I feel like the weariness of hundreds of years of feuds is sitting on my shoulders."

"It's only a few acres in dispute," said Deirdre, who had heard about this problem many times before. "Why don't you just let him have it, and end all this madness?"

"Not that land," said Greniston. "It's special."

"Yes, it must be," said Deirdre, with just a touch of dryness in her voice. In all the time that she and Greniston had been together, he had never once asked her to Far Tauverly. She felt a twinge of jealousy toward this Miss Fields, who had already visited the mound and the manor house that she had only imagined. Yet she was glad that perhaps a new woman had entered Greniston's life.

Maybe she can be the one, the right one, Deirdre thought. *God knows, I never was.* Partly, she knew, that was because of her profession. The side of Greniston that was Leo Hawker, brilliant playwright, had no problem with dating an actress on the London stage. She had been the star of several of his plays, his inspiration. But Lord Greniston of Greniston Manor could never have married an actress. Lord Greniston of Greniston Manor could not even reconcile himself to being a playwright. His true identity was an absolute secret, known only to herself, Greniston's agent, and Mr. Steadworthy, the family solicitor.

"I couldn't stand the publicity," Greniston always said, when trying to explain his secrecy. "If it came out that I was Leo Hawker, the place would be swarming with reporters wanting interviews. It would put me right off my work."

"Ummmhmmm," Deirdre had always replied skeptically. "Playwrights don't usually have the paparazzi problems. Just us stars, you know. Are you sure it isn't really that somewhere in that stuffy old aristocratic mind of yours, you don't quite think writing's a fit profession for a gentleman?"

"Perhaps it's not," Greniston had grumbled.

"Ah. And does that mean that acting's no fit life for a lady?" By then, they'd be off and running, into the thick of another verbal fray.

Let s not return to that, Deirdre thought.

"It's about Arthur," Greniston blurted out suddenly. "As sure as you and I are standing here. The new play, you see, it's about King Arthur."

Deirdre sensed that Greniston was drawing near to the heart of what was really bothering him and wisely said nothing. As Greniston stared moodily at the river, struggling to put words to his thoughts, she found herself remembering the first time she had seen him. It had been at a party, celebrating the opening night of Leo Hawker's new play, *Shiva s Dance.* Deirdre had been so moved by the play and its cry of defiance to the Gods on behalf of humanity that she had almost not gone to the party. Then, at the last minute, she'd decided to go just long enough to have one drink.

The first voice she had heard upon entering the crowded flat was Greniston's, booming out imperiously.

"No wonder this Hawker fellow never shows his face," Greniston was saying, "after baring his soul like that in public! It's indecent, don't you agree?"

155

"I certainly do not!" called out Deirdre, approaching from across the room. "I think it's the only play in the last ten years to even consider such subjects intelligently."

"Oh, is that so," retorted Lord Greniston, obviously delighted to have found a worthy combatant. "I'm sure Leo Hawker would be pleased to hear such a review, especially from so lovely a source."

"Physical beauty has absolutely nothing to do with intelligence," she had said stiffly.

"Oh, is that so? If that's true, my dear, why did you obviously go to such lengths to arrange your hair so becomingly? And that sapphire brooch, it's just the shade of your eyes, accents 'em admirably. But I'm sure you know that."

"I fail to see what the color of my brooch has to do with the quality of Leo Hawker's writing," she had replied, made all the more uncomfortable by the realization that he was the handsomest man she had seen in a long time. She knew that, even in argument, they made a striking couple: two dark-haired aristocrats pacing around one another.

"You could play the part of the temple dancer in this new play," Greniston had remarked. "Some Indians do have blue eyes. And you have the right look, the right sad fire."

Made uncomfortable by his scrutiny, she had said "Excuse me. I must go speak with the hostess."

As she walked away, she had heard Greniston thundering again, in his imperious voice, "Obviously, no one goes to the confessional nowadays. Why bother, when they can just write a play?" Then he exploded with laughter, seemingly more amused by his own wit than anyone around him was.

"Who is that man?" Deirdre had asked someone.

"Oh, that's Greniston, Lord of the Manor somewhere down in Somerset, don't you know. Probably invested in the play, and they had to give him an invite. Obnoxious, isn't he?"

"More like impossible," Deirdre had said thoughtfully.

He must have asked who she was, too, because, three weeks later, he rang her up.

"I don't suppose you'd care to go for a stroll in the park with me, would you?" he'd asked, before even introducing himself.

And so had begun her three-year love affair with the man she later discovered was Leo Hawker. Now that that love affair had been over for a year and more, she found herself walking beside Greniston/Hawker in the new role of friend. She wondered if she wanted the part.

"Yes, it's King Arthur," Greniston sighed now. "I can't get to the core of the story. Keep going dry, somehow. The story won't let me in. I can't get to it."

"Then why don't you let it get to you?" suggested Deirdre gently. Greniston looked puzzled. "It works for me with parts, when I get stuck," she continued. "I stop trying to be in charge of the part and let the part be in charge of me. It's the only way I can get past a certain point." Greniston looked troubled, but she knew he was listening carefully. "Sooner or later, Gren, you're going to have to surrender to something. If you ever want to meet anything bigger than yourself, that is."

"But the world's full of people surrendering to something," Greniston said. "I've seen it in the English Class structure, in the Church, I saw it everywhere I turned in the East. They've surrendered, all right, but to what and at what price? Something's having 'em all for lunch. But I suppose you think there is something higher, something worth surrendering to?"

"I know it," said Deirdre quietly. "I can't put it into words; you'll have to find it for yourself. But when you do, you'll know it's right, because it will summon you to the best of yourself and ask you to do only what is good and courageous. You'll know it's right. I only hope you won't be too stubborn to submit to it. Don't you see," she added earnestly, "that all your plays are full of the ache for just such an encounter? You're a spiritual man, Gren. I've always known that. Maybe someday you will, too."

Greniston looked at her dubiously. They walked on together, through a small park that hugged the side of the river bank. A light rain had begun to fall again, surprisingly chill, even for an English spring. Out on the river, a tour boat went slowly past, its shivering passengers gazing drearily out at the sites the guide explained through his megaphone. A grapefruit rind and some bread floated on the gray, choppy waters as gulls swooped and disputed them.

"It's a bleak old world," Greniston muttered, gazing at the scene.

"Sometimes," acknowledged Deirdre. "Doesn't have to be always, though. Depends on your point of view. You need to get out more, not be so isolated. Humans need someone, or something, outside themselves to love."

"Oh, 'love,'" scoffed Greniston, "that poor, abused word! Spare me the dripping sentimentality of the world's greeting card companies and every cheap, two-bit, fake guru who 'loves' the world all the way to their bank account! Spare me - "

"Oh, shut up!" exclaimed Deirdre. Greniston looked at her with surprise. "You really are one of the most depressing men I have ever known! You mount into your own ego, and you go on and on about obvious problems that everyone else has known about for years and think we should all be fascinated because you, the mighty Greniston, just happen to have finally discovered them! Well, stop it! Just, stop it!" They had indeed come to a stop in their walk, by a park bench where a drunk gazed at them with some interest.

"Yes, the world has its tawdry side," Deirdre continued, "but there are other things in it. There is real love, you know. A quiet thing, often unseen, but as real as the ground beneath your feet, damn it! Perhaps it's even been offered to you, and you never even noticed, so wrapped up in having your own way were you. You always want your own way, Gren; that's your biggest problem. You bossed me around—as much as I would let you. You boss the meanings in your plays around, you boss the characters around, you take every little word and shape it to your will. And you've always been bright enough, and charming enough, and rich enough to get away with it! You like to think it was your brilliance that wrote your plays, but I've got news for you, it wasn't! Not that alone. Because if it was just you alone, no one would have come after the first play; people would never be as moved as they are by your work. Oh, don't you understand, you stubborn man, that something greater than you, call it a muse, call it inspiration, has been trying to speak through you ever since you started writing? You surrender to it part way but never completely. And if you find that 'your' writing's gone dry, well perhaps it's because your muse has finally gotten fed up and moved on to someone else who will surrender to it more and give it more of the credit! We don't own these things, you know."

Greniston felt that in all the years he had known her, he had never seen Deirdre so clearly as he did in that moment. *Do I have to lose her in order to really find her?* he wondered. *It seems too cruel a price.* Yet he knew that it was precisely because it was over between them, because her own life had moved on and she no longer needed him so very much, that Deirdre felt able at last to speak so freely.

"You said I bossed you around," he said softly. "Was I really such a tyrant?"

"Sometimes," said Deirdre. "Especially when you asked me to give up acting and marry you."

"I can't believe I ever asked that of you!" Greniston exclaimed. "It would be like asking a thoroughbred never to run!"

"Well, don't be too hard on yourself. It didn't work, after all."

Almost shyly, Greniston asked, "Would you have married me, if I hadn't put that condition on it?"

Deirdre did not answer that question, but she did say, firmly, "It's over, Gren."

"Oh, God," exclaimed the drunk who had been watching them for quite some time. "Does it have to be over, luv? 'E looks an allright bloke, beneath the poshness."

Both Deirdre and Greniston had scarcely noticed the old man's existence. Now they both turned to look at him. He was leaning forward on his park bench, watching their discussion as intently as if he'd been given a front row seat at Wimbleton. He had stuffed his shoes and clothing with bits of newspaper for warmth, and his slightest move caused a rustling sound.

Deirdre addressed her next remarks to the old man, finding it easier to say what needed saying to him rather than to Greniston.

"Yes," she said gently, "it is over. We missed our timing, him and me. Life has moved on. But I hope very much that if he meets another woman—when he meets another woman—he won't miss the timing with her, too."

"Nobly spoke," murmured the tramp, wiping his eyes on his rustling sleeve, "nobly spoke."

"I will think about what you've said today," Greniston said to Deirdre. "I actually listened, for once," he added with a rueful smile. "And I hope we can part as friends."

"Oh yes," she said, offering him her hand in a firm shake.

"That's best," murmured the tramp. "Leave thinkin' the best of each other."

"Well, then," said Deirdre, "Good-bye." Not trusting himself to speak, Greniston merely nodded and raised his hand in a sad wave.

With a last smile, Deirdre turned and started to walk away. Then she stopped and called over her shoulder, "Good Luck with your Miss Fields!"

"She's not 'my' Miss Fields," Greniston protested.

Deirdre shook her head. "Can't hear you! So I guess I'm going to have the last word, for once!"

Greniston caught a last glimpse of her rare grin. Then she turned and was gone, hurrying up the steps that led to Oxford Bridge.

I will never see her again, he realized, *not as a lover. Oh, we may, in some unforeseen way, meet again as friends. But I will never see this Deirdre again, never hold her in my arms again.* He realized that although their affair had ended over a year ago, it was now that it was finally over. He felt a strange combination of raw sorrow and relief that something he hadn't even known was unfinished was at last resolved, and he was released from it.

Deirdre had reached the top of the bridge. For a few seconds, he could still see her, an elegant dark-haired woman in a raincoat, moving through the crowd. Then she disappeared, absorbed like a drop into the flow of humanity. She was gone.

"Don't take it too hard, Guv," the tramp remarked. "At least you parted well." Greniston smiled wanly.

"Got a light, Guv?" the old man asked, pulling from his pocket a cigarette that looked like it had seen better days.

"Surely," Greniston said.

The tramp bent close to him as he lit his cigarette. Greniston noticed that although shabby, the old fellow was clean enough, and he had a deep red rose in his lapel.

"There was so much I wanted to say to her," Greniston sighed, "so much I'm sorry for, so much I still value in her."

"She knew, mate," the tramp said. "She knew." He looked at Greniston shrewdly and then added, almost in a whisper, "Don't give up. You have great things yet to do."

Greniston snorted. "I doubt that," he said, "but thanks all the same." He turned and began to walk away in the opposite direction from Deirdre. Then the strangeness of the old man's remark struck him. He looked back to ask him what he'd meant by "great things yet to do," but the tramp was gone, as if he had melted right into the shadows beneath the bridge.

***

"Hey there, youngster, where do you think you're going?"

Wyatt looked innocently up at the conductor.

"It's me Dad's lunch," he said, pulling a sandwich out of his satchel as proof. "He forgot it on the kitchen table, and Mum said, 'Oh, wun to the twain and catch him, he'll be ever so hungwy water if you don't!'" The conductor was not a Far Tauverly man, or he would never so easily have succumbed to a young Walmsley's earnestness.

"All right, get on with you then," he said. "But mind you hurry up. This train's due to leave in one minute, thirty-two seconds."

"Yes Sir. Thank you, Sir," said Wyatt sweetly. He dashed onto the nearest car, and hid in the lavatory. When he judged, from the clatter and speed, that they were well away from the station, he emerged and began his search for the Chalice Thief. He had followed the man for nearly a mile along Marip Coombe, the wooded stream that cut through Far Tauverly and then headed northwest through open fields until it came to Norton-Thryerby Station, which was no more than a whistle-stop platform for the Westbury-Bristol run and the train stop closest to Far Tauverly, next to Tweeverton.

Wyatt had been impressed by the man's knowledge of the best way to escape the village unnoticed, an art at which he had previously felt himself to be unequaled, even by Osgood.

Too bad he's a wealtor, Wyatt thought. As far as he could figure out, "wealtor" was a term for some kind of super villain. *He would make a tewific Sentinel of the Kingdom. Maybe I can turn him fwom his wife of cwime.*

Wyatt spotted the thief sitting in an otherwise empty compartment. He was reading a magazine. The bag with the stolen chalice in it was on the seat beside him.

Wyatt entered the compartment and said cheerily, "Hewo!" The man looked up briefly. He nodded but did not speak.

Wyatt settled himself happily on the opposite seat and began to unpack his sandwiches and comic books. In a characteristic moment of largesse, he opened the box of chocolate McVitey wafers and offered it to the thief. Wyatt was never one to be stingy, even with an arch fiend.

"They're excewent," he assured the man.

His fellow-traveler hesitated, and then, with the barest trace of a smile on his thin, sad face, he reached forward and took one chocolate covered wafer. He nibbled it cautiously, like a squirrel, Wyatt thought, and then nodded, as if to say, "Yes, they are quite good."

"Have as many as you wike," Wyatt said magnanimously, putting the open box on the seat beside him. "Just weach over and help yoursewf."

Again, that thin little scrap of a smile lightened the man's face, briefly. Then he returned to his magazine in a typical boring, grown-up way. Wyatt sighed and ate one of his sandwiches. He would have preferred to chat.

As the train clattered past fields and hamlets, Wyatt considered his situation: only an hour before, he had witnessed a crime of real magnitude, and now he was illegally on board a train bound for he knew not where, sitting but inches away from a man who was both a foreigner and a thief, and he had only twelve pence in his pocket. He felt that things were going rather well.

His first thought had been to follow the man. When he realized that he was not headed for a car but for the train stop, Wyatt had been impressed. It was very clever of the man not to bring a car into Far Tauverly, where every new vehicle was a subject of interest and conversation. His immediate attention had been taken up with finding a way to get on to the train; now that he had done so, he wondered what to do next.

It was when they entered the tunnel that the brilliant idea came to him. It was very dark in the tunnel, very dark indeed. A plan began to form in Wyatt's mind. By the time they reemerged into the daylight, he was ready for action. His wispy, flaxen hair was even more fluffy than usual, a sure sign that he was excited about something. Trying hard to sound casual, he said to the man, "Excuse me, are you going to be on this twain for awhile?"

The man nodded. "Well, could you watch my stuff, pwease? I have to find the loo." The man nodded again.

Wyatt slipped out of the compartment. He wasn't sure where to find what he needed or, indeed, exactly what he needed, but he knew that if he just kept looking, the answers would come to him. When he was in this inspired state, things always did just come to him.

He wandered down the corridor, keeping an eye out for the conductor. Then his gaze fell upon a tea trolley. The steward was nowhere in sight. Wyatt looked the trolley over and thoughtfully helped himself to several towels, which he stuffed under his sweater. Then his eye fell upon a bottle of mineral water, a plastic bowl full of butter pats, a bottle of thousand island dressing, and some lemon wedges. As Michelangelo saw the statue in the stone, so Wyatt saw his inspiration in these objects.

A few minutes later, he popped back into the compartment. He had taken off his sweater and carried it bundled up under one arm.

"I'm back!" he announced.

162

He settled himself back into the seat across from the man and began to eat McVitey wafers. He gazed out the window, evidently absorbed by the passing scenery. In fact, he was craning his head so that he could see as far down the tracks as possible. When he saw that they were approaching another tunnel, he was ready. He stood up and clutched his rolled up sweater to his stomach like a pillow.

"I . . . I don't feel so good," he said tremulously. "I think I'm going to thwow up!"

He was pleased to note that the man looked alarmed. Wyatt lurched toward him, just as the train rushed into the next tunnel. Under cover of darkness, Wyatt leaned heavily against the man and produced a series of awful retching sounds. With one hand, he fumbled with the zipper of the canvas bag the man had left on the seat. By the time the train clattered out of the tunnel, Wyatt was back in his own seat, looking breathless and shaken.

"I'm ever so sowwy," he said, wiping his mouth with the back of his hand. "Too many McVitey wafers."

He looked apologetically at the mixture of lemon juice, salad dressing, and crumbled cookies that he had smeared on the man's coat in the darkness. He hoped that the lemon juice would give it just the appropriate acrid smell and that the overall mess would look so disgusting that the man would be disinclined to examine it closely.

His admiration for the thief increased when the man did not have a typical grown-up tantrum about the incident. He just quietly took the canvas bag and headed for the loo to clean up, as Wyatt had hoped he would.

As soon as the thief left the compartment, Wyatt fell to his knees, and dragged the chalice out from under the seat where he had kicked it in the darkness. With any luck, the thief would be fooled by the weight of the substitute chalice he had made from the mineral water bottle and the plastic bowl and stuffed into the bag in the darkness. Hopefully, he would have no reason to open it until he reached his destination. Wyatt felt it best not to count on this, however. He stuffed the real chalice into his own knapsack, along with the Super Heroes comic books and his sweater. He hesitated. Then, in a noble gesture, he took one comic book, *Superman and the Black Comet*, and left it on the man's seat, next to his magazine. Perhaps the story, in which good so clearly overcame evil, could inspire the thief to change his ways.

Wyatt darted into the corridor and headed in the opposite direction from the loo, just seconds before the thief returned. Realizing that he now needed to hide from both the conductor and the thief, he decided it was best to get off the train at the next stop, wherever that was. It turned out to be a little village called Farley-in-the-Wolde.

It was with relief that Wyatt saw the train pull out of the station. From his vantage point behind a luggage rack, he saw that the thief was back in his seat. Wyatt was delighted to see that the man was reading the comic book with that sad, meager smile on his face. Wyatt reasoned that he could not yet have missed the chalice, or he would never have been sitting there so calmly.

Once the train was safely away, Wyatt stepped boldly out onto the platform and burst into tears. "There, there, what's wrong, mate?" a porter asked him.

"I . . . I don't know where I am," said Wyatt truthfully. "This isn't the wight stop!" He wailed brokenheartedly.

"What's the trouble here?" an elderly lady with blue-tinted hair asked.

"Poor little blighter seems to have missed his stop, Mum," the porter explained.

"And where were you supposed to get off?" the old lady asked kindly.

"Far Tauverly. My Gwan was to meet me at the station. But this doesn't look like the right place!"

"Indeed, it is not," exclaimed the porter. Far Tauverly's over forty miles from here. You've gone right past it, lad."

"I suppose we should call his grandmother," the old lady said. "She's sure to be worried."

"She's not on the phone wine," Wyatt put in, sensing trouble.

"Oh dear. Well, your parents, then, in case she calls them. Where did you get on the train?"

"Westbury," said Wyatt, hoping that that was in the right direction. He sniveled and simulated some very effective hiccups. He was actually beginning to believe his own story and felt quite sorry for himself.

"We'll ring your Mum in Westbury, then," the porter said. "Your Gran is bound to try to reach her."

"You can't," Wyatt wept. "She's on her way to Reading, to see my Dad. He's in jail," Wyatt added in an awful whisper, "for bank wobbewy. So she went to visit him. That's why I was to go to Gwan's for overnight."

Wyatt could sense that the porter had his doubts about this, but the old lady bought it, hook, line, and sinker.

"You poor dear," she gushed, "and such a lively looking lad! Well, I suppose the best thing is to put you back on the next train for Far Tauverly."

"There's no stop right in Far Tauverly, strictly speaking," the porter said. "Folks either get off at St. Marip's or at Tweeverton."

"T . . . T . . . Tweeverton," Wyatt gulped, "that's where she meets me."

"It is the likelier one," the porter acknowledged.

"Well, I shall buy your ticket and see that you get safely on the train," the old lady said. "I shall speak to the conductor, as well, so that he sees you safely off at Tweeverton."

While they waited for the train, the old lady bought Wyatt an ice lolly and told him some stories about Jesus. He didn't mind; he quite enjoyed the one about the loaves and the fishes. It seemed to him that his own life had just that magical way of providing what was needed at the moment, so why worry?

As she put him on the train, the old lady stuffed a ten pound note in Wyatt's pocket.

"I know young boys need to eat, so get yourself a nice lunch in the buffet car," she said.

Over roast chicken, peas, and mashed potatoes with double gravy, Wyatt Walmsley, Super Agent of the Independent Kingdom of Greenstone, considered his day so far: the true chalice was in his knapsack, he had met and foiled an arch fiend, had two train rides for free as well as an excellent lunch, and now was about to have a ramble around Tweeverton—and it was not yet one o'clock. Who knew what might happen next? Who needed to? Something surely would, and that was good enough for him.

CHAPTER TEN

"*Alo, Bonjour, Guten Tag, Shalom*! Hey, it's true, you've reached me, Filipo! *Quelle domage*, I'm not *chez moi* right now, but hey, you can leave your message after the music, the poem, and the beep." There followed a brilliant guitar passage from Albeniz; then Filipo returned, reading a poem by Miguel de Unamuno.

Gwen sighed. She had hoped to reach Filipo; still, it was good just to hear his voice. When the beep finally came, she left the number of the Greenstone Arms and asked him to call her as soon as he could. Of all the people she knew, Filipo seemed the most likely to figure out a way to help Logan. She knew that from the other side of the world, he might perceive a solution she couldn't see close up.

She hung up feeling a bit disgruntled. The timing of things wasn't working out today. She had hoped to sleep in, talk to Filipo, then spend a gentle afternoon in Tweeverton, doing some shopping and visiting its twelfth-century cathedral. After speaking to Swindon earlier, she had managed to go back to sleep, but her doze had been restless, troubled again by dreams she couldn't quite remember. And now, in—she glanced at the clock—four and a half hours, she was going on a date she had never exactly said yes to. The afternoon stretched before her, too long to ignore, too short for any serious sight-seeing.

Coffee, she decided, *That's what I need, and lots of it. Even English coffee.* She got up, dressed herself casually in tan corduroy slacks, a white turtleneck sweater, and sneakers. She decided that her eyes were so puffy from her overindulgence the night before that makeup was beside the point. Grabbing a scarf and her raincoat, she went out in search of caffeine.

Three cups later, standing in front of the bakery, which doubled as the Far Tauverly cafe, she began to feel much better. The throbbing in her head had retreated, and she realized that the clouds had lifted, the sun was out, the wind was soft, and the day was extraordinarily lovely. There was no sign of Logan. Perhaps he, too, was just stirring into life.

I know what I'll do, Gwen thought, *I'll go to Greniston Manor, to see Lord Peter's diaries and that portrait the Vicar mentioned, the one that has the shield on it. It's just as well Lord Greniston's out of town, too. I don't really feel up to meeting him today. But I bet Mrs. Fitzpatrick would let me in, at least to look at the portrait. I guess it's a little bit pushy of me to ask, but what have I got to lose?* She purchased a scone to munch on her way and set out for Greniston Manor.

The woods were in the full glory of springtime. Everywhere Gwen looked, she saw color: the green of new leaves, the yellow of daffodils like scattered gold beneath the trees. Everything sparkled in the sun as if newly made. It was the first truly warm day since she had come to England, and she relished the reprieve from the pervasive chill.

A light that was both silver and gold gleamed on the swaying treetops, and above them, the mist of the day before had parted to reveal a high, blue sky that seemed as boundless as the hopes of youth. A few billowy white clouds sailed like galleons, high and far on the sea of the air. Suddenly, the old, old world seemed full of bright promise, as if great, new things might be about to happen.

Gwen felt moved to poetry.

> "'Whan that Aprille with his shooures soote,
> The droughte of Marche hath pierced taw the roote,
> Than longen folke to gooen on pilgrimages . . .'"

Gwen paused in her recitation. She couldn't remember exactly how the next lines of *Canterbury Tales* went, and anyway, the *oo*'s and *awh*'s of Middle English suddenly struck her as an extraordinarily silly way to talk.

"Ahm gooen aloong tha rood ta Grenistoon Mahner," she said, and found herself giggling. It occurred to her that in spite of all the coffee, she might still be just the tiniest bit drunk from the Drambuie the night before. If so, it was a pleasant feeling—so pleasant that she found herself now moved to song.

"Heigh-ho, nobody home! Meat nor bread nor money have we none, still we will go wandering . . ."

It was a wonderful old song, an English folk song that she remembered from high school glee club days. Some of the words eluded her, but she decided that really, the stirring melody was the thing and walked on, humming the tune and tossing crumbs of scone out for the birds.

Soon, she found herself once again at the gates of Greniston Manor. The stone lions gazed down at her benignly.

"Bit of scone, old thing?" Gwen asked, offering one of them a crumb. The lion, evidently lost in thoughts of its own, did not reply. Gwen ate the crumb herself and peered through the iron scrollwork of the gate. There seemed to be no one about. The park-like lawns sparkled emerald in the sunshine. Nearby, some sparrows were having a fiesta of chatter in a flowering Hawthorne tree, but of people, there was no sign.

Gwen tried the gate. Slowly, silently, it swung open at her touch, as if pulled back by invisible hands.

As she stepped onto the Greniston land, Gwen felt as if she were walking right into an illustration from some wonderful old book of tales, something she had often longed to do as a child. It would not have surprised her, in her tipsy state, to see a unicorn peering out from among the trees or to come upon a knight in armor, or a group of Tudor ladies out to pick violets. A person from any time might appear, she thought, for there was nothing in the scene to indicate what century it was. For hundreds, perhaps thousands of centuries, wild roses had flowered, just as they were now. Larks had built their nests near hidden streams, pouring their joyful songs into the air, just as they were now. The beetles, ants, hedgehogs, and otters had scurried about their pressing business, just as they were now. The noble trees had grown quietly, inch by silent inch, and had fallen to lightening or storm, to be replaced by others and, at last, by those that rustled near her now. The Roman legions had come this way, in all their pomp and glory, and had disappeared, and then had come kings and armies, priests and dynasties, all so mighty in their time, yet all now passed quite away, all now but a delicate dust, while here still bloomed the snowdrop and the columbine. It seemed to Gwen that if there was any truth to be found in life, the place to search for it was here, in Nature, for It endured.

She now rounded the curve that brought the first clear view of Greniston Manor. "How beautiful!" she exclaimed. By night, the manor had seemed almost foreboding to her. Now, in the bright April sunlight, it looked like the most welcoming place she had ever seen.

She had learned from the Vicar that although there had been Grenistons on the land "as far back as anyone can remember," the current house dated to 1485. The old, central portion was built of gray stone, with high gables and mullioned windows. Wings had been added on either side of the original manor in the eighteenth century. Whatever architect had designed them had done a masterful job, for although the additions were models of the elegance and restraint of the mid 1700s, they did not clash with the original home at all, for they were built of the same stone and complimented the core in line and proportion. The wings stood like two staunch companions on either side of the oldest section, with a faint sense of protectiveness that Gwen found very warming.

The house faced southwest, so that sunlight warmed the gray stone. The simplicity of the building was further softened by ivy and by the high beeches that framed it from behind.

The drive was brick, half-wild with grass and myrtle, designed to curve into the woods and approach the manor house from the side, so that the wide expanse of front lawn stretched unbroken from the front steps for at least a quarter of a mile, to where Gwen now stood. It was a view of epic proportions, and Gwen was struck by the thought that this was a home for people who were large of heart and gallant of mind and were generous enough to entertain a hundred guests at dinner and not think twice about it.

How much this place has seen, Gwen mused. According to the Vicar, Henry the VIIIth and Elizabeth I had both stayed at the manor more than once, and Bonny Prince Charlie had found sanctuary there in his flight from the Roundheads.

She tried to imagine what the place must have been like in its heyday. With a large family in residence, complete with visitors, servants, gardeners, peasants to farm the fields, horses, hounds, hawks, and other livestock, the manor house and its outbuildings would have been almost a small city, in a sense, its own kingdom, where the noble, boisterous tribe of Grenistons had entertained royalty almost as equals.

No wonder Lord Greniston is a bit arrogant, Gwen thought, *growing up as the heir to all this.* She walked on. As the road curved, she left behind the vista of the manor and entered more woods. Here, too, she found heroic proportions. On either side, the drive had been planted with lime trees. Their trunks grew straight and true for over thirty feet, then met overhead in an arch of new green. It was a road to be taken at the gallop, a road for messengers to ride down, crying, "Make way! Make way for the King's business!" or, more likely, "The Greniston's business, Make way!" She wondered how many valiant lords and ladies had traveled the same path she walked on now and what their heroic missions had been. She could almost hear the thunder of their horses' hooves and the jingle of their bridles.

Perhaps, King Arthur himself was here once, she thought. "*Perhaps, long before the manor house was built, this was the site of Camelot, or Lancelot's castle, Joyous Garde. Perhaps Arthur knew and loved these very woods and walked upon a forest track where this drive is now. Perhaps he stood and wondered about the future right here, on this very spot where I now wonder about the past . . . and perhaps he truly is buried in that mound, . . . not dead, but sleeping, waiting to do more great deeds. . . . And Merlin, perhaps his spirit, too, haunts this place, . . . perhaps it was his cry I heard, for I did hear something, . . . perhaps it is all true, . . . but if it is true, then what do they want, Arthur and Merlin? Why have they called me to this place?*

"What do you want?" Gwen called out aloud, as if the woods could answer her. There was no reply. Yet from her own heart, she received a clear message of what she wanted: to live a life that was not puny, careful, and comfortable but was courageous, bold, and had some meaning to it. A great life, yes, a hero's life.

Her wish was so strong that it seemed to fly from her, up, up, into the high, daring sky of spring blue, swift as an arrow shot from the bow. Though unspoken, she had the strangest feeling that her thoughts had been heard, that her prayer for a hero's life had been witnessed, as if it was not merely a wish but an oath that she had taken.

"I promise," she said, "as God and this place are my witnesses, that my life will not be wasted."

After she spoke, the woods seemed especially still. She felt like her pledge had somehow been heard and noted, though by what she was not quite certain.

Then, a magpie chattered, a breeze stirred her hair, and she felt like just herself again, Gwendolyn Fields, somewhere between drunk and hungover, but happy, walking along a tree-lined drive on a beautiful day in spring. She soon reached the end of the drive. About thirty feet away was the East wing of the house. She saw a kitchen-looking door that seemed much more approachable than the main entrance. The door was slightly ajar, but she saw no one nearby.

"Hello?" she called out. From somewhere beyond the threshold, a young female voice giggled.

"Hello?" Gwen called out again.

There was a flurry of whispers, more giggles, and hurried footsteps. Robert appeared in the doorway. His brown hair was disheveled, and his shirt not entirely tucked into his trousers.

Oh dear, Gwen thought. It was hard to say which of them was the more embarrassed.

"Oh, it's you, Miss," Robert exclaimed. "I'm ever so sorry, but Lord Greniston isn't here, he's in London."

"Is Mrs. Fitzpatrick at home?" Gwen asked, although under the circumstances, it seemed unlikely. Robert had the grace to blush, slightly.

"No, Miss, she's gone to Tweeverton for the day. Won't be back 'til evening. No one here but me, and, er, me. Anything I can be helping you with?" Gwen hesitated. "It's no trouble if you need something, Miss, really."

"Well, actually, I came because I want to see the portrait that I understand is in the Greniston gallery. *The Yellow Portrait*, I think it's called. And there are some diaries I hoped to look at, too."

"Oh, old Lord Peter's stuff? You want to look at that? I'm sure Lord Greniston wouldn't mind, Miss; he's always glad when anyone's interested. I'm sure you'd be welcome to read those diaries from cover to cover. Not very racy stuff, though, if you know what I mean. Not that I've read 'em, exactly. But I'm sure you're welcome to 'em, and I'm sure Mrs. Fitz would say the same, if she was here."

"You really think so?"

"Oh, absolutely. I'll take you to the portrait gallery myself . . . ," he glanced over his shoulder at the kitchen door, "but let's go in the main entrance."

"Good idea," Gwen murmured. A few moments later, Robert led her through a huge entrance hall and up a stone staircase to the second floor of the manor.

"It's at the end of this corridor, Miss," he said, "you can't miss it."

"You're sure this is all right?"

"Don't worry, Miss, I'm sure Lord Greniston would welcome you."

Privately, Gwen thought it was rather handsome of Robert to say so, since he, like everyone else in Far Tauverly, had probably heard every detail of their encounter on the street at least three times.

"Thank you," she said, "but actually, it's your privacy I'm concerned about. This is your home, too, and you have company."

"Don't worry about that, Miss." Robert grinned. Then his face suddenly sobered. "I just realized, Lord G. wouldn't like it, if he knew . . . ." Robert glanced in what Gwen supposed was the direction of the kitchen and his giggling visitor.

"No need to elaborate," she said quickly. "It's not the sort of thing I'd mention. After all, it's me who's intruding, into your private time."

Robert's relief was patent. "Thank you, Miss," he said fervently. Then, with a grin, he added, "Well, best be getting back to see what's cooking—so to speak." He suggested that Gwen let herself out whenever she was ready to go. "After all, Miss," he explained, "you don't look the type to steal the family silver, now do you?"

Gwen assured him that she wasn't, and he hurried back down the stairs, whistling.

At first Gwen wasn't sure she wanted to stay at all. In spite of Robert's assurances to the contrary, she still felt she was invading his privacy. Then she realized that the manor house was as big as some hotels.

There must be a hundred rooms here, she thought.

She walked down the corridor toward the portrait gallery. She seemed to be in the oldest part of the house. The stone floor and high-ceilinged stone walls gave it very much the feeling of a castle. From the amount of dust around, she deduced that poor Mrs. Fitzpatrick was hard-pressed to keep so vast a place clean. Probably, Lord Greniston's living quarters were in the lighter, airier rooms in one of the wings. The corridor she was now in definitely looked much older than the rooms she had seen the other night.

Her tipsiness had vanished, she realized, and had left her curiously alert and clear. She stood before the tall oak doors that led to the portrait gallery. Although Robert had assured her that no one else was home, she felt she should knock. After waiting for a moment, she opened the doors and stepped inside.

In crossing the threshold into the gallery, she might have stepped back in time five hundred years. She found herself in a large room, perhaps fifty feet long, with ceilings at least twenty feet high. The walls and floors were of stone, not plastered, which gave the room the feeling of an old church or Abbey. She noticed a great fireplace and a massive oaken table, at which were placed some regal-looking chairs upholstered in faded garnet velvet, with lion's heads carved on the ends of the arms. The stone floor was softened by several oriental rugs in shades of rose and gold and cobalt. All along the west wall was a series of diamond-paned, arched windows that opened onto a view of the back lawns far below and, beyond, the forest. Across from the windows, portraits of the Grenistons were placed so that they seemed to be gazing out the windows at the rustling woodland they had loved and protected for so many centuries.

Gwen gazed at the first portrait. It was not an oil painting, but a brass rubbing from the effigy on a tomb. Sir Richard de Greenstone, 1136. He looked solemnly back at her, steadfast and rather grim in chain mail, a broadsword at his side. Next to him was a similar rubbing of his wife, Lady Anne de Greenstone. There was something gentle about her; she had died young, if the likeness was true. In her slender fingers, she held a five-petalled rose, and at her feet was a little dog.

The portraits seemed to be arranged in chronological order, for the next was another rubbing, of Sir Boyne de Greenstone, 1173. He looked a jollier fellow than his father. One by one, Gwen stopped in front of each of the portraits. She had the strange feeling that she was introducing herself to a family that was looking her over rather carefully and that it would be very bad form to omit greeting even a single one.

By the time she had reached Sir Humphrey Greniston, 1443, Gwen had a strong sense of the Greniston clan. Sir Humphrey's portrait was three-quarter length, painted in rich colors upon a wood panel. He had the dark hair, strong chin, and laughing eye of so many of his family. Even more noticeable than the physical traits passed down through the centuries were those of character; face by face, the Grenistons proclaimed themselves to be a courageous, intelligent, stubborn tribe, humorous, generous-hearted, and bold. Here and there, the stubbornness turned a touch severe or the courage a shade arrogant; here and there, a gentler strain appeared, mostly by marriage, but about all of them, there was a sense of honest goodness and strong character.

At last, she came to the portrait she had been waiting for: Lord Peter Greniston. "Hello, Lord Peter," she said, feeling that she was greeting someone who already felt like an old friend.

The portrait smiled back at her. This Lord Peter was a few years older than the man she had seen in the museum. But his smile was just as charming, and the light in his eyes was just as brave and bold.

The picture had been cleverly painted to copy the very room in which it stood. Except for the walnut frame, one might have thought, at first glance, that Lord Peter himself was standing there, in a suit of daffodil-colored velvet, one arm resting casually on the mantelpiece, so perfectly did the wall in the painting blend with the wall behind it, so well had the artist captured the soft, peaceful light of the room.

There, as if leaning against the real wall, was Lord Peter's shield. It did indeed show a lion rampant, holding a daffodil. Gwen glanced back at Lord Peter's face and could not help feeling that he was smiling right at her.

Gwen moved on, looking carefully at generation after generation of Grenistons. She looked with interest at the present Lord Greniston's parents. The man was in military uniform; the lady beside him wore a silver-white ball gown that set off admirably her silver white hair. They both seemed to be in their fifties. The man's thin face was quiet and worn; the woman's was very strong of feature. They gazed lovingly into each other's eyes, oblivious to the two children who stood in the background. One of the children was a rather severe-looking girl of about twelve.

That must be his sister, Julia, Gwen thought. Then she looked carefully at young Greniston and laughed. He was the only person in the portrait who was smiling, and even at that age, his dark hair was unruly, and his eyes sparkled with wit.

She moved on to the last portrait there so far, although there was room for many more. It showed Lord Greniston as a man of about thirty, she reckoned. He, too, wore military uniform, but his officer's cap was set upon his head at an almost mocking angle, and the light in his eyes was troubled. Like all of his ancestors, he seemed to gaze through the arched windows at the forest beyond. Gwen, too, turned to look toward it. The treetops swayed in the wind of spring.

It dances to a slower music than we do, she realized. There were oaks in that forest that had been four hundred years a-growing. Millions of years of wind and rain and flood had shaped those hills and streams, slowly, carefully, as the potter shapes the clay upon the wheel. The life within its tapestry was interwoven down to every leaf and lady bug. It had taken millions of years to weave a lace that fine, yet it could be destroyed in a day, the ancient trees felled, the creeks filled in and paved over with concrete. It could be destroyed so quickly, as quickly as a name being signed on a contract.

Gwen saw as never before how fast life had become, compared to the timings of nature. She thought of the way she dashed to work each morning, gulping her coffee as she searched for her shoes, hoping to make each green light, then rushing around the office, jumping to answer phones. It had nothing to do with the rhythm of the seasons or the sigh of the wind in the distant trees, which she could faintly hear through the panes.

174

How separate from this earth we have become, she thought. A line from Housman came to her mind: "The happy highways where we went, and cannot go again."

She knew that life in Lord Peter's time had not been all May picnics and weaving of garlands. It had surely been full of pain and brutal struggles, yet she wondered if it had also been more human, in some ways, at least,.

It's gone now, though his time is gone, she thought. *Yet perhaps we can recapture a bit of the best of it, and bring it forward into this time, now.* She moved to the oaken table at the center of the room and sat down in one of the chairs with the lion's heads carved on the arms. She knew, somehow, that Lord Peter himself had sat at that table, in that chair, in that very room. She picked up the first of the leather-bound volumes on the table, Lord Peter's journals. Carefully, she opened the old book, and began to read.

In the year of our Lord sixteen hundred and forty three, by the Grace of God, do I Peter de Grenistone, write these words. Indeed, I do not know but that they may be the last that ever I shall write, so dark are our times become. The soldiers have been here twice today, searching for Father Thomas. Fortunately, the priest's hole is so cleverly concealed that I doubt the Roundheads will ever find it. Still, it gave me some sobering moments when they felt the wall and tugged the tapestry just inches from the hidden lock. I swear, tis dangerous for me even to write these words, yet I must have some friend in whom I can confide all, and Thou, Dear Booke, art that faire friend to me. To all others, even my Sara, I must seem strong and without care, even as befits a Grenistone.

No day goes by without some fighting: Roundheads and Cavaliers, back and forth, and then the waves of criminals, who, in their wake, take advantage of the confusion for their own ends. No road is safe, no stillest hour of the night is without alarms. The food is scarce, and now to make all worse, the plague hath broken out in St. Marip, and again in Tweevertynne. (I pray it does not reach us.) Some say tis the end of the world, and no hope to be had. Therefore, some do devote all time to prayer and moaning, others to seize what pleasures they can, in these our last days, perhaps. But I say, Steady on, to our purpose let us cleave, for we are men, not weepers or brutes. Yet what is the purpose worth cleaving to? I can not say tis the life of our foolish king, tho I fight for him in secret, gainst the Roundhead troops. Alas, our Bonnie Prince Charlie is but the lesser evil of the two! (I could be hanged for what I have just writ, for all that I have risked my life a hundred times on the fool's behalf! But by Heaven, I will speak my mind, at least within the confines of my own soul!) Then I ask myself, is it the Grenistone name and the Grenistone lands I fight for, so that our patch of earth be left in peace, tho all have gone mad around us? Well, yes. . . . And yet, I do believe, there's more. Do I fight for mine own honoure, that I might feel clean when I do die? Yes, . . . and yet, I think I serve at hearte another master, harder to name . . .

.

We are mysteries even to ourselves, it seems.

I must confess that sometimes death seems very near. And yet, for all its constant shadow, it still do be needful to remember small things - a bit of lace to make Kathlyn Travey a wedding veil, for the lass do be determined to wed Andrew Golightly, war or no, and indeed, from the look of her she had best marry him soon, for bread do be a-baking in that oven. And who's to say that a third maid is not to look as a Queene on her bridal day? Yes, I must remember to get some lace in Tweevertynne Tuesday next; if I sell the remaining pewter mugs, I can get something Spanish and very fine. Twill suit her dark hair very well, especially if Sara can get her to wash it, so that the strands do shine. Yes, on that dark gloss, the white lace will look like a dust of snow upon a dark brown river rock, gleaming in the water's flow, and we must let the lass have her moment of beauty, at least one, before the dark days close round us again. Also in town, I must contrive a discreet way to get some satin, for the last banner was shot through by a Roundhead cannon ball. Though we go into battle masked, yet we must declare our Honoure. Now, who can I buy from who will not blab?

And so Lord Peter's journals continued. For him, it seemed, the great questions of life were ever interwoven with its homeliest details; he would speculate about the meaning of a church sermon, then make a note to mend a fence or buy sugared almonds for a child; life was all cut of the same cloth for him. He survived the war and survived the plague, for the journal described his subsequent journey, "upon the King's Command," to go to London, "there to receive honoures and landes." Lord Peter seemed to have found London a tragic place.

So many be hungry in the very streets, and they sleep against the cathedral walls without blanket or cape to call their own, like featherless chicks all fallen from their nests, but when I told the king, he bade me not speak of it, yet I did speak, which pleased him ill, I think. Tho he still gave me honoures at Whitehall next day. What a mistake that place is, was ever so much treasure spent in service to such bad taste? I would not minde our sovereign to spend fortunes on display, had he some sense of art and elegance. I almost left before the ceremony, but tho I did not want the honours, I did want the land, for my children to use well. So there it is. But I must say, it suits me not, this fussy town life, with all its manners and its chat, but nothing to do! How can a man feel clean at day's end, if he has not stretched mind and sinew in some hard, good work?

Hard work was clearly Lord Peter's joy. Not for him the role of indulgent Lord of the Manor. Judging from the journals, he seemed to have plowed fields and mended fences alongside his peasants. Indeed, some entries made him sound like the hardest worker of all.

Marche thirtieth, the Year of Our Lord sixteen hundred and fifty three. Rose about four for prayers. Went fishing at dawn, caught three good trout for cook. From seven to nine instructed Master Thaddeus in Greek; I fear Homer is not to the lad's taste. Nine a.m., chapel with the family. From ten til luncheon, discussed orchard plans with Pritchard. A grand lunch of trout and sorrel soup. Went riding after, to check fences Knobbly Hill way. Guests to sup, and fine daucing. Margery Kenellton was there, bouncing through the cotillion as merry as May., Her petticoats revealed a dimpled knee, and I did enjoy the view, tho none can compare to my dear Sara, who fortunately knows not jealousy's darts. The musik was very fine, we daunced til nearly eleven of the night. Then Aubrey came in to say there was trouble with a calfing. I came to see, and oh, God's Sorrow, the little creature was trying to come out sideways; I have never seen the like, nor had Aubrey neither. At first we feared to lose both mother and calf, but with some coaxing hours, the wee creature at last came free, and a fine calf too, and the mother safe as well, tho weak. I held the little creature in my arms (another good coat ruined, Sara will have words for me), and upon its forehead a white blaze like a star, and thru the barn door was shining the morning star. Aubrey said, "Sir, let us call him 'Morning Star,'" and I did agree. We toasted the wee one's birth with stout, and so to bed for an hour or two. A good day.

The next entry was dated but a week later, Easter of that same year.

All are at the feasting, save me; I have slipped away to this dear quiet room, to gaze at the greenwood budding. The house is all a bustle. Earlier, a hell-fire sermon from Father Thomas, which pleased all save me. The servants seem to rate a sermon by how many shocks it gives 'em, about on a par with a good bear-baiting. A bear-baiting of the soul; tis what a sermon often is. But I sometimes long for quieter fare that speaks to the soul deep. A Breton minstrel passed thru here Wednesday last, and I heard in his musik as much of God as ere in any sermon. He played wondrous well upon a harpe strung with metal in the olde fashion, musiks both sad and glad. Then he told a tale that he had heard in Wales, about a King whose hearte was filled with longing, for what he could not name. Yes, what is it that we longe for, as we pass through this dusty world? I care not much for the Bible, tho twould shock poor Father Thomas to hear me say it. Indeed, I believe his poor old hearte almost failed him when he asked our little Katie how she liked her Bible studies, and that pert little miss, not yet seven years old, wrinkled her nose and replied, "Not so much." Father Thomas staggered back, clutching the cross he wears round his neck as if a demon had spoken to him through her, while Miss Katie continued, "I like the stories, about the burning bush and all. But God seems awfully mean. Jesus is much better; I would like him to visit us."

"But my dear child," Father Thomas exclaimed, "He comes to visit you at every mass."

Katie shook her head in disbelief. "But I have never seen Him there," she protested, a valid point, I thought.

At this moment, Sara thought it was wise to lead the girl from the room. It was as well that Father Thomas did not hear Katie's further comments about St. Paul, who is not a personal favorite of hers. They shocked her mother well enough, so that Sara felt it would be wise to whip her, for her own salvation. I would not hear of it. "Why should honesty ever be punished?" I asked. At that, Sara threw up her hands and said, 'She's as much a Grenistone as you are. Impossible, all of you!" and she fled the room in tears. I fear my dear Sara finds our family ways trying at times; she has ever been one to put her thoughts in neat piles, the way she does with folded laundry, with lavender tucked in between, to make all smell sweet. An excellent thing with lavender, but is it right for thoughts? Yet Sara is an admirable wife, gentle, kind, and true, and a veritable command general of the pantry as well. Cross her on a cleaning day, and you feel you should salute, and smartly, too. Ah, Sara, I must plant some more roses for you, along the herb garden wall, since you like them so well. Perhaps that new strain Pritchard heard of, they say it comes all the way from Persia and blooms as red as ruby. But back to the Breton minstrel and his tale of longinge (My thoughts, you see, ramble over the days like a wild clematis vine, everywhere at once. No wonder it drives Sara mad sometimes!) I recognized that longinge, it put me in mind of the psalms: "Teach me to know mine end, Lord, what it is, for I am but a stranger with Thee, and a sojourner." Or again, Henry Vaughn: "There is in God, some say, a deep yet dazzling darkness, as men say night is dark, because they can not see the day. Oh, that to that darkness were I come, to merge Eternally with Him, Him bright, and me invisible and dim." I told these poems to the Minstrel, and he liked them right well, indeed, put them to memory on the *spot. He promised to return, another day, another year, with the poesy set to music. I hope right well he does, and sent him on his way with more gold in his pocket than Sara would care to know about.*

Well, dear Booke, I shall be glad when this Easterday is over, and we are back to work, there is much to be done. The first shearing came in last week, and I went to watch Dame Cranderwell spin it; eighty three years old, yet she spins better than the youngest maid on the land. Around and around her spinning wheel went; it made me wonder of the stars, and this goodly earth, which they tell us does spin like a top in the sky. I find it hard to imagine, yet something does make the seasons return, and the sun come and go. I suspect that this is the book for me to ken, not the Bible, but the stars, and the streams, and why roses grow better if you plant garlic near em. Tis full of mysteries, even a garden plot is, and surely it is writ in God's own hand. And yet, for all that, we men are different; we are not like sparrows and gilly flowers, "for I am a stranger here, and a sojourner." What part in these questions does our Lord's passion play? A great one, I am sure, yet I doubt I'll find the answers from Father Thomas, bless his Faithful Hearte for all his loyal years. Well, I hear the maid calling me; the meal must be ready, and I must go.

Dear Booke, enough of my heretic thoughts, upon this Easterday. I must remember to send goodly portions of meat to Charles, the ploughman's son, he that be ill, poor lad. Perhaps I can take the provender to him myself, and thus escape the evening service; one sermon in a day is enough, after all. Like Sara's spring tonic, a little sermon goes a long way! Ah well, the maid has found me out. She stands upon the threshold, torn between her awe of me and this solemn room full of portraits on the one hand and the sense of mission imposed upon her by her mistress on the other. She hath been dispatched to bring me back alive, I see. Therefore, to Whoever, to Whatever, I pen all these foolish wordes to, Adieu, again, Sweet Friend, for now.

The bells of St. Aethelrood's tolled four o'clock. Gwen heard them, but as if from a great distance. She knew that she needed to leave, if she was to get ready for her reluctant date and be on time to meet Geoffrey Swindon. Yet she lingered, not wanting to leave the portrait gallery.

She had not discovered anything about Lord Peter's prophecy, but there were three and a half volumes of his journals still to go. Besides, she felt that she had already come across a great treasure: the life of a man. She thought of how he had signed the last entry: "To Whoever, to Whatever, I pen all these foolish words to." He could never have known that his words would be read over three hundred years hence by a traveler from America. Yet she felt as if the journals were a letter, sealed and addressed to her, waiting, all these years, for her to find them. Perhaps others, reading the journals before her, had felt the same sense of intimacy, as if Lord Peter was right there in the room with them, speaking in the most honest way. Gwen felt moved as she sometimes was by Shakespeare, amazed at how another life can reach its hand across the centuries and touch one's own. She knew that she had much to learn from Lord Peter; what she could offer him, she was not as sure. Listening, perhaps. For it seemed that Lord Peter had needed a good listener in his life. On the one hand, he had been the least lonely of men, woven into life at every turn, busy, bustling, involved with the Greniston lands down to every leaf and foal and christening. Yet within it all, there was the pensive man, who asked deep questions and met no one to discuss them with, save a passing Breton minstrel. Perhaps she could at least send the message back across the centuries: "I hear you, Lord Peter, your questions make sense to me." And perhaps he would know. Normally, Gwen would have thought such an idea quite far-fetched, but since coming to England, she seemed to have entered a realm where time did not work the way she thought it did. Right now, her own century seemed a thousand years away to her, and Lord Peter's as close as her own breath. Who knew how things really worked? She thought she had come to England to find adventure, but perhaps she had also come to be a friend and listener to a man from three hundred years ago.

The bells tolled a quarter past the hour, and Gwen knew that, now, she really must leave.

"I'll be back," she said to Lord Peter, as she gathered up her things. His elegant face smiled kindly back at her. She had the distinct impression he was glad to have had her as his guest.

***

Luan Tey was just entering the Cavendish Museum in Bristol. He had stayed on the train until the end of the line and then spent several hours sightseeing. Already, he had visited two churches, a park, and the zoo. Like many another tourist, he carried a canvas overnight bag with him. And like many another tourist, he bought postcards, fish and chips, cups of tea. Everywhere he stopped, he made a point of acting confused about the money, or directions, so that the clerks would remember him, if anyone came asking questions. ("Sure, he was here, skinny foreign bloke with sunglasses. Spending the day in Bristol he was.")

Now, at 4:15 p.m., right on schedule, Luan Tey entered the Cavendish Museum, a restored eighteenth-century house. For a few minutes, he followed the guided tour. Then he quietly glided back to the room they had just left, slipped under the blue velvet rope, and let himself out by a side door, into a tiny, shadowed alley, where a car was waiting.

The car sped swiftly along the back roads to Bath. It came to a halt by a small, circular park. A man got out, no longer dressed in a navy windbreaker and black slacks, but in the white uniform of a butler. He carried a large bag of groceries, in which, underneath some celery and a bag of noodles, was a squashed black canvas bag.

A few minutes later, Luan Tey stood in his employer's elegant study.

"Ah," a cordial voice said, "you're back. Did you get it?" Luan Tey nodded. He set down the bag of groceries and began to unpack it. Not for the first time, he wondered why his employer was so interested in the chalice. He felt a curious reluctance to deliver it into his hands, but then, business was business.

As always, Luan Tey found himself faintly shocked by Miller's appearance. At first glance, there was, of course, nothing to be shocked by. The man wore the most elegant clothing London and Rome could supply: understated, impeccable. His sandy, slightly graying hair was trimmed and sculpted into conservative perfection. His even features were wonderfully forgettable; his calm, intelligent voice held the perfect balance between melody and command. His was an appearance designed to glide through seas of wealth and power as smoothly as the finest yachts glide over the rocky depths of the Adriatic, the only sound being that discreet hum of the ever-present engines of money, well-oiled and purring. Even his name, Miller, seemed well-designed. Anonymous, quiet, yet a fit name for one so busily engaged in grinding down the lives of millions to extract a little more cash.

None of this impressed Luan Tey anymore. He had seen his employer at moments when his intelligence and power were as dead as a switched-off light bulb. Then, his features and sandy coloring were as bland as pudding; then, he had all the charisma of an empty Styrofoam cup. Luan Tey alone saw this. Luan Tey alone knew the great secret of his employer: he was *no one*. Oh, he thought he was impressive, with his bank accounts and his art collections, but it was evil that had loaned him the cunning to amass those riches. Evil powered him, as gasoline fuels an engine. Without evil, his employer was nothing much, just a bland, moderately intelligent man

181

without even any scruples to call his own. Evil used him, because it was convenient for evil to do so. When evil was done with him, it would crumple him up and toss him aside, like a used paper bag, and find another, fresher customer. After all, there were so many waiting for the opportunity.

Therefore, Luan Tey was not impressed by his employer. He was impressed by the evil that looked out of his eyes and pulled his strings. And yet, of late, even that did not frighten him as once it had. After all, he had seen it looking out of the eyes of so many: torturers, soldiers, drug dealers, crowds of otherwise nice people who went momentarily berserk, and, most often of all, looking out of his own eyes in the mirror. It is hard to remain impressed by anything one sees so very often. Luan Tey had, after all, committed his first murder at the age of seven, for five yen and a chocolate bar, in the back streets of Saigon. He had known since childhood that possession by evil spirits was real. Movies like *The Exorcist* held no terror for him; he found it far more frightening to walk down any quiet suburban street in any city of the world and wonder just how much hunger or fear it would take to push the inhabitants into cruelty. No, evil was an old, old acquaintance of his. Lately, it was goodness he found himself wondering about. If evil was so powerful, why did it have to work so hard to maintain its grip on people? Perhaps there were forces greater than evil, after all.

Luan Tey's eyes met those of his employer. For an instant, evil itself seemed to glare at him out of Miller's eyes, as if it sensed his doubts of its power and was angry. Luan Tey stared coolly back. Then the dark intelligence in Miller's eyes receded; the moment passed. Luan Tey took the celery out of the grocery bag and put it on the table. Next he pulled out the black canvas bag and handed it to Miller.

Eagerly, the other man ripped open the zipper. Luan Tey knew something was wrong as soon as the bag was opened. The chalice was not wrapped in the black felt as it should have been but in what appeared to be a red-and-blue-striped sweater.

Miller unwrapped the sweater. Onto the table tumbled a bottle of mineral water, the neck of which was poked through the bottom of a plastic bowl. It formed a crude kind of chalice. Miller stared at the object.

As for Luan Tey, he did something he had not done fully in all his twenty-four years: he laughed. Not a cynical laugh, but genuine, clean laughter that welled up from somewhere deep within him, somewhere he hadn't even known existed. No sound could have been more shocking in that room. The bodyguard's hand went to his gun, as if the laughter was an enemy he should shoot.

Miller drummed his fingers on the tabletop, struggling to regain his composure. When he had control of his anger, he spoke again.

"I think you'd better explain yourself," he said, cordially, evenly.

"Only when we are alone," Luan Tey said firmly. His employer looked at him closely. Then, with a gesture, he dismissed the bodyguard and assistant.

"Sit down," he said to Luan Tey. He poured a glass of brandy for each of them. Normally, Luan Tey did not drink. However, he sipped the brandy slowly, because he knew that to do so would buy him a few more seconds to think, and every second counted right now.

The important thing, of course, was to protect the flaxen-haired boy he had met on the train. Luan Tey could not imagine how that little boy had known he had the chalice or why he had stolen it, but that Wyatt was the thief, Luan Tey had no doubt. No one else had been within two feet of him, all day, but the boy had, when they went through that tunnel. Besides, the sweater in which the improvised chalice had been wrapped was a child's size, and he thought he remembered the boy carrying it. Yes, the child was involved, and this Miller must never know. Why it suddenly seemed important to him to protect one small life, when he had damaged so many, Luan Tey had no time to analyze just then, although he was soon to ponder it much.

"I sense, I am followed in Far Tauverly," he began. Miller looked startled, but gestured for him to continue. "In the museum. I know it, I feel it. Someone is behind me." This had not been the case at all, but in retrospect, Luan Tey wondered if the boy had been in the museum, watching him. He continued, coolly improvising in a manner that would have impressed Wyatt very much. "Then I see a movement, reflected in the glass case in front of me. I say nothing, I do not look around, I think fast. Someone is there, but they do not sound the alarm when I open the case. Maybe they are a robber too. . . . They will rob me when I leave, take the chalice after I have done the hard work. So, what to do? I leave the real chalice in the museum case, but I move carefully, so they can't quite see what I do. I seem to steal the fake you sent with me, after all, it looks just the same, this forgery you have had crafted. That way, I think, if someone robs me when I step outside, they will get the fake, and think they have the original."

"Brilliant," said Miller. "Brilliant thinking on the spot."

More brilliant than you know, Luan Tey thought to himself, *and more on the spot.* Aloud, he continued, "I cross the fields, I get on the train, all as planned. A man comes into the compartment. Blonde, very innocent face . . . "

"How old a man was he?" Miller interrupted.

"Not yet thirty," Luan Tey said truthfully enough.

"Go on," said Miller.

"When the train goes through the tunnel, I am pretty sure the young man steals the chalice. I let him. He has a fake, what harm is done? Better for us if your enemy thinks he succeeds; then he will give himself away." Miller nodded in acknowledgment of the wisdom of this.

"As for me, I continue as planned, to sightsee, to lay the false trail. I don't even open the bag, in case someone is watching. But I suspect a substitute has been made; the weight is so slightly different. That is why I laugh, when at last you open the bag. My theory is correct. And the young man, he had such an innocent face."

"I see," said Miller thoughtfully. "But no one could have known you were even going to Far Tauverly, except someone from here, someone close in. . . ."

Luan Tey looked Miller in the eye. "Exactly," he said quietly. Then he sipped his brandy with the calm of a loyal servant, who knows he has done well by his master. Behind his impassive mask of a face, however, Luan Tey's mind was racing: Did Miller buy his story? How easily could one tell the fake chalice from the real? Why did he want this chalice, anyway? He felt his story had bought him a little time, but not much. How much, he wondered? All the while, as the questions whirred through his mind, Luan Tey sipped his brandy and looked blank.

He could tell that calculations were whirring through Miller's mind as well. Who knew of the plan to steal the chalice? Who would have betrayed him and to whom? Could Luan Tey be trusted?

"Should I return tonight and get the real chalice?" Luan Tey asked. Given his story, it seemed a logical question.

Miller thought about it. "Yes," he said pleasantly.

"I also want to be the one to find the young man on the train," Luan Tey added, "a matter of professional pride."

"I understand," said Miller equably. "But don't kill him. Bring him to me, alive, at least barely. Other than that, you have a free hand."

The phone rang. Miller answered, listened, frowned. Then he sighed, like a patient man who has simply been too inconvenienced. "There'll be hell to pay when the papers get a hold of this," he remarked, still calm, still collected. "Well, get the lawyers working on it."

He hung up. Luan Tey wondered what the call was about: an oil spill in the Pacific, an incident at a chemical plant in Turkey, a dirty deal in Washington? Whatever it was, misery on a vast scale would be its byproduct, yet Miller handled it as a minor irritation, compared to his concern about the missing chalice. Luan Tey filed this fact away for future consideration. He finished his brandy and stood up in a way that implied, "If that is all for now . . ."

"Yes, of course," Miller said, waving him away. Blandly, slowly, Luan Tey gathered up the black canvas bag, the sweater, and the improvised chalice, as any good butler would, removing a mess.

"Tell cook not to over steam the asparagus this time; we have a dinner party for twenty tonight," Miller remarked, as Luan Tey left the room.

What a strange world I live in, the butler thought as he left. When he was a few steps down the hall, he gave a very small, very cautious sigh of relief. He had left the room alive, and that was a good beginning. He didn't think Miller entirely believed him, but he had cast enough seeds of doubt to leave Miller uncertain about everyone in his employ, and that would buy him time. He needed time. He had a lot to do in the next few hours: save his own skin, find that boy from the train, discover why this chalice was so important. But first, he had to tell cook not to oversteam the asparagus. Yes, he lived in a very strange world.

Back in the elegant drawing room, Miller wrote something on a pad of paper. As Luan Tey had cleared the table, Miller had noticed a name, written in laundry ink, on the collar of the sweater. Now he wrote the name, and looked at it thoughtfully: "Wyatt Walmsley, Grade Three."

He picked up the phone.

CHAPTER ELEVEN

Now there's a classy bird, Davey Lee thought appreciatively from his perch in an oak, high above the forest path. Rather wistfully, he watched Gwen pass by below.

"Nice, very nice," he murmured to himself. "A bit cool, a bit shy—type that needs a delicate treatment. Not likely to react well to me leaping down from the trees like Tarzan. No, that lady is a single stem of white orchids, sent by private messenger. Got 'special handling' stamped all over her. Bet she's worth it, though."

Davey wasn't the only one who noticed Gwen go by. The Sentinels of the Independent Kingdom of Greniston gave the low, wood-dove call that meant "Let the stranger pass, all is well."

Woods are full of those kids, Davey thought speculatively. *Wonder what's up?*

They weren't just playing, those kids. There was a note of real seriousness beneath their Robin Hood games. They were guarding something, protecting something, a treasure. Davey Lee had always had a good nose for treasure. In a ballroom full of evening-gowned beauties, he could tell at a glance whose pearls were real and whose were paste. Let him slip into a posh townhome at dead of night, and he knew within seconds where the safe was hidden. He simply had an instinct for treasure, for the genuine article. And he felt treasure nearby now, treasure in a big way. The kids knew something about it, but not all, he suspected. His Gran also knew something, but she didn't yet know what she knew. She was sleeping now, curled up in the caravan as neat as a mouse in its hole, peaceful for the first time in many days. She seemed relieved simply to have gotten to the source of her Calling and content now to wait for more information. Davey quite agreed. It didn't do to rush these things.

He settled more comfortably onto the branch and closed his eyes. Being thirty feet above the forest floor didn't bother him at all; he was as confident as a cat snoozing on a ledge. A light rain began to fall. Davey did not stir for that any more than a robin would have. He felt the drops upon his face, felt the rough bark beneath his bottom and along his spine, smelled earth and rain and spring. He let himself grow so still that he and the forest began to interweave. Tendrils of his thoughts went out, into the woods, seeking information, and bits of the forest came into him with every breath

186

he took. His roguish young face took on an ancient look. He could have been one of any of the centuries of Romani folk that had passed that way, known those woods; for an unspoken alliance between the Grenistons and the people of Rom went back very far indeed.

Motionless on his perch, he seemed to sink into a deep stillness in himself, and into the green mystery of the forest as well. He sank into the life of the woods as a stone sinks into deep water, and it closed around him without a ripple. He was no longer watching the forest; he was within it.

In an elm, not far away, Osborne, Sentinel of the Independent Kingdom of Greenstone, whispered to Charles, his fellow Sentinel, "Gypsy in that tree." Charles nodded. "Aye," he whispered back, "but Osgood says he's all right; he has right of passage." Osborne nodded, satisfied, and resumed his watch.

***

"Reverend Mother, I don't know what to do. I'm consumed by this . . . sin. I know I must be loathsome in the eyes of God. I pray every night to be cleansed of this. I've done every penance I can think of. If it wasn't a worse sin, I'd throw myself in the sea to be free of this! And nothing works! Just when I believe I've scourged this attachment from myself, the smallest thought of him makes my love well up anew."

The young nun glowered at the Abbess, half-appealing, half-defiant. The older woman, who was by no means so old, looked at the younger with compassion. As the young nun paced about the cell, the Abbess sat very still in her carved oak chair. She rested her chin on one pale, white hand, and followed the young woman's pacing with a luminous, gray-eyed gaze. The nun suddenly stopped before her, her eyes almost frenzied. "Dame Juilianna," she cried, "they say our God is a God of love, but it sometimes seems to me that love can lead us to ungodly places!"

"But what do you want of me?" the Abbess asked in a soft, clear voice. "You must listen to the voice of your own conscience. This matter is between you and God."

The younger woman laughed nervously. "I expected you to be shocked; yet it is I that am, by your words. What of the vows I made? I swore to be the Bride of Christ. How can I have these feelings toward a mortal man?"

"Then make a choice."

187

"What choice can there be? My choices have all been made—for life!"

Gwen leaned forward in her seat, enthralled by the dialogue between the Abbess and the young nun. Beside her, she sensed Swindon stirring restlessly.

"It's a bit talky in this part," he whispered, "but the action picks up soon. Worth the wait."

"It's already fascinating," Gwen whispered back, hoping he would take the hint and let her focus on the play.

Gwen had known "Wholly Writ" would be a good play, but she had never expected it would be this amazing. She felt as if she was back in time, as the Abbess said: "Choice? What choice did you have? The choices of a girl who entered the convent at fourteen? A choice is only real when it is made with the whole of oneself. But you scarcely knew yourself when you made those vows."

"But I can't break them! That would be evil!"

"I say it would be evil to hold you to them if your heart is in doubt."

The Abbess rose. The sudden movement, after her stillness, was arresting. She gazed not at the girl but into the deep distance, as if addressing God Himself. When she spoke again, her voice that had been so soft and calm now rang out with fierce courage.

"The human heart and the human mind can speak to God directly," she cried. "They need no confessors, no priest."

The young nun backed away from the Abbess, as if afraid of her.

"But you, the Abbess of a great convent, how can you believe that?" she asked in a whisper.

"God hears us whether we whisper or cry out," the Abbess remarked dryly. Then she added, "I do not *believe* what I tell you; I *know* it, from my own experience. Just as I know that God has made His love in many forms. But it is not the form that matters; it is the motive for its expression. And only you know your motives."

Sitting in the darkness of the theater, Gwen nodded her agreement. *Yes,* she thought, *yes, that's the way it is.* She caught her breath when she saw what the Abbess and nun did not: the figure of a man standing in the shadows of an archway, listening. She knew from his garb and stance that he was the envoy, sent from Rome to investigate Dame Julianna. She wanted to warn her, "He's listening. He can hear every word you say." Then she realized that even if the Pope himself had been standing there, and the Abbess had known it, she would not have changed one word of what she was saying.

"Do you mean," the young nun asked, "that individual conscience is more important than the laws of the Church?"

"Yes," said the Abbess.

From the archway, the envoy leapt forward, a company of armed soldiers at his heels.

"Heresy!" he cried. And the curtain fell for the intermission. Stunned, Gwen sat staring at the stage as the lights slowly came up.

"It's marvelous, isn't it," said Swindon. "Of course they say that Deirdre O'Connell, who played the Abbess in London was even better than this actress. But this one's good, she's very good."

Gwen felt that she could not bear to chat about something that had moved her so deeply. Not just yet, at least. Perhaps sensing her mood, Swindon quickly said, "Would you like some wine?"

"Yes, please," Gwen said, perhaps too quickly, she realized. She wanted a few moments to herself, to be with the effect the play was having on her.

"What would you like? White, or Red?"

"Oh, anything, thank you very much," she said with a smile, trying to be polite.

"Perhaps Merlot? Or Shiraz?"

Shiraz, shut up, whatever, just go, Gwen thought. Then she felt rather ashamed of her irritation with Swindon. Aloud she said as graciously as she could, "anything you choose will be fine."

Once Swindon had left on his errand, Gwen drew a deep, grateful breath. She didn't want to move, she didn't want to talk. From Swindon's description beforehand, she had not expected to be so moved. A play about an English Abbess in 1703 had sounded intellectual to her. But now, instead of intellect, she had met a mystery. She wondered who Leo Hawker was, and how he could write with such passion about the human soul.

All too soon, Swindon returned, two glasses of white wine in hand.

"I opted for chardonnay," he said. "Not really supposed to bring wine into the theater proper, but I tipped the usher."

The lights flickered in warning that the intermission was almost over.

"Just in time," he continued. "I did so much want to talk, but the line at the bar was enormous. I can see you're very moved by this," he added. As he handed her the glass of wine, his hand lingered over hers. "We'll talk later," he whispered as the curtain rose.

Fortunately, Swindon was quiet once the performance resumed. The second half of the play was concerned with the trial of Dame Julianna. She was arrested for heresy and taken to Canterbury. Most of the action of the play took place either in the Archbishop's chambers or in Dame Julianna's prison cell.

Her sole champion was a young nobleman named Sir Patrick D'Archer. At first, he seemed a frivolous fellow, dashing, handsome, dressed in the height of fashion, and surely more interested in the latest court intrigue and his own witticisms than questions of theology. Yet, as the plot progressed, he revealed a deeper side that reminded Gwen oddly of Lord Peter Greniston. This young Sir Patrick was not the same man, yet there was a strain of Lord Peter in him. Antagonist to Sir Patrick was the papal envoy, also young but as intense as the aristocrat was flippant, as cold as Sir Patrick was kind.

As earnestly as Sir Patrick defended her, it was clear that Dame Julianna was doomed. Inexorably, the play moved toward the moment when she was sentenced to be burned at the stake.

"Do you have any words in your own defense?" the Archbishop asked.

"I will not defend myself to mere men, when I know that I am clean in the eyes of God," Dame Julianna said coolly. "Make no mistake, however," she added with a smile, "I am no mad Jeanne D'Arc, whose ravings you can dismiss as devils. No, I am as sane and ordinary as you are. The sole purpose of my life has been to serve the teachings of Christ. Whatever failings I have in this regard, they have nothing to do with the charges the Church brings against me. I am a soul responsible to the God who made me and not to a roomful of men, however high-placed they may be."

Amazingly, on the morning of her execution, her cell was found to be empty. The door had remained locked, the barred windows were untampered with, guards had been posted in the hall all night—yet Dame Julianna was gone.

"Witchcraft!" cried the envoy.

"A miracle," replied Sir Patrick joyously.

The theater went completely dark. When the lights on stage came up again, three figures were seated there: the papal envoy, no longer so young a man; Sir Patrick, also in his middle age; and a woman in her late thirties. The envoy spoke first.

"I thought she had escaped by her own witchcraft," he said in a voice that rang with hatred, "but later I understood that could not be true. God would never allow such evil to go unpunished! Then I knew—He took her directly to His own justice and damnation! No other explanation is possible." With a triumphant smile, the envoy blessed the audience, as the stage darkened around him.

Next, the spotlight came up upon Sir Patrick, who, now in his forties, reminded Gwen of Sir Peter more than ever.

"I sent spies, messengers, and all manner of seekers to try to find news of her. All my attempts to convince her to escape had failed, so I do not think it was solely by her own choice that she left that wretched cell, though I thank God each day that she did. To this day, no one has ever discovered how she was freed. From time to time, my agents bring me word of someone who might be her, that she was seen in France, or again, in Ireland. But I am never sure. It has been over twenty years since last I saw her, yet her luminous presence often seems far more real to me than all of this." He gestured with one elegantly gloved hand, as if to indicate and dismiss both his world on the stage and the world of the audience watching. "Yes," he repeated, "far more real than all of this." Darkness engulfed him, too.

Next, the light came up on the woman. Only when she turned to look directly at the audience was it clear that she was the young nun of many years before, dressed now in lay garb.

"I took her advice," she said, "the only advice she ever gave me, to follow the voice of my own heart. I left the Church and married the young man I loved so much—whom I love to this day. I wanted to speak in Dame Julianna's defense at the trial, but she would not let me. She actually had me barred from the proceedings, so that I 'would come to no harm by my tongue,' as she put it. But so many years have passed, and perhaps now I can speak freely."

The woman leaned forward, confidingly, and continued in a softer tone: "Now I'm going to tell you something I've never told a soul, not even my dear Ned. I saw her. Nearly seven years ago, it was. It was near Dorset; we live there now. By sheer chance—or so it seemed at the time—I took a path I'd never used across the fields. It was in the spring. No one in sight, save only the land, the sky, and me. Then far down the path, I saw a figure approaching. As she came nearer, I saw it was a woman in a faded blue cloak. And she was singing, singing as she strode across the fields, singing without a thought of who might hear her, singing as if she sang for God alone. And then I knew, long before I saw her face, who it was. She drew nigh. As astonished as I was, she seemed not at all surprised to see me, though she recognized me at once. She looked at me with her clear gray eyes, as radiant as ever. I started to speak; I felt I had so much to say to her. But she, wiser than I, put her hands to her lips. She blessed me and then strode on, singing. I have tried so many times to remember the words she sang, but I cannot, only I know the spirit of freedom was in it. I watched her for a long time. I could hear the faint music of her singing even after she disappeared over the crest of a hill." The woman paused. "Indeed," she said, "it often seems to me I hear it still."

Slowly, the light on the woman's face faded. The stage was dark for several seconds before the house lights came on. Even then, the audience sat stunned for a moment, as though caught in a spell, before they burst into thunderous applause.

"Let's leave quickly, before the rush," Swindon whispered. "I have somewhere in mind for a late supper."

Twenty minutes later, Gwen found herself seated in an elegant, modern restaurant that, in her current mood, impressed her not at all.

"I can see you're moved," Swindon said. "Tell me everything you feel about it."

The last thing Gwen felt like doing was talking. Fortunately, at that moment, the waiter arrived with their soup. Gwen glanced at Swindon and wondered, *What am I doing here with this man? How could I have been so charmed by him a few days ago and now feel like getting away from him as quickly as I can?*

Part of the reason for her distance was, she knew, the play. It had put her in touch with depths in herself she didn't meet every day, depths it was clear she and Swindon couldn't deal in. *That's not his fault,* Gwen realized. She resolved then and there to never go on another date with him during the remainder of her stay, no matter how hard he pressured her. It simply wasn't right to let him treat her like royalty and then sit there feeling irritated at his very presence.

"I'm so glad you liked the play," Swindon continued. He paused to taste the wine and nod his approval to the steward. "The critics acclaimed it as Leo Hawker's greatest masterpiece to date."

"I doubt that Dame Julianna would have cared what they called it."

"I beg your pardon?" Swindon asked, looking a bit confused.

Gwen blushed at her own rudeness. She tried to speak gently, and yet be honest. "I just meant that it seems odd to mention the critics, when so much of the thrust of the play was 'be true to thyself' and never mind what others say."

"Oh yes, I see," said Swindon. But Gwen wasn't sure he did. She wondered if he had been as moved by the play as she was or if he had just feigned enthusiasm to please her, glad that his date was sensitive and had good taste. She suddenly found herself wondering what Geoffrey Swindon was really like, beneath the elegant clothes, the perfect car, the Cordon Bleu restaurant, all in the best of taste, yet chosen, she suspected, to impress. What would he be like if he didn't care about impressing anyone? She decided to try to find out. She was, after all, his guest. She owed it to him to make the best of the occasion. Perhaps they could salvage the evening after all.

"I wonder if you do see," she said boldly. "I mean, you have perfect taste in everything; you've ordered the best dish on the menu and chosen the perfect wine to accompany it, I have no doubt. But I can't help suspecting that if you had no one to please but yourself, you might be just as happy sitting down to a plate of sausage and mash."

"Would you prefer sausage and mash?" he asked worriedly.

"No, no," exclaimed Gwen, "that's just the point! Never mind what others like! What does Geoff Swindon like?"

Swindon looked confused. Gwen felt certain that he was wondering what she would like to hear him say about his own likes. *Damn it*, she thought, *this is like trying to grasp water.* With a certain yearning, she thought of Lord Greniston. She couldn't imagine him shifting his views to please anyone. His assertiveness might be annoying, but at least you knew where you stood with him. She suddenly felt very sorry for Geoff Swindon, who obviously needed to win approval from anyone he liked.

"You don't need to impress me, you know," Gwen said warmly. "Just be yourself. That's what I'd like most of all."

Swindon blinked and looked rather overwhelmed. "Do you really mean that, Gwen?"

"Of course I do! Let's be simple and honest and not stand so much on ceremony."

Swindon looked enormously relieved. "I can't tell you how much it means to me to hear you say that, Gwen. The truth of the matter is; I fear I've been flying under false colors. I didn't just ask you on this date to see *Wholly Writ*. I had something on my mind I wanted to talk with you about, but I've been stalling all evening, uncertain how to bring it up."

"Well," said Gwen, thinking of Logan and his tax problems, "there's something I'd like to talk to you about, too."

"Not really?"

"Oh yes." They looked at each other and laughed with relief.

Swindon raised his wineglass and proposed a toast: "To clearing the air!"

"To clearing the air," Gwen heartily agreed. As they clinked their glasses, their fingers touched for an instant, and Gwen felt again the thrill of attraction she had first felt for Swindon. He seemed once more to be the confident, elegant man who had taught her to play darts with such ease and made her feel like the most desirable woman in the world.

"You go first," Gwen said.

"Oh no," Swindon replied, "ladies first."

"Ah, but you're the host."

At that moment, the waiter arrived with the main course. Gwen looked down at her plate and realized, *Oh damn, it's veal.* She had been so lost in the after-effects of the play that she hadn't realized what Swindon had ordered. Now she looked down at the perfectly grilled meat. Visions of baby calves, tethered in tiny pens and force-fed fatty milk, filled her mind. She never ate veal. Yet she felt that she could not risk hurting Swindon's feelings, after he had treated her so well, and they had finally got the evening on a good note. The poor calf was already dead; the kindest thing to do on this occasion would be to eat the meat. Swindon was already sampling his portion enthusiastically.

"The sauce Veronese is delicious," he told her.

Gwen nodded, cut off a tiny piece of the meat, and popped it into her mouth. It was no good; she would rather have been offered a goat's eye at a Bedouin feast. Her mind flashed on Annie, the wild young heroine in

Henrietta Amberly's *Kinsfolk in Cracow*, the one who was born and raised in the forest and refused to eat the "vile food slain by man." Gwen lifted the pearl-pink, damasked napkin to her lips and managed to spit the piece of veal into it unnoticed.

Swindon chatted amiably on about French sauces, obviously waiting until he had her complete attention to introduce the topic on his mind. Gwen contemplated how to dispose of the rest of her meat. Perhaps she could distract Swindon and, while he was looking the other way, slide the entire medallion of veal into her beaded evening bag. Too risky, she decided, the juices might ooze through later in the evening. It then occurred to her that the plate was garnished with a large leaf of lettuce. She could cut off bits of veal and discreetly shove them under the lettuce. That would at least make it look like she was eating something. A few feet to her right was a potted palm. Perhaps she could cough some additional pieces of meat into her napkin and then find a way to transfer them to the plant.

She had become so preoccupied with all these plans that she scarcely realized Swindon was now just about ready to launch into the honest, heartfelt conversation toward which she had urged him. He looked earnestly at her, just at the moment that she spat several pieces of veal into her napkin. As delicately as she could, she placed the napkin on her lap and smiled.

"Before we really get into our talk," she said, "I wonder if I could ask you one favor?"

"Certainly," said Swindon, "name it!"

"It's probably just a silly American taste, but I find that I would really like a glass of ice water with a slice of lime in it."

"Of course," said Swindon. "That sounds most refreshing. I'll join you. Now, where is the waiter?" He looked around, but the waiters seemed all to have vanished, as if by common agreement. "I'll be right back," he said, heading for the kitchen.

It was just what Gwen had hoped for. Hurriedly, she shook her napkin out over the roots of the potted palm, raining tiny bits of veal down upon the soil. Then, made daring by necessity, Gwen cut off a larger chunk of meat and transferred that to the palm as well. It looked obvious, sitting there, so she tried to cover it up with a sprinkling of soil. She glanced up and met the fascinated gaze of an elderly Pakistani gentleman seated at the next table. He had evidently been watching her for some time. Now the man turned and remarked to his dinner companions, "I wouldn't order the veal, if I were you. I think it may be a bit off, this evening."

Just then, Swindon returned, proudly bearing two champagne glasses of ice water garnished with lime.

"Lovely," said Gwen.

"It's absolutely refreshing," Swindon said, sipping his drink appreciatively. "A perfect addition to our meal."

"Just an impulse," Gwen replied.

"Now then," Swindon said, putting down his glass, "it's time we spoke freely. Don't you agree?"

"Oh yes."

"I knew you would," Swindon said warmly. "And there is so much to tell you, I scarcely know where to begin. But I think the best place, the core place, would be to start with the island."

"The island?"

"Yes. A little while ago, you asked me what I'm really like, on my own terms. Well, the one place on earth where I feel free, where I feel like myself, is on the island." Something in the intensity of Swindon's voice disturbed Gwen.

"What's it like, this island of yours," she asked, trying to keep the conversation light.

"It's a marvelous, marvelous place, off the coast of Scotland. All mist and mystery. I've never taken anyone there, but I'd like to show it to you, Gwen."

"Why, why, I'm honored that you feel that way, Geoff, but you see, I won't be in England very long. . . ."

"I know that you will love it as I do," Swindon continued, as if she had not spoken at all. "Up until now, it's been my island. But from now on, it will be *our* island."

Swindon leaned forward and placed his hands protectively over hers. He gazed into her eyes with an expression of absolute devotion.

Oh dear, thought Gwen. *Oh dear*.

"Geoffrey," she began carefully, "I'm glad you can be honest with me, but don't you think this is all a little - "

"Sudden?" he finished for her, smiling. "I can understand how you would feel that way, but don't worry, it will be fine, I know it will. I knew the moment I met you that you were the woman I wanted to spend my life with, just as I knew the moment I saw the island that it was meant for me. That's why I bought it and had a house built on it. A house fit for but one lady on earth. For years, I thought I'd never find that lady, but now I have, and her name is - "

"Stop. Please stop," Gwen interrupted. "Geoff, this is very flattering, but I must remind you, you scarcely know me."

Swindon laughed, dismissively. "I knew you the moment I saw you. Your heart shines in your eyes."

"Now, really," said Gwen, uncomfortably.

Swindon lifted his hands from hers, lightly, elegantly. "Never mind," he said easily. "We'll speak no more of it for now. I can understand that you need time to contemplate this." He smiled, very charmingly. "Please forgive me, Gwen, if I've startled you. I know you'll see how right this is when you've had time to consider it. But my confidence about us must seem a little overwhelming to you just now; I apologize. Now, what would you like for dessert? I can highly recommend the crème glacé."

A waiter appeared at Swindon's elbow. "A telephone call for you, Mr. Swindon. Will you take it here? "

"I'd prefer a private office, if one is available."

"Of course, Sir. Right this way, Sir."

"Please excuse me," Swindon said to Gwen. "I just don't want my business concerns to intrude upon our time together any more than it has to. I'll be right back."

Relieved to be alone for a moment, Gwen took a large gulp of her ice water.

"A brandy might be better, under the circumstances."

She looked up and again met the gaze of the elderly Pakistani gentleman at the next table. His dinner companions were engrossed in a conversation of their own, and he seemed to have been eavesdropping on hers for some time. He looked at her sympathetically.

"You might be right about the brandy," Gwen replied. "But I suspect I need to keep a clear head."

"Forgive the intrusion, but are you sure you feel quite safe with that young fellow? He looks a bit of a hasty character to me."

"Oh, I'm sure I'm safe," Gwen said. "But thank you for being concerned."

197

"Well, if the lad gives you any trouble, just scream, and I shall impale him nicely with my salad fork."

"Thank you," Gwen said. "That's gallant and reassuring of you."

The man's friendliness had indeed helped to calm her. When Swindon came back, Gwen found the confidence to request firmly that they forgo dessert and head back to Far Tauverly.

"Of course," Swindon agreed instantly. "It's been a full day, hasn't it?"

***

It wasn't until they were gliding along the highway that Swindon asked, "What was it you wanted to talk to me about?"

In the darkness, Gwen blushed. Under the circumstances, she couldn't imagine asking Swindon about money, even on someone else's behalf. It would seem like taking advantage of his declared affection for her, and that was the last thing she wanted to do.

"It was nothing," Gwen replied, wishing only for the drive to be over.

They rode on in silence. For once, Swindon seemed content to leave her to her own thoughts, probably confident that she was pondering his declaration. She supposed that was the right word for it; it hadn't been a proposal, although it had implied that. Certainly, phrases like "the woman I want to spend the rest of my life with" suggested marriage to Gwen.

If only Mrs. Gordon could hear about this, Gwen thought with a smile. The situation did indeed sound like a plot from one of her more gushing books—a little too implausible, Gwen felt, for Henrietta Amberly, but right up Daphne Dalton's or Sabrina Southampton's alley: "A penniless travel agent from Denver is swept into whirlwind romance with English millionaire, and in a matter of days finds true love, and a life of ease and comfort."

She supposed it would be a life of ease and comfort to be married to Swindon. For just a moment, Gwen tried to imagine what it would be like never again to have to worry about the rent; to go on as many shopping trips as she liked, in the most exclusive shops of London and Bath; to vacation anywhere she wished; to see, at last, the isles of Greece and the Cathedral of Notre Dame; to see Rome from a penthouse overlooking the Appian Way; and celebrate Christmas at a cabin in the Swiss Alps, not to mention visiting the island Swindon had spoken of, a private island off the coast of Scotland.

It was heady stuff, imagining life with Geoffrey, and she was attracted to him physically; she was acutely aware of that sitting next to him in the car. Her mind and heart and common sense wanted to end their date as quickly and kindly as possible. Her body entertained other thoughts, responding to his presence in spite of her better judgment. Yes, she was definitely attracted to him. And she was not really upset by the suddenness of his declaration; she had always felt that true love could happen in a moment, that it could come upon a person like an act of God. No, what disturbed her was the feeling that Swindon was not drawn to her, a real person, but to some fantasy, some imaginary woman that he wanted her to be. It made her ill at ease and increased her sense that she never knew exactly where she stood with him. One moment, he seemed confident, charming, very much his own man. The next moment, he seemed to be all too eager to please, molding himself to suit her in a way she realized she couldn't stand. She felt very uncertain who Geoff Swindon really was. It wasn't an intriguing uncertainty, she realized, but a disturbing one. She was very relieved that she had already decided not to go out with him again.

Just as this resolve was fresh in her mind, Swindon asked, "Penny for your thoughts?"

Flustered, Gwen said the first safe thing that came to her mind. "I was thinking about the play and wondering about Leo Hawker. Yes, I was wondering what kind of man he must be, to write so wonderfully well."

"He's a mystery, evidently. They say he's a recluse. Refuses to be interviewed or photographed. Even the directors of his plays don't get to meet him; he just talks to them over the phone." Swindon sounded disinterested in the playwright.

"Oh," Gwen replied.

Well, she thought, *that topic was a dead-end*. The drumming of the rain on the roof of the car and the clacking of the windshield wipers seemed very loud. It was with great relief that she saw the lights of Far Tauverly in the distance .

"I thought we could leave for the island tomorrow," Swindon remarked amiably. "I'll pick you up around one p.m. We can spend the night at a charming inn I know of in the border country and reach the island before nightfall the next day. Or, if we wish to drive straight through, we can be there before midnight. I can have a boat waiting."

Gwen could scarcely believe her ears.

"Pack some warm things," Swindon added. "Of course, we can stop on the way and get you some additional sweaters and a rain slicker—whatever you need, whatever you want."

"Geoffrey," Gwen protested, "I'm afraid there's been a terrible misunderstanding. I can't possibly go to this island with you. Not tomorrow or any other time."

Swindon pulled the car off to the side of the road and turned to face her. He seemed intensely close to her in the darkness. The rain drumming on the car seemed to form a tent around them; there might only have been her and him for a hundred miles. She was acutely aware of the perfectly chiseled line of his cheekbones and the scent of his expensive aftershave.

"You must understand," Gwen said firmly, "I'm only visiting Far Tauverly. In two weeks I'll be gone, back in America."

Geoffrey laughed. "You don't ever have to go back, now. I'll take care of you. I'll take care of everything."

"No, you don't understand," Gwen said, trying to be kind, yet make her meaning clear. "You don't know me. I don't know you. This isn't right. It's—it's a bit mad, really, to move so fast. I don't like the way it makes me feel."

With no warning, Swindon leaned over and kissed her. It was a surprisingly effective kiss. Had his ardor stopped there, Gwen might not have minded so much, but in the next instant, she found herself pinned to the seat, as Swindon began to unfasten zippers, buttons, and snaps with amazing speed.

"Geoffrey, stop!" Gwen exclaimed, torn between fear and laughter at the absurdity of the situation.

"It will be all right, you'll see," Swindon whispered in her ear, having somehow managed to pull her dress down around her shoulders.

"I'll see no such thing!" snapped Gwen. "Now let go of me, this instant! I am not kidding!"

It was the voice she had often used in her teaching days to quell a roomful of adolescent troublemakers, but it had no effect on Swindon. *This is getting serious*, Gwen realized. Swindon's grip on her was surprisingly strong, and there was, she realized, no one within earshot to hear her scream. She contemplated what basic aikido move would be the most effective in the rather cramped circumstance of the front seat of a sports car and then decided a much more primitive gesture was in order. With all the force she could muster, she raised her knee and slammed it into a strategic part of Swindon's anatomy. The groan that followed was singularly satisfying. Gwen managed to open the car door and leap out. She kicked off her high heels and ran through the rainy darkness toward a line of trees. Once safe within their welcoming shadows, she crouched down and tried to breathe as quietly as possible. Wistfully, she wished that the elderly Pakistani gentleman were there, ready to defend her with that salad fork.

Swindon had recovered himself enough to stagger along the roadside. "Gwen!" he cried. "Please come back!" He sounded heartbroken, and Gwen was glad that she had not done any more serious damage to him. She didn't want to injure him; she just wanted him to go away.

Now his tone changed. There was real anger in his voice as he continued to yell "Gwen! Miss Fields! Come here!" It was the imperious voice of a spoiled child whose pet refuses to come when called. But this child had the strength and cunning of a full-grown man. *He might know some martial arts himself,* Gwen realized. *It's just the sort of thing he might think would impress people. And he's very strong.* She decided she did not fancy a contest of skill with Swindon just then. She remained crouched among the dripping trees for what seemed like hours, although it was actually only a few minutes. At last Swindon, cursing, trudged back to his car, slammed the door, and drove off with an angry screeching of tires.

Gwen breathed a deep sigh of relief. She managed to refasten the various buttons and zippers that Swindon had partially undone, but her shoes, she realized, were somewhere near the road, where she had kicked them off. She didn't really enjoy the idea of trudging to Far Tauverly, a good mile away, in her delicate silver high heels, but the muddy ground was too cold and slimy to think of going in her stocking feet. She began to scan the roadside.

It's a good thing there's no one here to see me, she thought. She didn't want to imagine what she looked like, with her pale yellow silk dress drenched and clinging to her like cold plaster in places it was never meant to cling, and her hair soaked and sticking to her face and neck.

She saw one shoe gleaming in the mud. She had just bent over to pick it up when she heard a deep, jovial voice call out, "Why, Miss Fields, did you lose something?"

Startled, Gwen looked up. A car had pulled up, and a man peered out of the open window at her—a dark-haired, serenely dry man, who gazed at her with that mixture of arrogance and kindheartedness that could belong only to the Lord of Greniston Manor. Greniston's laughing eyes seemed to take in every detail of her bedraggled appearance.

"Like a lift?" he asked.

CHAPTER TWELVE

Gwen was so relieved to see him and not Swindon gazing at her that she exclaimed "Greniston!"

"None other," he replied cheerfully, peering out at her through the drenching rain. "I repeat, would you like a ride? Or do you prefer to walk on such a pleasant night?" Gwen ran to his car and got in.

"Thank God it's you," she said.

"I often do—thank God it's me," Greniston quipped. "But why do you?"

Gwen smiled but did not reply directly.

"I've just had a very . . . confusing encounter," she said. "I know it must look incredibly strange, me running around in the rain like this, but I just can't explain it right now. I hope you don't mind."

"Not at all," replied Greniston. He looked at her with concern, then added, "You can be as enigmatic as you like, dear lady, but I won't permit you to catch pneumonia in my car. You're drenched to the bone! If you look in the back, you'll find a plaid blanket."

Gwen gratefully wrapped the blanket around her shoulders, while Greniston took a flask from the glove compartment.

"Drink," he said. Gwen took a hefty gulp, only to burst into a fit of coughing and sputtering.

"Not used to Scotch whiskey?" Greniston asked casually.

"No," gasped Gwen. When she trusted herself to speak again, she added, "I like wine, sometimes, and brandy. Well, I'm not sure I like brandy, but it looks so beautiful in the glass, and you can just take little sips. And your English ale is very good. But when it comes to drink-drinks, I usually order something that doesn't taste so bad, like a White Russian or a Brown Squirrel—or is it a Nutty Squirrel? I never do get that name right. I had some Drambuie last night—enough, I think, to last me the rest of my life. You English are a hard-drinking lot, you know. I've had more to drink here in a few days than in the last six months back in Denver. . . ."

Gwen stopped, realizing that she was babbling. The shock of the last hour seemed to be catching up with her. She expected Greniston to respond with a provocative comment on the unsophisticated tastes of Americans, but he merely looked at her and said, "Are you warm enough?"

"Yes, thanks," she replied. Perhaps it was the plaid blanket, perhaps it was the small amount of whiskey she had actually swallowed, but whatever the reason, her teeth had stopped chattering, and she felt a sudden need to yawn and settle back into the car seat.

"Miss Fields," her companion said gently, "I don't want to intrude on your quiet, but there is one thing I must say. I'm really very sorry about how I acted when I met you and Swindon on the street. You certainly shouldn't have been placed in the middle of an old feud, and anyway, I acted like an ass. Can you forgive me?"

"Actually," said Gwen, "your attitude toward Swindon might make perfect sense. Right now, I find myself wishing you'd slugged him."

"Oh, really?" Greniston replied, trying not to sound as pleased as he suddenly felt. Then, glancing at Gwen's disheveled appearance he added, "I take it you and he had a, um, misunderstanding. Are you all right?"

"I'm fine, thanks. Mr. Swindon may not be feeling as well."

"Sounds serious."

"Well, I'm not going to be seeing him ever again, if that answers your question."

Greniston found himself unreasonably delighted by this information and had to make a concerted effort to repress the rather silly grin that seemed determined to spread over his face.

"You had a dinner date or something, didn't you?" he asked, confident that he had struck just the right nonchalant, just-making-conversation note. He would have been surprised to see that Gwen, on her side of the car, was now repressing a pleased smile at his curiousity. She nodded.

"Food must have been bloody awful to send you running all the way back to Far Tauverly in the rain."

Gwen laughed. "Actually, the food was excellent. I just didn't eat much of it. Now I'm starving, but I'm sure the inn's kitchen is closed by now."

"True. Probably just a couple regulars in there, dozing over their ale until last call. But I'll wager Mrs. Hodges would allow us to raid the larder."

"Do you think so?" Gwen asked hopefully.

"Not to worry," said her companion. "I'll simply woo her with the full force of the Greniston charm. Meanwhile, you can go upstairs and change into something dry and warm. Then we'll have a sort of picnic by the fire. Only if you want to, of course."

"I do want to," Gwen replied. "And that will be two good things that happened tonight."

"Oh—and what was the other?"

"I saw the best modern play I have ever seen."

"Really?" Greniston found himself very curious as to what modern play this young American woman would like so much. *The Fantastiks*, in its seven thousandth revival? *Our Town*? He could imagine her liking *Our Town* but was sure it would not be new to her. More likely, something by Andrew Lloyd Weber. He wanted to know and yet was half-afraid to hear the answer, in case she ruined the enchantment she seemed to be casting over him by naming something inane. Curiosity won out.

"What was it?" he asked.

"*Wholly Writ*, by Leo Hawker."

Inexplicably, Greniston was seized by a fit of coughing.

"Are you all right?" Gwen asked with concern.

Greniston nodded. "Swallowed wrong. Just pass the flask," he managed to wheeze. A gulp of alcohol restored his equilibrium somewhat.

"Not only was it the best modern play I've ever seen," Gwen continued, "but I'd say it was one of the best plays of any time. It doesn't quite compare to Shakespeare, of course."

"Of course," Greniston murmured.

"But it does touch greatness."

"Do you think so?" Greniston asked skeptically.

"Absolutely! You must not have seen it, or you couldn't question that."

"Oh, I've seen it," Greniston replied, "several times." Instantly, he cursed himself for revealing that. This Miss Fields had a disarming way of getting him to let down his guard.

"Really? Then, you must think a lot of it, to have seen it more than once."

"No, it was just, er, coincidence."

"But weren't you moved by it? You must have been; I saw a copy of it in your music room. That's what gave me the idea to want to see it at all. I hadn't heard of it before then."

"I see," said Greniston in an odd voice. He almost sounded as if he was trying not to laugh. Gwen felt he really was one of the most unusual men she had ever met.

"I can't remember when something has touched me so deeply," she continued. "I felt transported, somehow, . . . not just to another time, but as if the play came along like a safecracker and opened parts of me that are usually hidden somewhere under lock and key. . . . It's so hard to put into words. I suppose this isn't making any sense."

When Greniston spoke, his voice now sounded as earnest as her own. "Believe me, Miss Fields, it makes perfect sense. And any playwright would be more than honored to receive such praise. It would be water in the desert to Leo Hawker to hear a reaction such as yours."

"Do you really think so?"

"I know so. And please don't misunderstand, I don't think Hawker is a bad writer, I just have mixed feelings about his work. I do think that *Wholly Writ* is his best play. But he hasn't stretched to all he can do yet. He can be a real lazy bastard when he wants to."

Gwen looked at Greniston with surprise. "You speak as if you know him."

"I do," Greniston muttered under his breath. The comment had just slipped out, barely audible, but Gwen leapt upon it like a hound that scents the hare.

"What?" she exclaimed, clearly thrilled. "You know Leo Hawker?"

In the privacy of his mind, Greniston cursed himself thoroughly. He couldn't believe how careless he'd been. Aloud, he said, "Well, 'know' isn't really the right word. He's an old friend of the family, really. Used to get together with my parents, when they were still alive. But I hardly ever see him anymore; lives nowhere near here."

"Where does he live?" Gwen asked, evidently acutely interested in any scrap of information about her new hero. "And what is he like?"

"Oh, he lives—on the Isle of Man," Greniston invented on the spur. "And he's old— in his eighties by now, I'd say."

Was it his imagination, or did Miss Fields seem just the tiniest bit disappointed to hear her idol's age? Evidently, though, she loved Hawker for his mind alone, for she rallied quickly.

"It's funny," she mused, "I'd somehow pictured him to be a man in his forties, well-traveled, and not just a writer but a man of action, somehow."

"He may have been, once," Greniston said, almost bitterly, "but not now. I can assure you, Miss Fields, that he spends most of his time holed up in his study, reading the great works of others and praying for inspiration of his own."

"I don't believe it!" Gwen retorted with fire in her eye. "Old he may be, but a man who could write a play like that would never languish his days away!"

"You'd be surprised," Greniston said quietly.

Gwen blushed. "I'm sorry," she said. "I realize that you know him, and I don't. It's just hard to believe." She paused, then said, "Lord Greniston, I don't suppose . . . , I mean, I wonder . . . , that is, is there any way I could meet Leo Hawker?"

"Oh God," said Greniston quickly, "no, no, no! I'm afraid that would be quite out of the question. He's a total recluse. Probably wouldn't even let me in the door anymore."

"You see," continued Gwen, who evidently was not one to drop an idea easily, "I thought that if he is suffering from some kind of temporary setback, perhaps what he needs is encouragement."

"It's just not possible," Greniston said firmly. Gwen looked so crestfallen that he added, against his better judgment, "but if you'd like to write him a letter, I'll make sure it gets to him. I'm under oath not to reveal his address to anyone, but I'll make sure the letter gets sent."

"Really?" Gwen's face was shining with gratitude.

"I assure you, Miss Fields, that when you hand your missive to me, you may feel as confident as if you were putting it into Leo Hawker's own hands."

Gwen sighed contentedly, like a child who has been promised a treat. As for Greniston, he was relieved to turn onto the main street of Far Tauverly.

"There's the inn," he said, happy to change the topic, for he had begun to experience the awkward sensation of being jealous of himself.

***

The delicate, subdued clatter of fine china and crystal wine goblets, . . . laughter, and well-modulated, well-educated voices, . . . in the background, strains of Handel. Miller's very late, very exclusive dinner party for twenty was proceeding well.

Luan Tey served the dessert liqueurs and the cocaine in the blue drawing room. Then he returned to the kitchen, asked his assistant to take over for him for a while, and headed upstairs with the air of a man on an errand.

It attracted no particular notice when Luan Tey let himself into Miller's private suite. Of all the staff, he was the most likely to be sent there to fetch something.

Once inside Miller's study, he locked the door behind him and pulled on a pair of surgical gloves. He deactivated the infrared alarm system that sent a spider's web of unseen rays across the room and headed for the wall safe. Only Miller was supposed to know its combination, but little was hidden from Luan Tey. His slim, golden fingers turned the knob, the tumbrels clicked into place, and the door swung silently open.

He ignored the sack full of one hundred pound notes, the priceless Minoan statuette, and the diamond pendant, rumored to have been a gift from Lorenzo de Medici to his mistress. He reached beyond all these and pulled out a plain brown envelope and a spiral notebook, such as might be purchased at any five and ten. These he took over to the desk. He sat down in Miller's chair and spent several minutes reading the contents of the envelope and the notebook.

Luan Tey was not a praying man, but by the time he finished reading the little notebook, the phrase, *God help us all*, was the one thought in his mind. He gripped the edge of the desk until his knuckles turned white, as if his whole world had suddenly become unsteady.

He had known this feeling once before, in Nicaragua. He had been standing on the balcony of the fifteenth floor of an apartment building, when an earthquake started. One moment, everything was solid, and the next, the floor rippled like jelly beneath his feet. Across the street, other high-rise buildings danced and waved like ribbons in front of an electric fan, and the cars on the street rose and fell like flotsam on choppy waves. It had only lasted for a few seconds, but it had taken him weeks to overcome the panic it left in him. Nothing afterwards, not making his way out of a building that seemed to be collapsing in slow motion around him or the screams and the sirens and the fires, had been as frightening as those brief moments of the quake itself, when it seemed that the very laws of nature were melting, and the substance of matter itself was being played with.

That terror was nothing compared to what he felt now, sitting in Miller's quiet, elegant study. For a moment, he could not believe that the desk was still there, the floor was still there, and the Royal Water Music tinkled in the distance.

He had long known his employer to be one of the most evil men on the planet. Up until now, he had always thought of that evil as intelligent, if nothing else. Now he realized it was insane. Absolutely insane, beyond even its own self-preservation.

He looked at the wire-bound notebook sitting so innocently on the desk. If Miller thought he could manage the power contained on those pages as suavely as he could order a cook not to oversteam asparagus, he was out of his mind. Mad, yes, the man was mad, with the boundless arrogance of the human race that thought that because it could conceive of something, it was therefore fit to handle the power of it, to gamble with it, even, for its own advantage.

And now, the key to a more concentrated power to destroy than was contained in a ton of plutonium or in all the chemical warfare arsenals in the world was in the hands of a fluffy-headed little boy, wandering somewhere in the southwest of England.

He hasn t a clue what he stole, Luan Tey realized. *Only Miller and I know all the facts.* He was sure of it. His employer worked by the old Roman motto, "Divide and conquer." It was second nature to him to include no one in the whole of his plans. The facts and formulas in the notebook would have been only theory, except to someone who knew of the existence of that chalice. And the chalice itself would be only another artifact, except to someone who knew of the notebook and certain other odd facts that Luan Tey had come across, here and there, over the last few weeks. *Yes*, he realized, *only Miller and I know how this all fits together.*

For a moment, he wished it was an hour ago, wished it as desperately as he had ever wished for anything. He did not want the responsibility of knowing what he now knew.

This should have happened to a good man, he thought wryly, *to someone who would not have hesitated to do what is right.*

And yet a good man, he realized, would never have been in a position to find out what he now knew. Only someone on intimate terms with evil, a member of the devil's own household, so to speak, could come across such secrets. And only someone intimate with evil could have a chance of defeating it at its own game.

Perhaps I am the perfect choice, he thought, with a thin smile. He had to decide what to do, now: accept the hero's role so unexpectedly offered him and do his best to defuse Miller's plans or try to forget every shred of what he had discovered.

Whatever I decide, he thought, *no one will ever know but me. I am alone.* He would choose, yes or no, and it would happen as quietly and unnoticed as a twig snapping beneath one's foot in a forest.

He made his choice. Then he got up, replaced the notebook and the envelope back in the safe, and began to make his plans. His face was more masklike than ever. On the course he had chosen, he could not afford to be distracted by feelings. In the next few hours, he would need to muster every scrap of skill, instinct, and cunning he had ever learned and use them as automatically as a machine. It was no longer a matter of just saving his own skin and that of a flaxen-haired child with an innocent face, but of saving the world—if there was time.

What I need now, he thought, *are a magic comb, bottle, and rose.*

He had once seen, on a street corner in Jakarta, a shadow-puppet show, in which the hero and heroine, pursued by demons, had tossed behind them a series of magic obstacles: a comb that became a forest, a water bottle that became a sea, a rose that became a mountain of thorns. In the end, the demons had caught up with them and had to be battled. But the magic obstacles had bought them time. Time, Luan Tey felt, was what he needed most of all right now.

He took a notepad and pen from his pocket, and began to write: "Gone to get real cup. Beware false servants. Ask Leston about Bolivia. Ask Helge about the Swiss bonds."

Luan Tey smiled to himself. Not for nothing had he silently noted the transgressions of Miller's henchmen over the years, saving them up like cash in a high-interest account. That Miller doubted him by now was certain. But perhaps he could toss in just enough suspicion of others, as well, to slow Miller down a little. He would not know who he could trust, whom to send in pursuit.

A few minutes later, from behind a curtained doorway, Luan Tey watched the party in the blue drawing room. He had sent a maid in to hand Miller his note.

Annoyed at the interruption, Miller moved to the side of the room and opened the folded paper. A moment later, he looked up, a mixture of shock and anger on his usually bland face.

"Tell the butler to meet me in my office," he told the maid.

But by that time, Luan Tey had slipped from the room. Moments later, he backed one of Miller's own cars down the alley behind the townhouse. To his right, he could see, dark and brooding beneath a clouded moon, the circular park the old woman had told him was haunted. Perhaps she was awake right now, a few doors down, doing her crosswords. He saw no sign of the ghostly charioteer, condemned to circle the park endlessly, but felt he might well have been there.

He pulled the car onto the street. He put his foot on the gas and set off at full speed for Far Tauverly.

***

At the Greenstone Arms, Gwen and Greniston were finishing the late-night meal Mrs. Hodges had been glad to provide. Unfortunately for the gossips of Far Tauverly, they had arrived at the inn just as Mrs. Hodges was closing, and there was no one around but her to see that Gwen had left several hours earlier in the company of one man and now returned escorted by another, and those the two wealthiest bachelors in the county. If Mrs. Hodges noted this, she gave no sign but merely took in Gwen's soaked appearance and suggested they find "a nice table near the fire."

Gwen hurried upstairs to change. She decided to opt for warmth rather than glamour and put on the same corduroy slacks and white sweater she had worn to Greniston Manor earlier that day. Then she did a quick repair job on her makeup, ran a comb through her damp hair, and hurried back downstairs.

Mrs. Hodges had worked wonders. A snowy white cloth had been laid on one of the inn's rough tables and set with china and silver that was definitely not everyday. There were candles in brass holders as well, and a bouquet of daffodils from the inn's back garden.

Greniston rose to greet her, smiling warmly. He pulled back a chair for her and said, "Miss Fields, you look lovely. Downpours suit you, you know. You should wear them often. Almost every time I meet you, it's in the pouring rain. I'm beginning to think you aren't human at all but some sort of visiting pixie or water sprite. Are you really staying at the inn, or are you actually accommodated at a local spring?"

"Definitely at the inn," said Gwen with a smile.

"I'm not convinced," Greniston replied. "There's something deuced ethereal about you. However, I hope you're substantial enough to dine. I don't think I gave you much chance to eat last time we dined together. I seem to remember dragging you off and forcing you to play the piano. Cruel host! However, this time I hope you will feast your delicate frame to its full."

"You bet," said Gwen, wasting no time in buttering a piece of Mrs. Hodges' excellent bread and stuffing it into her mouth.

Greniston watched her approvingly. "I do appreciate a woman who isn't coy about her food," he said. "Nothing puts me off my own food like watching someone else poke anorexically at theirs."

Gwen laughed. "No problem here. But have you known so many starving ladies?"

"Just one. But then, in fairness, she had to. For her job."

"Was she a fashion model?" said Gwen, trying to sound only mildly interested.

"An actress. But that's ancient history now. Let's do justice to this excellent roast beef."

In the kitchen, Mrs. Hodges sipped her daily pint of ale, which she always had while washing up. As was her custom, while she stacked dishes and polished silver, she sang old Cole Porter tunes and, from time to time, twirled across the brick floor with surprising grace for a rather portly, not entirely sober, middle-aged lady. Unfortunately, Gwen and Lord Greniston could not see her Ginger Rogers impersonation, but they could hear her through the open doorway.

"'I've received an invitation to a situation that simply reeks . . . of . . . class,'" Mrs. Hodges trilled.

Across the table, Greniston's eyes met Gwen's. He smiled. As Mrs. Hodges' unintentional concert continued, they didn't say much. Gwen didn't mind; she sipped her ale and enjoyed the warmth of the fire. Greniston, too, seemed quite content to slather amazing quantities of horseradish sauce onto his beef and swallow it without so much as blinking.

"'To the beat-beat-beat of the tom-tom,'" Mrs. Hodges continued, "'Da da dum dum dum da da dee . . .'"

She seemed to quite enjoy her washing up, and perhaps the ale as well, for when she at last poked her head round the door, her cheeks were considerably pinker than they had been before.

"I'll leave you both to lock up, shall I?" she said. "Just turn the little knob sideways, and close the door behind you, and if you'll be so good as to damp down the fire when you go?"

"Of course," Greniston assured her.

"Well, good night, then, my dears." Mrs. Hodges disappeared up the stairs, gently humming "A Foggy Day in London Town."

The inn seemed wonderfully quiet, then, just the drumming of the rain outside and the crackling of the fire within. Gwen was glad that she felt no pressure to make conversation. Greniston, too, seemed content to gaze peacefully at the fire, evidently lost in thought. Gwen watched the flickering light playing over his features. As she had been with Logan, on the first day they sat together in that same room, she was struck with the closeness of the past. She could easily imagine Greniston in the rough cape of an early Briton or the uniform of a Roman centurion, sitting just where he was now, gazing into the firelight of centuries gone by . . . , yes, or a Greniston of Arthur's time: a weary, noble-faced man in a cloak of reddish-purple wool. She saw the scene so vividly, it was as if she had been there. And as she had with Logan, she had the feeling that she had known Greniston a long, long time.

He looked up and met her gaze. His thoughts seemed to have lead him deep into himself, and now he gazed at her from that depth, as if from the heart of himself, and Gwen found herself thinking, *I have loved this man for so long.*

In the morning, in the sunlight, she would wonder how she could feel that way for someone she had met only days before. She would even blush a little, remembering how silly she had thought Swindon, telling her that her heart shone in her eyes, and that he already knew she was the woman for him. Yet here she was, gazing at Greniston, feeling as if she had always known him, as if she was meeting a love already old and tested, now reunited and fresh, like new flowers on an old, old tree.

It's the wine, Gwen told herself, *it's the firelight, the candlelight, the stillness of the night. I can't let myself take this too seriously, but oh, it is lovely to feel this way.*

As for Greniston, his thoughts had fewer words. He only knew that when he looked into Gwen's hazel eyes, he felt suddenly a great hope, as if a treasure he had thought lost forever had been restored to him. It seemed to him fitting that they were in an inn, for he felt they were like two travelers, reunited on the road, safe at last after much misadventure.

Somehow I know her, he thought. *I know her of old.*

And Gwen, gazing back at him, felt that all the sweetness, of life was gathered in his features. Minutes before, this man had been just a passing part of her life. Now, in a moment, he seemed to be at the heart of it.

A log on the fired snapped. They both jumped.

"Have some cherry flan. . . ."

"Why not try this cheese . . . ?"

They spoke at once and then laughed, suddenly shy with each other.

"Rain's stopped," Greniston remarked awkwardly.

"Perhaps we could take a walk," Gwen suggested, as if it was the most natural thing in the world to go for a walk at two a.m.

"Capitol idea. I'm sure Mrs. Hodges won't mind if we leave the door unlocked for just a few minutes."

Perhaps the intimacy of the firelit room had been so potent a wine that they could handle only a few sips of it at a time. Outside, in the fresh wind, each relaxed a little.

"The clouds are blown back over there, you can see the stars," Gwen remarked. "I think it's the Pleaides."

"Yes," said Greniston. But he was not looking at the stars. He was gazing at Gwen's face as intently as if some new, yet recognized, constellation had appeared on his horizon, and he wanted to memorize every star of it.

"Let's just walk to the bakery and back," suggested Gwen. "It's pretty chilly out."

"All right," Greniston agreed. In his present mood, he would have been glad to walk to the Andes, if she had wanted it. As they stepped around a puddle, he quite naturally put his arm around her, to steady her balance. He did not take it away as they walked on.

Gwen's heart was singing. *I love this man*, she thought. She knew it was ridiculous. She knew she barely knew him. But her heart kept singing *he has his arm around me!* That simple thing seemed like enough, and more than enough. She registered every sensation of it: the steady feel of his arm, the smell of his aftershave, the warmth of his body next to hers.

"How many spring nights, just like this, have softened the streets of Far Tauverly?" Greniston mused. "I wonder if King Arthur himself saw these same stars near here, on a night just like this one, perhaps."

"Surely he did," said Gwen. "On a night like this, it's almost as if he might appear. . . ."

"Some say he will," Greniston remarked.

They were at ease with each other again, talking about legends and Arthur like old friends. Indeed, they got so interested in their conversation that they walked from the inn to the bakery and back seven times before Gwen suggested, "It doesn't seem so cold after all, let's go around the block."

"Good idea," agreed Greniston, as if it would be an adventure. And so it was, for in her company, he felt as if he was seeing the streets of the town he had known all his life for the first time. Everything was new and fresh, because she was there.

It was under an apple tree, its first pink buds appearing, that they paused. In the quiet, they heard the bells of St. Aethelrood's toll out four a.m.

"We've talked almost all night!" exclaimed Gwen.

"Yes."

"We really should be getting back," she said. Yet neither moved.

Once again, they found themselves gazing deeply into each other's eyes. very softly, very deliberately, Greniston leaned over and kissed her. Then he wrapped his arms around her and held her very close, as one would hold a treasure, lost once, that one means never to lose again. In the tree above them, the first bird of the morning began to sing in the predawn darkness. On and on, it poured out the sweetness of its song, like a benediction upon the man and woman standing there.

As long as I live, Gwen thought, *I shall keep the joy of this moment. No matter what happens in the years to come, I shall remember this.*

Then the peace was rent by the flashing light of a police car and the sound of voices.

"What the devil?" exclaimed Greniston.

"They've pulled into the museum driveway," Gwen said. "I hope the sisters are all right!"

Greniston grabbed her by the hand, and ran toward the lights. As they drew closer, they saw that both Althea and Lettice, in nightclothes and curlers, were in the yard, talking excitedly with two policemen.

"Oh, Lord Greniston," Lettice exclaimed, "I'm so glad you've come! We sent a message, but Robert said he didn't know where to find you!"

"What message? What's happened?" Greniston demanded.

"It's the chalice," Althea explained. "It's been stolen!"

CHAPTER THIRTEEN

"It was really very mysterious," trilled Lettice, who was now beginning to enjoy her little adventure, her nerves marvelously restored by the presence of Lord Greniston. "I woke up in the night, I had a kind of . . . of realization. . . ."

"More likely it was gas," Althea muttered under her breath.

"And feeling restless," Lettice continued, regally ignoring her sister's comment, "I felt myself drawn to the kitchen. There, as I was getting a glass of water, I looked out the window and saw a movement in the bushes. So I went to the backdoor, just to see. You know, I thought it might be one of the children—the Walmsley children—running around in the middle of the night. They sometimes do, I fear, and of course, they really oughtn't to, out in the damp in their nightclothes and all - "

"Very true," agreed Lord Greniston politely, "but about the chalice . . ."

"Oh, yes, of course," giggled Lettice, "I was straying from the point, wasn't I?" (In the background, Althea rolled her eyes.) "Well, you see, when I peeked out to see if the children were there, that was when I noticed it was open."

"It?" Greniston prompted gently.

"Oh, yes, how silly of me! The door to the museum was open! Not widely, but ajar, . . . well, I'll show you. We shouldn't be standing here in the chill anyway. Come to the museum!"

Lettice led them down the drive. By the time they reached the bright red door of the museum, the first light of dawn was gleaming over the treetops.

"Yes," said Lettice, "the door was ajar, just as you see. We tried to return it to its exact position, you see, so that - "

One of the policemen interrupted, naively hoping to aid the cause of brevity. "And so, seeing what you thought was a movement, you went to investigate and discovered that the chalice was missing?"

"Oh no!" gasped Lettice, horrified at the mere thought. "No, I called out . . ."

"Screeched like a moor hen is more like it," murmured Althea.

" . . . and Althea came running. And then she, courageously, but very rashly, I must say, charged out the door and into the museum. I begged her to wait until we'd called for you," Lettice nodded graciously to the policemen, "but she wouldn't hear of it. She risked life and limb."

"Don't be silly," Althea interrupted. "I was armed."

"Yes, dear, but only with an umbrella from the hall stand."

"A perfectly adequate weapon in skilled hands," Althea said crisply.

"I think," suggested Greniston, "that we might enter the museum. I shall go in first, to make sure all is well."

As soon as he declared it safe, all the others came crowding in. Greniston and the policemen turned their attention to the open glass case. Greniston gave a low whistle of surprise.

"This looks like a very professional job," he said appreciatively. "It doesn't have that Walmsley touch, somehow. I must confess, those kids were my first thought as culprits, but that glass case—it's been sprung open without a scratch. Mind you, I wouldn't put it past Osgood to have learned to pick locks like a pro. . . ."

Greniston knelt thoughtfully by the case, and examined the floor for clues.

"We'll need to dust the area for prints, of course," he murmured.

"Just what I was thinking, Sir," replied the older of the two policemen. "And we'll need to file a report."

"How exciting," said Lettice.

"Too exciting," sniffed Althea. "It will be in all the papers then, and the reporters will come."

Lettice's expression turned to one of dismay. "But they will trample the tulip beds," she exclaimed. "I know they will! And my Prince Albert Specials are just coming into bloom, such a fine, pale yellow, and oh, dear, it will be so distressing. . . ."

"Perhaps something can be worked out," said Lord Greniston. He looked hopefully at the two police officers. "Surely we don't need to bother the outside world with this little incident," he began, in the reasoned, gently humorous tones that had so often helped him make a point in parliament.

"Oh, I don't know, Sir," said the first policeman. "We must send in our report. Orders is orders, you know."

"Yes," the second one agreed, "and as soon as it goes out on the police radio, the reporters can pick up on it if they want to. They listen to it, you see. Nothing we can do about that, freedom of the press and all." He shook his head. "Besides, Sir, this is the theft of a National Antiquity.

218

Wouldn't do to hush that up. I'm afraid this could be big, Sir, very big. Best go through the proper channels."

Greniston sighed, realizing that he was up against two of Tweeverton's finest, incorruptible by bribe or threat.

Well, he mused, *if we must go through channels, let s go through the highest.* He turned to Althea and said, "I wonder if I might trouble you for the use of your telephone?"

"Of course," she replied. "You can come into the house this way. It leads to the kitchen."

Through the open door, Gwen and the others blatantly eavesdropped.

"Averton? Greniston here. . . . Yes, yes; it is almost five o'clock in the morning, but this is business, old boy. . . . No, I haven't been out robbing trains! If I did that, not you nor all your boys at the yard would ever catch me. Been a theft, though, the chalice. You know, you saw it in the museum when you came to visit. . . . Yes, that 'old thing.' It happens to be the pride of Far Tauverly. Any chance we might convince the local constable it's all right to keep it out of the press for a few days? You know how these things are. . . . Well, yes, it is an important antiquity, I suppose, but it will turn out to be a schoolboy prank in the end, I'll wager. We'll find the ruddy thing fastened to the church tower in the morning, some kind of dare, you know. . . . Exactly, . . . no point in littering the landscape with reporters and gawkers. . . . Enough inconvenience already. . . . Exactly! . . . Well then, if not seventy-two, how about forty-eight? . . . Have it all cleared up before then, of course. Fine, yes. . . . It's the Tweeverton police. . . . No, station here in Far Tauverly. . . . Yes, I'll ring you first thing. Ta-ra, old bean, and give my best to Connie."

"It'll be kept quiet for up to forty-eight hours," Greniston announced when he returned. "Give us more than enough time to solve it," he added to the policemen.

"Right you are, Sir," one of them agreed.

"We'll show 'em what the local force can do," the other added with a grin.

"We'd better get cracking, though," Greniston continued, "make the best use of our time."

"Perhaps a cup of tea?" Lettice suggested.

Greniston looked up, as if surprised to see her still there.

"Ladies," he exclaimed, "how rude of me! Forgot all about you! No, thank you, you've done more than enough already. I think you and Althea should get some rest, we may have questions for you later. And as for you, Miss Fields," he added, "it's high time you got a bit of shuteye as well. Perhaps one of these officers would be good enough to run you back to the inn in the squad car."

"Oh, I can walk," protested Gwen.

"It's barely light out, I wouldn't hear of it, Miss," said one of the policemen.

"Neither would I," growled Greniston. He put his arm around Gwen in a proprietary manner and walked her out to the car. She knew that he would not kiss her in front of the wide-eyed policeman and the early risers of Far Tauverly; he was far too private a man for that. Nonetheless, he opened the door for her and then gazed down at her with frank tenderness in his warm, brown eyes.

"I'll call you later," he said.

That was all, but to Gwen it said everything. He did not regret the kiss beneath the apple tree. He wanted to see her again. He said he would call, and he was a man of his word. It was enough, it was everything. Those few simple words, and the way he lingered, smiling down at her, clearly remembering the moment when their lips had met, just as she was.

She rode back to the inn in a dream of happiness, arriving just in time to lock the door and do the dishes from their supper before Mrs. Hodges woke up. Once up in her bed, she fell into a deep, sweet sleep.

When she awoke again, to a morning of radiant sunshine, her first thought was *I'm in love! I'm in love with the Lord of Greniston Manor, and he kissed me!*

She glanced at the clock on the bedside table. It was only eight o'clock, but she felt as refreshed as if she'd slept for hours. She supposed it was a little too early to expect Greniston to call, so she got up, had a bubble bath, danced a little jig of happiness as she brushed her teeth, and spent more time than usual on her hair and makeup. Then she sat back down on the bed and glanced at the clock: eight forty-three. She realized that Greniston, who had been up later than she, might be just now falling asleep. She imagined him asleep. His dark hair was surely tousled, giving a bit of a little boy look to his rugged features. He was probably a sprawler, she decided, taking over the whole bed and the covers as well. She wondered what kind of pajamas he wore—white ones, perhaps, with burgundy stripes.

But he might not wear any pajamas, she realized. She smiled as she considered that possibility.

Just then, there was a knock on the door of her room.

It's him, she thought joyfully.

When she opened the door, she found herself face to face with a bouquet of flowers. A muffled voice from behind the bouquet, which filled the entire doorway, said "Delivery from Bristol Florist's, for Miss Gwendolyn Fields."

Her heart leapt. *He sent me flowers*, she thought, thrilled. It really was an impressive bouquet of deep red roses and snow-white lilies.

"There's a note with the flowers, Miss," the delivery man said. He set the bouquet down on the dresser and handed her an envelope.

"Thank you so much," said Gwen, reaching into her purse to give the man a tip.

"Oh, I'll be back, Miss," he said with a smile. "There's fifteen more bouquets to come, out in the van."

"My goodness," said Gwen. After the delivery man left to get the next bouquet, she opened the envelope. The letter inside was several pages long. She read only a sentence, before she realized that the note was not from Greniston but from Geoffrey Swindon. She glowered at the bouquet on the dresser with sudden dislike. So many roses and lilies, lovely, but a touch overdone, really. . . .

The delivery man returned, this time bearing an arrangement of Birds of Paradise. Behind him was Sarah, the maid, carrying a lacquer vase full of Japanese mums.

"I'm sorry," Gwen said, "I can't accept these flowers."

"What, Miss?" The delivery man looked surprised.

"I simply can't accept them. I . . . I am not on friendly terms with the gentleman who sent them, and it wouldn't be right. So please, take them back to the florist's with my apologies."

"Are you sure, Miss? They're all bought and paid for already, we can't use them over, against the law, that is. Shame to throw 'em all out."

Gwen thought for a moment. "Is there a hospital nearby?" she asked.

"There's one in Tweeverton, that's the nearest," put in Sarah.

"Fine. Take the flowers there, then, to be given to anyone who might like them. And I'd appreciate it if your shop could let Mr. Swindon know where his flowers were sent."

"Certainly, Miss. What about the letter?"

Gwen looked at the missive in her hand with some distaste.

"I'll keep it," she said. "I suppose I owe it to him to at least read it. And I'm very sorry to have caused you so much extra trouble," she added to the delivery man. She handed him what she hoped was a generous tip.

"Oh, there's no need for that," he replied. "It's been taken care of already. More than adequately."

"I'm sure," Gwen replied. "But I insist." The man tipped his hat with a trace of a smile, and said "Very good, Miss."

As she closed the door, Gwen caught a glimpse of Sarah, her eyes as round as saucers. The news of the refused flowers would probably be all over Far Tauverly before noon.

With a sigh, she sat down on the edge of the bed and began to read Swindon's letter.

"My Dearest Gwen," it began, in a fast, shaky hand. "Can you ever find it in your heart to forgive me? My behavior last night was inexcusable, I know, and I have suffered many moments of bitter regret since then, counting the minutes until I could send an apology to you. . . ."

Gwen paused. A hurried glance showed her that the letter was eighteen pages long. She felt that however sincere Swindon's feelings were, she couldn't stand to read that much apology right now, especially when it was clear, after last night, that she and Geoff Swindon had no possible future together.

I'll read it later, she decided, putting the letter on the dresser. She glanced at the clock. Nine-eleven. Lord Greniston was just as likely to be asleep as he had been half an hour ago. For a moment, she allowed herself to imagine what kind of flowers he would send her, surely, someday. . . .

She could see, very clearly, how it would be. A day of breeze and sunshine. They were walking across the lawns of Greniston Manor.

"There's something I want to show you, Miss Fields," he said. "You see, it came to my mind today to send you flowers, . . . so I drove to Bristol, to the finest shop for a hundred miles, . . . and they had roses, and freesias, . . . but they were all cut flowers, and I knew that for you, only living flowers would do. So here, here is your bouquet. . . ."

They had turned into a small, walled garden. They passed under a rose-covered archway, and she saw before her a profusion of columbines and bell-flowers, rhododendrons, roses, mums, and pinks, it being, evidently, all seasons at once in her daydream. The air smelled heady with the mingled perfumes of so many blooms; she could hear the homey drone of bees. . . .

"Are you going to pick me a daisy?" she asked.

Greniston shook his head. "No, you fey sprite of the woodlands, the garden is your bouquet! Yours, forever, but only on the condition that you stay by my side always, to tend it."

He took her in his arms. Their lips met. . . .

And outside on the street, a car backfired.

Startled from her reverie, which she realized could have been straight out of *Fandango in Florence*, by none other than Henrietta Amberly, Gwen found that her spirits were marvelously restored. Smiling, she glanced at the clock. Nine fourteen.

I'll go for a walk, she decided. *Maybe Logan's out by now, and we can get some coffee. No*, she amended, *tea*, for she felt quite English that morning.

Leaving careful instructions with Mrs. Hodges that if Mr. Swindon called, she was out for the day, but that if Lord Greniston called, she would be back within the hour, Gwen stepped out into the sunshine of one of the most glorious spring days she had ever seen.

***

The Lord of Greniston Manor was having quite a different morning. When at last he had arrived home, at six thirty, he had felt wide awake and keen to write, just as he had, he realized, on the evening Gwen had come to dinner. He went to his study and, without even bothering to take off his raincoat, had begun to jot down notes for later development. From time to time, he had glanced up at the bust of Shakespeare and murmured "She's quite a girl, Will."

Around seven fifteen, he had dozed off, sitting in his chair. His dreams were all of Gwen: Gwen at the mound, Gwen on the staircase of Greniston Manor, wearing some kind of long, white dress, her auburn hair flowing around her shoulders, with flowers entwined in it. She smiled and reached out to him, as if in welcome. Then, suddenly, Deirdre stood between them on the stairs. She wore something dark and smart-looking and smoked a cigarette in a long, ivory holder. She flicked the ash of it on the stairs, then said, almost casually, "You never could write, Gren, unless there was a woman in your life. You don't think you do it all on your own, do you? *Wholly Writ* is as much my play as yours, for all it bears your alter ego's name on the cover. The cadence of my speech is there, my imagery, my thoughts that I freely shared with you and that you grabbed and called your own. Just as Gwen's thoughts will be in the next one. Her life, her poetry, her beauty; that's what will drive you to write, my dear. Will she even get the recognition of a dedication, I wonder?"

Greniston woke with a start. The clock said nine-twenty. He found himself sitting at his desk in a damp, wrinkled rain coat and an unaccountably bad mood. Bits of the dream began to come back to him, and his mood did not improve.

"Never wrote a play on my own, did I?" he growled, as Deirdre's words came back to him. "Preposterous! Oh well, never mind, it's just a dream."

Telling himself this several times did not seem to help his mood at all. Hopefully, he picked up his notes of the night before, feeling that these, surely, would be encouraging. It had been good work, he knew that, yet no sooner did he read one line of his own notes, then thoughts of Gwen filled his mind; it seemed that her eyes, the tilt of her head, the lilt of her voice, were interwoven into every syllable. He was not sure how this made him feel.

"Ah, Will," he sighed, "is there no escape from these women? They just walk right into your mind and start rearranging the mental furniture without so much as a by your leave."

In the distance, a phone rang. (Greniston refused to have one in his study.) Eventually, the ringing stopped. Greniston heard hasty footsteps, then a tentative knocking on the study door.

Probably Robert, he thought, disgruntled, *coming to tell me that's Miss Fields on the phone. No doubt she's just finished the play for me.*

"Oh, Sir, you are here!" exclaimed Robert, poking his head through the door. "Mrs. Fitz thought you were still in London. Colonel Averton insisted you were back."

"That Averton who's calling?" Greniston asked.

"Yes," said Robert, and Greniston found he was oddly disappointed. "Colonel Averton, of Scotland Yard," Robert continued, sounding quite impressed. "He's on the line now, Sir."

"Oh, very well," Greniston grumbled, "I'm coming. I can see that you weren't expecting me," he added, eyeing Robert, whose hair was uncombed and whose trousers had been pulled on over his pajamas. It didn't occur to Greniston that his own appearance was not much better.

His call with Averton did not improve matters. "No, I haven't found the criminal yet, nor the bloody chalice!" he exclaimed, struggling to keep from yelling. "I didn't find out about this little escape until five o'clock this morning, a mere four and a half hours ago. . . . Yes, I know that matters can only be hushed up for so long. . . . Yes, I will ring you as soon as I've learned anything new."

He hung up cursing. "Well, there's no thought of getting some civilized sleep now," he muttered, feeling quite put upon. "I shall have to go confront whichever sniveling Walmsley stole that damn chalice and get it over with. But first I need some coffee."

He headed for the kitchen, where he found Mrs. Fitzpatrick, prim and well-groomed, already putting on the kettle. For some reason, he found her punctual neatness as annoying as Robert's messiness had been.

"I don't want tea," he said, glowering at the kettle. "I want coffee."

"There is none," said Mrs. Fitzpatrick pertly. Unlike most people, she felt no awe of Greniston, probably because she remembered changing his diapers.

"No coffee?"

"No. Since you are the only one who drinks it, and you were not expected back so soon, I did not have any in store yet."

"Well, what kind of a reason is that?" growled Greniston. "I hope that at least there are kippers?"

Mrs. Fitzpatrick shook her head. "There is toast," she replied, "or oatmeal."

"Oatmeal!" exclaimed Greniston. "You know I think that stuff is only a poor substitute for library paste!"

"I take it you'll have toast," the housekeeper said dryly.

Several cups of Earl Grey tea mollified Greniston's ire somewhat. He looked almost human as he spread orange marmalade on his toast.

"Althea and Lettice expressed great gratitude for your behavior last night," Mrs. Fitzpatrick remarked. "They said you made them feel quite safe and secure."

"How on earth did you hear about that already?" asked Greniston, his mouth full of toast.

"Tom, the milkman," Mrs. Fitzpatrick replied. "The Pennington sisters had told him all about the theft. I trust Miss Fields is well?" she added.

"Miss Fields?"

"Yes. He said that they had said that she was there as well. Quite a comfort, in her quiet way, that's what they told Tom."

Greniston groaned, realizing that, thanks to the Pennington sisters and friendly Tom the milkman, who was second only to Logan in the dispersal of news, the fact that he and Miss Fields had been together the night before was probably all over Far Tauverly by now.

"I'm sure she's fine. Sound asleep right now, if she has any sense."

"So should you be," said Mrs. Fitzpatrick.

Greniston shook his head. "Off to see the Walmsleys."

"Not in those clothes, you aren't," said the housekeeper, eyeing his wrinkled attire.

"Damn," said Greniston, realizing that he did indeed look a mess.

"I trust Miss Field's enjoyed Lord Peter's diaries," Mrs. Fitzpatrick added. "So nice to see someone take an interest in them."

"Lord Peter's diaries?" Greniston felt confused and more in need of coffee than ever.

"Yes," said Mrs. Fitzpatrick patiently. "When she was here, yesterday. Robert told me she came to read them. I'm sure she must have mentioned it to you."

"No," said Greniston grimly, "she did not."

The fact that their evening had been cut short by the theft of the chalice and that she might not have had the time to mention her visit did not occur to him just then.

"Oh well," the housekeeper said, "I'm sure she will. Of course, Robert knew it would be perfectly acceptable to let her in."

"Indeed," Greniston remarked, in a tone that, had Mrs. Fitzpatrick been more alert, would have warned her that an explosion was coming.

"Such a lovely girl," she trilled, "Not at all what one imagines Americans to be, although, of course, I'm sure they're not all - "

"She was in this house without my permission!" Greniston thundered, the confusion and irritation that had been mounting in him all morning suddenly finding its vent. The fact that Mrs. Fitzpatrick and Robert both felt free to assume Gwen was intimately welcome at any time did not help matters. He suspected half the village would have them engaged before nightfall.

"I suppose she'll be moving in next!" he yelled. "God! Women! They take over your mind, your house! Probably fancies herself the next Lady Greniston and just came over to try the place on for size! Already on the phone with the decorators, I'll warrant, picking out new wallpaper."

"I hardly think so," said Mrs. Fitzpatrick. "Miss Fields does not strike me as a gold digger."

Greniston shook his head. "You don't know women, Mrs. Fitzpatrick."

"Oh really?" she replied archly. "I was under the impression that I had been one for several years."

This remark was lost on Greniston, who had just added to his own wrath by spilling marmalade on his shirt.

"You needed to change it anyway," Mrs. Fitzpatrick said. Greniston swore.

"Go take a bath," Mrs. Fitzpatrick sniffed.

Half an hour later, Greniston, bathed and changed, but not shaved, headed toward the Walmsleys. As he walked down the drive, he carried on an earnest conversation with himself.

"This is moving too fast," he said in reasonable tones. "The village probably has us almost married by now, though we scarcely know each other."

Even as he spoke the words, he remembered the evening before, in the inn, when she had looked into his eyes, and he felt that he had always known her. It had been a powerful moment, so powerful that it almost frightened him in the cold light of day. He had the sense of being swept away on currents he could not manage. Even now, he found himself wondering if she was awake yet; remembering her face, her smile. . . .

"Granted," he said aloud, "she has a certain charm. A great deal of charm. In fact, the word *charm* doesn't do it justice, somehow. She has soul, she has spirit."

Again, his thoughts drifted to remembering many moments of the evening before, including the kiss. Indeed, his thoughts lingered upon that.

"All right," he said aloud, "I kissed her. But surely she is not so naive as to build castles in air from a mere kiss. She might have, though. I don't want to lead her on, in any way; she is too fine a person to toy with. It might be better if I went back to London until her little holiday is over. She'll be disappointed, of course, but it would be the kinder thing to do."

At the thought of leaving town and never seeing Gwen again, Greniston experienced a literal ache near his heart. "Well," he said, "that might be going too far. No need to break things off utterly, but I'll just make sure she understands that this is, after all, a holiday romance, a fling, a bit of magic on life's journey. She's a mature, experienced woman, she'll understand that this plan is for the best. I'll settle it with her as soon as I've dealt with the Walmsleys."

Oddly enough, this well-reasoned plan did not improve his spirits at all. Greniston found that he did not like himself very much that morning. He felt unclean, as if in belittling the depth of his feelings for Gwen, he had betrayed not only her but himself as well. *It's that damn dream*, he realized. *Hit a nerve. Deirdre seems to have kept her ability to zero in on the core of things, even in my memory.*

He had reached the road to Far Tauverly by now. Turning on to it, he half expected to see Gwen. *She has a habit of appearing from amongst the trees when you least expect her*, he mused.

He saw several squirrels and two magpies but no Miss Fields.

Well, of course she isn't out, he thought. *It isn't pouring rain! She wouldn't dream of coming out on a pleasant, sunny day like this.*

The thought that the day would come when he would never see Gwen again, dripping wet or otherwise, shocked Greniston.

"Damn it!" he muttered. "Has she already made such inroads into my heart that I can't imagine life without her?" He couldn't even tell if he was happy or displeased about the fact, and his own confusion irritated him most of all. In a fouler mood than ever, he strode on toward the village. *I hope all the little Walmsleys are home*, he thought. *I feel in a mood to savage several of 'em!*

***

Anne Walmsley stood in her front yard. The baby, Amanda, she held in her arms. Rutherford clung to her skirts. Both children were crying, loudly. Mrs. Walmsley was crying, too, but silently. From inside the house came muffled curses and the sound of slamming doors.

At that moment, Gwen came along Milsom Road.

228

"Hello, Mrs. Walmsley," she called out cheerfully, "have you seen Logan today?"

Mrs. Walmsley shook her head.

Drawing closer, Gwen exclaimed, "What's wrong? You look terribly distressed!"

Before Mrs. Walmsley could answer, Gwen heard the sound of breaking dishes from inside the house.

"It's all right, luv," Mrs. Walmsley said. "He's just blowing off steam. It's the foreclosure. We're evicted, you see. We've got three days to get out, nowhere to go, and absolutely no money."

"But how can they do that to you?" Gwen exclaimed. "Surely it isn't legal!"

"I'm afraid it is," said Mrs. Walmsley wistfully. "It's not like we haven't seen it coming, you see. We're months behind on the rent, and there's late fees besides. I suppose Mr. Swindon felt he simply couldn't wait any longer."

"Swindon?" Gwen exclaimed.

"Why, yes," Anne Walmsley said mildly, "he's our landlord. I thought you knew—everyone seems to."

"No," Gwen said, "I certainly didn't. I thought your landlord must be some firm in Bristol or Bath! How can Swindon do this? He doesn't need the money right away!"

"Well, to be fair," Mrs. Walmsley said, "he's waited a long time. It does seem rather hard, since Bob offered many times to work the debt off. He even offered to work on the condos Swindon's going to build at half-rate to pay it back, but . . . "

"Did you say 'condos'?" Gwen asked.

"Why, yes. On the Greniston land, you know, although I suppose we should say the Swindon land, but old habits die hard. It's set to begin in a matter of days, as soon as the paperwork clears the courts."

"We'll see about that," Gwen muttered darkly. Her attention was reclaimed by immediate problems, however, when Mrs. Walmsley suddenly began to sob as loudly as her children.

"I'm sorry, dear," she said. "It's just that you being so concerned, it seems to have opened the floodgates, somehow. You see, on top of it all, I'm so worried about the children. They're barely in the house these last few days, and I know they are playing truant. Just this morning, two men from the

229

school board came asking about Wyatt. They said it was a 'routine check,' but it really was very odd. They didn't look like school people to me, and they weren't very nice, somehow. I'm afraid Wyatt's in some real trouble this time. I can feel it."

"I'm sure everything will be okay about that," Gwen said soothingly. She suspected that Anne Walmsley had not yet heard about the stolen chalice, and she did not want to break that news to her on top of everything else. Lord Greniston, she felt, would know how to handle it in a much more efficient manner. She was much more concerned about the Walmsleys' housing situation and the sound of a none-too sober Mr. Walmsley, hurling crockery and slamming doors.

"Well," Mrs. Walmsley said, drying her eyes, "thank you for listening. Sometimes it helps just to say things, you know. But I suppose I should pack, now. Although where we'll take it all, I don't know."

Privately, Gwen thought that by the time Mr. Walmsley got done, there wouldn't be much left to pack.

"There's got to be something we can do," Gwen mused aloud, "someone who can help."

Even as she spoke the words, the solution came to her mind.

"I've got it!" she exclaimed. "I know of a place you can stay, right here in Far Tauverly!"

"You do?" Mrs. Walmsley looked doubtful. "There's few that have room for so large a family as ours."

"The place I have in mind has plenty of room," Gwen assured her. "I know it will work, so, yes, do start packing. I'll be back before noon to tell you the details. And don't worry, everything is going to be all right, I promise."

"Yes, but truly, this is not your problem," Mrs. Walmsley said. "You needn't go to so much bother." Yet in spite of her protests, she dared to look a little bit hopeful. As if sensing her encouragement, both Amanda and Rutherford stopped crying, as well.

"It's going to be all right," Gwen said firmly. "I'll be back as soon as I can. You start packing."

She turned and hurried in the direction of Greniston Manor. She knew Lord Greniston would want to help the Walmsleys, especially after seeing how kind he had been to the Pennington sisters last night. And he had all that room in his home, whole wings of it unused. . . .

Greniston's heart skipped a beat when he saw Gwen coming down the road, right toward him.

So she does come out in the sunshine, he mused, thinking how pretty she looked, in the blue dress, with her auburn hair loose around her shoulders.

Don t go overboard, old man, he reminded himself. *She s leaving in a week or two. Anything between us could be only a brief encounter, at best. You ve got to let her know the terms. Tell her you may be called out of town at any moment, casually mention a mistress and seventeen illegitimate brats in Katmandu or Leeds, put it any way you like to make the point, but get it over with. Damn it, why has she chosen this morning of all mornings to look more charming than ever? Never mind, it has to be done.*

He strode purposefully toward Gwen. "It won't do to let things go too far, Miss Fields," he blurted out.

"Ah," Gwen interjected, "Then you know already. No, of course it won't do; it's preposterous, isn't it? I knew you'd agree."

For once in his life, Greniston found himself speechless and quite deflated. He had never expected her to be so quick to end things. Not, of course, that there was any *thing* to end. Yet he had thought she'd at least shed a tear or suggest, perhaps, that they make the best of the time left to them. What would be wrong with that, after all? Yet here she was, sounding as crisp as a bank teller discussing funds. He felt quite shocked.

"Amazing," he said.

"It's more than amazing," Gwen said, "it's shocking! And of course, it's obvious what must be done. Whatever our emotions about this might be."

At least she s conceded we have them, thought Greniston.

"What's needed now is practical action. You agree, don't you?"

"To be honest," replied Lord Greniston, "I confess I was thinking along the same lines you are, but I'm a little taken aback to hear you put my feelings into words, and so clearly, too."

"Taken aback?" asked Gwen, astonished. "Why ever would you be taken aback? It's the only decent reaction to have."

"Indeed!" exclaimed Greniston. He suddenly felt rather wounded. Really, she didn't have to be quite that businesslike about it all. After all, they had kissed.

"Well, so it's settled," said Gwen, looking pleased. "Will you come with me to invite them?"

Lord Greniston stared at her, more confused than ever. "Invite them?"

"Yes! That's what we've been talking about, isn't it? Of course, I forgot, you've had no sleep, everything's probably really confused right now. Let's go invite them to the manor house, and then I'm going to find you some strong, black coffee. They'll be so pleased. You don't know how much this will be appreciated."

"Wait a minute," Greniston growled, "Just what the devil are we talking about?"

"Why, the Walmsleys, of course!" Shocked at his angry tone, Gwen noticed for the first time that, really, Lord Greniston did not look quite as she remembered him from the night before. For one thing, he was unshaven. For another, there was a brooding, almost peevish look in his dark eyes. With misgiving, Gwen realized that he was not now gazing at her with that tenderness he had displayed but a few short hours before.

"The Walmsleys?" Greniston now exploded, "What the devil do the Walmsleys have to do with our relationship?"

Equally confused, and with just a touch of her own outrage beginning to rise, Gwen replied, "What does our relationship have to do with the Walmsleys?"

"Slow down," said Greniston, "and tell me from the beginning what this is all about."

You must be exhausted, Gwen realized, *to have forgotten already*. She felt relieved to have reminded herself of the reason for his odd behavior. Sympathetically, she said, "You know. About the Walmsleys coming to stay at Greniston Manor."

"What?" thundered Greniston.

"But you agreed it was a good idea, not five minutes ago," protested Gwen, bewildered. "You said you knew about it. You said you'd been thinking along the same lines as I had."

"I never said any such thing!" exclaimed Greniston. "And anyway, why the devil should the Walmsleys come to Greniston Manor?"

"Why, because of the eviction!"

"Eviction! So Swindon finally did it, the bastard!" Slowly, it began to dawn on Greniston what Gwen had been talking about all this time. His first reaction was one of delight. *So she doesn't feel so ruthless about us*, he thought happily. It was absurd, the way his heart seemed to be doing a little tap dance of relief and joy all around his rib-cage. In a much gentler tone, he said, "Well, I'm sure it's a low blow for the Walmsleys, but right now I think we should concentrate on us. . . ."

Gwen looked pleased at this, but said, "Well, yes, of course we should. But first, you do need to invite them, you know." She paused, looking at Greniston's face, which seemed to have gone quite pale beneath his five o'clock shadow.

"You are going to take them in—aren't you?" she faltered, suddenly uncertain.

"Take them in?" thundered Greniston. "A bunch of snot-nosed peasant brats running wild in Greniston Manor? It's unthinkable! Surely you can see that. I have my work," Greniston caught himself and left the sentence unfinished.

Gwen looked at him in shocked silence. Several lines of thought, all distressing, seemed to be running through her mind at once. For one thing, it began to dawn on her that if Greniston had not been referring to the Walmsleys when they met, he must have been talking . . . about them. Just what had he meant by, "It won't do to let things go too far, Miss Fields?" For another thing, she realized, uncomfortably, that she might have been just a wee bit highhanded in being so sure he would be willing to take in the Walmsleys. Yet, somehow, seeing this only made her want to deny it all the more. Most of all, she felt angry at both herself and Greniston, that neither of them seemed to be acting like the magical people they had been the night before. Right now, she wasn't sure she even liked the scowling, unshaven man who stood before her.

"What's unthinkable," she retorted, "is your attitude! I cannot believe that you, of all people, would so callously dismiss the plight of the Walmsleys! I believed in your honor," she continued, mounting into a frontal attack that she knew, somewhere inside herself, to be exaggerated and unfair. Yet the biting words came, with a life of their own. "In good faith, I promised the Walmsleys that help would be coming before noon, that there would be a place for them to stay. I will leave it to you, Lord Greniston, to crush their hopes! You march up to that door and tell Anne Walmsley that no help is coming! To think that I believed you were a true descendant of Lord Peter! You and Swindon, you think you're so different, but you're just alike. You're neither of you what you seem! Men! I've never been so disappointed in anyone in my entire life!"

Whether, at that moment, it was Greniston or herself she was so disappointed in was not quite clear to Gwen, which upset her all the more.

She looks quite spirited when she is angry, Greniston thought. Oddly enough, as Gwen's fury mounted, his own seemed to dissipate. He had to admit to himself that there was some truth in what she had to say, although in her present mood she reminded him of a sergeant major he'd known in his military days, Reginald Simpson. "Ready Reggie," they used to call him, because he was ever ready to reorganize whole battalions when a bright idea struck him. He could see that Gwen was cut of the same cloth. *What had happened to the ethereal, regal lady who was my companion last night?* he wondered sadly.

He must have missed the conclusion of her arguments, he realized, for now she turned away from him and strode toward the village.

"Where are you going?" he called out, bemused.

Instead of answering, she yelled an enigmatic parting thrust over her shoulder: "And you didn't send the flowers!" Then she disappeared around a bend in the road and left him standing there, quite bewildered.

***

"No, that won't do," said Geoffrey Swindon.

"Indeed, Sir," the clerk murmured, lifting a well-penciled eyebrow. "A member of the Royal Family was quite pleased with that blouse, just last week."

She sniffed. The staff of Clerendon's, Bristol's most elegant and exclusive ladies' clothiers, were not accustomed to being told their merchandise 'wouldn't do.' Nor were they accustomed to showing garments without an appointment, and certainly not at nine forty-five in the morning, before the shop was even open for business. At first, when the elegantly dressed young man had appeared on the doorstep, the clerk had coolly suggested that he call later to arrange an appointment—in several days time, perhaps. To her surprise, he had stepped right past her into the foyer and pulled out a wallet fat with hundred pound notes.

"I realize I'm inconveniencing you," he said, "but I know you have the best, and that's what I need. My mother and sister shop here. Swindon's the name. I'll be glad to pay your staff overtime, whatever arrangement is needed. This is, well, a bit of an emergency, you see."

"In that case," murmured the clerk, "surely Marks and Spencer's would do?" Her tone managed to imply that well-bred families did not have emergencies of any kind.

To her surprise, the young man did not wilt before her gaze but grew quite flinty himself.

"Name your price," he said, thrusting the wallet in her face, as if he actually expected her to grab a few hundred pounds out of it. Just as she was about to order him to leave or call the police, if need be, he tilted his head to one side and added the single word, "Please." There was such desperate appeal in the way he said it that she weakened.

"Is it really so important, Mr. Swindon, that you go shopping today?" she asked, her tone a bit gentler.

"Oh, it is! The timing is crucial! It's more important than you could possibly imagine!"

Without waiting any longer, he brushed past her into the shop.

"Ah, look at this!" he exclaimed, taking from the rack an evening cape of royal blue velvet, with buttons of real sapphire. "This is perfect for her! It's regal, and she's the Queen of the Island, you see." He clutched the cape, as if afraid someone might snatch it away from him.

This young man is not well, the clerk thought. Aloud, she said soothingly, "Have a seat, Mr. Swindon, and we'll send for some tea. There will be plenty of time to look at everything."

That had been an hour ago. Now the clerk calculated what Swindon had spent already: seventeen dresses, at no less than three hundred pounds each, cashmere sweaters, silk blouses, and evening gowns as well as a complete set of practical wear—woolen slacks, raincoats, hats—for all occasions.

This must come to at least £15,000, the clerk realized. She thought of her own commission from it, and felt a little dizzy.

"I shall clothe her in the colors of sand and sea, and the morning star shall be her diadem," the young man was murmuring to himself. He was making the clerk quite nervous. Sometimes he talked to himself in a kind of reverie; the next instant, he would be totally alert and shrewd, looking at a skirt and muttering, "Won't do; it's fake crepe de Chine. Show me another one."

Now, as she was tallying the final bill, Swindon looked at her and asked earnestly, "She'll like this, don't you think?"

"Any lady would be delighted to receive such a wardrobe, I assure you, Sir. Now, where should it be delivered to?"

"I'll take the cape with me," said Swindon, still holding it protectively in his arms, "but have the rest delivered to this address." He tossed a slip of paper onto the counter. "And I want it to arrive the day after tomorrow. That's very important!"

The clerk glanced at the address, and then exclaimed in surprise, "But this is near the Orkney Isles!" Somehow, she had pictured the clothes arriving at a London townhouse or a country home in Devon, not the wild coast of Scotland.

"It's not the Orkney Isles. It's a private island. I own it. So, what do I owe you for this little foray?"

"£16,323," the clerk replied, trying to keep her voice even.

"Fine," the young man said, casually counting out twenty thousand pounds in cash. "The extra is for delivery costs—and a little something for you, for your trouble."

"But Mr. Swindon, that is far too much. There's no need, really!"

He seemed not even to hear her protests. Tenderly, he gathered the blue cape in his arms and headed toward the door. Just as he left, he turned and said softly, "She'll be back for her bridal dress—custom made."

The door clicked shut behind him. Staring after him, the clerk felt oddly disturbed. Instead of feeling overjoyed about her commission and the tip, she felt almost as if she had witnessed a crime and should report it to the police.

Yet what would I say? she reasoned. *That a Mr. Swindon came in, spent buckets of money, and acted oddly? That's not against the law. Yet all the same, something's not right. Well,* she decided, *keep your nose out of it, my girl. You got your cream from it, and that's a fact. So leave well enough alone, I always say.*

CHAPTER FOURTEEN

The omelet sizzled in the cast-iron skillet, perfectly golden, bursting with diced onions, tomatoes, three kinds of cheese, seven spices, and a secret ingredient. Its fragrance wafted out of the kitchen, and into the hallway. Gwen, just entering the inn, stopped, sniffed, and looked puzzled.

I was just thinking about Filipo, she thought, *and that smells just like his cooking. I can't believe Mrs. Hodges makes Basque omelets! It must be something else, or my memory playing tricks.* She remembered all the times that she and Filipo had talked late into the night, and he had prepared them a midnight feast of omelet, washed down with Beaujolais..

What I wouldn't give to talk with Filipo now, she thought.

Her anger at Greniston had dimmed enough by now for misery to take its place. Everything that had seemed so bright and promising when she awoke that morning was now tarnished: Greniston was not the man she had thought him to be; she was not the woman she had been in his company; Swindon was even more of a rat than she had realized; and the Walmsleys had nowhere to turn, after all. In spite of this list of woes, or perhaps because of it, she realized that she was hungry. She pushed open the swaying door to the kitchen.

"Hi, Babe," a familiar voice called. "We're looking at two more minutes tops until this thing's ready!"

"Filipo!" exclaimed Gwen, "Am I dreaming?"

"Yes, and in your dream it's breakfast."

Filipo grinned at her from the other side of the massive kitchen table. He wore one of Mrs. Hodges flowered aprons over his crumpled traveling clothes.

"What—what in the world are you doing here?" stammered Gwen delightedly.

At that point, Filipo bounded around the table and swept her into his arms.

"Hey, I came to see you, Babe! I got your message on my machine. Sounded to me like you really wanted to talk. But every time I tried to call back, I'd miss you. I thought, hey, for what we're spending on phone bills, I could get a ticket! And then I thought, why not? Let Joe"—Filipo's most advanced student, Gwen remembered—"take the lessons for a while. Do him good to be on the other side of the agony. And I got some friends in Brittany

I feel like visiting, and I'll stop here on the way. And you know, there was a cancellation on the next flight to London. I been traveling for almost twenty-four hours." He paused, took in Gwen's pleased but still stunned expression, and added, "I can run down to the pay phone and call, if you've got your heart set on telephones."

"Oh, Filipo, I'm so glad to see you," cried Gwen, returning his hug and patting his shoulders, as if to reassure herself that he was real.

"Now sit down and have some food, *Carissima*," Filipo ordered. "You look like you could use it."

Obediently, Gwen pulled a chair out from the table. It was only then that she noticed a familiar figure, sitting in the corner, drinking, could it be, at nearly eleven a.m., tea?

"Logan," she said happily, "have you met?"

"Yes," Logan replied, "we've been chatting for quite a while, awaiting your return."

"Yes," Filipo said. "He drinks tea, I drink cognac, which would you prefer?"

"Tea, a good strong cup, with honey and cardamom, the way you make it."

"Fortunately, I have some cardamom right here in my backpack. Also some garlic, gracias Dios! That Mrs. Hodges, she's a very gracious lady, most kind to let me use her kitchen, having only just met me, although we do have to be out before eleven fifteen, for the lunch crowd. But you know, she's got things to learn about spices. Where did she go, anyway? She was here a moment ago. Oh well, maybe she'll be back in time to help us finish this."

Privately, Gwen thought that Mrs. Hodges probably wasn't prepared to face the wonderful chaos that always attended Filipo's cooking. The usually immaculate counter was littered with greasy spoons and dripping bowls. Whatever kitchen Filipo entered, he seemed to fill every corner of it instantly.

As her friend rummaged around, hunting for the tea pot, Gwen looked at Logan. He had gotten up from his seat and now stood by the window, holding his tea cup. He looked awkward, as if he were at a vicarage tea party and wished it would end.

He looks so uncomfortable, thought Gwen. *I do hope he likes Filipo. I'm sure Filipo likes him. Maybe he feels left out. I'll have to make sure he knows his friendship is just as important as it was before. But it isn't just that, he looks really worried, and different, somehow. Something's happened.*

"Okay," Filipo announced with loving command, "it's ready, so eat!"

"Perhaps I should leave," murmured Logan. "You two old friends obviously have a lot to talk about." He set down his tea cup and reached for his cap.

"Nonsense!" cried Filipo. "Are you kidding, you would break up this obviously destined threesome? We've been together what? Twenty minutes? Twenty thousand years? It's like we've known each other a long time, can't you feel it? We three are meant to eat at this table together. It's Kismet. Besides, even if you were a total stranger, you should join us. True friends, true love, it only expands things! It opens doors, it doesn't close them. Hey, in a house where love is, you can fit a hundred around a table the size of a postage stamp! You could have a meal the size of a bean, yet everyone gets a portion! And anyway, how could you leave without tasting my omelet?"

Filipo clasped his hand to his heart and staggered backwards across the kitchen, murmuring, "You wound me, Logan. What good is a chef without stomachs to receive his creation?"

"Yes, please stay, Logan," Gwen added. She reached out and took him by the arm. "Come and sit beside me. I want you and Filipo to get to know each other, and besides, you and I need to talk. So much has happened!"

"Oh yes," Logan agreed rather mysteriously, "it has!"

"Well then, that's settled," said Filipo. He put an enormous plate of omelet and buttered toast on the table, along with a bottle of cognac.

"Now, everyone drinks," he said, "to all of us, to old friends!"

***

It took Logan over half an hour to extricate himself from the friendly breakfast. He left Gwen and Filipo doing the washing up (and placating a rather flustered Mrs. Hodges), pleading his neglected mail route as an excuse to leave. He did not, however, turn toward the post office but instead headed quickly out of the village and down the road toward the Greniston land. As he hurried along, he muttered to himself.

"It's the only way," he said, "I couldn't possibly let the children suffer the consequences. Reform school, foster homes. If this case goes unsolved, and the police and social services people start poking into the Walmsleys' situation, there's no telling where it will end! Althea and Tom

239

both said Lord Greniston only has twenty-four hours before the news gets released, and part of that time is already gone. Everyone in town is sure it was those kids, they'll be the first ones questioned—as if they didn't have enough problems already! Officials will get involved, probably declare the Walmsleys unfit parents just because the kids skip school—sign of good parenthood, to let them, say I! But it can't happen, it can't be investigated. No, there's only one way around it: I shall have to say that I stole the chalice."

Logan stopped on the woodland path and looked regretfully at the unopened bottle of Watneys in his jacket pocket. Only six hours earlier, he had taken a solemn vow of, "if not Abstinence from Spirits, at least Restraint." He already felt severely tested in this regard; it had been no easy matter to leave his glass of cognac unfinished.

"After all," he mused, gazing fondly at the Watneys, "this is a medical emergency. My mental health's at stake."

He reached into another pocket and found the bottle opener he always carried. At the first sip of ale, his thoughts miraculously began to clear and slow down. He settled himself onto a rock by the roadside and took a second sip.

Logan felt relieved to be alone. On any other day, he would have enjoyed showing Gwen's friend around Far Tauverly. He liked him already; a generous, good-hearted man, this Filipo seemed to be. The truth was, on any other day Logan might also have been jealous of Filipo, clearly Gwen's friend of many years. But today, Logan had other things on his mind. Today, he realized, he needed quiet. He had gone to the inn hoping to find Gwen but now realized that it was just as well she had unexpected company. What he had to do now had best be done alone.

The police will want to know why I stole it, he realized. *I shall have to think up a good story.*"

Story. At that shining word, he paused, remembering his experience of the night before.

It had all begun at around eleven. He had finished his last pint at the Greenstone Arms. It had seemed that Gwen would be out later than she had planned, so he decided to go for a walk. At first he had only intended to go as far as the church, but something magical seemed to be abroad; he found himself walking farther and farther toward the Greniston land. Then, a voice in his mind whispered: *Why not visit the mounds?*

On so lovely a spring night, when the wind was stirring in the budding trees, the idea held an irresistible appeal. True, it was pouring rain off and on, but for Logan, who, between farming and mail delivery, had spent more time in rain than out of it, this was scarcely a consideration.

How still the forest had seemed. By the time he reached the mounds, the rain had eased. He felt the wind upon his face; cold with the memory of winter, sweet with the promise of spring, a combination he had always loved. The waxing moon appeared from behind the clouds, and by its light, he saw the daffodils that encircled the mounds. The sight of spring flowers blooming at night had always touched him. Perhaps it was the knowledge that their display continued even when there was no one there to see it that so quietly moved him.

"Oh God," Logan whispered, "grant that I may be able to do right by beauty such as this, before I die. Grant that I may somehow find fit words, in poem or story, to do homage to this world You have made."

Had Logan not uttered that small prayer and lingered for a moment at the edge of the clearing, his life might never have taken the turn it now did. But because he did pause, appreciating the night, he suddenly glimpsed a blur of motion out of the corner of his eye.

"Claire?" he called aloud. He had not seen the form that passed, just on the edge of vision, well enough to recognize it. Yet something about it had brought Claire to his mind. There was no reply to his call, yet Logan was sure he had seen something. He stepped closer to the place he had seen the movement. There was no one there. But there was, caught on a branch of a lilac bush, a blue chiffon scarf that he recognized as one Claire often wore, borrowed, no doubt, from her mother's wardrobe. The scarf was in his hands, but of Claire, there was no trace.

She can't have just vanished, Logan thought. *And it's not safe for those kids to be running around at this time of night.* He peered behind the bush, into a dense tangle of wild rose vines. And then, by some trick of the moonlight, he saw what he had never seen before in all the years he had visited the place: an opening in the earth, a kind of tunnel, it seemed to be. He got down on his hands and knees and peered into the darkness of it.

"Claire?" he called out softly. Suddenly, from behind, two strong young hands grabbed his arms.

"Intruder!" a stern voice cried. "In the name of The Kingdom of Greenstone and the Brotherhood of the Shining Mound, we arrest thee!"

241

Logan looked over his shoulder. He found himself the prisoner of Osborne and Charles. Both carried homemade spears and wore crude tunics that looked like they had been fashioned out of old bedsheets. Yet the expression on their faces was absolutely serious, and Logan found himself loathe to destroy the game that clearly had them in its grip.

"No intruder am I," he responded, "but a wandering bard, a humble wayfarer, who seeks audience with Lady Claire. Would you deny me the hospitality of your kingdom?"

Clearly, how to handle such a question had not been within the brief given to the two sentinels. They exchanged a worried look, then Osborne said sternly, "Hold the prisoner here." He scrambled into the dark mouth of the tunnel and disappeared. Charles gripped his spear, made, Logan realized, from an old mop handle, and tried to look intimidating.

I'll just go along with this for a while, Logan thought, *and find out what they are up to.* A moment later, Osborne reappeared, with Osgood, Wyatt, and Claire at his heels. They were all, Logan realized, in costumes of some sort. He could not see them very clearly in the darkness, but he had an impression of generous amounts of old draperies and aluminum foil crowns. The result was oddly effective; he felt as if he really was in the presence of royalty.

Charles came to attention and announced, "His Majesty, Osgood the First, and the Most Royal Court of the Shining Mound."

Osgood looked at Logan severely. "Trespasser!" he intoned.

"Trespasser," Logan chuckled, "You're a fine one to be talking, my friend, out here on the Greniston land in the middle of the night."

"Silence!" cried Osgood. "This is not the Greniston land. Nor is it the land of Swindon" he paused here to spit at the mention of that name, and all the others followed suit, then he continued "Nay, it is not his! This is *our* land."

"How do you figure that?" Logan asked, genuinely curious.

Unexpectedly, it was Osborne who blurted out the answer to this question. "Because we love it," he said earnestly.

Logan felt he could not dispute this as a higher claim than tradition, or greed. "Well," he said, "if I trespassed, it was unintentional. I was merely walking here, thinking it was but the Greniston land I trespassed on, when I caught sight of the Lady Claire. Concerned for her safety, in so dark and desolate a setting, I attempted to follow her."

242

"And then the Sentinels seized you," said Osgood, with some satisfaction. He thought the situation over, chewing his lip. Then he said, "Logan Knowelles, for that you have long been a friend to this Kingdom," the others nodded vigorously at this, "and for all that you are a man of honor, whose High Intent was to come to the aid of a Damsel you feared was in Distress, We are moved to be lenient with you."

"Thank you very much," murmured Logan, with just a touch of irony in his voice.

"You have discovered the secret entrance to our High Chamber," Osgood continued, "and from this there is no turning back. However, in respect of your high . . . um . . . "

"Courage," suggested Osborne in an undertone.

"Yes, your High Courage and Noble Heart," Osgood continued, "We offer you a choice: to remain here at the mound, our prisoner forever, or to become a true and loyal citizen of the Independent Kingdom of Greenstone, Realm of the Shining Mound. How do you choose?"

It was on the tip of Logan's tongue to say, "I choose to head home to a nice warm bed," but something stopped him. He understood, as never before, the power adults have over children. In an instant, just by reacting in a sensible, grown-up way, he could ruin the fragile beauty of the children's game as surely as he could take that scrap of old lace curtain Claire wore about her shoulders like a cape and rip its delicate weave. But why do that? The children were doing no harm, as far as he could see, and, actually, they were probably as safe at the mound as they were at home in bed. They knew their way around the woods so well it was like a big house to them. Perhaps their games had gone too far. He wondered by what stratagems they had all escaped their home to meet here and if their parents were worried about them. Not too worried, he decided, if they even knew about their absence. Anne and Bob seemed to have decided long ago to let their children run free, like a yard full of wildflowers, content as long as they reappeared, undamaged, for the next meal. All this passed through his mind as he gazed at the rag-tag little court gazing back at him so solemnly in the moonlight.

They need some guidance, he decided, but *not now, not in the full magic of this midnight spell. If I have to talk to them like a grown-up soon, I'll do it by daylight, in their parents' kitchen. But not here, in the heart of their little kingdom. I'll play the game on their terms for a while longer.*

"I choose to become a Most Loyal Subject of the Shining Mound," he replied aloud, hoping he had gotten the language high-flown enough to suit the occasion. A sigh of satisfaction came from the children.

"Very good," said Osgood. "Let the ceremony begin."

"Oh, you've got a ceremony for this, do you?" Logan asked with interest. "Do I swear an oath or something?"

"That comes later," Osgood replied. "First you must spend your night upon the mound."

"Spend the night?" exclaimed Logan. "Out here? But I'll catch pneumonia! It's one thing to go for a stroll; it's quite another to sit all night in the damp and cold. It's going to rain again before morning, and it's bloody cold out here."

"Oh, stop whining," replied Osgood the First. "We've all done it."

As Logan watched, the others brought several old quilts out of the tunnel that led to the mound. One of these they spread on the ground; the others, with the aid of sticks poked into the ground, they fashioned into a crude tent.

"And we have Tom the Milkman's down sweeping bag," Wyatt explained eagerly, "the one that got whipped up when he went camping in the Wake Distwict. No one wanted it at the wast jumble sale, and he said we might have it. You wap yoursewf in it wike a cape, you see, and it's weally ever so warm."

"Good thinking," acknowledged Logan.

"Has the Knight been bathed in the waters of the sacred spring?" Osgood asked solemnly.

"Now, just a minute," said Logan, as gently as he could. The thought of stripping in the chill air and trying to bathe in the spring of the farther mound, whose stream was like a trickling water faucet, was too much for even his willingness. However, even the Independent Kingdom of Greniston seemed prepared to make some concessions to the weather; Claire went to the spring and got a cupful of water, which she brought back and dashed in Logan's face.

"He has been bathed, Your Majesty," Osborne intoned.

"Then let his vigil begin." Osgood turned to Logan, who was still wiping his face, and intoned, "Logan Knowelles, now will you spend your night alone upon the Shining Mound, in prayer and vigil solemn, for the good and cleansing of your soul. The dreams you dream here will be for you alone; what you see here you must speak of to no man, nor lady, for as long as you shall live. At the sound of first birdsong, we will return. Then you will swear your oath of fealty and be allowed entry into the mound."

Charles, Osborne, and Wyatt had formed a line along one side of the mound. Charles had a muffled drum made of an old stew pot covered with a torn sweater, on which he began to beat a slow, solemn rhythm, using a cracked wooden spoon.

Claire stood apart, on the mound itself. She lifted a penny whistle to her lips, and began to play an odd, haunting melody. It startled Logan to hear music coming so freely from a child he had never heard speak.

He wondered what combination of fairy tales, television programs, and sheer imagination had contributed to the ritual the children were enacting. He was sure they had been inspired by many sources, yet he had the uncanny feeling that most of all, it was the place itself that had moved them. It was as if some ceremony had, long ago, often been enacted here, and the children had somehow tapped into the memory of it and were replaying their own version. He felt that he would never forget how they looked just then, so young, yet so ancient, standing so solemnly in the moonlight, with the muffled drumbeat and Claire's strange, sweet music the only sounds.

At his side, Osgood said, "Come forward with me, Logan the Brave." The music stopped. A sudden breeze circled the mound, rustling the oak leaves and rippling the children's makeshift capes. Osgood led Logan to the tent on the crest of the mound.

"Here will we come to greet you, at dawn," he said simply.

"At dawn," the others echoed in a whisper. Without another word, they formed a line and, to the soft beat of Charles' drum, marched away into the darkness.

Logan found himself alone upon the mound. Almost at once, the moon slipped behind the clouds, and a cold rain began to fall. Logan sought the refuge of the makeshift tent. Once he had the down sleeping bag wrapped around his shoulders, he did feel surprisingly cozy.

It would be daft to stay here all night, he thought, *yet I don't want to hurt the children's feelings. It's an honor, being initiated into their world, like this. I'll stay, at least for a little while. . . .*

He must have dozed off. When he woke again, with a start, it was to the sound of someone calling his name.

245

Can it be dawn already? he wondered. But the voice that spoke was far too deep to be a child's.

"Logan of Somerset," it cried, "Logan the Brave! Step forth!" Mystified, Logan crawled out of the tent. At first, he saw only darkness and the dim shapes of the encircling oaks. Then, within the circle the daffodils traced around the mounds, a pale golden light began to rise, as if from the earth itself. It rose and expanded until it formed a dome of sparkling, golden mist over Logan and the place.

Can this be happening? Logan thought, amazed. Yet he felt no fear. Now, within the dome, figures began to appear, as if condensing out of the mist itself. He saw men and women in the garb of ages long gone by. Behind them, more and more figures began to appear, until Logan had the sense of being in a vast, high room, with tiers of seats on every side and row upon row of faces gazing intently down at him. Whenever he tried to look right at any of the faces, they seemed to disappear, only to magically reform just at the edge of his vision. Wherever it was that he found himself, it was a golden place, a good place. The air smelled sweet and clean, with the scent of flowers he could not quite name. He had the sense that there was music, the loveliest music he had ever heard, yet when he tried, he could not quite catch the melody of it, though the sounds returned as soon as he stopped trying to hear them.

Most of all, he was struck by the sense of excitement, as if the figures gathered in the golden mist had met for some very important, joyful reason. As he watched, five figures stepped out of the crowd and came toward him.

"How can this be?" he marveled. To his amazement, he recognized all of them. They looked just as he had always imagined they would in his many long nights of reading old tales in the back room of the post office. There was Amergin, High Bard of Wales, dressed in a cape of red feathers and carrying the golden apple branch that marked his noble office. And there was Taliesin, storyteller of legendary skill, "He of the Shining Forehead," as he had been called, with a star of light upon his brow. The lady next to him, dressed in the robes of an Arabian princess, could only be Scheherazade. "Shining Face," her name meant, and her features did indeed shine with wisdom, and kindness, and the wit of someone who, every night for a thousand and one nights, had had a new tale to tell—and forever after, too, no doubt. Next to her stood a laughing-faced man in priest's garb, holding up a shamrock in one hand. This, Logan knew, must be St. Patrick, dear St.

246

Patrick, who, when he came to Ireland to convert the heathen, had spent more time listening to old myths and poems than he had preaching the gospel, until at last, feeling guilty, he had consulted the angels that lived with him, and the angels themselves had encouraged him not only to listen to the tales but also to write them down, "to save forever." And last of all, though Logan could scarcely believe it, came Gwydion, Bard and Wizard of Wales, who had always been his especial hero. Gwydion of the Golden Hair and the Golden Smile, trickster, healer, poet and rogue. Gwydion, whose fate it had ever been to endure the worst sorrows men and Gods could devise and yet emerge smiling. He was smiling now, as he approached Logan.

"Logan of Somerset!" he cried gladly, "Logan the Brave! Welcome!"

"Welcome!" echoed the thousand voices of those gathered around, sighing like a wave of the great sea, like wind moving through a vast forest.

"You have summoned us," Gwydion continued.

"Summoned you?" exclaimed Logan. "But how?"

"By your love of Story," Amergin replied.

"By years of longing for our realms, when the world scoffed," said Taliesin.

"By your good heart," added Scheherazade.

"By the prayer you uttered upon this very mound," said St. Patrick.

"By the kindness you have shown children, who are dear to us," added Gwydion, with a sparkle in his eye.

"Have no fear," Gwydion added, seeing the amazement on Logan's face. "We mean you no harm. Yet we come in response not only to your need but to our own as well."

"Your need?" exclaimed Logan.

"Oh yes," said Gwydion sadly.

"This world—both your world, and ours, for they are but one that's interwoven—is in most desperate peril," explained Scheherazade.

"Yes," said St. Patrick, "you live in the darkest of times, my friend. The dangers for all that lives are greater than you know. Someone must take up the cause of good, must be its champion, as Knights were champions in the days of old."

"But, but you are great champions," said Logan. "What do such as you need with me? I'm kind of an idiot, really."

Amergin waved these words aside with a lofty gesture. "Our time is over," he said wistfully. "Our hands can never again take up sword to defend or elixir to heal. Our speech is heard no more by those of your day, who do not believe."

"All we can do," Taliesin added earnestly, "is seek to inspire the living. Those few who will listen, as you always have. "

"The moment is coming soon when we will need a true champion among the living," Gwydion put in, "someone of faithfulness and valor, who will not shirk from doing great deeds, whatever the cost. And we hope, Logan of Somerset, Logan the Brave, that this champion will be you."

"Me?" Logan exclaimed. "I don't see what use I could be!"

"Oh, you can," St. Patrick assured him.

"So, what do you say?" asked Gwydion, "Will you help us?" Under his breath, so that only Logan could hear, he added, "Be bold, lad, I'm with you!" Then Gwydion stepped back, waiting for his answer.

Logan had the sense that not only Gwydion but all the storytellers who stood before him and all the rows and rows of watching faces gathered round on every side cared mightily how he answered. He could not imagine why, but he felt them all leaning forward, hoping, praying, yet leaving the choice up to him.

"Of course," he said. "I will help you any way I can."

"It will be dangerous," Amergin said.

"I have given my word," Logan replied.

"Are you sure?" St. Patrick asked.

"By my life and honor," Logan said, "I will help you however I can. I swear it."

There were no cheers in the vast room, but there came a sigh, a delicate sigh, like held breath released, the sigh of something that dares, to hope, to live again.

When Gwydion came up to him, Logan saw that there were tears of joy in his dark blue eyes. "Well spoke," he whispered.

"And now," Gwydion cried aloud, "the Gifting!"

"The Gifting!" the others cried joyfully.

Now there was music—merry, spirited music. The Storytellers led Logan to a table on which were five glasses, each filled with a different colored liquid.

"Each of these wines contains a different magic," Gwydion explained. "Here is the Yellow wine of Wisdom, and the Green Wine of Healing Ability. The red wine will give he who drinks it Good Fortune for all

248

of his days. The blue wine gives Endurance, the strength to withstand all tests."

The wines gleamed in their glasses, as if lit by fire from within. "What about that clear wine on the end?" asked Logan, pointing to a glass that held a substance as humble as rain water, compared to the rest.

"Oh, that," said Gwydion, "that is the Clear Wine of Poetry." He shrugged. "Whoever drinks that will live haunted by the mystery of things, forever putting beauty into rhymes, going deep into things, far out to things, high up to things, feeling at home everywhere, and nowhere."

"You may take one sip from one glass," Scheherazade said, "and whichever wine you choose, the magic it endows will be with you forever after."

"Choose well, Logan of Somerset," said Amergin, smiling.

"Choose well," echoed St. Patrick and Taliesin. It seemed a solemn moment, yet out of the corner of his eye, Logan noticed that St. Patrick was biting his lip, as if struggling not to laugh, and Scheherazade was casting him a warning glance that only seemed to make his struggle worse.

"Choose," said Gwydion, his face unreadable.

"Well," said Logan, "this is a great gift, and one it would not do to take lightly. Common sense tells me that the Red Wine of Good Fortune is nothing to sneeze at. And my conscience tells me that I should choose Wisdom, or the Ability to Heal. God knows, the world needs both those things. Or, I suppose I really should choose the Blue Wine of Endurance. It sounds like I'm going to need it, and I don't think I'm a very strong person on my own, really."

At this point, St. Patrick snorted, yes, actually snorted, with ill-suppressed laughter.

"Shut up, Pat," Taliesin hissed good-naturedly. To Amergin he added in an undertone, "He always does this."

"But somehow," Logan continued, a bit confused by the behavior of the bards, but struggling on, "my heart pulls me to that Clear Wine of Poetry. It's not that I don't appreciate the other Gifts," he added worriedly, "I do. But it's Poetry, it's the Mystery of things that's brought me to this moment, and it's that Mystery that causes the love of God in me, the way the sun and rain cause a flower to bloom. It looks like rain water," he added fondly, "clean and quiet, like the droplets running off a holly leaf. Yes, that's the one for me, the Clear Wine of Poetry."

Now a great cheer did rise up among all the watchers gathered round. There was happy laughter, too, and music brighter than ever. St. Patrick, wiping tears of delight from his eyes clapped Logan on the back, and Scheherazade put a garland of flowers on his head.

"You chose truly," Gwydion explained, smiling himself. "You would have gotten the Gift of whichever wine you chose, but because you named the one that was truly in your heart, you now may take one sip from each glass."

"You mean," said Logan, the truth slowly dawning on him, "that the game was rigged?"

"Only for the Good," Gwydion replied sweetly.

And so he, Logan of Somerset, Logan the Brave, Logan the Daft, perhaps, took one sip from each of the wines. The Red wine of Good Fortune was as sweet as nectar; Wisdom and Healing tasted faintly medicinal, like comfrey tea and mint, and the Blue Wine of Endurance was first as bitter as gall, yet turned to the flavor of rose water in his mouth. But the Clear Wine of Poetry had no taste at all, only a freshness that seemed to reach his very soul, as rain reaches buried roots.

Then, to his sorrow, the golden mist and the watching faces began to fade; the mysterious music grew dim.

"No!" he cried, "please, come back!"

"Someday," a thousand voices softly called, "someday!"

"Your heart will tell you when you are needed," Amergin told him.

"And what to do," Scheherazade added.

"The time will be soon, very soon," cried Taliesin.

"Be strong," said St. Patrick, "like the old Irish heroes, who called themselves 'Conn,' because it means 'The Hound.' Hounds of God, they wanted to be. Be thou, Logan, as loyal as a Hound to Goodness, be Thou as Swift in God's Service, as Sure in Scenting God's Truth, as loud in calling out God's word as a Hound that gives chase! Logan Conn Deos, Logan the Hound of God, shall Thou ever be to me!"

One by one, the bards were fading, slipping into the golden mist that itself was fading. Now only Gwydion remained. He was pulling a traveling cloak over his shoulders, a cloak of blue as dark as a night sky that seemed spangled with living stars, twinkling upon the cloth.

"There's one more thing," Gwydion said, "now that you've tasted our wine, I hope you won't drink quite so much of yours. You'll need a clear head for what's to come."

"Not another drop of spirits shall pass my lips," Logan began, ready to promise anything in the midst of the magic he now felt.

"Don't go too far," Gwydion said. "A drop or two of ale never hurt anyone. Just use it for celebration, not for escape. Oh, and don't be surprised if tests and trials come to you now—they generally do after such encounters." Then he laughed his joyful, ancient laughter and added, "I ought to know! Hung from the tree of Ys, cast into the ocean depths, exiled to the wilderness. Yes, I ought to know, for here am I, to tell the tale!" The light in his dark eyes sparkled like sunlight on dark waves. "Good bye, Logan the Brave," he cried, "Logan the Poet! I shall see you again, but for now, farewell."

The darkness of his cape seemed to fade into the darkness between the trees, the cry of his farewell seemed to blend with the sighing of the wind, until Logan found himself again alone upon the mound. It was not yet dawn, but in one of the oaks, the first bird of the morning poured out its song.

"Greetings, Logan, Subject of the Shining Mound," called a pure young voice behind him. Logan turned and saw the children gathered a few feet away, watching him.

"Good dreams?" Osgood asked.

"Good dreams," Logan replied. He remembered little of the ceremony that followed, so dazed was he by the events of the night before. He swore an oath of fealty, to protect the mound and all that lived there. Then Wyatt seemed to be trying to feed him some soggy scrambled eggs and cinnamon toast, saying, "But you need to eat, Wogan," while Claire nodded in the background. Charles and Osborne had insisted he kneel so that they could put on his head a foil circlet just designed as the proper attire for a Bard of the Kingdom.

"Now you must see the mound," Osgood intoned.

On any other morning, Logan's curiosity would have been all aquiver at the prospect. On this day, however, his thoughts were so full of the vision he had just seen that he simply said matter-of-factly, "Oh, all right."

He had a little trouble crawling through the tunnel, being neither as small nor as agile as the children, but he made it in the end. He found himself standing in a cave, a room, really, for it was certainly man-made. It was much bigger than he would have expected and poorly lit with candles the children had brought. He had the impression there were cloth hangings on the walls, and dried flowers. He was about to examine the place more carefully, when his eye lit upon an object, sitting in state, on a crude table in the center of the chamber.

"Wait a minute," he exclaimed, "that's the chalice!"

"Yes," said Osgood proudly, "but recently returned to its proper home."

"I took it," Wyatt said proudly.

"You took this chalice from the museum?" Logan asked, feeling himself definitely reentering the cold light of day.

"No, the man fwom the twain did that! But I took it fwom him and bwought it here! Gwand, isn't it?"

"Oh my God," said Logan, shakily taking a seat on one of the cloth-covered crates that served as thrones. "When did you do this?"

"Just yesterday," said Wyatt proudly.

Logan thought fast. With any luck, the Pennington sisters might not even have missed the chalice yet. Perhaps he could return it, and no one the wiser.

"It really should go back to the museum," he said.

"No!" the children protested fiercely.

"It wath in danger there," Wyatt explained, speaking so excitedly that his spit flew in all directions. "The golden man, the man fwom the twain . . ."

Logan felt he had had as much mingling of fantasy and fact as he could handle, at least for the moment. Some game about golden men and trains was beyond him.

"Calm down," he said gently. "Now that you've taken it, I don't suppose it will hurt anything for it to stay here a little while longer." To himself, he thought, *I'll just speak to the Pennington sisters; they'll be understanding, and then I'll find a way to get the chalice back that doesn't upset the kids too much.*

He rose and bowed solemnly to Osgood. "Your Majesty, I am deeply grateful for the honor paid to me this day by your Kingdom. But now I fear that I must attend to my duties in the village, lest my absence cause alarm and a search be mounted."

"Of course," said Osgood graciously. "We understand the problem very well."

As he walked back to Far Tauverly, Logan was not overly worried about the chalice. *I'll speak with Althea and Lettice right away,* he thought, *and with Gwen. She's had experience with children, she'll know how to handle the situation.*

That settled, he allowed his mind to return to the mysterious events of the night before, events which seemed to have filled him with great peace and well-being.

It wasn't until he ran into Tom, the milkman, outside the post office that Logan heard the full story. "And Scotland Yard knows about it?" he asked faintly.

"Absolutely," Tom assured him. "Heard it from Lettice herself, not ten minutes ago. Twenty-four hours, Lord Greniston has, and then the professionals and the press and everyone'll be in on it. Send in television crews and all, I shouldn't wonder. Of course, everyone knows it was those Walmsley kids that did it. . . ."

"Oh, no," exclaimed Logan. "I mean, I scarcely think they'd have the skill."

Tom shook his head knowingly. "Don't underestimate those kids. Clever as a cartload of monkeys, they are. I just hope they give it up willingly, so the police don't have to be too hard on 'em. That's a family that doesn't need any more trouble."

"That's for certain," Logan replied. His first thought had been to talk to Gwen. So much had gone on in the last few hours that he needed help to think clearly. Upon entering the inn, however, he had met not Gwen, but Filipo.

And so the morning had proceeded, until now, when he realized that whatever action he took, he would have to decide upon it alone. Standing in the morning sunlight on the road to the Greniston land, feeling tired, chilled, and unshaven, he wondered about the bards, the storytellers he had met but a few hours before: *Had it all been merely a dream?*

"No," he said aloud, "it was real. It is real. And whatever it was that I met there, I know it was truth itself. It was the brightest, noblest thing I've ever seen, ever felt. It lives, and it has found refuge, somehow, at that mound. But how sacred will it remain if reporters start traipsing all over it? I must act quickly and trust that if the chalice is returned, Lord Greniston can keep the investigation quiet. Surely there need not be a big brouhaha in the press, if I go willingly? I wonder how many years they'll give me? Stealing a National

Treasure—it's got to be good for twenty years, at least. Twenty years! I'll be eighty when I get out, if I last that long. Twenty years without seeing any friend, without wandering the green fields—without ale! Perhaps I can say I found the chalice in a ditch or something. No, that would never do. The Yard would never stop until they'd found the thief. The news would leak, the press would come. God, I can just see the tabloid headlines now: 'Space Aliens Steal and Return Mystery Chalice.' Curiosity seekers would flock. No, they want a thief, and they shall have one. And better me than those kids. I've had my life."

Logan started to take another sip of Watney's, then paused with the bottle halfway to his lips. *I can t*, he thought desperately. *I can t go to prison now, not now, when it s all just begun! Whatever happened in the mound, it was real! I ve waited all my life to encounter something like that, and Gwydion said, promised, that he would return, that I would be charged with great deeds to do. I can t give up that! And yet, perhaps this is my great deed to do: to create a diversion so that the kids are safe and the mounds are left in peace. Is this what Gwydion meant? Perhaps I ll never know. But what I do know is what I must do.*

Resolutely, he stood up. He looked at the bottle in his hand, and thought, *And I don t need this to help me do it.* He poured the remaining ale out on the grass. With a determined stride, he headed again toward the mounds.

Well, he thought wryly, *if I go to jail for theft, I won t have to worry about back taxes or a place to live anymore.* He laughed. Then he realized that he had just supplied himself with the perfect motive for his crime.

"That's it!" he exclaimed, delighted. "I stole the chalice to try to sell it to some collector so that I could pay my back taxes. Genius! There's actually some truth in it. Perfect!" He smiled, and thought, *Now the real challenge faces me. It s going to be no easy matter, wresting that chalice from the Independent Kingdom of Greenstone!*

***

"Too bad Logan had to leave in such a hurry," remarked Filipo, as he and Gwen sipped their cognac in the garden behind the inn.

"He's definitely not himself this morning," Gwen said.

"I'm not sure you are either," Filipo remarked gently. "This argument with Greniston that you told me about has upset you more than you care to admit."

The bells of St. Aethelrood's tolled twelve noon. "I suppose I really must go tell the Walmsleys the bad news," Gwen said reluctantly. "I promised I'd be back by noon. There's no point in putting it off; Lord Greniston's not likely to change his mind."

She must have spoken more bitterly than she intended to, for Filipo crossed his arms and looked at her coolly.

"What's wrong?" asked Gwen warily.

"Nothing," said Filipo. "I'm just amazed."

"Amazed? At what?"

Filipo shook his head admiringly. "There must be something really special between you and Greniston."

"Why on earth do you say that?" asked Gwen.

"The level of trust," replied Filipo. "You've known the man less than a week, and already he's given you *carte blanche* to invite people to live in his ancestral home."

"Well, . . . he didn't exactly give me *carte blanche*," Gwen admitted.

"Okay, we won't quibble over words. But he obviously has immense trust in you, and there's clearly already a deep understanding between you. I mean, if he didn't explicitly give you permission to invite them, it's because he didn't have to. Clearly, you have the kind of communion that enables you to know that it would be perfectly okay to invite a family of—nine, isn't it?—plus some pets, I gather, into his home, without asking first."

"Well, okay, I didn't ask," Gwen acknowledged. "But damn it, he should have offered it! Calls himself Lord of the Manor, and then he doesn't even know what's going on in his own village! He never even uses two thirds of that manor, anyway."

"Now wait a minute, Babe," Filipo said, "slow down. I'm on your side, remember? But what actually is the situation here? Perhaps you'd better explain it in detail."

"Well, like I said, I found out that the Walmsleys were being evicted and had nowhere to go. And it just sort of . . . came to me that they could stay at Greniston Manor. I was sure Greniston would agree, so I promised the Walmsleys they'd have some place to go inside of four hours."

"Ah," murmured Filipo. "Ever one for the cautious approach, that's my Gwen."

255

"And then," Gwen continued, "I ran into Lord Greniston on the street, and actually, he didn't agree. In fact, he was a real bastard about it. So I gave him a piece of my mind."

Filipo burst out laughing. "I see," he said. "You invited a bunch of strangers to live in his home, and when he wasn't thrilled about it, you told him off." He shook his head wonderingly. "You've got a style all your own, Gwen. If I was a girl trying to romance a man, it would never occur to me to go about it like that!"

"Who's trying to romance him?" asked Gwen defensively.

Filipo raised an eyebrow. "Oh. Perhaps I am mistaken. But we'll go into that later."

There was an uncomfortable pause. Suddenly Gwen started to laugh, ruefully. "I really went too far, didn't I?" she asked.

"Well, look on the bright side: Think of the hundred or so other villagers that you didn't invite to share his home."

"Oh, Filipo," wailed Gwen, caught between laughter and tears, "what have I done? I've promised the Walmsleys something I had no right to promise, and I've really insulted Lord Greniston!"

She looked so dismal that Filipo said, "Buck up, kiddo, it's not the end of the world!"

"Lord Greniston will never speak to me again."

"Somehow, I doubt that, *Carissima*. But right now, why don't we go to the Walmsleys' and tell them the actual situation, and take it from there? Who knows, this Greniston fellow may be willing to reconsider, if we approach him right."

"Never," said Gwen mournfully. "I've ruined everything, forever. But you're right, we should go tell the Walmsleys, before they get their hopes up anymore."

As they neared the Walmsleys', her step grew slower and slower.

"I can't believe I got myself into this," she sighed.

Before they could even open the front gate, Mrs. Walmsley came running out of the house toward them.

"Miss Fields!" she cried. "Lord Greniston was just here!"

"Oh no," Gwen whispered to Filipo, "he's already refused them, before I had a chance to explain!"

"Miss Fields, I don't know what to say to you," Anne Walmsley continued.

256

"I'll bet," Gwen agreed. "I don't know what to say to me either. Or to you. Mrs. Walmsley, I'm so—"

"A true gentleman," the other woman interrupted happily, "that's what Lord Greniston is! But I know," she added with a wise look, "that you inspired him. How can we thank you?!"

"Thank me?" said Gwen.

"I'd invite you in for tea," Anne Walmsley continued, "but we're packing the china right now. Lord Greniston is sending Robert, at three, to begin moving our things. I can hardly believe it," she added. "When you said you knew of a place we could stay, I never dreamed it would be Greniston Manor! Why, I've never even seen the inside of it! And Lord Greniston himself coming to invite us!"

"Ah, so everything is clear for you to stay there?" Filipo asked, since Gwen appeared to be speechless.

"Yes, we can stay as long as we need to get back on our feet. And Lord Greniston said there would be some work for Bob as well. I've never known a day to go from bad to good so quickly!"

"*Mirabile*, isn't it, how such things can happen? By the way, *Ma Donna*, please allow me to introduce myself: Filipo Alejandro Vargas de le Reyna, a visiting friend of Gwen's, and at your service."

"Yes," said Gwen, who finally seemed to have recovered the power of speech, "and Filipo, this is Anne Walmsley." She added, fervently, "I am so, so glad that everything worked out!"

Mrs. Walmsley smiled. "Ah, but you always knew it would, didn't you? Well, I don't mean to rush you, but I must get back to packing. But I'm sure I'll be seeing you soon, at the manor house, no doubt. Now, if I could only find those children! It's funny. First those men from the school board wanting to see them, and then Lord Greniston asking after them, too. He wouldn't say why, but he's gone toward Knobbly Hill looking for them. They sometimes play at the Roman ruins there. I hope they haven't done anything too terrible, but I must say, their escapades seem minor, now that we've got a home to go to! This is indeed a happy day!"

"Thank God!" Gwen sighed, as they walked away.

"Yes," mused Filipo, "all's well that ends well, for the Walmsleys."

"Oh, yes, of course. But I was thinking of Lord Greniston, too. Thank God that he is a gentleman, after all! He may not ever speak to me again, but at least he hasn't let himself down." Her face was such a naked mixture of relief and sorrow that Filipo had to hide a smile.

"I don't think you've seen the last of Greniston, *Carissima*," he said. "It sounds to me like your temper did him a world of good, and when he calms down, he'll realize that. I bet you'll be dining together before the week is out."

Gwen shook her head. "I don't think I'll ever see him again, Filipo! And all because I acted like a stubborn fool! I just don't think!" Her chin trembled, and tears began to spill down her cheeks.

"Hey, hey," said Filipo, pulling a large, polka-dot handkerchief out of his pocket, "here now, let us stop weeping over milk that isn't necessarily spilt yet! That milk may still be safely in the bottle, no matter what you may think. There, that's better. Now, to take your mind off love's ups and downs, why don't you show me these famous mounds?"

"The—the mounds?" Gwen asked, still perilously near tears.

"Sure! It's a beautiful day, I'm in the mood for mystery, and perhaps we'll round up some stray Walmsleys on the way."

"Well, all right," said Gwen, rubbing her eyes and brightening a little. "There's a good chance, actually, that the children are somewhere in the woods."

***

From his hiding place in the Walmsleys' tree house, Luan Tey watched Filipo and Gwen head down the road toward the Greniston Woods.

It had been an eventful morning already. First, at three a.m., he had stolen the false chalice that he had left behind at the museum. By stealing the chalice Miller thought to be the real one, he had hoped to spread a little more confusion. Later, he would send a message to his employer saying that the chalice had already been gone when he reached the museum. Miller would not know who to trust.

After the theft, Luan Tey had searched the rainy streets of Far Tauverly for a hiding place that would conceal him but also allow him to keep an eye out for Wyatt. The tree house had presented itself as a perfect sanctuary. Through a crack in the boards, he had watched the eviction notice be delivered to the Walmsleys. Then he had heard, if not seen, Mr. Walmsley's reaction. After that, he had caught his breath when two of Miller's henchmen, Totino and Schmed, had arrived on the family's doorstep, looking for Wyatt. They had claimed to be from the school board.

It chilled him to see them there so quickly; it meant that somehow, some way, Miller knew far more than he had expected. Fortunately, the mother had not seemed to know where any of her children were, and Totino and Schmed had left, for the moment, at least. Next, Luan Tey had seen Gwen and Anne Walmsley's encounter and Gwen's subsequent fight with Greniston. After she left, Greniston had stood in the road for several minutes, evidently lost in thought. Then he had burst out laughing and walked up to the front door of the house. A few minutes later, he left, with a radiantly happy Anne Walmsley waving in his wake. Then Gwen had returned, accompanied by this new man, and now they were off again. In all this coming and going, Luan Tey had caught no glimpse of Wyatt, or the real Chalice. Now this auburn-haired woman, who seemed to be having such a busy morning, had said she might know where the children were. He decided to follow her.

***

"'The way that can be named is not The Way,'" said Filipo. "Wonder what old Lao Tsu would have thought of these woods. Funny how this mist has come up. It was sunny when we left the Walmsleys. Now there's all these pockets of mist between the trees, and it's very still. . . ."

Filipo came to a halt in the middle of the forest path, and began to feel the air with his left hand held up near his head.

"What are you doing?" asked Gwen.

"Ley lines," he answered matter-of-factly. "Searching for 'em. Yep, I knew there was one. Feel it? About three feet above the ground. It's a blue one."

"Is this one of your psychic things?" Gwen asked cautiously, remembering very well her friend's delighted interest in everything from astrology to water dousing and herbal medicine.

"I keep telling you, Babe," Filipo said good humouredly, "these aren't 'my' things, they are the planet's things. A ley line is a line of energy. They crisscross the whole earth. Maybe they are like her veins, I dunno, but I can feel them, and, sometimes, I can see them. There are ones it's good for us to be near and ones we should leave alone. This one feels good. Some people say the fairies travel along them. I bet people have had . . . experiences . . . around here."

"Experiences? What do you mean, *experiences*?" asked Gwen.

"Oh, you know," replied Filipo, who was preoccupied with following this line that was clearly real to him but that Gwen could not see at all, "in some places, it's easier to connect."

Gwen remembered her own experiences that day in these woods with Logan—not only the cry she had heard in her dreams but how close the past had seemed.

"Maybe you're right," she whispered, feeling that the mist itself seemed to be watching them.

Filipo gave her a quick, searching look, but all he said was, "Hmm. Let's get to those mounds before this stuff gets any thicker."

Even the sound of their own footsteps was muffled by the misty stillness. Gwen barely recognized the trail. The path turned a corner and, suddenly, the outlines of oak trees and the mounds themselves loomed toward them, much closer than she had expected them to be.

"Listen!" whispered Filipo. "Voices!"

Gwen froze, listening. Filipo was already creeping forward. He paused, listened again, then waved for her to join him.

"They sound so close," he said, baffled, "but there is no one here!"

Indeed, the mound was deserted, so quiet beneath its veil of mist that not even a leaf stirred. Yet within that mist, disembodied voices seemed to converse.

"I can't quite make out what words they are saying," whispered Gwen, her own voice tight with fear. "Yet they seem right beside us."

"Yes," agreed Filipo, who looked as if even he had gotten a little more "connection" in this magic spot, than he had bargained for. "It's as if they are coming out of the air, or the ground beneath our feet."

Suddenly relief flooded Gwen's features. "That's Wyatt's voice!" she exclaimed, "Wyatt Walmsley! I'd know that lisp anywhere!"

"And there's a deeper voice. It sounds like your friend, Logan." They moved cautiously closer.

"I think those voices are coming out of the mound itself," mused Filipo. "They have found a way to get inside the mound!"

"That means there must be an opening somewhere," said Gwen. "But I haven't seen anything like that. . . ."

His head tilted to one side, Filipo began to walk back and forth across the misty clearing, listening intently.

"Over here," he said, "near these bushes. I can't see the opening, but I can hear the voices very clearly. Sounds like they're arguing." Gwen crept closer, and listened.

"The Independent Kingdom of Greenstone absolutely refuses to allow the theft of its treasure," intoned a haughty voice that Gwen was sure was Osgood's.

"Theft! You're fine ones to talk about theft, you lot!" The voice was clearly Logan's.

"It wathn't theft," put in an unmistakable voice, "it wath the withful wecwaiming of our own object! I keep telwing you, Wogan, I thowed it fwom the thief who took it, the man on the twain!"

"Wyatt, there's no time for games right now. Give me that chalice! Whether you understand it or not, I am trying to help you!"

Now, Osgood cried "Sentinels! Seize him!" Following this were the sounds of a scuffle.

Suddenly, Logan seemed to burst out of the bushes, spattered with mud, cradling something in his arms. An instant later, Osborne and Charles also shot out of the hidden entry to the mound and tackled Logan from behind, each grabbing an ankle. Logan toppled onto the damp grass. He looked up and met Gwen's gaze. His jaw dropped.

"Well, well, well," said Filipo, eyeing the object in Logan's arms, "there's that chalice!"

Speechless for the moment, Logan simply stared at his friends, as the remaining Walmsleys emerged from the hidden entrance.

"Miss Fields!" gasped Wyatt, as soon as he saw her.

Osgood stared fiercely at Filipo. "There is an Intruder in the Woods," said Osgood solemnly. Only Claire seemed unperturbed.

"It's not what you think," said Logan to Gwen and Filipo, "whatever you think it is."

Wyatt ran forward and grabbed Gwen's arm. "Oh, pwease, Miss Fields," he begged, "don't wet him do it!"

"Do what?"

"Say he stow the chalwice, when it was me who did it, except it was weally the man on the twain, and . . . "

"Silence, Sir!" thundered Osgood.

"No!" protested Wyatt hotly, "I won't be quiet! Ith's too important! Wogan can't go to the powice to pwotect us. . . ."

Years of teaching had left their mark on Gwen. She clapped her hands, glowered fiercely enough to intimidate even Filipo, and said sternly, "Now settle down, all of you! Tell me what is going on here, and speak one at a time, please. Logan, you first."

"I stole the chalice," said Logan, managing to rise to his feet as he spoke. "I stole it, and now I'm going to confess and hand it over to the proper authorities. And that's all there is to it."

Filipo snorted with laughter. "Forgive me," he said, "but you, a thief?"

"No one stole it," interrupted Osgood. "It was simply returned to its true home, here, at the Shining Mound, by us, The Royal Family and Sole Citizens of the Independent Kingdom of Greenstone. Now, Sentinels, seize the chalice!"

"Not so fast," said Gwen. "We're going to get to the bottom of this before anyone does anything, and anyway, seizing is not polite. Now, Logan Knowelles, there is no way you stole that chalice!"

"Oh, yes I did," said Logan, as if reading from a script. "I took the chalice, and I'll take the consequences. I did it in order to—to fence the goods and pay my back taxes."

Filipo laughed harder than ever. To Gwen he said, "Don't you see? It's crystal clear! The kids took it, and Logan is trying to protect them. A noble gesture, but it won't work, Logan. You may be a great storyteller, but you're a terrible liar. One hour of questioning by the Yard, and they'd have found twenty holes in your story."

Logan looked desolate, which simply added the final confirmation to his innocence.

"Don't worry," Filipo added. "We'll get the chalice returned, in a way that implicates no one. I already feel a plan cooking; but all in good time."

Gwen looked severely at the children. "I don't know what's going on, but you seem to have caused a great deal of trouble. Your mother is very worried about you, and Lord Greniston is looking for you, too. "

"Oh, no," blurted out Wyatt, "They musthn't come looking here! Thith ith the Kingdom, The Secwet Kingdom, the . . . "

"Silence, Knight," cried Osgood. "Too much has been said already!"

"On the contrary," replied Gwen, "not enough has been said at all."

"Gwen, please," exclaimed Logan, "surely you can deal with the children later? Right now, we have a crisis on our hands. This chalice must come to light soon."

"Agreed," said Filipo. "But have no fear, what's been stolen can be replaced. Just leave that to me."

With quiet authority, Filipo took the chalice from Logan.

"Don't worry," he said. "By nightfall, this chalice will be back in that little museum, with no one the wiser as to how it came there."

Filipo looked positively pleased at the idea of this reverse burglary. Secretly relieved, Logan still protested, "If it just reappears, there will still be questions. Everyone in town thinks these kids took it. There will be questions."

"I wouldn't worry too much," said Filipo. "The Walmsleys seem to have found a staunch ally in Lord Greniston. In fact, they are soon to be residents of Greniston Manor." Logan's jaw dropped.

"It's true," Gwen assured him. "Swindon finally evicted them, but Greniston has offered them a home for as long as they need one. They are moving today."

"What?" exclaimed Osgood. "We're going to live at Greniston Manor?"

The other children exchanged astonished looks.

"It's a long story," Gwen said, "which I will tell you on the way to your new home. But we really must go now, before anyone else comes looking for you. You don't want them to discover your entrance to the mounds, do you?"

The vehement chorus of "No"s that followed this comment assured Gwen that she had some leverage.

"Then you must come along, and quickly, too," she said firmly.

The others looked willing enough, but Osgood hesitated. "We cannot leave the chalice in the hands of a stranger," he said, glaring at Filipo.

"I promise you—I swear it, on my sacred word of honor," said Gwen, trying to find the kind of language that might appeal to Osgood, "that you can trust this man. He will return your chalice to its proper resting place at the museum. He is one of my dearest friends, and, and—a Knight Errant in search of Adventure. Destiny has led him from lands far across the ocean, so that he may be of service to your realm at just this moment."

Osgood considered this and then nodded slowly, evidently satisfied on that point. In the face of the massed strength of three grown-ups, he seemed to accept the inevitable return of the chalice—for the moment, at least. However, he clearly took his duties as monarch seriously, for he now said, "There's still the mounds. We cannot leave them unguarded, especially now, when the woods are full of strangers. There must be at least one Sentinel posted here."

Logan glanced from Osgood's face to Gwen's. Sensing a Battle Royal in the making, he quickly said, "Your Majesty, as the newest member of the Independent Kingdom of Greenstone, I gladly offer my services as sentinel. I will faithfully guard the mounds until midnight, longer if needed. Is that satisfactory?"

"Well . . . ," Osgood hesitated.

"Yes, it is," said Gwen, giving Logan a grateful smile, "eminently satisfactory. Now come on everyone—to Greniston Manor!"

"Yes," said Osgood, attempting to regain some measure of authority, "to the manor!"

With a happy cheer, the children headed across the mound in the direction of the manor house. Gwen looked back over her shoulder and said to Logan and Filipo, "Good luck! And please be careful. I'll see you both later."

Then she and the children headed down the path and quickly disappeared into the mist.

"Send ale," Logan called wistfully after them, feeling that he had at last earned a pint. "I'm recovering from a nasty shock."

Now that only Logan and Filipo remained, a measure of stillness began to return to the mounds.

"Quite a place," Filipo said. "And I bet it was really something to be inside that mound." Logan nodded. "That was a really stupid idea," Filipo added amiably, "to say you were the thief. But the motive—the motive was impeccable. I salute your honor. But now, to practicalities. I'm going to go replace this old cup before it causes any more trouble. I'll meet you back here when I'm done. Might take a while, though."

"That's quite all right," Logan assured him. "I actually welcome the chance to be alone here for a while."

"In that case, *mon ami, adios*," said Filipo with a bow. He turned back toward Far Tauverly. The mist closed behind him, and Logan was left to his musings. He never noticed the slender figure that slipped out from the shadows of the trees and followed Filipo as silently and swiftly as the mist itself.

CHAPTER FIFTEEN

The sound of the vacuum shattered what was left of Lord Greniston's concentration. His search for the young Walmsleys at Knobbly Hill had proved unsuccessful, so he had returned home, hoping to piece together what meager clues he had about the chalice theft in the calm of his study, but calm had scarcely been the word for what he met.

"Damn it, Will," Greniston sighed wistfully, looking at the bust of Shakespeare, "you who know of more things in heaven and earth than are conceived of in my philosophies, do you know how to convince an Irish housekeeper that the arrival of a band of wraggle-taggle brats and their parents doesn't necessitate a major cleaning?"

Shakespeare did not reply concerning this point. His insights into kings, rogues, jesters, noble Moors, and star-crossed lovers were well-known to Greniston, but what the bard might have made of Mrs. Fitzpatrick and the Walmsleys remained unknown. Now Greniston heard the housekeeper's voice, albeit from several rooms away, raised in imperial command to Robert: "Now mind you move that dresser quietly, we're not to disturb Lord Greniston."

At that point, Greniston threw down his pen with a reluctant chuckle. "It's all her fault, Will!" he exclaimed, "that Miss Fields! Inviting the Walmsleys to stay, no less, to share—or is that shatter?—the sanctuary of my hearth and home, the peace of which, it is true, I have rarely noticed but will now miss acutely, I am sure. Good God, Will, they even have an infant! Hope she gets over it fast!"

Greniston sipped his Earl Grey tea, now cold, and sighed. Then he got up and began to pace around his study, talking to Shakespeare the while: "If Miss Fields thinks it's such a good idea that they move in here, why doesn't she come along and take care of them?"

He paused in his pacing and mused, "Not a bad idea, that! She can wipe their snivelly little urchin's noses, take them for happy nature rambles, brew their revolting little cups of bostom, change their nappies—I believe that's the term—counsel the parents, walk their bloody dog, and generally keep the whole tribe of 'em out of my hair!"

Greniston grinned, more and more delighted with this plan the more he contemplated it. "No, Will," he continued, "it's not a bad idea at all. Of course, she wouldn't see the delicate justice of it. She would think I actually wanted her to stay here so I could be near her. And then she might be worried about what I might want in return: the Lord of the Manor has designs on the innocent young governess. Yes, I'm sure she has read her share of Gothic novels, from Jane Eyre to—curses be upon her!—Henrietta Amberly. So, if she did move in here, she'd be waiting every moment for Heathcliff—or should it be Rochester? Which one is more appropriate? Must look it up in the Brontë-saurus—to ravish her in the hours of the night. God, it's so American; everything reduced to a hackneyed plot, a soap-opera!"

Had the bust of Shakespeare been able to speak, or had Gwen been there, either of them might well have reminded Greniston that both the Brontës had been as English as English could be and that, indeed, many of Will's own plays could well have been graced by lurid paintings from Henrietta Amberly's own cover artist: a full-color rendering of Richard III seducing Lady Anne over the coffin of her late husband, say, or of Romeo climbing onto the balcony as a well-endowed Juliet bent down to watch his progress.

Now Greniston paused in his monologue and met the level, marble gaze of Shakespeare. "Who am I fooling?" he sighed. "She wouldn't think like that at all. And the truth is, I do want her here. It's only been a few hours, yet I miss her, Will. And she was right, this morning, when she called me a pompous ass. Although—did she call me that, or did I? Well, it was in the air, that's for certain." A faint smile played upon Greniston's lips as he remembered his encounter with Gwen. "She's like a lion cub when she's angry," he mused. "Fearless, yet adorable, somehow. At least, in retrospect, after one has bandaged up the major wounds and removed the odd claw or two she left impaled in one's ego. Yet, was it only last night, Will, that she and I kissed in the moonlight? Well, perhaps it was partly cloudy, but the kiss was the key point; that kiss certainly wasn't the first thing on her mind this morning, though. Wonder if she even thought about it since."

At this point, Greniston frowned, his feelings a little more bruised than he would have cared to admit, even to himself. "Americans probably don't think about such things," he muttered. "They just kiss, gush, and move on. All part of the soap opera of life. . . ."

Will made no comment on any of this, but something about his quiet gaze made Greniston blush when he met it.

"You're right, that was unworthy of me," he said in an embarrassed tone. "And it was definitely unworthy of Miss Fields . . . of Gwen . . . , who,

I am sure, does not bestow her kisses lightly. Oh, Will, who's fooling who? She was the first thing on my mind this morning, then I backed off from it, like I always do when things get too close. Deirdre always reminded me of that . . . like that time in Nice. . . . We'd spent a splendid week together, . . . so splendid that things would seem to be leading, inevitably, to that little march down the aisle. . . . It's not for nothing they call it a march; there's a distinctly military side to the female of the species. . . . They strike up the march, and there she is, waiting for you at the altar, Ready Reggie, in lace gloves. . . . Yes, Deirdre was right, I've always bolted when even the thought of that loomed nigh. Yet, with Gwen, the thought seems to have come up after just one kiss! Egad, Will, I'm in deep trouble here. And on top of everything, I've made a complete ass of myself about the Walmsleys. Of course, they need a place to stay. Well, they're here now, but she may never know about it. She may have already packed her bags and left Far Tauverly forever."

It was a sobering thought. So sobering that Greniston actually stopped in his tracks and wondered if he should dash to the accursed telephone on the far side of the manor house and ring up the inn, to speak to Gwen. But before he could even put down his tea cup, there was a loud knock at the door.

"It's her!" he exclaimed, fairly leaping across the room. "She's returned to give me a further piece of her mind! Thank God!"

Greniston flung open the door to his study and found himself gazing not at Gwen but at old Mr. Steadworthy, the family solicitor. For a moment, he felt quite disappointed, then he burst into laughter.

"Is there something amusing about my appearance?" the elderly solicitor asked crisply. "A collar stud missing? A smudge on the nose, perhaps?"

"No, no," Greniston assured him. "I was just expecting, or hoping to expect, well, someone quite different, that's all. But of course you are most welcome, come in, please. . . ."

Mr. Steadworthy stepped rather stiffly into the study, his bowler hat in one hand, his briefcase in the other.

"Have a seat," Greniston said. Steadworthy looked rather pointedly around the study, until Greniston realized that there was not a single chair, save his own, that was not covered in books and papers.

Greniston shoved the papers off the nearest seat and said heartily, "There you go, just make yourself at home. I'll ask Mrs. Fitz to fetch us some tea."

"That won't be necessary," said Mr. Steadworthy coldly. "My business here will be very brief."

Lord Greniston raised an eyebrow. He had never seen the old man so crusty.

"Now then," he replied in placating tones, "you must at least have some refreshment. Come all the way from London. Can't think why you didn't just ring me on the phone."

"I did. Seventeen times, in the last two days. Ten of those times, Mrs. Fitzpatrick said that you were away, and she did not know where to reach you. The remaining seven times I was told that although you were back, you had given absolute orders that you were not to be disturbed, 'even if Atherton or God Himself rings,' was, I believe, the phrase."

"Oh." Greniston looked nonplused. "I'm sorry," he said. "I didn't even think to say that a call from you would be an exception."

"That is just as well," Steadworthy replied. "I should not wish any call of mine to take precedence over a message from the Almighty."

Greniston shifted uncomfortably in his chair. Before the stern, unwavering gaze of the family solicitor, he felt like a small boy caught smoking his first cigarette behind the school yard. In this case, he was not certain what he had done wrong, but he got the definite impression that he had brought dishonor upon his name, his family, and his lands.

Trying to make amends for his nameless crime, Greniston said, "Since I've forced you to make this trip, you must let me at least feed you well. I insist." He went to the door, and thundered into the hall: "Mrs. Fitz! Tea for two! And those biscuit things!" He glanced back at Mr. Steadworthy and then added gruffly, "Please!" To the solicitor he added, "Very fortifying, her biscuits are."

Sighing deeply, Mr. Steadworthy said, "You really haven't read them, have you?"

"The biscuits? Really, Steadworthy," said Greniston, a bit too jovially, "I've heard of reading tea leaves—but biscuit crumbs? Might be worth a try, of course. I saw a man in India once . . . "

"Damn it, Sir," exploded Mr. Steadworthy, "is nothing serious to you?" The old man pounded the arm of his chair so violently that Greniston was afraid he might injure his frail bones.

"Mr. Steadworthy," he said gently, "clearly you are upset. I seem to have offended you somehow. I assure you, it was unintentional. Please, tell me what it is I've done to distress you."

The old solicitor struggled for a few moments to regain his composure and then spoke, in formal tones, words that he had obviously considered at some length: "Lord Greniston, it is with deep regret that I must terminate an association that I have enjoyed with your family for over fifty years, but there is no other honorable course."

"You're quitting?" Greniston asked, his face white with real shock. "You can't quit, Mr. Steadworthy. You don't quit, it's not in your character. Why, it's like hearing the sun say it's going to stop shining, or the Earth saying it's decided to turn to mush."

"I shall see you through this current crisis, of course," Mr. Steadworthy interrupted, as if Greniston had not spoken at all, "but that's the last."

"Current crisis?" Greniston asked.

"The matter about which I sent four letters and and made seventeen phone calls," Steadworthy said dryly. "The land dispute with Swindon."

"Oh, that," said Greniston, "well, of course, that's been dragging on for years now, hasn't it? I did read one of those recent letters; it's around here somewhere." He glanced casually at the chaos of papers on his desk, then gave up the search. "It'll never come to anything," he said confidently. "Tempest in a tea pot."

"I hardly think you would be so sanguine if you had read the most recent letter I sent you," the lawyer replied.

Greniston poked around the desk again and then pulled out a special delivery letter, unopened.

"I'll just read this now," he said meekly. "Good thing you're here, anyway, in case there are any questions."

"Quite," replied the lawyer.

"Dear Lord Greniston," Greniston himself began to read, "I am writing to you with some anxiety, fearing that my previous three letters have unaccountably gone astray. I fear that this means we have lost even more time, a loss we can ill afford. Let me therefore state bluntly: Geoffrey

Swindon intends to take the issue of zoning for land usage before the Far Tauverly town council on Tuesday, May 7th, at nine a.m. As you know, for him to build the condominiums he has in mind, on the land commonly known as the Greniston Wood . . .'"

Greniston looked up from the letter, and muttered darkly, "Condominiums, indeed! He can't even build a bloody sand castle on that land. He doesn't own it!"

"His lawyers are making quite a good case to the contrary," Steadworthy remarked, "and despite my repeated warnings, you have neglected to contest his recent claims in court. Now the matter has grown far worse, as most things do with neglect. If Swindon does obtain a zoning change and the support of the villagers, there is every chance that the courts will award him ownership of the land as well."

"The villagers will never support this!" thundered Greniston.

"I fear very much that they may," said Steadworthy. "Far Tauverly has a severely depressed economy—perhaps you had not noticed—and the jobs and income that such a building project would involve, not to mention the influx of Bristol commuters, which would mean more business in the shops, is something the villagers can scarcely afford to say no to, even if they might wish to do so."

"Preposterous!" Greniston exclaimed. His further comments were interrupted by the arrival of Bosley, the butler, with tea, Mrs. Fitzpatrick's biscuits, and sandwiches and lemon cake besides.

"Ah, that looks most inviting," said Mr. Steadworthy, who seemed to be growing calmer and calmer as Greniston grew more and more upset.

Greniston, on the other hand, seized a sandwich and bit into it as if he wished it was Swindon's neck instead of mere bread and cheese. Struggling to remain civil, he glanced at the butler and said, "Weren't you away for a few days? Enjoy your holiday?"

"Actually, Sir, it was a funeral I attended," Bosley remarked smoothly.

"Oh my God," said Greniston contritely, "how boorish of me! I am sorry."

"That's quite all right, Sir, I would scarcely expect you to remember," Bosley said, rather ambiguously.

Steadworthy gave Greniston a significant look and then continued fastidiously to put exactly a teaspoon of strawberry jam on a biscuit. After

Bosley finished slowly fussing with cutlery and doilies and left the room, Greniston exclaimed, "Hearing set for May 7th! But that's only four days from now!"

Mr. Steadworthy, his mouth full of biscuit and tea, merely nodded.

"How did things come to such a pass?!" Greniston thundered.

Steadworthy took his time, patting his lips carefully with a napkin before replying, "Perhaps I should be asking you the same question. In many areas, beyond the scope of a mere court hearing. For instance, the welfare of this place."

"Oh, come, come, you can't seriously say that the economy of Far Tauverly and the perfidy of Geoffrey Swindon are my fault!"

"In part, yes," the solicitor replied. "All the other generations of Grenistons have done their best to look out for the village, to find ways to bring money into it without disturbing the weave of things. You have, I admit, always been generous in donations to the church, and the museum, and particular families in need. But you have shown no interest whatsoever in the deeper issues."

"The villagers have always known they could turn to me for help," interrupted Greniston.

"Perhaps," sniffed Steadworthy, "but people do have their pride, you know. Not everyone who needs assistance relishes the thought of begging for a loan, hoping you are in a good mood that day. And it is far easier for you to be the beneficent Lord of the Manor, doling out alms here and there, than to actually provide people with a means to support themselves."

"I've been busy," growled Greniston. "Military service, diplomatic corps, three terms in Parliament, trivial things like that!"

"They can indeed be trivial," murmured Steadworthy.

"And then I do have my work."

"Ah, yes, playwriting," Steadworthy mused. Apart from Deirdre, he was the only other person who knew the true identity of Leo Hawker.

"Your tone implies that writing is but a child's game," snapped Greniston.

"On the contrary," said the older man sincerely, "I have the highest opinion of your writing. But I happen to agree with Auden when he said something like

'Put your life into your art, yes;

272

Hope that your poems will save you from hell;
But what of the poems that you might have written,
Had your life been lived well?'"

Greniston looked so shaken by this that Steadworthy softened. Slightly. "I don't mean to say that your life has not been good," he explained. "Indeed, for a lesser man, it has already been an exemplary existence: honors at Cambridge, brilliant and sometimes courageous service to your country in many capacities, accomplished author, and a benefactor, if not an instigator, in local affairs. Yes, many could say you had already earned the right to rest upon your laurels—all this in a man barely forty."

"I'm glad you don't find me a total blot upon the Greniston escutcheon," muttered Lord Greniston.

"Certainly not. As I said, yours has already been an exemplary life— for a lesser man. But you are not a lesser man. From you, one would hope for more."

"What more?" asked Greniston.

"Greatness," Steadworthy replied.

"Greatness?" said Greniston, as if trying out a word in a foreign language. He smiled ruefully. "It is not a word associated with our modern times."

"You write of it in your plays."

"My plays are set in other times. I fear true greatness would go unrecognized in this era."

"The truly great do not care for recognition," the lawyer replied.

"Virtue is its own reward, is that what you mean?" Greniston asked thoughtfully.

The older man smiled. "Something like that."

Greniston rose and went to the windows. For several minutes, he stared moodily out at the misty lawn. Meanwhile, Mr. Steadworthy nibbled a slice of lemon cake, looking, as he did so, remarkably like an elderly field mouse. When he was finished, he brushed all the crumbs into the palm of one hand and took them to the windowsill for the sparrows to find.

Greniston spoke at last. "I suppose that your exit from my employment is to do with this lack of greatness?"

"In a way," said Steadworthy. "The Greniston lands and the Greniston name are not something you earned in your own right. They were

273

given to you as an inheritance, in trust. I am sad to say that you seem to be more interested in what you can get from this inheritance, than in what you can give to it."

"I'm afraid I don't see your point," said Greniston coolly. "I've never been one to squander the family funds."

"No," said Steadworthy, "that I'll grant you. But you have used the wealth and privilege to which you were born to provide yourself with a buffer from the needs of those around you. I know you are very aware of the needs of those at distance," the lawyer added, before Greniston could interrupt him, "and I applaud your charitable and largely anonymous good works in Africa and the Orient. I have not forgotten that side of your character, my boy. But what about matters closer to home? You have looked the other way while the state of Far Tauverly has grown steadily worse. You might have tried to help, in a big way, but you didn't. And you have let Geoffrey Swindon nurse some family grudge against you until it's grown to real hatred. Yet there was a time, as lads, when the two of you were friends. You can't tell me otherwise, because I remember it. You could have done the noble thing, years ago, and tried to sort this foolish feud out, man to man. Perhaps you two could finally be the ones to end an enmity that's been brewing for centuries. Instead, you have more and more, of recent years, sequestered yourself away, in a private world of writing, refusing even to read your mail or answer your phone, until at last things have indeed 'come to this pass,' as you so aptly put it. Now a goodly portion of the Greniston lands and perhaps the very character of Far Tauverly are in jeopardy. I cannot respect such an attitude, and what I cannot respect, I cannot serve. Unless you are prepared to take up your responsibilities in a fashion more worthy of your name, I fear I must give you my notice. I'll do my best for you at the Town Council meeting, of course, but there's an end to it."

Greniston continued to stare moodily out at the land, the Greniston land. Without turning around, he said, "What would I need to do to win back your services?"

"For a start, you could come with me to this meeting next Tuesday and plead your case."

"Plead my case?" exclaimed Greniston, outraged, "There is no bloody 'case!' The Grenistons own this land free and clear. Whatever documents to the contrary Swindon has come up with are just some kind of forgery!"

"That well may be, but they seem to be convincing the courts nicely, so far."

"Impossible!"

"I wish it were. But the fact is that the condominium blueprints are drawn, a building crew has been engaged, and work will begin the very hour a court finally gives its approval. We would have a chance to appeal, but I can tell you even now that it wouldn't be worth the effort. When finished, the buildings should have an excellent view of your front lawn. The mounds I believe Swindon intends to leave intact, as a sort of park at the center of the complex. He does mean, however, to bulldoze the oak grove and carve out an ornamental duck pond. And then, of course, there will be parking lots."

"Parking lots!" sputtered Greniston. "This is unbearable! Am I to be harassed by gawking commuters, polluting the weekend peace with their lawn mowers and their picnics? Bloody intrusion - "

"Enough, Sir!" retorted Steadworthy, losing his own temper at last. "Has nothing I have said made any impression upon you? Do you never think of anything save yourself? An intrusion upon your privacy indeed! It will be far more of an intrusion to those two-hundred-year-old oak trees! But they, of course, have no voice to complain! They must rely upon yours to speak for them! You can't let them down! I will not stand by and see you jeopardize all that has been given to you because of your foolish pride and your refusal to face the facts! You have a responsibility to the people here, and to the land."

"What am I supposed to do," interrupted Greniston, "go around organizing nature walks, so that people can appreciate 'the land' you keep droning on about? 'The land' would be doing just fine, if it weren't for that idiot, Swindon!"

"For your information,' Steadworthy said icily, "idiots like Swindon are taking over England and just about every other country with land left to grab as well! If they have their way, every village on earth will become a bland, commuter haven, and every forest a shopping mall. This will surely happen, unless men like yourself, Lord Greniston, take up the cause of a better way of life, not based solely on greed, and champion it. I had thought you would, I had thought you were the man for it. But I see now that I was wrong."

Steadworthy sighed. Suddenly all the fight seemed gone from him. He looked old, sad, and drained. He picked up his hat and briefcase and walked slowly to the door.

"I will inform you of Tuesday's outcome by mail, and my secretary will send you a list of excellent solicitors to choose a replacement from," he said quietly. "Good bye, Lord Greniston."

The old man's hand was on the door before Greniston cried "Steadworthy! Wait!" The solicitor turned, a gleam of hope in his old, birdlike eyes.

"This seems to be my day for hearing home truths," said Greniston ruefully. "And I can't say that I receive them graciously. But you're right, right in everything you've said. I've become a self-absorbed ass, and oddly enough, you are the second person to tell me so today. The third, if you count me talking to myself. The truth is, I don't like myself very well just now. But that is no reason to take it out on you. I do want to fight this thing. Will you stay in my employ, and help me?"

Greniston held out his hand. For a moment, neither man moved. Then, with a great sigh of relief, Steadworthy seized Greniston's offered hand and shook it vigorously.

"Delighted to help," the old man said with a twinkle in his eye, "delighted to."

***

As Filipo walked toward Far Tauverly, he was assailed by a rare feeling—rare, at least, for him—that of caution.

It isn't going to be so easy to return this chalice as I led Logan to believe, he thought. *There's a lot of attention focused on it now. I feel like the one fox in the neighborhood, and every hound's loose. They'll smell the thing in my pocket, if I don't act fast. And I'm a stranger and therefore suspicious. People have already seen me around the place, the museum's closed now, and no doubt under surveillance by Tweeverton's boys in blue . . . hmmm . . .*

Filipo paused in the road, considering all the factors. From where he stood, he could not yet see any house, only dense, mysterious forest, looming at him out of the mist.

It could be any century, right now, he thought, *and I could be anyone. Yes, and I could be anyone, . . . anyone at all. . . .*

He smiled to himself. "This is going to be good," he mused aloud.

He continued walking until he reached the edge of the village and caught sight of St. Aethelrood's. He was operating on sheer instinct now, and instinct told him that, in the church, there might be something useful for the plan forming in his mind.

There's a note on the door, he realized as he approached. *Wonder what it says?* He opened the note, which was addressed to Emma Beatty, and read: "Dear Mrs. Beatty, please leave jumble sale clothing in basement. So sorry I couldn't be here, have driven up to Bristol, to see about some yew clippings. Sincerely, Rev. Sterling."

Filipo chuckled softly to himself. He looked up at the mist-hidden heavens and murmured, "Gratzia Deos! Jumble sale clothing, couldn't be better!"

He opened the church door and stepped quickly inside. Then he stopped and sent out the radar of his instinct, listening, scanning.

No one else here, . . . at least, no people. . . . Definitely a church with a presence . . . but that's not my business, right now. . . . Where's the basement? Must be over here, down these stairs. . . . Where are the lights?

Finding the switch and proceeding carefully down the narrow, curving stairs, Filipo found himself in what was clearly the church storage room. Choir robes and costumes for Christmas pageants, including wise men's crowns, cotton wool beards, and a tattered pair of angel's wings, were piled in one corner. On a large table were several cardboard boxes marked "Jumble Sale."

That Mrs. Beatty could appear at any moment, Filipo mused. *If she does, I'll present myself as a hobo, just looking for a warm jacket. . . . Better ditch my own coat, make it convincing."* Filipo took off his raincoat and Basque beret and added them to the jumble sale items. *So, . . . what have we here? . . . Hmm, nice tweed cape . . . and that wool cap. . . .*

A few minutes later, an elderly Scottish gentleman emerged from St. Aethelrood's. He wore a tweed cape and a weather-worn, shapeless wool cap. Much of his face was hidden by bristling white whiskers, shaggy eyebrows, and a thick pair of spectacles. Whistling "Scotland the Brave," he limped jauntily down the church steps. He walked with the aid of a mahogany cane, whose handle was carved with an elephant's head.

As he drove up to the Rectory, the Vicar was surprised and somewhat flustered to see a stranger studiously admiring the Norman front of the church.

"Oh dear," the Vicar muttered under his breath, "why do they always come when I'm out? People get the wrong idea, they think I'm never here! They don't understand about yews; it's so rare to get a chance at a really good clipping."

The Vicar hurried toward the stranger. "Good afternoon," he called out. "Can I help you?"

There was no response from the old gentleman, who continued to peer nearsightedly at the stone carvings by the door. "Hello?" Not until the Vicar was close enough to tap the visitor's shoulder did the old man seem to notice him.

"Och, ye moost be the Vicar," the stranger said, in an almost incomprehensible brogue. "These auld Norman churches are a true delight! Saw one yesterday near Truro, but doesn't hold a candle to this one. Nice clipping you've got there," he added. He bent down and peered through his spectacles at the twig the Vicar held. "Och! Yew!" he exclaimed with pleasure. Wonderful stoof, yew! Don't tell me you're the yew artist," he added, gesturing toward the enigmas that dotted the lawn. "Marvelous work! True act of devotion!"

"Why, why thank you," stammered the Vicar.

"Yes, well," the Scotsman said, clapping him on the back with amazing heartiness for so old a gentleman. "Carry on, laddie! Och, I probably shouldna call ye that, you bein' a man o' the cloth and all, boot everyone seems like a lad when you get to be my age, you know."

"That's quite all right," the Vicar assured him. "At fifty three, I welcome any assurances of youth that come my way."

"Och, you'll be good for ninety," the Scotsman said. "Well, I must be on my way. So I'll leave 'yew' to it—get it? I'll leave 'yew' to it? Och, well, never mind." Limping, but vigorous, the stranger headed back toward the road.

"Won't you stay for tea?" the Vicar called out. But the Scotsman, who seemed to be a bit hard of hearing, was already headed toward town, whistling "The Bluebells of Scotland" to himself.

Nice chap, the Vicar thought. *So rare to find someone who appreciates yews. Leave 'yew' to it? Ah, a jest, now I get it! Leave 'yew' to it, yes, quite amusing.*

Chuckling to himself, the Vicar entered the church.

***

Mrs. Fitzpatrick beamed as she opened the massive front doors of Greniston Manor.

"Miss Fields! You've brought the children! Their parents will be so relieved Come in, all of you, please!"

Rather awed, the Walmsleys stepped over the threshold. None of them had ever been inside the manor house before.

"We're going to live here?" Osgood exclaimed. "Why, it's bigger than the church!"

"Look, real swords on the wall," cried Wyatt.

Mrs. Fitzpatrick looked pleased. "It's so nice to have young life about the place," she said. "Why, I remember when Lord Greniston himself was the same size as this little fellow." She smiled at Wyatt. "And what a lot of trouble he was! Though I'm not sure his sister wasn't even worse, but that's another story." She turned her attention to the children. "Now, then, I expect you'll be wanting to see your parents. Robert is helping them settle into the West Wing."

"This house even has wings!" said Wyatt in awe. "It can fwy!"

Everyone laughed, to his annoyance.

Just then, the door to Greniston's study opened, and his voice boomed out, "Mrs. Fitz, dear Mrs. Fitz, can you find a room somewhere for Steadworthy? He's kindly agreed to stay the weekend and help me sort out this land business." Then Greniston strode into the hall.

It was exactly what Gwen had hoped for, to encounter him again. Yet now that she found herself face to face with him, her one thought was to bolt and run. The careful speech of apology she had prepared seemed to have vanished from her mind. Somehow, she had imagined meeting Greniston alone, in some intimate corner of the manor. Now she found herself in a hallway crowded with the Walmsley children, Mrs. Fitzpatrick, and a rather distinguished looking elderly gentleman, who had just appeared in the doorway of Greniston's study. To make matters worse, the expression on Greniston's face seemed neither pleased nor angry. He glanced at her impassively, as if utterly unaffected by her presence.

"Miss Fields," he said, flatly.

"Lord Greniston," she replied, trying to sound equally formal and failing miserably.

Robert chose that moment to come strolling down the corridor, humming to himself. When he saw her, his face lit up, and he called out,

279

"'Lo, Miss Fields!" as if she were an old family friend. His warmth only made Greniston's coolness the more obvious.

"I only came to bring the children," Gwen blurted out, "I really must be going now," she added, backing toward the door.

Before she could escape, however, Wyatt went up to Lord Greniston, took his hand, and said gravely, "Thank you ever so much, Word Gweniston, for wetting us wiv in your wing."

Everyone laughed, and the tension eased.

"An associate, Greniston?" the elderly man asked.

"Oh, yes," Greniston replied. "Excuse my manners, I must introduce you all! Everyone, this is Mr. Charles Steadworthy, the family solicitor, and an old and trusted friend. Mr. Steadworthy, these are the Walmsley children: Osgood, Osborne, Charles—another Charles, like yourself—Claire, and Wyatt. There are two more, Amanda and Rutherford, but being of tenderer years, they are, I believe, hanging upon the skirts of their poor mother, sweetly shredding her sanity. They have all done me the honour to be my guests for a while."

"Word Gweniston took us in because Swindon convicted us," Wyatt explained.

"Evicted us," Osborne corrected.

"Whatever," Wyatt continued grandly. "We are to stay here as wong as we need! In a wing!"

"I see," said Mr. Steadworthy thoughtfully. To the children, he added, "Well, I'm very pleased to meet you all." He looked at Gwen. "And this fine lady is?"

"Gwendolyn Fields," Greniston said, his voice betraying nothing.

"An honour," said the lawyer, with a courtly bow.

"Well," said Gwen, after offering him her hand, "now that the children are safely here, I'm sure Mrs., Fitzpatrick can manage, so I'll be going."

"Weren't you going to stay to tea?" asked Greniston casually, as if such an arrangement had already been agreed upon between them. Before Gwen could reply, he turned to Mrs. Fitzpatrick and said, "I know you have just supplied Steadworthy and me with a magnificent tea, but now here's a whole new crew, all hungry, I'll wager, and I've some things to discuss with Master Osgood here that might go down a little easier with some cream buns on the side. And to tell you the truth, mulling over legal matters makes a man ravenous. I dare say Steadworthy could find room for a taste of Wendsleydale and some really good wine?"

"Indeed," the old gentleman agreed.

"Well, let's retire to the kitchen," Greniston said, "and raid the larder. This way, Miss Fields."

Mr. Steadworthy lingered behind for a moment with Mrs. Fitzpatrick.

"There seem to be quite a few changes at Greniston Manor," he remarked.

"That there are," the housekeeper replied with a smile.

"You know, Mrs. Fitzpatrick," the lawyer continued, "that Miss Fields, . . . I haven't seen a young lady like that in thirty years, at least. I can't quite find the words for it, but there's a rare quality about her."

"I was thinking the same thing myself," said Mrs. Fitzpatrick. "It's a pleasure seeing her here; she seems to belong in this place. And it's a pleasure to see Lord Greniston have some company, if you know what I mean."

"Indeed I do," replied Mr. Steadworthy with a smile, "indeed I do."

CHAPTER SIXTEEN

Filipo gazed through the kitchen window at the two elderly ladies, setting out their meager tea.

Must be the Pennington sisters, that Gwen mentioned, he thought. *The plump one looks easy-going, but the thin one, she'll be a challenge for . . . for . . . hmmm. . . . What is my name to be?*

A few seconds later, Althea and Lettice were startled by the sound of a thunderous knocking at the museum door.

"Oh, not another policeman!" exclaimed Lettice, almost in tears. "All those questions, I can't bear it!"

"Just ignore it," said Althea. "They'll give up and go away." Instead, the knocking grew louder.

"It almost sounds like someone is kicking on the door," said Lettice incredulously.

"I'll kick him," snapped Althea, who had had just as much visiting as she could stand, whether it was in the cause of justice or not. Grabbing a broom as a possible weapon, she charged through the door to the museum with Lettice following fearfully behind.

When she reached the outer door of the museum, Althea opened it a crack and yelled, "Go away! The museum's closed!"

"Clothes?" replied the man outside. "No, I don't want any clothes, lassie! Ah'm here to see the museum!"

In utter exasperation, Althea flung open the door, raising her broom like a spear. "Don't you understand?" she cried. "The museum is closed! Now go away!"

"Hay, d'ye say? That broom looks like straw to me. Good thought to bring it to the door. Never know who might be there. Has there been trouble in these parts?" the man asked.

He managed to push past Althea and into the museum, brandishing his walking stick.

"No need to worry now!" he cried. "Let any miscreant get within ten feet of you bonny ladies, and they'll feel the wrath of the Scots. You're safe now, me hinnies!"

"How did you get past the policeman?" asked Althea sharply. "There's one stationed outside."

"What's that ye say?" the man asked, leaning toward her.

"The po-lice-man," Althea began.

"No fleas, d'ye say," the Scotsman replied. "Nay, I've goot no fleas. At least," he added, looking rather worriedly down at his tweed cape, "Ah doona think so."

Before Althea could question him further, he pointed at one of the glass cases and exclaimed, "Look at that, would ye! A collection of signet rings! And that one's an 18th C. Carloon, I'll wager!"

Neither Althea or Lettice had the least idea what an 18th C. Carloon might be, but they were both pleased by this stranger's obvious appreciation of the museum.

"And joost look at that," he continued, bending over the case. "A colonial governor's ring, used in Malta in the Victorian era! And so well dusted it all is, too!"

"Well," said Althea, softening in spite of herself, "we do try to keep the place up. Are you a collector of signet rings, Mr. . . . ?"

"McCloud," the man replied. "Dr. Douglas McCloud. And no, ladies, I'm not a collector, merely a deep appreciator of antiquities." He gazed around the museum. "Wonderful place, wonderful. I am reminded of the private collection of Sir David Peavey of Argylle. But just between us, his prehistoric flints could never match the assortment I see displayed on the wall there. Just between tha three o' us, ye understand. Doon't let it get out."

"Certainly not," murmured Althea, wondering who Sir David Peavey was.

"We're ever so pleased you appreciate our little museum," Lettice put in, "but perhaps you could come back tomorrow? You see, we were just sitting down to our tea."

"Tea?" exclaimed the old gentleman. "Why, what a gracious invitation! Lead the way! Hope there might be time for a dram of sherry first. Of course, ye'll allow me to make a contribution to the museum's hospitality fund! Cooldn't eat a bite if I didn't," he added, pulling a handful of pound notes out of his wallet and thrusting them at Althea.

The two sisters exchanged a glance, well aware that the money in his hand could feed them for two weeks.

"Oh, 'Thea," Lettice whispered, "I'm not sure we should accept; it isn't quite right, you know. . . ."

"We'd be very pleased to have you stay," said Althea firmly, accepting the money while mentally calculating the possibility of a lamb pie on the morrow. "Come right this way to our kitchen, you can enter the house through the museum." To herself, she added, *It's not true that all Scotsmen are tightfisted.*

As he followed the ladies toward their kitchen, Dr. McCloud, also known as Filipo Antonio de Reyna, noticed the empty display case, where the chalice had obviously rested.

The job's two-third's done, he thought to himself, with a smile.

An hour later, the half-empty sherry decanter sparkled in the candlelight, enjoying the first sojourn it had made to the dining table in ten years. The Pennington sisters had brought out not only the sherry bottle but also the damask tablecloth and the best china for the occasion.

"And I think we can justify the candles," Lettice had said, "since it is late afternoon and so very misty out."

Now the remains of an eclectic meal were spread upon the table. The sisters had been hard-pressed to muster a substantial feeding for three and, in the end, had simply produced the entire contents of their larder, arranged as invitingly as Lettice's style and Althea's wit could muster. There were sardines, pickled onions, wheat bread, digestive biscuits, hard-boiled eggs, sliced apples, some beets, and a hastily prepared macaroni salad. It looked like the beginning, or the end, of perhaps five different meals.

"What a royal picnic that was!" exclaimed Dr. McCloud. "The combination had a mysterious ordering, a piquancy. In fact, I am reminded of a supper partaken at the Rajah of Pravesh's winter palace. I knew him in the old days, you know, joost after Independence. I was but a yoong laddy, and what a good friend he was to me. Did his own cooking, you know, an eccentric fellow. No one else would have thought of combining green olives, honey, and almonds in the same curry, but the results were truly memorable. Very similar to the feeling of this repast."

The sisters exchanged a worried glance, wondering if their guest could possibly be sincere in his praise. Dr. McCloud, with a sigh of evident satisfaction, said, "Sherry and beets—I moost remember this combination! I'm sure it's an elixir for the blood! Beets for iron, sherry for zip, probably ups the red blood count like nobody's business!"

"Wait 'til you see the sweets," exclaimed Lettice.

"I'm not sure there are any left," Althea remarked. "You know Wyatt found the hiding place again." A rare expression of affection softened her features.

"Ah, but there are a few," said Lettice triumphantly. "I put the remains of the box on top of the bookshelf in the other room. I'll just go get them."

"I'll come with you," said Althea. "You know you're afraid of heights."

While the sisters went to get the candies, Dr. McCloud was left to himself for a few minutes.

As long as I'm here, he thought, *I might as well draw them out about Greniston. I bet they know the life history of everyone in town. Not that I'll pry, bien sur. But Gwen seems serious about this man, whether she knows it yet or not. A little character check is in order, I think.* He glanced at the clock. *Hmmm . . . seven-thirty. Been here a while, pretty dark out now. Don't want that young cop coming in to check on the sisters and finding me here. He'll wonder how I snuck past him. I'd better get this reverse theft over soon. But there's time for a little more chat."*

The sisters returned to the table, proudly bearing a china dish of hard candies.

"Och now, would 'ee look at that!" exclaimed their guest. "Toffees, lemon drops, haven't had those since I was a wee laddie! Even some chocolate swirls—the infinite variety of our meal continues!"

He held up a raspberry sour to the light, as if inspecting a gem.

"Quality," he announced firmly, "that's what these have. A thing fast vanishing in our world! Why, even some of the noblest old families aren't really quality anymore."

"That is certainly not the case in this area," Althea said proudly. "Our current Lord Greniston has held fast to the old values."

"Not that he isn't stubborn as an ox," Lettice put in.

"Just like his Grandfather," Althea agreed. "He was a stubborn man. But good, and true, and generous."

"And this young laddie, Grenedine, Grenedier, ye'd say he's of the same ilk?" Dr. McCloud asked. "So many yooung folk seem ta be goin' downhill now-a-day."

"Not Lord Greniston," Althea maintained. "It isn't generally known," she added confidingly, "but he does a great deal to keep this museum afloat. And two years ago, when I needed my gall bladder removed -"

"Och," interrupted Dr. Douglas sympathetically, "pesky things. Better off without 'em!"

"Yes, well, when I did need it removed, I was afraid I'd have to go to the general hospital in Bristol, all among strangers. No money for a private one, you see. But then, one day, right through the mail slot came a bank draft that more than covered an operation right nearby in Tweeverton! It was sent anonymously, but I'm sure it was Lord Greniston."

"Oh yes," said Lettice, "of course it was. Just like what his father did for Mrs. Sanders in 1972, when - "

"That was in 1971, dear," Althea interrupted.

"Oh no, it was 1972, I know, because - "

"Excuse me, ladies," their guest managed to put in, "but I wonder if I might use the, er, necessary room?"

"Oh, certainly," Althea replied, "It's right at the top of the stairs."

As he limpingly ascended the steps, Filipo heard the argument continue.

Once inside the safety of the bathroom, Filipo locked the door and opened the window. He tested the eaves trough within his reach; it seemed well able to bear his weight. He swung out of the window and, clinging to the eave with both hands, climbed around the house with an agility that would have surprised the Pennington sisters. Once he reached the wing with the museum in it, he climbed lightly down the vines and crept in the window he had unobtrusively unlocked while examining the case of signet rings. He took the chalice from under the tweed cape (which he had kept on during their meal, pleading a chill) and replaced it in the broken case. Then he crept back out the window, leaving the shutter slightly ajar.

A mere three minutes later, Dr. McCloud limpingly descended the stairs and reentered the drawing room.

"Ladies," he announced, "I hate to cut short an evening of such rare pleasure, but glancing at your hall clock, I saw that the time had quite gotten away from me. 'Tis nearly eight fifteen, and I fear I've overstayed my welcome! Besides, you know, I'm visiting friends in Bristol, and they'll be worried if I'm not back soon."

"Must you go?" asked Lettice, with real regret.

"I fear so," said Dr. McCloud, as he put on his wool cap. "But I can't recall when I have enjoyed an evening more!" Suddenly he stopped. "What was that?!" he exclaimed. "That noise!"

"What noise?" Lettice asked nervously.

"Sounds like it's coming from your museum," their guest said.

"Oh no," said Althea, "not more trouble!"

Lettice wrung her hands nervously and looked near tears.

"Have no fear, ladies," Dr. McCloud cried, lifting high his walking stick, "You are safe! The Honor of Scotland defends ye! Now, I recommend a policy of stealth. I will enter the museum silently and surprise the culprit at his own game."

"Shouldn't we tell the policeman," said Lettice nervously.

"No time," Dr. M cCloud replied. "We must act!"

He crept through the door that led from the house to the museum, Althea and Lettice at his heels. Then, as Lettice switched on the lights, he cried, "Cease your felonious activity, you villain!"

There was no reply.

"The window," Althea exclaimed, "It's open!"

Lettice screamed. "The chalice—it's back!"

"That what they stole?" Dr. McCloud asked with interest. (He had, of course, heard the full story of the theft over supper. Three glasses of sherry had eroded Lettice's memory of the fact that the event was to be kept secret outside of Far Tauverly.) "Can't imagine why they took that," he added, "when that Carloon signet ring is right to hand, so bright and bonny."

"But who has returned it, and why?" asked Althea. "Really, this is very odd."

"And we didn't even hear a thing," fretted Lettice. "We were so busy with our, our bacchanalia, sherry and all! Oh dear, I shall have palpitations of the heart, I know I shall. Of course, it is such a relief! Now we can ring Lord Greniston, and he can ring Scotland Yard, and it won't have to be in the papers!"

"Papers?" said Dr. McCloud. "Never read 'em. Bad for the nerves. Look like your own nerves are a little piqued, let me find you a chair, lass. Marvelous herbal remedy for nerves, by the way. Comfrey leaf, or is it burdock root? Well, it's one of 'em."

Ignoring their guest, Althea turned to Lettice. "I'm going to call Lord Greniston right away. You know, it could have been the children who returned it, but didn't want to say."

"I suppose so," Lettice agreed, "although I hate to think it was any of them who took it in the first place."

"So do I," admitted Althea, "but whoever has returned it, we must let Lord Greniston know."

Seeing the ladies were no longer quite so shocked by the appearance of the chalice, Dr. McCloud decided to make his escape.

"Och, well, I'll be off then, leave you to sort out your little mystery."

"But the police will wish to question you," Althea protested. "It will only take a moment. Their car is right outside on the street."

"Card? Calling card?" Dr. McCloud asked. "Sorry, can't give ye one, don't use em anymore. Lovely custom, though. "

He stood for a moment, musing, perhaps on calling cards, perhaps on burdock root. Then, suddenly, he roused himself from his reverie, and said, "Well, ladies, now I really moost be going."

Althea breathed a sigh of relief. *Let the police stop him if they want,* she decided.

Dr. McCloud paused in the doorway and bowed deeply. Then, humming "The Pride of MacFairne," he wandered into the shadows of the backyard.

"He isn't headed toward the street," Lettice said.

"Too much sherry," Althea replied crisply.

"I could do with another glass of sherry myself," Lettice said wistfully.

"Nonsense," sniffed Althea, "we've the dishes to do."

***

Filipo and Logan headed through the rain toward Greniston Manor. Filipo made a beeline for the windows of Greniston's study, out of which a welcoming golden light spilled.

"We'd better go around to the main door," Logan said. Unlike Filipo, he wasn't certain they would be welcome at the manor house, but he was so relieved to know that the chalice was safely returned that he hadn't protested too much at the idea.

"I want to see this Greniston for myself, *amigo*, and there's no time like the present," Filipo had explained. Now he ignored the front door suggestion and, bounding the last few steps to the windows, tapped on the glass.

Greniston looked up with a bemused expression, then came over and opened the window.

"Hello," he said affably, gazing out at them as they stood in the pouring rain, "out for a stroll? Logan I recognize, but who are you?"

"Filipo Antonio de Reyna."

"Ah, yes, Miss Field's friend. Heard all about you at tea. Welcome to Greniston Manor. You're soaking wet, you'd better come in. Meet you at the side door."

A minute later, Greniston opened a nearby door and gestured for them to come in.

"I'm right in the middle of something," he said. "Can't chat. But you're more than welcome to come in and get warm. In fact, why not stay the night? Everyone else is. Steadworthy, my solicitor is here for the weekend, the Walmsleys just moved in, and Miss Fields is going to stay for a few days to help them settle in."

Filipo and Logan exchanged a quick, pleased smile at this news.

"But that still leaves the East wing free," Greniston rumbled on. "Twenty-seven rooms there, ought to suffice. Take your pick. Take as many as you like."

"Thank you!" exclaimed Logan. "I hope we aren't putting you out, though."

"Nonsense," their host replied. "Can't have the Bard of Far Tauverly, and Guest, catching pneumonia out in the rain. Especially on such a happy night. Just got some good news: that bloody chalice is back where it belongs! Don't know how, don't know who, but it's back in its little glass case. Pennington sisters rang up about it half an hour ago. The Yard might send a man down to ask a few questions, but no reporters, no big investigation. Thank God! So you've caught me in the best of moods!"

By this time, they had reached Greniston's study. He handed a bottle of brandy and two glasses to Filipo. "You'll need something to warm yourselves up," he said. "And you must have something to read." He looked over the nearest book shelf. "Let's see," he mused. He pulled out a volume and handed it to Filipo, saying, "You might enjoy this."

Filipo glanced at the title: *Three Centuries of English Armour: Seven Hundred A.D. to one Thousand A.D.*

"A good read," Greniston said with evident sincerity. "Once you get into it, you can't put it down. And for you, Logan, old friend, how about this?"

He handed Logan a first edition of *Campbell of Islay's Collected Tales of the West Country*.

Logan touched it reverently. "There are only five copies of this in the British Isles," he said. "Are you sure?"

"Meant to be read, meant to be read," said Greniston firmly. "And now, I must bid you good night, much to do. Pick out your rooms and pull the bell ropes. Eventually, young Robert will appear to make up the fires, bring you dry clothes, supper, whatever you need. There's some excellent stew, had that for supper myself. Goodnight."

Abruptly, but pleasantly, Greniston ushered them out of his study, and closed the door. Logan and Filipo shared a welcome nightcap in the hall, and then headed toward the East wing, to choose their lodgings.

***

It was with considerable interest that Luan Tey had watched Filipo's transformation into Dr. Douglas McCloud. He had also witnessed, from a safe vantage point in Lettice's prize peach tree, this mysterious Scotsman's acrobatic journey from the bathroom window to the museum and back, which he had no doubt involved the return of the chalice, the real chalice, to its place of honor beneath Lord Peter's portrait.

He thought it regrettable that so much creative skill would be wasted, but he had no choice. He could not allow either chalice, and especially not the real one, to remain in the museum long enough for Miller's men to find it. He was sure that they were by now watching the area as keenly but, he hoped, not as skillfully as he was. As soon as the old women in the house turned out their lights, as soon as the village grew quiet beneath the cover of night and rain, he would make his move.

***

At that same hour, Gwen sat in the portrait gallery of Greniston Manor. On the floor nearby, Claire and Osborne were engrossed in making their own crayon portraits of Lord Peter.

What a day of surprises it's been, Gwen reflected. Twenty-four hours earlier, she had been hiding from Swindon in a ditch. Then she had been rescued by Greniston. They had kissed. The chalice had been stolen. She had had a fight with Greniston. Filipo had arrived. The Walmsleys had been invited to the manor. She and Filipo had found Logan, and the chalice, at the mound. The chalice had been returned, and her friends were safely recovering from their adventures in the East wing (this she had learned from Robert).

Most memorable of all, though, had been tea with Lord Greniston. Gwen paused in her thoughts, smiling to herself.

Filipo was right, she realized. *We were dining together before the week was out— before the day was out!*

Her mind lingered over every detail of the meal. There had been other guests there, of course. All nine Walmsleys, in fact, and Mr. Steadworthy, not to mention Mrs. Fitzpatrick and Robert and Bosley coming in and out. Yet for her, Greniston, at the end of the table, might have been the only one in the room.

He had spoken but little to her, at first, being largely occupied answering the constant flow of questions from young Walmsleys—questions about everything from *petit*-fours (a new experience for them) to knights, castles, and the tapestry in the front hall. Yet, from time to time, Gwen had felt Greniston's gaze upon her. When she looked up, the brown eyes that looked back at her were sparkling with warmth and tenderness, as they had been in moonlight the night before.

He can't have just forgotten our fight, Gwen thought. *I must be imagining things.* Yet, every time their eyes met, there was that warmth, that friendliness.

Then Greniston had said, "I was hoping Miss Fields might be willing to accept the hospitality of Greniston Manor for a few days. For as long as she likes, for that matter."

Gwen had nearly choked on her sandwich as Greniston continued: "The house can certainly accommodate one more, and with so many other guests, I'm sure she'd feel safely chaperoned. What do you say, Miss Fields? You can still come and go as you please, but why not make this your home base? You could take your meals here, and I'm sure the children would adore spending some time with you."

"Oh, that would be such a help," Anne Walmsley exclaimed. Then she looked embarrassed. "Please excuse me, Miss Fields," she said. "You're on your holidays and all."

"I'd love to spend some time with the children," Gwen replied truthfully. "In fact, perhaps one day they might like to come to Stonehenge with Logan and me. If the two little ones stay with you, I think we can fit the rest in the rental car."

"Nonsense," Greniston interrupted. "Robert will take you all in the Rolls. Might as well travel in style. Take 'em to Stonehenge, take 'em to Timbuktu, take 'em wherever you like, Miss Fields."

"Would that be all right with you?" Gwen asked Mrs. Walmsley. Anne Walmsley had looked worried.

"I'll take very good care of them," Gwen had assured her.

"Oh, it's not the children I'm worried about," Anne Walmsley explained, "it's Stonehenge, so old and historic."

Greniston had roared with laughter. "Now, don't you worry! Those stones have withstood Normans, storms, two world wars, and poking scientists! I don't think your little clan will disturb them."

Privately, Anne Walmsley thought that world wars and conquering Normans were one thing, but Wyatt and Osgood were quite another. For a moment, her mind was filled with images of the two of them actually finding a way to knock the granite posts and lintels over, while crowds of horrified tourists ran for cover. However, the prospect of an entire day of relative peace was too tempting to resist.

"Well, perhaps in a day or two, when things have settled down," she agreed.

"Right," Greniston said. "Because come to think of it, I've some things to settle myself around here." He looked at the Walmsley children with mock sternness. "No one leaves town until this chalice case is cracked."

From Claire to Osgood, each child gazed back at Greniston in total innocence. Greniston sighed.

"I see they mean to present a united front," he said. "Suspicious in itself. I shall have to interview them one by one, see where their stories don't match."

Gwen blushed furiously as he spoke, realizing that at that very moment, Filipo was doubtless returning the chalice.

"You look quite furtive yourself," Greniston said jokingly. "Don't tell me you are the chalice thief!" Gwen shook her head.

"Well," Greniston said, "you are going to be my house guest. Mrs. Fitz, perhaps you can find a suitable room for Miss Fields? Robert, you go to the inn and get her things."

"Oh, that's all right," Gwen had said. "I'd rather do that in person and explain to Mrs. Hodges."

"Fine," her host replied, "but don't go now. Nasty weather, all mist and rain. Fond as you are of the damp, I'd rather think of you safe and dry between these walls. Wait until morning; I'm sure we can find you some things to get through the night with here. And now, if you'll excuse me, Steadworthy and I have some dreary legal documents to look over. I'm sorry, Miss Fields, that I can't be a more gracious host. But perhaps you might enjoy reading some more of Lord Peter's diaries. Robert can make a fire for you in the gallery."

Greniston and Steadworthy left the table. Gwen's heart was dancing. Greniston didn't hate her. He had invited her to stay in his own home. She had seen the pleased smile that had passed between Mrs. Fitzpatrick and Mr. Steadworthy when Greniston had assumed her acceptance. And Robert, while serving her a cucumber sandwich, had winked. She was glad to know that she had allies.

After tea, she took up Lord Greniston's suggestion and headed for the portrait gallery. Claire and Osborne came along to keep her company. It was very pleasant, sitting in that friendly room, reading Lord Peter's description of a visit to Chichester. Her only concern was for Logan and Filipo. When the phone rang in the distance, she dashed down the hall to the staircase and leaned over, eavesdropping.

First, she heard Greniston speak with Althea Pennington. Then he dialed Scotland Yard. "Atherton," he boomed happily, "It's back! No, an anonymous donor, so to speak. Yes, quite a relief, isn't it? Of course, of course, send a man up in a day or two. But we can keep it out of the press now, surely? Right, so distressing for the sisters. Well, thanks old bean, ta-ra."

From her vantage point on the stairs, Gwen gave a sigh of relief. Filipo's plan, whatever it was, had worked. She was just about to try to call him at the inn, when Robert came bounding up the stairs to let her know that he and Logan had both arrived.

"Wet as water rats, the both of 'em, Miss. Lord G. invited them both to stay. Mrs. Fitz is ever so pleased, says the house is filling up, just like in the old days. Anyway, they went straight to bed, those two. Logan asked me to give you this note. They was both sound asleep before I even brought their supper trays. Logan's in the Yellow Room, and that Mr. de Rain . . . "

"De Reyna," Gwen corrected.

"Right, him. He's in the Blue room."

"I'll see them in the morning, then," Gwen said, quite pleased.

"Oh, yes, I'm sure you will. Mrs. Fitz is already planning a breakfast to end all breakfasts, and everyone had better be there, I tell you! Poached eggs, ham, kippers, coffee, tea, three kinds of toast and five kinds of juice, fresh cream! I bet they don't eat so good at Buckingham Palace!"

"Probably not," Gwen agreed.

Logan's note said simply, "All is where it should be," but that and the knowledge she would see both her friends at breakfast were quite enough to end any worries she might have had. She returned to the portrait gallery with a happy step.

As she picked up the next volume of Lord Peter's diaries, Osborne looked up from his drawing, and said, "Will you read to us from those books?" so winningly that Gwen could not but agree. For over an hour, she read passages to the children: Lord Peter's struggles during a year of drought, his oldest son's near-fatal fall from a horse, the same son's recovery and pilgrimage of gratitude to Canterbury, the discovery of a geode full of amethyst while plowing a wheat field. It was all told in Lord Peter's fresh and colorful style, and Claire and Osborne seemed riveted by it. But of King Arthur and the mounds, there was no mention. Wistfully, Gwen took out her copy of Lord Peter's prophecy and read it aloud:

"'When the stranger comes to the lion's gate
And woods with Merlin's cry resound
When Knobbly Hill doth tremble and shake
Then must the treasure swiftly be found
A throne, a crown, a speaking sword
A golden lady, a silver lord
Twelve true jewels to shine and meet
Where gold springs from the ground

Then Arthur from ancient sleep shall wake
Deep in the greenstone mound
And rise to battle for England's sake
Summoned by a grail found
Encircled by gold
This is the time –
Light set free for all mankind

Yet, if no jewels be gathered there
This have I seen in waking dream:
Brightest light turns darkest night
Nor leaf, nor creature, nor human face
In this nor any other place –
World's despair.'"

Gwen sighed, wondering if she would ever unravel the meaning of the rhymes. When she glanced up, she saw that Osborne had at last fallen asleep under the table, but Claire was wide awake and gazing at her intently.

No sound broke the stillness, save the drumming of rain on the roof, the crackling of the fire, and Osborne's even breath. Claire came and stood beside Gwen and pointed to the paper with the prophecy on it.

"You want me to read this again?" Gwen asked.

Claire nodded, vigorously.

Slowly, Gwen read the lines again. She had the curious sense of being listened to, not only by Claire but by all the portraits on the walls as well. It felt as if the ghosts of the Grenistons were looking over her shoulder, yet she felt no fear; she was sure they only meant her well.

Claire listened intently to the prophecy, frowning at first. Then, suddenly, her face cleared. She dashed back to her paper and crayons and began to draw something as fast as her little hands could move. A few minutes later, she eagerly presented the result to Gwen. What exactly the drawing was meant to represent, Gwen could not quite tell. There seemed to be a necklace, of two strands. The outer strand was yellow; the inner had beads of many colors. Inside of the inner strand were stick figures of people.

"The colors are very beautiful," Gwen said cautiously, "but I'm not quite sure what it is. Is it a necklace?"

Disappointed, Claire shook her head. She pointed to the prophecy again, and then to the drawing, and looked at Gwen with an expression of urgent appeal.

"You want me to read it again?" Gwen asked. "Not tonight, honey. It's too late, and we should all go to bed. Come on; let's see if we can wake Osborne."

Undeterred, Claire tugged at Gwen's arm, and pointed at the prophecy.

"Not tonight," Gwen said, gently but firmly. "But I'll read it to you tomorrow. I promise. Now come along, it's time for sweet dreams."

***

Not too far away, in Far Tauverly, Davey Lee hunched in the shadow of the little alleyway that ran between the post office and the greengrocer. He wished the rain would stop, but there was no sign of that. He also wished he could light a cigarette, but he didn't dare risk it. The brief flare of the match, the faint scent of tobacco on the night air, might give him away.

The bells of St. Aethelrood's tolled one a.m. Davey had been watching from his hiding place for two hours. Across the street, in a parked car, were two men, also watching the quiet street. Davey had been tailing them all day. He didn't know what they were up to, but he knew it was no good. Not the kind of minor, interesting no-good that he himself quite enjoyed dealing in, but deep, serious evil. He could smell it.

Ordinarily, he would have looked the other way. Some things, he had learned, it's better for a bloke not to know about. But this time, it was different. This time, his Gran was involved. His instinct told him that the same thing that had drawn his Grandmother to the village had drawn these men as well. He didn't understand how the same place on earth could attract someone as good and sweet as Annie Lee and as rotten as those two slick men. But it had, of that he was sure. And it all had something to do with the chalice everyone in town was whispering about, and those kids in the woods—and the woods themselves.

"Salesmen, just passing through from Bristol," that's what the two in the car had told the old girl at the inn. *Salesmen! In a pig's tiny eye*, Davey had thought, as he sat eavesdropping from the bench outside the window. The village was filling up with people who didn't fit, including that little yellow-skinned fellow he'd seen tailing the Spaniard in the woods. The Spaniard was all right, Davey had decided; he seemed to be a friend of the elegant, auburn-haired bird. The yellow one, he couldn't figure. But the two in the car over there, he knew were rotten. They had left the pub at closing time and had been crouched out of sight in their car ever since. Davey wanted to know what they were waiting for.

It just didn't add up, any of it. Even Gran was acting strange. He had expected that after taking a few hours to recuperate, she would find the source of her Calling. Instead, she had replied serenely, "It will find me, soon enough. Just wait."

For the last two days, she had spent her time resting up, like she was waiting for something big. It made Davey Lee restless, so he had decided to figure a few things out on his own, and that hunt had led him to this stakeout in a rainy alley.

Suddenly, he heard a new sound, distinct from the drumming of the rain. It was the crack of a single twig breaking, in the darkness across the street.

Then things happened very fast. The little yellow man came running out of a dark, wooded driveway carrying something in one hand. The two slimy men leapt out of the car and stood in his path. They both had guns.

What was strange about what followed is that it was silent. The yellow man stared at the gunmen. He didn't seem surprised to see them, just frightened. The gunmen looked at him as if they knew him, too. One of them held out his hand and gestured impatiently, as if demanding the shiny object the little man held. The little man shook his head. One of the gunmen raised his arm and fired. There must have been a silencer on the gun; it made no sound above the drumming of the rain. He could see from the way the little bloke clutched his arm that he had been hit.

It happened in silence, like a dream. Davey Lee realized that was why the two men had risked driving into town in a flashy car and letting themselves be seen at the inn. It didn't matter. What they had to do that night no one would ever know of. It would happen as silently as a dumb show; they would shoot the skinny yellow one, stuff him in the trunk of the car to ditch somewhere far away, and make off with what he had done, the hard work of stealing. *No ethics*, Davey Lee thought with disgust. Besides, there was something terrible about the thought of a life being snuffed out so tidily and quietly, as if it didn't even merit a last yell of defiance.

Now the little bloke staggered and dropped the shiny object. It clattered on the cobblestone street and rolled right toward Davey's hiding place. One of the gunmen started to run after the goblet, or cup, or whatever it was; the other aimed to fire at the little guy again. On his face was an expression of cool enjoyment.

When he looked back on it, Davey felt it was probably that expression that had spurred him into action. Theft he had no problem with, but cruelty outraged him. Without stopping to think further, he flung himself onto the man who was diving after the goblet and kicked the gun out of his hand. The other gunman spun around, but fortunately, the little bloke recovered himself enough to seize the moment and hurl himself at him so that his aim went wild. The shot shattered a window of the greengrocer's, which clearly had been in nobody's plan. A light went on at the inn. With a look of panic, the gunmen raced to their car and took off. Horrified, Davey saw that they were headed right for the wounded man, who had fallen to his knees in the street.

Davey leapt forward and pulled the man out of the car's path. The gunmen sped away with a squeal of tires. More lights were coming on now, and down the street, a man's voice called, "Who's there? What's all that bloody racket?"

As gently as possible, Davey slung the wounded man over his shoulder. The man groaned and managed to say, "The chalice . . . "

"Don't talk," Davey advised, running as fast as he could for the shelter of the alley.

"The chalice, . . . don't let them find it," the little man insisted, "please."

He sounded so desperate that Davey relented. He eased the man down into a patch of shadow and searched the ground. Yes, there it was, under a dumpster. He pulled the object out and looked at it with disgust. So this was that chalice everyone was gabbing about. Not even silver. It was too bulky to fit in any of his pockets, and he needed his hands to carry the other man to safety. Yet he felt loathe to leave the cup there for those other bastards to come back and find.

He looked around for a hiding place. *The dumpster? Too obvious. There's no place, damn it.*

On the roof above the post office, a cat meowed. Davey looked up and saw an orange Tabby rubbing against the chimney. Davey grinned.

"Thank you, Brother Cat," he whispered.

The roof was a low one. It was the work of a moment to hoist himself up by the eaves and toss the cup into the chimney. It wasn't the best hiding place, but it would have to do. Chances were that if the gunmen came back, they would think he had the chalice with him, anyway.

What have I gotten myself into? Davey wondered. Well, there was no time to sort that out now. He heard more voices, down the street.

"Time to go," Davey muttered. "Afraid this'll hurt, but just hang on, mate."

He hoisted the wounded man over his shoulder again and staggered down the alley.

It was rough going through the village streets. Davey was more afraid of running into the gunmen again than of meeting any villagers. He breathed a sigh of relief when at last they reached the edge of the woods. As soon as they were a few feet into the shelter of the trees, he stopped, gently leaned the other man against a tree, and began to tear apart his shirt to improvise a tourniquet.

He thought the fellow had passed out; he had lost so much blood. But in the darkness, he heard him whisper, "Who are you? Why do you do this?"

Davey grinned. "Good question, mate. Let's just say I had a Calling to be at a certain place, at a certain time. Now shut up, and let me help you."

***

The clock on the bedside table said three a.m. when Gwen woke with a start. She wasn't frightened, only alert, as if someone had spoken her name, quite nearby. Yet there was no one in the room with her. She listened and heard only the sound of the rain and the sighing of trees in the wind. The old house creaked now and then, like a ship sailing into the high seas of a wild spring night.

Yes, the weather outside was wild, but inside, the house felt peaceful.

Here I am, a traveler in a strange house, Gwen realized, *yet I can never remember feeling more at home.*

Certainly, she had not felt at home in her apartment back in Denver. She thought of it now, that 650 square feet she had called her own, and it seemed as distant as a motel room in which she happened to have left a few things. Yet in this vast house, most of the rooms of which she had never glimpsed, she felt more at ease than anywhere else she had ever been. She knew that this was partly because Filipo and Logan and so many others she had come to care about were gathered together under one roof—including Greniston, of course.

Of course, she smiled in the darkness. She was just about to doze off again, when she saw something very strange. The door to her room, which she had left slightly ajar, slowly opened a few inches wider. Through the opening slipped a little circle of light, which wavered and danced upon the floor. The light was a soft, pale yellow, about five inches across, like a little halo.

Is it a ghost? Gwen wondered. She felt no fear of the little light, only curiosity.

It moved closer to her, right to the side of the bed. Then, to her surprise, at the edge of the light, on the floor, she saw toes. Five pink toes. Then another five, and then the outline of two small, bonny feet and the ragged hem of a flannel nightgown, then a small, pale face, surrounded by a tangle of long, red hair, bent close to hers.

"Claire!" Gwen exclaimed.

For a moment, the circle of light wobbled madly over the bedclothes and the walls. Then, with a click, the lamp on her bedside table was turned on, and the flashlight—for that was what it was, Gwen realized—that Claire carried was turned off.

"It's okay, Claire," Gwen said gently. "Couldn't you sleep?"

The girl smiled and gave Gwen a rolled up piece of paper that she had been carrying in her other hand.

"It's another drawing," Gwen said, looking at it. "Is this what you got up in the middle of the night to give me?"

Claire nodded.

"Well, it must be important to you then. Let's look at it."

As she glanced at the girls face, she saw that she was shivering.

"You must be freezing," Gwen said, "with no robe and no slippers. You'd better get under the covers with me, while we look at your picture."

Gladly, Claire clambered up onto the old bed and snuggled under the down comforters. Gwen held the picture to the light. It seemed to be a refinement on the theme the child had drawn earlier that night. There was again a kind of necklace of yellow beads. Inside the necklace, in another circle, were tiny people. They were no longer just stick figures. Gwen could recognize them now. There, that one must be Logan, she could tell from the scarf at his throat, and the brown lump at his side, that must be a mail satchel. Wyatt she identified by the pale cloud on his head, very like his flaxen hair, actually. There were Osborne, Osgood, and Charles, and Claire had put herself into the picture. And there was Filipo, she recognized him by the pancake on his head, which was probably meant to be a beret. And there, she saw with a blush of delight, were she and Greniston, hand in hand.

All around the outer edge of the necklace the paper had been colored dark brown, as if things were surrounded by a dark fog. Yet within the yellow necklace, the background was pale yellow, like the light of a candle flame. And near each of the figures were blobs of color: a lump of turquoise near Logan, a circle of emerald green sitting on Greniston's head, a cloud of golden orange around Filipo.

It was a messy, rather confusing picture, but obviously, great care had gone into it. Gwen imagined Claire, with her crayons and her flashlight, hiding in some corner of the manor, working for hours on the drawing and then making her late night journey through the dark corridors of Greniston Manor to find her.

"This picture means something very important to you, doesn't it, Claire?" she asked.

The child did not nod in reply, for, Gwen realized, she was fast asleep beside her, her lips slightly open, her sweet breath rising and falling in deep, even sighs.

Let her sleep, Gwen thought. *We can talk about it in the morning.*

She put the picture carefully beside the bed and turned off the light. Soon she, too, was drifting toward deep, untroubled dreams. For a moment, she thought she heard a woman's voice, very kind and soft, gently saying, "There now. There now. Sleep."

Yes, Gwen thought drowsily, *sleep*. And then she did.

Outside, the wind and rain continued. The wind sighed over the lawns of Greniston Manor, the rain fell steadily upon the trees and fields and upon the ancient house, as it had for centuries of springtimes.

Within, the rooms and halls of Greniston Manor felt surrounded by a tent of rain, and within it, peace filled the rooms. Everyone was deeply asleep now, from Robert in his quarters to the quietly snoring Greniston, stretched out on the couch in his study, a pen still in his hand. All was peace, all was stillness. Yet within that stillness, something joyful stirred. The silent manor was filled with a kind of glad expectancy, the feeling of a house on Christmas eve, or before a wedding, or when a longed for journey is about to be undertaken. Perhaps it was the spirits of generations of Grenistons feeling their ancient home filled with life again, at last. Yes, it may just have been that they woke while all else slept. The shades of many a valiant lord and lady, so glad after centuries of waiting to feel that, again, great events were on the move, unseen as yet but more real than much that can be seen.

CHAPTER SEVENTEEN

Gwen gave a glance of grateful farewell to the room at the inn and, humming to herself, she closed her suitcase. Then she glanced at her watch: eight-fifteen. Robert wasn't due to pick her up for another half hour. She decided to take her luggage downstairs herself and wait outside in the sunshine.

After the mist and rain of the day before, the morning sun made everything seem dazzling, fresh and new. Sitting on the bench outside the inn, Gwen felt that she and the Walmsley children couldn't have chosen a better day for their first outing together. Filipo was coming along as well "to help orchestrate the chaos," as he put it. They weren't going so far as Stonehenge today but instead to Bristol. The children had clamored to go to the zoo, and Gwen hoped to fit in a visit to St. Mary's Cathedral, where Coleridge had married young Anne Southey. As for Robert, he had said, "I don't mind where we go, Miss, as long as there's not a packing case nor a feather duster in sight."

Gwen's plan was to keep the children away from Greniston Manor as long as possible. Mr. and Mrs. Walmsley were busy settling into their new home and cleaning up the old one. Greniston and Mr. Steadworthy were sequestered in the study, searching through boxes of old family papers for documents relating to the land. In the kitchen, Mrs. Fitzpatrick and Bosley were in an ecstasy of planning. Lord Greniston had declared a formal dinner to be held on the next day. *House full of guests, might as well make the most of it, as they did in the old days*, he had reasoned. Dinner for seventeen, it turned out to be, including the Pennington sisters and the Vicar and his wife, to be invited from the village.

Now there was no seeming end to the lists to be made, the walnuts to be chopped, the linen tablecloths to be ironed, and the silver to be polished. To rise to so momentous an event, extra help had been engaged; Mrs. Hodges to help cook and two girls from the inn to clean and serve. The mere sight of a tray full of Waterford crystal on a sideboard that morning had convinced Gwen that the Walmsley brood had no place within five minutes of Mrs. Fitzpatrick in action, so the expedition to Bristol had been hastily proposed and agreed to by all.

It's going to be fun, Gwen realized. Normally no fan of zoos, she suddenly found, to her surprise, that she relished the thought of so ordinary an outing. Between mysterious cries in the night, haunted mounds, missing chalices, and love's ups and downs, the last few days had been extremely intense. She didn't want to run away from the adventure her life had become, but she found that the thought of a few hours reprieve, looking at penguins and elephants and buying balloons and ice-lollies, would be most welcome. She resolved to take the children for a huge lunch somewhere after the zoo. They would probably enjoy a Wimpy's bar far more than anywhere elegant, and that kind of meal she could afford to treat them. She wondered if she could be ruthless enough, after lunch, to leave the children with Robert, while she and Filipo slipped away to see the cathedral. She decided that she easily could. There might even be a nice, modestly priced dress shop in Bristol. She felt like getting something new, a pale pink blouse, perhaps, to go with her gray skirt.

While she was thus pleasantly musing, a piece of paper fluttered past and came to a stop against her foot. She picked it up, glanced at it idly, and caught her breath in shock.

"GRENISTON OUT," the paper proclaimed in crude, black letters. Next to it was a cruel drawing of a man, presumably Lord Greniston, hanging from a gibbet.

"Come to the Town Council meeting on Tuesday next and get what's rightfully yours," she read. "Why should a few rich bastards have land that should belong to all of us? Building in Far Tauverly means MONEY for us all, STEADY MONEY. Don't let anything stand between you and what you want! Be at the meeting, and vote for SWINDON'S PLAN."

Beneath this, there was another drawing. On the left, it showed a likeness of Greniston, his face contorted in an ugly leer, devil's horns on his head. His left foot was raised in the act of crushing a miniature Far Tauverly. This picture had an X drawn through it and, beneath it, the word "NO!" To the right was a sketch of Greniston Manor in flames, as a rain of pound notes descended on a crowd of villagers nearby. Beneath this was written "YES!"

Disgusted, Gwen ripped the paper up and put it in the nearest trash can. As she did so, she realized that similar fliers were stuck on car windshields and tacked to phone poles up and down the street. It shocked her to realize that on that beautiful spring morning, someone had been busy spreading venom.

And without even the courage to sign a name! she thought furiously. She doubted that Swindon could have come up with propaganda so crude; it

303

didn't seem his style, somehow. She wondered who in the village could be so hateful, and then felt ashamed that she was calling people's faces to mind, one by one, wondering if they could have done it. She rubbed her hands on her skirt, feeling that she had touched something unclean.

What really bothered her about the flier was not its suggestion to approve Swindon's plan. She could understand the villagers wanting to bring money to Far Tauverly, even though the thought of destroying Greniston Woods made her sick at heart. What bothered her was the hatefulness of what she had read. Someone had enjoyed making those crude drawings, enjoyed thinking of the anger, greed, shock and fear they might cause. She sighed deeply. There were some things you just couldn't escape, no matter how far you fled from them.

The glorious day seemed a little less bright to her. She looked forward all the more to the Bristol outing, to spending a day in the company of children and the comforting presence of Filipo. Thinking of the children reminded her of Claire's visit to her room last night. When she woke in the morning, the little girl was already gone. She hadn't yet had a chance to ask her about the mysterious drawing she had given her in the middle of the night. Thinking of the contrast between the evil sketch she had just thrown away and Claire's bright, lovely picture made her smile wryly. You could call them both drawings, but there the similarity ended.

"Miss Fields," a man's voice called. Gwen turned eagerly, expecting Robert with the car. Then her expression changed to one of concern. *Oh dear* she thought, *how awkward.*

***

"When is she coming?" Wyatt asked, for the fifteenth time in as many minutes.

"I don't know, *poquito*," Filipo replied, a worried frown on his face. He had known Gwen to be late before, but it wasn't like her to leave her luggage unattended, sitting out in front of the inn. At first, he had thought she had just stepped back inside for a moment, but Mrs. Hodges, just preparing to head to the manor house and start cooking, said she hadn't seen her for over half an hour.

"I'll tell you what," Filipo said to Robert, "you stay here with the kids. I'll walk down the street and see if she's in any of the shops."

With a long-suffering sigh, Robert nodded in agreement. As Filipo walked away, he heard Robert say, "If you kids will be quiet, I'll treat you all to cinnamon buns from Grundley's."

"With cocoa?" Osgood asked shrewdly.

A search of the main street revealed that no one had seen Gwen for several minutes. "She was sitting on the bench, in front of the inn," Jim, the greengrocer said, "and it was eight-fifteen. The church bell had just tolled the quarter hour. But when I looked again, a few minutes later, she was gone. Didn't see much else, I'm sorry to say. A bit preoccupied." He gestured toward the large pile of broken glass in the center of the store.

"I saw that," said Filipo. "What happened?"

"Vandals, must've been," said Jim. "They didn't steal anything, just broke the window for the sheer deviltry of it, I guess. Ruined five dozen peaches, though, all full of glass splinters. And they were lovely peaches. Real waste, in a world where folk are starving. I'd rather have given the peaches away than seen them wasted." He shook his head sadly. "I don't know what this world's coming to, I truly don't. I've lived in Far Tauverly all my life and never saw naught like this. Between the window and those foul pamphlets, it's a dark morning, I am sorry to say."

"What pamphlets?" asked Filipo.

Jim reached into the waste basket and pulled out a piece of paper. "This," he said. "Found it on my door this morning. A dirty business, and that's a fact."

Filipo glanced over the flyer with distaste, then threw it back in the trash. With a sympathetic nod, he left the greengrocer to his clean-up and stepped back onto the street. There was still no sign of Gwen.

Maybe she's at the post office, he thought. Logan had declined the outing to Bristol, saying that he needed to deliver the mail "at least one day out of three." Now it struck Filipo that Gwen might have gone to greet him and gotten enmeshed in a longer conversation than she had intended. It was easy to do that with Logan, he had already discovered. Hopefully, he strode across the alley to the post office and knocked on the door.

"Come in," Logan's voice called out cheerily, "not locked."

Filipo stepped inside. Logan was on his knees in front of the fireplace, poking a yardstick up the chimney.

"Welcome." he said warmly to Filipo. "Thought you'd all be on the road by now. Just excuse me one moment, I want to light a fire, it's gotten quite damp what with last night's rain and all. But I can't get the flue open, there's something stuck up there."

He gave another vigorous poke of the yardstick, and a cloud of soot came billowing down, and something fell with a loud clunk into the fireplace.

"Whatever is that?" sputtered Logan, peering at the object. Suddenly he gave a horrified cry and leapt backwards. "It's back!" he exclaimed.

"What's back?" asked Filipo. He, too, bent over the fireplace and then exclaimed, "What the hell?"

For there, amidst the ashes, lay the Far Tauverly Chalice.

***

Several minutes later, a hastily convened conference was being held in the little post office. Between the disappearance of Gwen, and the reappearance of the chalice, Filipo had decided it was best to call the manor. Greniston arrived a few minutes later, looking grim and concerned.

"If Swindon's laid a hand on her, I'll have his hide," were his first words.

"Hey, we don't know that anything bad has happened to her, let alone that this Swindon *hombre* is involved," said Filipo, although his own misgivings were growing by the minute.

"I'll lay odds ten to one it does," said Greniston darkly.

The matter of the chalice was quickly settled, or rather postponed, by Greniston. A phone call to the Pennington sisters informed him that they had not yet entered the museum that morning; however, when Lettice went to look, her discovery of the again-empty case could be heard not only over the phone line but across Milsom Road as well. Once she had calmed down, both sisters agreed that since the chalice had already reappeared across the street, there was no need to inform the police; indeed, if Lord Greniston would be willing to keep the goblet until it stopped wandering around, they would be most grateful.

"That's settled," said Greniston, hanging up. He stuffed the chalice into his raincoat pocket. "Now we've got to find Miss Fields. Has anyone called the police?"

"No, we called you first," Logan began to explain.

He was interrupted by the arrival of Robert, the young Walmsleys, and Sarah, the maid from the inn.

"Mrs. Hodges said you'd better talk to Sarah, here," Robert said solemnly, nudging forward the girl, who promptly burst into tears.

"Now then, Sarah," said Greniston, who felt that between Lettice and this, he was getting more than his fair share of feminine hysteria that morning, "calm down, and tell us what's the matter."

"It's all to d-d-do with the letter, Sir," Sarah sobbed. "I'm ever so sorry, ever so sorry! I k-k-know I shouldn't have done it!" Here her weeping became so violent that speech was impossible.

"Get that girl some water," growled Greniston. "Pour it into her mouth, or over her head, I don't care which."

A glass of water and a few kind words from Logan restored Sarah enough for her to continue.

"You see, I was cleaning Miss Fields' room, Sir, this morning, right after she checked out. Not that it n-needed much cleaning, she left it very nice, a real lady, no damp towels on the bathroom floor from her . . . "

"*Bien sur*, I'm sure it was immaculate, *carisima*, but get to the point," urged Filipo, eyeing Greniston's growing scowl.

"Well, you see, Sir, there was a letter. An open letter, that had fallen behind the dresser. I found it when I was dusting. I didn't mean to read it, truly I didn't. But it w-was open, not even in the envelope, and I could see from the signature it was from Mr. Swindon, and s-so . . . "

"You read it," said Logan, not without sympathy for such sore temptation.

"Yes, I did. You see, I couldn't help being curious, her having sent back them flowers, and all."

"Of course," said Filipo. "She told me about that letter. Said it was almost twenty pages of apology, about a misunderstanding between them. It upset her, and she didn't finish reading it. Then she probably just forgot about it, in the rush of packing."

"Oh dear," exclaimed Sarah, weeping anew. "She shouldn't have forgotten, Sir, she really shouldn't have!"

"And why is that?" asked Greniston.

"Well, Sir," said Sarah, warming to the drama of the tale, despite her own tears, "because it only started out to be an apology. B-but about halfway through, it began to sound very angry. Mr. Swindon said that if he couldn't have her, no one would, and th-that it was all your fault, Lord Greniston, that you had cast a spell on her."

"Sounds adolescent to me," said Greniston, who did not look totally displeased at the part about casting a spell.

"M-maybe so, Sir, but then it got worse, really crazy."

"What do you mean?"

Sarah leaned forward and lowered her voice, as if she had come to the dramatic part of a ghost story. The Walmsley children, seated on the table and window sills, leaned forward as well. "He began to write all crazy, about how she was the Queen of his Island and the Lady of his Kingdom, how once she was on the island everything would be clear to her, and she would n-never want to leave."

"The island," said Greniston, "I wonder. . . . He does own an island, off the coast of Scotland."

"He said that she was to meet him this morning at eight thirty, in front of the inn. That he would be there first thing, to pick her up, and 'take her away from this madness forever.'"

"And she was out there," Greniston realized.

"But not to meet Swindon, to meet me with the car," said Robert.

"*Madre de Dios*! She never did finish the letter; just forgot about it, and walked right into his plan!"

"But surely," Logan pointed out, "Swindon would not have forced her to go with him."

Sarah shook her head doubtfully, "I don't know," she said, "you should have seen the handwriting. Madder and madder it gets, gives me the chills, just looking at it."

"Do you have the letter?" Greniston demanded.

"Yes, here it is, Sir." Sarah fished the letter out of her apron pocket. Greniston seized it and scanned the pages swiftly. When he finished, his face was dark with rage, but his voice was cool and controlled.

"I'm afraid Sarah is right." he said. "The man that wrote this letter was definitely unbalanced. I would guess that Swindon is fully capable of forcing Miss Fields to accompany him."

"Oh no," exclaimed Logan, sinking into a chair, "she's been kidnapped!"

A significant look passed amongst the Walmsley children. They might have missed out on the Bristol Zoo, but they were in the thick of a kidnapping, which was far better, anyway. That Gwen was in real danger may have occurred to them, but the intrigue was irresistible. They were sure that Lord Greniston was about to rescue her.

"You're going to get her back, aren't you Lord Greniston," Osgood said proudly.

"You're damn well right I am," Greniston replied. He turned to Sarah and demanded "How long ago did you find this letter?"

"About eight-thirty, Sir."

"Well, why didn't you warn Miss Fields? You knew she was standing in front of the inn."

"Well, yes Sir, but when I g-g-got out there, she was gone. S-so I thought she must have stepped away for a moment, so then I took out the garbage and came back, and everyone was wondering where she was. So, I told Mrs. Hodges everything, and she found Robert and sent me over here."

When Sarah had finished, her round young face looked rather wounded. She really did feel she deserved a little thanks for having been brave enough to admit her guilt.

"Don't you worry, Sarah," said Logan, patting her arm, "you've done very well. Without your help, we wouldn't know where to begin to look."

"Yes, of course," said Greniston abruptly, "you've done as you should. But you had better get back to the inn now, I'm sure you are needed there."

Reluctant to have her brush with adventure end so quickly, Sarah allowed herself to be escorted back to the inn by Robert.

"Now then," said Greniston, taking command, "when Robert returns, he will take the children back to the manor." A collective wail of protest rose from the Walmsleys.

"None of that," said Greniston firmly. "Besides, I've got jobs for all of you. You will be my eyes and ears at the house. If Miss Fields manages to escape from Swindon, the manor house may be the first place she heads for. So I want you all on duty there, watching and waiting for her return. I want your sentinels at every tower window, to spot her the moment she draws near. Osgood, I want you to help Robert answer the phone. She may try to ring the manor, if she gets the chance."

"Right, Sir!" said Osgood, saluting smartly.

"Good man," said Greniston. "Now, Logan, I think it's best if you stay here in the village, keep your eyes open for any leads. Swindon may not have taken her as far as the letter leads us to believe. It may all be a cunning way to leave a false trail. If Gwen is nearby, she may well try to reach you. I'll be calling you here myself, to check in."

"Right," said Logan crisply. He stood tall and alert, his long-ago military training rising to the fore in this crisis.

"Also," Greniston continued, "I'd like you to call the Tweeverton police. You needn't mention the chalice, but tell them everything else that's happened, and get them moving. If Swindon is taking her to that blasted island, he'll likely be heading north, on the M5."

"Right away," said Logan, his hand already on the phone.

"What about you?" Filipo asked Greniston.

"I am going after her myself."

Filipo raised a quizzical eyebrow. "Surely the police can handle it better. . . ."

"I can't sit around here and wait for a phone call while she is in danger!" Greniston exploded. "I'm going to do what I can!"

Filipo smiled to himself. He wouldn't have wanted Gwen to be with a man who said any less.

Greniston charged toward the door, calling gruffly over his shoulder, "Thought you might want to come with. I've got the Austin, it's faster than the Rolls."

"*Absolutamente*," Filipo replied, hurrying after him. "I'm right with you, *compadre*."

***

God I feel awful, Gwen thought. Her head felt like it was being crunched by a giant nutcracker. She opened her eyes and quickly closed them. The light felt like daggers. Every cell of her body ached, and her mouth tasted foul.

What happened? she wondered. Slowly, she realized that she was in a car. A car that was going very, very fast. *I was standing outside the inn, waiting for Robert to pick me up* ...Gwen opened her eyes, and glanced at the driver. Swindon. Swindon, not Robert, was driving.

But I was supposed to be taking the Walmsley children to Bristol, to the zoo, Gwen groggily remembered. She did not have to look in the back seat to know that no Walmsley children were present. There was no whispered conversation, no rustle of Cadbury bars being unwrapped, no one enthusiastically opening and closing an expensive window until it broke, no kicking, shoving, or requests to stop. *Just me and Swindon*, Gwen thought, *and I don't know why. I was standing by the inn ... Swindon pulled up in his Jaguar. He rolled down the window and told me to get in ... said I wouldn't need my luggage. I refused .... He got out of the car, came to stand behind me ... we argued ... then he grabbed my arm ... I yelled, but just at that moment, there was no one on the street.* Gwen paused, trying to remember more. There had been a sickly sweet smell, something being held to her face. ... .

"You bastard!" she exclaimed aloud, "You chloroformed me!"

Swindon looked over and said cheerfully "Ah, you're awake!"

"You bet I am," said Gwen. "And you've got some explaining to do!" Her voice, she realized, sounded strange. Her mouth and throat felt puffy. She wanted to sound noble and strong, like the Abbess from "Wholly Writ." Instead, she feared, she sounded more like Wyatt Walmsley.

"You can't just go around chloroforming people," Gwen said. "It's not like in the movies! It's dangerous stuff! And it only lasts a few minutes. You have to keep reapplying it to keep a person unconscious for long – "

"I know," Swindon interrupted kindly, reaching over to pat her hand. "I've stopped to reapply the cloth several times. I researched it carefully, you see. I knew that although you had agreed to come to the Island, you might change your mind, turn coy. I came prepared."

"The Island?" Gwen exclaimed. "I never agreed to go to your island!"

Swindon smiled tolerantly. "Actions speak louder than words, my dear," he said lightly. "You were there outside the inn, waiting for me. Just as I asked you to be in my letter."

"Your letter," Gwen said with dismay. The crazed, passionate letter she had not read more than a few sentences of, before tossing it aside to look at later.

Swindon looked at her sharply. "You *did* read my letter, didn't you?" he asked.

Guiltily, Gwen shook her head. "But I was going to," she added quickly. "I just needed some quiet time to really give it my full attention."

"I doubt that," Swindon replied, his voice suddenly cold.

For a few minutes they drove on in miserable silence. Then Swindon said "If you weren't waiting for me, why were you in front of the inn?"

"I was waiting for Robert. Greniston's driver. I promised to take the Walmlsey children to Bristol, to the zoo. Robert was going to drive us there."

"But why did you have your luggage with?" Swindon asked.

311

"Well," Gwen said, trying to think of a non-hurtful way to answer but coming up with nothing that wouldn't cause him further pain, "I was moving out of the inn. I'm going to stay with … a friend … for the rest of my time here."

"Greniston?" Swindon asked, in a small, tight voice.

"Yes," Gwen answered. Then, trying to soften the blow, she added "He's having a weekend party, you see. Several people will be staying there. Including a friend of mine who has just arrived from the States. And the Walmsleys have moved there, for the time being. So it just made sense for me to stay there, too, since I'll be bringing the children back to the manor house."

Gwen paused, hoping that Swindon would say something, anything, to ease the tension of the moment. He remained silent, only the his white-knuckled grip on the steering wheel and the grim set of his jaw hinting at his distress. And yet, without a word being said, his pain filled the car. It was as if his anguish permeated the air that surrounded them both.

"I'm sorry," Gwen said softly. She was glad her voice was returning to normal; she didn't want her next words to sound ridiculous. "I'm sorry I didn't read your letter. I'm sorry you got your hopes up. I never meant to mislead you. But we have no future together. I'm sorry you have to find that out like this, but it's true."

Still Swindon made no reply. His face was masklike, focused only on the road ahead.

"I'm angry that you drugged me," Gwen said. "That was a terrible thing to do. But I don't want to cause you pain. Now that you know this has all been a terrible misunderstanding, please turn the car around. Please take me back to Far Tauverly."

Unexpectedly, Swindon began to laugh. Jagged, joyless laughter. Then with a kind of mad nonchalance, he exclaimed "It's rich; it's really rather marvelous! It's the irony, you see, the marvelous irony! Greniston sends the hired help to collect his prize, and she falls into my lap, instead. Ah, perhaps it's even better this way. Don't you see, it's a sign, a sign from the Fates that our union is destined to be! They caused this misunderstanding so that we would be brought together. Yes, this confirms it. It is predestined; we are meant to be together! Don't you see?"

"I can see how you feel that way," Gwen replied gently. "But I don't feel the same, Geoff, I really don't. Please take me back now."

In response, Swindon drove faster than ever. They were on a country road, Gwen realized, with deep ditches on either side. There was not a farm house in sight, just open fields and gathering fog.

"I planned our route carefully," Swindon said, "so that we could stick to the quiet roads, and be alone together."

Gwen had felt a little nauseous ever since regaining consciousness. Now she felt bile rising in her throat.

"Geoff," she gasped, "please pull over."

"All in good time," he said. "I have some isolated stops planned for us."

In reply, Gwen leaned forward and vomited on the Jacguar's sumptuous leather interior, the gear shift, and Swindon's dove grey Armani slacks.

"Sorry," she said. "But you'd better pull over, because I may need to do that again. After effects of chloroform," she added pointedly.

Swindon ignored her. Gwen tugged at the door handle.

"The lock is controlled by the driver," Swindon remarked.

I'll just have to wait for the right moment, Gwen thought. *In the meantime, I shouldn't antagonize him anymore. He could drug me again. He could tie me up. God knows what he might do. I need to keep him talking.*

"What's it like, this island of yours?" she asked, trying to sound pleasant and at ease.

"Why, it's *The Island,*" said Swindon, as if there were no other place on earth the two of them could possibly go. Then he smiled. "Of course, you don't know, since you didn't finish the letter. It's all right, you don't need to apologize, I'll tell you about it now. It's the island, my island, off the coast of Scotland. It's like another world there, another world entirely—you'll see. There will be no one there but us, and the sea, and the gulls. It's a real sanctuary. From the sea, it just looks like an outcropping of rock. The cliffs are a hundred feet high, on every side. It's only from the air that you can see that the center of it is a green, protected meadow. That's where the house is, our house."

"If you can only see the meadow from the air, how did you ever find it?" Gwen asked.

"Ah," said Swindon, "that is a tale! It was with Greniston, oddly enough!"

"Greniston!"

"Yes, years ago. We were friends once, when we were boys. We went to different schools, of course, and in any case, he's six years older than I am. I'm thirty-four. There weren't any other boys in Far Tauverly my parents wanted me to associate with, though, and Greniston never made friends easily, especially back then. So, on holidays, and during the summers, we spent a good deal of time together. We had some good times; we truly did."

A look of yearning for those long ago summer days came over Swindon's face. Gwen tried to picture the two boys, one so fair, the other dark, rambling through the freedom of the Greniston lands and woods, perhaps even invading the vast attics of the manor house in their games. Greniston would have taken the lead, of course, and Swindon would have been glad just to be included.

He worshipped Greniston, Gwen realized. In her mind's eye, she saw clearly the lonely, nervous child that Swindon had been, thrilled to be with the bold, creative, older boy, so confident, so full of life and careless charm.

"It changed, of course," Swindon continued. "When Greniston was around sixteen, and I was ten. He started bringing friends from school home to visit on his vacations, friends of the right sort, friends of his own age. I was never quite the right sort, you see, no matter how hard I tried. And then, of course, our families had never really gotten along. They didn't mind too much when we were boys, but as we grew older, they expected us to go our separate ways. There is some old feud, I don't really even know the details, but it mattered terribly in our grandparent's day. Besides, my family is just 'new money.' Oh, we've owned the land since who knows when, but we always just scraped by until Father made a killing in the South African diamond mines. He built our new house. He tried to buy a title, too, but that didn't work. So we were never really considered quite acceptable by Greniston standards. But we didn't fit in with the working class, either.

"Of course, it was natural, too, that the adoration of a much younger boy, like me, would grow stale after a while. To be fair, I don't think Greniston ever quite noticed the change happening, you know. He was so busy and brilliant at school, and then, at sixteen, he had definitely discovered girls, which was still another world to me. Yes, as I look back on it, it seems quite reasonable that he drifted away, but I took it hard at the time."

Beneath Swindon's reasonable analysis, Gwen could glimpse the confusion he must have felt, not understanding why his hero suddenly had no time for him. Mentally, she winced with sympathy, she could imagine how painful it would be to feel included in Greniston's warmth and then suddenly have him seem to turn cold.

"But it's the Island I'm telling you about," Swindon continued, "and that's a happy story. You see, Greniston's father liked to go fishing in Scotland. Sometimes, during summer holidays, Greniston and I were allowed to come with. Old Lord Greniston usually stayed with a friend of his from his RAF days, a Colonel McBride, who had a house on Loch Leryness. And this Colonel McBride had a biplane. It was an antique, really, from World War I days, but he kept it in perfect running order. From time to time, he'd take young Greniston up for a ride in it, because he was keen to fly. We boys were never allowed to go near the plane on our own, though, but of course we did; it fascinated us. When the two men were off fishing, we would sit in the plane. It was often just out on the lawn, in front of the house. We pretended we were fighter pilots, and sometimes Greniston would imagine he was St. Exupery, delivering the African mail. He was fifteen, and he had just discovered the St. Exupery books. We used to sit in that plane, and he'd read passages from *Night Flight*, and *Wind, Sand, and Stars*. I tell you, Gwen, when he read those words, it was like being right there. We peered out over the edge of the plane and felt that we saw beneath us the curve of the earth and the lights of faraway cities that we longed to visit, instead of heather and Colonel McBride's dogs, watching us suspiciously.

"Well, one day, we were sitting there, and Greniston said, 'You know, I could fly this thing.' I must have protested—I'm sure I did—but it was too late, the idea had caught him. 'I've been watching McBride very carefully, every time we go up,' Greniston said. 'I know exactly what he does. It looks very simple. I don't know why they make such a fuss about pilot's licenses. Anyone can do it.' I'm sure that I said something like 'we should ask for permission,' but Greniston wouldn't hear of it. 'I'm taking her up, right now,' he said. 'Do you want to come, or not?' Well, of course I would rather have died than appear cowardly in his eyes. I stayed, come hell or high water. And somehow, we got off the ground. 'We'll be back before anyone knows we're gone,' Greniston yelled. It was amazingly loud, up there, between the wind and the engines.

"The plane tilted this way and that—he found it harder to steer than he'd imagined—I was terrified, I had never been in any airplane at all, before. But it was glorious, as well, to see the green treetops spread out before us and Loch Leryness, like a piece of ice blue satin. Even McBride's house looked tiny, like a toy house, and the dogs yipping on the lawn looked smaller than ants. They looked so ridiculous that Greniston and I began to laugh a bit hysterically, drunk with the freedom of it all. Then we looked down again and saw Colonel McBride and old Greniston staring up at us, fishing poles in hand. They seemed to be yelling and gesturing wildly, but they looked so tiny, so insignificant. It had never occurred to me before that adults could look so insignificant. 'I think they want us to land,' I said. Greniston shrugged. 'In for a penny, in for a pound,' he laughed. It was what he always said when we were in trouble. 'We're in for it already, might as well enjoy it.' And he turned the plane to the west and headed for the open sea."

A faraway, enchanted look had come over Swindon's face.

"As long as I live, I shall never forget that flight above the sea," he said softly. "It was late afternoon by then. Everything was bathed in a soft, golden light; a pale gold light, like champagne. It shone upon the water, and the clouds. We could see the faint curve of the earth and the whole stretch of the coastline. Far beneath us, gulls wheeled and cried. It was absolutely magical. Greniston had discovered that he could shut off the engine for a few seconds at a time, and we could glide on the wind. Except for the wind, we hovered in a kind of unearthly stillness then. It was splendid, it was peaceful; and yet, so very sad, somehow.

"Greniston must have felt the same way I did, because he said, 'One gets so caught up in it all, when one is down in it; the streets, the houses, the people, they all seem so important. But up here, it makes one feel there must be something else that's really important, something much bigger than all that littleness. It's something, something my father and your father and Colonel McBride have forgotten; maybe they never found it at all. But we'll find it, won't we? And once we do, we'll never forget. But I wonder what it is and where we can find it. It's not down there, not at Colonel McBride's, or Greniston manor. No, it's somewhere else we're always longing for, somewhere farther even than those clouds...' He had put into words exactly how I felt, but could never have expressed. But then, he had always been good at that.

"It was when we were up there, coasting on the wind, that we saw a little string of islands beneath us. Most of them were nothing but jagged rock, sticking straight up out of the sea, but the largest had a meadow in the middle of it; from the sky it looked like a patch of deep green moss, so smooth and rich, in that golden light.

"'I bet you can't even see that from the ground,' Greniston said. 'That meadow's a perfect place for a house. No one would ever even know you're there. A private fortress, by the sea.' Right then and there, I decided that I would build a house on that island someday, and Greniston could come and stay there whenever he wanted to.

"We were losing altitude by then, so Greniston decided to turn back on the engine. It sputtered terribly. 'Petrol,' he said, 'I never thought about that.' We made it back safely, but just barely, coaxing the plane along. We came coasting over the roof of McBride's house with an inch or two to spare and landed on the front lawn, wrecking havoc with Mrs. McBride's prize rhododendrons. I don't think the plane was ever quite the same, either.

"Of course, there was hell to pay. Old Lord Greniston always seemed more like a Major than a father, and I think his discipline was pretty severe, although Greniston never talked about it. As soon as we landed, his Dad grabbed hold of him, and cuffed him on the ear, hard. He started to drag him toward the house, saying 'By God, young man, you've gone too far, this time!' Then he and McBride both noticed me. I was only nine, and I suddenly felt quite terrified. 'As for you,' old Greniston began, 'I'll deal with you next.' Greniston interrupted him, saying,

'It's not his fault at all. He didn't want to go up at all, but I didn't give him a chance to get out.'

"I cried, 'That's not true!' but Greniston's father was already dragging him toward the house."

"And did he get a caning?" Gwen asked, horrified at such a form of punishment.

"Oh, yes. He wasn't at supper that night. And a grim supper it was, the disapproval of the adults as thick as smoke. I didn't get a caning; perhaps old Greniston thought it would be going too far, with a boy not his own, but he definitely gave me the cold, silent treatment. And the next day he told me, 'You'll have to amuse yourself today. My son is confined to quarters.' Well, as soon as the men left for their fishing, I snuck upstairs, into Greniston's room. He moved very stiffly and looked pale, but he put a brave face on it. He actually apologized for risking my life, asked me to forgive him! Then he joked that the next time he stole a plane, he'd check the fuel gauge first. Then he said, 'You wouldn't have any food, would you? I'm on bread and water indefinitely.'

"Well, of course, I scurried downstairs, and took some chicken salad sandwiches and an entire raspberry pie as well as a bottle of real ale. I think I thought that Mrs. McBride would never notice. Well, if she did, she kindly never said so. So Greniston and I ate contraband provender, and read Sherlock Holmes stories."

Swindon smiled at the recollection. "Anyway," he said, "that's how I found the island."

"I see," said Gwen. She felt that she did indeed see a great deal more than she had before, about both Swindon and Greniston. So caught up had she become in the vividness of Swindon's memories that she had almost forgotten where she was and the danger she was in. Swindon soon reminded her of that. His voice lost the warmth that boyhood memories had brought to it and turned hard.

"Yes," he said grimly, "I remembered that island. And years later, after Dad died, and I had made something, really made something of his investments, young as I was, I didn't just build a house there, I bought the whole bloody island. And I built a place, as grand in its way as Greniston Manor. On a smaller scale, suited to the setting, a replica, exact in every way, of a fourteenth-century French chateaux. A jewel, in that wild setting. You'd never know it has central heating or electric lights, it is all so well concealed. There is no phone, of course, no servants. Enough food stored to last a year or two, a true fortress. Every stone of it had to be flown in by helicopter; it's the only way to reach the meadow at the center, short of real climbing up those cliffs, with ropes.

"And I worked for it! Not like Greniston, who just inherited his wealth. Everything I have, everything I know, I worked for; the right clothes, the right people, the right taste in wine. He's never had to think twice about any of that, he was born into all the right things. But no matter how hard I've worked to acquire that same rightness, it's never been quite good enough, not for him, or anyone like him.

"I thought that when he came back from the RAF, and the diplomatic corps, things would be different, that since I had made something of myself, he would be proud to call me his friend. His parents were both dead by then; there was no family pressure to remain aloof. Yet he did. Countless times I invited him, to dinner parties, hunting trips; every time, he declined. Oh, very courteous, the refusals always were, but formal, like he was writing to a stranger.

318

"Then, one evening, I ran into him, at a party in London; a smart set, I didn't even know he ran with. He didn't say much all evening, left early. But just before he left, he took me aside, and said, 'I'm sorry to see what you've become, Geoff.' That's all. No friendship, no recognition of a job well done, just 'I'm sorry to see what you've become.' I shall never forget that, never!"

Swindon's face was pale with fury. His thin hands gripped the steering wheel so hard that his knuckles showed white beneath the skin. Despite the growing fog, he drove faster than ever.

I've got to get away from this man," Gwen realized. *I've got to get away before we reach that island. There's no phone, no one can see the house from the shore. God knows how long it would be before I found a way to escape.*

She didn't know how Swindon planned to get them from the mainland to the island, but she was sure it would be well-planned and that she had better make her move before then.

It's a long way to Scotland, she reasoned. *Sooner or later he has to stop for gas, or to go to the bathroom, or something. When he does stop, I'll be ready.*

It was easy to think that, but she knew it would not be easy to do. She had studied a little aikido, and taken a self-defense class in Denver .But applying the moves she had learned to a deranged man who was driving a car in the fog down curving country roads with deep ditches was not as easy as overcoming an assailant in a supportive group. And the thought of using self defense on a stranger out of instinct was one thing, but the prospect of possibly really injuring someone you knew, who had kissed you and bared his heart to you, even if he was a rat, was very different. Especially when one had far too much time to contemplate it ahead. She thought about trying something now, but once again she realized that the challenge of struggling for control of a speeding car was not so easy to face when you were actually in the passenger seat.

At the back of her mind remained the increasingly forlorn hope that Greniston would rescue her. Then, for the first time, to her horror, Gwen realized that Greniston might put an entirely wrong construction upon everything. If someone had seen her get into the car with Swindon, Greniston might think she had actually chosen to do so. It had all happened so fast, someone just glancing out a window might not realize she had struggled.

319

Yes, she thought, *Greniston might think that the fickle American tourist had changed her mind and gone off with the flashier suitor, not even bothering to take her luggage. But Filipo and Logan, they would know I wouldn't go off like that. But they might not know where to search, unless someone found that letter.*

Please" Gwen prayed, silently, fervently, *someone find that letter, read it, call the police."* She shivered, at the thought of what might happen, if no one did.

"Are you cold?" asked Swindon, suddenly solicitous. "If you look in the back seat, you'll find something to keep you warm. It's in the large box, next to the picnic basket."

Gwen reached over and opened the box, expecting to find a travel blanket. Instead, her eye met blue—the deep, radiant royal blue of a velvet cape.

"It's lovely," she exclaimed, startled by the sheer beauty of the thing.

"I knew you'd like it," Swindon said happily. "I thought of you as soon as I saw it. Go ahead, put it on, it's yours. And that's just the beginning."

Gwen put the cape back in the box. *I can't accept it,* she thought. *It would be like accepting Swindon's mad plan.* Aloud, she said, "I'm not really that cold. I'll put it on later."

For a moment, Swindon looked utterly crestfallen. Then he rallied, saying, "Yes, that's best. Save it for the island. But you like it, don't you? And you will like the island, won't you?"

He looked at her with the earnestness of a small child seeking reassurance, and Gwen felt sick at heart to see such naked need.

"Geoff," she said gently, "it doesn't matter if I like your island, or not. Or if anyone else on earth does, Greniston included. What matters is that you like it. That's enough."

Swindon looked at her, aghast. "Oh no," he said, "no, no, no. You must like it, that's the whole point; you must, you will, I know you will."

Gwen sighed, realizing that the damage and need for approval in Swindon was too deep for mere reason to cure.

When the moment comes, I'm going to risk injuring this wreck of a man, she thought. *I will if I have to.*

Suddenly, it all seemed overwhelming: the misery of the man beside her, the danger of her own situation, the uncertainty of what Greniston knew or thought, the fact that she was cold but could not bring herself to put on the cape, the need for violence that she had to face. Without warning, she burst into tears.

When she reached the nose-blowing stage, several minutes later, she realized that Swindon had stopped the car. Her first feeling was one of panic; she had vivid memories of the last time she had sat in a parked car with him.

Swindon, however, made no move to touch her. He sat on the far side of the front seat, looking at her with an unreadable expression on his pale, elegant face. The intensity had gone out of his eyes. He looked hollow now and quite worn out.

"You really don't want to go with me, do you?" he asked quietly.

Gwen shook her head and cautiously, softly said, "No, I really, really don't."

Swindon sighed and turned his face away. For several minutes, he looked out the window, and Gwen had the distinct impression that he was fighting back tears of his own. When he looked at her again, however, he had regained his composure.

"Well, then," he said evenly, "I'll take you back."

The shock and relief on her face must have been very evident, because Swindon managed a rueful smile and said, "Don't worry, Miss Fields, I won't change my mind. I know I get carried away sometimes, but I'm not a raving lunatic. I suppose there's no point in saying it," he added, "but I am sorry about all this. When I saw you standing outside the inn, I thought, to my joy, that you had read the letter and actually wanted to come with me. Even when you seemed unwilling, I thought, 'She's just pretending to resist. Women do that.' And then, when I discovered you hadn't read the letter, why, it seemed to be too strange of a coincidence. I was sure it was a sign that we were meant to be together. I thought you would be fine once you got used to the idea. But now that I see you so distressed... The last thing on earth I want is to cause you unhappiness, Miss Fields. I'll take you back."

Then, to Gwen's surprise, both doors in the front seat swung open. "You are my prisoner no longer," said Swindon, with a trace of his old wit. "Before we start the long journey back, why not get out and stretch your legs a bit?"

Gwen thought that was one of the best ideas she had ever heard. When she stood up, she found she was shakier than she had realized, but a few breaths of misty, cold air helped to clear the dizziness.

She gazed around. As near as she could tell in the fog, they seemed to be in a patch of woods. The road made a sharp bend, and she could not tell what lay ahead, but to the right she could just make out the shapes of trees, and she heard the sound of gurgling water. The thought of a little stream where she could wash her face and hands was wonderful. She took a few more steps away from the road, before she realized that the fog was too dense between the trees to find anything. Still, she lingered for a moment, wondering if she should allow Swindon to drive her to the nearest town or just run away, then and there. He seemed sincere in his resolve to take her back, but his mood swings were so sudden that there was no telling what he might do five miles down the road. On the other hand, the other alternative, running away, was almost as uncertain. The road they were on seemed deserted. She might walk for a long way before seeing a house or hitching a ride. Meanwhile, the fog was growing thicker and colder by the minute, and she had no protection except her flimsy sweater. Yet her instinct recoiled at the thought of getting back in the car.

Gwen did not have to consider her choice much longer. She heard a cry, and turned back toward the road in time to see Geoff Swindon meet a part of his destiny—not in the form of a tryst on a Scottish Isle but of a Brinsley's ice cream truck, twenty minutes late on its run from Chichester to Porlock, and trying to make up for lost time.

***

"Curse this bloody fog!" said Greniston. "It was clear in Far Tauverly, but the farther north we go, the worse this gets!" He steered the Austin expertly along the narrow, curving road.

"Still sure they're on the back roads, not the highway?" he asked Filipo.

The other man shook his head. "I thought I was sure, but all I know is that my instinct seems to say 'this way.'"

"Mine too," said Greniston. "Curse this damned fog. Keeps us crawling along in pea soup."

Crawling was not the word Filipo would have used to describe their pace. His own fearless driving style had met its match in Greniston. More than once, he found himself clutching the dashboard, murmuring, "*Madre de Dios!*" while they swerved to avoid a tree or fence that suddenly loomed toward them out of the fog.

"What's that!" cried Greniston now. Down the road several hundred feet, cutting swathes of color through the gray air, was the flashing light of an ambulance.

"Looks like there's been an accident," said Filipo grimly. Greniston did not even reply but simply drove faster than ever.

***

For Gwen, the past half-hour had passed in a blur. She had turned back from the roadside just in time to see the ice cream truck crash into the Jaguar. The impact had thrown Swindon across the road and into a ditch. It had also flung open the back door of the truck and sent gallon after gallon of ice cream tumbling into the road.

She had run immediately to Swindon. He looked so pale and still, lying at an odd, discarded angle in the ditch that she had feared he was dead, but when she bent over him, his eyes fluttered open.

"Cold," he murmured.

"I'll get you something to keep you warm," Gwen said. "Just stay alive!"

As she ran back to what was left of the car to search for a blanket, she saw the lorry driver. He had climbed out of the cab of his truck and now stood beside the wreck, holding his shoulders in a dazed manner.

"You should get out of the road," Gwen called to him. "Someone might hit you in this fog." (Not until later did she realize the irony of the remark.)

The only thing she could find to cover Swindon was the blue cape. She placed it over him as gently as she could and was reassured to see his lips form the words "thank you."

At that point, the lorry driver wandered off the road and headed toward the fog-shrouded woods.

"Come back!" cried Gwen, but the man seemed not to hear her. She patted Swindon's hand reassuringly, then dashed after the driver. He was a big man, but she managed at last to steer him toward where Swindon lay.

"Now you stay right here," she said, as if addressing a seven-year-old.

The man nodded meekly. As soon as she turned her attention back to Swindon, though, he got up again. He wandered back into the road and tried to scrape some spilled strawberry swirl back into its carton.

323

"Just look at this mess," he fretted. "The strawberry, the fudge marble—all wasted! It really is too bad!"

"You're in shock," Gwen said gently. "You need to sit still."

"But I must clean up the mess," the driver protested, as she led him out of the road.

Gwen thought, *Someday, I hope I can look back and see the humor in all this.* She ended up sitting in the mud at the roadside, holding both men by the hand—the lorry driver to keep him from disappearing into the fog, Swindon because she felt that if only she did not let go of him, he would not let go of life. He looked very white lying against the dark, damp earth, with the blue cape that had been meant for her now covering him.

How am I going to go for help, Gwen wondered, *when I can't leave either of these men? Not that I would know where to go for help, anyway*, she realized, gazing at the fog-shrouded landscape. *Oh, please, someone, come driving by!* When she recalled how empty the road had been for many miles, she didn't have much hope of that. And then, like the answer to a prayer, the wavering beam of a bicycle light appeared out of the fog. Then the bicycle and the man riding it appeared: a middle-aged man, with a kind face, in a bright yellow rain slicker, whistling "Eine Kleine Nacht Musick" to himself. He paused in mid-note at the sight of the wreck, screeched to a stop, and seemed to take in the accident and the survivors in a single glance.

"Going to ring for help, luv," he said briskly. "Just hang on for a few more minutes." Then he disappeared into the fog again, peddling very fast.

Looking back on it, Gwen realized that she, too, must have been in shock, because she had no sense of how long she continued to sit there, the lorry driver on her right, Swindon on her left; she just had the sense of blankly sitting there, as if she always had been and always would be.

Then, suddenly, there was noise and people everywhere. An ambulance and two police cars burst out of the fog, lights flashing, and sirens wailing. Voices issued curt, loud orders. Someone wrapped a blanket around her and put a cup of hot, sweet tea in her hand. Someone else led away the lorry driver, who seemed intent on explaining to everyone that they needed to scrape the ice cream back into the cartons, otherwise his pay would be docked for the cost of it.

Other people came and very gently lifted Swindon onto a stretcher.

"I need to ask you some questions, Miss," a policeman said.

Gwen shook her head. "Not now. I need to find out if Swindon's going to be all right."

"Your boyfriend, Miss?" the policeman asked sympathetically.

Gwen shook her head. "That will never be," she said, "but I have to help him as much as I can."

"He's still alive," the policeman assured her. "They're taking him to hospital now. He's in good hands, Miss, and I do need to ask you some questions."

Dimly, Gwen sensed that the policeman was asking her to describe exactly what had happened. She also noticed that two other policemen were trying to measure tire tracks on the road, their efforts considerably hampered by a great deal of slushy lime sherbet and French vanilla.

"How fast would you say the lorry was traveling, Miss?"

Gwen replied with a question of her own, "What hospital are they taking him to? I should go with."

"Certainly, Miss, in just a minute. Now - "

Gwen strode past the policeman, toward the ditch. The paramedics had left the blue cape lying in the mud. Swindon had wanted to give it to her so much. Only an hour before, she had been loathe to accept it. Now she felt that she could not leave it lying there; it was not decent. The royal blue cape now seemed to her like the emblem of the best of Swindon, mixed up with mud and fog and fear, it was true, but worth salvaging. With the policemen at her heels, patiently trying to ask his questions, she knelt down and picked up the blue cape, carefully folding it over her arm.

It was then, when she turned back toward the road, that she looked at, really looked at, what was left of the car. The magnificent silver Jaguar, with its custom-ordered paint and its leather upholstery, now looked like a tin can that someone had crushed under their heel. The back was not as damaged as the front, although one of the back doors was ripped off entirely. (She hadn't even noticed that, when she had gone to get the cape.) The entire front half of the car, however, was crushed like aluminum foil against the front of the lorry.

If I had come back to the car a few seconds sooner, she realized, *or gotten out a minute later; if Swindon and I had been sitting in the car, instead of standing near it, we would be crumpled in there as well, crushed, like old foil.*

Everything began to spin, and her knees gave way beneath her. The policeman's voice, asking if the lorry had approached on the right or the left side of the road, grew fainter and fainter.

Suddenly, she felt strong arms around her and heard a deep, familiar voice saying, "The devil take your questions! Can't you see this lady is in shock?"

"Greniston," she whispered.

She felt his grip tighten around her, as if to say, *I am here. Everything will be all right, now.*

And another familiar voice said, "Don't worry, Babe, it's all gonna be okay."

What happened next was a bit of a blur to Gwen. They rode to the hospital, in a town somewhere on the moors, whose name she did not know, and then she waited with Greniston and Filipo for what seemed like hours in an emergency room, until at last a cheerful young nurse appeared and said, "Mr. Swindon's going to be all right. He's got a pretty severe concussion, as well as a broken leg and several cracked ribs, but he will pull through. He's very groggy right now, not up for visitors, but his mother and sister are on their way here, if you would like to wait and see them."

"That won't be necessary," said Greniston, who seemed to understand, without having to have it explained, that Gwen had just needed to know that Swindon would survive. Now he put his arm firmly around her, and said, "It's high time we got this lady home."

She was dimly aware of him leading her out of the hospital and of Filipo offering to drive the car so that Greniston could sit in the back with her. Now all the shocks of the day seemed to catch up with her at once; she felt herself falling into an exhausted sleep. The last thing she heard was Greniston telling her, "It will be all right now; we're going to take you home."

She smiled. *Home.* He had said the word as if it included her—and that was everything.

CHAPTER EIGHTEEN

"Face it," Logan told his reflection, "You're over the hill." The features that looked back at him from the rather muddy pool did nothing to disprove the comment. The eyes were bloodshot, and the skin beneath them was puffy from too much brandy and not enough sleep. Worst of all, the whole face wore a guilty, hang-dog expression. Logan found it difficult to meet his own eyes; the thought of confronting anyone else's was too much to bear. A need for retreat had sent him to Shalimar.

"The Abode of Love," that was what *Shalimar* meant in Persian, or so he had read in a book. The tangled garden he found himself in now might not have been a place of love, but it was certainly one of solitude. Although he was on the Greniston land, only a quarter of a mile from the manor house, Logan felt as if he was on the far side of the globe. Aside from the chirping of solidly English sparrows and robins, there was nothing to say he had not wandered into some Arabian Nights Dream.

Shalimar House and the gardens around it had been built by Tommy Greniston, the younger brother of the current Lord's grandfather. Not having inherited the title or the responsibilities of the estate, young Tommy had devoted himself to the army. His was an undistinguished career; he had risen to the rank of Major through his reliable blandness as an officer and considerable family influence.

The true passions of Thomas Greniston's life had been archeology and travel. The army had given him ample opportunity to pursue both. During the thirty years of his service, he had been stationed at posts from Luxor to Damascus, Bangkok, Delhi, and Peking. On his many leaves, he had wheedled and bought his way onto digs with Flinders Petrie and Howard Carter, yet somehow, he always managed to participate during a season when nothing extraordinary was found.

His might have been called a career of "almosts." He dug with Carter in the Valley of the Kings during one of the seasons when he did not discover King Tut's tomb, he served with T. E. Lawrence in Cairo three months before his desert campaigns began, and he met and dined with Mahatma Gandhi when he was still a well-mannered young lawyer in an English suit. Glory and danger did not thrive near Thomas Greniston; instead, he had an uncanny knack for being at historic places before history was made there and for meeting great people and conversing with them about nothing more momentous than the weather. His mere presence seemed to ensure that nothing extraordinary would happen. Yet to him, it was all thrilling. Many a drink in many an officer's club, from Poona to Pretoria, had come his way by him saying, "I knew Lawrence, of course. Served with him in the Middle East, actually." He would then pause, until his companion realized that a shot of something potent was needed to wet the whistle for what was clearly going to be an amazing tale. Yet, once Tommy was settled in with his gin and tonic and, if possible, a rather good cigar, the buyer would be treated to nothing more marvelous than the fact that "Lawrence was deuced fond of apples," and Tommy's brief memory: "Never could get good ones in Cairo, though, he always said. Nothing like a Dorset apple, he always said. Had to make do with Syrian ones, though. Used to cut 'em in to eighths with his pocket knife. Gave me a piece, once. Nice fellow." Then, with a nod and a smile, Tommy would wander off to another table, leaving his listener with the vague sense that things had not quite worked out as expected.

Indeed, the phrase "not quite worked out as expected" might well have been the motto for many episodes in Thomas Greniston's life, including his one excursion into marriage. At the age of forty, he had astonished everyone by wooing and wedding young Maude Ellen MacGregor, daughter of a Colonel then stationed in Delhi and the belle of the regiment. She was twenty years younger than Tommy, three inches taller, and due to receive a considerable inheritance from her mother's side of the family. No one could understand what she saw in Greniston.

Perhaps she couldn't, either. A year after they married, she returned to England, alone. Having no family of her own there, she settled in at Greniston Manor, ostensibly to wait patiently for Tommy's retirement and return. In fact, she proceeded to lead her own life with a gusto that shocked even the Grenistons. She disappeared for weeks on end to London, where she ran with a racy crowd the family held in deep disapproval. When she was at the manor, she played dance records so loudly that the crystal chandeliers rattled, and she sped about the countryside in an azure-colored roadster. She smoked cigarettes in public, and even, it was said, went to lectures about communism and the Irish Freedom Front.

One thing that could be said in her favor was that she was loyal. Not faithful, perhaps, in the technical sense, but whatever her affairs were, she managed to keep them discreet, and she would never hear a word said against "good old Tommy."

During World War II, she surprised everyone, including herself, by serving with great distinction as a London ambulance driver. Indeed, there were those who remarked that she saw more action than Tommy did, since he sat out the conflict safely stationed in Ceylon.

After the war, to the family's great relief, Maude moved to a smart flat in Bristol and took up painting. When Tommy finally retired from the army, at the age of fifty five, he repaired to Greniston Manor with two foreign servants, one of whom, his mother remarked nervously, was "quite black, dear," to which Tommy replied, "I noticed." He also brought with him a seventeen-year-old dancing girl from Bali.

"Thank God," were Maude's first words when she found out. "I was afraid old Tommy might want to resume married life, and to tell you the truth, I haven't the time for it anymore."

"You'll divorce him, of course," the then current Lady Greniston had said, sympathetically.

Maude had shrugged. "I don't see why, after all these years. Too much paperwork. I'm quite happy for him, actually. That dancing girl is beautiful; I'd love to paint her."

She did twelve different paintings of the girl, in fact, including one of her and Tommy lying together on a Persian carpet, both quite naked, except that the girl was wearing a toe ring and a smile, and Tommy, a fez.

The rest of the family were not as tolerant as Maude. When Tommy announced his plan to build his own house on the land, at some distance from the manor, the relief was unanimous.

He called the house Shalimar, after the famous gardens in Kashmir. Certainly, there were traces of that locale in its design, as well as of Cairo, Thailand, China, and just about every other Eastern post where Tommy had been stationed. This combination of oriental styles resulted in a rather fairy-tale result; the house looked like something from an old Dulac illustration for the *Rubaiyat*. It was small, compared to the manor house, but with three floors and twelve rooms, it was quite large enough to shelter Tommy and his little retinue.

The gardens around it were enclosed by a wall and modeled after those of Mogul India. There was a reflecting pool, a row of cypresses, roses imported from Shiraz, and peacocks strutting on the lawn. Exotic plants like frangipani and fuchsia bloomed in the house's miniature solarium. Some flowers, like the wild orchids Tommy had brought himself from the center of

329

Bali, did not survive, even in the shelter of a greenhouse. Neither did Tommy. After so many years abroad, perhaps he, too, had become an exotic transplant. After only three winters at Shalimar, he passed away of pneumonia one cold November day. The servants disappeared before he was buried, along with several of the more valuable antiquities collected during his travels. As for the dancing girl, she seemed stricken with genuine grief. She stayed in the empty house, refusing to eat, until, to the family's shock, Maude arrived in her roadster and took the young widow to live with her, in Bristol.

Legally, Shalimar House and all of Tommy's money went to Maude. She, however, had insisted that the cash go to the dancing girl, who eventually returned to Bali, a still young, beautiful, and extremely wealthy woman. She remarried after a few years and named her first two children Maude and Tommy.

As for Shalimar House, it was never inhabited again. For over forty years now, it and its gardens had stood neglected. Everyone in Far Tauverly knew its story, but no one ever visited the old place except Logan. Normally no lover of things Eastern, he found an odd peace in the half-wild gardens. He never went into the house—local superstition held that it was haunted, and anyway, the doors were locked—but he enjoyed the gentle melancholy of the setting.

Only traces of the original garden survived here and there and poked through amid the tangle of oaks and elms and wildflowers. The seven-foot wall that surrounded the house and its three acres had long since been overgrown with ivy and clematis; only here and there did its crenelated top (modeled after the Red Fort, at Delhi) or a trace of its band of blue tiles (replicas of those in the Mosque at Isfahan) peep through the vines.

The marble fountains (copies of those in the palace of the last king of Morocco) had not jetted forth their glittering spray for decades; their fluted basins were now full of dead leaves. The reflecting pool by which Logan now knelt was filled only with rain water.

The old place is falling apart, Logan thought, *like me*. He left the pool and made his way along what remained of a stone path to a small garden behind the house. Here, at either end of a long-neglected yew alley, stood two statues Tommy Greniston had brought back from Bali. These were not replicas but rather the real thing, blatantly stolen from an overgrown jungle temple south of Chandrapradesh. At one end of the yew alley, which was perhaps eight feet wide and twenty feet long, stood an almost life-size statue of Krishna. It was carved of some smooth, gray stone with a bluish cast. On either side of Krishna, carved of the same stone, stood two young maidens. Krishna stood between them, one leg crossed in front of the other, head to one side—a relaxed, youthful pose. His arms were raised, and his fingers were lifted as if he was playing the flute, but there was no flute to be seen in his hands. Logan had never been able to decide if there once had been a flute in his grasp, carved of some other stone, or if the sculptor had always intended the instrument to be invisible, even as its music was silent. The two slender maidens had their heads tilted, clearly listening to the melody. One had her hand raised, as if beseeching whoever drew near to approach softly, so as not to disturb the song.

On all of their faces was an expression of calm and playfulness. Their full lips curved in gentle smiles; their eyes seemed to gaze at some distant, profound horizon. "O, Mortal," their expressions seemed to say, "if only you could see what we see, hear what we hear—and perhaps," the curve of their smiles seemed to add, "you can."

At the other end of the yew corridor was a statue of Shiva, dancing within a circle of flame. Logan found this statue a bit formidable, yet he had examined it enough to know that Shiva's face, too, bore an expression of imperturbable peace and the trace of an eternal smile.

Across the length of the yew alley, Krishna and his consorts and Shiva gazed at each other. To his own surprise, Logan had, over the years, grown quite fond of the gods. He had seen them in every season: when autumn winds and winter rain seemed not to chill their nakedness at all, and when summer roses clung to the consorts graceful forms like draped velvet and butterflies danced on the fiery ring surrounding Shiva. When the elm trees behind the yews were in full leaf, their branches met overhead, and the light that filtered through their canopy was of a pale, aqueous green—a moving, stirring light that played over Shiva and made him seem more than ever to be dancing, forever dancing, just as the sighing of the summer breezes seemed to be the music that Krishna was forever playing.

Over the years, Logan had gotten into the habit of going to this secluded spot to sort out his troubles, the way other people went to sit in the quiet of St. Aethelrood's on a weekday afternoon. Logan had never felt quite comfortable in the church, although he appreciated its beauty. Somehow, he couldn't associate Christ with the pale, immaculate statue near the altar, whose well-groomed hair and beard had prompted the current Lord Greniston to grumble, "Looks like an advert for some damned shampoo." Logan had to agree. He felt certain that Christ had been a rough-hewn, down-to-earth man—the sort who could have downed his pint at the inn and challenged any takers to arm wrestling, yet who had a fire of God in his eye that stopped you in your tracks when it blazed forth. A big, restless, rugged sort of man he must have been, who didn't like sitting indoors too long.

Logan deeply appreciated a conversation he had overheard some weeks before between Wyatt and the Vicar. The Vicar had been trying to explain to Wyatt why it was not suitable to use the altar as a hiding place during hide and seek.

"This is God's house, you see," the Vicar said.

Wyatt had looked skeptical. "Isn't God a lot bigger than this?" he asked.

The Vicar sighed and decided not to try to explain metaphysical doctrine to a Walmsley.

"It is also Jesus' house," he had continued, hoping that this idea would be more accessible to the youngster.

"Too bad," the boy replied.

"Whatever do you mean?" the Vicar had asked nervously.

"Well," said Wyatt, looking around, "it's not vewy comfortable. There's no beds or sofas, and no telly."

"Jesus would not watch the telly," the Vicar said.

"Maybe not," Wyatt had agreed. "He'd pwobably wather be outside."

The Vicar, who felt that he was rapidly losing his grip on the conversation, murmured, "Outside?"

"Sure," said Wyatt. "In the Bible, he's always outside, having picnics and things."

"Picnics?"

"Wiff the woaves and the fishes," Wyatt explained patiently. "Or he's at the beach, or walking awound, or pwaying in some garden. He even died outside."

"Ah, but He didn't really die," the Vicar began, hoping to inject at least some morsel of solid theology into the dialogue.

"I know," said Wyatt, who did indeed know his Bible stories, rating them right up there with Super Hero Comics. "He wose on the third day and pushed away the stone. And went outside," he added triumphantly, "to work in a garden! That's where the Mawys saw Him. So I guess it's okay if His house isn't too comfortable; He pwobabwy doesn't use it too much. He might not even come inside to use the bafwoom. I don't, always," he added, confidingly.

At this point, the Vicar had suggested hastily that Wyatt leave before Osgood and the others discovered his hiding place.

Logan, who had been helping Althea bring the Ladies Guild flower arrangements in the side door, had quite agreed with everything that Wyatt had said. It seemed to him that if Christ ever did turn up in Far Tauverly, He would probably enjoy a ramble on the Greniston land.

Now Logan sighed at the thought.

"*If Jesus did turn up right now,*" he thought, "*I'd probably be afraid to look Him in the eye. What a fool I've been, filling my head with dreams and fantasies til I don't know what's real anymore. But I've been reminded of what's real. Oh yes, reminded very well! Plain old Logan Knowelles, good for a pint and a joke and not much else, that's what's real! 'You stay here, in case she rings,' that's what Greniston expected me to do, while Gwen was in real danger! He just found something to keep me busy with, to pacify me, like he did with the kids! I fell for it at the time, though when I look back on it, I don't know how I could have! Keeping me out from under foot, like I was a troublesome child! And me old enough to be his father, almost!*"

Logan paused and sighed. Krishna and his maidens looked unperturbed by his fuming. "What a bitter old fool I must sound like," he muttered aloud. "I can't blame Greniston for not taking me along to pursue a kidnapper! I wouldn't be much help. It just made me feel so old, and useless, and bloody left out! Damn it, I should have gone with him, not Filipo! I know Swindon; I know the ley of the land here. Filipo's just a... a foreigner!"

Logan blushed with shame, even as the words left his lips. "I didn't mean that," he said quickly. "I like Filipo. He seems like a very fine man, and he's been Gwen's friend a lot longer than I have. He seems used to action and things like that. Why shouldn't Greniston have asked him to come with? It was the right choice, and the fact is, Logan Knowelles, you're just plain jealous!"

He sighed again and wished that he did not feel quite so hung over. When Greniston had finally called the evening before, to let him know that

Gwen was safely back at the manor, his first thought had been one of sheer relief. The tension of waiting, so suddenly over, had left him feeling drained.

I'll have a drink, he had thought when he hung up. *Just one, in keeping with my promise to Gwydion, of course.*

There was only whiskey left in the cupboard. Against his better judgment, Logan had poured himself a stiff shot. The first sip did indeed soothe his nerves. But by the time the glass was half empty, a bitter bravado began to rise in him. Little hurts and fears he had swept under the carpet of his thinking now came to the fore.

"She could have called me herself," he thought reproachfully. "Surely she would have known I'd be worried. But then, now that Filipo's arrived, she doesn't have as much time for me. And then, of course, there's Greniston..."

A few days before, nothing would have made Logan happier than to think that Gwen and Greniston might fall in love. If that happened, he reasoned, they might marry, and she might stay in Far Tauverly. Now he realized that even if that daydream did come true, she would want to spend a great deal of time with Greniston. They might well travel, spend part of the year in London, and after all, the quaint, local postman who was amusing company for an American tourist might not do as the confidant of the next Lady Greniston.

Even as these thoughts rose up in him, Logan knew they were untrue. Yet knowing that didn't seem to make it any easier to fight them off. Perhaps feeling spiteful and nasty was better than letting himself look at the deeper feeling, which was, quite simply, that he felt old.

"Face it, Logan," he had told himself, "you fooled yourself that you were going to have adventures, be a part of things, but it was all just sheer imaginings." Without even thinking, he poured himself another drink.

If I imagined that, he thought, *what else have I been imagining? Gwydion, bards, a holy charge to do great things? I've imagined it all! The daft ravings of an old fool. Dreams, that's all!*

Indeed, the events on the mound seemed to him as if they had never happened. They had no more to do with real life than some story read in an old book. *What a fool I've been*, he thought again.

The phone rang. It was Robert.

"Lord Greniston wants to know if you'd like me to come round with the car," he explained, "since it's raining and all."

"The car?" Logan had asked, realizing that his speech was now none too clear.

"Lord Greniston said to remind you that you're part of the house party. He's having Mrs. Fitz keep some supper warm for you," Robert added.

"I'm afraid I can't make it tonight," Logan had managed to say, realizing that he probably couldn't make it to the door in his present state. "Behind on the mail. Lots of shorting, er, sorting, to do."

There was a pause, during which Robert seemed to be conveying this information to Greniston. Then he said, "Lord Greniston suggests that you send the bloody mail to Kingdom Come and hurry to the manor for a nightcap. But he says that if you feel you must be dreary, laudable, and responsible that you at least not forget the dinner laid on for tomorrow night. He says to be at the manor no later than five, for 'revels and music before we sup.' You know how he talks. Said I was especially to tell you that if you need a ride or anything, you've only to ring."

"Thank you," Logan managed to say, mouthing the words very carefully.

After he hung up, his first thought was, *They are only being kind. Greniston, Gwen, the lot of them. They don't want me there, they are just being kind.*

The thought of being included from pity stung Logan worse than the fear of being left out. Before he knew it, he had downed another glass of whiskey.

You're drunk now, lad, he realized, when his hand had difficulty getting the glass to his lips. *Your vow is broken for sure. But then, what does it matter, a vow made to shadows?* "Shadows to shadows," he said, lifting his glass in a shaky toast.

Then he had proceeded to drink, steadily and joylessly, until there was nothing left in the bottle and had passed out at the table. He was paying for it today.

"This is the worst hangover of my life," Logan remarked to the more sympathetic looking of Krishna's maidens. "And that's saying something."

He shook his head gingerly and instantly regretted even that small movement. "What's the use," he said aloud. "I've let down everything! I've dishonored Gwen's friendship by my doubts and jealousy; I've broken my vow to Gwydion. If he is real, he'll never want to deal with me again now."

"I'm not going to that dinner tonight," he decided, "I can't face anybody in this shape. After all, a man's got to keep his dignity."

"True enough, old bean. A man's got to keep his dignity."

Logan spun around, wondering who on earth could have been eavesdropping on him. A second later, he braced himself for the skull-splitting pain the movement should have caused him, but no hurt came. In fact, he suddenly felt amazingly lucid and refreshed.

"Tied one on, didn't you, mate?" the voice said sympathetically. For a moment, there still seemed to be no one there. Then, an instant later, Logan saw a man in military uniform standing next to one of Krishna's consorts. The man had one arm around the statue's shoulders and paused to glance at her attributes appreciatively.

"Happens in all the right places, don't she?" he asked with a wink. Then, reaching into his shirt pocket, he pulled out a little packet of herbs. "Just dissolve these leaves in hot tea," he said, "and it'll give your hangover the old caybash. Got 'em off a Parthian trader, and wondrous well they do work."

Logan stared at the man, wondering who on earth he was. He looked about fifty, cheerful and fit, if a bit rotund. He wore the white shirt, shorts, knee socks, and pith helmet of a British officer in the tropics. The stripes on his chest and the swagger stick under his arm proclaimed him to hold the office of Major, although there was no essence of command in his round, sunburned face or his friendly brown eyes.

"You look startled," he said to Logan, "and well you might be, me forgettin' my manners and all. Allow me to introduce myself, mate: Major Tommy Greniston. But you can call me Tommy."

"Where did you come from?" Logan asked.

Thomas Greniston, if that was indeed who stood before him, laughed. "Why, the officer's club." He peered more closely at Logan. "New here, ain't you? You look quite green around the gills, lad. Takes newcomers that way, sometimes, the heat and all. Not to worry, you'll soon come right."

Heat was not a feature Logan would have put to Far Tauverly's climate. Yet now that the Major—Tommy—mentioned it, the air did seem quite sultry, . . . odd, . . . and there was a heaviness to the sunlight that filtered down through the . . . surely, those weren't elms. They looked like some tropical, jungle tree . . . and was that frangipani, blooming along the garden wall, where only a moment before, there had been an ivy vine?

I must be dreaming, Logan decided.

Tommy settled down on the grass beside him. "Don't mind if I join you, do you? A lovely spot, these Maharani's gardens. Locals don't come here much; say it's haunted. I wouldn't mind running into the lady's ghost, tho. They say she was a real prize. Died young, poor girl. If you look through the branches of that baobab tree, you can see a corner of her summer house, just there. . . ."

At first, Logan thought he was seeing the familiar outlines of Shalimar House. Then he realized that the glimpse of domed roof and decorated balcony were subtly different. Everything was slightly different. Somehow, the wall around the garden was surely higher than before and was of some pink stone. . . . The trees above were much taller than he remembered, and among their overhanging branches, he caught the orange flash of a parrot's wings, and he could have sworn he heard the distant chattering of a monkey. The breeze that stirred the garden smelt of dust, manure, spices, and jasmine, all mingled into a strange, heady combination. From beyond the now-pink garden wall came the sounds of village life, but the village was not Far Tauverly. He heard the lowing of cattle and a woman's voice calling out wares in some unknown tongue. It all sounded faint and faraway, though this garden was as still, in its way, as the gardens of Shalimar House, and just as in the Shalimar gardens, there stood the statues of Krishna and Shiva. But between the statues, instead of a yew corridor, there now was a long, narrow rose garden with wine-red roses in full bloom.

"'My luv is like a red, red rose, that's newly sprung in June.' Robert Browning, wasn't it? Or was it Bobbie Burns? Never could keep those two straight," Tommy mused, "but it's nice poetry, anyway. Now then, as you were saying, 'A man's got to keep his dignity.' That was how you put it, wasn't it?" Logan nodded.

"I've never had much myself," Tommy said, "Dignity, that is. At least, not in the eyes of others. Bit of a buffoon, really." He shrugged. "I can be philosophical about it now, but there were times when it stung, I can tell you! Family never thought I amounted to much. The enlisted men snickered at me behind my back, the other officers smiled to my face. Even poor Maude was disappointed in me. Just too boring for her, really."

Tommy shook his head. "Enough to drive a man to drink."

"It could do that," Logan agreed.

337

"Yes," said Tommy, "hard to feel the fool. For me, it all came to a head when I was just about to retire from the service. . . . Nine more months I had to go. . . . It hasn't happened yet, but it will, of course. . . ."

Logan looked confused.

"I see you still think of time as a line," Tommy said sympathetically. "It's more round, really. You see, today I'm fifty, but I remember very well what I did when I was fifty-four."

"I must be dreaming again," mused Logan.

"Not exactly. But don't worry about it, takes getting used to. Anyway, as I said, this happened in '47, when I was fifty-four. Stationed northwest of Delhi, then. Things were dodgy, very dodgy, what with Indian Independence right around the corner, and all the fighting between Pakistanis and Hindus, and everyone mad at the British. You never knew where trouble would break out next.

"Well, I was due for retirement in nine months, like I said, so I hoped I might be able to just glide through my time without encountering any real danger and then take an extended holiday in Bali on my way back home. And yet, even as part of me wanted to lay low and not make any waves, another part of me couldn't stand it. *Thomas Randall Greniston*, I thought to myself, *you've lived for fifty-four years, and been in the military for thirty five, and you've never done one really brave or dashing thing!* It rankled me. I felt not useful, somehow, not a man. But then, I was accustomed to a faint self-disgust by then—the background noise of my life, really.

"I fully expected to serve out my time without incident. And then, It started. Funny, how you remember things. There I was, sitting in my quarters in my pajamas and dressing gown, drinking my morning chai, perusing a map of Bali. Then, in comes young Lieutenant Oberly, absolutely spruce and in uniform at seven a.m. I used to wonder if he slept in uniform, at attention. Anyway, he came in without knocking, very unlike him. And he said, 'It's started.' That was all he needed to say; we all lived in fear of 'It' starting at any moment. 'It' being the violence that seemed to have a life of its own at that time. It might break out as a Muslim crowd attacking a Hindu temple, or a Hindu crowd retaliating against a street of Muslim shops, or a mixed crowd setting fire to a British government building, or a group of our soldiers panicking and firing into a crowd, any crowd, with unreasoned cruelty.

"Up until then, the madness had passed us by in our little backwater of a post, but we all knew it was only a matter of time before it reached us, too. It didn't even occur to me to ask how 'It' had started. It would have been as pointless as asking what kind of twig had started a forest fire. We were all dry kindling, in those days, everyone in India. There was a violence loose on the land that, like a fire, didn't care what wood it fed on, as long as there was tinder in its path.

"These kinds of thoughts went through my mind very quickly, as Oberly stood there. Then my gaze happened to fall on a red geranium I had planted in an old tea tin and was trying to grow on my windowsill. It looked so homey there and so at odds with the threat coming toward us. Then I heard, in the distance, that odd, impersonal roar of a crowd, rushing through the streets like a wave. I knew that people I knew might be faces in that crowd: the shopkeeper I bought tobacco from, a flower seller I always greeted—perhaps my own servant, Hasim, who, come to think of it, I hadn't seen in over an hour. I wasn't shocked. I didn't hold it against them any more than you hold it against someone if they catch cholera when there's an epidemic in the city. You just hope your own resistance is strong enough to keep you from catching it, too.

"'Right,' I said to Oberly, 'what's the plan?' He flashed me a grateful smile. I think he'd feared that because I outranked him, I might try to take charge. We both knew that that would be absurd. Although only thirty, he'd been stationed at Calcutta and Bombay and had experience with this sort of thing.

"'Well, Sir,' he said carefully, still deferring to my supposed rank, 'Laughton and I have mustered what troops we can, and we'll head toward the bazaar. That's where it started. Haze is organizing reserves at the barracks. Unfortunately, we can't send for help; the lines are already down. But we thought, Sir, that you could take the ladies—fortunately there's only Mrs. Haze and Mrs. Hewbridge, the rest went to Simla three days ago, thank God—and head into the countryside, lie low 'til things cool off, and try to find a way to get a message through to Debpanapoor, that's probably the closest. If you think it's a good plan, of course, Sir.'

"We exchanged an eloquent glance. We both knew it didn't matter a monkey's toss what I thought of the plan; I certainly didn't have a better one. We both also knew that any green recruit could have done as well at shepherding the ladies. It wasn't a job you gave to a valuable officer. He wanted me out of the way, Oberly did, it was too bloody awkward, taking over command with me right there, yet he knew he had to. I decided to make it easy on him.

"'Right,' I said crisply, as if I'd actually just been given the most crucial part of a mission. 'I'll take a jeep, and head northwest. Send someone to get the ladies packed, and try to get them not to take too much luggage.' I added dryly. 'We won't be attending too many formal dinners in the hills this season.' Oberly grinned, as I'd hoped he would, and we parted with a jest.

"Just a few minutes later, the ladies and I were bouncing along the dirt road that inched its way up the hills behind the town. The landscape was parched, the earth hardened to bone-pale smoothness. The sky, too, had the pale blue quality of a bleached-out old photograph. In the valley below, the post was already marked by plumes of smoke, and when the wind shifted, we heard the sounds of distant fighting.

"Young Mrs. Haze was a wreck, poor thing, worrying about her husband, who was somewhere down in the fray. Mrs. Hewbridge, on the other hand, seemed far more concerned about the lack of a parasol than her own spouse's fate. 'Really, Amrita,' she chastised her maid, 'you should have remembered to pack it.'

"The servant said nothing, just kept her face hidden behind the pink veil of her sari. I suppose she was used to Mrs. Hewbridge's recriminations. She had with her a child of three or four. Male or female, I couldn't tell. It kept its face buried in her skirts, whether in fear of riots or Mrs. Hewbridge, it was hard to say.

"I really hadn't counted on the servant and child when I'd hastily put what provisions I could find into the jeep. Probably Mrs. Hewbridge hadn't thought of them as passengers, just part of the luggage.

"'Oh dear,' Mrs. Hewbridge exclaimed at every bump in the road. Considering that she was far and away the best padded among us, I found it hard to be sympathetic. I had never liked Emily Hewbridge. At forty-seven, she still cultivated the voice and coy mannerisms of a young girl, though her features were those of a Roman matron. Her chief enjoyment in life was complaint, and so, in a funny sort of way, our escape afforded her the prospect of a really good time, there being no dearth of discomforts. If she wasn't exclaiming at the rutted road, she was bemoaning the lack of a parasol, or the fact that the water from the canteen tasted odd, or that I seemed a sorry choice for a protector: Why hadn't they sent young Captain Gregory.

"Meanwhile, young Mrs. Haze kept sobbing into her handkerchief, occasionally finding the strength to say 'Oh, poor Robin,' before she dissolved into tears again. It was only fifteen miles to the nearest village, but it seemed like fifteen hundred.

"It was a quiet little puddle of a place that had scarcely heard of telephones, let alone had one. News of the trouble hadn't reached them yet and perhaps never would have, if we hadn't arrived. The villagers were all concern, murmuring soft commiserations at the red face of Mrs. Hewbridge, outraged in its sunburn, and the constant tears of Mrs. Haze.

"The place boasted three trees and a bush, a miracle of vegetation, after the landscape we had just passed through. There was also water: a thin brown trickle of a creek, dribbling down the hillside, as if some God had spat tobacco juice there and never bothered to wipe it up.

"'What an awful place!' Emily Hewbridge exclaimed. She stared at the huts the villagers lived in. 'You can't expect us to stay in one of those,' she said firmly. Fortunately, I had brought a tent, which, although not nearly as comfortable as the village huts, had the virtue, in Mrs. Hewbridge's eyes, of being British. With a good deal of help from Mrs. Haze, who snapped out of her tears quite nicely once she had something to do, I got the tent set up and the food and water unpacked.

"All this while, a plan had been forming in my mind. It seemed to me that the ladies were safe enough for the moment, far safer than they would be driving around in what was clearly an army jeep. The best idea seemed to leave them there, while I pressed on to Debpanapoor, some twenty miles further, where I knew there was a telegraph line, unless the fighting had spread that far. I broached the plan to Mrs. Haze, who instantly agreed, with amazing spunk. 'Emily won't be pleased,' she said, 'but you leave her to me. If I were you, I'd just get in the jeep, and bloody well go.'

"I decided that she was right. I gave her my extra pistol, along with a brief lesson on how to use it. As I pulled away from the campsite, I heard Mrs. Hewbridge exclaim, 'Where is he going? What does he think he is doing? What . . .'

"Mrs. Haze interrupted, 'Now listen to me, you old bat. I'm sick of your complaints and hysterics! If we are going to survive together in this tent, you are going to keep your big mouth shut, otherwise I can't guarantee what use I'll put this pistol to.'

"There was actually—note it for the history books—a moment of stunned silence. I confess that as I drove away, I was grinning. I made it to Debpanapoor without incident. They had had some trouble there but nothing nearly as serious as us. I was able to telegraph Delhi from there, in the hope of reinforcements. I felt a great sense of relief. I had done what I could. After a brief meal with the lieutenant, I headed back toward the village where I had left the ladies.

"It was sunset by then. The sky was purple, smudged with gold. The air, still hot, was softened by the movement of a breeze. It was odd to think of such a dollop of beauty being ladled onto a landscape so filled with violence. I pulled over to the side of the road to enjoy the changing sky. Then, behind me, in the jeep, I heard a sound. I spun around, pistol in hand, and there, peering at me from underneath a tarp I'd thrown in the back when we unpacked, was the servant, Amrita, and her child. Evidently, she had hidden back there when I left the village and was only now risking being seen."

Tommy Greniston paused and took a sip of the gin and tonic that he was now, somehow, holding. Logan realized that the time of day had adjusted in keeping with Greniston's tale. It was now twilight in the garden where they sat. Not the misty lingering of a Far Tauverly twilight, but the sudden twilight that comes to hot lands like a benediction after the fierceness of the day. The tangled trees were filled with soft, lavender shadows; the vault of the sky overhead was amethyst near the horizon, fading to a pale sea-green above. Here and there, very faintly, the first stars began to appear. From somewhere beyond the garden walls, certainly not from St. Aethelrood's, a muezzin gave the evening call to prayer. His distant cry leant a note of infinite longing to the scene.

Tommy Greniston sighed. "Ah," he said, "I'll tell you, I've seen beauty in many forms, in many places. But never anything like what was in the face of that serving girl and her child, when I saw it. The veil from her sari had fallen back, and in the twilight there, I saw her clearly for the first time. I tell you, she could have posed for a Renaissance Madonna, her features were that sweet. It was most of all her eyes that caught me. Big, lustrous eyes. They gazed at me, so steady, clear, and trusting. She pointed to the North and said something in a dialect I couldn't understand at all. 'No, no,' I explained, 'there's more fighting there.' She ignored this, and continued pointing to the horizon, speaking in the most beseeching tones. Then the child stirred beside her, lifted its head, and looked at me.

"I am sure I gasped with surprise when I saw its face. I was shocked by the sheer beauty of it. It was a little boy, with the pure features that make any child beautiful. But, as with its mother, its really extraordinary beauty lay in its eyes. They absolutely gleamed with light. The expression in them was at once so young and yet so ancient. For all their innocence, those eyes looked as if they would be surprised by nothing, as if they had already anticipated and forgiven anything that could possibly happen.

"Their gaze stopped me, I can tell you. Looking at those ancient eyes in that young, young face, I remembered something I had heard an old Rabbi in Bombay say: that at any given moment, there are only thirty-six truly good people in the world, and upon their continuing goodness, the fate of the world depends—but they don't know who they are.

"I felt sure that I was looking into the eyes of one destined to be one of those thirty-six good people. Somehow, that child seemed to have a destiny, had something vital to do here on this earth. Oh, I don't mean a famous destiny, not the destiny of a Christ or a Buddha, but one of the anonymous destinies, one of the lights of this dark world, whose mere existence stands between us and utter destruction, like a wall of tissue paper, holding back a flood.

"I met the mother's gaze again. Her eyes seemed to say, 'You see how it is.' I nodded. It sounds daft, I'm sure, that I felt these 'knowings,' just from the look in a child's eyes. Well, perhaps it was daft, but to me, at that time, it was as real as anything I had ever met. I started the jeep again and drove in the direction the mother wanted. It no longer bothered me in the least that this was not a rational plan. I was in the presence of a mystery, and the mystery knew what it was doing.

"Our journey together lasted seven days. I sometimes feel as if I remember every instant of it, so vivid an impression did it make upon me. I remember how we traveled by night on deserted roads, with the Milky Way above us like a sea of scattered jewels. We rested in the daytime, hidden in what patches of undergrowth we could find. There was danger. Three times we skirted the edge of fighting. Once, on a lonely stretch of road, I had to threaten bandits with my pistol. Who would have thought it? Old Tommy Greniston, playing the hero! We passed as well the traces of violence: a burned village, a railway station abandoned and looted. It was there I was able to find some petrol.

"It was just at dawn when we finally said good bye. The jeep had run out of fuel at about midnight, the night before. By dawn, we had reached a hilly, wild area, far from any fighting. The air was cool, the hillsides softened by grass and pines. Here and there we even came across streams of sweet water. From the lightness in her step and the gladness in her eye, it seemed that Amrita recognized the area, although whether that was because she had been there before or because she, like me, was in the current of a mystery and knew that it had led her to where she needed to be, I will never know.

"I will always remember that dawn. We were near a line of poplar trees that rustled in the wind. In the grayness, one bird had begun to sing. Its music was so pure, it made my heart ache just to hear it.

"Amrita pointed into the hills and made clear with her gestures, if not her words, that she and the boy could go on alone now. It seemed that our little sojourn as Madonna, Child, and unlikely Joseph was at an end.

"Her face shone with gratitude. She made a deep *namaste*. The boy looked at me out of his ancient, peaceful eyes and smiled just a little. Then, with a last wave, they walked on and soon disappeared into the misty distance.

"My return to the post was uneventful. Most of the local fighting had died down by then. I walked cross-country for two days; then caught a lift the rest of the way with a Red Cross lorry. I had come up with a really good story about being jumped by ruffians on the way back to Debpanapoor. At first, I said, they had intended to hold me for ransom, then they had thought the better of it, taken the jeep, and dumped me in unknown country, and it had taken me days to find my way back. In that time of unbelievable truths, it was a plausible enough lie; it served not only to keep me out of trouble but to buy me several good drinks at the club as well.

"Of course, I never forgot the real story. And I've never told it to another soul, except to you, just now. For one thing, I knew what the other officers would make of it. 'Took you for a good one, Tommy,' they'd say. 'A little native skirt decides it's time to head for her hometown, and all she has to do is bat her eyes at you, and you're turning AWOL, to drive her to her doorstep! That's rich! Mystic child, indeed; probably some wandering beggar's bastard, that's all.'

"And so it would have gone. I couldn't bear to have their smudged thoughts fingering my memory, so I never told 'em. It might well have been all in my imagination, but as much as I have doubted my own perceptions afterwards, at the time I was certain, and I will never regret having trusted that certainty.

"Never found out what happened to Amrita and the child. It's only in fiction that you get all the loose ends nicely trimmed; in life, it's almost always mostly unknown. You never know what your efforts amounted to, you only know whether you tried your best or not. Something wants it that way, I've come to suspect.

"One thing I know for certain, though: there's great mysteries at play in this world. Think of it like a river: if you just paddle around near the bank, you think it's all pretty tame and predictable, but if you get out into the middle of the river, you discover there's mighty currents out there that pick you up and carry you along with them, like a little leaf before their power, yes indeed. When my life touched Amrita and the child's, it pulled me out of the shallows and into the center of that river, into the great mystery currents, for just a little while.

"Ah, but that's everything, that's Life, lad! 'A man's got to have his dignity,' wasn't that what you were sayin' when I came in? Well, I don't know, it seems to me there's more important things. Bit of an overrated business, this dignity stuff. Life, lad, life, that's the thing! But can you get to it? That's the question!"

Tommy Greniston paused, his head tilted to one side, and looked at Logan in the most engaging manner. "Seems to me," he mused, "that one of those mystery currents is tugging at you. Why resist? Going to let a hangover and a bit of wounded pride keep you from life?"

Tommy paused to light a cigar. It was night, now, in the garden. Moonlight silvered the edges of the Maharani's abandoned palace. The scent of night-blooming flowers was heavy on the dark air.

Tommy breathed in deeply. "Ratrani, that's called," he said, "Queen of the Night. . . ." The smoke from his cigar, which was an excellent one, mingled with the scent of the flowers.

"What a funny old world," he reflected. "It's a place of longing, that's what this place is. You'd think life would be the easiest thing in the world to get to, bein' as we're all born into it. But it isn't, not the deep life, not the one we're always longing for. I tell you, lad, if you get a chance to

345

touch that life, even for a moment, don't let anything stop you, even yourself! Funny thing is, the closer you get to what you are longing for, the more full of longing you will be. Something wants it that way, I suspect. And never will you be able to put it into words any more than you can put this marvelous night wind into a box and keep it on a shelf somewhere. No, life's the part that's always dancing—even I, daft old Tommy Greniston, know that."

For several minutes, Tommy gazed pensively at the moonlit garden. Then he said to Logan, "People have got history all wrong, you know. They think it's made up of a few great men and women who were born great, not cut out of the same cloth as the rest of us poor wretches. But it's not true. I've met quite a few heroes, and as near as I can tell, they're imperfect, struggling fools like you and me. The main difference between them and most people is that they get a taste of the big currents, out at the center of the river, the mystery currents, and they decide that they don't ever want to come back to the shallows, so they find themselves doing whatever it takes to stay with those currents, and that struggle changes them in ways they could have never predicted.

"That's their courage; not that they are born better than most, but that they keep flinging themselves toward life, however it appears to them. Most of 'em didn't know they were great at the time, you know. Listen, you think of some big names, like Beethoven, Shakespeare, Buddha, King Arthur—there's a nice local Far Tauverly lad—they didn't know that anyone was going to remember 'em or call them great, centuries later! Mostly their own folk thought they were pretty weird, and they themselves thought so, too, sometimes, but they had a longing in them that wouldn't give up. And do you know what else? Most of the great folks who actually make a difference in this world have been unknown—the anonymous ones, the thirty-six good people who don't even know who they are themselves.

"Cause history's not like people think. People think that history's the part they know about, the part that gets written down in books and remembered." Tommy shook his head. "That's the least of it! No, most of the real heroes have been anonymous. What good did it do for the world, you might say, if no one knew about their good deeds?

"Ah, but listen; *something* always knows. There's no moment of life here, no passing thought of some old fart at a garden party in Bristol, no breath of a sleeping baby in Lima, no fanning of a butterfly's wings on a branch in a tree in the heart of fifty thousand acres of jungle somewhere in

Uganda that doesn't get recorded, noted down. It's all in the record, lad, it's all in the record. And do you know what? You help make that record, the days of your life. Oh yes, you do. All the goodness that ever happened on this planet is in that record, and all the evil. And I'll tell you, it's a near thing, the balances of it! You know, when I was a lad, they used to get very concerned about the air quality in the cities. People still burned a lot of coal in those days, and if the conditions were right, and the fog and coal smoke combined, it could make a 'real pea-souper.' If you went out in it, it could kill you, if your lungs weren't good. So they'd warn people, stay at home today, if you possibly can.

"I gather this kind of worry about air pollution is pretty general in your world, now-a-days. But what about the *goodness* pollution? Do you know, in the realm where I live now, you can actually see the general level of greed and cruelty and despair in a place, like a fog in the air! On the other hand, you can also see the amount of goodness, generosity, kindness. Things like that are shining and clear. No one comes on your telly thing nowadays and says, 'Levels of greed are dangerously high today, and levels of patience are poor.' But by God, they ought to! And you see, everything you do goes into those general levels—every thought, every act, even the private moments of courage or generosity that you think no one will ever know about—they're all there, in the record of the world. So don't ever give up, lad! So you were a fool yesterday? Yesterday is gone! But your next thought could be a shining one that helps to keep the balances livable. Because the balances between good and evil are a near thing on this planet right now, I tell you. We need all the shining thoughts we can get, the anonymous ones most of all. Tend to be cleaner, actually, the anonymous ones."

Tommy Greniston paused, leaned forward, and looked searchingly at Logan. "This make any sense to you, old bean?"

Logan nodded. "Oddly enough, yes."

Tommy smiled and looked rather relieved. "Hope so," he murmured to himself. "Wouldn't want to botch this mission!" Then he added brightly, "Well, old boy, I've got to be going. It'll be day soon." As he said this, Logan realized that it had been getting lighter for some time, the garden was now full of the misty freshness that comes just before dawn.

Tommy glanced at his watch. "Got to check back in at HQ," he said, "then I've got a breakfast date with a farmer near Dubuque, and then an urgent appointment with a little girl in Zanzibar at two thirty two p.m. exactly. Hope the winds are in my favor.

"However, just before I go, I thought you might like to see some of the unknown great ones. Might beef you up a bit, let you know you're not alone and all that. Now, just you take a looksee at that grove of mimosas over there, . . . that's right, . . . just relax your gaze, look softly."

Logan gazed at the shadowy trees. A pale golden mist began to fill the air, like the one he had seen around Gwydion and the bards. Looking into it, he began again to see row upon row of tiered faces, like the faces of an audience in some vast auditorium. Each was human and unique, but they all shared an expression of intensity and longing, as if they urgently wished to get some message across to him but could not speak it. Faces from every time and place were there: a Masai warrior, a twelfth-century Geisha, a confederate soldier, a Victorian housewife, an Eskimo hunter, a scribe of Egypt, a Jewish scholar from old Krakow, a young girl from Tahiti, a wise old woman of the Iroquois tribe, a gallant youth from Renaissance Florence in a golden tunic and dark red cap. Face upon face: faces of beggars, faces of Kings, faces of mothers and soldiers, of clerks and cooks, of poets and ditch diggers, even faces of thieves and cheats who had somehow done more good than evil, in spite of themselves.

Not a one was a famous face. You could have passed any one of them in a marketplace of their time and scarcely noticed them. Yet, all together, they were unusual faces, unusual because of the light in their eyes. Logan found himself remembering what Tommy had said: "They got a taste of the big currents, the mystery currents, and they struggled to stay with them." Yes, as different as the faces were, they all had that quality in common, that sense of having been touched by something greater than life in the shallows, greater than just themselves and their selfish concerns. And now they all seemed to share the understanding that Life, every Life, every second of it, was a bigger and more important thing than most people ever understand. It was this knowledge they seemed to long to convey to Logan by the sheer earnestness of their gaze. He felt the power of all their eyes looking at him, as if saying, "It matters, what you do; it matters, how you live. Every instant of it matters, and you have another instant, with every breath you take." "Be Great," their eyes seemed to say. "You must try, and try, and try, again."

As if reading his thoughts, Tommy Greniston said, "Yes, we want you to try. We're out of the game, now, you see. Out of your game and into another. Our record is written, but yours is yet unfinished. You can still choose, lad! Our time in your realm is done, we can only look on from the wings, but you, the living; you're center stage, now. You write the lines, so write some great ones, lad. Why not? It's such a short scene, each life; why not make it really count? We'll give you everything we've got—courage, inspiration, loyalty—but now, it can only turn into actions through you, who are alive. You ones who have the stage, whilst others wait to appear. You can't believe the help that we would give you, if only you would try."

Tommy's voice was fading, now. The golden cloud of faces was slowly fading, too. Logan strained to see as many of them as possible, before the vision faded. He caught a glimpse of someone who might have been Amrita and of her wondrous child, grown up. He saw another face he was sure was Emily Hewbridge. Perhaps she had distinguished herself by later valor, in spite of being an old battle-ax. What had Tommy said? "Every breath a new chance to try again." It gave Logan great hope to see Emily Hewbridge there, sixty years a pain in the neck to one and all, and yet she, too, had met a moment that won her entry into that noble company.

If she can do it, I can do it, Logan thought. Emily Hewbridge smiled, as if in agreement.

The vision faded to a golden shimmer on the air. He faintly heard Tommy Greniston saying, "Quite enjoyed our chat, old bean. Must be off to HQ, ta-ra . . . "

And then, Logan found himself sitting in Shalimar gardens, in the midmorning sunlight of an English spring day—and another voice was calling "Logan? Logan?"

He turned and saw Gwen, standing by the statue of Shiva. "I've been looking for you everywhere," she said. "Are you all right?"

"Never better," Logan replied, slowly. "By the way, what day is this?"

***

Half an hour later found Gwen and Logan happily ensconced at a window table in the Tweeverton Tea Shop. Logan was reassured to know that it was still Saturday, May third, the same day he had started out on before his encounter with Tommy Greniston. Gwen relaxed in to the cheerful normalcy of the place: flowered chintz curtains, the smell of toast and cinnamon rolls, the clinking of teacups, and the voices of housewives chatting as they took a break from their shopping expeditions. The setting offered a welcome relief from the intensity of their lives over the last few days.

As Logan devoured a bowl of shortcake with hothouse strawberries and clotted cream and drank his way through four cups of strong coffee, Gwen nibbled her watercress sandwich (she seemed, recently, to be cultivating a taste in everything British) and filled him in on every detail of her 'kidnapping' and rescue.

"I'm sorry I didn't get to talk to you last night," she added at the end of her narrative. "I fell asleep in the car before we even got back. I slept for fourteen hours, they tell me."

"Well, of course you did," Logan replied understandingly. "You had a nasty shock to get over."

"All the same," said Gwen firmly, "I don't want our friendship to fall into disrepair, just because of unexpected events."

If Logan had any lingering doubts about Gwen's feelings for him, they were dispelled by the staunch way she said this and reached across the table to clasp his hand.

"I looked for you everywhere this morning," she added. "When you weren't at the post office or on your route, I felt sure you would be on the grounds somewhere. That was a wonderful old place I found you in." She added curiously, "I never even knew it was there." She sipped her coffee, and said, "I'm glad I found you so that we could talk, and also because I don't think I would have ever been able to get back into a car again without your help."

Their expedition to Tweeverton was Gwen's way of jumping back on the horse that threw her. After the accident with Swindon, she had feared she would never have the nerve to ride in a car again, let alone drive, so she had resolved to take her rental car at least as far as Tweeverton, before her fear hardened any more. She felt Logan was the perfect companion for such a journey because, as she had explained to him, "you won't laugh at me or get impatient if I burst into tears before I even start the engine." Logan had nodded sympathetically; although he didn't mind being driven, he hated to drive himself. Perhaps because of his moral support, Gwen had made it as far as Tweeverton without incident. "Let's quit while we're ahead," she had suggested, once they reached the neighboring town. Now, as they enjoyed their snack, her relief was palpable.

"Is Swindon going to be all right?" Logan asked.

"They think so," Gwen replied. "I called the hospital this morning. They said he would need to stay there for at least two weeks. His concussion is worse than they thought at first, and the broken arm needs traction for a while. But the doctors think there's no permanent damage. I didn't talk to Swindon," Gwen added. "He was asleep when I called. It's just as well, really; I don't know what I'd say to him."

"I can think of a few choice things," Logan muttered.

Gwen shook her head. "Don't be too hard on him," she protested. "He didn't kidnap me, not exactly. He honestly thought I had read his letter and was waiting at the inn to meet him. When he finally understood that it was all a misunderstanding, you should have seen his face. I never saw a man look so desolate. He instantly offered to take me back, as soon as he understood."

Gwen paused, her face growing pale as she remembered the shock of the accident. "But you will press charges?" Logan asked.

"No. But I spoke with his mother, and told her that I would take legal recourse, unless she guaranteed that Swindon would get serious counseling for as long as is needed. He is very unstable emotionally, much more so than shows on the surface."

"How did she take it?" asked Logan, rightly suspecting that the appearance-conscious Swindons would view psychiatric care as a real stigma.

"She wasn't what I'd call pleased," Gwen said dryly, "but I managed to convince her that counseling would be better than a jail sentence. To tell you the truth," she added, "I think the shock itself has done a lot to bring Geoff back to reality. Let's hope so."

"Yes," said Logan, reflecting on his own experiences of—could it be, just that morning? "He's young, he has so many moments yet to come. He must understand that there's still a chance for him."

Gwen looked surprised at the note of compassion in her friend's voice. *Something is definitely going on with Logan these last few days*, she thought.

Logan met her curious gaze and smiled. "A lot has happened since last we spoke," he said. Carefully, he described to her his strange experiences of the last few days, from his "dream" on the mound to his encounter with Tommy Greniston that morning. He remembered the Walmsley children's instruction that he was to tell no one of his experiences during his initiation to their kingdom, but he felt that Gwen would be an exception to this rule, even in their eyes. And there were parts of his experiences that he did not speak of, any more than he would have pulled a just planted seed from the earth to show to anyone. In time, when all that had happened to him was not so new and fragile, he knew he would be able to tell her more, and of all the people on earth, she would be the one he could confide it to. He told her enough, though, to give her a vivid picture of his encounters with other realms.

"It's all part of the same mystery," she said. "The cry I heard, what's happened to you, the chalice being stolen, what the children are up to in the woods. . . . It's all interwoven, somehow. It's as if two worlds that usually live side by side but never touch are actually interplaying for a while, and I wonder why."

For a moment, the mystery of the events in which they had been caught up seemed to surround Logan and Gwen, even at their cozy table in the busy teashop. Then a waitress laughed nearby, and they felt themselves brought back to the resolutely ordinary world of cheese sandwiches and neighborhood chat.

"Let's enjoy this while we can," suggested Logan.

"Yes," Gwen agreed. "I have a feeling the Mystery is just catching its breath and is soon to return, stronger than ever."

After they finished their tea, they spent a pleasant hour exploring the Tweeverton church, St. Mary of the Meadows. Here they encountered nary a ghost, only a friendly verger and a nun trying unsuccessfully to shepherd a party of schoolchildren through the peaceful aisles with some degree of quiet. Watching the children, Gwen remarked, "I hope Filipo and Robert are okay. They volunteered to take the Walmsley children to the Bristol Zoo today, since it didn't work out yesterday."

"I salute them," said Logan solemnly.

After their peaceful exploration of the church, Gwen decided to find a beauty salon. She wanted to get her hair done for the special dinner that evening. Once she found a place to her liking, Logan went off on a search of his own to the florist shop near the train station.

"We have several lovely 'Get well' bouquets," the clerk said brightly. "This one comes with pink carnations, yellow daisies, and a heart shaped balloon that says 'Get Well Soon!' Or, for only fifty pence more, you can send pink sweetheart roses, with a white stuffed bear holding an umbrella that says, 'Sorry you're under the weather.' And the bear is crying; he has a glass tear on his cheek! It's very sweet."

Logan couldn't imagine Swindon enjoying either the balloon or the bear. "I think three blue irises, three white freesias, and some ferns," he said.

"And how should the card read?" the clerk asked.

Logan paused. He couldn't send the flowers anonymously. Swindon might think they were from Gwen, with disastrous results. On the other hand, he couldn't sign his own name. Swindon would never understand why Logan Knowelles would send any comfort to him. He might even take it as a kind of mockery. Logan considered something cheery, like "From your pals in Far Tauverly," but that, too, fell flat. Geoff Swindon knew perfectly well he didn't have a single real friend in Far Tauverly, or anywhere else, for that matter.

"Put: 'With sincere best wishes for your recovery and future from Tommy G. and Emily Hewbridge,'" he said at last. *Let it remain an enigma,* he decided, *that s best.*

After a pleasant ramble through two bookstores, Logan met Gwen outside Chez Patrice. Her hair was covered with a blue scarf, but from the smile on her face, she seemed quite pleased with the result.

"I'll unveil it tonight," she explained, "with the dress and everything—the grand entrance effect."

Logan smiled. "Could all this attention to beauty have anything to do with the presence of a certain Lord Greniston?" he asked.

Gwen blushed. "Well . . . perhaps. Yes, actually, . . . but don't you tell a soul!"

"Aha!" replied Logan, "I knew something was brewing! But mum's the word." To himself, he thought that Gwen's radiance rang clearer than any words could, and that, clearly, events between herself and Greniston were progressing nicely.

As they walked back to the car, the church bells tolled out three p.m., and Gwen remarked, "Well, I'm not on that flight to New York."

"New York?" Logan exclaimed.

Gwen nodded, a twinkle in her eye. "Yes, and my travel agent back in Denver had it all planned out so nicely, too. Lovely girl, name of Gwen. You'd like her. She had me scheduled to depart Gatwick airport on flight 704 to America, my little holiday in England being over."

"Oh my," said Logan, "you must like Greniston a great deal."

Gwen laughed. "I believe I do," she said. "But you know, he isn't the only reason I'm still here. It's the whole story, you might say. You are part of

353

it, and King Arthur, and Sir Peter, even Geoff Swindon, in his way. It just feels like we're all brought together for a purpose, and whatever that purpose is about, it isn't finished yet. I thought about it quite a lot, and I decided I couldn't just leave in mid-story, so to speak."

"Of course not," agreed Logan.

"I'm glad you agree," said Gwen. "I've been wondering if my choice was crazy. I've never done anything like this before. Oh, I've done impulsive things, like moving to Denver or coming on this trip in the first place. But this is the first time in my life I've ever done anything adventurous when I had the time to think it over, when it was really my choice. Usually, when I have time to think about things, I play it safe. This time, it's different. There is nothing I'm running away from or rebelling against. It's just my choice to be mad." She smiled. "It's a great feeling. Despite the fact that I don't know if I can get any money back on the plane ticket, my charge cards are just about up to the hilt, and after this house party at Lord Greniston's is over, I don't know where I'll stay."

"Have you got any cash?" Logan asked.

Gwen checked the contents of her wallet. "Seventeen pounds and forty-three cents."

"Don't worry," Logan said quickly, "You are welcome to stay with me for as long as you wish to. Either at Kestrel Farm or at the post office. You need never be without a home and meals, not as long as I've got a roof over my head." Reflecting that, given his tax situation, that might not be too much longer, he added, "If we have to, we'll break into Shalimar House and live there secretly."

"Or inside of the mound," Gwen suggested.

"Or in the Walmsleys' tree house!" Their eyes met, and the two friends found themselves laughing.

"I don't know how I can feel so carefree," Gwen said, a few minutes later, wiping her eyes. "But I do. I don't even know how to explain it, really. It's just that I have the strangest sense that all I need to worry about is staying with this mystery, and the rest will take care of itself."

Logan smiled, in complete agreement.

***

At Greniston Manor, the Lord of that noble house had barricaded himself in his study. In a futile attempt to protect himself from the Walmsley children, just returned from Bristol Zoo and dangerously armed with all-day suckers shaped like hippos, and from Mrs. Fitzpatrick and Mrs. Hodges, who were in a frenzied ecstasy of last-minute planning for the night's dinner, he had actually dragged a sofa in front of his study door. He had reckoned without the resourcefulness of young Wyatt, however. A strange thumping, which seemed to come from inside the east wall of his study, alerted him to the fact that all was not well with his citadel.

"What the devil is that?" Greniston demanded of Shakespeare, as he slammed a handful of papers down on his desk. "How can a man be expected to write in the midst of this infernal racket?"

The bard refrained from comment. The thumping continued, louder than before.

Feeling rather absurd, Greniston went to the wall, and thundered "Who's there?"

Somehow, he wasn't surprised when a muffled voice exclaimed excitedly, "Hewwo? Ward Gweniston?!"

"Wyatt! What are you doing in the wall?"

The explanation that followed was far too garbled to understand through stone and plaster. *How can he be in the wall?* Greniston wondered, baffled. Then he remembered that behind a bookshelf, long unused, was a dumb waiter that connected his study—once a breakfast room, decades before—with the basement below.

Better get him out of there, Greniston thought quickly. *That contraption hasn t been used for twenty years. I ve no idea if the cables are still safe.*

"Be right there, Wyatt," he bellowed. He tried to slide the oak bookshelf away from the wall, but it was far too heavy. "Like trying to move the bloody rock of Gibraltar," Greniston muttered. He began flinging books off the shelves, until, at last, the cumbersome old piece of furniture was light enough to move. He reached the dumb waiter and tugged the stiff door open, grazing his knuckles on the lock. Out tumbled Wyatt, hippo lollipop in hand and wearing a fluorescent orange baseball cap that said "Support the Bristol Zoo." His jacket was adorned with a veritable chain mail of buttons, endorsing everything from whales to rain forests to the zoo's "Junior Guides of the Wild" program.

"Ward Gweniston!" Wyatt exclaimed, waving the sucker within an inch of Greniston's face. "I'm ever so gwad to see you! We had a fabuwous day! We saw the penguins, and Osgood almost got bitten by the tiger, and we

355

went to a Wimpy's bar! Charles had too many burgers and thwew up! It was gweat! And wook what I got!"

Out of his pocket, Wyatt pulled a little canister that, when turned upside down, emitted a sound vaguely like the mooing of a cow.

"Oh dear," said Greniston.

"No, it's not a deer," explained Wyatt, "It's a cow. Claire got a sheep, Osgood got a pig, and Osborne and Charles both got geese. It's smashing when you hear them all at once!"

"I can hardly wait," remarked Greniston dryly, imagining all too clearly the peace of Greniston Manor broken at odd hours of the day and night by the cries of a tiny barnyard.

"We pwayed them for Fiwipo and Wobert all the way home, almost. When we got to Baff, Fiwipo said we should stop for a while, because we might wear out the sounds, and we wouldn't want to do that before you had a chance to hear them, too."

"Did he now?" asked Greniston, "My, that was generous of him."

"Ummhmm," replied Wyatt, his attention now caught by Greniston's study.

"What a wot of books you've got!" he exclaimed. "Do they have good pictures?"

"Not most of them," Greniston acknowledged.

Wyatt scanned the mass of papers on the desk. "What's all that?"

"Oh, something I'm writing."

Wyatt looked appalled. "But you aren't in school anymore! You don't ever have to wight anything, ever again!"

"I'm a strange man," Greniston acknowledged.

"I guess so," Wyatt agreed cheerfully. He sat down in the swivel chair at Greniston's desk and began to spin around in faster and faster circles.

Greniston grabbed the back of the chair and brought it to a halt. "I've enjoyed our little visit," he said, "but now I've got work to do."

Wyatt ignored this hint and gazed with fascination at Shakespeare's bust. "Who's that?"

"William Shakespeare. Now . . . "

"I've heard of him," Wyatt said happily, "'Womeo, Womeo, wherefo art thou Womeo!'"

"Quite," said Greniston, "but you'd better be going, now."

"Oh, I almost forgot," Wyatt exclaimed, "I came to tell you something!"

"Aha! And what was that?"

Wyatt paused, and wrinkled his brow. "I forget," he said at length.

"Well, I'm sure it will come back to you later," said Greniston. He succeeded in steering Wyatt to the door, only to realize that it was barricaded by the sofa.

"Why did you do that?" Wyatt asked, "Were you expecting burglars?"

"Mongol hordes, actually," his host replied. "Why not go out this way?" He led Wyatt to the French doors and let him out into the garden, a form of exit the boy found "weawy super."

After Wyatt was gone, Greniston gave a deep sigh and surveyed the damage: the books he had flung from the shelf lay in a disordered heap on the floor. His hand was bleeding from its scrape on the dumbwaiter, and the blood had gotten onto his shirt. The remains of Wyatt's hippo lollipop lay on his desk, stuck to the pages of his manuscript, and Shakespeare now sported an orange baseball cap from the Bristol Zoo.

The boy was only here for five minutes, Greniston thought, stunned. He started to take the cap off of Shakespeare, then thought the better of it.

"Actually, Will," he said, "it looks quite fetching on you."

Surveying the wreckage on his desk, Lord Greniston sighed. *Life*, he mused, *let it get its foot in the door, and there's no telling what will happen!*

Now, in the hallway outside his barricaded door, he heard Mrs. Hodges and Mrs. Fitzpatrick conversing. "He's got the door closed. I suppose we really ought not to disturb him," Mrs. Hodges said regretfully.

"No, I daresay not. We'll just have to decide about the cheese ourselves," Mrs. Fitzpatrick replied. "I say Stilton. It's always been a favorite of Lord Greniston's."

Mrs. Hodges sounded doubtful. "Awfully strong for some folk. I was thinking of a nice Havarti, or an Edam."

In an uncharacteristic burst of truly festive extravagance, Mrs. Fitzpatrick said, "Let's have all three!"

"Do you think so?"

"Yes, indeed. With the fresh grapes and pears and the table water biscuits, it will be just the thing to follow the trifle."

"On glass plates," said Mrs. Hodges. "I do love the look of fruit on a sparkling glass plate! So elegant!"

"Absolutely," agreed Mrs. Fitzpatrick. "Well, I'm glad that's settled! And we didn't have to bother Lord Greniston at all! Now, we must go help Meggy with the radish roses. She just can't get the hang of them."

"Ah," said Mrs. Hodges, "it's all in having the radishes cold enough, before you start to trim, I've found. Soaked in ice water, that's the way."

The ladies voices faded away, happily discussing the finer points of ornamental radishes. Greniston smiled to himself. *Nice to hear them so happy,* he thought. *They feel useful, that's the thing. Never realized how much Mrs. Fitzpatrick likes these dinner parties. She must have felt bloody underused, all these years.* He looked at Shakespeare and mused, *Everyone wants to feel useful, don't they Will? Not just useful doing grim good works because they think they ought to, but useful doing what they're good at, what they love to do.*

As he stood there, it seemed to him that Greniston Manor itself felt glad and useful for the first time in a long time, with rooms long unused suddenly occupied, china and crystal that had been gathering dust on shelves now being polished, the great hall that for years had held nothing but history now scrubbed and buffed and prepared for new memories to be made in it. All around him, he could hear the quiet—or not so quiet—hum of life happening. Somewhere within the walls of Greniston Manor, decorative radishes were being sculpted, young Walmsleys were being wrestled to the ground like lion cubs and combed and washed. Somewhere, old Steadworthy was fussing over his collar studs. In the distance, he heard Logan saying, "My, my, sounds just like a sheep, doesn't it?" And if Logan was back, he realized, then so was Gwen.

He smiled, even more broadly than before, at the thought that she, too, was within the walls of Greniston Manor. Yes, at that very moment, she was somewhere in the house, arranging her hair and trying on different dresses. Anyone passing the study door at that moment would have been surprised to hear the Lord of the Manor burst into song.

"Life is a many-splendored thing," he paraphrased. "It's the radish that gets sculpted, and the joy a good cheese brings! It's the presence of young Wyatt, in a house with wings! It's the mooing, not so serious, of a canned cow quite mysterious, it's the marvelous refrain, of Miss Fields drenched with rain . . ."

Still singing, loudly and tunelessly, Lord Greniston slipped out the French doors and headed across the lawn. Halfway past the flowering cherry trees, he stopped and gazed at the cloudy sky, as one who is overcome by inspiration. Then he began to search his pockets for pen and paper. He found a pen but nothing to write on. Scarcely pausing to consider it, he began to jot down notes on his shirtsleeve. He continued to amble around the lawn, pausing every few minutes to jot down more notes, occasionally bursting back into song, and seemingly oblivious to the fact that a light rain had begun to fall.

CHAPTER NINETEEN

As the distant bells of St. Aethelrood's tolled six, Gwen surveyed herself in the mirror. For a moment, she almost didn't recognize the woman who looked back at her. The floor-length, rose-colored dress made her seem taller than usual, and the wonders worked by an inspired hairdresser in Tweeverton had brought out a striking beauty she had never known her face possessed.

"I need a fairy princess hairstyle," Gwen had told Irene at Chez Patrice, "to go with a fairy princess sort of dress. It's rose-colored silk, with a scooped neck and long sleeves. It fits fairly tight to the hips, then it flares out to the floor. It made me think of an illustration in a book I had as a child. *The Twelve Dancing Princesses*, it was called. I've never worn the dress; I've never gone anywhere fancy enough. I don't know what made me bring it to England, but now I'm glad I did. Only, I don't know what to do with my hair."

"Don't you worry, luv," Irene had replied, "I know just the look you need."

The result was a loose chignon, pulled onto the crown of her head, with strands that escaped here and there and curled delicately around her face and neck. On top of the chignon, Irene had insisted on placing what she called "coiffure jewelry," a thin golden wire decorated here and there with tiny golden leaves and chips of rhinestone. By daylight, looking in the beauty parlor mirror, Gwen had feared that the affect was a little overdone, too obviously not real gold, but Irene had insisted that she at least try it with the dress.

"You wait and see, luv," she said. "You'll look just like one of your dancing princesses."

Now Gwen had to admit that Irene had been right. In the softer light of evening, the rhinestones and tiny gold leaves seemed almost to float upon her auburn crown of hair and were the perfect touch to the regal dress. She decided she needed no other jewelry and applied a minimum of makeup. That and her rose-colored, low-heeled pumps, dyed to match the dress, and just a whiff of "Evening in Paris," and she felt she was ready to assess the results.

Is that really me? she thought, looking at her reflection. She smiled, knowing that it was not merely Irene's wizardry that had brought such a glow to her cheeks, such a light to her hazel eyes. It was the presence of Greniston, in that very house.

With a last pat to her hair, she headed out of the bedroom and down the corridor toward the stairs. On the way, she passed the door that led to the minstrel's gallery, which overlooked the great hall. The door was ajar. Curious, Gwen opened it and looked in. There seemed to be no one there, but the view from the gallery was wonderful. Below her, the great hall gleamed with candlelight. Garlands of roses and gardenias were festooned along the walls, and their fragrance filled the place. A fire was lit in the great granite fireplace. Down the center of the hall, a long table was set up, covered with white, linen cloths and set for seventeen guests. From the minstrel's gallery, Gwen noticed details of the hall she had not seen before, like the carved faces of jesters, kings, and lions along the molding and the troubadour's harp that sat near the tall, leaded windows at one end.

It's like a room out of a fairy tale, Gwen thought. As she watched, Greniston entered the hall along with Robert and Bosley. They did not notice her standing in the shadows above. Gwen felt she had never seen Greniston look so handsome. He was wearing a tuxedo, and the formal dress seemed utterly natural to him. Robert and Bosley were also attired in their best, formal butlers' uniforms, right down to white gloves on their hands and tiny pink rosebuds in their buttonholes.

"Now remember," Lord Greniston said, "whichever of you serves the wine on Mr. Walmsleys' side of the table, I want you to serve him the sparkling fruit cider. Don't say anything about it. Simply pour his glass from that bottle only. It's the same thing the children will be drinking, so that they can feel included in our grown-up toasts. Walmsley will probably object when you begin to pour, so you must quietly say, 'It's a vintage you might prefer, Sir,' and let him see the label—and his wife, who will be seated next to him—but no one else. It will take some discretion, but I'm sure you'll be up to it. He's gone on the wagon, you see, and we've got to honor that, without making him feel self-conscious."

"Very good, Sir," murmured Bosley.

"Yes," agreed Robert, in hushed tones. The grandeur of the occasion seemed to have inspired in him an almost religious awe.

"Good lads," said Greniston. "Now then, where are our guests? Mrs. Hodges will be in a frenzy of concern over her water chestnut soufflé if they don't arrive soon! Ah, I think I hear them now!"

The first to burst into the room through the great double doors were the Walmsley children, clearly scrubbed within an inch of their lives and dressed in their Sunday best. There was a gleam of mischief in Osgood's eye, but the rest looked as awed by the occasion as Robert was. On their heels came their parents: Mrs. Walmsley, looking actually quite striking in a long dress of amber-colored jacquard, her brown hair no longer pulled back in a mousy pony tail but flowing to her shoulders and brushed until it shone, and Mr. Walmsley, with the strained but proud bearing of a man who has but recently gone cold sober.

"Welcome, welcome!" cried Greniston jovially. "Mrs. Walmsley, you look absolutely lovely, like a lady of old from some pre-Raphaelite drawing! Let me show you to your seats!"

I never dreamed he could be so gracious, marveled Gwen from her vantage point. *And what a kind thought that was about Mr. Walmsley's wine.*

Intrigued by this new side of Greniston, Gwen decided to remain in her hiding place to see how he would greet the other guests.

Filipo and Mr. Steadworthy entered next: Filipo wearing an embroidered Basque shirt and vest, and Mr. Steadworthy in the pinstriped suit he had worn the day before, but with the addition of a rosebud boutonniere.

"Grand!" Greniston exclaimed at the sight of them, clapping Filipo on the back and shaking Steadworthy's hand vigorously. "Have a drink! Have several!"

Next, Logan appeared, looking rather shy and quite dashing in the same burgundy velvet dinner jacket and paisley ascot he had worn for their private dinner a few days ago.

"Logan!" Greniston cried. "Come in, come in!"

Logan hesitated in the doorway, seeming to feel suddenly out of his element in the formal setting. Greniston seemed instantly to notice this and, softening the normal boom of his voice, walked over to Logan and gently said, "I'm sure your bardic eye is taking in the atmosphere, isn't it? Let me show you some of the fine points of the room. The harp, for instance—a soul like yours is sure to appreciate that!"

Warmly, Greniston took Logan by the arm and led him over to the troubadour's harp. Logan's gaunt features glowed with that look of adoration that signals love at first sight.

"It, it's magnificent," he sighed.

"Yes," Greniston agreed. "Been in the family over seventy years, but still quite playable. Try a strum or two."

Reverently, Logan reached out and played a delicate chord upon the metal strings.

"Why, it's in perfect tune," he exclaimed delightedly.

"Yes, an old custom of the Grenistons," replied his host, "to always have a harp on hand, and always keep it in tune, in case a minstrel appears. Fortunately, Mrs. Fitz has a good ear for that sort of thing, although she can't play. "

"Neither can I," said Logan wistfully.

"Oh, you never know 'til you've tried," said Greniston.

"But they say it's one of the hardest instruments to learn."

"Idiots," Greniston responded grandly, waving away this objection with one hand. "I'll wager you and this harp were made for each other. Perhaps, later, you'll try it out? But in the meantime, let's get you a seat and a glass. Now then, where is Miss Fields?"

As he spoke, the Grandfather clock in the hall chimed half-past the hour.

"I'll go fetch her," offered Logan. "After all, a lady should have an escort."

"Just the thing," agreed Greniston heartily.

Gwen slipped out of the minstrel's gallery, and, a few moments later, met Logan on the stairs.

"By all the Saints," he exclaimed, "you look a vision, My Lady!"

"Does it . . . do you think . . . Lord Greniston will like it?" Gwen asked.

"He'd be a fool if he didn't," Logan said sincerely. "Believe me, you look a fitting lady to this manor!"

Gwen blushed, but Logan only smiled and, offering her his arm, said, "Shall we go to dinner, then?"

For an instant, Lord Greniston truly did not recognize the lady who entered on Logan's arm. She looked like some queen from one of the old family tapestries, come to shimmering life. Then, the truth dawned on him.

"Miss Fields," he said at last, not taking his eyes from her.

"Lord Greniston," she replied, gazing back at him.

For once, Greniston seemed stunned into silence. He had expected Gwen to look lovely, but in that dress and with jewels entwined in her crown of auburn hair, which so set off the slender beauty of her neck, and with such a sparkle in her luminous, intelligent eyes, she looked more exquisite than even he could have imagined. He simply stared, drinking in the sight of her.

A conspiratorial smile passed between Logan and Filipo. Robert gazed at Gwen so intently he dropped a sauce spoon. Mrs. Hodges beamed, and a significant look was exchanged by Mrs. Fitzpatrick and Mr. Steadworthy. Osgood nudged Wyatt and whispered, "Looks gorgeous, don't she?" Claire smiled, dazzled.

At last, Greniston seemed to gather his wits enough to say, "Please, Miss Fields, come and sit here, on my right."

As she crossed the room, he continued to gaze intently at her. Gwen could not resist a small surge of happiness at the fact. *Yes*, she thought to herself, *I think this dress will do.*

"Now our little party is almost complete," said Greniston, as Gwen took her seat. "I invited the Pennington sisters as well."

Filipo nearly choked on his wine but recovered himself quickly. "Those are the elderly ladies who run the museum, aren't they?" he asked, trying to sound casual but exchanging a worried glance with Gwen and Logan.

"Yes. Invited the Vicar and his wife too, but they regretfully had to decline. Previous engagement at the Bristol Oxfam Society. Ah, there are our guests now!"

Everyone turned to greet the Pennington sisters, and it was a tribute to their entrance that not only the men but the ladies as well stood to acknowledge them, as if they were royalty.

Althea and Lettice had outdone themselves. Cedar chests and boxes long packed with mothballs had been dragged out of closets; indeed, perhaps even the costumes of the museum had been foraged through.

The results their search had achieved were oddly enchanting. Althea wore a floor length gown of midnight-blue velvet that had been the height of fashion a mere half century earlier. True, the material had seen better days, but by candlelight, who was to know? To complete the outfit, she had wrapped a length of burgundy chiffon (formerly a parlor curtain) around her shoulders and fastened it at the bosom with an ornate brooch. Her dark, silver-streaked hair she wore upswept, with a garnet necklace resting upon it like a crown. The overall effect was very like that of a portrait of Elizabeth the

First. The burgundy chiffon softened Althea's sharp features, and her upswept hair revealed a neck that was, Gwen realized, absolutely swan-like.

She must have been a beauty in her day, Gwen thought. Then she realized, *But that's silly. She's far more beautiful now, at eighty, than she ever could have been at twenty*. Every wrinkle around the eyes represented hard-won human experience. There was a lifetime of kindness and wisdom in that face that made a woman of thirty, or even of fifty, look a bit of a child in comparison. It struck Gwen that Althea was like a silver rose, just now flowering into the full grace of her long, rich life.

As for Lettice, she was equally stunning in her own way. Wisely, she had not tried to emulate Althea's rather Elizabethan approach. Instead, she had aimed for a more Greek affect. Two damask tablecloths had united to form a long, draped gown that gave an unexpected elegance to her rounded form. All the real jewels the sisters still possessed, the garnet necklace and the brooch, had vital roles to play in Althea's attire, so Lettice had turned to the garden for her adornment. A bit of lace, some ivy, and some early yellow primroses formed an entrancing cap upon her fluffy gray curls. Woven in and out of the white crocheted shawl she wore over her shoulders were snowdrops, hyacinths, and narcissus. The effect had a gently sylvan charm, and she smelled marvelous. If Althea looked like an elderly Titania, from *A Midsummer Night's Dream*, then Lettice had the flavor of a rather mature Celia, from *As You Like It*. This resemblance was not lost upon Lord Greniston, who paraphrased a greeting with the lines:

> "Thus 'nature presently distilled
> Helen's cheek, but not her heart,
>   Cleopatra's majesty,
>   Atalanta's better part. . . .
>   Thus these Rosalinds, of many parts,
>   By heavenly synod were devised,
>   Of many faces, eyes, and hearts.'"

Althea nodded in regal acknowledgment of the compliment. Lettice blushed and said "Oh, Lord Greniston, you say such things."

Filipo caught Gwen's eye and shrugged helplessly when he saw that the sisters were to be seated on either side of him. As he pulled out their chairs, he murmured, "Delighted to meet you," his Basque accent perhaps a bit thicker than usual.

"This is very odd," twittered Lettice, "but I can't help feeling we've met."

"That's unlikely," said Greniston. "Mr. De La Rayna is a friend of Miss Fields, just arrived for a visit in Far Tauverly. Please, allow me to introduce you. Ladies, this is Filipo Alejandro Vargues de la Reyna. Filipo, this is Lettice, and this, Althea Pennington."

"Charmed," said Filipo, kissing Lettice's hand, which sent that lady into a flurry of delicate giggles.

"I know who you remind me of!" she suddenly exclaimed.

A silence fell over the table. Gwen and Logan exchanged a glance. Filipo and the Walmsley children seemed to be holding their breath.

"It's—it's—oh, now, what was his name? From the films, you know, he always played a hero?"

Filipo gave a sigh of relief. "Ah," he said teasingly, "Charles Boyer, perhaps? Or Robert Donat? Maybe even Bogart." He tilted his head to one side, looked deep into Lettice's eyes, and said, "'What's a classy dame like you doin' in a joint like this?'"

"Oh, my goodness," said Lettice, adjusting her shawl and scattering a few snowdrops in the process.

Filipo turned now to Althea. He took the hand she offered and raised it respectfully to his lips. When he raised his gaze to meet hers, he was relieved to see the hint of a twinkle in her sparkling gray eyes.

"I think it's Olivier, rather than Leslie Howard, playing that master of disguise, the Scarlet Pimpernel," she said. "'Is he in heaven, or is he in hell, that damned elusive pimpernel?'"

Filipo replied, "'They seek him here, they seek him there, those Frenchies seek him everywhere; when he arrives, let evil beware.'"

Althea's lips curved in a warm smile as he held her chair for her, and she whispered, "Don't worry, M'sieur, your secret is safe with me, for I know you to be an agent of good. Any house guest of Greniston's could be no less."

"Gracias, *Dona* Althea," murmured Filipo, as she took her seat.

"Well," cried Greniston happily, "now that we are all well met, good friends, let our revels begin! I propose we start with a toast to the culinary wizards who have prepared the feast of which we are about to partake. To Mrs. Fitzpatrick and Mrs. Hodges!"

"To Mrs. Fitz and Mrs. Hodges," everyone echoed, lifting high their glasses.

And so began the most marvelous gathering Gwen had ever attended.

By the time the distant bells of St. Aethelrood's tolled nine o'clock, the softness of the candlelight and the warmth of the wine had woven the guests together as if they had always been old friends.

". . . and so I said to him," Mr. Steadworthy was saying, "'Sir, a judge of the court you may be, but a judge of men's souls, never! I thank God my client faces an assessment far wiser than your own!' At that point, the whole courtroom stood up and cheered. Jury acquitted the fellow, of course."

Mr. Steadworthy's cheeks were flushed with excitement as he related this long-ago legal triumph.

"And quite right that they should have," commented Althea. "I remember the case very well."

"You do?" Mr. Steadworthy looked surprised and pleased.

"Oh, certainly," said Lettice. "It was in all the papers. I believe we even saved some clippings. You being the Greniston's solicitor, I mean, it practically makes you a local man."

"Why, thank you," said Mr. Steadworthy, genuinely pleased at this ultimate compliment.

On the other side of the table, Logan and Mr. Walmsley were deep in a conversation about wood, a topic in which it seemed they both had a passionate interest, though in different ways.

"Hazelwood, now there's a lovely stuff to fashion a walking stick from," Mr. Walmsley was saying fondly.

Ah! Hazel!" cried Logan, "A sacred wood to the Celts, you know. Why, the only way to capture the salmon of knowledge is with a hazel nut, upon a silken line."

"Is it now?" responded Mr. Walmsley. "Well, I wouldn't know too much about that, but I can tell you that those twelve holy trees of the Druids that you mentioned are a very interesting choice. What were they again?"

"The willow, the birch, the alder," began Logan in loving tones, "the larch, the rowan, the oak, . . . "

"Ah, oak!" interrupted Mr. Walmsley, "Now there's a wood for you! A king of woods, in fact! For beams or doors, there's none better."

Greniston caught Gwen's eye and smiled. "Good to see them all so at their ease, isn't it?" he said.

"Oh yes," said Gwen, meaning it with all her heart. That the guests were so comfortable was due in large part to Greniston's skillful hosting. Without seeming to, he had found a way to draw out the best of each person, making sure that everyone, even the children, had a moment to tell a story or a joke that was appreciated by all. Not only was Greniston gracious to his guests, Gwen realized, but his warmth was so contagious that they became gracious to each other. Differences of habit or "class" that might have prevented them from conversing elsewhere melted in the warmth of Greniston's presence. It was a marvel to her that the same mind that could be so laser-like in its devastating wit could, when aimed at a wider target, zero in on people's deepest hidden strengths and dreams and create an atmosphere in which they could form magical combinations.

She suspected, for instance, that given Anne Walmsley's shyness and Althea's surface haughtiness, they scarcely greeted each other when they passed on the street. Yet tonight, she had seen them discover a mutual interest in sewing and quite glow together, discussing darts and gussets. She had watched Mrs. Walmsley's confidence expand as she spoke about something at which she was competent, and Althea's stiffness soften in the pleasure of discovering someone who shared a skill. Now they were planning a project together: a new altar cloth for St. Aethelrood's.

This is how life should be, Gwen thought, surveying the table. *People feeling safe to be themselves, bringing out the best in each other, being more together than we can be one by one. And it's Greniston, and the spell of Greniston Manor, that have made it possible.*

She raised her glass, and cried "A toast!"

"A toast," everyone echoed happily.

"To our host, a Greniston worthy of his name!"

"To Greniston!" the guests all cried, rising as one, lifting their glasses high.

As they cried out the ancient name, it seemed to Gwen that they were honoring not only the current lord but all the bold and large-hearted Greniston ancestors who had gone before him. "Greniston!" How many times, she wondered, had that cry been uttered in that very hall? A call to battle, to courage, a proud declaration of nobility, but most of all, as a cry of fierce joy, joy at being alive and able to proclaim it.

368

"Greniston!" she cried again, "Greniston!"

Then Greniston raised his glass, and proposed, "To our guest with the heart of Basque fire—to Filipo!"

"To Filipo!" all agreed.

More wine was poured by Robert. Filipo raised his glass and said, "In the words of the great poet, Federico Garcia Lorca, who, although he was not technically a Basque, was one in spirit . . . "

"Here, here," agreed Greniston.

"And—to the children!" Greniston added, smiling wistfully at Gwen.

"To the children!" all agreed, lifting their glasses to the Walmsley brood.

Before Filipo could resume, Wyatt seized his glass, which, Gwen noted, seemed now to contain real wine instead of sparkling juice—indeed, all the little Walmsleys' glasses did—and cried, "To Wogan!"

"Yes," said Greniston, "To Logan, the Bard of Far Tauverly!"

"To the Bard!" the company echoed.

"Tell us a story," Osborne added, when all had drunk Logan's health.

"A story! A story!" everyone echoed enthusiastically.

Logan looked pleased, but embarrassed. "Well . . . I, I don't know," he murmured.

Sensing his awkwardness, Greniston instantly took the situation in hand. "I'll tell you what," he said, "It's awfully formal, sitting at this huge table. We seem to have reached the nuts stage of the meal—so to speak—so why don't we all take our chairs and gather around the harp over there. Let the children sit close in, and we'll arrange ourselves in the shadows nearby. That way, Logan can feel as if he's sitting in some forest nook, spinning a tale for the Independent Kingdom of Greenstone—as I'll warrant he's often done."

Even as Lord Greniston spoke, Robert began to rearrange the chairs and candles.

"Get Mrs. Fitz and Mrs. Hodges back in here," Greniston added, "and Bosley, and those girls who are helping, Meggy and Nell, and you, too, Robert. You've all worked hard enough, and with magnificent results. Now pile yourselves some plates of food and sit with us to listen."

Soon the hall was rearranged, with chairs gathered in a gentle arc at one end. The harp stood splendid against the tall, diamond paned windows, now filled with darkness. An oak chair, its arms carved like lion's heads, its seat and back upholstered in ruby velvet, was set out for Logan. Cushions were spread on the floor for the children. Robert skillfully arranged the candles so that a soft pool of golden light fell around Logan and the children but left the others in shadow.

"But I can't play the harp," protested Logan as he sat down.

"No, but I'll wager it can play you," said Greniston. "If ever two beings were made for each other, it's you and that harp. Don't worry, we don't expect you to rattle off a concerto, just strum a little in the background, like Homer did on his lyre, while he recited his *Odyssey*. Your voice will supply the rest of the music. You know," he added, "there's scarcely a one of us here who hasn't heard an old tale from you over a pint at the inn or strolling through the woods. It isn't any different now, except that we're all together. But it is safe, so be at ease, good Sir Logan, be at ease."

Looking at least a little less shy, Logan gazed at the faces of the children gathered round him. In the stillness of the moment, they could clearly hear the drumming of rain on the roofs of the manor house, on the lawns, the woods, and on the mounds.

Gently, lovingly, Logan's hands touched the harp strings and played a chord that shimmered and lingered on the air.

"Well, what's it to be?" he mused, "a tale of Love or Valor, of Fairy Realms or Great Kings, of Rogues or Saints?"

"You could finish the story you were telling Gwen in the woods that day," suggested Osborne. "The one about the king who chased the white deer, and got lost. . . ."

"How did you know about that story?" Logan asked, "I don't remember you being there."

The Sentinel of the Independent Kingdom of Greenstone shrugged, his methods of stealth clearly a matter of professional pride.

"I see," said Logan with a smile. "Well, that is a good choice, for it's an old tale, and an old tale's best for a night like this, . . . an old, old tale, from an old, old time . . . and yet a tale that 'twas ever new. . . . So, come with me now, to a time long ago, to the time of Arthur Pendragon, Arthur, King of the Britains . . ."

As Logan spoke, all self consciousness gone as he lost himself in the story, Gwen wondered how many bards, over the centuries, had told their tales and sung their songs, perhaps in that very room. Gazing at Logan's hollowed, wise face, she felt that he could well have been a bard of Arthur's court. And the faces of the others, she realized, seemed just as timeless. Filipo could easily have been some rugged knight errant, visiting from Brittany. Robert looked every inch the young squire, eager to prove himself. Mr. and Mrs. Walmsley could be the loyal Stewards of the castle, while the Pennington sisters and Mmes. Hodges and Fitzpatrick seemed like the older ladies in waiting, the steady heart of the court. In the shadows, Gwen glanced at Greniston, beside her. She felt that his face had an undeniably kingly cast.

It's not just us who are listening here, Gwen realized. She had the feeling that this was one of those moments when time overlapped itself, somehow, when past, present, and future could meet and intertwine. Out of the corner of her eye, she had the sense of other figures lining the walls: gallant courtiers and ladies of days gone by, knights and minstrels of old. When she turned to look, the figures slipped away, like sea-foam fading into sand, only to reappear at the edge of sight when she stopped trying to see them.

"Now Arthur's great sword, Excalibur," Logan was saying, "What became of it?"

"It was returned to the Lady of the Lake," Osborne replied.

"Ah, true, true, so say some. . . . Yet some say that it came, somehow, into the hands of a great king named Macsen. . . ."

Logan gazed now into the darkness beyond the windows. The soft glow of the candles and the flickering light from the fireplace played upon his sad, gaunt features. His hands found chords upon the harp of their own accord. His eyes gazed far beyond the listeners gathered near, as if out there, through the ancient windows, in the realm of dark and wind and wild, he could see the tale he told being played out. . . .

"A great king, and good was he, who ruled in ancient Avonlee. . . . Yet ever sad of heart was he, for he had no lady by his side, no fair queen to be his bride. . . . This worried his counselors true and wise, that yet no lady had found favor in Macsen's eyes. . . . 'Sire,' his ministers at length did say, ''Tis every king's duty to wed. Sons you must have, to take up the crown, when you, alas, one day are gone.' Yet still the king their suit denied, saying, 'Only she my heart's eyes see, will I take as my Queen and Bride.' Ah, but then, but then, change came to this most stubborn of men, change in the autumn of the year, when leaves are scarlet, and skies grow drear. . . ."

By now, Logan seemed to have settled upon a series of three chords, which he repeated softly as a background to his tale. In that simple music, Gwen could hear the rustling of leaves in the autumn wind and the beat of horse's hooves as the king and his men now went out a-hunting. "Then caught they sight of a mighty white stag, . . . it's antlers full seven foot span, its coat as pure as purest snow. . . . Such a creature had ne'er been seen by mortal man! 'Onward,' cried Macsen the Bold. 'Whosoever catches it shall win his weight in jewels and gold! Onward my men, make earth to thunder, and fields to ring; let loose your arrows, make bowstrings sing!' Then onward, indeed, leapt all the men, each urging on his steed. Yet one by one, they fell away, so great the white stag's magic speed. At last, only Macsen alone kept on the chase, and his great gray struggled to keep up the pace."

Now Logan came to the part of the story Gwen remembered very well: how King Macsen followed the magic stag into the enchanted forest until he was lost and knew himself to be on the edge of the fairy realms.

"Then a drowsiness came over the king, as if by enchantment by some fairy ring. . . . Down from his horse he weary came, loosing the bridle, letting go the reins, . . . and then the king lay down his head, oak leaves and earth did serve for his bed. . . . And as he slept, he dreamed a dream, a dream most rare, ah, fairest of dreams, that came to him there. . . ."

A hush came over the room as Logan described the magic journey of Macsen's Dream: how the king felt himself rising to the treetops, how he looked down and saw his body lying asleep in the glen and his gray horse beside it, how he rose and rose on the wind and flew far and far, across forests and fields, across mountains and distant lands, until the wind put him down on the beach of a strange and distant shore . . . and up to the shore came gliding a magic boat. Into it got Macsen the Bold, without a moment's hesitation. Across the waves the little boat sped, carrying him toward an island across the water. On the island was a castle, which Macsen headed toward as soon as he landed. Its golden doors opened of their own accord for him, and he found himself in a great room, where twin brothers, princes, were playing chess with gold and silver pieces upon a crystal board. They looked up and nodded to Macsen, as if they knew him, as if he had been long expected, and said "Pass, friend." Then Macsen passed on to the next room, and there he met an old, old man with a long white beard and a staff, who also nodded to Macsen as if he recognized him and said "Pass, friend." Then Macsen strode into the third and innermost room, where he beheld the most beautiful lady he had ever seen. Her hair was like golden light, she was dressed in a shining white gown, and was seated upon a throne of gold. At the sight of him, she leapt up with gladness in her eye, as if she had waited long and long to see him, in all the world, him. And Macsen felt an answering joy in his own heart, for he knew that this lady, and no other, was meant to be his bride.

At this point in the story, Greniston reached over in the darkness and took Gwen's hand. He held it very firmly, as Logan continued.

"He reached to take her in his arms, but Alas! At the very moment they might have touched, the lady, the castle, the island, all vanished, like a mist upon the air . . . and the king awoke, as from a dream, to find himself back in the magic wood he had started from, with no fair lady there. Heavy indeed, his heart was then, as he slowly returned to his kingdom and men. Searches he ordered, to find his true bride, that she might be brought, to dwell at his side. 'Search far, search near,' the great king cried, 'Search for a day and search for a year, and when you have found her, bring that lithesome lady here, for she is my darling, my jewel, my dear!'

"Then searched his men, o'er land and sea, but of lady and castle, none did they see. . . . Sad passed away the year and a day, one by one, the searchers returned, and lonely in his greatness, Macsen still yearned.

"'Twas only a dream,' his advisors then said, 'Take some other lady to thy throne and bed.' Then spoke out Macsen, angry and bold: ''Twas no dream, but truth, that I to you told!'"

Logan's voice rang out now, confident and royal as Macsen's own had surely been. For an instant, it seemed to Gwen that there was another figure behind him, a man with pale golden hair, in a dark blue cape spangled with stars, who smiled and touched Logan's shoulder, but it was only there for an instant, and then Gwen wondered if she had seen it at all.

As Logan continued, there was a wonder in his face, as if something new was being revealed to him even as he spoke the words of the old, old tale, as if the story he told was now somehow his own, as well as Macsen's.

"'Twas no dream,' brave Macsen cried, 'I swear to thee! 'Twas a message and a mystery, sent to me! To its truth shall I be true, whate'er others say, whate'er others do!' Then the King declared that he himself would go searching for a year and a day, so all alone, he set forth, riding west, ever west. Through field and forest, his path led on, far from, the world of men, into the realm of eagle, bear, and fawn. Spring passed, and summer, and he felt the autumn's chill, and then the winter's cold drew nigh. The time of his search had all but gone by, hungry, alone, and in despair, Macsen the Sad was like unto die. . . .'"

"'Perhaps it was but fantasy,' the king now thought, 'as all my councilors did say to me, and yet 'twas truth, this I do know, for my own heart doth tell me so! I would rather die searching and longing for a vision true than return to the cold comfort my heart could but rue. Onward, onward, search I, onward, I'll search, to live, or to die!'

"And even as Macsen spoke these words, he came to a beach on a strange shore, . . . the very beach he had seen in his dream! And a little magic boat came speeding toward him across the waves. He stepped into it, and it took him to the island, where he saw again the castle. . . . Again he strode boldly through its golden doors, and again, he met the twin princes, playing chess with pieces of gold and silver upon a crystal board, . . . and again they looked up and said 'Pass, friend.' . . . And again, the old man nodded and bade him pass, as well, . . . and again, he went to the innermost room, . . . and there, with golden hair, upon a throne of gold, there was the lady of his heart, the one true wife for Macsen the Bold! She ran to him and he to her, and this time, when they embraced each other, they stayed real and solid in each other's arms! Great was their joy! Married they were that very day, and for many a year, his bride with him did stay. Light was she and lovely, and Fair Elyn was her name. . . . She was of the Faery Realms, and their wisdom she brought to Macsen's land, of where to build roads so they disturbed not the Faery bands, of healing arts, and sacred wells, and places where the nature spirits dwell. . . . And many gifts she gave to him, and chiefest of these, 'twas Arthur's sword, Excalibur. . . . Held in trust by the Faery Folk, it could fell an oak tree at one stroke, . . . and upon the sword there was this spell: It could only be wielded by one who loved and lived well, who feared not combat, yet longed in peace to dwell, whose heart was kind, whose speech was true, who never shirked from what he had to do. Such a one was Macsen, this Elyn knew, and the sword unto him was her love gift true. Long and well ruled they side by side, Macsen the Bold and Elyn, his Fair bride. But he grew old and she aged not. Alas, came the time when he did die, and then, Fair Elyn, she sighed a great sigh and vanished as dawn mist into the air, with all her great arts and her golden hair. Back with Excalibur, now went she, back to the island in the sea, back to a place beyond space or time, Elyn, Fair Elyn, time out of mind. . . . And here ends this tale of Bold Macsen's Dream, of a king who was true to more than what seems. May all who search truly remember him now and cleave to their longing, their heart, and their vow. . . ."

When Logan finished, a deep quiet lay over the room. All seemed touched to the core by the tale of a long-ago king and his Elyn Faer.

At length, Osborne said, "Does everyone except Fairy folk have to die?"

"Aye," said Logan, "At least, their bodies do. As for their souls, ah, now, that's another tale. . . . But come soon or come late, we all must say goodbye to this old world, that's been our home."

Logan closed his eyes and began to sing the old Irish song, "The Parting Glass." His voice and the haunting melody were well matched.

> "But since it falls, unto my lot,
>   That I must ride, and you must not,
>   Then drink to me the parting glass,
>   Good night and joy be with you all. . . ."

There was stillness in the great hall then, the stillness of the ages. Logan let the moment last. Then, at the perfect instant, he began to sing another Irish tune called "Rosin the Bow." This, too, was a song of farewell, but to a melody so jaunty and defiant that, soon, everyone in the room was smiling and tapping time as Logan merrily sang:

> "I fear that my death is approaching,
>   That cruel relentless old foe;
>   Yet I'll laugh in his face when he finds me,
>   Sayin' 'Have a drink with old Rosin the Bow!'
>   And when I am dead and I'm buried,
>   And into me coffin I go,
>   Then pour down a hogshead o' whiskey,
>   As a drink for old Rosin the Bow!
>   Yes, I'm done with this world of sorrows,
>   And now to another I go;
>   Be there angels or devils to greet me,

Let 'em drink with old Rosin the Bow!
Have a drink with old Rosin the Bow, friends,
Have a drink with Old Rosin the Bow!"

When Logan finished, Mrs. Fitzpatrick, whose Irish soul was stirred to its depths, sighed and said wistfully, "Ah, if only we had a fiddle player, we could dance a rare reel, now!"

"Why, dear lady," said Mr. Steadworthy, "if I had but a fiddle, I'd be glad to give you a hundred reels!"

"You can play?" Mrs. Fitzpatrick exclaimed.

"Indeed I can. In my youth, I was much taken with folk music—English, Scottish, and Welsh, as well as Irish. I determined to learn to play the fiddle, and indeed, I play it often, to this very day. What a pity I did not bring it with me!"

"But we have a fiddle!" cried Greniston, "In the music room! There's a drum in there, too, and a flute. Fetch the instruments, Robert! And Filipo has his guitar here, as well! Mrs. Fitz, you shall have your reel—and waltzes and pavanes as well. Let's see if we can move the table back to make some room for dancing!"

To cries of "Bravo!" and "Well done!" from the ladies, the men joined forces to lift the great oak dining table and carry it to one side of the room.

By the time they finished, Robert, assisted by several excited young Walmsleys, returned, bearing many instruments including a 1903 Antonius Violin.

Steadworthy's eyes lit up. "A fine instrument," he said, tuning it. He fussed over the strings and bow but at last declared himself ready to start.

Turning to Mrs. Fitzpatrick, he said, "Dear Lady, what shall it be?"

"Well," said the housekeeper, "Lord Greniston and his partner should start off the ball. That's proper."

"Of course," agreed Greniston, pulling Gwen to his side.

"And the dance," mused Mrs. Fitzpatrick, "the dance should be, oh, Jesus, Mary and Joseph, there's so many grand tunes to chose from! Well, well, let it be—"Crowley's Reel'!"

"Excellent!" cried Mr. Steadworthy. Fearlessly, he struck the first notes of the lively melody. Gwen was not certain how to dance a reel, but Greniston seemed to know, or at least not to mind improvising, and she followed his lead. Gradually, other couples came on to the floor with them: Filipo and Althea, Mr. and Mrs. Walmsley, Robert and Lettice. Mrs. Hodges beat time on the drum, and Mrs. Fitzpatrick played the spoons with rare zeal. Logan seemed a little shy of dancing, but he clapped time and seemed to be enjoying himself immensely. As for Bosley, he grabbed Meg by one hand and Nell by the other and pulled them both out on to the floor at once. The children danced as they pleased, weaving in and out among the couples.

No sooner had Mr. Steadworthy struck the last note of "Crowley's Reel," than Mrs. Fitzpatrick called out "Cherish the Ladies!" and without pause, the music continued. Tune after tune slipped happily from the old man's gnarled fingers. Watching the joy on his face, Gwen thought, *Only an old man could be so young.* For only someone who had lived and suffered much could have brought such sweetness and verve to his playing.

When at last Mr. Steadworthy called for time out to drink a glass of claret and flex his fingers, Filipo began to play tangos and waltzes. Then Mrs. Fitzpatrick called for "The Star of the County Down," which Logan began to sing, strumming a few background chords on the harp. As soon as he heard the old melody, Mr. Steadworthy could not resist it. His fingers were back on the fiddle, playing along. On and on, the dancing went. The partners changed, the melodies glided from reel to waltz, from Spain to Ireland to Brittany, but the music itself never stopped any more than rivers stop flowing or winds stop in the sky. It seemed to bubble up out of old Mr. Steadworthy like the fresh water that poured from the ancient spring on the mound. The church bells tolled ten, and then eleven, and still the candles burned bright and the dance went on.

Now, Mr. Steadworthy seemed to play not pieces he remembered but simply as he was moved to play. The music took on an ancient feeling. The melody seemed as old as Arthur's time—older, old as the human heartbeat, . . . older, as old as the spinning of planets and the twinkling of stars. Now it seemed to pull them all into one common dance. Looking back on it, Gwen never understood how they each knew their places in the nameless dance, but somehow they did. Without needing to say even a word, they formed two facing lines across which partners clasped each other's hands, weaving in and out, Robert now dancing with Gwen, then Logan with Althea, Greniston with Claire. They seemed to weave around and about each other like threads in a living tapestry. Gwen had the feeling, stronger than ever, that generations of Grenistons were there with them, lining the walls, smiling and clapping in time—generations of Grenistons so full of life that nothing, not even death, could keep them from a good dance.

And then, as effortlessly as it had begun, the ancient dance came to a close. Breathlessly, the company sank gratefully into their seats and reached for their glasses. In the quiet that followed, Logan began softly to sing the slow Scottish aire, "The Piper's Lament."

Suddenly, Claire appeared on the now empty dance floor. Her eyes were shining, and she began to move to the sad music as naturally as a tree branch might move to the wind. So effortlessly did she bend and spin in the candlelit darkness of the great hall that she seemed but a bit of milkweed, floating on a night wind's current. The old Scottish tune came to a lingering end, but Mr. Steadworthy, unable to resist one last tune, struck up a wild jig which sprang from the fiddle as lovely and sudden as a lark's headlong flight out of rushes, straight toward the sun. Claire seized Gwen's hand and pulled her out onto the floor.

Never in her life had Gwen felt so free as she did at that moment. The wild, sweet melody that now poured forth seemed like a music she had always known. *If King Macsen's longing had had a music, it would have been this*, she thought.

There was defiance in the music, and loveliness; it was the music of a spirit that will never be broken, but will love life and dance with it to the last breath, and perhaps beyond.

Gwen forgot the others watching there, forgot Claire, forgot herself. There was only the music and the longing to be with it. How long she danced, she did not know, only that, at last, she and the melody seemed to have stopped. There was a moment of stillness, then Greniston cried, "To Miss Fields! To Fair Lady Gwen!"

"To Lady Gwen!" the others echoed, "To Lady Claire! Your healths!"

Pleased but embarrassed, Gwen stood hand in hand with Claire. She blushed as Greniston came to her side and murmured, "Well danced, Lady!" He gazed into her eyes so deeply that she wondered if he was going to kiss her, even there, in front of everyone. But what the Lord of Greniston Manor might have been moved to do, she was not to find out, for suddenly Wyatt exclaimed, "Wook, evewyone! It's the man fwom the twain!"

CHAPTER TWENTY

"The dancing was lovely," a roguish voice called down from the Minstrel's Gallery, "and the story was grand! And I do enjoy a room full of well-decked-out ladies!"

"Who the devil is that?" thundered Greniston, peering up at the three figures standing in the shadows above.

"Davey Lee's the name," the voice replied. "This is my Grandmother, Annie Lee, and the bloke with his arm in a sling is Luan Tey."

"That's the man fwom the twain," Wyatt exclaimed excitedly. "The one called Wuan Tey! He's the one who stole the chalice! I told you it wath twue!"

"Gypsies!" gasped Mrs. Fitzpatrick in alarm.

"Have no fear," said Mr. Steadworthy, moving to her side.

Davey laughed. "No need to worry, Guv," he called down to Greniston, "we're on a mission of peace. You've nothing to fear—from us, at least."

"What is that supposed to mean?" demanded Greniston. He turned to Wyatt and added, "And what do you mean, 'the man who stole the chawis—I mean, damn it, the chalice? I thought you lot were mixed up in that somehow! I have a growing list of questions about that wandering cup!"

"So have I," murmured Althea, glancing at Filipo.

"It's about that bloody chalice that this bloke wants to talk to you," called down Davey Lee.

"I've a good mind to ring up the Yard and let him talk to them about it," growled Greniston. "I don't know who the devil you are or what you are doing in my home—and I'm not sure I want to!"

"Oh, come on, Guv, be reasonable," countered Davey amiably. "This here's a wounded man, arisen from a bed of pain, 'e 'as, just to help you out. And you propose turnin' 'im in to the coppers." Davey shook his head and sighed deeply. "Fine 'ospiltality that is! I tell you, I don't know what the English gentry are comin' to, and that's a fact! And to think of the silver and other valuables I could have lifted since I been 'ere, and didn't, out of respect for your hospitality, even if you didn't know you was offering it! Wasted opportunity, it now seems. Enough to bring a grown man to tears."

Greniston was about to suggest several other methods of bringing unwanted visitors to tears, when Logan came to his side and lightly touched his shoulder.

"Ever have the noble been known by their generosity," he said gently. "A true Lord grants hospitality to all who beseech it, be they invited, or no." It was clear that the spell of the evening was still upon Logan. There was a faraway look in his dark blue eyes, and he spoke as a wise old bard daring to advise even a king might have done.

"Consider King Conor of Ireland," he continued, "of whom it was said that if all the brown leaves of autumn were gold, and all the white waves of the sea were silver, yet still he would have been giving them away to those who needed, and that not man nor lady nor child nor even a mouse nor a hound ever left his table hungry nor sad nor in need of help, he was that generous. Now there was a leader. . . ."

"Hmmm," said Greniston, "You have a point there." Smiling now, he turned back toward the gallery and called up in his booming voice, "Travelers of the Road! Cousins of the Dusty Feet! Hospitality is granted thee! Come down and join us, and welcome, too!"

"That's more like it, Guv," answered Davey approvingly. "Down in a jiff!"

Greniston turned to Mrs. Fitzpatrick and Mrs. Hodges and said "Ladies, I wonder if I could trouble you to provide a snack for our new guests. Perhaps some sliced meat and some of those delicious dinner rolls? And come to think of it, everyone might be ready for a second course, after all that dancing! Let's lay on cheese and fruit and raspberry trifle all around. And some strong coffee, I have a feeling we'll need clear heads for this."

"Clear heads and locked cupboards," sniffed Mrs. Fitzpatrick, who was still not pleased at the prospect of gypsies at her table.

"Och, now you must understand," Greniston said to her in his most soulful tones, "your cooking is so mouthwatering, I'd not be refusing the devil himself—my dear pegeen."

"Oh, go on with you," the housekeeper replied, smiling in spite of herself. She and Mrs. Hodges hurried toward the kitchen.

By the time Davey and his companions reappeared at the door to the great hall, the oak table had been pulled out from the wall, and the second feast of the night was being laid out. Grinning, Davey Lee sat down at the head of the table without being asked and dug into the roast beef.

"'Ave a seat," he said graciously to Greniston, between mouthfuls.

Annie Lee, not Greniston, sat quietly down beside him, and gave her grandson a warning glance, as if to indicate that he should mind his manners, at least a little bit. As for Luan Tey, he lingered in the doorway, looking dazed and unsteady on his feet.

"Come and sit by me," Wyatt said proudly, taking him by the hand and leading him to a chair among the children.

Osgood eyed the sling on Luan Tey's arm respectfully, and then asked in a casual tone, "Pirates or Bandits?"

"Fools," Luan Tey replied, with the ghost of a smile.

Greniston looked at this new guest with reluctant concern. "Whoever the devil you are—and I suspect that is the appropriate phrase—you look peaked. Look like you could use a side of beef and a gallon of brandy. Or at least some of Mrs. Hodges excellent consommé."

Only when all were seated, and Luan Tey had been provided with a strong drink and a cup of broth, and trifle and coffee had been served all around did Greniston say, "Now, then, what's this all about?"

Half an hour later, Greniston almost wished he had not asked. His head was reeling.

"I'll take some brandy now, Mrs. Fitz," he said. "Now, let me see if I've got this straight: you kids, because of Lord Peter's prophecy, decided that you needed to guard the Far Tauverly Chalice as part of the Greniston treasure?"

"Right," said Osgood.

"Which is why Wyatt happened to be doing guard duty in the museum when this gentleman" - he nodded at Luan Tey - "arrived to steal that same chalice?"

"Wight," said Wyatt.

"A fake was left in place of the real chalice, and Luan Tey left, thinking that his little substitution would never be noticed. And so it might not have been, were it not for the vigilance of the Independent Kingdom of Greenstone. But as it was, little Wyatt here followed him, stole the real chalice on the train, leaving a crude substitute in its place, and brought the original back to the mound. Meanwhile, Luan Tey returned to his employer, whom he still refuses to name, and the counter-theft was discovered. Other agents, it seems, were dispatched to steal the replica in the museum, which Luan Tey had claimed was still the real one. And this theft was noticed."

"Right," said the Pennington sisters, in unison.

"Even as the Tweeverton police and I began to search for the bloody thing, Logan got the shock of his life, finding it in possession of the children."

"Right," said Logan, with a heartfelt sigh.

"Then you two," Greniston nodded at Gwen and Filipo, "came upon the scene, and decided to help."

"Right," said Gwen.

"Wishing to protect the children from any scrutiny, Filipo decided to make the chalice reappear at the museum, as mysteriously as it had vanished. Disguised as a Dr. Douglas McCloud, amateur antiquarian, he charmed his way into the Pennington household and found an opportunity to return the real chalice."

"*Bien sur,*" said Filipo with a grin.

"I knew he looked familiar," Lettice whispered.

"That same night, Mr. Tey here, having observed Filipo's antics, returned to the museum to re-steal the cup our friend had just so lovingly returned, because it was important, for reasons not yet explained, that his employer's other agents not discover either cup." Luan Tey nodded.

"I must say," Greniston put in, "your employer sounds most unpleasant. I'd consider a career change, if I were you. Anyway, Mr. Tey stole back the chalice. I'll tell you, that old cup hasn't seen this much excitement for centuries! But he was almost instantly attacked by some of his fellow employees—you lads need a union, or something—who were lying in wait for him. They shot you, and you were then rescued by this rogue" - Greniston here indicated Davey Lee - "who had been tailing these other men . . ."

" . . . on grounds of suspicion and a general intuition that something was up," supplied Davey Lee obligingly, as he helped himself to more trifle.

"And wishing to dispose of the chalice and turn your attention to the wounded man, you tossed the cup into what turned out to be the chimney of the post office, where it was found the next morning, to his horror, by our local postmaster."

"Right," Logan chimed in fervently.

"Meanwhile, Miss Fields had disappeared, and the chalice seemed trivial in comparison, so I dealt with it . . . "

" . . . by putting it in your raincoat pocket, Sir," finished Robert, who had just returned from fetching that article from the hall closet. "And here it is," he added dramatically, placing the chalice on the center of the table.

"Right," said Greniston.

Luan Tey picked up the chalice, examined it closely, then nodded. "Real one," he said.

"Mrs. Fitz, a little more brandy, please, "said Greniston. "And no one—no one—say anything more, just yet. My brain cells have gone into temporary overload."

As Greniston sipped his drink, allowing the story to settle in his mind, the others gazed at the chalice sitting at the center of the table. The dull gray metal on the outside of it looked as crude as ever, but the silver/gold metal inside the cup and the bejeweled border of tiny figures gleamed in the candlelight more magically than ever.

"Well," said Greniston at length, "you've all been quite busy lately. And to think that all I thought was going on was a child's prank and a simple kidnapping and rescue. Silly old me. But now, my eyes are opened, and I find I have some questions. First, though, there is something that must be cleared up. Osgood, old man, I fear I have sorely misjudged you. I suspected you and your cohorts of stealing this thing; now I see that I couldn't have been more wrong. You were instead trying to protect it." Greniston reached across the table and extended his hand to the boy. "Will you, on behalf of your kingdom, accept my sincere apologies?"

"Certainly," said Osgood, in a manly tone, shaking the offered hand vigorously.

"Good," said Greniston. "Now then, there's two other matters I'd like to clear up. One concerns you," he added, looking at Luan Tey. "I don't mean to pry, old chum, but just where have you been recovering from your wound? In this good lady's wagon, I suppose, camped on the Greniston land, while these other henchmen, or whatever they are, scour the woods for you, endangering - "

"Not at all, Guv," interrupted Davey, pouring himself a brandy. "'E's been mending right 'ere in the comfort and safety of your own house."

"In this house?" exclaimed Greniston, for once too amazed to bellow.

"That explains the voice I heard in the night," Gwen mused, "a woman's voice…"

"And my missing duck," said Mrs. Hodges, triumphantly.

"There was a roast duck that just vanished from the sideboard yesterday," Mrs. Fitzpatrick explained. "We had plenty to spare, so it didn't matter really, but I couldn't imagine what had become of it. I fear," she added rather sheepishly, "that I, too, suspected the children."

"That's alwight," said Wyatt magnanimously. "It is the sort of thing we might do, you know."

"Missing ducks, voices in the night. Or is it missing voices and ducks in the night? Whatever it is, don't tell me that part just now," murmured Greniston rather faintly. "It's all quite fascinating, I'm sure, but let's stick with the main thrust of the plot for a while. Humor me, I'm a simple man, not steeped in skullduggery, as you all seem to be. Now, you, Davey Lee, our Romany friend, you rescued Luan Tey and started to carry him to your Grandmother's wagon."

"Right you are," said Davey, "but it was raining and cold, and 'e didn't look like 'e'd make it that far, losin' blood by the buckets, 'e was. So when I saw the lights of your house, I thought, 'That's a bit of all right,' and I headed for this place, which was closer by half a mile. Figured there was bound to be a couple extra rooms in a big old lookout like this one, and no one the wiser. So I fixed 'im up as nice as I could in one of your spare bedrooms and lit out to fetch Gran. But she had gotten her Calling and was already on her way. Just about fell over me on the front lawn."

"Yes, that's something else I'd like to come back to," put in Greniston, "your Grandmother and her 'Calling' and how it happened to bring you here in the first place. But for now," he added hastily, as Annie Lee opened her mouth to speak, "let's stick to the main plot: the three of you have been stowaways, as it were, in Greniston Manor, whilst nursing Mr. Tey back to health?"

"Exactly," said Davey Lee.

Greniston peered suspiciously at Luan Tey. "He doesn't look very healthy to me," he said. "He looks bloody awful. He needs to see a doctor."

Luan Tey shook his head.

"'E won't do it, Guv," Davey explained. "And 'e is mending very well, all things considered. Gran knows what she's doin', most times. His fever's broke. I think he'll pull through."

"We'll see," growled Greniston. "I still think a physician is in order. However, he does look well enough at the moment to answer my most pressing question: What's so bloody important about this damned chalice, and why does everyone want it?"

"Because," said Luan Tey quietly, "the fate of the world depends on it."

There was a pause, in which they could all hear very clearly the drumming of the rain on the roof and Luan Tey's labored, shallow breath.

"I might have known you'd say something like that," Greniston mused. He turned to look at Wyatt. "Are you sure you don't write his lines? In fact, did you write the plot for this whole escapade?" Wyatt shook his head.

"Hmmm," said Greniston, "I'm still not convinced. Plots and counterplots, a pair of chalices—as if one wasn't trouble enough—that dart around the countryside like butterflies in Maytime, mysterious intuitions and Callings. . . . It's too bloody implausible." He looked at Gwen. "If your Henrietta Amberly concocted a plot like this, her agent would tell her to sober up."

"Not if her agent had heard Merlin's cry," Gwen replied. "It's hard to explain, but there is more going on here than what we usually call 'real.' And yet, it is all real. That's where we usually make our big mistake, you see," she continued earnestly. "We are so sure that the everyday world of concrete and business and facts we can measure and boss around to our liking is the 'real' one, the only one, that we miss most of what's actually going on around us. But I'm coming to see, more and more every day, that there is much more to life than most of us think." In the shadows, Filipo smiled with satisfaction.

"Things that even I might have dismissed as nonsense just a couple of weeks ago," Gwen continued, "I now seem to be encountering again and again. Something is going on here that is more than we understand. It's as if something has gathered us all here to play our parts in—in some kind of great story. If you look at it that way, there is nothing implausible about these events at all. Mysterious, yes, but who says mysteries aren't real?"

"Not I," said Greniston softly, looking at her with greater appreciation than ever. "Well, you have made your point, and eloquently, too. But it still doesn't explain why the 'fate of the world' depends on this battered old cup."

"That is something I can tell only you, Lord Greniston," said Luan Tey. "I need to speak with you alone."

"'E means it, Guv," put in Davey Lee. "Had a fever for forty hours, babbled like a bay about findin' you the whole time. Single-minded bloke, 'e is. As soon as 'e come to 'imself, 'e said we had to take 'im to see you, couldn't wait another hour. And 'ere, as you see, we is."

"Hmmm," said Greniston, "very well, Mr. Tey, we'll talk in my study. This way."

"Oh, Lord Greniston," protested Lettice, "are you sure that is quite wise? He looks a desperate character."

Greniston smiled. "Desperate characters interest me," he said. "But thank you for your concern, Miss Pennington. I'm sure I'll be quite safe, though."

Then Greniston kissed Gwen lightly on the cheek, bowed to the rest of the company, and led Luan Tey from the room.

"Oh, my goodness," exclaimed Mrs. Hodges, when the door had barely closed behind them, "what does it all mean?"

"Well, luv," said Davey, "I don't know what's so important about that ruddy cup, but I can tell you this . . . "

At this point, Annie gave him a warning glance, but Davey winked, and continued, "that little Burmese fella is the reason the greengrocer's is now missing a window. It wasn't vandals that took a shot at it, it was hired killers, after that Luan Tey!"

Cries of "No!" and "You don't say!" echoed around the table. Everyone pulled their chairs closer to hear what threads of the story the Gypsy might have.

Muttering something about the "baffoom," Wyatt slipped away. He sauntered casually toward the doors, pausing on the way to take a handful of cashews from the sideboard and to examine a tapestry. Once outside the door, however, he flung the nuts aside and raced down the hall as if his life depended on it.

***

"This is almost too fantastic to be believed," Lord Greniston said. "And yet, you don't strike me as a man much given to exaggeration."

Luan Tey managed a dry little smile. "Not usually."

Greniston looked at the chalice he held in his hands. "You are telling me that this metal contains an extremely rare element called 'sedasium'— that's what you called it?"

"Yes. You can read that for yourself in the British Museum report. Sedasium appears as a trace element in the silver the cup is made from. That is what gives the outside metal that odd, dull sheen. The inside is, as you know, coated with electrum."

"And you are telling me that this sedasium, if processed from its raw form, is a catalyst that may increase the potency of plutonium almost a thousand times?"

"That's right."

"And how much of the stuff does this chalice have in it?"

"If returned to its raw state—if that were possible—and converted correctly? Enough to destroy China, Japan, and half of Russia." Greniston put the chalice down on his desk, very carefully and very quickly.

"In its natural state, the metal is harmless," Luan Tey assured him. "Only when it has been refined in the most sophisticated laboratory with the formulas my employer has discovered and combined with other key ingredients could it have that effect. The chalice holds the key to that infernal effect."

"It makes me shudder to think of it in the clutches of the young Walmsleys." He gazed at the chalice, sitting on top of his papers. "It isn't really a very pretty metal, with that stuff in it," he mused.

"Powerful things are not always pretty, Lord Greniston," his companion replied. "Certainly, it is rare. The only known vein of silver with sedasium in it is in the African country of Zaire. And that has recently been made unreachable by earthquake."

"Hence, your Mr. Miller's interest in this chalice."

"The chalice, and the secret it contains," said Luan Tey. "From Miller's papers I have learned that he is convinced there must be another such vein of sedasium-rich silver in this district. That is why he is so eager to buy Swindon's land."

"It's not Swindon's land," thundered Greniston. "It is my land, and it is not for sale!"

"So I have heard in the village," said Luan Tey. "Mr. Swindon is of a different view."

"I can't believe that even Swindon would be mixed up in something this bad!" Greniston sighed.

"Oh, he knows nothing of the sedasium," Luan Tey assured him. "He really thinks Miller wants the land for real estate. That is why he wants the woods. Not to build commuter homes, as he tells your villagers, but to sell to Miller."

"Who I am sure is offering him a fat price."

"Not a lean one. Although, the main profit for Mr. Swindon is that if he sells the land to Miller, then he will refrain from exposing certain unfortunate deals Swindon has made in the past."

"Blackmail," said Greniston. "A great many things are beginning to fall into place. The pressure of that kind of threat could drive many people around the bend, and Swindon has always been a nervy type. . . . Yes, this explains a great deal. But how did Miller ever know about the chalice? It's an obscure treasure, to say the least."

"Yes, but Mr. Miller is a collector of art objects. Not, I do not think for their beauty, but for the power they represent."

"Surely his lust for power would be better served by amassing Swiss bank accounts and private arsenals," said Greniston.

"Oh, he has those. The power in the artwork is different. It is human power, Lord Greniston. Powerful emotions, powerful inspirations go into the making of great art. Miller is a man who can smell power, the way a shark smells blood. When he sees power, he wants to possess it. All the paintings, the statues he owns, they seem like slaves to me. They would never want to be owned by a man like him; he stands against everything that created them. But of course, a statue cannot get off its pedestal and walk away."

"This chalice seems to have been doing a good job of bouncing around England," Greniston commented.

"It has moved people to move it. It has a lot of power. I am not sure, but I think that Miller first came across it simply mentioned as an artwork, perhaps in one of the journals he receives. And he remembered it when his private researchers discovered the uses of sedasium."

"So he wants this land, and he wants this chalice, very badly," Greniston said.

"More than that," the other man replied, "he wants the Greniston treasure. Of course, in researching this place and the chalice, he learned of Lord Peter's prophecy and the mention of a treasure. He is convinced that this treasure exists and that it contains other objects made of sedasium-rich silver, just like that chalice. Miller has an unerring instinct for destruction. He knows, is absolutely certain, and willing to risk lives on it, that the ancient treasure was made from elements on this land. Capturing the treasure is like a talisman for him. Miller always has to have some sort of talisman to go forward on a project. He's perfectly capable of wasting millions of dollars, waiting months, even years, to find some relic, some symbol that tells his mind it's now clear to proceed. If it's a 'sacred' object, even better. I think his greatest pleasure in life, if you can call it that, is perverting a sacred object by linking it to one of his demonic projects. So, if he has the treasure, he knows he'll get the live 'treasure' of sedasium. That's how Miller's mind works."

Greniston was amazed by Luan Tey's diagnosis of Miller's madness. The little man seemed to take a dark pleasure in describing it so precisely.

"I see," said Greniston. "And if he found that . . . if one cup contains enough of the catalyst to destroy a continent or two. . . ."

"Whoever possessed such an infernal 'treasure' and was mad enough to use it, or sell it to those who might want it, would be—what is your English phrase?—'top dog' of the world."

"But surely no one would ever consider unleashing such destruction," Greniston reasoned. "Why, it would be suicide!"

Luan Tey shrugged. "The human race is suicidal," he said simply. "Consider the evidence of every nuclear warhead and biological combat laboratory that already exists. All sedasium does is up the ante."

Greniston sighed, recognizing the truth of what the other man said. "So, Miller thinks the ancient treasure is buried on my land and that the land is riddled with raw sedasium."

"He believes the treasure is hidden beneath the mounds or hidden in your house."

"In my house? Grand." Greniston poured himself a glass of brandy. "Fourth glass tonight," he joked, "and it seems to be having no effect at all. Must be the sobering effect of these awful facts you keep telling me. Well, besides yourself and Miller, and now, unfortunately, me, how many people know about all this?"

"No one, I think. Not all the facts. You see, part of Miller's genius is that he keeps his sources of information insulated from each other. The chemist who developed the conversion formula for sedasium is 'out of the way,' you might say. The employees who know that Miller wants the land

and the chalice don't know why. And even if they did, they don't have access to the formula, unless they kill Miller for it. I think only I have all the facts."

"Does Miller know you know this?"

"I think he can't be sure."

Greniston nodded. "So Miller has already sent new errand boys here to get the chalice—the ones who shot you. And those charming gentlemen may even now be skulking in the corners of my house, seeking treasure."

Luan Tey nodded. "Or seeking you or anyone else here they think might be my accomplice."

"I'm calling the Yard," said Greniston, reaching for the phone.

"Out of the question," said Luan Tey, putting his hand over Greniston's and holding down the receiver. "You cannot risk it. There is no one who can be trusted."

"Don't be ridiculous!" exploded Greniston. "I've known Atherton since we were both fifteen, and he's as right as rain."

Luan Tey shrugged. "He may be. But I can assure you, Lord Greniston, there will be those near him who are not. Mention the name Miller, and there will be those who do not need to know all the facts to smell a profit to be had by protecting him. A call might even come from very high places to insure his safety. If your friend Mr. Atherton is honest, and you tell all this to him, you may well be signing his death warrant. A bomb planted in his car and blamed on some terrorist group, a heart attack after a game of golf—these little things happen every day, do they not?"

"Oh, for God's sake," scoffed Greniston, "things aren't like that at the Yard!"

Luan Tey smiled very sadly. "They are like that everywhere. Let me tell you a terrible little story, Lord Greniston. I read this in the British prison at Kowloon. It had an excellent library, and I had time on my hands. I read this in a history book. It seems there was once, a few hundred years ago, a Queen of Spain with a cruel nature. She had built a special audience room with a floor of crystal tiles. Underneath this clear floor was a huge aquarium of sea water, filled with sharks and octopus and sting rays—monsters of the deep, real oddities she had her conquistadors bring back from far off places. The people walking across the floor could see the monsters very clearly. Yet the court business went on as usual. Picture it, Lord Greniston: the elegant officials taking snuff—itself a new discovery—the ladies in lovely gowns making small talk, the tinkle of glasses, the low murmur of sophisticated chat. Everything went on so, until someone displeased the Queen. Suddenly, that person found that the crystal tile beneath them, controlled unseen behind velvet draperies, gave way beneath their feet, and they fell into the dark waters beneath the floor, to be devoured by monsters. Everyone else was expected not to notice, while the business of the day went on. And all the while, the poor fool in the water struggled, perhaps beating the floor beneath the very feet of those he or she had thought to be friends. Possibly some of those 'friends' laid discreet bets on whether the victim would drown or be devoured first. Servants appeared, closed the crystal tile, discreetly pushing down a tentacle, perhaps, or a hand grasping toward the air, and then mopping up any traces of sea water with fine linen towels."

Luan Tey paused, letting the story sink in. "Believe me, Lord Greniston," he then continued, "the behavior of those courtiers who had seen this demonstration in action was far more careful than the demeanor of those for whom the idea was still a titillating novelty. The difference between you and me is that I have seen that floor open up beneath the feet of the man standing next to me. For you, the crystal membrane between you and the monsters is still intact. Oh, you are a smart man, well read about the problems of the world. Maybe you can quote genus and species of every monster in the water. But for you, they are still something that lives on the other side of the tiles, far way, in Africa, maybe, or Viet Nam. Even, perhaps, in Belfast, London, or Manchester. But not here, not in your orderly world, with your old school chums who are as right as rain. But the dark water, the monsters, they are all right here, inches away, all the time. Even at Scotland Yard, even in Far Tauverly. Even inside us."

Greniston had walked to the French doors as Luan Tey spoke. Now he stood there, gazing out at the night. Many feelings were stirred in him: fear, sorrow, even a foolish annoyance that the other man thought he knew so little of the world. Yet he knew, uncomfortably, that it had been several years since he had dealt first hand in the realms Luan Tey described. If he was not naive, he was indeed protected, by money, by choice.

Greniston thought, *Yes, this sad little man is right. That dark world is just a few inches away. You can t depend on crystal floors or the whim of royalty to keep you safe from it. Only your own character can do that.*

He looked at his own reflection in the windowpane. For a moment, it seemed to him that his reflected features on the glass were all that stood between him and the enormous darkness without. He tapped the window, as if testing the strength of his own face. Then he turned back to his guest.

Now that he was emptied of words, Luan Tey looked drained. He sat slumped in his chair. Recent pain and worry had clearly taken their toll on him, but beneath that, Greniston saw the marks of an even deeper despair. He suspected that the man felt himself to be not just one of the courtiers who had watched his world give way, but one of the very monsters of the deep. Looking at his face, a line from Virginia Wolf came to mind: "the feeling of being far, far out to sea, and alone."

Greniston felt that he had never seen a lonelier face. He suspected that Luan Tey felt himself to be so steeped in evil that he was outside the human circle and could never return to it.

He might be, Greniston thought. He had met those who were. Yet he found himself hoping that this man was not. Within his bitter words, behind his mask-like face, Greniston sensed a desperate cry for redemption.

"How old are you?" he asked Luan Tey.

"Twenty-four."

Greniston restrained an exclamation of shock. He had assumed the man before him to be at least forty. He sighed. "Since you don't want me to call the Yard," he said, "I assume you have a plan?"

"Yes. I get in touch with Miller. I leave enough doubts behind me that he won't know who to trust, so he will listen to me. I tell him that I have found the Greniston treasure and that I will sell it to him for the right price. But that he must meet me here, on the land somewhere, alone. He might not come alone, but he dare not bring too many."

"And then?"

"Then we deal with him." The way Luan Tey spoke the words it was clear what he had in mind.

"No," said Greniston. "I'll not be party to the murder of an untried man, vile though he may be." Luan Tey shrugged impatiently at this nicety.

"But what I will do," Greniston continued, "is consider tricking him into discussing his plans for the treasure, when he thinks no one but you is there to hear. If we can tape what he says, or if I simply hear it, we will have evidence that cannot be ignored. I know it is an inefficient plan and fraught with problems," he added, as Luan Tey opened his mouth to protest, "but it is the only one I am willing to consider, and if you want my help, you're going to have to take my scruples along with it. I'm sure you've cursed the bullet that got you a thousand times, because without it, you could be handling it on your own. As it is, though, you can barely stand, let alone defeat an armed man. I think you're in no position to call the shots. I am, and I intend to think this over before I agree to anything. This is too dangerous not to be careful about. For all I know, you could still be working for Miller, and all this is some scheme of his. Though, I confess, I doubt it. But I'm still not sure I shouldn't ring Atherton. I'm going to think this over. I promise to have reached a decision by dawn. Until then, you are now one of my official guests."

"Guest or prisoner?" asked Luan Tey.

"Ah, well, there's often a fine line between the two, isn't there?" Greniston asked. "Particularly when one is visiting relatives. At least you have the good fortune to be among strangers. Now, I have *carte blanche* to inflict my eccentric hospitality on you, and here is what I command: You will have a peaceful night's sleep in a proper bedroom, and you will see a doctor if that fever returns. Now, before going to the paradise of clean sheets and hot water bottles that Robert will provide for you, you are going to drink a nightcap of my personal brandy, a brew so ancient that merely to inhale it is to drift toward the spell of Hypnos."

Greniston poured Luan Tey a drink and handed it to him with an authority that brooked no interference.

"And let's find you a book or two, in case you want to read in bed." Greniston perused the piles of books on the floor. He still had not had time to replace the bookshelf from the confusion of the afternoon. "Hmmm . . . *Screwtape Letters*. You'd enjoy that. . . . *Chronicles of Narnia*—why not? Ah, Joseph Conrad! Now there's a great soul for you; and one not unacquainted with ocean depths himself. Here is a quote I return to often, listen to this: 'It was for me to find fit words for his meaning: he was one of us.'"

Though he spoke lightly, Greniston tried to throw the words to Luan Tey as he would have hurled a lifeline to a drowning man. In his mind, he prayed, *Grab the line, lad, grab the line, and hang on. Don't give up yet. You still get my vote as part of the human tribe.*

He looked up from the page directly into Luan Tey's eyes, as dark as any monster-ridden sea water, the loneliest eyes he had ever seen. "One of us," he repeated, his gaze unwavering, "one of us." Then he smiled and added, "I'll tell you something, my unhappy friend, if I had been in your

Queen of Spain's court, I'd have grabbed the bitch and held her hostage on her own wicked floor, until the old bag made some changes around there."

A faint smile curved Luan Tey's lips. "Lord Greniston," he said, "I believe you just might have." That was all. Greniston could not tell if his words had offered the man any comfort. They had sunk into the depths behind those dark eyes like seeds cast into midnight water. He did not know if they would grow into anything that could ever reach the light.

"Well, old chum," Greniston said, "You've a good night's sleep to get, and I've a house full of guests to soothe. Best be on our way."

After both men had left the room, the door to the dumb waiter inched open, and Wyatt Walmsley crawled out. His young face bore the thoughtful expression of one who has heard a great deal more than he bargained for.

***

As St. Aethelrood's bells tolled three a.m., Filipo paused by a hawthorn tree to light another Gauloise. He did so not merely to enjoy the cigarette but to see if the flash of the match or the scent of the tobacco on the air caused any stirring in the underbrush. Not the least movement was visible, however, confirming his intuition that, except for Davey Lee patrolling to the north, he had the grounds to himself. This knowledge did not ease his tension. Whatever this business was, there was danger in it. He had recognized that in Luan Tey's face the moment he had stepped out of the shadows of the minstrel's gallery. He had seen it again in Greniston's face when he returned to the hall. However jovial their host's manner was, there had been a new tautness in his jaw as he said, "It seems a bit of a mystery has come up. I hope you all don't mind being involved."

"Oh, no, not in the least," everyone had instantly assured him.

"Excellent!" Greniston had replied, beaming, as if they were all acting out some elaborate country weekend game he had planned for their amusement. "Now, at present, I can't tell you everything, but I must impress one fact upon you: Please do not leave the manor house. If you were not already planning on staying the night, I hope it will not inconvenience you too much to do so." Here, Greniston had glanced at the Pennington sisters.

"Of course not," Althea had assured him, "but is it really necessary?"

"Without wanting to cause undue alarm, I'm afraid it is. There is a good chance that anyone leaving this house could be followed and even harassed by unsavory characters—to put it mildly."

A gasp of rather thrilled fear rippled around the room. "Please believe me," Greniston had continued, "when I tell you that there could be real danger. It is far safer for us to stick together within the safety of these walls. No, I'm sorry, I simply can't tell you any more just now," he had added, to deter the host of questions he saw rising around him. "I have given my word of honor not to. However, I can tell you this: Tomorrow we are going to have the greatest treasure hunt Far Tauverly—and possibly Britain—has ever seen."

"A treasure hunt?" Osgood asked, his eyes sparkling.

Greniston nodded. "It appears there may be more truth to the old legend of the Greniston Treasure than I previously believed." The Walmsley children exchanged a triumphant glance.

"If the treasure exists," Greniston continued, "there is a good chance it may be hidden somewhere in this very house."

A chorus of fascinated "reallys," and "you don't says" echoed among the guests. Greniston held up his hand for order. "It is more important than I can currently explain to you that we find that treasure, if indeed it is here. I hope that you will all be willing to help hunt for it upon the morrow . . . "

Greniston here was interrupted by an enthusiastic chorus of agreement. "I expected as much from such staunch friends as you," he said, when the excitement had quieted a little. "Therefore, I suggest we all repair to our beds, so that we may be fresh to hunt in the morning."

The guests had headed to their rooms in an almost festive mood. Yet Filipo had not been surprised when Greniston had pulled him and Davey Lee quietly aside and asked if they would be willing to patrol the perimeter of the house until morning.

"Sure thing, Guv," the Gypsy had said, "but what exactly are we lookin' for?"

"I don't know," Greniston had sighed. "Be on the alert for anything. If something, however small, strikes you as the least bit odd, come and get me at once. I shall be patrolling the inside of the house, since I know it best. Here, you had better take these pistols."

Mrs. Fitzpatrick had come up to Greniston then and said, "Now, Lord Greniston, I know when something's up, and something's up here. I am not going to pry, but I am going to let you gentlemen know that hot coffee and fresh rolls will be available in the kitchen all night long, for whoever needs them."

"That's handsome of you, truly," Greniston had said, "but surely you need some sleep."

"Actually," Mrs. Fitzpatrick had interrupted, "I've lived through a war and seventeen teething babies, including yourself! I've known more sleepless nights than you have known quiet ones! So just you let me do what's needed, and don't interfere."

Grinning, Lord Greniston had saluted smartly, and said, "I stand corrected."

"Quite right," Mrs. Fitzpatrick had retorted with a sniff.

Now, several hours later, Filipo and Davey both had good cause to appreciate the housekeeper's generous offer. A cold rain had fallen on and off through the night, and the cups of steaming coffee she insisted on giving them every time they passed the kitchen door had proved most welcome.

Filipo finished his cigarette, turned up his jacket collar against the rain, and continued his guard duty.

Unknown to him, others were awake at that hour as well. In a seldom-used storage room of the manor, High Council of the Independent Kingdom of Greniston was under way. At that moment, Wyatt, Sentinel of the Kingdom, Recoverer of the Chalice, and Super Agent extraordinaire, was just finishing his report to the assembled council.

" . . . and so you see, that's why he told Ward Gweniston it's a matter of wife and death— because it twuly is!"

"Yes," said Osgood, his eyes gleaming with the zeal of one who has at last met events worthy of his genius. "On one hand, we have an international evil villain, his awful henchmen, and world peril. On the other hand, we have the Independent Kingdom of Greenstone!"

"Greenstone!" the others echoed, in a none-too-muffled shout. Only Charles looked worried. "Shouldn't we tell Lord Greniston that Wyatt heard?"

"Shhh," interrupted Osgood. "Arch villains may even now be eavesdropping upon us! We will tell the grown-ups nothing," he added in a whisper. "They have their duty, and we have ours. We will watch and await developments."

At that same hour, the Lord of Greniston Manor was holding High Council of his own. He stood in the portrait gallery, the beam of his flashlight trained upon Lord Peter's face. Greniston gazed speculatively at his noble ancestor's visage.

"What the devil should I do?" he asked. "Hard for me to believe all this is happening. Last week, my biggest concern was getting Robert not to run the lawnmower when I was trying to write. Now, I'm worried about fending off world destruction. 'Is this an improvement?' one might well ask. Part of me wants to run away. I mean, for God's sake! Weapons, fear, violence, I want no part of it! Yet it comes with the world we are all born into. I've just been forced to see it a little more clearly, that's all. Saying we never made the mess doesn't make it go away, does it? We either leap in, and do our best to help put things to rights, or look the other way—if we can."

Greniston began to pace up and down the length of the dark gallery, gesturing now and then with the hand that held the flashlight. "It would be easy to call the Yard, have Atherton take this out of my hands. Even sounds like the sensible, the right thing to do. But what if what Tey says is true? What if Miller can bribe himself out of trouble? What if I call the Yard, and because of that, Atherton gets killed, and Miller ends up free to sell his madness into the wrong hands? What then? I wouldn't sleep well for it, I tell you."

Greniston stood before the portrait again, and said, "But what if, on the other hand, I try to handle this my way, and someone gets hurt—Logan, or the Walmsley children, . . . or Miss Fields. Yes, what if Gwen gets hurt, or killed, because of a choice I make? I don't think I could bear it."

Lord Peter made no reply. He gazed at his descendant with the ghost of a smile on his elegant face. "Damme, Sir," muttered Greniston, "I believe you know where the treasure is! If only you could speak!"

"Hello?"

Greniston spun around to see Gwen standing in the doorway of the gallery, holding a candle. "Gwen," he exclaimed, "What a delight to see you! There's nothing wrong, is there?" he added worriedly.

"No, no," said Gwen. "I just thought you might like some company. I couldn't sleep, and I went down to the kitchen to get some tea. Mrs. Fitzpatrick told me you were, um, watching the house."

"Well, I would like some company, as a matter of fact—if the company is yours."

Suddenly, Gwen felt rather awkward. In her impulsive wish to see Greniston, she had not stopped to think that she was wearing a flannel nightgown and an old quilted blue robe. On her feet were a pair of fuzzy bedroom slippers, designed to look like huge lion's paws. (These were a birthday present from a niece in Chicago.)

Gwen padded across the stone floor to Greniston's side.

"What remarkable footwear." he murmured. "I wish I had a pair just like that."

"You could wear them if you ever return to the House of Lords," Gwen suggested. "The wig, the robes, and a pair of these. But in pink, I think."

"Definitely pink," Greniston agreed. "But I think they would show to better advantage at Ascot, for the opening day of the races. Top hat, gray tails, and those. It would probably rate me a photo on the cover of several tabloids: 'Aristocrat reveals terrible family curse.' . . . 'In sixteen forty three,' Lord Greniston revealed, in an exclusive interview, 'my Great-Great-Great-Great-Great and a few more greats Granny had an affair with an alien life form from Loch Ness. Ever since then, the tragic genetics of this liaison have appeared in the feet of the eldest son of the family. For generations, we have tried to cover this curse with Wellington boots, but I have decided to come out of the closet, or rather, the boots, and be proud of my mixed ancestry.'"

Greniston cut himself short, smiled, and said amiably, "This is a silly conversation we're having, isn't it?"

Gwen nodded. "I don't mind."

"Good. I could use a bit of silliness right now. Oh, Miss Fields, dear Miss Fields, talk to me of silly things, of shoes and ships and sealing wax, and whether pigs have wings."

"We could. But why not be really silly and tell me what's going on around here?" asked Gwen, sweetly.

Greniston smiled ruefully. "That, Dear Lady, I cannot do. Whatever I told you might endanger you, even more than you already are."

"Thank you for the concern," Gwen said sincerely, "but I'm not a Victorian doll who needs to be protected from the dark side of life."

"Of that, Miss Fields, I am well aware," Greniston said with a smile. "I see the twin fires of liberated woman and Irish ancestry in your hazel eyes, and I bow before their might. But this situation I would shield even myself from, if I could. I am now the unwelcome possessor of knowledge some might kill me for. It is not an honor I wish to share with anyone, and certainly not with someone that I hold so dear. Besides, I truly have given my word to reveal nothing."

"Well, then you must honor that, of course," said Gwen.

Saying that simple sentence, and meaning it, was one of the hardest things she had ever done. Had it been Logan who was burdened with a painful secret, or even Filipo, she would probably have had the truth out of them within an hour. Greniston was different, and not only because she could see she didn't stand a chance of budging him, once his mind was made up. He was a person who needed to have his privacy respected, even in times of trouble. To leave him alone, even when everything in her ached to help, would, she realized, be one of the hardest parts of knowing him, if their relationship continued.

"Penny for your thoughts," Greniston said. "You look quite solemn."

"Oh," said Gwen, a bit flustered, "I was just wondering if there was anything I could do that would actually help."

"Just be with me," said Greniston. "That's a greater help than you know."

"All right," said Gwen brightly. "What do you say we continue your night watch? You can show me the manor by candlelight."

"Capitol idea," said Greniston.

They left the room, and all was quiet in their wake. In the darkness, Lord Peter's portrait gazed, as it always did, out the windows, toward the woods. Yet on this night, he seemed to smile just a little more than usual— the pleased smile of a matchmaker whose plans are working out.

For the next two hours, Gwen and Greniston wandered through the corridors of the manor, conversing in whispers. Perhaps because the presence of the past was so strong in the old house, Gwen found herself telling Greniston about Lord Peter's diaries, which he admitted that he had only skimmed.

"But you must read them," Gwen exclaimed. "They are your heritage! They explain so much, not just about Lord Peter, but about what it means to be a Greniston."

"For instance?"

"Well, like what a proud family yours is," Gwen said. "They remind me of the de Coucys, that fourteenth-century French family, whose motto was "*Je ne suis de roi ni, Je suis de Coucy!*""

"I serve neither king nor," Greniston translated, "I am of the Coucy's! Sounds pretty snobby to me."

"At its worst," Gwen agreed, "but at its best, it speaks of brave people who didn't wait around for some government or society to tell them how to live. They did what they thought was right, and to hell with what anyone else said about it! And they bent their knee to no man, not even to popes."

"I take it you approve of this independent behavior," Greniston said.

"You bet I do," replied Gwen. "Human beings were meant to stand on their own two feet and make their own choices—that I am sure of."

Greniston smiled. "Interesting you should bring it up now. '*Je suis de Greniston*' has a ring to it, I must admit."

As they patrolled the halls of the manor, Greniston felt he was learning a great deal about Gwen, from what she chose to tell him about Lord Peter.

She admires courage in a man, he realized, *and generosity, kindness, a mystical strain, humor. . . .* He wondered if he could measure up. And yet, he knew that those ingredients were in him by nature and by inheritance, like an old treasure buried away that needed to be brought to light and polished, but that were, for all their disuse, still genuine at core.

St. Aethelrood's bells tolled five a.m. "Gwen, let me show you something marvelous!" Greniston exclaimed. He seized her hand and led her down a hallway. "There's no time to waste," he added, "This way! Quickly!"

He led her through an old wooden doorway and up a narrow, winding staircase. The light from his flashlight wavered on the stone walls. The steps were worn with centuries of use. Evidently, many generations of Grenistons had climbed up and down this very staircase. Gwen was sure they were in the oldest part of the manor house, but beyond that, her sense of direction was quite muddled, and the twists and turns of the stairs were not helping to clear it. She felt dizzy and out of breath, but Greniston's grasp on her hand was firm, practically dragging her up the stairs.

"We're almost there," he said encouragingly.

Sure enough, a moment later, he thrust open a wooden door at the top of the stairs. Cold, fresh air came rushing through it.

"This way," Greniston cried.

The first sense Gwen had was of being pulled out of something narrow and confining into a vast open space. *The roof*, she realized, *we're on the roof.*

They were indeed standing on the roof of a high, round tower. Above, the vast dome of the sky arched above them. The rain had stopped, and here and there the clouds were blown away to reveal pockets of stars.

"It's wonderful," Gwen exclaimed, spinning around, trying to take in the whole sky at once.

Greniston smiled. "It will be dawn soon, just wait."

A faint light was indeed growing in the east. Somewhere in the darkness below, a single bird began to sing, pouring its melody of piercing sweetness into the stillness.

Gwen looked over at Greniston, who was leaning against one of the parapets that encircled the tower, gazing into the distance.

In a few minutes, she thought with certainty, *that man is going to kiss me. And oh, how much I want him to.* Yet she savored the moment before it happened. For the kiss that was about to happen would change everything, like crossing the border between two countries. So far, her path and Grenistons had crossed in the land of strangers. Their first kiss had been but a greeting in that land. Now, when they kissed again, they would have stepped into the land of those who acknowledge that they love, and nothing would ever be the same again. From that moment on, they would travel together, for a long time or a little—that remained to be seen—but the journey would be acknowledged between them. Gwen longed for that moment, and yet appreciated the pause before it, as she gazed at Greniston, that separate life, that wonder.

"Look, Gwen!" he said, pointing to the east.

She had been so engrossed in his features that she had forgotten about the scene around them. Now she turned and gasped with wonder. The horizon was tinged with peach, wine, and pale gold, yet higher up the last stars still twinkled in a vault of violet-blue. Below, the deep green of distant trees and the green and gold of fields began to emerge from the darkness.

"When the weather's right, you can see three counties from here," Greniston remarked.

"It's amazing," Gwen said. To the west, she saw the rustling treetops of Greniston Wood and, beyond, the Norman tower of St. Aethelrood's. To the south, rolling fields, a gleaming patchwork of green and gold. To the east, the distant lights of Tweeverton and the silver thread of the highway, and to the north, forest and shadow.

"Sometimes you can just catch a glimpse of the Bristol channel in that direction," said Greniston.

A wind rose and sent the broken clouds sailing across the sky, so that here and there across the landscape, spatterings of rain fell.

Never before had Gwen seen so clearly how land is sculpted and smoothed, like the contours of a living thing. The first shaft of bright, clear sunlight broke upon that land, and the solitary singing bird was joined by a host of others, until the whole sky seemed full of their music.

Gwen's eyes met Greniston's. He gathered her into his arms and pressed his lips against hers.

Yes, thought Gwen, *yes. Yes to Greniston, yes to love.* The wonder of his face had become to her a gateway through which she glimpsed all that was great and beautiful. In saying yes to him, she felt that she was somehow saying yes to life itself. She responded totally, without reserve.

How long they might have stood there, complete in each other's arms, it was hard to say. But one of the small, wandering rain clouds passed overhead and drenched them both with rain.

Gwen laughed, and Greniston said fondly, "Well, my dear, I suppose no date with you would be complete without a little rainfall. Come," he added, "the day's begun, and we have much to do."

Mrs. Fitzpatrick, busily preparing a huge breakfast of eggs, toast, bacon, and kippers did not bat an eye when Gwen and Lord Greniston came into the kitchen, he still in evening dress, she in her nightclothes, and both soaking wet. Neither did Filipo and Davey Lee, who, having finished their night watch, were eagerly awaiting the meal.

"Good morning, Lord Greniston," Mrs. Fitzpatrick said matter-of-factly. "Morning, Miss Fields. Would you like your eggs scrambled or poached?"

"Just coffee for now, thank you," said Gwen, "I'd better change."

She was so joyful that when she spoke even those everyday words, she practically sang them. Davey caught Filipo's eye and grinned. As he later described it to Annie, "Love was in the air so thick and sweet, you could 'ave spread it on your toast instead of marmalade."

As for Filipo, he felt he had never before understood the appropriateness of the phrase "in love." Now he saw how true it was. Gwen and Greniston did not simply love each other; they were *in* love. Just as a boat is borne along by mighty currents, they seemed to be living in the current of love itself. Love shone out of their faces until it seemed to fill the room they stood in. Filipo felt a surge of joy at the fact. Joy for Gwen but also simply at seeing that in the old, battered world, such love could yet appear, as fresh as the dawn of time.

Then the room seemed to darken, as if a cloud had passed over the sun. Luan Tey stood in the doorway.

"That wasn't much sleep you got," Greniston remarked. "Still, seems to have done you good. Have a seat, have . . . "

"Have you made up your mind?" Luan Tey interrupted.

Greniston nodded. "Go ahead and send your message," he said. "We'll handle this on our own."

CHAPTER TWENTY-ONE

Still lay the mist upon the roofs and towers of Greniston Manor, upon its quiet lawns and gardens, and upon the mounds deep within the Wood. Still lay the mist upon the quiet streets of Far Tauverly and upon the Roman mosaic and noble beeches at Knobbly Hill. The day that had dawned with golden sunrise and silver sprinklings of rain had settled into a silent mistiness, unbroken by any breeze.

In the great hall of the manor house, Logan Knowelles sat by the mullioned windows, gazing out at the lawn. His gaunt hands rested tenderly on the harp he had played the night before.

He would not have been surprised to see Gwydion appear out of the mist, or Tommy Greniston, with a gin and tonic in hand. Just as the mist gathered closer and closer around the house, so did the immaterial presences he had encountered in the last few days seem to be gathering closer and closer around him. He had the strong sense that the dream world and the everyday world of time and objects were meeting and interweaving, more and more.

"Logan?"

Lord Greniston stood in the doorway, holding a pot of coffee and a plate of scones.

"Mrs. Fitz continues to fortify the troops," he explained. "Mind if I join you for a quick break?"

"Of course not," Logan replied. It struck him that he had never seen Greniston so calm and steady in himself. He thought of Gwen and smiled.

"Found any treasure?" Greniston asked, as he sipped his coffee.

Logan shook his head. "I've searched the room for hidden doors, cubbyholes, anything, but found nothing."

Greniston sighed. "If only we knew exactly what we were looking for! Could be plates or swords or candelabras."

"But made of the same metal as the chalice. . . ."

"Yes. But then what do we make of this?" Greniston asked, pulling from his pocket a copy of Lord Peter's prophecy:

"When the stranger comes to the lion's gate
And woods with Merlin's cry resound
When Knobbly Hill doth tremble and shake
Then must the treasure swiftly be found

A throne, a crown, a speaking sword
A golden lady, a silver lord
Twelve true jewels to shine and meet
Where gold springs from the ground."

"All these references to a speaking sword, a throne, a crown, . . . and a golden lady and a silver lord? All of it sounds like pieces of a treasure."

"And it needs not only to be found but also fitted together at the right time and place, like a jigsaw puzzle," mused Logan.

"Yes," sighed Greniston, reading on:

"Yet, if no jewels be gathered there
   This have I seen in waking dream:
   Brightest light turns darkest night
   Nor leaf, nor creature, nor human face
   In this nor any other place—
   World's despair."

"Everything seems to hinge on those 'jewels' gathering—if we believe the prophecy, that is," Greniston continued, deeply puzzled.

"Do you?" Logan asked curiously.

"Had you asked me that three weeks ago, I would have surely said 'no.' But somehow, ever since Miss Fields came and found 'the lion's gate,' my ideas about everything seem to be changing before my very eyes. So perhaps there is something to it." Greniston shook his head and added in an undertone, "God knows, it may be the world's despair, indeed, if I don't handle tonight well."

It did not surprise Logan to hear Greniston speak seriously of such a dark possibility. It made sense that great evil was drawing near; why else would so much goodness and power also be gathering, unless it was about to be greatly needed?

He strummed a chord upon the harp, and half-spoke, half-sang:

"Then in combat mortal, the brothers twain,
   The fair twin and the dark did struggle,
   And all the gathered court did fear, lest the gentler brother
   would soon be slain.

So close, so close, did wrestle they,

That which was which grew hard to say."

Greniston smiled appreciatively. "A great theme of world folklore, freely adapted by Logan Knowelles."

Logan shook his head. "Better not to put a name to it. Who knows who 'writes' a story? So many things come together, . . . old tales heard long ago, . . . faces of people around us, the sound of wind in the trees, . . . the Muse, whispering in one's ear. It seems quite arrogant to stamp a name on the end result and say 'I wrote this, I and I alone.' It just misses the whole point."

"Oh, come now," said Greniston, looking unexpectedly annoyed by Logan's comments, "are you going to dismiss all skill with words and say that Shakespeare, for instance, was just a sort of bulletin board for the Muse's messages?"

Logan stood his ground. "Yes, in a way. There could be worse jobs."

He spoke with such certainty that Greniston was sobered. "Don't you credit the artist with any skill, then?"

"Oh, yes, I do," Logan replied. "The skill of a weaver, the skill of one who loves the colors and textures of human lives and who wants others to appreciate them as well. Who knows which threads to use in a certain story and which to discard, and who knows how to combine them to bring out the hidden design. There's great skill in that. As long as the artist doesn't fool himself that he is responsible for the fact that silk or wool exists, or pretend that because he makes good use of scarlet threads, scarlet is his creation. That would be like the flute taking credit for the music that comes through it."

Greniston looked more sober than ever. "So you would have all artwork be anonymous, then?"

Logan nodded. "That would be best, wouldn't it? But since in this world you can't get around laws and copyrights, well, let writers take pen names and keep themselves secret and humble."

Greniston smiled. "Like 'A. Weaver,' for instance?"

"Yes," said Logan earnestly.

Greniston looked with new appreciation at the other man's gaunt, weathered face and the intelligence gleaming in his dark blue eyes.

I've known him all my life, he realized, *yet never knew these depths were in him. If nothing else comes out of this bloody treasure hunt, this moment is treasure enough.*

"I take it you don't agree?" Logan ventured, noting Lord Greniston's thoughtful expression.

"On the contrary," his host replied, "your thoughts have given me some real gems."

***

Elsewhere in Greniston Manor, the treasure hunt was yielding other unexpected results.

Gwen and Mrs. Walmsley were on their hands and knees, crawling down a narrow passageway they had discovered behind the guest suite that had become the Walmsleys' living quarters.

"Why would anyone build a passageway you have to crawl down?" Gwen had mused, trying to hold her flashlight high enough to see by. "If I ever go into the secret passage business, I'm going to make 'em a good seven feet high."

In the darkness behind her, Anne Walmsley laughed. "And at least five feet wide."

"Look!" Gwen exclaimed, "It comes to an end up there! And there's a chest, an old sea chest!"

Excitedly, they scrambled the last few feet toward the chest. "It's locked!" Gwen exclaimed in disappointment.

"Yes, but look how old and rusty that lock is," mused Anne Walmsley. "Shine the torch on it, I'll see what I can do." She pulled a hairpin out of her French braid. "Osborne locked himself into a pair of handcuffs last Christmas," she explained, "and I got him out with one of these."

Deftly, she inserted the hairpin into the lock and wiggled it back and forth. Sure enough, a few seconds later, her efforts were rewarded with a sharp click.

"We can open it now," she said, suddenly speaking in a whisper.

"Yes." Both women hesitated.

"Of course, this chest is far too recent to be from Arthur's time," Anne Walmsley commented.

"But anyone in recent centuries could have put the treasure into it," Gwen pointed out. She took a deep breath. "Let's find out."

Gwen propped the flashlight against the wall and reached forward to help the other woman lift the heavy lid of the chest.

An instant later, both women screamed. Something gray and hissing rushed past Gwen's face.

"It's on me, it's on me!" Anne Walmsley cried, beating at the air with her hands.

Shaking, Gwen found the flashlight and held it up. There, on her companion's lap, was something long and pale gray. It looked dry and ashy.

"It looks like a snake," Gwen whispered. "Don't move."

Anne Walmsley answered with a petrified squeak that seemed to indicate that moving was out of the question.

Thinking fast, Gwen slipped her belt from around her waist.

"I'm going to get it to bite this," she said.

"Then what?" asked Anne Walmsley in a taut whisper.

"Then I'm going to beat it to death with the flashlight," Gwen replied, trying to sound more confident than she felt.

Moving very slowly and carefully, Gwen lifted the belt and dangled it teasingly above the gray snake. The snake lay sinuously on Anne Walmsley's lap and ignored the belt. Gwen brought the belt closer, brushing it against the snake's skin.

"It isn't moving," the other woman said. "Perhaps it died of fright. I almost did."

Gwen lowered the belt even closer to the snake. The reptile trembled and then, to her amazement, crumbled into dust.

"What in the world?" she exclaimed.

"There's another one! On the floor behind you!"

Gwen spun around. There was indeed another snake there. She lifted the flashlight as high as she could in the cramped space and saw at least ten snakes, all curiously inert.

"Wait a minute," she said, "those aren't real snakes."

"They're paper," Anne Walmsley added, finding the courage to touch one. "Trick snakes, like you get in a novelty shop."

Gwen reached into the chest and pulled out a canister.

"Amazing exploding snakes," she read from the label. "Scare your friends with these amazing lifelike cobras!"

The two women looked at each other and burst into laughter. Anne Walmsley said, "Trick snakes indeed! Just wait 'til I get my hands on Osgood! You can mark my words that he's behind this!"

"I don't think so," said Gwen slowly. "Remember, when we found this passage, it looked like it hadn't been opened in years and years."

"That's true," Anne Walmsley acknowledged.

"And the snakes, they're all old and faded and turning to dust, almost."

Anne Walmsley peered more closely at the canister. "Acme Novelty Company," she read, "and the date on it is twenty five years ago! Who could possibly have put this here?"

Gwen shone the flashlight into the chest. On top of its contents was a yellowed piece of paper that read, in a child's printing, "RRR Greniston and Geoff Swindon: Their Secret Treasure. BEWARE!!!"

Beneath that was a crude sketch of a skull and crossbones. Then a more elegant hand had written, "The contents of this chest are the private property of the Brotherhood of the Quest. DO NOT disturb them, upon pain of the ancient Pharaoh's Curse!"

Gwen thought about the date. Swindon would have been nine, Greniston fifteen—the same year they had their flying adventure in Scotland, the last year they really spent time together. She could imagine the two boys using the hidden passageway as their secret hideout, dragging the old sea chest into it, meeting there, probably by candlelight. Swindon would have been totally immersed in the game and Greniston, the older, more amused by it, yet kind enough to invent adventures for the younger boy and himself still lad enough to enjoy them secretly.

She lifted the warning paper and peered at the contents of the chest: two model airplanes; a Union Jack with what appeared to be real bullet holes in it; an unopened box of Callard and Bowser's Toffee, stale now for over two decades; and half a pack of ancient Player's cigarettes. She closed the chest, suddenly feeling she was invading the privacy of those long-ago boys. Treasure the chest did contain, but not the one she and Anne were searching for.

"It's sad to think of Lord Greniston and Geoff Swindon not getting along anymore," Anne Walmsley reflected. "It seems they were so close, long ago. And Lord Greniston is such a good, generous man."

"You would call him generous, then?" Gwen asked, trying to make the question sound casual.

"Oh yes," her companion said warmly. "Not only has he taken us in, but he's offered Bob permanent work here, at a handsome salary. And the best part of it is that it's things that really need doing around here—carpentry, stonework, fence mending—things that take some real skill, that Bob is good at. I can't tell you the difference it's made in him already. He feels proud of himself for the first time in a long time. "

"I can imagine," Gwen said quietly. "I'm glad," she added.

Anne Walmsley smiled. "This might even help him stay sober. His drinking never got out of hand until times got so bad for us. Oh, he tied one on once in a while, but it used to bring out the jolliness in him. But when he got to feeling useless, that's when he got bitter when he drank. Lord Greniston told him he might not lick it overnight, but he had to see that Bob was trying to stay sober, and he said that if he needed any help, any counseling, he would pay for it, as an investment in a valuable worker. Somehow, he managed to say it in a way that saved Bob's pride—man to man—and that seems to have really helped. I'm hopeful for the first time in a long time."

Anne Walmsley paused, as if weighing her words, and then added rather shyly, "He's a good man, your Lord Greniston."

From the way she said "your Lord Greniston," and the way she smiled, it was clear that she wished the best for Gwen in her romance.

"Thank you," said Gwen, appreciating not only the sentiment but also the delicacy with which it was expressed.

What passed between the two women was a small moment, of simple warmth, yet Gwen suspected that without the adventure of the amazing snakes, it would never have happened so easily between them. As they crawled back up the passageway, she decided that she definitely had found treasure there, even if it wasn't the one she had thought she was looking for.

***

Davey Lee lay back on the burgundy velvet sofa and sighed contentedly.

"Nice digs this Greniston's got," he said to himself, "very nice indeed." He adjusted the cushion behind his head. Let others search for the treasure, he reasoned. He was resting up, saving himself up for events that his instinct told him were soon to come.

A bloke could get used to this, he thought, surveying the comfortable library he had come to rest in.

Never a great one for books, he still enjoyed the sight of the shelves of leather-bound volumes, the walnut paneling, and the warmth from the pink marble fireplace.

He reached languidly for one of the cold beef sandwiches Mrs. Fitz. had made for him and opened the volume on his lap.

Put me to sleep that much quicker, he thought. *Besides, always wanted to find out about this Sherlock Holmes bloke.* Hound of the Baskervilles, *that ll do.*

***

In another part of the manor house, Claire Walmsley bent over her drawing, her small fingers urgently coloring a design of great importance. Across the kitchen table from her sat Filipo, smoking a Gauloise.

The Basque looked at the little girl with concern. The other Walmsley children were, mercifully, all searching for treasure in the rambling attic of the manor. Claire alone seemed curiously disinterested in the search. Instead, she had spent the whole morning working on a drawing. Once it was finished, she had presented the artwork to Gwen and looked at her expectantly, clearly waiting for a response.

"It's beautiful, Claire," Gwen had said sincerely. "It's like the others, isn't it? That necklace shape." She had looked worriedly at the child, who gazed so earnestly back at her.

"I know this means something important to you," she had said, "but I just can't figure it out. Grown-ups can be very dull sometimes, you know. Isn't there any clue you can give me?"

Claire had sighed and pointed to the southwest. She didn't seem to be pointing at anything in the room but at something beyond the walls.

Sadly, Gwen shook her head. "I'm sorry, Claire," she had said, "I just don't get it."

Claire had looked near tears, obviously deeply frustrated. Now she was making yet another drawing on the same theme.

"Poor little dear," said Mrs. Fitzpatrick, who, along with Mrs. Hodges, was busily peeling several pounds of potatoes destined to become part of a barley soup. "It must be terribly frustrating for her, not being able to speak."

"Does she know how to read and write?" Filipo asked.

Mrs. Hodges shook her head. "She's only just six, you know. And it would take a special training, wouldn't it, to teach a child that doesn't speak. They don't have that in Tweeverton. And then, you know, the Walmsley young ones are truant as much as they're there. Not that I blame them. Such a long ride for the Far Tauverly young ones to be bussed to another town every day. No, I imagine Claire's picked up but a few words, at best. Not that she couldn't learn to read. She's as smart as they come, you can see it in her eyes."

"Would you like to learn to read and write, Claire?" Filipo asked. The girl looked up. Her interest seemed negligible. Filipo got the sense that it was the spoken word she loved—Logan's stories, people's voices. Writing she probably associated with school, and all that was dull and confining.

"If you knew how to write," he suggested, "you could write Gwen a letter to explain the picture."

Claire stared at him. Understanding kindled in her sparkling blue eyes, and a smile of delight spread across her elfin face. She thrust a purple crayon at Filipo, as if to say "Great! Teach me now!"

"I'm sorry, *Carissima*, it takes time to learn. But you know, Gwen is a teacher. I bet she could teach you."

Claire nodded enthusiastically. Then she handed Filipo her latest drawing. He examined the picture carefully. "Now, let's see," he mused. "These are people. That's Logan, isn't it? And there is Gwen. That one must be Wyatt, I can tell by the hair. Hey, there's me, with the guitar! *Gracias* for including me, *Senorita*! Yes, it seems everyone is there, sitting in a circle, and around the people is a necklace of green and yellow beads, and inside the circle is a big light shining on us. Is that right?"

Claire nodded, watching his face—hoping, straining, for him to say more.

"I'm sorry, little one, I don't understand," he said gently. Tears of disappointment sprang to Claire's eyes.

"Hey, hey," said Filipo, "not to be so distraught, *Bellissima*! Hey, I tell you what, I'll keep your picture with me. Can I do that? Because sometimes things come to me slowly. Maybe later I look at it, and presto! I understand it, all of a sudden. Okay?"

The child nodded, but it was clear that beneath her smile, she felt very discouraged.

Mrs. Hodges and Mrs. Fitzpatrick exchanged a knowing glance.

"It's just too bad, Mabel, that you are still full from breakfast," Mrs. Fitzpatrick said with a sigh. "I do need someone to taste one of these cherry tarts, to make sure they came out properly."

Mrs. Hodges shook her head sympathetically. "I know you do, Kathleen, but I can't eat another bite, I'm that full."

Mrs. Fitzpatrick looked appealingly at Filipo. He, too, shook his head. "My stomach's too crowded already. If I sample that tart, delicious as it looks, the cherries will quarrel with the eggs from breakfast, and they'll both crowd out the toast. Sorry."

"Oh dear," sighed the housekeeper, "there's got to be someone who can taste these tarts. It would never do to send food to Lord Greniston's table untested. And I'm not so sure about the crust on these."

Her eyes lit upon Claire, who had been looking eagerly at her for some time. "Claire! Do you suppose that you could possibly try one of these tarts, even a mouthful, a morsel? You'd be doing me such a favor, child, to let me know if 'twill do." Claire nodded.

"She says she can, Mabel," Mrs. Fitzpatrick said with relief.

"Saints be praised," Mrs. Hodges replied, already bustling to set a place and pour a glass of milk for the girl.

Claire's eyes sparkled with delight at the sight of the cherry tart, its latticework crust baked to a golden perfection, its ruby red filling still bubbling. The seemingly endless supply of food at Greniston Manor was clearly a miracle to her.

The two women looked on fondly as Claire dug into the pastry, her worries over the picture momentarily forgotten. With a smile, Filipo slipped out the door, carrying the drawing with him. According to the careful schedule that Althea had made up for them all, he was due to begin searching in the hallways of the East wing in exactly ten minutes. Greniston's study was on the way. He decided to stop there and show Claire's picture to him. Perhaps Greniston, being more familiar with the Walmsleys and the place, would understand the meaning the girl so clearly ached to convey.

The door to the study was ajar, but when Filipo poked his head in, he found no one there except the marble bust of Shakespeare and, on another shelf, the statue of an Egyptian cat, silently gazing into the deep distance.

Filipo put Claire's drawing down on Greniston's crowded desk. *I'll leave him a note*, Filipo decided. As he hunted for a pen, his eye fell upon a sheet of writing on the desk. An unforgettable line leapt out at him. He paused, while honor and curiosity engaged in a brief, very brief, tussle in his mind. Then he picked up the paper and read on. As he read, his jaw dropped, and his eyes grew round with amazement.

"Oh ho," he said aloud, "so that's who he is, our mysterious Lord Greniston." Chuckling to himself, Filipo put the sheet of paper back exactly as he had found it. He took Claire's drawing with him when he left, evidently wishing to leave no trace that he had been there at all.

***

Filipo was not the only one searching for Greniston. Consulting Althea's schedule, Gwen noted that the Lord of the Manor was due to be searching for treasure in the first floor sitting room. When she got there, he was nowhere to be found. She was about to leave, when a movement in the background caught her eye. She looked again and saw that in a far corner of the room, Luan Tey lay asleep on a sofa. Annie Lee, was looking down at him, humming to herself, now and then making odd, quick gestures. Gwen had the instant feeling that she was intruding upon something private and rather unnerving. She turned to go.

"Come, come," Annie Lee called out. Rather reluctantly, Gwen approached.

"I am just healing this man," the old woman explained. As she spoke, she moved her hands through the air around the sleeping figure with the gestures of a sculptor smoothing damp clay.

"What exactly are you doing?" Gwen asked, curious.

Annie's reply was indirect. "He has seen terrible things, done terrible things. Maybe it is too late for him. But he is part of what called me here, so I have to try. You see, all the pictures of our life, our patterns, are here"—she swept her arms out, describing an egg shape around herself. "This part gets wounded, just like the rest does. This man is in very bad shape, very bad. He needs many healings, but I think I may only get the chance to do just this one. Maybe I can give him a fighting chance. Of course," she added in a stern voice, "you must never, never, never try to heal someone unless you have the gift or the training. If you don't, you might catch all the diseases you take out of others, and that could eat you in the end. Remember that."

"The part that you are healing, is it his . . . *aura*?" Gwen spoke the word uncomfortably; to her, at least until recently, auras had been one of the strange things Filipo took seriously, and she found hard to swallow.

414

Annie shrugged, as if unfamiliar with the word. "It's his lights and colors," she said.

"You mean you really see lights and colors around him?" Gwen asked earnestly. "You really do? And this tells you how to help him?" Annie nodded.

"I wish I could see that," Gwen said wistfully.

The Romani woman smiled. "Maybe someday you will."

Ten minutes later, Gwen, still thoughtful after her encounter with Annie Lee, knocked on the door of the study.

"Excuse me," she said to Mr. Steadworthy, who opened the door, "I was looking for Lord Greniston."

"He isn't here, my dear," the old man said warmly. "I just got here myself. Why don't you come in and wait for him?"

Feeling rather pleased at the opportunity at last to see Greniston's inner sanctum, Gwen stepped into the room.

"Have a seat," suggested Mr. Steadworthy. "Better not sit at the desk. Lord Greniston is quite particular about keeping that for his use only, but perhaps the armchair by the window?"

"Thank you," said Gwen. She couldn't help noticing that Mr. Steadworthy quickly put his own open briefcase on top of the desk, almost as if to conceal whatever papers lay there. And yet he had just said that Greniston was fussy about keeping the desk to himself.

"I'm just searching for some family papers, in hopes of finding some clue about this treasure business," the solicitor explained. "No luck so far, I fear."

Gwen settled into the armchair and gazed curiously at this room in which Lord Greniston seemed to spend so much of his time. She was sure that were it not for the unusual conditions of the treasure hunt, neither she nor Mr. Steadworthy would ever have been there without their host.

He sits in this very chair sometimes, she thought. *He gazes out at just this view—well, at whatever the view is behind that mist.*

She looked around the room, drinking in every detail of what Greniston had chosen to have near him in this most intimate place, from the bust of Shakespeare to the Egyptian cat, the faded Persian carpet with its pattern of rose and blue, the crowded bookshelves, and the old maps on the walls.

I want to remember this room forever, she thought, *so that if someday I am far away, I can imagine him sitting here, here, where he is most himself.*

It was then, sitting in that quiet room, that Gwen admitted to herself that she wanted to marry Greniston. That she loved him, she knew full well, but up until then she had lived moment to moment, glad simply to see him again, joyful if his eyes lit up at the sight of her. Now she allowed herself to realize that she wanted his presence never to end.

It's mad, she thought, *I've known him for only two weeks. Yet I feel as if I've always known him, and I do want to marry him.*

It was so simple, compared to any other relationship she had ever been in, compared to the relationships of most of the people she knew. So often, it seemed as if two people who loved each other ended up negotiating an armed truce as they tried to juggle careers, freedom, bank accounts, and that elusive word, fulfillment. How much, she realized, people talked about their relationships. What she felt for Greniston seemed very quiet compared to all those words. Because of him, she felt released into the best of herself. She wanted never again to do anything petty or mean or bitter, because the love that filled her was large and generous and sweet.

Watching her from the shadows, Mr. Steadworthy smiled. It had been a long time since he had seen a face so touched by love. During the war, he had seen it often: the husband, the wife, the parent, the friend, lifted to nobility by hardship and deep feeling. Since those days, ever more rarely.

"It's growing a bit dark, with the mist and all," he said gently. "I hope you don't mind if I turn on one of the lamps."

"Not at all," said Gwen, who had been so lost in thought that she had all but forgotten the old gentleman.

Mr. Steadworthy switched on a desk lamp with a shade of peach-colored glass. Its light gave a soft, friendly glow to the room. Gwen couldn't help gazing curiously at the unruly pile of papers, so ill concealed on the desk.

"Lord Greniston seems to do a great deal of . . . of work here," she remarked.

"Oh, yes." Mr. Steadworthy hesitated, and then added. "He actually does work very hard, you know. I sometimes feel that he tries to present himself as a more frivolous person than he really is." There was a pause.

Gwen cleared her throat. "Without meaning to pry—well, that's not true, I am prying—er, what I'm trying to say is, exactly what work does he do?"

"Ah. Don't worry, my dear, I can understand a young lady wishing to know such facts about a gentleman in whom she takes an interest," the solicitor assured her. "The truth is, Lord Greniston is a man of many abilities. He was in Parliament for several terms, you know, and is still keenly involved in various research committees, to gather facts for those presently in office. And then, there are his charity projects. But of course, you probably know about those already."

"No," said Gwen, "not at all."

"Well," said Steadworthy, warming to his topic, "that I know of, Lord Greniston is involved in the administration and funding of at least five substantial projects, from an orphanage in Sri Lanka to a pensioner's home in Bristol. Indeed, I should say that Lord Greniston has a difficult time saying no to anyone who approaches him in need."

"I had no idea," said Gwen, pleased and impressed. "He's never mentioned any of this."

"Just like him," said Mr. Steadworthy, with almost parental pride, "to hide his light under a bushel."

"The Greniston fortune must be considerable, to fund so many causes," Gwen remarked.

"Not really. Oh, the inheritance is more than adequate to maintain this estate, but Lord Greniston earns a great deal of what he gives away."

"Oh really? How?" asked Gwen, trying to make the question sound light and failing utterly.

Mr. Steadworthy grew suddenly agitated and glanced, embarrassed, at the papers in his hand. "He, er, manages his investments very wisely," the old solicitor said hurriedly. "A keen sense of the market."

Somehow, Gwen found it hard to imagine Greniston having a keen sense of the market.

"You see, Miss Fields," the lawyer continued, "I fear I have said too much as it is. Lord Greniston would be quite upset if he knew I had told you even as much as I have. He may not seem like it, but he is actually a very modest man. But I have spoken because I feel that a young lady in your situation, without the benefit of parents present on either side, to make sure the association is a suitable one, needs to have some assurance that she is in good company. Yet I cannot say more about Lord Greniston's circumstances without violating his trust in me as his solicitor and an old family friend. I hope that you can take my word for it if I assure you, on my word of honor, that everything Lord Greniston is involved in is honest and above reproach."

"Of course," said Gwen, who was touched by the old man's concern. "And I hope you will take my word that I will never mention this conversation to Lord Greniston. Whatever else he may choose to tell me about his life, I'm sure he'll reveal in his own good time. What you have told me gives me the peace of mind to wait."

"Well then," said Mr. Steadworthy, looking quite relieved, "I doubt that you shall have to wait too long, my dear."

***

Davey Lee was far from enjoying the sleep he had anticipated. He finished the last page of *The Hound of the Baskervilles*, his eyes shining with admiration.

"What a mind!" he said aloud, "what a brilliant mind!"

And he smiled, as in his own bright mind, an irresistible idea began to form. . . .

***

Some twenty minutes later, the Lord of Greniston Manor left the stables of his estate, once home to the finest line of Arabians in England, now long unused. He hoped that the recording equipment he, Robert, and Mr. Walmsley had improvised there would be sufficient to track his own movements and record whatever Miller said.

The meeting between Miller himself and Luan Tey was set for ten that evening, at the mound. Greniston wanted the business handled on his own land but well away from the house.

What bothered him most about it all was the unknown character of Miller. From what Luan Tey had told him, the man seemed to be a curious nonentity. Evil surrounded him, like the layers of sarcophagi around a mummy, yet beneath the gilded boxes and the layers of linen, there seemed to be nothing there at all, just empty air. He would have to wait until they met to see how the man's character might be played upon to reveal itself. He hoped that at least Luan Tey's estimate of Miller's greed and paranoia was accurate and that he really would come alone that night.

All in all, it was about as reliable a plan as trying to patch a punctured tire with a piece of scotch tape. However, Greniston still had a few ideas of his own to put into place before the night was done. Glancing at his watch, he realized that it was almost time to do so. High Tea was to be served in the great hall in ten minutes.

As he approached the house, he thought of Gwen. *She is somewhere within those very walls*, he mused, surprised at how much joy the knowledge gave him. The whole house seemed made anew, because somewhere within it was Gwen. And he himself felt made anew at the thought of her, as if, because she was near, he was able to be more, to do more. He had known her so brief a time, and yet, he realized, he could not imagine his life without her.

When all this is over, he thought, *she must stay*.

As he drew nearer, he saw her standing in the doorway, looking out into the mist and twilight, as if, perhaps, it was him she watched for.

He wondered how many generations of Greniston men before him had been so greeted, and if they had felt as glad as he did as they drew near their home.

"Home." It was not a word, he realized, that he had been in the habit of applying to Greniston Manor. "The House" was how he had thought of it for years. Yet now, with Gwen standing in the doorway, the light behind her delicate figure, "home" was the only word that seemed to fit. He felt as if he was returning after a long absence.

He hurried the last few steps toward her, and scarcely realizing how it happened, they found themselves in one another's arms. It seemed to Greniston that he could not hold her close enough.

Never mind chalices and jewels, he thought, *here is my treasure*.

Mr. Steadworthy, watching from the study window, smiled approvingly. Davey Lee, who stood at his side, said, "I'd say them two is in love. Does me 'art good to see it, that it does. I'd wish such love to come to everybody, though perhaps for some, it ain't so likely."

"Oh, you never know where Cupid's arrow will strike next," the older man replied with a smile.

The bell sounded for high tea. From the many nooks and corridors of Greniston Manor, the treasure hunters began to make their way toward the great hall, where candles were lit, and the table was generously spread.

Outside, in the growing shadows of evening, a wind rose. It tugged away the mist from the landscape and stirred the budding branches of elm and larch. It was a searching wind that roamed over the landscape, touching everything. It circled the walls of Greniston Manor and set the ivy there rippling; it crossed the lawns and entered the wood. It passed ancient trees and new green shoots, and wherever it passed its movement was like a signal that seemed to awaken a secret life within the woods.

The wind blew stronger now, and the forest rustled and creaked and stirred with the feeling of something long asleep now called into wakefulness.

Tethered near Annie Lee's caravan, Chieftain sniffed that wind and whinnied joyfully. He tossed his noble chestnut head and pawed the earth, as if to say "I am here! I am here!" His lustrous eyes gleamed with the gladness of one who senses a moment and a purpose he was born for drawing near at last.

CHAPTER TWENTY-TWO

"We shouldn't be in the least discouraged," said Althea Pennington, as she spooned a helping of Yorkshire pudding onto her plate. "A few hours of searching have barely scratched the surface of so vast a residence. I am still convinced that the Greniston treasure is real and probably close at hand."

"I quite agree," said Greniston heartily, "and I very much appreciate the zeal you all brought to the hunt and your willingness to help tonight's little plans along as well."

A chorus of comments - "Of course! Count us in!" and "Couldn't do otherwise!" - greeted this remark. Greniston smiled. It had indeed been gratifying to see the keenness his guests had brought to turning Greniston Manor into an armed fortress, even if they did not know the reason why. Under the circumstances, he felt that they were reasonably well organized to defend themselves, should the need arise. Bob Walmsley, Davey Lee, Bosley, and Robert were to patrol the first floor, armed and at the ready. On the second floor, the Pennington sisters and Mr. Steadworthy would stand guard, while Mrs. Walmsley, Gwen, Annie, and Logan kept watch on the third and attempted to keep the young Walmsleys confined to the portrait gallery.

Filipo, Greniston had asked to accompany him to the mounds that night. Luan Tey had been less than pleased about this, but Greniston had stood firm.

"I have trusted your motives and your word in this affair," he had said. "Where Filipo is concerned, you must trust me. I don't know much about his history, but I can tell he has been around danger. I intend to confide in him concerning this matter—that is, if he is willing."

"*Bien sur*," Filipo had replied, calmly lighting a Gauloise.

"And it's my firm belief we may need his help before this night is out," Greniston added.

Luan Tey had given Filipo a searching glance. The feeling of that cold, unrevealing gaze upon him made even the Basque, who had been stared down by experts in his day, shiver inwardly. He did not, however, display this unease to the other man. Instead, he had taken a long drag on his cigarette and stared back at him. In the blue smoke that curled between them, the two gazes had seemed to meet and measure each other. In the end, it was Luan Tey who looked away first, with a faint smile on his lips. It was hard to say whether he accepted Filipo as an ally or merely the inevitable. Whatever the case, Greniston had been satisfied.

He was glad that that had been settled before this meal; now there remained only two more allies to recruit: Steadworthy and Gwen. Steadworthy he took to one side while Bosley was clearing away the sandwich plates.

"I'd like you to keep this for me," he said, handing the solicitor a sealed letter. "It explains what is going on here tonight. Don't read it yourself, the contents could endanger you. However, if I have not returned by morning or if this house is in any way attacked, I want you to deliver this letter instantly to Atherton, of Scotland Yard. His home address and number are on this slip of paper. Please do not hesitate to use them, if you see the need; I trust you not to panic over trifles. Ring him first; then get Robert to drive you to him in the Austin."

"Very good," said Steadworthy calmly, as if Greniston had simply informed him of a minor change in some document.

"You will also need to take with you the tape recording of the night's events. Walmsley, Robert, and myself, have attempted to set up a sort of walkie-talkie device to record the information, which I will also be hoping to record with a small cassette hidden in my pocket. God only knows if the thing will work; it's all jerryrigged with bits and pieces we found around the house, but we have to try. This tape, if it works, may be the only solid evidence Atherton will have. If anything happens to me, I want to know that it will reach him. The bloody thing is in the stable, set with a lamp timer to begin recording at nine. Here is the only key to the stable. I entrust it to you now."

"Thank you," the older man said gravely. "Your plans seem to be most efficient. I confess I have only one qualm."

"Ah, and what is that?" asked Greniston with concern.

"Leaving the others, especially the ladies, should there be any trouble here."

Greniston smiled. "Don't worry, old friend," he said. "You have heard me speak once or twice of the priest's hole, where the Grenistons used to hide their clergy during Cromwell's day?"

"Yes indeed," the lawyer said.

"Its hidden entrance is, of course, known only to the Greniston's. Family secret and all that. I will show that entrance to Miss Fields." Mr.

422

Steadworthy smiled. The implication that Gwen was practically considered to be a Greniston was not lost on him. "Should there be any trouble here, she is to shepherd everyone into the hiding place and wait for help to arrive." Unnoticed by either man, Wyatt had sidled nearby and was listening intently from behind a carved Victorian screen.

"That relieves my mind as much as is probably possible, under the circumstances," Mr. Steadworthy said.

Not five minutes later, Gwen hurried after Greniston as he strode down one of the corridors of the old part of the house. "But what exactly is a priest's hole?" she asked rather breathlessly.

"Had 'em in the old days," Greniston said over his shoulder, "when Catholic priests were outlawed. Families like the Grenistons that wanted to keep to their faith or perhaps just defy authority, hard to tell with our lot, used to build hiding places in case any inspecting soldiers showed up for dinner. Some families even installed underground passageways leading from the hiding place to some distant point on the land."

"Does this one have a passageway?" Gwen asked.

Greniston nodded. He seemed preoccupied, his thoughts clearly on events to come. "Whatever you are doing tonight," Gwen said, "I want to come with you."

"Absolutely not!"

"Why? Because I'm a woman? I can assure you that I am quite capable of keeping my head in a crisis. And of defending myself."

Greniston snorted. "A delicate blossom like you?"

Before even thinking her response through, Gwen grabbed Greniston from behind and prepared to bring him to his knees in an aikido slam. To her surprise, however, she found herself neatly flipped to one side and pinned against the wall.

"It appears we share a skill," said Greniston sweetly.

"That," she replied, breathing hard, "was merely round one."

"We'll see," he said, smiling at her in an infuriatingly condescending manner. Gwen discovered that even in the midst of intense love and concern, she could feel a strong desire to throttle Greniston.

"You had better go flying off into the teeth of danger tonight," she muttered, "before you meet an even greater danger at my hands."

Greniston laughed, obviously enjoying her pique. Fortunately, they seemed to have reached their destination by then. "It's in here," Greniston said, opening the oak doors to the portrait gallery.

As always, Gwen was impressed by the stillness of the room and its curious sense of being inhabited, even when it was clearly empty. Greniston pulled some matches from his pocket and lit the candles left on the table from the night before. Out of the gloom, rich colors in the old portraits sprang to life: the red of a velvet cape, the gold of a painted medallion. In the diamond paned windows, Gwen saw a faint reflection of herself and Greniston. Beyond them lay the darkness of the windy night, and somewhere in that darkness, the woods, the mounds, and the unknown future. In that world beyond the window, all was wild and in movement. Over that windy darkness lay the diamond pattern of the leaded glass. In between the two slipped the reflections of herself and Greniston and the bobbing light of the candles they carried. It gave Gwen the sense that they were indeed poised between two worlds: the one elusive as air, unseen, yet as real as the wind; the other as solid and fortifying as the stones of Greniston Manor.

"What I'm going to show you now," Greniston said, "none but the Grenistons and their priests have ever seen." All traces of the teasing that had been in his voice but minutes before had vanished. He sounded as serious as Gwen had ever heard him.

"If we need to use this secret passage as an escape route, then a great many people will know your family's secret," Gwen pointed out.

"Hopefully, it will not come to that, but if it does, we shall simply have to hold a mass christening," Greniston replied, with just a trace of a smile.

"And what about me? Must I be christened after this?" Gwen asked quietly.

Greniston gazed deep into her eyes. "There are other sacraments which change a name," he said. "Gwen, will you . . . "

Just then, the distant bells of St. Aethelrood's tolled eight o'clock.

"Good God!" he exclaimed, "I'm supposed to be meeting Filipo in the study, now! Come, I've much to show you, and quickly, too."

He strode over to Lord Peter's portrait and reached behind it. The whole paneled section of the wall behind it began to creak slowly open.

"It's like something out of the movies!" Gwen exclaimed.

"Or else the movies are like something out of Greniston Manor," her companion observed. "When you reach behind the portrait, on the left side, you'll feel a slight unevenness in the wood, as if the molding has been mended there. Press that rough spot, and the wall swings open on hidden hinges. My ancestors brought a craftsman all the way from Italy to devise it. Now, come along."

He stepped into the dark passageway beyond. Gwen followed, grateful that this hidden corridor was tall enough to stand up in. By the wavering light of their candles, they made their way for a few feet, then the passage turned sharply to the right and stopped at an old wooden door with an arched top. The handle and lock were of iron and looked very old indeed.

Greniston reached into his pocket and pulled out an equally ancient key. Handing his candle to Gwen, he fitted the key into the lock and carefully turned it. With a soft creak, the door swung open.

"Lady Gwendolyn," he said, "I invite you to enter the secret heart of Greniston Manor."

He took back the candles from Gwen and held them high to reveal a room perhaps twenty by thirty feet long. The walls were high, and near the tops of them were small, arched windows.

It was a wonderfully simple room: walls and floor made of some pale, cream-colored stone; three pews of golden oak, unadorned with any ornament; and, at one end of the room, a simple stone altar. On either side of the altar were two tall, freestanding silver candelabras. On the altar itself, where one might expect to find a cross, there was instead a small bouquet of snowdrops in a glass vase. Gwen realized that the flowers and the fresh white candles must have been put there recently, and that none but Greniston could have put them there. She wondered if he often visited this mysterious room.

Greniston had been watching her intently. "Well," he said, "what do you think?"

"It reminds me of some lines from Leo Hawker," Gwen said, "How does it go? 'God cares not for gaudy display, nor the weighty words the Pharisees say: Nay, God holds dear the silent prayer sent when none are near; ever does God love and see, the Heart's white chapel of simplicity.'"

To her surprise, Greniston agreed without demur. "Yes, those words might have been written to describe this very place."

Set into the wall behind the altar, Gwen noticed a curious carving. She drew closer to look at it. It was of a different stone than the walls around it, almost pure white, and flecked with specks of some silvery metal that sparkled faintly in the candlelight. Carved on it was a five petalled rose. Rising from the rose was a double helix of vines, which intertwined five times. Above that, as if it had emerged from the vines, was carved a small bird, which seemed to be flying straight upward, toward a distant, eight-rayed star. The carving was simple, almost crude, yet it managed to convey the sense that the stubborn little bird was flying not merely across the sky but across galaxies, if need be, to reach that particular, far-off star. Gwen was not sure why, but the carving brought tears to her eyes.

"No one knows quite how old it is," Greniston said. "Older than old, it seems. It's from this that our family motto comes: 'Silent and Faithful, by the star.'"

Looking at the carving, Gwen noticed something odd: along one side of the stone was a deep gash.

"Strange, isn't it?" Greniston said, following her gaze.

"It's almost like a wound, as if someone had thrust a sword into the stone and pulled it right out again."

Greniston nodded, seeing in her face the thoughts that were already occurring to her. "The sword in the stone. Yes. The Grenistons claim that this is the very stone from which Arthur pulled the sword Excalibur. And the legend says that when Arthur returns, in England's greatest hour of need, the stone will be silent no longer, but will sing."

"Sing?" Gwen shivered, suddenly.

"Yes. But enough of legends for now, there are things I must show you. Over here"— Greniston went to the wall opposite the door—"you will find that if you count down from the middle window until you reach the twelfth stone from the top, and tap on it three times, a doorway is revealed."

Even as Greniston demonstrated this, a section of the stone wall swung open to reveal another passageway.

"This passage leads to the cellars of the manor," he explained. "From there, it goes underground for about half a mile, and emerges in the woods. More than one Greniston has used this method to escape from unwanted callers, I can assure you. There is no time to take you the length of it, but it is safe; I examined it myself, earlier today. I'd suggest bringing electric torches rather than candles, though. Bit drafty in there."

"Torches it will be," Gwen said.

"Right. Well, we'd best be going back. I'm already late for my meeting in the study."

Greniston's step was brisk and sure as he led her back to the portrait gallery, showing her how to close the hidden space behind them. Gwen felt his mind had already left her side, leaping ahead toward events to come. He did return to her for a moment, when he placed the iron key to the chapel door in her hands.

"Keep this safe for me, My Lady," he said. Then he kissed her lightly on the cheek, turned, and with swift steps, left the room.

Gwen found herself alone in the portrait gallery, holding the key to the very heart of the manor. Something told her that she would need to use it before the night was through.

***

"Nine o'clock," said Althea crisply, consulting the Victorian watch she wore pinned to her bodice.

Osgood watched her with new appreciation. She had just called Robert to attention for dozing on sentry duty, and Osgood felt he could not have done a better job of it himself.

The burden of command was something he could sympathize with. Althea's situation was now not unlike his own, he realized. She, too, had the job of trying to turn a rag tag assortment of raw recruits into crisp, crack troops. She wasn't half bad at it, and Osgood felt that a promising general for the Independent Kingdom of Greenstone had been lost in her. Too bad she belonged to that damned race, the grown-ups.

He had obtained temporary release from the portrait gallery by pleading a need to go to the bathroom.

"I'll take him," Althea had said. "I need to check on everyone, anyway." She had nominated herself as acting Commander in Chief of the evening's operations, and no one had felt like disputing the appointment.

"What on earth is the child wearing?" she had asked.

"It's Lord Greniston's sweater," Mrs. Walmsley explained. "He said Osgood might wear it earlier today, and now I can't get it off of him."

Althea eyed the shapeless brown turtleneck, which hung almost to Osgood's knees, with distaste. "Well," she sighed, "if it keeps him quiet." To Osgood she said, "Come along, then, and no fooling about!"

"Yes, ma'am," he had replied meekly.

Osgood had been impressed by the firmness of Althea's grip upon his hand and by the way she had checked the bathroom window for access to drainpipes—none—before leaving him alone in the room.

He knew he would have to work quickly to outwit so shrewd a guardian as Althea. As soon as the bathroom door was closed, he pulled out the bundle he had managed to conceal beneath the bulky sweater and set to work.

Two minutes later, he emerged, smiling sweetly, to accompany Althea on the rest of her rounds.

On the ground floor, all was well, with Robert, Bosley, and Mr. Walmsley guarding the inside of the house, and Davey Lee making circuits of the outside every fifteen minutes.

The second floor regiment, however, presented a looser deportment. Lettice sat by the fire, snoring gently.

"Just as well," Althea remarked. "Keep her out of the way."

Mrs. Hodges, knitting in the chair next to Lettice, nodded in agreement. As for Mr. Steadworthy and Mrs. Fitzpatrick, they were engrossed in a chess game.

Althea cleared her throat. "I hope you won't forget to check this floor."

"Every fifteen minutes. I do remember," the old solicitor told her patiently. "As you see, I have the cooking timer from the kitchen, so kindly lent to me by Mrs. Fitzpatrick, right here at my side. In another eleven minutes, the buzzer will sound, to alert me of my duties."

"Very well," said Althea. She turned to Mabel Hodges. "And the signal, in case of trouble?"

"Three shrill toots on this," the other woman replied, holding up a police whistle, which she wore about her neck, on a piece of red yarn.

Althea nodded. Evidently, the second floor squadron passed muster—barely.

"I shall return after I escort this young man to his station," she said.

"Take your time, dear," Mabel Hodges replied, with hopeless comfiness. Althea sighed. Osgood sympathized with her frustration; some people simply could not grasp the military flavor so vital to a smart operation.

Back in the gallery, all seemed peaceful. Rutherford was asleep on a pile of quilts in the corner. Their Mum sat nearby, sewing, like she always did in the evenings. Miss Fields was sitting at the desk by Lord Peter's picture, reading some old books. Logan sat across from her, gazing out the windows. The Gypsy was rocking the baby to sleep. As for the members of the High Council, they were playing with a train set by the fireplace. Osgood joined them. Wyatt looked up questioningly. Osgood smiled and nodded. "Fifteen more minutes," he whispered.

***

Gazing out at the darkness, Logan felt that Gwydion was near, very near. He sensed that his own part in the night's adventures was drawing near. He felt calm. He would be shown what to do. He needed only to be ready. A line from Hamlet came to his mind: "The readiness is all."

Anne Walmsley yawned over her sewing and rubbed her eyes. A log shifted in the fireplace. Gwen turned a page of Lord Peter's diaries. Suddenly, the stillness was rent by a horrifying scream. Instantly, Logan was on his feet.

"What on earth?" Mrs. Walmsley exclaimed.

The scream came again, this time followed by low, gurgling laughter.

"It's coming from somewhere down the hall," Gwen said in a small, tight voice.

"Right," said Logan, cocking the loaded pistol Greniston had given him. He strode to the door and flung it open. Gwen and Mrs. Walmsley were right behind him.

"I'll stay with the children," Annie Lee said quietly.

The scream came again. It sounded like a man, not so much in pain as already driven mad with pain. It pierced the stillness and echoed through the halls of Greniston Manor, ending in a long drawn out cackling sob. From the floors below came the sound of doors slamming, voices, and hurried footsteps.

"Where is it coming from?" someone cried.

"Down this way!" came a voice.

"No, this way," someone else yelled.

In the quiet of the portrait gallery, the children looked at each other and then at Annie Lee.

"It's now or never," Osgood said. He looked at Wyatt. "Are you sure you remember how?"

"Of course!" the Superagent of the Kingdom scoffed. "I was wight behind the tapestwy. I saw it all. Watch."

429

He dragged a chair to Lord Peter's portrait, climbed onto it, and fumbled around behind the painting. The wall slid back, to reveal the dark passageway.

"Blimey," whispered Osborne, clearly impressed. Claire's eyes sparkled. Beside her, Charles looked worried.

"Grab the torches, and let's go!" ordered Osgood. He glanced at the Gypsy, surprised that she had not yet sounded the alarm to the other grownups. But then, he mused, perhaps she was not a grown-up—just a tall, old child. He did not protest when she followed them into the passageway.

It took five minutes for Gwen and the others to discover that the bloodcurdling screams were coming from the third floor bathroom and a few more minutes to discover the child's cassette tape player, fastened to the back of the toilet with duct tape.

"It's Wyatt's," said Anne Walmsley, looking down at the blue plastic tape player, decorated with pictures of Mickey Mouse and Goofy. "I should have recognized the screams right away. It's a tape Wyatt and Osgood made for a play at school. A ghost story, it was. The boys spent weeks taping sound effects from old films on the telly. Boris Karloff's on that tape, and Christopher Lee and Vincent Price."

"But if the children left this here . . . ," Gwen began. No more needed to be said.

"Gone!" Gwen exclaimed breathlessly from the doorway of the gallery, not really surprised, although they had sprinted down the corridors at breakneck speed. The others crowded behind her.

"But how, dear?" Lettice asked anxiously.

"The secret passageway that Lord Greniston showed me earlier," Gwen said. "One of the children must have followed us."

"Thank God the babies are safe!" Anne Walmsley exclaimed, hurrying to Amy and Rutherford, who were sleeping side by side on their quilts.

"The Gypsy is gone too," Mrs. Fitzpatrick said darkly, as if her worst fears had been realized.

"She may have gone after the children," Gwen said. "And so am I, before they get too far."

"I'm coming with you," announced Logan.

Althea rallied and reassumed command.

"Yes," she said decisively, "you two go get those children. The rest of us should return at once to our posts."

Mr. Steadworthy considered this. It did seem to him that the escape of the Walmsley children was not the sort of emergency Lord Greniston would have felt necessitated notifying the Yard.

"Yes," he agreed, "that seems the best plan."

Davey Lee did some considering of his own as he headed back outside, nominally to continue his guard duty. He was pleased to see that the evening was stirring into motion at last.

"'The game is afoot, Watson,' he murmured to himself, "and I've a plan of my own to tend to."

***

The real stroke of genius, thought Osgood, as he marshaled his troops down the last stretch of the underground passageway, *was recording twenty minutes of blank tape before the screams started*, thus giving him time to be innocently back in the gallery. That had been Wyatt's idea. Osgood did not begrudge its brilliance; he knew his own limits. He excelled at boldness and strategy, but Wyatt had flights of inspiration that elevated outwitting adults to a real art form.

Wyatt passed him now, the last to scurry out of the tunnel and into the safety of the woods.

"To the mound!" Osgood cried to them all, "Run like the wind!"

Quite a ways behind them, Gwen and Logan had just left the Greniston Chapel.

"It's odd," Logan said breathlessly, "that they stopped to light candles."

Gwen nodded in agreement. She and Greniston had used only the candles they had brought with them and had left the room in darkness, but when she and Logan had dashed through the chapel, both of the silver candelabras had been ablaze with light. She had noticed something else strange, as well: in the glass vase that had before held only snowdrops, there had been daffodils as well. Well, there was no time to figure that out now. Yet, as they ran headlong down the ancient stone steps that led to the cellars of the manor, she heard behind them the echo of a young man's joyful laughter—a bold young man who had, in his day, been fond of light, and danger, and daffodils.

Silently, Greniston passed Filipo the brandy flask. They had been keeping vigil near the mound for two hours now, and an unspoken comradeship was being woven between them, as they waited, concealed in the shadows of the oak trees. Luan Tey, on the other hand, sitting alone and in plain view on the mound, seemed to grow more and more isolated.

Filipo glanced at his watch: ten o'clock. Miller was late. If he meant to send gunmen to take them by surprise, they would surely be in place by now, yet Filipo had no sense of anyone waiting in the darkness behind them. He felt only the presence of the mound itself. He gazed at the, by now, familiar scene: the clearing, surrounded by a chain of daffodils that gleamed faintly in the moonlight. It reminded him of something he had seen, something important, yet he could not quite remember what. He searched in his pocket for another Gauloise, then paused with the cigarette halfway to his lips.

"*Dios Mio*," he whispered in the darkness. Suddenly, everything was clear to him.

***

Gwen and Logan emerged from the underground passageway and found themselves in an unfamiliar part of the woods.

"Now the question is," said Gwen, "where are those children?"

"Ten to one they headed for the mound," Logan replied.

Gwen groaned. "Exactly where we don't want them to go! And which way is the mound from here?"

She and Logan searched the darkness for some clue to their whereabouts. Suddenly, Logan exclaimed: "Gwen! Look!"

Gwen turned in time to catch a fleeting glimpse of an elfin figure running into the shadows.

"That was Claire," Logan said, "I'm sure of it. Come on!"

Logan headed into the forest, looking more than ever like some noble hound, his gaunt features totally focused on tracking the scent of their elusive prey.

At that moment, the Sentinel of the Independent Kingdom of Greenstone peered into the darkness. The night wind tugged his flaxen curls, making them wilder than ever. He felt the wind on his face and smelled the scents of damp earth and fallen pine needles. He listened to the thousand sounds of night: the creak of branch and sigh of leaf, the squeak of mouse, and the stirring of the robin in its sleep. He heard the delicate plop of one red

432

ash berry, falling from a nearby branch onto last year's dead leaves on the ground below. He did not have to think about the wealth of information that assaulted him through sound and smell and sight. He absorbed it through the whole of himself and knew that all was well, and the woods were as they should be. Safe as well was the new sound that came toward him: the light tread of footsteps. He recognized the person approaching to be Claire, Priestess of the Kingdom, Seer and Knower, Councilor to the Monarch, Osgood the First. All the same, he called out, "Who goeth there? Decware thyself!"

Claire appeared, smiling in the moonlight, and made the hand signal that was her version of a password. Wyatt bowed gravely in acceptance of this sign.

"Doth the visitors appwoacheth?"

Claire nodded.

A herd of elephants, Wyatt felt, could not have made much more noise than Gwen and Logan did as they drew near, trying to be stealthy. He and Claire exchanged an indulgent smile.

"Gweetings, Visitors!" Wyatt called out, as the adults came into view. "The Cwown of Gweenstone wecognizes Thee, and gwants Thee safe passage to its High Council woom."

He pulled back the branch of a hawthorn tree to reveal what seemed to be the opening to another tunnel.

"Another underground passage?" Gwen asked warily.

"Yes!" said Wyatt excitedly, momentarily forgetting his formal role as sentinel. "There are wots of them awound here! This one weeds wight to inside the mound! And Cwaire—I mean, The Pwophetess—says you and Wogan are to come inside, that you are destined to be here to night!"

"Yes," said Logan, "we are."

Not five minutes later, he found himself once again inside the mound. The chamber had clearly been prepared for a special occasion. Kitchen candles which Mrs. Fitzpatrick's careful housekeeping might soon miss burned in holders made of old soup cans. By their flickering light, he saw that near the roof of the cavern, a wreath of dried branches and flowers encircled the room like a crown. The scent of dried rose, lavender, and gilly flower as well as of the candle wax gave the place a clean, churchlike smell. The stone walls were covered with even more bright crayon drawings than before, including drawings of each brave knight's shield. Tonight, there was a crate in front of each shield. The crates were covered with bright cloths, made to look as much like thrones as possible.

There was even a makeshift throne for Logan and a space on the wall for his shield, as the newest member of the Kingdom. On the floor, Logan saw a new, additional threadbare oriental carpet, its once crimson pattern so faded that Mrs. Fitzpatrick, in her recent frenzy of cleaning, had declared it fit only for the next church jumble sale. Evidently, the carpet had met with a detour on the way from the manor to St. Aethelrood's.

Every effort had clearly been made to make the chamber as splendid as possible. The Royal Court itself was in full regalia, each member carefully adorned in a homemade robe and foil crown.

It was a scene delicately poised between splendor and comedy. Logan felt that splendor won, by a hair's breadth. He saw that Gwen, seeing the place for the first time, looked awed in spite of herself. Annie Lee, sitting on the ground next to Osgood's throne, seemed gently amused by the pageantry.

"Greetings to the Independent Kingdom of Greenstone, to its Monarch, and Most Royal Court!" Logan cried in a ringing voice. "Lady Gwen and myself are honored indeed, to be invited to your presence."

Osgood accepted the greeting with a solemn nod. "Be seated," he said, the words as much a command as an invitation.

"We don't have time for this," Gwen said, kindly, but firmly. "You need to come back to the manor house with us now!"

"That will not be possible," Osgood replied, dismissing her words with a truly regal wave of his hand.

Meanwhile, Charles put down some cushions that Logan recognized as having been 'borrowed' from a sofa in the Walmsleys' new quarters.

"Bring refreshment," Osgood ordered.

"Now wait a minute," said Gwen, a little less patiently this time. "This is a very dangerous situation. You need to come back with us right now."

Claire appeared, carrying a tin tray on which were proudly arranged some broken pieces of chocolate, an orange, and, in a truly regal touch, a bottle of wine and two jelly glasses. Evidently, the Walmsleys' exploration of Greniston Manor had reached the wine cellar.

Gwen noted that the label read "Montrechat, 1974." Someone had a good instinct for a vintage. *Probably Osgood*, she thought. In spite of her frustration at wanting to get the children back to the house safely and quickly, she had to admire the grandeur of their hospitality.

"Let's humor them a bit," Logan whispered to her. "Might be quicker in the long run."

"You do the talking, then," Gwen whispered back, "I'm losing patience with this."

"We thank your Majesties for your hospitality," Logan said in grand tones, "and yet we wonder why it is we have been brought here."

"Your words seek out the heart of the matter," Osgood gravely replied, "even as . . . even as . . . "

"Even as the hunter's arrow finds its mark," Osborne suggested in a whisper.

"Yes," said Osgood, recovering himself quickly, "even as the hunter's arrow finds its mark. High adventure, matters of life and death, do concern us this night. In these most High matters, the Crown beseecheth your help."

"But how can we help you?" Gwen asked, intrigued in spite of herself.

"That will be explained in good time," Osgood replied with dignity. "First, it is necessary that all three of you, Logan, a member of this Kingdom, and Thou, Lady Gwen, and Thou, Lady Annie de Lees, do greet this Court, and state your motto and by what devices upon your shields you shall be known, as gentle knights do ever do, when visiting a strange kingdom."

"Logan," Gwen whispered, "we really need to get the children back to the house." She looked appealingly at Logan and Annie Lee, realizing that she would need the help of both adults to shepherd five unwilling Walmsleys back through the long tunnel. Neither her friend nor the Gypsy, however, seemed inclined to interrupt the play in progress.

"This is where we are supposed to be," Annie said quietly. "We too have our parts to play. Can you not feel it?"

The truth was, Gwen could feel the same tug at her intuition that had brought her to England in the first place, stronger now than ever, encouraging her to remain at the mound, to surrender to whatever the weave of events had in mind for them all.

"My motto," she found herself saying, "is 'Let the Good Prevail,' and my shield is . . . a golden daffodil, upon a field of green."

"And Thou, Bard Logan, of the Forest World?" Osgood asked.

"My motto is 'Where the Story Leads Me,' and my shield is a silver harp upon a field d'azure."

"And Thou, Lady Annie De Lees?"

The Gypsy paused, considering. "My motto," she said at length, "is between God and me, and I will speak it for no man. My shield is a comfrey leaf, upon sky blue."

Osgood nodded. "So they have spoken, so let them be known," he intoned. "Welcome to these three, by Arthur, and by Greenstone!"

"By Arthur! By Greenstone!" the other children echoed.

"Now the sacred trust of our kingdom is to be revealed to you," Osgood said solemnly. Wyatt and Charles took two candles from the rustic table by Osgood's throne. Osborne pulled back one of the old bedspreads that served as tapestries on the walls, to reveal an arched opening that seemed to lead to a smaller cavern.

"Enter!" Osgood commanded. Standing nearby, Claire nodded and smiled, as if trying to assure the others that everything was all right.

Gwen stepped through the arch. The first thing she saw, as Wyatt held high his candle, was the gleam, everywhere, of treasure.

"The Greniston Treasure!" gasped Logan beside her, as an uncut ruby the size of a hen's egg rolled past his foot.

Proudly, the children led the three adults into the second chamber. This room was perhaps half the size of the first and seemed to be a natural cave rather than a manmade barrow. Everywhere Gwen and Logan looked, they saw piles of gems, objects of silver and gold, and crowns, lances, bracelets, buckles, and daggers fashioned of the same dull metal as the Far Tauverly chalice.

"It's a king's ransom," Gwen whispered in awe.

"And the Greniston Treasure is real," Logan murmured.

"'Twas Arthur's treasure before it was ever the Greniston's," said Osgood firmly. The other children nodded in agreement.

As Logan and Gwen surveyed the riches with wonder, gingerly touching an emerald brooch or a golden coronet, as if to reassure themselves that what they saw was real, Annie moved to the shadows at the far end of the cave, where she heard the sound of trickling water. A spring flowed out of the rock and trickled down the side of the chamber into a fissure in the floor, some three feet long and two feet wide, through which she caught the glint of moving water.

"There must be an underground river down there," Gwen said, standing beside her now. "And look, where the water begins, the roots of a tree reach down. This must be right under the tree at the end of the mound, the one they call Merlin's Oak. You can hear its spring above ground, too."

Osborne nodded. "This is Merlin's Spring," he said, "and Arthur's Treasure."

"You have known about all this all along," Gwen said to the children. "Why didn't you tell Lord Greniston about the treasure? You knew he was searching for it."

"This treasure belongs to King Arthur Pendragon," Osgood said staunchly. "The Greniston's were just supposed to keep it safe, in trust, like Lord Peter's poem says."

"But the Gwenistons forgot," Wyatt put in.

"All the grown-ups forgot," Osborne added.

"But we remembered," said Charles. At his side, Claire nodded.

"We have kept the trust," said Osgood proudly. "We have kept Arthur's treasure safe for his return."

He spoke with the simple pride of a job well done. Gwen imagined the children stumbling across the entrances to the mound in their play, clearing tunnels filled with rubble perhaps for centuries, and stumbling across the treasure. She realized it must have been a sacrifice for them to guard it so well, given their family's constant need for money. Yet she was sure that every jewel was exactly where they had found it, kept intact for their legendary hero. They had not even used the crowns and chains for their own costumes but had fashioned their regalia from cardboard and foil. Looking at their steadfast faces, she felt they had probably never even been tempted to use any of the wealth there, so great was their young honor.

"But your Majesties," said Logan, "why reveal this to us now?"

"Claire told us it is time," said Osgood simply.

"She is the Prophetess," Charles explained. "She speaks to us in drawings and in signs. We understand her."

"Yes," added Osborne rather loftily, "the grown-ups do not, but we understand her, always."

"And now the pwophecy cometh twueth," said Wyatt excitedly. "For 'The Stwanger hath cometh to the Wion Gate'—that's you," he added, for Gwen's benefit.

"And Knobbly Hill doth tremble and quake," chimed in Osborne and Charles.

"And tonight is the night of greatest danger," said Osgood. "Tell them, Sir Wyatt, what Thou knowest."

Excitedly, Wyatt related all that he had heard Luan Tey tell Lord Greniston from his hiding place in the dumb waiter.

When he finished, Gwen felt stunned. A metal that contained a capacity more powerful than plutonium, international criminals. . . . At first, the story, like the jewels piled high before her, seemed too fabulous to be real. Yet she knew it was real.

Logan seemed not so much surprised as relieved. "So it is all true," he said, almost joyfully. "Everything that's been happening has a reason."

As for Annie, she held her hands a few inches above a shield formed of the curious gray metal that was potentially so powerful. She felt a fiery warmth emanating from it.

"It makes me afraid," she said.

Gwen could sympathize with that. It was not herself and the others that she felt afraid for, though, but Greniston, who was perhaps, at that very moment, facing the evil that wanted the treasure. And so, she realized, was Filipo.

No wonder they didn t want me mixed up in this business, she thought. Yet she was glad that she knew, now. Her mind was already racing, wondering what she could do to help with the encounter that was taking place, she realized, just a few feet above their heads. As her own thoughts struggled to grapple with the facts, she decided to find out what plan the children had in mind, for she was sure they had one.

"Your Majesty," she said to Osgood, "right glad are we that you have confided in us. Now tell us, we pray, what do you need us to do?"

"Wake up Arthur," said the King of the Greenstone Realm.

"Wake up Arthur? You mean *King* Arthur?" Logan asked.

"Who else?" Osgood replied.

"The legends do say that Arthur is not dead but only sleeping," Logan said.

"And that he will awaken and return at England's hour of greatest need," said Gwen. "Well, this hour could qualify not only for England but for the world. But how will Arthur hear us?" she asked the children.

"Because he's right in there," Osgood explained patiently. He pointed at the gently trickling spring. "There is another cave on the other side of the spring. It's all sealed up, we haven't been in it. But Arthur is in there, with all his true knights. Sleeping. Claire saw them."

"Claire saw them?" Gwen exclaimed.

"Yeth," Wyatt interjected, "she sees things. Twough walls and all."

"You mean, she sees things that aren't really there," Gwen suggested gently.

"No," said Osgood pointedly. "She sees the things that *are* really there."

"And the things that are *going* to be," Osborne added. "Sometimes she sees those, too."

Gwen opened her mouth to protest, then thought the better of it. Given all the extraordinary things that had happened to her in the last few weeks, she felt she was in no position to dismiss the children's claims.

"It's very possible," Annie said. "Some have this gift."

Claire now signaled rapidly to Osborne, in what seemed to be a private sign language they had devised.

"Slow down, Claire," he said, frowning, as he tried to follow the movements of her thin white hands.

"She says she knows that you and Logan are to help wake up Arthur, because the Shining Man told her so."

"'The Shining Man' . . . ," Logan's thoughts turned to his own recent visions, and the memory of a golden haired bard, surrounded by light. "Does she mean Gwydion?"

Claire nodded emphatically, then looked expectantly at Osborne.

"She said that the Shining Man told her that Logan must tell Arthur stories of his great deeds," explained Osborne. "That will make Arthur long to be great again, and he will wake up."

Logan nodded as if this made perfect sense to him.

"She doesn't know why you and Annie have to be here," Osborne added to Gwen, "she just knows that you do."

This is all happening too fast, Gwen thought. Part of her wanted to run back down the underground passageway to the manor and tell Steadworthy to call Scotland Yard. Greniston had told her he had the number. That would be safe; it would keep everything that was happening in the realm of facts and real, physical evidence. That would be the rational

439

choice that one would expect a thirty-two-year-old former school teacher to make in a crisis. Yet another part of her was certain that the mysteries her life had touched recently were real and that it was those mysteries that she was here to deal with. She had to decide which path to take, and the safety of the man she loved, and of dear friends, and of children, depended upon the choice she made now.

"Does anyone else know of the entrances to the mound?" she asked.

Osgood shook his head. "They were both covered with stones and bushes. But Claire saw them, and we cleared away the stuff."

If no one else knows of the entrances, she thought, *then the children are as safe here as anywhere else, especially if Logan and Annie stay with them. Let them try their summons of King Arthur, and more power to them.* She knew that she could not just sit with them. She found herself in both worlds; the mystery realm and the land of facts. She had to do something to help Greniston and Filipo. *As soon as they are all engrossed in Logan's stories*, she decided, *I'll slip away, up to the mound.*

What she would do when she got there, she did not know. She felt, though, that it would be a good idea to have a weapon. A silver dagger with a hilt carved like a horse's head had caught her eye amidst the treasure. When no one was looking, she picked up the dagger and slipped it into her sweater pocket. She did not think that King Arthur would begrudge her the loan of it, under the circumstances.

***

Greniston wasn't sure what he had expected Miller to be. Whatever it was, it wasn't this innocuous man, who, except for the extremely fine cut of his clothes, could have stepped off of any London/Guildford commuter train rather than out of the shadows surrounding the mound.

If Miller was surprised to see Greniston and Filipo standing on the mound, it lasted only an instant. He gave Luan Tey the most fleeting of reproachful glances. In his greed to possess the sedasium, perhaps Miller had allowed himself to trust the man. Perhaps not. Whatever the case, he recovered his balance almost instantly.

Smooth, thought Greniston, *very smooth.*

"I've come about the artwork," said Miller affably.

He spoke as if Greniston was the manager of some posh Mayfair gallery with whom he had an appointment.

"Mr. Tey has evidently taken you into his confidence in this matter," said Miller lightly.

"Not really," Greniston interrupted, deciding to throw as much confusion into the situation as possible, on principle. "But I saw him skulking around the place. I knew what he was looking for. I've known about the treasure for years, you see. But it just so happens that I like things left where they are." Greniston decided to leave it at that, uncertain exactly what Luan Tey had said to Miller about the supposed treasure and its location.

"How did you know we were to meet here tonight?" Miller spoke so lightly, so pleasantly, that his tone almost tripped Greniston up. Almost.

"Simple, really," said Greniston with a smile and a shrug, wondering at the same time what the devil he was going to say. "Servant problem. Someone on my staff's been making long distance calls without my permission. Deuced annoying. It's not the expense so much as the deception; I'm sure you'll understand that. One likes to know whom one can trust, doesn't one? So I set up a system to have the outgoing calls taped. And your Mr. Tey made the mistake of calling out from my hall phone. I have every word he said, that you both said, for that matter, on tape."

For a moment, Greniston had the satisfaction of seeing Miller unnerved, as he tried to remember exactly what had been said in his conversation. *He's uncertain*, Greniston thought. *Good. Now, if I can only keep him off guard.*

As if sharing the thought, Filipo now stepped forward. "Perhaps it's time I introduced myself," he said. He paused, took out his cigarettes, and thoughtfully lit a Gauloise. "I am called *El Nino*, an affectionate little nickname given to me because of the aftereffects of my work. I am an associate of Lord Greniston's, and of . . . "—Filipo took a long drag on his cigarette and picked a name he had seen in a recent *Newsweek* article on international financiers—"Hokirii Tonamuto."

"Tonamuto?" Miller exclaimed.

"Even so," said Filipo with a shrug, studiously removing a fleck of tobacco from his tongue. He hoped that dropping the name of the Japanese industrialist might inspire enough fear in Miller to up the ante.

"I did not know Tonamuto had an interest in artifacts," Miller replied, struggling to keep control.

"He doesn't," replied Filipo. He gazed at the surrounding oak trees, allowing the full implications of the comment to sink in.

Bravo, Filipo, thought Greniston. It struck him that were it not for the threat to the world Miller posed and the threat to Gwen, whose safety he wondered about every moment, he could have almost enjoyed this parley.

"*El Nino* here has an unusually penetrating appreciation of antiquities," Greniston said. "No matter how drab the piece, he is able to see the value in its very substance. Always seems to recognize the use even some battered old cup could be put to and to be able to find a buyer for it. So when I overheard your little tête-à-tête with Mr. Tey, I immediately contacted him. Seems my dreary old family cup holds the key to blowing up a planet or two. Mustn't leave it just lying about anymore, it could excite the servants."

"So . . . ," Miller's voice had become a hiss. "It's not possible! Who? Who approached you? Schwartz? Calderon? But they only knew of the process, not of the deposits! No one had all the facts but me!"

Good, good, thought Greniston, moving as close to Miller as he dared and praying that the system he and Bob Walmsley had rigged up would actually record the conversation. *It's nice to get some names, old boy,* Greniston thought. *Just keep talking. Just get a little more unnerved. . . .*

"It was you," Miller cried, turning to face Luan Tey, "It had to be you!"

Luan Tey opened his mouth to speak, but before he could, Greniston burst into song: "It had to be you," he warbled, in his loud, tuneless baritone, "no one else would do, for skulking around in the dew, blowing up the planet so blue . . ."

Inspired, *El Nino* now chimed in: "Yes, it had to be you, for the arts of betrayal, putting Herr Miller in jail, no one else would do. For at lying and theft, you are simply the best, yes . . ."

"It had to be you-u-u . . . ," Greniston and Filipo finished together.

"But it wasn't," Filipo added lightly. "Signor Tey told me nothing. I have sources of my own, you see."

Miller stared at them. "You are mad, both of you," he said with disgust.

Filipo ignored this remark. "I assure you, Signor, Tey and I are strangers to each other."

"Ah!" exclaimed Greniston. "Strangers in the night, exchanging gunshots, snipers in the night, who have just one shot . . ."

"Shut up, you fool!" snapped Miller.

442

"Why should I?" asked Greniston. To himself, he thought, *If I can bait him just a little more, something will snap. He'll let down his guard, say just that one sentence that will really incriminate him. . . .* Aloud, he continued, "Why should I be quiet? It's my land, and my treasure, and I feel like singing. I'm in the mood."

El Nino's eyes lit up. "I'm in the mood for crime," he sang, "simply because you're near me."

Greniston picked up the tune: "A bit of murder if you've the time, after all, who can hear me?"

"Enough!" In one swift movement, Miller knocked the gun from Luan Tey's hand, grabbed the little man from behind, and held a knife to his throat.

Greniston was shocked, but Filipo remained cool. "Have that knife up your sleeve all the time?" he asked. "You must be great at card tricks, *amigo.*"

Miller did not reply. A change had come over his face. Gone was the suave, blank businessman. In its place was evil. Absolute, impersonal, evil— ruthless, ancient, and very, very, smart.

"Kill him," whispered Luan Tey. "It doesn't matter if I die. Use this chance, kill him!"

Miller brought the knife closer to the man's throat, just close enough to bring a faint trickle of blood to the surface.

Greniston's heart sank. How cunning, how shrewd of Evil to use this man as its hostage. Had Miller seized Gwen, or a child, or Filipo, his own choice would have been clear. But to confuse him with a man who was himself a murderer, who seemed to want to die? That was cunning, very cunning. Yet Greniston remembered the look in Luan Tey's eyes the night before, as they stood in his study—the look of an astronaut, whose line to his ship has been severed, who finds himself drifting into the vastness of space, alone, alone, alone. Only a few hours before, he had tried to throw a lifeline to that loneliness, to tell the man that he was "one of us." Was he now to sever that lifeline at his own convenience?

"Kill him," Luan Tey urged, "it doesn't matter if he kills me."

Greniston shook his head. "Afraid that's out of the question, old boy. Couldn't barter with your life. After all, you are one of us."

For an instant, he saw a flash of hope in the other man's eyes. Perhaps Luan Tey was fated to die that night, but at least he could die feeling like a member of the human family. *And so will I*, thought Greniston, glad of his own choice.

The Evil that looked out of Miller's eyes laughed with pleasure. "Very good, Lord Greniston," It said. "I was counting on your Honor. It is often so useful to me in my own affairs, the honor of men. But I must ask you—as a point of honor—why is this man, Luan Tey, included in your compassion, while I, it seems, am not? Surely that is not right."

Greniston looked Evil in the eye. It was a long glance. "The difference between you and Luan Tey," he said carefully, "is that he is still a battleground between good and evil—like most of us poor devils. But you, Mr. Miller, have quite given over the field to darkness. Of your own free will, you joined the ranks of greed and cruelty so long ago that 'you' aren't even there anymore; you are simply a puppet for Evil to use. That's all you are, anymore, Evil's puppet, and when it is done with you, it will toss you away and find another creature for its use."

"Perhaps even you, Lord Greniston," the Evil replied.

Greniston shook his head. "Between you and I there is an insurmountable barrier."

"And what is that?" the Evil asked.

"My will."

Evil laughed. "We'll see." A glance came out of Miller's eyes that flickered over Greniston and Filipo like the tongue of a snake, testing the temperature of what it saw.

"Now, then, gentlemen," Evil said affably, "let's talk."

***

Logan saw them all: Gwydion, Taliesin, Amergin—the great bards stood near. St. Patrick was there, as well, and Scheherazade, and heroes of times gone by: Brian Boru, Fergus, Finn McCool, King Alfred, Boadicea, and more great men and women of every age; now they were gathered round, standing behind the children that encircled him, faces in a golden mist. Faces of the great and the unknown were there: soldiers and poets, healers and farmers, hunters and troubadours, saints and tricksters, ladies and knights, beggars and kings, milkmaids and queens. The faces of all who, in their lives and in their ways, had stood and worked for good. Now they gathered in— young faces, old faces; faces from Ireland, Baghdad, Cathay; faces from Ethiopia and ancient America; and faces from Far Tauverly's own history, Lord Peter's face among them, and Tommy Greniston's.

Silent they were and waiting, as they had waited, some of them, for centuries. What a yearning was in their eyes.

"Fail us not," their eyes pleaded to the living. "Oh, you who find yourselves upon the crest of time, fail us not."

The power of their yearning flowed into Logan and, with it, their courage and goodness. He felt fortified with the strength of thousands, as he whispered, "Arthur! Arthur Pendragon, we remember you!"

"Yes!" the children echoed softly, "we remember you!"

"Arthur, Arthur Pendragon," Logan whispered again, "Life remembers you! Do you remember Life? Remember the fields of your youth, Arthur; the forests rustling, green and deep, where owl and deer their watch do keep; the hidden glen where dwells the stag, far from the fretting hunt of men!"

The words seemed to spring to his lips. He did not plan the rhymes or images; they came to him. He saw it all in his mind's eye like a living tapestry.

"Remember, Arthur, the long summer hours, the sound of bees 'midst wild flowers, remember the mists of autumn, the asters bright beside the path, and all the mysteries September hath! Remember the crunch of frost beneath thy horses feet, and in the still mountain air, the eagle's wing beat; remember holly berries, brilliant, red, and the river water dripping from the otter's sleek head; remember the small birds fluffed against the cold; remember the snake, so wise, and so old; remember the spring's water, more potent than wine, remember wind rustling through the wild ivy's vine. . . ."

As Logan spoke, it seemed to him that now the spirits of Nature were joining the throng of bards and heroes that stood near, adding their plea and their strength to the cry. The sylphs of the air were there in garments of mist, the spirits of oak and birch and willow, and the yellow angel of the daffodil, and the elves that love to dance afield on moonlit nights, and fairies, sparkling in and out like match-struck jewels—all were there, pouring their persuasion into his voice.

"Arthur! Arthur, remember the Fairy Realms, for they remember you! Arthur, King Arthur, whose heart is pure, whose word is true, the Realm of Fairy beckons now to you!"

"Arthur, Arthur," the children echoed fervently.

"Arthur, King Arthur," Logan continued, "remember the Mother who gave you birth, a noble Princess, whom men call Earth. She calls to you

445

now in sore distress! Arthur, hear, in your kingliness! Thy Lady Mother sickens unto death! Help her, Arthur, while she still has breath! And Merlin, too, we call to Thee! Thy magic men have ceased to see Merlin in the cavern, Merlin in the well, and in the sacred tree. Merlin, may our summons set thy ancient spirit free! By the rowan and the oak, by the willow and the hazel tree, Merlin, oh Merlin, we call to Thee! By the wind in the heavens and the white-froth wave of the blue-green sea, Merlin, oh Merlin, we call to Thee!"

Logan paused. It seemed to him that Arthur and his knights might truly be on the other side of the stone cavern wall, stirring from their long sleep, listening, slowly remembering; as if Merlin's enchanted spirit truly was woven into the roots of the tree and the trickling of the spring. He began to speak again, louder now:

"Arthur Pendragon, leader of men, the world has need of your fire again! Our times are darker than even your own; the good are few, and stand alone! Arthur, remember: Gawain and Galahad, Lancelot and Merlin, Bors and Pellinore, and many more! Remember thy good companions, thy fellow travelers upon this turning globe; remember the beauty and valor of women, remember the pure-faced children, and the good monk in his rough, brown robe! Remember the thrill when adventure draws nigh, the thunder of hooves and jingle of bridles, how brave the banners fly, riding out on true quest, on a clear winter's night, when frost blooms from the horses' noses, and Orion sparkles in the midnight sky! Remember the challenge, the joust you so loved, the weight of shields, your standard wind-snapping above; the test of wit and nerve, heart and sinew; the jolt when sword or spear met true; the longing you had, to do all you could do! Arthur, remember the companions, fighting beside you! Their courage, their daring, their wit—the world has sore need of it! I summon their spirits, call out their names: Galahad, Gawaine, thy mother, Igraine. Sir Leon de Grance and Lancelot, who traveled from France . . ."

As Logan cried out the names, he felt that he could see the faces of those who had borne them, down to the laugh lines around one's blue eyes and the scar on the hand of another. Loyal men were they, not perfect, but great of heart. These were not the handsome knights of movies and the Victorian poets; these were rough and ready men, for whom a bath most often meant wading into a stream with their clothes on, and luxury was having a servant pick the lice from their hair. Most of them had never known how to read or write. They stank of leather and sweat and the dust of the

446

road, were quick to quarrel and as quick to mend the quarrel, deep in love, rare in speech. Crude men, some might say, yet they had an elegance of heart that put the modern age to shame and a kindness rare in this world for many a year. To a man, they burned with inspiration. Arthur's dream shone out of their eyes; their lives were transformed by it, lit up from within by their spirit's fire.

Logan saw the faces of the women, too. He had never known there were so many women at Arthur's court. That older woman with the wise, dark gaze, was she Arthur's sister, Morgan Le Faye? And that slender lady, with long blond hair and a crown of gold, was she Guinevere? Instinct told him that she was, yet she looked different than he would have ever imagined: a mature woman, in her thirties, with a face that, though beautiful, was deeply marked by laughter and pain. Intelligence gleamed from her clear, gray eyes. She looked honest and kind and humorous, and no man's fool. Though slender, her hands and feet were large and made for work; she looked tall and strong, as capable of giving a foe a right hook to the jaw as of weaving a delicate tapestry. Everything about her spoke of all that is forthright and clear. If, indeed, she was Guinevere, then whatever had happened between Lancelot and her could never have been a matter of sneaking deceit, of that Logan was sure. She looked capable of telling even a king to mind his own bloody business. But of telling a trashy little lie? Never.

The faces of other women rose before him: young maidens, their hair unbraided, garlands of flowers on their heads like crowns; women of middle years, their eyes as bright with courage and purpose as any knight's; old women, their faces wise, some gracious, touched by patience; and others, defiant to the last, but all shining with life. . . .

Life, Logan realized, was what all the faces had in common. They shone with the knowing that every instant of life, every breath drawn are more precious than any treasure and that Life is a great and purposeful thing, all of it—the joys and the griefs, the pleasures and the wounds. The quest, the mystery that Arthur had given to these lords and ladies they had kept alive for centuries, and now seemed to be offering it back to him, summoning him to Life through the voice of Logan.

"Arthur!" he cried, "Remember your good companions!"

He looked at the faces of the Walmsley children, of Gwen and Annie Lee; they, too, seemed to call silently to Arthur.

"Arthur! Arthur Pendragon!" he cried. "Rise to meet your new companions!"

***

"Gentlemen, I can offer you so much," the voice that came out of Miller said reasonably. "We're all men of the world, here . . . "

"Not of the same world," Greniston interrupted.

Miller shrugged, as if amused by Greniston's fine distinctions. "As you wish," he murmured, with a trace of silken condensation in his voice.

Greniston felt his temper rise dangerously near the boiling point. *Careful, old boy,* he thought to himself, *that's just what he wants you to do—get angry, terrified, he doesn't care which, as long as he gets you rattled. Don't give him the satisfaction, lad.*

Aloud, he remarked to Filipo, "This is getting tiresome. Too bad we didn't bring a chess set."

"*D'accord,*" Filipo said. He glanced thoughtfully at the gun he held trained on Miller. "Although perhaps we do have a game in progress. And soon I may be driven to remove a black pawn from the board, out of sheer ennui."

"Kill me, and he dies," Miller reminded them. The knife he held to Luan Tey's throat gleamed in the moonlight.

"You can't hold that knife to his throat forever," Filipo said with a yawn. "Sooner or later, you'll fall asleep. It's a boring way to spend a day or two, but, *eh bien,* we can outwait you."

"Ah, yes," Miller replied, "boredom. Of course, you and boredom are old friends, are you not?"

Greniston watched Filipo brace himself for the ordeal he knew was to come. For over an hour, now, the Evil that looked out of Miller's eyes had tested them both, probing for their innermost weak spots. With expert, safecracker's hands, it had turned the tumbrels of their deepest weaknesses— greed, fear, ambition. It had seemed to know exactly where their fault lines lay, and it had played upon them, trying to get what it wanted from them: a treasure, which, as far as Greniston knew, might not even exist.

Again and again, Miller's cunning pitted them against some darkness in themselves. A few minutes ago, he had almost captured Greniston in his own arrogance. Cunningly, knowingly, the Evil voice had said, "Oh, come, come, Lord Greniston, don't be so naive. You and I know that weapons of destruction aren't going to disappear from the world. Isn't it better that their use lies safely in the hands of educated men, intelligent men, like me, like yourself—men who have the welfare of all at heart? Better that we should bear the burden of destructive knowledge than leave it to be discovered by fanatics. Frankly, Greniston, I think it is a duty for us to take the power up."

To his horror, Greniston had found himself almost seduced by the implications of that voice. "You are one of the elite," it seemed to say, "one of the real leaders of this world. . . ."

Revulsion had overcome him. How could such appeals to stature still sway him? He thought he had outgrown his aristocrat's arrogance long ago.

Perhaps I am what Miller finds me, he had thought, *a snob, a disgusting creature. Perhaps there is no heroism in me to draw upon.*

Yet he knew he had to try.

"'S'blood, do you think I am easier to be played upon than a pipe?'" Greniston had said, quoting from Hamlet. "'Call me what instrument you will, though you fret me, you cannot play upon me.'"

The words were full of bravado, but as he spoke them, he had felt utterly alone. He felt as if he was stepping out onto an empty abyss. Yet he had to do it. And as soon as he took that first step, he suddenly felt courage and certainty such as he had never known before flow into him.

What is helping me? he had marveled.

Now Greniston saw that Miller had just faced Filipo with his own worst demon.

"Yes," Miller hissed, "you know boredom, and boredom knows you." He spoke now with a strange dark poetry that Greniston realized sounded like Filipo's own voice. How cunning, how terrible, to attempt to destroy a human with his own voice.

"Yes, boredom has followed you around the world, like an invincible hit man," Miller continued. "You change countries, change cities, but sooner or later it finds you. You look out the window some morning, and there it is across the street, looking up at you. . . . It's got your place staked out again. Then, one day, you come home to find out it's moved in with you, the roommate you never wanted. It haunts the rooms of yet another cheap apartment . . . and then it comes in closer, doesn't it, *amigo?* It moves under your skin and into your mind, and then you realize it isn't just boredom that's with you but its ancient twin, despair. . . . What does any of it matter? It's all pointless, empty, . . . galaxy upon galaxy but an accident, . . . your own awareness but an accident of evolution, without a meaning, . . . empty. .

. . You know that this is the truth of it, you've known it for years. . . . It always finds you in the end, the emptiness. . . . It all comes down to nothing, in the end, nothing."

The nothingness that lay behind the boredom was Filipo's greatest fear. Greniston could see it unmasked now. Filipo probably concealed his despair from his friends, from Gwen, even from himself sometimes, but Evil had found it out and laid it bare.

Don't give up, Greniston thought fiercely. Yet he knew this battle was Filipo's to fight.

It's hopeless, Filipo thought. *Miller is right*. Yet from somewhere deep within him, some seed of sheer stubbornness said, *Try*. He remembered the words of a Red Cross medic he had known once: "It's only when the mission seems impossible, and you try to do it anyway, that real life begins." From the depths of himself, Filipo summoned images of life, as if weaving them into being from nothingness.

"It is not all nothing," he coolly replied. "For how do you explain the reoccurring mystery of a five-petalled rose?"

"Nothing . . . ," the Evil replied.

"The love between a man and a woman?"

"Nothing . . ."

"The longing of the human heart for God?"

"Nothing . . . "

Slowly, a grin came over Filipo's face. He began to sing: "'I got plenty o' nothin' . . . '"

Greniston chimed in gladly, "' . . . and nothin's plenty fo' me!'" Despite the knife at his throat, Luan Tey began to laugh.

"As the fool said to Lear, 'Nothing will come of nothing, my lord,'" Greniston said.

"'But it ain't necessarily so,'" Filipo warbled in reply. "'It ain't nessa, ain't nessa, ain't necessarily so-o-o . . . '"

"Silence!" Miller yelled.

"Oh, come, come," Greniston replied, "where's your sense of humor, man? Or could it be," he added with a shrewd smile, "that we've found your little weak spot? Don't like to be laughed at, do you, old bean?"

"He can't stand it," Filipo agreed. Turning to Miller he said, "*Nothing*? It's only yourself you describe with that word. Powerful you may be, but it's a tawdry, empty power. You have no wit, no style. Hey, a dandelion has more magnificence than you, for it is filled with life. Hey, even death can lead to life, if one dies well. But you, you are up to nothing much."

Filipo paused. Moments before, he had felt alone and terrified. Now, a great mirth filled him, as if the spirits of all the jesters and wags since time began was flooding into him, adding their humor to his own. Laughter bubbled up from deep within him, like the water from some ancient spring.

"But I, on the other hand," he mused, "feel witty. . . . 'I feel witty, oh so witty, . . . '"

Handing his gun to Greniston, Filipo began to dance around the mound. The sight of the muscular Basque, twirling about and trying unsuccessfully to sing in a falsetto, was too much for Luan Tey. It was unbelievable to him that these two men could mock not only Miller but also the Evil he served, yet they were—and enjoying themselves, too. Laughter came over him again.

"Find it funny, do you, you little fool?" snapped Miller. Deliberately, slowly, he drew the knife across the other man's throat again, drawing fresh blood.

"How humorous will it be, Lord Greniston," Miller continued in a whisper, "When I hold a knife to the lovely throat of Miss Fields?" Greniston stared at him, all laughter drained from his face.

"Oh yes," laughed Miller, "I had several hours in which to do a little research on you and your situation. Would you be able to jest if she whom you love were beneath my knife? Or perhaps one of the Walmsley children? Claire, then? No, she would not be amusing, she cannot cry out. Perhaps little Wyatt, though?"

"You'll never get near them!" Greniston said.

Miller laughed. "Not tonight, perhaps, . . . but soon. Whenever I choose, in fact. And don't think that I haven't left instructions for my revenge, if any harm comes to me tonight. Men will do a great many inventive things for money, even if that money comes to them from beyond the grave."

Suddenly, it was very quiet on the mound. "I'm tired of this game," Miller said. "I'll have that treasure now, Lord Greniston."

***

Ten feet away, beneath the mounds, Logan made his last appeal. He had told every story he knew of Arthur and his knights: the pulling of the

451

sword from the stone, the quest for the Grail, the Fisher King, Sir Gawain and the Green Knight, the wonder of Camelot, the Lady of the Lake. With all the love and poetry he could muster, he had recalled Arthur's life to him. Now was the moment.

"Arthur, King of the Britains, the Once and Future King," he cried, "These are your deeds! Remember yourself, remember your Quest, and rise to be great again! Arthur!"

The children joined in the appeal, calling again and again, "Arthur! Arthur! Arthur!"

As for Gwen, she was suddenly propelled into action. She did not know what was happening on the mound above, she only knew that Greniston and Filipo needed her, now. She sprinted across the cavern and into the tunnel, scrambling to the surface. She took in the scene without even pausing to catch her breath.

"Unhand that man!" she yelled at Miller, brandishing her dagger. She only partly understood the look of shock on Miller's face. It was only later that she realized that the children, Logan, and Annie Lee had been close on her heels, seeming to emerge from the earth itself, all shouting, "Arthur! Arthur Pendragon!" at the top of their lungs. The Walmsley children waved their homemade spears, and Claire carried a grail banner, which flapped wildly in the rising wind.

Then everything seemed to happen at once. From the dark woods came the sound of mighty hoofbeats. A huge war steed burst from the trees and thundered onto the mound. Its mane and bridle gleamed with white fire. It glowed like the ghost of a horse, yet the weight of its stride was sure and mighty. And upon its back rode a man in gleaming golden chain mail—a king—whose golden crown was studded with emeralds, whose shield was emblazoned with a dragon rampant upon a field of stars.

"Arthur!" the children cried joyfully, as the gleaming apparition burst upon the mound.

Miller stared at the oncoming rider, and in his shock, loosened his grip on Luan Tey. Greniston leapt forward and pulled the man free. With the speed of wickedness itself, Miller darted forward to grab Wyatt, but before his hands could quite touch the boy, the horse and rider were upon him. The horse reared up, its gleaming hooves pawed the air as it whinnied and tossed its gleaming mane. Its rider stood in the saddle and lifted high his right arm, in which he held a shining spear that gleamed as if made of light itself.

"For God and the Good!" the rider cried in a deep, ringing voice that shook the night air like the tolling of great bells. The spear whistled through the darkness, and an instant later, Miller crumpled to the ground without a sound. He lay very still, face down upon the earth.

In the stunned silence that followed, horse and rider paced back and forth on the mound. Clouds of steam puffed from the horse's nostril, the leather of the saddle creaked, and the bridle jingled.

In a voice that rang with gladness, the rider called out, "Companions! Gather! Avaunt! The battle begins and calls to us!"

At first, there was only silence in reply. Then a wind began to circle the clearing, sighing through the branches of the oaks, lifting the children's' banners and capes. From the darkness between the trees, another horse and rider stepped forth, a ghostly rider formed of light. Then another, and another. . . .

"Gawaine!" the kingly rider cried. "Lancelot!"

"Arthur!" they exclaimed in glad reply.

Arthur, Gwen thought. *Yes, it is he, the Once and Future King, returned at the hour of greatest need.*

Ladies appeared now as well from the shadows, all mounted on palfreys and dapple grays, as if prepared to ride forth on a great quest.

"Nimue!" Arthur called in greeting, "Gwenevere!"

Whatever had happened whilst they lived, there was nothing but warmth in the look that passed between Arthur and his Queen now. Perhaps many matters heal themselves in so long a sleep.

"Bors! Pellinore! Elaine!" Arthur called out the names, as more and more riders began to gather, encircling the mound. Among their number, Logan saw not only knights and ladies of Arthur's court but also Gwydion, Taliesin, Tommy Greniston, even Emily Hewbridge, wearing a pith helmet and mounted on an army corps camel. There were other figures he did not recognize, as well: a Zulu warrior, an elderly Chinese gentleman mounted on a white donkey, a Bedouin princess on a white Arabian pony, a Peruvian peasant riding a llama, a pharaoh and two ancient Egyptian ladies on the backs of sleek lionesses. There were three Samurai and a veiled Geisha. He glimpsed St. Patrick, his face, as ever, alight with laughter, riding in the company of what seemed to be Robin Hood and his Merry Men, while nearby was Scheherazade accompanied by a Roman Centurion, and a cowboy from the Wild West. He saw a Hopi medicine woman and a piper from a company of Scots guards; a Greek maiden and Lord Peter Greniston, dashing in his Cavalier's uniform, sharing a chariot; and a musician from ancient Ethiopia. There were a Yankee Colonel and a Confederate lady and a black field hand, all riding side by side like old friends. Near at hand, a rabbi dressed in the garb of turn–of-the-century Poland struggled to keep a huge pile of books on his lap and still hold the reins of the shaggy pony he rode, who seemed inclined to wander onto the mound itself.

"Mirabai," the Rabbi whispered to the beautiful Hindu woman beside him, who was mounted upon a black panther, "help me with this *meshugginah* beast!"

The lady reached over and, with one gentle touch of her delicate hand, stilled the pony's fretting.

More and more ghostly riders arrived, circling the mound, filling the forest beyond. Arthur rode back and forth before them, reviewing his assembled troops. As his mighty steed cantered around the clearing, the sound of its hooves on the earth was very clear, as the thousand riders gathered there now grew quiet and looked up at their leader. With easy assurance, Arthur spurred his horse to the crest of the mound. He lifted his arm, and the chain mail that covered it seemed to ripple with white light.

"Comrades of the Quest!" Arthur cried in ringing tones, "Well met! Well met, you faithful ones, who have kept the Light alive! Long and long, some of Thee have waited! Now is thy moment, now is thy time!"

A sigh of joy passed through the gathered company, as a wind moves over treetops.

"Yes, Companions!" Arthur continued. "Now is the darkest hour! Now are we summoned by Merlin's cry to ride into battle once more! But it is a different battle this time, for we ride forth not to attack, but to inspire! Our swords will meet no clash of steel, our arrows pierce no hearts. We will be unseen by most, being to them at best but a whisper in their dreams, yet a whisper that can move a few to greatness, do they but hear! Companions, go now. As rain hurries to the parched earth, so must you ride into the world, seeking ever the places where you are most needed! Invisible you may be, yet your presence will haunt the world with courage, and hope, and the resolve never to give up! The world has sore need of such valor; there are hearts that wither for lack of it now! Speak to their dreams, inspire their thoughts! It

454

matters not if they never know from whence the inspirations come, so long as ye kindle their hearts with hope! Wherever evils grows, we shall grow a greater good! 'For God and the Good,' that is our Quest! Are ye with me, great hearts, or nay?"

"With you!" a thousand voices answered as one voice. Arthur laughed in pure joy. "Then soon, soon, shall we ride forth! But stay a moment. We must greet our newest knights."

The King of the Britons rode up to Greniston and Filipo, who stared at him, dumbfounded. Arthur gazed back at them—a measuring, man-to-man look.

"Glad to see you two up off your asses and useful at last," he said grimly, but with a faint smile on his face as he spoke. "Well done tonight," he added.

Next, he rode up to Annie Lee. To her, he bowed his head gravely, as if greeting fellow royalty. "So how do I smell?" he asked, with a wink.

"Pretty good," the Gypsy replied, "for someone who's been around a while."

Arthur laughed. When he reached Gwen, the King reined his horse to a stop, and looked down at her, his hands folded on the saddlebow.

Gwen was never able to describe exactly the features that gazed down at her then, save that it was the strongest face she had ever seen, and the light that looked out of its eyes seemed ancient in experience yet young in valor and joy. The proud, seasoned face of the king softened as it looked at her. Leaning forward, Arthur whispered gently, "Thank you, my Lady. Without you, this moment would never have been woven."

Before Gwen could reply, Arthur rode on, to Luan Tey, who stood in the shadows. No one ever knew what passed between them; the king spoke too quietly to be overheard.

Last of all, Arthur greeted Logan and the Walmsley children, who stood clustered together, gazing at him in utter awe.

Smiling broadly, Arthur pulled his sword from the scabbard and, lifting it high, cried out, "Witness now the knighting of the Faithful!"

Passing his sword over their heads as he spoke, Arthur called out their names: "Bard Logan, Lady Claire, Sir Osgood, Sir Wyatt, Sir Osborne, Sir Charles! From this time forward, be ye known to all the world as true knights of Arthur's Court, for true your hearts have proven!" In a gentler tone, he added, "Fear not, dear friends, we shall meet again. Upon my Honor, I avow it."

With that, the King turned back to face his ghostly troops.

"To the four corners of the globe, we now ride forth!" he cried. "We shall meet again someday, to take our ease in courts of gold and compare our tales. But for now, enough of such long disuse! The trumpet sounds, the time is nigh, Great Hearts! We are called to Life and the Quest once more!"

An answering cry of gladness rose up from the gathered company. "Hurrah! Avaunt!" a thousand ghostly voices called. A thousand ghostly faces shone with the joy of being called to action and to purpose again. A thousand ghostly riders sat poised and ready, taut as arrows fitted to the bow, waiting only for the final command to ride forth.

"For God and the Good!" Arthur cried, in a voice that seemed to echo to the very stars. "For God and the Good! Onward!"

"Onward!" the company cried in response. And suddenly, all the riders turned, and, as if they were one life, urged their mounts forward. They surged out from the mound in every direction, a wave of golden light flowing out into the darkness, as unstoppable as life itself. "Onward!" they cried in voices of wild joy. "Onward!"

Arthur's horse reared, and suddenly, there seemed to be two horses and two riders there—one formed of golden light, the other strangely familiar. The golden horse and rider leapt forth into the night, leaving behind them only the echo of Arthur's last "Onward!"

And there, on the crest of the mound, was Davey Lee, mounted on Chieftain, both of them daubed with phosphorescent paint and looking shaken.

"What happened?" Davey asked, in a croaked whisper.

"I was about to ask the same question of you," Greniston replied gently, noting the other man's white face and expression of shock.

"All I know," Davey said slowly, struggling to recall his own actions, "was that I got inspired by this Sherlock Holmes bloke—*Hound of the Baskervilles*. I knew a bit more about your meeting on the mound than I let on. Talks in his sleep, that Luan Tey does, especially with a fever. So, I thought you might need some extra help. Then I came across this Holmes story in your library, and there was already the legends of Arthur hereabouts, and it all kind of came together in me mind."

"So you decided to paint yourself and that horse with phosphorescent paint and thunder into the situation like 'Arthur of the Baskervilles'?"

Davey nodded. "Thought it might have a shock value, Guv, and stir things up in your favor." He paused, and shook his head confusedly. "That was me plan, but what really happened, I'm not sure. I remember slipping away from guard duty and daubing Chieftain and meself with the paint. Got it at the Tweeverton hardware store, earlier that day."

"I had expressly requested that no one leave the grounds," Greniston muttered.

Davey shrugged, as if to say that it was taken for granted that no rules ever applied to Romani folks a anyway. "I got the paint smeared on," he continued, "and rigged meself up a cloak." He looked rather ruefully at the blanket fastened at his throat with a safety pin. "I borrowed one of your ancestors' spare crowns," he indicated the baron's coronet which sat, not quite straight, on his dark, curly hair. "Found it just lying about in one of the library cases. Thought no self-respecting ghost could begrudge me the loan of it," he explained. "Anyway, I got meself all fitted up, thought it might do the trick, between darkness and the element of surprise. I got as far as the rowan tree on the other side of this oak grove, and suddenly, something seemed to come over Chieftain. He reared up, and I felt ice-cold, like someone had poured a bucket of snow right into my veins. Chieftain bolted at top speed for the mound, and that's all I remember, until now—except that I thought I saw . . . just for an instant, . . . but it couldn't have been . . . "

"Perhaps it was," replied Greniston. "We all saw it too."

Suddenly, from the edge of the clearing, Filipo gave a cry of dismay. "*Dios Mio!*" he exclaimed, "Miller's body is gone! And so is Luan Tey!"

The others spun around, staring at the spot where Miller had fallen. There was no trace of his body or of the spear that Arthur—if Arthur it had been—had hurled at him. And Luan Tey had vanished as swiftly as a shadow soaked into the night.

"Given us the slip," Greniston muttered. "I can't believe it! Maybe the two of them were in league all along!"

Annie Lee cleared her throat. "I assure you that Mr. Miller was dead. I felt his pulse; his heart had stopped. There was no wound of any kind," she added, "but on his face was a look of fear I could not smooth away. I am sure that Mr. Tey has taken his body away to spare you the trouble of being involved with the death. He knows how to deal with such situations. And you will find the pledge of his good faith there, upon the mound."

The others looked and saw two chalices, the true and the false, gleaming side by side there. "True," said Greniston softly. "Had he meant us harm, he would surely have taken the true one. Instead, it would seem we are in Mr. Tey's debt."

***

And then, as if there had been sufficient magic for one night, the whistle of the four-twenty-seven express, bound for Bristol from Tooten Waverly, echoed through the predawn darkness. Close upon it came the steady, reassuring note of the church bell, tolling the half hour.

Just then, Mr. and Mrs. Walmsley emerged from the mound, looking spattered with mud and out of breath. "The children!" Mrs. Walmsley exclaimed, rushing toward her brood as if hoping to gather them all into her arms at once.

"When Logan and Miss Fields didn't return, we decided to follow them down the secret passageway," Mr. Walmsley explained. "We would have been here much sooner, but when we got to that little chapel, something, I don't know what . . . "

"There was music," said Mrs. Walmsley, "music like none I've ever heard. It seemed to come from the stone above the altar, as if it was singing, somehow."

"Never heard anything so lovely in all my life," said Mr. Walmsley. "We stopped to listen for what we thought was a moment, but now I think it must have been hours."

"Yes," said Mrs. Walmsley, "it was as if the music caught us in a spell. Then, all of a sudden, it was over, and we came running here."

"I can see," mused Greniston, "that we're going to have quite a large christening to organize. Half of Far Tauverly seems to be in on the family secret now." He smiled, as if not displeased. "However, before we alert the Vicar, I suggest we head home for breakfast—and some brandy."

Gwen slipped her arm through Greniston's as they walked back to Greniston Manor. First light was softening the landscape to a misty gray, and the beginnings of bird song stirred among the trees as the little party made its way across the dewy lawns, each quiet, as if musing over the mysterious events of the night before, disinclined to speak of it yet glad to be with others who had shared the experience.

"We don't keep very regular hours, do we Miss Fields?" Greniston asked Gwen. "This seems to be the second night in a row that you and I have welcomed in the dawn. Or is it the third? Ah, I shall appreciate that brandy, and then," he added gratefully, "to bed."

"More likely to bath and a shave," Gwen corrected gently. "Have you forgotten? The hearing about the land starts in less than four hours."

CHAPTER TWENTY-THREE

"This is a very serious course of action," the solicitor said gravely. "Are you quite certain, Mr. Swindon, that you wish to pursue it?"

The pale figure in the hospital bed smiled wanly. "Quite certain." The faint sunlight of early morning filtered through the blinds, accentuating the grimness of the room.

"Once this motion is notarized and duly entered into the court records, there will be no turning back, you know," the solicitor said. "Speaking frankly, your recent injuries and shocks may be coloring your reason. I would strongly advise you to wait. I can still obtain a postponement of the hearing, given your health."

"Oh, for God's sake, Barkley," Swindon interrupted wearily, "just do what I've asked. Just do it."

"Very well," the other man replied stiffly.

***

Later that morning, the same solicitor entered the county courtroom in Tweeverton. The Judge had not yet entered, but the room was crowded and already in an uproar.

"Let's get this over with," someone yelled. "Everyone knows the land's Swindon's! Got the deeds to prove it, 'e does! Get the paperwork done, so we can bloody well start buildin' them condos and get some money movin' around here!"

"Right!" echoed many other voices.

"Bill Saxton, shame on you!" cried Mrs. Hodges, standing on one of the benches so as to be heard above the crowd. "That's been Greniston land time out of mind, and well you know it! Where's your loyalty?"

"Hear, hear," other voices echoed. "Grenistons have always been loyal to us, after all!"

"Hah!" someone else retorted. "Loyal to their own pocketbooks, more likely!"

"Outrageous!" exclaimed Althea Pennington, brandishing a rolled umbrella as if it were a sword.

Insults flew back and forth across the room like grenades, fists were clenched, feet were stamped. Barkeley, Swindon's solicitor, peered through the mayhem, looking for one particular face.

He recognized old Steadworthy. He had considerable respect for the man, for all his fussy, old-fashioned ways. And that unshaven, disgruntled-looking man Steadworthy was talking to had to be Greniston. He looked every inch the Lord of the Manor. It was not, however, these faces that the solicitor sought. There—that auburn-haired woman standing off to the side—that must be Miss Fields. She certainly fit Swindon's description of her, yet her appearance surprised the solicitor. He had not expected to see such intelligence looking out of her eyes or such gentleness in her manner.

She isn't a gold-digger at all, Barkley realized. *She is . . . a lady.* It was the only word that fit. He shook his head in wonderment. The case was proving to be far more interesting than he had anticipated.

***

Standing on the sidelines, Gwen watched the growing confusion with misgiving. Everything was happening so quickly that she found it hard to think clearly. They had arrived at the manor house to discover that everyone there had heard the same mysterious music that had enchanted Anne and Bob Walmsley. They had seemed confused, like people waking from a dream. Evidently, Miller had gone alone to the mound, and no trouble had come to those at the house. There had been no time to exchange stories of what had happened, only to drink strong coffee and hurry to the hearing. After the mysterious events of the night before, Gwen found the angry crowd in the courtroom to be crude, almost cartoon-like. Yet the situation was real, she reminded herself, and had to be dealt with.

Moments later, to the cry of "All Rise!" the Judge entered the court. He was young, for a judge. The Tweeverton/Far Tauverly district was his first appointment, and this hearing his first case of much importance. He was not looking forward to it at all. He would have preferred to be trout fishing on the River Beck, where he was usually to be found on a fine spring morning like this one.

He sat down with what he hoped was dignity. He could never be sure. The ridiculous wig and long robes always made him feel like a fool. He glared at everyone over his wire-rimmed glasses, trying to appear formidable.

One of the solicitors approached him from the side, thrusting some papers at him. The judge caught a few words: something about how a last-minute development changes everything. They always said things like that, these pushy solicitors from London. Trying to intimidate him.

"All right, all right," said the Judge, waving the man aside.

Steadworthy began the statement for the defense. As the old man's voice droned on, quoting minute regulations and a tiresome list of legal precedents gleaned from the last three hundred years of local history, the Judge found his mind wandering. Ah, to be seated now by the River Beck in the leafy shade of an elm, while the clear water flowed over the smooth brown stones, and somewhere in the shadows, a trout eyed his lure. Yes, that was the life, undisturbed by all this crowd and clamor.

" . . . for it is of prime importance that the land is undisturbed, and the wilderness remains unspoiled. . . ."

The Judge looked up, summoned from his reverie by these words, so sympathetic to his own thoughts. He wasn't sure what had happened in the last few minutes. Lord Greniston now seemed to be speaking in his own defense, while Steadworthy stood by with a long-suffering expression on his face.

" . . . this ancient land," Greniston rumbled, "with its irreplaceable oak forests, and its crystal streams . . . "

"Streams, did you say?" the Judge chimed in.

Greniston looked surprised at the interruption. "Yes, certainly. There are several streams which run through the Greniston land. . . ."

"Objection," Swindon's solicitor said. "The land *in question*. And your Honor, if I might take this moment to bring to your attention . . . "

"Streams," mused the Judge, dreamily. "Any trout in 'em?"

Greniston exchanged a confused glance with Steadworthy, who shook his head in equal bewilderment.

"Why, yes, I believe there are considerable trout there," Greniston said.

"Ah," replied the Judge, as if this was by far the most cogent point yet presented, "proceed."

"Yes, well, as I was saying, your Honor," Greniston continued, "it is of prime importance that this irreplaceable land remain undisturbed . . . "

"They don't like disturbance," the Judge remarked. Seeing Greniston's bewildered face, he added, "Trout. Can't abide a fuss."

"Enough of this," muttered a disgruntled voice from the crowd. "Just decide whose land it bloody well is, and get on with it!"

Once again, Swindon's solicitor was at the Judge's side, urging him to look at some papers.

"Oh, very well," the Judge snapped, as he turned his attention to the folder so rudely thrust upon him. Meanwhile, the debate in the room continued.

"It's Greniston land, right and proper," Mrs. Walmsley was saying hotly.

"Right you are, my dear," added the Vicar.

"In a pig's tiny eye it is," snarled Bill Saxton, who appeared to be the ringleader for the opposition. "That land's been in question for hundreds of years."

A near riot of exchanged insults followed, which only a full minute of gavel pounding managed to quell.

In the unwillingly silence that finally followed, the Judge adjusted his glasses and said calmly, "It is my happy duty to inform you that the land in question belongs neither to Lord Greniston nor to Geoffrey Swindon."

"What?" thundered Greniston. "What the devil are you talking about?"

Majestically ignoring this, the Judge continued, at his own slow pace: "The documents originally submitted did indeed substantiate Mr. Swindon's claim to the land . . . "

"The devil they did," muttered Greniston.

" . . . but he has seen fit to deed that land over to a third party—a Miss Gwendolyn Fields."

A murmur of shock rippled through the courtroom. For once, even Greniston was struck speechless.

"I understand that the lady is present here today. Miss Fields, will you please approach the bench?"

Dazed, Gwen stepped forward. The intensity of the last twenty-four hours was beginning to catch up with her. "I'm afraid I don't understand," she said.

The Judge smiled kindly at her. "It seems that Mr. Swindon has felt it best to deed the land in question over to you, Miss Fields. I take it this comes as a surprise?"

"Totally."

"Well, Mr. Swindon has enclosed a personal note to you which may help to explain his action. You are welcome to take a few moments to read it now, if you wish."

Gwen opened the envelope the Judge handed her.

"Dear Miss Fields," the note inside began. "After all the trouble I have caused you, I feel that the least I can do is to offer you a bit of the land that drew you to England in the first place. You love its woods and mounds for their own sake, perhaps even far more than either Greniston or I ever will. Therefore, it is only right that they should be in your keeping. I hope you will see fit to accept this deed as a parting gift from one who will forever remain your true admirer. I doubt that our paths will cross much in the future, but I shall always wish you well, whatever course your life takes. Sincerely, Geoffrey Swindon."

Reading these words, Gwen could only feel that Swindon had risen to the best of himself in writing them. Yet she felt she could scarcely accept the gift of acres of land from a man whose flowers she had refused just days before.

"This is very generous," she began, "But I feel I can scarcely accept so great a gift. . . ."

"I'm afraid it's a *fait accompli*, my dear," the Judge replied.

"Mr. Swindon has already legally signed the land over to you," his solicitor explained, "as if it had been left to you in a will. If you wish, in turn, to give it to someone else, that is, of course, your prerogative, but legal steps would need to be taken. For the moment, it belongs to you whether you like it or not. I suggest," he added, "that you accept it."

"And just how much land have I been given?" Gwen asked.

"Ah," said the Judge, pulling a map out of the sheaf of papers, "everything within the red lines, my dear."

Gwen met the second shock of the day. The area outlined on the map included not only the mounds but the entirety of Greniston Woods and a large expanse of open fields.

"My goodness!" she exclaimed, "it's huge. Why, this must include . . . ."

"Almost half of the Greniston property," the solicitor finished for her. "Some eighty-three acres of first-rate, ideally located land, to be exact. Should you ever decide to sell it, Miss Fields, you would find yourself very comfortably provided for, very comfortably indeed."

"Oh, I could never do that!" Gwen exclaimed.

"Nonetheless," the solicitor said with a smile, "it's nice to know these things."

"What the devil is going on up there?" Greniston thundered, his patience at an end. "Does she have the land or doesn't she?"

"She does," said Gwen, turning to face him.

A hush fell over the court. Gwen felt acutely aware of all the faces looking at her: Filipo's, Logan's, and others, full of support; Greniston's torn between relief and wounded pride that Swindon had dared to present so great a gift to her; and other faces like Bill Saxton's, speculating faces, clearly wondering what the relationship between herself and Swindon had been, wondering if she could be bought or bribed or threatened.

"In light of this unexpected turn of events," Mr. Steadworthy was saying to the Judge, "I move that this hearing be adjourned to allow Lord Greniston and Miss Fields to confer about this surprising new development."

"Granted," said the Judge, pounding his gavel.

Gwen turned toward Greniston, but before she got three steps, Bill Saxton's voice called out, "Wait a bloody minute! What about us! We've been counting on this building project. We've got mouths to feed at home, and I for one would like to know if it's going to happen or not! So what about it, Luv, what are you planning to do with the land, now that you've got your mitts on it?"

Greniston lunged toward Saxton, only to be held back by Filipo, who murmured, "Steady, pal, you don't need to add assault and battery to your list of woes."

At the same time, the Judge leaned forward and said to Gwen, "You are under no obligation to answer anyone's questions."

"It's all right," said Gwen, "I want to."

She turned to face the crowd, and a hush fell over the room. For the briefest moment, her mind flashed back to her first entry into Far Tauverly, a stranger in the village. She had experienced lifetimes in a matter of weeks. Was all that had happened already somehow present in that first moment, like a seed waiting in the earth? "You must understand," she began, "that I've only owned this land for" - she glanced at the clock on the wall - "twelve minutes. So there is a great deal I need to think about. It's a responsibility I never dreamed would fall to me. . . ."

"Cut to the chase, Sweetie," one of Bill Saxton's mates yelled, "Are you taking up Swindon's building deal, or not?"

"Certainly not," Gwen replied coolly. Greniston smiled triumphantly.

465

"She'll leave it to be Greniston land, every inch of it!" snapped Althea Pennington.

Gwen took a deep breath. "Not necessarily," she said.

"What the devil?" exclaimed Greniston, rising from his seat.

Gwen felt she could not bear to look him in the face, or anyone else, for that matter. She felt that what she was about to say would please no one, yet it had to be said.

"It may well be," she began, "that the best thing to do is to deed this land over to Lord Greniston, so that it belongs to him legally as well as historically."

"I should say so," growled Greniston, somewhat appeased.

"And yet," Gwen continued, "although I have been here only a short while, it's clear to me that the economy of Far Tauverly is struggling and that anything that brings jobs into the area would be welcome."

"Bloody right," muttered several voices.

"At the same time, it's clear that there are parts of the land that must remain forever undisturbed—most especially the mounds and the woods. We would never want to build condos or a shopping mall over them."

This statement was greeted by boos and hisses from Bill Saxton's crowd. "What's wrong with shopping malls?" an old woman in the back muttered.

Wistfully, Gwen wondered what one of Henrietta Amberly's heroines would do in a situation like hers. *Their* stories often resolved with the heroine inheriting unexpected millions. For *them*, things always worked out like a fairy tale. Glancing at Greniston's dark face, she was not sure that things would work out so smoothly for her. The temptation to make the deed over to him then and there was very strong, yet she knew that if she did so, it would be for the wrong reason, out of the fear of losing him, rather than because she was sure it was the right thing to do. A line from an old poem came to her mind: "I would not love thee half so much, my dear, loved I not honour more." She clung to the thought like a lifeline.

In a shaking voice, she continued, "I know this must seem totally unsatisfactory all the way around," she said, "but you see, I need time to think about this. Somehow, by chance or fate, this land has been thrust upon me. I never expected to be in such a situation, but now that I am, I mean to be very careful. I want to do what is best for everyone; Lord Greniston, those who need jobs, and the land itself, if I possibly can. I don't have a quick solution to sort it all out, but in my experience, quick solutions bring quick disasters on their heels. So I need to think about all this, and I refuse to be forced into a quick decision about it—by either party. That's all I have to say for now," she finished, in a voice that had grown so soft the listeners had to strain to hear her.

Greniston leapt from his seat and charged toward the door. Gwen caught just a glimpse of his face as he stormed past her, but that glimpse was enough to confirm her worst fears: his features were set in an icy mask of control far worse than any rage. Their eyes met for an instant, and in that instant, he managed to look through her as if she were not there at all.

Gwen fought back tears. Mr. Steadworthy appeared at her side, offering her a very clean, white handkerchief. She felt Logan take her arm on one side, and Filipo on the other.

"Come away now," Logan said. "Tweeverton boasts a couple of decent pubs, and I'm sure we could all use a pint—or two."

As they started for the door, Bill Saxton muttered, just loudly enough to be heard by all, "Aye, the conniving little wench! Romanced both Swindon and Greniston, no doubt, just to see what she could get out of it! Not even from around 'ere, bloody little foreign tart!"

A flush of shock and outrage rose in Gwen's cheeks. She looked around for something to hurl at Saxton, preferably something large, like a chair, when, to everyone's surprise, Logan stepped up to the man and grabbed him by the collar.

"Now you listen to me, Bill Saxton," he said, speaking very slowly and distinctly. "You're a sneaky, crafty, cowardly little worm of a man, and you always have been. I'm Far Tauverly born and bred, and I've as much right to speak for it as anyone here. I don't have a problem with one word Miss Fields has said here today. As for any aspersions on her honor, you utter one more syllable like that, and I will personally beat the living piss out of you. And I'll enjoy it, too."

When Logan finished, there was not a sound to be heard in the room. Everyone stared as if they could not believe that Logan Knowelles, town gossip and cadger of drinks, was actually threatening to trounce a bully half his age and twice his size. Bill Saxton himself looked incredulous. He tried to give a scoffing retort, but the sound died in his throat. Logan's dark blue eyes gleamed with a resolute fire never seen there before.

"I'd tell you to apologize," Logan added, "but an apology from you wouldn't be worth the lady's bother. Just remember, one more word out of you about her now, or ever, and you'll have me to reckon with."

"And me," said Filipo.

"And me," said Robert, Mr. Steadworthy, Davey Lee, and Mr. Walmsley, in one voice.

"And us as well," chimed in Osgood, Wyatt, Osborn, and Charles.

"And me," added the judge.

Bill Saxton blinked and looked from face to face. Then, muttering something that might have been an apology or possibly a curse, he slunk from the room.

***

A few minutes later, across the street at the Woolsack, Gwen was touched by a further show of support. Everyone from Mrs. Hodges to the Vicar came in to have a pint, as if to let her know she was still in their good graces. Even a few of Bill Saxton's crowd showed up to let her know that "'e went too far, Miss, that 'e did."

At any other time, Gwen would have been inspired by such a show of good heartedness. Yet now, what stood out the most in the circle of the friendly faces was the one face that was absent, the one face Gwen feared she would never see again. *Greniston*, she thought, utterly miserable. *Oh, Greniston!*

As soon as she decently could, Gwen whispered her apologies to Logan and slipped away from the gathering. Once outside, she headed toward the open fields that led to Far Tauverly, glad that there, at least, no one would see the flood of tears she could no longer restrain.

***

In another pub in Tweeverton, a conversation between old friends was taking place. At a booth in the Rose and Swan, Greniston sat nursing a brandy. It was his third brandy, but the food he had ordered was scarcely touched.

Perhaps it was the brandy, perhaps it was a lack of sleep, but he seemed to hear Deirdre's voice in his mind.

"Well," she said, "you certainly let yourself down back there," she remarked with annoying cheerfulness.

Get out of my mind, Greniston muttered gracelessly.

"Yes," Deirdre's voice continued, "You really let yourself down, walking out on Miss Fields, like that."

"Me, walking out on her?" Greniston exclaimed out loud, so that the waiter glanced nervously at the seemingly empty seat across from him.

"Hush, dear," Deirdre replied sweetly.

It seemed to Greniston that he could almost see her, sitting across from him. In his mind's eye, she was wearing a chic, lemon-colored sheath and a huge navy-blue straw hat, with elbow length blue gloves to match. In one hand, she casually held an ivory cigarette holder, which sported a jasmine-scented cigarette. From her dress and mannerisms, he deduced that she was in her twenties mode, the way she always was when she had a part in a Noel Coward play.

"Certainly you walked out on her," the Deirdre in his mind now said. "And at her hour of greatest need. All those wretched country people insulting her, everyone so sure they knew what needs to be done, and her all alone with the responsibility of it. I would have expected you to rush to her side, and say to one and all, 'Miss Fields has come by this property fair and square, and I support her in any choice she makes about it, for she is the love of my life, and I respect her judgment more than my own.'"

That's what you would have expected me to say? Greniston replied in his mind, in tones rich with disgust.

"Something like that." Deirdre's attention was momentarily distracted by his plate of food.

"What is that?" she asked in his imagination, poking at his plate with her own fork, a habit of hers he realized he had always particularly disliked.

It's supposed to be Shepherd's Pie.

Deirdre wrinkled her adorable nose. "Looks more like the shepherd's socks. Still, 'twill do ye good, lad. Eat." Then, seeing that he wasn't going to, she began to nibble at his bread. He had forgotten that in between her bouts of self-starvation, Deirdre had a hearty ability to enjoy food, especially when he himself was suffering and couldn't swallow a bite.

I swear, Deirdre, he muttered, *you could probably chow down at a funeral.*

"Indeed, I could," the Deirdre in his mind replied. "A proper funeral should offer cold meat, three salads, and the Guinness should flow unstintingly as God's Mercy. At least, that's how they do it in Dublin town, where folk know how to die. Miss Fields will probably still have you," she added, "if you approach her right."

"She still have me?" Greniston thundered aloud, forgetting himself.

Now he could see Deirdre's face very clearly in his mind. She had dropped her brittle, sophisticated act; it was the real Deirdre he saw now. In her blue eyes, he saw the soul of the Irish, the saddest, merriest race on earth, looking at him with all its centuries of mad, haunted wisdom.

"If you lose this Miss Gwendolyn Fields," this Deirdre said gently, "you'll never find another treasure like her. Is that worth sacrificing to your wounded pride?"

With that, Deirdre seemed to walk out of his mind, as quietly as someone making a swift exit, stage right. He found himself gazing at the empty seat across from him.

She always did find a way to have the last word, he thought ruefully, *and she was always right, too. I see that hasn't changed.*

Turning to the waiter, he said, "Coffee, please. It appears I need to wake up."

***

Gwen stood alone upon the mound. She had been crying for over an hour, but now her store of tears seemed spent. Her misery about Greniston had become a heavy lump of sorrow wrapped around her heart. She did not expect that it would ever lift, no matter how long she lived.

That she had lost him was clear to her. A proud nature like his would never forgive the insult she had caused him in front of just about every citizen of Far Tauverly.

"Oh, why didn't I think?" she muttered to herself for the hundredth time that morning. She did not for a moment regret her decision to consider the land carefully before acting. But she bitterly regretted her tactless expression of it. The graceful phrases she might have spoken now came effortlessly to mind: "The future of this land is of course something which I must discuss with Lord Greniston, who has held it in trust for so long." That would have saved his pride nicely. Or, "I'm sure that Lord Greniston as well as myself will take every consideration of the best step for all." That would have done. But no, she had blurted out the first things that came to her mind. "Forthright," she had always called that part of her character. She had even been proud of it. Now she saw that there was a fine line between valor and sheer thoughtlessness. She thought she had learned her lesson when she had impulsively invited the Walmsleys to Greniston Manor, but evidently not. This time, she did not think the damage would be so easy to repair. It seemed a bitter price to pay, to learn this home truth about herself at the expense of all future happiness.

Again, her eyes filled with tears. She looked at the mound and thought of how, just a few hours before, she and Greniston had walked away from it arm in arm. Then, everything had been possible. Like many another lover before her, Gwen wished with all her heart that she could turn back the clock but half a day.

She thought of some lines Filipo was fond of quoting: "The moving finger writes, and having writ, moves on, nor all your piety nor all your wit can cancel out a word of it."

Never had the old words seemed more vividly true to her. Yet, for all her sorrow, Gwen also felt a strange sense of satisfaction. She had chosen her own course of action. Up until now, it seemed to her that, underneath her "independent spirit" she had still always been trying either to please someone or to rebel against someone. Ever since choosing to come to England, she had stayed true to her own instinct, with no compromises. In the midst of all her loneliness, this fact felt somehow reassuring to know. And this moment, standing now upon the land, was where her own choices had led her.

I 'own' this land, she realized, the fact of it slowly beginning to dawn upon her. *Me, who never owned anything more than a second-hand VW bug with a bad alignment*, she laughed.

Yet, even as she thought the words, she knew they were not true. If anything, the land owned her. It belonged only to itself. She was there simply to care for it and protect it.

How am I even going to pay the taxes? she wondered. *I'm sure I don't have a job anymore.* She sighed. *I've lost everything*, she thought, *my old life, Greniston; yet I've gained this land to care for, and I've gained myself, somehow. Yet what am I to do? I don't even have the train fare to get back to the airport. And, oh, shit, my luggage is all at the manor; I can't bear the thought of going back there!* Not knowing whether to laugh or cry, she did both.

"Miss Fields?" She whirled around, her heart racing.

"I believe this is the only time I've met you here that one or both of us hasn't been soaked with rain," a familiar voice said, "although looking at your tear-stained face, it seems you've been trying to supply the moisture nature has failed to provide."

"Greniston!"

"It would seem so."

They stood, gazing at each other. All around them, the woods rang with birdsong. The sun shone radiant through fresh leaves, the high, windy sky was blue and clear.

If this is our last moment together, at least it will be a beautiful one, thought Gwen. *I shall always remember this: the feel of the breeze on my forehead, the scent of the hyacinths, and his face, every line, every curve, every shadow of his face. I should have known he'd be a gentleman and at least say good-bye.*

She felt that she should rise to some equally noble gesture. Struggling to hold back a fresh wave of tears, she blurted out, "I'm sorry," only to realize that Greniston had spoken the same words at the same time. For a moment, they stared at each other, and then, before she even knew what was happening, Greniston had rushed to her and gone down on one knee before her.

"Miss Fields," he said, "I've been the greatest fool that has ever lived, but I hope, I pray, that there is still time to repair that. Damn it, what I'm trying to say is, will you marry me?"

"Marry you?" Gwen asked faintly.

"It strikes you as absurd, I can see that," Greniston said ruefully. "I can't say I blame you, after the weakness you've seen in my character. But I swear to you, Miss Fields, Gwen, if you but allow me to prove it, I will protect and cherish you all the days of my life. I don't give a damn about losing this land compared to the thought of losing you."

Gwen hurled herself into his arms and clung to him so tightly it seemed that she would never let him go. For several minutes, no words were spoken. At last, when Greniston had disentangled himself from her lips and hair enough to speak, he murmured, "Am I to take this as a 'Yes,' then?"

***

Half an hour later, the sentinels on the roof of Greniston Manor were rewarded by a cry of "They are coming! Miss Fields and Lord Gweniston are coming!"

"How does it look?" cried Filipo, rushing to Wyatt's side.

"They appear to be hand in hand," said Logan, the most far-sighted of them all.

"Oh, I hope that bodes well," whispered Mrs. Fitzpatrick, who was clutching her rosary in one hand.

"Wait!" Logan said. "They've stopped. They're speaking. Ah, they're in each other's arms." A sigh of relief escaped from the gathered watchers.

"Saints be praised," said Mrs. Fitzpatrick. "Now I'd better go put on the kettle for tea."

CHAPTER TWENTY-FOUR

Some twenty hours later, Luan Tey stood on the deck of Miller's private yacht in the Aegean Sea. He checked his watch and nodded with satisfaction. Three minutes left. He would just have time briefly to admire the sunset, now staining the sky with extravagant streaks of wine and gold, before the yacht was blown to smithereens.

He did not attempt to escape the ship; he doubted that there was time for him to do so. Nonetheless, he smiled, as he gazed at the western sky, the smile of one who has completed a difficult job well and knows it. It had taken all of his skill and cunning to drag Miller's body to the car parked near the woods, sneak back to the flat in Bath and destroy all of the records there so that no trace of the formula or its purpose remained, and then devise a way to dispose of Miller's corpse. That, at first, had stumped Luan Tey, but as he gazed at his former employer's collection of statuary, inspiration struck.

He himself had escorted the packing case to Miller's private jet. "Roman statue, for the yacht," he had explained. "Not to go through customs," he added, for the pilot's benefit. This was nothing new; the amount of illegal artwork that Miller's connections smuggled over borders was considerable. It was almost routine, to bring one more such package to Greece.

"Must be life size," the sailors remarked as they loaded the case onto the yacht.

"Almost," Luan Tey had replied.

"Valuable?" another sailor asked.

The butler shrugged. "Some might say it's worth a lot of money. But it is as ugly as sin, I tell you."

The men had laughed at that and had suspected nothing when he told them to bring the yacht to the open sea and then return to shore in the motor boat.

"Mr. Miller is arriving later by helicopter, with a guest. A private meeting." The men had nodded. This, too, was nothing unusual.

As soon as he was alone on the ship, Luan Tey set about destroying every scrap of paperwork and computer file on board. He wanted to take no chances that any atom of Miller's terrible information would survive the explosion. Miller's body, he left in the packing case. It seemed an ironically fitting coffin.

He had a moment's regret at the destruction of so much artwork, including the actual canvas of Rembrandt's "David Playing the Harp for Saul." However, its beauty could not compare, for him, with the faces of a few people in a village called Far Tauverly. If he could manage to draw the trail away from them and secure some safety for their lives, he would sacrifice all the artwork in the world. He did not delude himself that this last action would redeem his life. Only an act of God could convince him that he could ever be clean or welcome in the world. He did not think that such an act was likely to . . .

The explosion was so violent that it sloshed the soup in the bowls of a fisherman's family, on a tiny island nearby. "Holy Christ!" the father exclaimed, as his wife and daughter crossed themselves.

He ran to his boat and rowed toward the wreck. Flames lit the darkening sky. He rowed back with a heavy heart.

"No one could have survived that," he told his wife. He was amazed, therefore, the next morning, when his daughter came running to him, saying "Papa! Papa! There's a man on the beach, and I think he's alive!"

The man was lying very still on a scrap of board that must have served him as a raft. *He must be dead*, the fisherman thought. Just then, the corpse stirred and moaned.

"Holy Christ!" the fisherman cried, "He is alive! Eirene, run, tell your mother! Get blankets!"

***

Three days later, Luan Tey awoke to find himself on a narrow bed in a small, whitewashed room. He was covered with bright blankets that smelled of goat. On the wall before him was a vividly painted picture of the Virgin Mary and a calendar with a picture of the Acropolis that said, "Athenopolis Insurance! We cover you in the best of luck!"

Luan Tey blinked. Wherever he was, it was probably not heaven and certainly not hell. He tried to sit up and fell back in a searing wash of nausea and pain.

I am alive, he thought with amazement, *I am alive!*

In the yard outside, he heard the bleating of goats and the sweet voice of a little girl, singing a nonsense song to herself.

I am alive, he thought again. And he wept with joy and pain, as one newly born.

***

And so it was that some three weeks later, Lord Greniston handed Gwen a postcard over breakfast at Greniston Manor.

"This looks like the Hagia Sophia," Gwen remarked, glancing at the photograph on one side.

"Yes, it's from Istanbul. No return address, but I think you'll recognize who sent it."

Curious, Gwen turned the card over. The message there was printed in a crude but careful hand. "Dear Lord Greniston," she read, "Thank you. Have no concern about business matters. All is taken care of." Following this, there was no signature, only a quotation: "Let the deep, deep sea keep him up."

"That's from *Lord Jim*," Gwen said. "Do you think . . . ?"

Greniston nodded. "I do."

"Thank God," Gwen said with relief. She and Greniston had seen the news of Miller's supposed death on his yacht; it had been front-page news on every paper for days. The stories claimed that Miller, his butler, and an unknown "Mystery Guest" had been the only people on board at the time. She wondered how Luan Tey had escaped, after all, and under what new name he would lose himself, in what distant city, hoping to start his life again as just one more face among so many. She hoped this fresh start would be under a better star than his first birth, but she realized, wistfully, that she would probably never know. Yet just the news that he was alive was happy indeed.

There had been many glad tidings in the last three weeks. For one thing, Mrs. Fitzpatrick and Mr. Steadworthy had eloped.

"Run off to Gretna Green like a pair of teenagers," Greniston had exclaimed in amazement, when he had found Mrs. Fitz's apologetic but patently joyful note on his desk one morning. "And she recommends Mrs. Walmsley to replace her as housekeeper!"

"That's an excellent idea," Gwen had said quickly. Actually, Mrs. Walmsley's housekeeping of even her family quarters left a lot to be desired. It was hard to imagine the whole of Greniston Manor under her care, but Gwen could see that, relieved of constant worry over where the next penny was coming from, Mrs. Walmsley had the ability to fill a house with gentleness and welcome, and that was worth more than all the perfectly polished silver in the world.

"You know those children will infiltrate every cranny of our privacy," Greniston grumbled.

"Children are supposed to do that," Gwen pointed out mildly.

Greniston sighed with mock martyrdom. "Well, dear, if you are happy with her work, I suppose I can't complain. And since Bob Walmsley will be here more or less full-time for good, it does make sense to have them all live here permanently, God help us." All complaint had melted as he looked into her eyes and added, "After all, the soon-to-be Lady Greniston should choose whatever bloody housekeeper she desires."

"Speaking of additions to the staff," Greniston had added, "I've been thinking that it's high time I hired Logan. He's been telling people he's the steward here for so long, I'm beginning to feel I owe him back wages."

"That would be wonderful!" Gwen said eagerly. "He can't continue as a postman forever."

"Exactly," agreed Greniston. "As Steward here, he wouldn't have to do any of the heavy work. Bob Walmsley and Robert can see to that. Logan can orchestrate, design a beautiful garden or two for them to plant, relax a bit, quote a poem, tell a tale, and be a bard in residence, that is, if he would want the position."

"Oh, I think he would," Gwen said fervently.

Greniston frowned. "I suppose he could live at Kestrel Farm," he mused, but it's awfully far away. . . ."

"Ummm . . . that might not be an option, anyway," Gwen said.

"What do you mean?" Greniston asked.

Hoping that Logan would forgive her, Gwen launched into the tale of Logan's tax problems. By the time she had finished, Greniston was wiping his eyes. "I swear," he said, "I don't know whether to laugh or cry! Only a Master of Avoidance could let it get this far! But why didn't Logan tell me long ago? I'll be glad to help him; it's not that big a sum!"

Thank God, thought Gwen. Aloud she said, "Well, he has his pride. He wouldn't want to just take a loan, no matter how generously you offered it, especially a loan so huge that you'd both know he could never repay it."

"True," admitted Greniston regretfully. "Still, there's got to be a way. I could call it an advance on his salary as Steward, but I want him to have that for spending money."

For a few minutes, Grenistons had stared moodily into the distance, his brow furrowed in thought. Then his face relaxed into a broad smile, and he cried, "I've got it!"

"Yes?" Gwen asked eagerly.

"It's your own idea, actually," Greniston replied. "Remember a few days ago, when you told me you thought Lord Peter's diaries should be edited and published? Well, who better to do the job than Logan? He knows the locale, the history, the folklore. He could edit the diaries with real sensitivity, and write a brilliant introduction, footnotes, select illustrations..."

"It's perfect for him!" agreed Gwen joyfully.

"If we can't find a publisher for it, I'll publish it myself," Greniston continued. "I'd like to see it happen. And I'll offer Logan an up-front sum that should take care of the taxes. That way, it doesn't deplete his regular salary, yet he can earn it . . . "

"And be happy doing it! Oh, thank you," cried Gwen, throwing her arms around Greniston.

For several minutes, no more words had been spoken. It was some time later that Greniston had remarked, "I still don't like to think of him living at that farm, it's too isolated. We can offer him a room here, of course, but that may not be isolated enough; he's a man that likes his solitude sometimes."

"Well," said Gwen, "There's Shalimar House."

"Shalimar House!" exclaimed Greniston, "Good Lord, I forget that place exists for years on end! Oh, no, that would never do!"

"Why not?"

"My darling," Greniston had said gently, "because it's surely a ruin of mildew and moths."

"No, it's not," Gwen had volunteered, "it looks pretty good inside, really."

"Aha!" Greniston had exclaimed. "So you and Logan have been indulging in a little breaking and entry!"

"It was more like bending and entry," Gwen had protested. "The lock was very rusty. Anyway, it looks quite good inside, if you see past the cobwebs and dust. Logan loves it."

"It's haunted," Greniston had cautioned.

"That's part of what he loves," Gwen had said.

Laughing, Greniston had thrown up his hands. "Very well, I know when I'm beaten! If Logan wants Shalimar House, he shall have it! I'll send in the painters and repairmen right away, and he can give his notice to Her Majesty's Postal Service."

For the second time in less than an hour, Gwen had thrown her arms around Greniston.

"Ah, my treasure," her beloved had murmured, after several minutes of eloquent, non-verbal communication, "forget this foolish wedding business, and follow the excellent example set by our elders—elope with me, this very day!"

Sorely tempted, Gwen nonetheless said, "It's only twelve more days."

"An eternity," Greniston had groaned, burying his face in her hair. "How can you be so cruel? Not only do you want a wedding complete with nut cups and in-laws and disgusting little cherubs carrying rings on pillows, but you insist on returning every night to that wretched cell of a room at the inn!"

"It is not a 'wretched cell,'" Gwen had protested, laughing. More earnestly, she added, "Please try to understand, in a place like this, people are old-fashioned, and they talk. Maybe it's silly, but I don't want there to be any scandal surrounding our marriage. I want everything to be as clean and fine and bold as the love we feel for each other! I intend to get married only once, and I want it to do it right."

"It's all right, it's all right," Greniston had laughingly interrupted, pulling her closer than ever. "I do understand, at least as much as a man can understand a fascination with decorum, lace, and engraved invitations. Just remember, once the wedding is over, it's my turn to set the tone, and I intend to whisk you off to the far ends of the earth and swathe you in ropes of Oriental pearl."

"And just where," Gwen had said sweetly, "are the far ends of the earth?"

"Oh no, you don't," her love replied. "Thy dewy eyes and honeyed lips shall not trick that secret from me! The honeymoon's to be a surprise, and that's that."

"But I need to know what to wear," Gwen had protested, only half teasingly.

"Fine. We're going to Thailand. Or is it Tierra del Fuego? No, that's right, it's Cape Town. Or Cairo."

"Egypt, or Illinois?" Gwen had asked with a sigh.

Her beloved had not replied.

Gwen's concern about what to wear on the honeymoon was not totally feigned. Her funds for buying a trousseau were not exactly unlimited; indeed, it was only thanks to the generosity of Trish and Mrs. Gordon that she had any funds at all.

It had seemed almost redundant to call Mercury Travel and formally quit, but Gwen felt that sheer courtesy demanded it. She had used the last of her traveler's checks to call from the inn.

Trish answered and, to Gwen's surprise, had been thrilled for her and very kind. She had even offered to send Gwen her last paycheck and call her landlord to let him know that Filipo would be back in a few weeks to move out her things.

"It's very good of you," Gwen had said gratefully, "after I just disappeared like that."

Trish had laughed. "Oh, we all had an intuition you might have found romance. Mrs. Gordon was so sure of it that she bet me fifty bucks you'd get yourself a husband, just like one of Henrietta Amberly's heroines. She'll be so happy for you. You've got to call her! By the way, she was so certain that you'd be staying in England that she's got a job all lined up for you over there."

"What?" Gwen had exclaimed. "What is it?"

"Oh, you probably wouldn't be interested in it, marrying a Lord and all."

"I'm interested, I'm interested," Gwen had interrupted. She didn't know how she could ever explain to Trish that as silly as it sounded, she didn't want to be entirely dependent on Greniston. She certainly could never afford to pay half the taxes on Greniston Manor, let alone on the land she had been given, which Greniston now amiably called "your land," and which she always amended to "our land." Yet she felt a need to contribute something substantial to her own expenses, although Greniston didn't want her to worry about it at all.

Fortunately, Trish didn't probe her motives too deeply. She seemed relieved that Gwen was interested. "It's a great idea, actually," she said. "It's very popular, right now, these literary tours: 'See Shakespeare's England,' or 'Visit Dickens' London,' that sort of thing. Mrs. Gordon felt that with your background in English literature and being over there and all, you could create the very best tours of their kind, for our agency, right here in Denver. You create the tours, and we'll find the clients. Mrs. Gordon is willing to invest, because she's sure it will make a profit. So am I, that is, if you're willing."

"Oh, yes," Gwen had said.

"Terrific," Trish had said. "Of course, you'll need to have a little office there and some tour buses, a secretary, drivers, mechanics, a few guides. They'd have to start on a per-job basis, but if it's successful, they'd have the opportunity to become staff."

Mentally, Gwen calculated how many jobs this might bring to Far Tauverly and decided it was good for twenty, at least. The jobs might not pay as much as the construction work, but they would last longer. It would be a start, at least.

"Of course, you're probably so busy with wedding plans," Trish had continued, "but if we could have something in place for a year from now, for next spring, say, that would be great. Of course, that would mean starting right away."

"Believe me," Gwen had said, "I can."

"I'll speak to Mrs. Gordon, then, and get an account set up to get you started."

And so, to her great relief, Gwen had found herself not only employed again and able to indulge in buying a modest trousseau but also able to fulfill her promise to Logan to do some traveling around England. He helped her evaluate pubs and inns in Somerset and Devon; together they went as far as Stonehenge, Tintagel, and Oxford. They even went on a three-day visit to Wales, a journey that seemed to fill Logan with a kind of mystic contentment, as he was at last able to see the little seaside village his mother had come from,

Yes, Gwen realized, many needs had been woven together happily in the last few weeks. Now, the arrival of the postcard from Luan Tey assured her than yet another life was finding a fresh start out of the strange events surrounding Merlin's cry. Yet there were still loose ends that concerned her, and not the least of these was Geoffrey Swindon.

***

At that moment, some forty miles away, Geoffrey Swindon gazed out at the rain that was drumming steadily on the green expanse of lawn. On sunny days, the grounds of Tinsdale's Rest Home were dotted here and there

481

with blanketed figures in wheelchairs and lovely young nurses in crisp white uniforms. There were only young and lovely nurses at Tinsdale's. Today, however, the lawn was deserted, save for the dripping rhododendron bushes and a rococo fountain, complete with nymphs and cupids, which continued to splash, rather foolishly, in the downpour.

Swindon sighed. The gray day filled his room with a sad half-light, but he did not move to turn on the lamp by his bedside table. The grayness suited his mood. Outside, in the hallway, he heard two nurses conversing in low, subdued tones. There were only low and subdued tones at Tinsdale's. Then the nurses moved on, and the quiet settled in again. That was what it was like here; one lay in one's bed like a stone at the bottom of the pond. Occasionally, there was a flurry of movement, then the stillness settled in around one again.

Swindon fumbled for a cigarette, lit it, and then lay back on the pillows. He was exhausted by even that small effort. Yet the doctors had told him that he was ready to go home.

"Movement is just what you need," Doctor Stansworth had said crisply. He, of course, had been the ruddy-faced, overworked young chief of staff at the county hospital to which Swindon had first been taken. The staff at Tinsdale's did not speak to patients like that. At Tinsdale's, there were only grave looks and sympathetic nods. That was what one paid so very well for, along with the unacknowledged infringements, like smoking in one's bed. Tinsdale's was a haven for those who wished to be ill. Swindon knew this very well.

When the time had come for him to check out of the county hospital, he had not been able to face going home. Every room, every hallway, every view of that house had been too full of thoughts of Gwen for him to endure. Not that she had ever seen his home, but he had imagined her in every part of it.

His mother and sister had been relieved when he announced his decision to check into the rest home.

"Much the better choice, dear," his mother had said. "Not that we wouldn't want to have you at home, but here, they can provide you with the care you need."

Privately, Swindon didn't see why two able-bodied women couldn't bring the occasional breakfast tray to his bed or at least tax their hands by writing a check for a hired nurse, but he said nothing. He didn't want their attentions, anyway; the care of strangers seemed preferable by far.

Still, his mother had lingered by his bedside with a worried look in her eyes. At last, she had said, "There's just one thing, dear: Are you quite sure that things will be all right at the office, with you being gone so long?"

Money, Swindon had realized. *All she's worried about is money.*

"Things can run themselves for a while," he had assured her. "Don't worry, Mummy dear, there will always be enough funds for the Swindons. If I never work another day, we will still be set for life. Even the consulting fees of three psychiatrists haven't made a dent in our finances."

If she caught the note of bitterness in Swindon's voice, his mother had ignored it. An ill-disguised relief flooded her features, and she said "Well, dear, if what you really need is rest, then perhaps it would be best if your sister and I went down to London for a while. That way we won't disturb you with our fussing little visits. I know how you hate fussing. And Tillie could use the change. All this has been so hard on her."

"Go," Swindon had replied, "Just go."

That had been three weeks ago. Now he found himself still at Tinsdale's. Dr. Abrams, the one psychiatrist on the staff he actually liked, kept telling him he needed to leave, get back into life.

"The muscles of your leg need use and so do the muscles of your courage," he kept saying. "You can still see me every week or so."

With an attitude like that, Swindon felt that Dr. Abrams' days at Tinsdale's must be numbered. Yet after every session with him, he did find himself thinking about checking out. The truth was, he just didn't know where to go. Home seemed out of the question. The island was an unbearable idea. He supposed he could set himself up with an elegant flat in any city in the world, but to what purpose? Hong Kong, Milan, London—they all seemed equally empty to him.

As for his business, he felt only a chill of fear at the thought of returning to it. Like everyone else, he had read the newspaper accounts of Miller's death, and like many, he had thought, *There's more to this than meets the eye.* Although the full story behind the explosion of Miller's yacht would probably never be known, Swindon's instinct told him it was a dark one. He sensed that in dealing with Miller at all, he had been, as the old saying goes, "flirting with the devil's grandmother." He wondered how many other of his business deals were actually far less savory than he had allowed himself to know. The mere thought of it filled him with disgust and a healthy touch of terror. He felt strongly inclined to sell out all his business affairs, to chuck it all. But what then? For the first time in his life, Swindon realized that, aside from making money by often dubious means, he had absolutely no skills. As far as he could see, he had no virtues, either. If he died tomorrow, no one, not even his family, would grieve. Many would be glad, and so, for that matter, might he.

The weight of his depression lay upon Swindon like fathoms of ocean water and held him to the hospital bed as if he was stranded at the bottom of a deep, deep sea. He thought about defying the heaviness of it all by lifting his hand to light another cigarette, but it seemed like almost too much bother.

Suddenly, outside in the hall, there was a commotion. "Hey, Babe," a thunderously loud voice said, "Is this Geoff Swindon's room? What's that? Be quiet? Why should I be quiet, this place is like a mausoleum, already! How can anyone get well in a morgue like this?"

A moment later, the door burst open. In strode a rough, cheerful looking man in a wrinkled beige raincoat, holding a bouquet of wild flowers mixed with deep red rhododendrons he seemed to have shamelessly just picked from the bushes outside. The rain-wet flowers dripped on the pale powder blue carpet.

"That's Swindon!" the man said happily to the nurse who stood beside him with a disapproving look on her perfectly made up face.

"I couldn't stop him, Mr. Swindon," she said apologetically.

"It's all right," Swindon assured her.

With a final glare at this visitor, the nurse left. The man, whoever he was, came over to the bedside and whispered confidentially to Swindon, "Are you sure she's not an android? They all look alike, the nurses here; it's like something out of an old *Star Trek* episode."

For the first time in what seemed like centuries, Swindon felt the trace of a smile on his face.

"Hey, where's a vase?" the man asked, waving the bouquet he held around so that raindrops and pollen showered down on Swindon's face.

"I'll ring for the nurse. . . ."

"No need, *amigo*, I'll find something; hah, perfect!"

His visitor thrust the flowers into the pitcher of water on the bedside table. "That'll do," he said. "But, hey, for what this place must cost, you'd think they could afford a few extra vases."

At that point, the nurse returned, wheeling in a tea trolley.

"That your breakfast?" the visitor asked with interest. He took one of the metal covers off the plate, then wrinkled his nose in disgust. "What's this?" he asked, staring at a bowl of watery brown liquid upon which a design had been drawn in cream sauce. A delicate flower made of radish and carrot curls floated on the surface.

"It's beef broth," Swindon explained. "The chef here is French. He decorates the food."

"*Dios Mio!*" the other man exclaimed. "That's not food for an invalid, that's some pre-schooler's art project! How do they expect you to get well, when they feed you tissue paper? What you need is a nice salad and some real soup! A Basque salad, with spinach, garlic, vinegar, olives, *bien sur*, and of course, freshly fried bacon, with the fat drizzled over the greens. And a hard-boiled egg, if you can get it! Of course, the egg has been stolen from a nearby farmhouse, and the farmer sets the dogs on you, and you escape; all this lends a certain *soupcon* to the recipe that nothing else can supply. And then, for the soup, you need a Basque stew! Onions, green peppers, lemon, lamb, and carrots, bubbling in a tomato sauce! To be served with red wine, just tart enough to make your eyes water, and French bread! And if the bread is hard to chew because you've lost half your teeth, that's fine, it just makes you appreciate the teeth you've got left all the more! Yes, Basque salad, Basque soup, that's what you need! Unfortunately, they could never serve you a meal like that in a place like this. For one thing, it needs to be cooked and eaten outside—the cool air of night, the scent of fallen pine needles, muscles aching after a day of hard work—that's all part of the recipe. And they can't supply those ingredients here; only life can supply those ingredients."

His visitor paused and glared again at the pallid-looking food on the plates. "Bah!" he said, "I know three-day-old infants who would turn their noses up at that anemic slop! Any Basque infant would, that's for sure! Food should be a holy thing; people should grab their food with need and gratitude! You know why? Because that food looks up at you from the plate and says 'Hey, you; I died so that you can live another day!' Now, that's holy!"

The man paused and began to rummage in the pockets of his raincoat.

"Fortunately," he said, "I have some garlic here somewhere. . . . Ah! Here it is!"

He pulled out an entire head of garlic and began to peel a clove, leaving scattered bits of its skin on the floor.

"Garlic is a natural antibiotic," his guest continued, "also very good against vampires. And this place seems full of vampires to me. You know how they work: keep their victims alive as long as possible so that, every day, they can drain them again." The man shook his head. "A bad business, but a common one. But hey, show a vampire a clove of garlic, and it runs like hell."

He turned to the nurse who stood a few feet away, glowering at him, and offered her the garlic he had just peeled.

"No thank you," she said icily. She hurried from the room.

"See what I mean?" his guest asked. He put a clove on Swindon's bedside table and popped one into his own mouth, crunching it with gusto.

Swindon was feeling rather dazed by this point. It seemed to him that he had seen this man somewhere before, but where? There was something oddly familiar about him.

"Excuse me," he said faintly, "but who are you?"

Filipo laughed. "*Madre de Dios*," he exclaimed, "how rude of me. Of course, you wouldn't remember. I was there at the accident. I am a friend of Gwen's."

Gwen. At the sound of her name, Swindon flinched. He had not heard it spoken since . . . since the last time he had spoken it himself, he realized, but seconds before the accident. God knows, he had repeated her name in his thoughts often enough since then, but hearing it aloud was like a knife lancing a wound. The pain of it flooded into him: her face, her beauty, her refusal, his shame at his own behavior. It was too much; he did not want to feel it. He closed his eyes.

His visitor seemed in no hurry to leave. In the stillness that followed, Swindon heard the striking of a match. Then the pungent scent of a Gauloise filled the room. Several minutes passed, then the man said, "Filipo Antonio Varques de la Reyna, that's my name. Call me Filipo, please." A few seconds later, he added musingly, "Speaking for myself, I wouldn't want to die in a place like this. No, I've always liked the feeling in that poem by Lorca—how

486

does it go?—'When I die, leave the balcony open, the small boy outside is eating oranges, when I die, leave the balcony open . . . '"

Receiving no response to this, Filipo continued to muse to himself. "Yes, if I have to die in a bed, which I hope I don't, but if I do, let it be in a room in the midst of a neighborhood that's crowded with life; let there be someone singing, and children playing, and an old woman complaining about her bunions, and chickens squawking, all of it, the lovely and the rough side of it, side by side, great gulps of life, like a wine, to be tasted down to the last instant—and beyond, if I've got anything to say about it! Life, that's what I want! Of course, to each his own. But I gotta tell you, my friend, to die in a place like this; it would be like dying surrounded by department store mannequins. I'd prefer to freeze in the Arctic—at least there'd be some living plankton for company! Not that you are going to die, of course. There's nothing seriously wrong with you, except ennui. Which can be terminal."

Filipo looked at Swindon. His eyes were closed. There was no indication that he had heard a word.

"Gwen really appreciated how you dealt with that land," Filipo remarked. "It was a noble gesture on your part, and she knows it. So do lots of people. She sends her thanks."

Or she would, Filipo reasoned, *if she knew I was here.*

"I got a note from her," Swindon said faintly. It was in the drawer of the bedside table. A brief, concerned, courteous note. He had not answered it.

"She's getting married, you know," Filipo remarked bluntly.

"To Greniston?"

"Yup. Seven more days."

Swindon was surprised that this not-unexpected news brought such a lurch to his heart.

Well, he thought, *so that is that.*

"You've got another visitor, besides me," Filipo remarked. "You've never met her, but she wants to meet you. She's waiting outside."

"So let her in," said Swindon, with a languid wave of his hand.

"She's not out in the hall. She's outside, on the lawn. Won't come in a place like this, says it smells bad."

"But it is pouring down rain outside," protested Swindon.

Filipo shrugged. "Refreshing to her. Hey, listen, she's a beauty. You oughta meet her. A woman like this, you meet once in a lifetime."

Intrigued in spite of himself, Swindon said, "Well, I suppose I could call for a wheelchair."

"Wheelchair!" scoffed Filipo, "You don't need that! Your leg's in a cast, you got crutches. Hey, you can lean on me. Here, sit up."

As Swindon gingerly swung his legs over the edge of the bed, he gave a gasp of pain. His ribs were still very sore.

"No time to find a raincoat," Filipo continued. "Here, just wrap this blanket around yourself, up over the head like a shawl, that's the way. Now, you've got a couple of casts on; have to wrap something around those." He glanced around the room, and his eyes lit upon the plastic liner in the wastebasket. "That'll do," he said happily, dumping the trash out onto the floor and ripping out the liner.

Once Swindon was sufficiently swathed against the rain, Filipo looked him over. "Maybe you do need a wheelchair," he said dubiously.

"I can walk," Swindon replied. "There's a crutch in the closet." Limping along after Filipo, covered in blankets and ripped plastic bags, Swindon felt that he must cut a very strange figure. It amused him, and for the first time in a long time, he felt like laughing.

Just as they stepped out of his room and into the hallway, a stern-looking doctor and two burly orderlies appeared.

"We understand there's been a disturbance," the doctor said quietly.

"What's that?"Filipo thundered. "Speak up, could you, Doc? You sound like an undertaker, you know, how they always talk."

"We understand . . . "

"No disturbance!" thundered Filipo. "Mr. Swindon is just going for a little walk. Wants fresh air. Look like you could use some yourself, by the way."

"I'm afraid a walk is out of the question; it is most inclement, and in Mr. Swindon's weakened condition . . . "

"The best thing for Mr. Swindon's condition is exercise. Not that you are going to tell him that, you damned vampire, encouraging people to be sick so your bank account can get fat and happy! Call yourself a doctor, but hey, you're a disgrace to Asclepius!"

Before the doctor and the orderlies could come any closer, Filipo grabbed a cart from the nurse's station and sent it speeding down the hallway toward them.

"Out of the way, parasites!" he yelled. Then he quickly steered Swindon through the doors to the back lawn, remarking, "Some people just aren't worth talking to."

Once outside, he did his best not to rush Swindon as he hobbled across the damp grass toward where Annie Lee stood waiting among the trees. He was pleased to see that his companion seemed to be enjoying himself, but he figured they had about twenty minutes before the cops arrived, and he wanted this interview to go well.

Swindon was shocked to see a Gypsy standing beneath the dripping trees, and an elderly one at that. Filipo's description had led him to believe the woman would be young and beautiful.

But she is beautiful, he realized, gazing into her sparkling, cornflower blue eyes. He leaned against a tree, out of breath.

"This is Annie Lee," Filipo said. "She's a healer. She wanted to meet you, because she needs an apprentice to pass her skills on to, and she thought you just might do."

Swindon laughed bitterly. "I can think of few professions for which I'm less suited. My specialty seems to be causing pain wherever I go."

"Let her be the judge of that."

Annie Lee proceeded to look Swindon over. She felt the texture of his skin, sniffed around him like a hound, gazed intently at his features and at the air around him. Swindon felt like a horse at a county fair being looked over by a prospective buyer. Oddly enough, he did not mind. As Annie considered him, he considered her.

A healer. Until glimpsing this old woman's serene and lovely face, it was a word he would have scoffed at—some kind of mumbo-jumbo—yet it was instantly clear to him that this person could be involved in nothing false. But what did her work involve? he wondered. Crawling around swamps at the full moon, picking herbs? Burning strange concoctions and chanting Romany incantations? He could scarcely imagine himself doing anything like that. Yet the thought of actually being able to ease pain, to mend what was broken? It seemed like a miracle to him, scarcely believable.

Evidently done with her examination, the woman whispered something to Filipo. He grinned, obviously relieved.

"She says you'll do," he said to Swindon. "She says you'll do because of what's wrong with you. You see, you have a weak resistance."

Swindon smiled cynically. "That would be hard for me to deny at this point in my life."

Filipo shook his head. "You don't understand, *amigo*. In itself, that weakness isn't good or bad. If you get around evil, it's bad *not* to resist. But if you get around goodness, hey, it's great to be weak to it; you won't resist what it wants you to do. Annie here can help you build the muscles you need to resist the rest. Listen, my friend, there's nothing wrong with what you are. What matters is what you do with it. You choose." Filipo couldn't help but remember the chilling dialogue with Miller and the clean influx of power he felt in choosing light and life.

Bitterness rose in Swindon, like an ancient venom. Later, he would understand that this was the beginning of his healing—that the very goodness confronting him had begun to bring his pain to the surface, the way a poultice draws out an infection. At this point, however, he only knew that he felt awful, dirty and spiteful.

"So, if I accept this offer," he said with a bit of a sneer, "she gets an unpaid servant. What do I get?"

Filipo looked at him sternly. "Redemption."

Just then, there was a commotion at the door of the nursing home. Doctors, nurses, and policemen emerged and headed across the lawn toward them.

"Uh-oh," said Filipo, "time to be running along! Hey, think it over. If you decide you want to do this, then be at the crossing of Edgeberry Lane and the Cirencester Road at three p.m. tomorrow. It's about three miles north of here. Ciao."

With that, Filipo and Annie ran into the trees, heading deep into the woods that lay beyond Tinsdale's grounds. Swindon watched the Gypsy's brightly colored skirt flickering amongst the trees until it disappeared. Who would have thought that so old a woman could sprint along like a deer?

"Mr. Swindon?"

He turned to face what seemed to be a mob of worried, disapproving faces.

One of the policeman said, "I understand there's been some trouble . . ."

"No. No trouble."

The policeman looked confused. One of the doctors opened his mouth, but before he could speak, Swindon said, "I was just enjoying a visit from two friends. Surely, that is my business?"

"Yes, of course," one of the doctors said, placatingly, "but in your condition, Mr. Swindon, it's best not to get overly stimulated. Come inside."

"In my condition," Swindon interrupted coolly, "it is best to fight for one's life."

***

At two-fifty p.m. the next day, a taxi dropped a young man off at the crossing of Edgeberry Lane and the Cirencester Road. It was an empty spot surrounded by open fields.

"Sure this is the place?" the cabbie asked.

The young man smiled and nodded. He pulled his wallet out of his pocket and started to count out some pound notes. Then he paused.

"On second thought," he said, "just take it all." He handed the cabbie all the money in his wallet.

"But this is way too - "

"Don't worry," said the young man, with a smile that quite lit up his pale, drawn face, "I won't need it where I'm going."

He got out of the taxi adjusting his backpack, as if unused to wearing one. The cabbie looked at him with concern. The young man seemed frail. He had a cast on his left wrist, another on one leg, and hobbled forward with the help of a crutch.

Hate to leave him out here all alone, the cabbie thought. Then he saw that there was another man he hadn't noticed at first, sitting against a turnstile by the side of the road, playing a guitar. The guitar player waved at the frail young man in greeting.

Well, if he's got a friend to meet him . . . ., the cabbie reasoned. Deciding to leave well enough alone, he turned his car around and drove back the way he had come.

Filipo looked Swindon over and nodded his approval. "Corduroy trousers, sweater, walking shoes—or should I say, shoe? Not bad. Only need two more things." Out of his pocket, he pulled a silk scarf and a gold ring.

"No true Romani is ever without a bit of silk and a bit of gold," Filipo explained. "Annie will probably encourage you to take a new name as well, but that's up to you."

Feeling a little awkward, Swindon slipped the ring onto one of his fingers, while Filipo knotted the scarf around his neck.

"*Bueno*. Annie's waiting down the road a bit, where the trees begin. I'll walk with you a ways."

"You're not coming with?" Swindon sounded quite crestfallen.

Filipo shook his head. "This is your adventure," he said kindly. "Besides, I promised to play guitar at Gwen's wedding. But hey, after that, I'll catch up with you at Appleby Fair, in August. Biggest event for all kinds of Travellers in England, that is. Annie's sure to take you there. I'm thinking that I'll head back to Denver after the wedding, clear things up there, and then come back here and hit the road. It's been too long since I've had a walkabout. England, Brittany, Spain, they're calling to me. So, hey, I think I'll be back in a couple of months, and I'll make you that Basque salad and soup. You'll be about ready to appreciate them by then."

"I'll look forward to it," said Swindon with a smile.

They walked on together a short ways, until they could just see Annie's caravan and Chieftain in the distance.

"Well, my friend," said Filipo, "this is as far as I go. It's your path, this one. But I wish you well on it."

With a firm handshake, Filipo turned and walked away. He did not look back.

Slowly, Swindon hobbled on. He could hear meadowlarks singing in the fields and smell the scent of new mown hay on the wind. The road ahead was empty, save for the Gypsy wagon under the distant trees.

And then, Swindon never knew quite how, an old man appeared on the roadside. He seemed to have stepped right out of the air. Yet he was a real enough old man, a hobo, maybe. He wore faded old workman's clothes and had a battered cap on his balding head. A ruby red rose was fastened in his ragged lapel. His was a thin old man, but he held himself erect and walked with a jaunty step. What hair he had left was white, very soft, wispy, and fine. He had as well a slight, well-trimmed white goatee.

Coming abreast of Swindon, the old man pulled a cigarette out of his pocket and said, "Gotta light, Guv?"

"Certainly." Awkwardly, leaning on the crutch, Swindon fumbled in his pocket for his lighter. As he leaned forward to light the cigarette, he felt the old boy's eyes upon him. Swindon looked up, and met that gaze. And he knew he was looking at the most mysterious face he had ever seen. The ancient, blue eyes looked at him with an infinite patience. They seemed to look into his soul, to measure every cell of his being. Yet their gaze did not recoil from what they saw. There was something very strange about this man, Swindon felt. He looked so old, so very old, and sad beyond telling, yet the light in his eyes was young and joyful. Clear eyes they were, that could see impeccably for a long, long way, like the eyes of a hawk, a Merlin. *Yes,* Swindon thought, *this is the face that Merlin would have, if he were alive today.*

"You will be absolved," the old man said. "The wind will scour you, and the rain will wash you. You'll come clean in the end, lad, I can see it."

As the old man spoke these words, Swindon felt an amazing lightening of his heart. The old man smiled and, with a nod and a tip of his cap, walked on.

For a moment, Swindon stood awestruck in the middle of the road. Really, he felt very strange. He turned to look after the old man—but no one was there. Only the empty road, gleaming in the sunshine, and the fields on either side, and the silvery songs of meadowlarks rising beneath the vast, open sky. And there, high, and far, near a passing cloud, he saw a hawk—a Merlin, perhaps—circling and soaring in the shining air.

A shrill whistle called Swindon back to earth. Down the road, Annie Lee was whistling and waving to him. Swindon waved in reply, and, with all the speed he could muster, went forward to meet her.

CHAPTER TWENTY-FIVE

"I'm so glad," Gwen said earnestly, several hours later. "It sounds like the best thing Geoff could do. Especially if Annie is willing to let him stay in touch with Dr. Abrams."

Filipo nodded. "Annie will take good care of him. You can be sure of that."

Gwen sighed contentedly and leaned back on the rose-colored sofa. She and Filipo were in the library of Greniston Manor. Gwen had realized, some four hours earlier, that Greniston had quite forgotten their dinner date. He was sequestered in his study, working on some project he was determined to finish before the wedding but refused to discuss. Gwen did not mind. She felt secure in the wondrous knowledge that they would have many, many dinners together to come; soon enough, she would spend every night beneath this very roof.

"Well, *Carissima*," Filipo said, sipping his sherry, "only four days left, eh?"

"Four days, eight hours, and three minutes," Gwen replied with a smile. "I wish you weren't going away," she added wistfully.

"Don't worry, I'll be back to play at your wedding," Filipo replied. "But in the meantime, I need to stretch my legs a little."

He did not add that he saw it was time for him to step aside to make room for the new life that was coming Gwen's way. He knew that they would always be friends. Both she and Greniston had assured him he would always have a home at Greniston Manor, and he knew that this was true. Yet he also knew that marriage would alter, though not end, their friendship. *Eh bien*, that was life. Whatever sorrow he felt was far outweighed by joy. He could not wish a better match for Gwen than the one she had made.

He reached for his guitar, never far away, and strummed a few measures of an old Portuguese *fado*. The haunting music lingered in the firelit room.

"You know," Gwen said, "there's still one thing you haven't told me. You said that you suddenly understood, that night on the mound, what the riddle of the Greniston treasure was. You said it isn't really the physical treasure we found in the mound. But you haven't told me yet what it is."

Filipo laughed. "Nor do I intend to! That's a riddle each must solve for himself. Once it dawns upon you, you'll know, *ma belle*. But I'll tell you this much: the clue really is in those pictures Claire drew."

He took another sip of his sherry, and Gwen sighed, recognizing well enough when her friend was in his "wild horses cannot drag it from me" mode.

"There's one more thing I need to ask of you," Filipo said. "Annie Lee has a vow to ask of you."

"A vow?" said Gwen, surprised.

Filipo nodded. "You remember how she said she got a Calling to come here, a Calling that meant something needed healing?"

"Yes, I certainly remember that."

"Well, it seems that this healing had many parts. Luan Tey was one part of it. Swindon is another. And the land itself cried out for a healing. Think of the wound it would have been to this poor old earth, already so insulted by the human race, if Miller's plan had succeeded, and she had found her scared places yet again raped and gouged to make more instruments of destruction. That's something you helped to avert, *Carissima*."

Gwen thought of the sedasium and hoped that she and Greniston had made the right decision about it. The chalice now restored to the Far Tauverly Historical Society was, in fact, a perfect fake, a fact not known even by the Pennington sisters. The real chalice along with the shields, lances, and other objects made of the potent metal had met a different fate.

After consultation with the Independent Kingdom of Greenstone, Gwen, Greniston, and the children, had met late one night in the mound. One by one, they had dropped each object of sedasium through the crevice that opened onto the underground river and listened as each one came to rest, far beneath the earth.

"The enormous energy in this metal is a gift from the Earth," Greniston had mused. "Perhaps mankind is not yet worthy to handle that energy. Let it return to the planet's safekeeping, until perhaps, one day, we are truly fit to handle it."

"So let it be spoken, so let it be done," King Osgood the First had solemnly agreed.

As for the rest of the treasure, the fortune of gold and silver and jewels, they had, for the moment, left it where it was, in the safety of the mound.

"That's your dowry," Greniston had said to Gwen.

"No," she had protested, "this is our land; we need to decide its future together."

To their surprise, Wyatt had contradicted them both. "Thith ith still Arthur's tweasure," he had said firmly, "to be used for the good of the Wealm."

Thinking about it, Gwen could see that this was right. She wondered what "the good of the realm" meant, and if it could include a few schemes to improve the lot of Far Tauverly. The tours she was organizing would provide a few jobs, but more were needed, even in so small a place. Already, a plan was forming in the back of her mind involving Kestrel Farm. Logan had always wanted to see the place filled with children, and the farm would make a wonderful school for those who lived near the manor, sparing them the trek into Far Tauverly. Gwen loved the thought of the Walmsley children learning nearby. Now that Arthur's spirit rode again in the world, his sentinels seemed to feel less worried about protecting his mound, although the woods were as much their Kingdom as ever.

"It's wonderful to see the children more light hearted," she had said to Filipo, "it's as if a wound has been healed."

Her friend had nodded his agreement. "Yet there is one more wound, Annie Lee said, that still needs healing. An old, old wound. She says it goes back to the time of Arthur."

"Arthur." It startled Gwen to hear that name spoken aloud. Since that night on the mound, none of them had said much about what had happened there. It was almost as if what they had seen there was so strange, so marvelous, that it could only be discussed under the most special circumstances. Sometimes, perhaps, they would all meet again and speak of it together. But not yet.

"Arthur," Gwen said carefully. "Yes, go on."

"Annie said that when she was in this house, she got pictures in her mind. Pictures of a great castle that was here, long ago. . . ."

"Camelot?" Gwen whispered.

"She didn't say. She only knew that there had been a castle here, and in it, many people. There were three in particular whose faces kept returning to her: a dark haired man, a king; a fair-haired man, a knight; and a lady with red-gold hair."

"Arthur, Lancelot, and Guinevere," Gwen said, not daring to speak above a whisper.

Filipo shrugged. "She said no names. Only that these three people once lived in this place and that there was both great love and great sorrow between them. There was some terrible misunderstanding that was not healed in their lifetimes. So bitter was the sorrow that it lived on in the bloodlines of their children."

"But Arthur had no children."

"Not by Guinevere. But Arthur—if he it was who Annie saw—had a bastard by his half-sister and perhaps other children as well, born, as they say, on the wrong side of the blanket. It was no shame for a king in those days, you know. As for Lancelot, he had a child by Elaine, or so the story goes: Galahad, purest of knights, who saw the Grail. Whoever they were, these two men passed down their feud to this day. Annie is sure that Greniston and Swindon are somehow the inheritors of that old bitterness."

"I see," said Gwen slowly, "and the old feud goes unhealed. But when we saw . . . Arthur and the others . . . there seemed no anger left between them."

"Not for them, perhaps. Whoever, whatever, it was that we saw. But the pain lives on in the blood. Annie Lee felt that you were the only person who could help to heal it."

Gwen looked shaken. The thought of trying to reconcile two such proud men as Greniston and Swindon was not an easy one.

"I'll - I'll try," she faltered, "if Swindon ever returns."

"He will. He must," said Filipo firmly. "It is part of his own healing."

"Then when he does," Gwen promised, "I will try to bring them together. I can't guarantee a miracle, but I can vow to give it my best effort."

Filipo smiled. "Annie knew you would say that. And now, *Carissima*, enough of such seriousness! Since your beloved seems to have forgotten both his dinner and yours, what do you say to a midnight snack *á la Basque*? I'm sure that under Mrs. Walmsley's generous if not tidy hands, the larder is full, just waiting to be raided."

"Let's go," said Gwen, taking him by the hand.

***

497

As Filipo was busy working wonders with leftover roast beef, scallions, basil, and a little red wine, the Lord of Greniston Manor was intent upon some artistry of his own.

"It's almost there, Will," he murmured, "almost there." He paused and rubbed his right hand, flexing the stiff joints. Lately, the words flowed into his mind so swiftly, his pen had trouble keeping up with the thoughts.

"A good problem to have," Greniston remarked, louder now.

He gazed thoughtfully at the bust of Shakespeare.

"What a fool I've been, Will," he said. "All these years, thinking it was 'me,' 'my' art, 'my' genius that wrote the good lines! Hah! It was Logan that opened my eyes . . . although, perhaps Deirdre was trying to tell me about surrender all along, too. And then, that night upon the mound. . . . One thing is certain, the world is a bigger place than I thought it was, but a few short weeks ago. Love is real, mysteries are real. . . . Great inspirations seek night and day to whisper in our ears, if only we would listen! Why settle for the ravings of one's own ego, when one can be a mouthpiece for something far greater than oneself? But you have known this all along, haven't you, Will?"

Greniston gazed fondly at the statue. He reached for his tea cup and sputtered when he tasted the stone-cold contents.

Good Lord, he thought, *how long has that been sitting there?*

He glanced at his watch. Twelve-forty-five. It couldn't be. He had thought it was seven, at the latest. Glancing out the windows, he noted that it was, indeed, pitch black. For a moment, he was vaguely troubled by the thought that he had forgotten or mislaid something. But what? He shrugged. No matter. He returned his attention to the writing before him, and, soon enough, the flow of words absorbed him. Outside, the distant bells of St. Aethelrood's tolled one, then two, then three. . . .

***

It was not until ten a.m. the next morning that Greniston remembered his dinner date with Gwen. In abject apology, he had invited her instead to a picnic lunch on the roof of the manor. Now they stood side by side on the top of the tower, leaning on the parapets.

Gwen was glad of the reprieve from wedding plans. As joyful as she was to be marrying Greniston, she sometimes secretly wished she had agreed to his suggestion of an elopement. She had had no idea how much work even a "small ceremony" could be.

"Shouldn't be much bother," Greniston had said airily. "Use the church for the wedding, then set up a few tables on the lawn, let 'em all eat, drink, and be merry, whilst I whisk you off to a distant corner of the globe."

"And where," Gwen began for the hundredth time, "might that be?"

"Have to wait and see," Greniston had said with a mysterious smile. "But it's somewhere you've always wanted to see. Of that I'm sure."

Gwen hoped he was right about that. He certainly hadn't been right about the ceremony not being much bother. She had never dreamed that even a small wedding could be so complicated. Wisely, she had decided to concentrate on the parts she enjoyed: designing her dress, which Anne Walmsley had almost finished sewing; choosing the music; and working out the service with the Vicar. When it came to nut cups and seating plans and menus, she decided to leave it to the Pennington sisters and Mrs. Hodges, who gloried in every last detail of the arrangements.

She was a bit saddened but not surprised that her best friend, Suzanne, would not be able to make it to the ceremony. The invitation had arrived too late for her to obtain leave from her teaching job in Tanzania, but at least Gwen had got to talk to her—a scratchy long distance connection that had seemed all too brief, although they had conversed for almost an hour.

She was more concerned that Suzanne couldn't be there, she realized, than she was about her own family. Perhaps that made sense; they hadn't been close for years. Her sister and older brothers had never been farther from Chicago than Disney World; perhaps a transatlantic flight seemed out of the question to them, except for a funeral. Her youngest brother, Sean, had surprised everyone by announcing at the last minute that he was coming; he was due to arrive the night before the ceremony. Since he was twelve years younger than her, Gwen felt she scarcely knew him as an adult; nonetheless, she was pleased that at least one member of her family would be there. In spite of Sean's arrival, she stuck firm to her decision that it be Logan who gave her away; he had seemed so honored when she first made the offer that she was not about to withdraw it, last minute blood kin or no.

"Penny for your thoughts," said Greniston now, standing beside her on the parapet and putting his arm around her.

"I was thinking about Logan," Gwen replied.

"Ah, he's looking happier by the day. Can't wait 'til he's trained his replacement at that postal job and moves into Shalimar House. Mind you, new job, new home—it's a lot of changes for him, but happy ones, I trust."

"Oh yes," said Gwen, "I'm sure of that. I think he'll miss delivering the mail a little bit, but only because he's been doing it for so long. He seems to be quite looking forward to restoring the Greniston gardens, though."

"Up to his ears in seed catalogues," Greniston remarked. "Consulting night and day with Lettice and the Vicar about lilies, ground cover, and, of course, God help us, yews."

"One thing I'm glad of," said Gwen, brushing a lock of hair from her eyes, "is that the villagers seem to treat Logan with more respect, now that he's soon to be working for you. Although mind you," she added rather hotly, "they always should have shown him that respect, because of who he is."

"Agreed," said Greniston. "But most people are impressed by rank more than merit, and that's a sad fact. The move to Greniston Manor doesn't seem to have hurt Bob Walmsley's stature in town, either."

"That it hasn't," agreed Gwen. Musingly, she added, "Do you think he's staying sober?"

"For the most part," Greniston replied. "Once or twice he's had the wretched look of a man with a walloping hangover, but then, a certain amount of hard drinking is the country way of life. For the most part, though, I do believe he's tea-totaling. And he is certainly doing a satisfactory job mending every fence on the land. Working young Robert to the bone, hauling up stones from the river bed," Greniston added with a slightly sadistic chuckle. "'Bout time somebody did."

As they leaned upon the parapets, gazing out across the landscape, by the golden sunlight of late May, they saw, far below, Osborne, Claire, and Osgood run across the lawn and disappear into the woods.

Gwen smiled. The Independent Kingdom of Greenstone, recently knighted by Arthur himself, was alive and well, as far as she could see. Yet she was glad to know that the children were also mixing more in normal activities since their move to the manor. Charles was often to be found tagging along after his father, proud to help mix a bucket of mortar or saw a board. Wyatt, on the other hand, had become attached to none other than Greniston himself and had more than once wormed his way into the inner sanctum of his study by sweetly promising, "I won't disturb your work, Ward

Gweniston; I will be as quiet as a church mouse, twuwy." And so he was, for at least five minutes on end.

As for Claire and Osborne, they had grown closer than ever to Logan. Gwen came upon them sometimes in the woods or gathered around the harp in the great hall. Osborne often seemed to be learning one of Logan's old tales by heart, and Claire, fascinated by the harp, was already able to pick out simple melodies on its strings. A bit of mystery hung over the three of them. Gwen felt that the strange events that had happened on the mound lingered close to them. When they looked up as she passed, there was often a faraway look in their eyes. She had the sense that they saw more than most folk did, and heard, perhaps, strains of the fairy music.

Osgood, to everyone's surprise, had grown quite interested in the Vicar's Oxfam fundraising. "The lad is far brighter than I ever realized," Reverend Sterling had told Gwen but a few days before. "Imagine, he turned up at the service last Sunday—I believe he had actually bathed for the occasion—climbed up into the pulpit with me, and took the congregation to task for not contributing more to charity. I believe some were quite shamed into donation. 'Out of the mouths of babes,' you see. Yes, a very bright lad, indeed; though I cannot seem to interest him in yew sculpture."

"Perhaps it's a taste for a more mature mind," Gwen had ventured, at which the Vicar had been pleased enough to blush.

Now, nestled close to Greniston, gazing out across the land, she felt glad indeed to see the happiness growing around them. Yet she knew that even here, in the idyllic English countryside, there was still a dark side to life. She would not soon forget the look of pure evil she had seen on Miller's face. Indeed, she had seen a scrap of that same hatred on Bill Saxton's face just yesterday. Running into him on the main street of Far Tauverly, she had summoned her courage and offered him one of the new jobs the tours were going to provide.

"We're going to need busses to drive tourists all over England," she had said. "That means drivers, and mechanics to keep them in good running order. It will be steady work, and the pay is good."

Bill Saxton had stared coldly back at her. "Swindon's plan would have brought big money into this town," he said scornfully. "Big money, fast money."

"I'm not so sure it would have," Gwen replied truthfully. "The buyer he had in mind wasn't honest with Swindon about his own plans. Besides, construction jobs don't last forever, you know. But the work I'm offering you will go on for years."

Unconvinced, Bill Saxton looked her up and down and spat, just missing her shoe. Then, with a last grunt of scorn, he had turned and walked away.

The incident had left Gwen shaken. Now she thought, *I guess there is no corner of the world, however lovely, that darkness has not touched.*

Yet even as she thought it, she remembered Arthur's charge to his ghostly troops: not to battle darkness directly, but "wherever there is darkness, to grow a greater good." She, too, was resolved to take up that quest. Far Tauverly seemed as good a place as any to start. If there were others who wished to join her in it, so much the better. But she would never be put off from her purpose, no matter what.

I avow it, she thought, standing on the parapets, the wind in her hair.

She moved even closer to Greniston. He looked down at her and bent close, his lips ready to meet hers, when the stillness was rent by the *thwack!* of a suction cup arrow hitting the stone ledge, just inches from Greniston's nose. The alarm this caused the lord and his lady gave rise to shrieks of wild laughter, followed by the patter of little feet careening down the tower stairs.

"Damn that Osgood!" Greniston thundered, removing the arrow from the ledge and flinging it off the roof.

"Now, you don't know it was Osgood," Gwen protested. "We just saw him running toward the woods, half an hour ago."

"Hah! I'd recognize that fiendish laughter anywhere! Children! I sometimes think they are sent to punish us for sins committed in some past lifetime!"

"I hope you won't feel that way about our children," remonstrated Gwen gently.

Greniston froze. "*Our* children?"

"Well, I mean, when we have them. Not right away, of course, but . . ."

"You want to have children?" Greniston interrupted.

"Certainly," said Gwen. "Don't you?"

"Actually," replied Greniston honestly, "it hadn't occurred to me."

He can't be serious, Gwen thought. And yet, she saw, he was.

502

With his most winning grin, Greniston turned to her now and said, "Can't we let the Walmsleys do the child-bearing around here? They seem to have really acquired the knack of it."

Gwen shook her head. "But my darling," Greniston protested, "there are already too many children in the world."

Aha, Gwen thought, *now he's finally going to tell me about the orphanages and the charities, and how he supports them.* She waited expectantly, but Greniston did not pursue this line of thought. Instead, he looked into the distance with a remarkably disgruntled expression on his face.

He looks like a child himself right now, Gwen realized. *This topic has really upset him.*

Taking his arm firmly in hers, she said, "I didn't mean to alarm you. And I would never want to force parenthood upon you, nor would I ever back out of our marriage. Not for any reason on earth. You are my choice, above all others, come what may. I want you to know that."

Greniston smiled gratefully at her, and said rather shakily, "It's not that I'm dead set against producing young 'uns; it's just going to take some getting used to."

"There will be time for that," Gwen said gently. "Time for many things."

This time, when they embraced, not even a renewed volley of arrows disturbed their concentration in the slightest.

***

Several hours later, Davey Lee sat beneath a Hawthorne tree. It was late night by then; the woods were still and dreamlike. He sat very quietly, not minding the damp and chill at all. Softly, to himself, he sang a scrap of the Romani Anthem: "Djelem, Djelem, . . . we travel on. . . ."

As soon as first light came, he tidied up the small camp he had made for himself. By the time he finished, only another Romani could have guessed that someone had been there.

The sun was sparkling on the treetops as he left the woods and headed across the lawns toward the manor house. He saw Gwen heading up the drive on foot. He liked the way she often walked from the inn to the manor instead of using a car, the way many would have. But then, he liked a lot of things about Gwen. In his opinion, she was a real Rani, a Queen, and he thought that Greniston was lucky to get her.

"Good morning," she called, cutting across the grass to greet him.

"And what are you up to, so fine and so early?" Davey asked. Gwen grimaced. "Wedding presents. It's not that I'm ungrateful for them, but there are so many of them, and they keep coming. In America, you don't open them until after the ceremony, but here, I gather, one is expected to have them all on display during the reception. Greniston won't be bothered with them, so it falls to me. Come and see."

Davey followed her into the manor house, to the great hall. The huge oak table was covered with a wide assortment of gifts. More packages had arrived by post the day before. Gwen gazed at it all with a trace of dismay.

"It's awfully nice of people, but we don't need half of it. Greniston Manor already has enough silver tea trays and crystal decanters to stock a department store. And most of it is from people I don't even know: cousins and friends from Greniston's days at university and Parliament."

"Thought it was supposed to be a small wedding."

"It was, but once my darling got used to the idea of any wedding, he got used to it in a big way. Not a day goes by that he doesn't say, 'Oh, and we must invite old so-and-so; it'll just be one more, no problem.' I've quite lost track of the guest list."

Gwen smiled. "Of course," she added, "some of the gifts are irreplaceable. Look at this." She handed Davey a scrapbook, handmade, it seemed, from bits of construction paper and yarn. It was filled with vivid drawings and a long poem, written in purple crayon.

"It's from the Walmsley children," Gwen explained. "It's a chronicle of my entire courtship with Greniston. And look at this," She pointed to a set of leather-bound books. "The complete works of Henrietta Amberly, my favorite romance novelist, rebound from paperback. It's from Mrs. Gordon, a friend of mine in America. Greniston choked with disgust when he saw it, but it is something only she would send. She can't make it to the wedding," Gwen added regretfully, "something came up with her family."

"That's a nice hunk of silver," Davey said, fingering a huge candlestick molded in the shape of a cherub holding a basket of fruit on one shoulder.

"That's kinder than what my beloved had to say about it," Gwen remarked dryly. "Some of this stuff is pretty awful. Although I really do like this crystal vase. Isn't it lovely, the way it catches the light?"

She refrained from mentioning that the vase was from Deirdre, who could not come to the wedding, being soon to depart for a filming in Morocco. She had, however, sent the vase by private messenger and, with it, a registered letter for Gwen. Gwen had been halfway through opening the letter when she saw, through the thin, elegant paper, that it contained but three words, each beginning with a capital R. She had paused, wondering by what bribery or influence Deirdre had managed to obtain the full name of R. R. R. Greniston. She knew that Deidre had not known it during her affair with Greniston, about which Gwen had by now heard quite a bit. She appreciated the feminine camaraderie that would want to arm her with this powerful information, and for several minutes, she had been sorely tempted to open the letter and read. Then, in an instant of triumphant integrity, she had thrown the paper into the fire.

If Greniston wants me to know his name, he'll tell me, she thought. Perhaps it was silly, but something in her wanted to respect this privacy as a reminder that however close she and Greniston became, however deeply they loved, they would still always be two honorable lives, entitled to their private places. It had not been easy to make the gesture, however, and she had to leave the room quickly, lest she be tempted to fish the letter out of the fire before it was consumed and read at least one of those three names. Woman to woman, she was deeply grateful for the information. The gesture was in itself a gift.

The crystal vase she could not dispose of. It intimidated her somewhat; bold and elegant, a fearless cascade of light that reminded her of Deirdre herself, who she had seen in a film about Elizabeth the First.

"It's so modern and simple," Gwen said, "it doesn't fit anywhere in the manor. I think I'll have to redecorate a room to do it justice."

"There's one room where it would look just fine," said Davey. "The Guv'nor's study."

With a slightly sinking feeling, Gwen realized he was right. The crystal vase would look right at home next to the bust of Shakespeare and the elegant Egyptian cat. For a moment, she wrestled with a twinge of jealousy at the thought of something so clearly Deirdre resting in her love's most inner sanctum.

Yet she has a place in his heart, Gwen realized, *and I wouldn't want it to be otherwise*. Then and there, she resolved to take the vase to the study that very day and instantly felt a great relief.

True love should open doors, not close them, she thought.

Meanwhile, Davey had been looking over the other gifts with an appraising eye. "Real quality, some of this stuff is," he said. "You shouldn't leave all this lyin' about. It's hard on a man whose fingers are inclined to be light, if you know what I mean."

Gwen felt that she did. A phrase of Filipo's came to her mind: "You can't change people. Just try to make the best use of what they naturally are." A quiet inspiration came to Gwen.

"You know," she said, "I really ought to sort this stuff out. Yes, I'm going to put all the gifts that—just between you and me—Greniston and I would never miss, over here on this sideboard. Like this . . . whatever it is."

"That's an eighteenth-century spittoon," Davey said. "Worth a bundle, that is."

"Maybe. But it's from a cousin Greniston can't stand. He's already threatened to give it to the Walmsleys. And, I don't know, it's a bit frilly for me, somehow. And so are those cherub candlesticks . . . and this heart-shaped box with the two turtledoves touching beaks as if they were kissing."

"Gagworthy, yes," agreed Davey, "but it's real silver. You could melt it down."

"We probably won't be getting around to that any time soon," Gwen said, "so I'll just put it over here, with the other rejects,"

"On the sideboard," finished Davey Lee with a grin. "I do get your drift. But I'm afraid I can't take advantage of your generous hint. I've taken a vow to not steal anymore. Not to line my own pockets, at least. But I could possibly help you find profitable homes for some of these items, if the funds made were to go to a worthy cause."

"I can think of several," Gwen said. "What a good solution."

Davey smiled. "By the way," he said, "Gran and I have presents for you too. 'Course, they ain't very showy compared with this spread." He reached into his jacket pocket and pulled out a packet of columbine seeds.

"Gran says the fairies like to be near them when they're in bloom," he explained. "And this is from me," he added, handing her a four leaf clover. "As long as you've got one of these by you, you'll never be fooled by a false enchantment. So just you keep that near you, and you'll be all right."

"That I will," said Gwen. She opened the locket she wore around her neck and put the four-leaf clover in one side of it, across, Davey noted, from

506

a picture of Greniston. The columbine seeds she put in a similar place of honor, next to the Walmsleys' epic poem.

"You'll be a lovely bride," Davey said. "I'm sorry I won't be at your wedding."

"But it's only three more days," Gwen protested. "Surely you can stay!"

Davey shook his head. "Something's Calling me."

"Calling you. I didn't know you shared your Grandmother's healing gift. "

"I don't. This is a different kind of Calling. Ever since that night on the mound, something is Calling, and Calling to me. Not like I'm supposed to go heal anything, this is different somehow. It's like a treasure that wants to be found, and it's tugging at my heart."

Davey's dark, sparkling eyes had a faraway look in them, as he gazed out the window. "It's so hard to put into words, yet it's real. Didn't you ever wonder how all those knights knew to come to Camelot? They didn't have newspapers or tellys to advertise it, yet people came from all over. I think something Called to them, just like something's Calling to me now. Something great, something new, is trying to happen in this sad, old world, and It's Calling to me, night and day. It's like a music that's so sweet, . . . yet it's just beyond what we can hear, . . . yet sometimes, just for a moment, you can almost hear it, . . . almost. I must find its source!"

There was a note of ineffable longing in the Gypsy's voice. "There's something we are born for, something we are here for, something we are meant to find, to do, as we travel through this world. Perhaps some find it by staying still, like them monks that sit and meditate. Perhaps, you, my lady, will find it by making a true home for many here. But me, I was born to wander, . . . and It's Calling to me, out there, somewhere on the roads and byways of this world, . . . Calling and Calling, and I must answer. . . . I'm sorry, but I must be on my way. I'll visit to help you with that school you mentioned starting, I'll always return for a while. But I'm not a settling down kind of person." He paused, then added, "You know, I think we are all Travellers. Even this beautiful earth and the other planets, it's like a caravan of wagons, travelling a star path. It's like the Romani flag – green on the bottom, for the earth, blue above for the sky, and in the middle, a red wheel, like the spoked wheel of a wagon, that turns and travels ever on. And some say the wheel is also community, the family circle of all Romani. But I understand now that I believe it's the circle of everyone. At least, that's what it means to me. Everyone. And what are we here for? Why are we here? Why, why, and yet again why, that's part of what's calling to me. Because there's a great mystery in it, a Great Something to be found."

Davey paused, and glanced at Gwen. She probably thinks I'm a right nutter, he thought. But Gwen was looking at him with total understanding. Davey thought he had never met anyone who listened to others so deeply, who so completely gave them her total attention. And that was a gift. It brought something out of people. It allowed them to find themselves.

"I understand having a Calling," Gwen said. "Something Called me here, after all. Promise me, Davey, if you find this Great Thing, the treasure that's calling to you, will you let me know?"

"By my heart, I will," Davey replied.

"Well then, Godspeed to you. You and yours will always have a home on the Greniston land if you need it."

"Thank you, Rani," he replied gravely. Then, before Gwen knew what was happening, he leaned forward and kissed her full upon the lips.

"Best luck a bride can have," he chuckled, "is a kiss from Romani lips."

"I thought that was a kiss from a chimney sweep – lucky for a bride to be kissed by a chimney sweep," Gwen replied.

Davey shrugged. With a wink and a grin he replied "Chimney sweep, Gypsy, handsomest man in the woods, same difference."

Then he stepped quickly to the open French doors, paused on the threshold to blow her another kiss, and then disappeared into the sunlight. From across the lawn, Gwen heard Davey's voice lifted in song: "Come all ye, oh wide ye awake, the piper's down from Dublin town, the gardener will open the gate, so early of a morning. . . . "

Then he whistled the ancient melody, joyful, yet haunting. As Gwen listened, the music grew farther and farther away, until it merged with the sigh of the wind and the chorus of birdsong. And then she knew that Davey Lee was gone away, wandering far, somewhere on the beckoning roads of the world.

***

Later that morning, Gwen had the happy task of driving into Tweeverton to pick up the wedding rings. As she drove past the train station, she recognized a familiar figure alighting on the platform.

"Mrs. Fitzpatrick!" she cried. Then, embarrassed, she amended her greeting: "I mean, Mrs. Steadworthy!"

"It's all right, dear," the older woman smiled, "just call me Eileen."

"Are you on your way to Far Tauverly?"

"As a matter of fact, I am," Mrs. Steadworthy said, with a twinkle in her eye. "There's a wedding I'm attending there this very Saturday, the first of June. Charles will be joining me on Friday, but I thought I'd come up a day early and visit with my old friend, Mrs. Hodges. I'll be staying at the inn."

"Why, so am I," said Gwen. "That is, for a couple more days."

"And quite right that you should, dear. It's nice to see a bit of ceremony preserved in these anything-goes days."

"I can give you a lift to Far Tauverly," Gwen offered, "if you don't mind running an errand on the way."

"Not at all." Mrs. Steadworthy got into the car, bringing a delicate trace of Eau de Joie with her. She wore a pink linen suit and a smart, white, straw hat with a silk rose on the brim.

"You look fantastic," said Gwen admiringly.

Mrs. Steadworthy chuckled. "Marriage agrees with me. And then, Charles is everything a woman could desire. I suppose everyone is still shocked at how we ran off together, aren't they?"

"Surprised," Gwen said, "but very happy for you both."

"Even Lord Greniston?"

"Well," Gwen said truthfully, "he was a little disgruntled at first, but he got over that. He thinks it's quite romantic, actually."

"And Mrs. Walmsley is working out all right?"

"Like a charm," Gwen lied blithely. The truth was that Mrs. Walmsley's housekeeping was proving to be the disaster Gwen had feared it might be. She was already resolved that she was going to use part of her salary from the travel agency to hire a couple of girls from the village to come and clean every week. But all in all, she felt that it was worth it. The meals Mrs. Walmsley prepared were delicious and healthy, and Gwen felt comfortable having her in the house. *Cleaning I can always pay for*, thought Gwen, *but a house full of happiness and high spirits is beyond price.*

Mrs. Steadworthy gave a sigh of relief. "Well, that's all right, then," she said happily.

***

Later, over a cup of Earl Grey at the Tweeverton Tea Shop, Gwen showed the older woman the rings.

"They were made to order," she said rather proudly. Hers was a delicate band of silver and gold intertwined, with the silver shaped to look like an ivy vine, and the gold, like leaves of holly. Greniston's was a plain, strong gold band, with an inscription inside. Mrs. Steadworthy peered through her bifocals. "I can't quite make this out. . . ."

"It says, 'An ever fix'd mark.'"

"Ah, Shakespeare. One of the sonnets, isn't it?"

Gwen nodded, and quoted, "'Love is not love which alters when it alteration finds, or bends with the remover to remove. O no! It is an ever-fixed mark that looks on tempests and is never shaken. It is the star to every wandering bark.'"

Mrs. Steadworthy nodded approvingly. "He'll like that."

They sat for a minute in companionable silence, watching the shoppers walk past the tearoom. At last, Gwen ventured to broach what was on her mind.

"Mrs. Steadworthy—Eileen—you've known Lord Greniston for a long time. . . ."

"That I have, dear, since he was four."

"Do you think that I will be able to make him happy?"

It was on the tip of Mrs. Steadworthy's tongue to say, "Of course, dear," but she didn't. That would not have been honest, after all. Instead, she said, "I don't think one human being can make another happy. Not in the long run. We make our own happiness, when you get down to it."

"Even in a marriage?"

"Especially in a marriage," said Mrs. Steadworthy firmly. "God spare me from those fools who think it is their partner's responsibility to make them love their own lives!" She took another sip of tea, and added, "Of course, if what you are asking me is whether you and Lord Greniston can have a good marriage together, then my answer is emphatically yes."

Gwen looked very pleased.

"In the end, you know," the older woman said, "marriage is what you make of it. Love doesn't just happen to you, you build it. And you and Lord Greniston will be all right together; you both have character. 'Tis true enough," she added wistfully, "that once in a while, one comes across a truly great love, a love that seems beyond reason, beyond time. But that, of course, is very rare."

She did not add that she suspected that Gwen and Greniston were just such a couple. *If they are*, she thought, *time will tell.*

Aloud, she said, "It's all love, when you get down to it. Love that finds you or love you find, love in a kiss or love in a prayer, love for one or love for many. It's what makes the world go round, you know. Literally."

Then she laughed, and said, "Och, Jesus, Mary, and Joseph, I do go on! Enough of this philosophy my dear. I've an old friend to meet, and you, I'm sure, have much to do!"

***

An hour later, as Gwen lay on her bed at the inn, holding the rings and daydreaming about the moment that she would slip Greniston's on his finger, there was a knock on the door.

Sarah, the maid, popped her head in, looking important. "A note for you, Miss," she said.

Opening the envelope, Gwen recognized the bold, sprawling hand of Greniston.

"If you wish to meet Leo Hawker," the note said, "come to the Sweet Maid Inn, in Claverton, at half past four today. Mention this to no one, and come alone." The last line was underlined so vehemently that the ink had splattered onto the note.

Leo Hawker! Gwen thought, thrilled. *Greniston didn't forget, after all!*

She called the manor to thank Greniston, but Robert told her, "'E's gone out, Miss. Didn't say when he'd be back. I think," he added mysteriously, "that it's about your wedding present."

Gwen spent the next hour trying to decide what to wear. At last, she settled on a plain blue dress and her silver locket. As she drove to the little village of Claverton, more than once getting lost on the back roads of Somerset, she tried to imagine what kind of man Leo Hawker would be.

I know he's old, she mused. *Old and slender, I think, rather than old and plump. Is he still handsome? Yes, but not in an ordinary way. Gray eyes, or brown? Gray, I think.*

Once she found Claverton, she had no trouble finding The Sweet Maid Inn, there being only four buildings from which to choose. She pulled into a parking spot just as the church bells tolled half past the hour.

When she entered the dining room of the inn, she was disappointed to see that the only person there was a middle-aged woman.

Leo Hawker must be running late, thought Gwen, sitting down on a bench to wait. Idly, she glanced again at the woman, who was sitting at a table a few feet away, rather noisily eating a blancmange.

There's something familiar about her, Gwen thought. Somewhere before she had seen that flowered dress, that huge, rose-bedecked hat, that slash of coral lipstick, those rhinestone earrings, that motherly smile.

"Henrietta Amberly!" Gwen exclaimed in total astonishment.

"Hello, dearie."

Gwen paused. The voice did not fit the face at all. Yet there was something familiar about that voice. . . .

"Care to join me?"

"Greniston?" Gwen whispered, amazement now contending with pure bafflement.

"The same." The person at the table pulled off the flowered hat and the platinum wig that lay beneath it, much to the shock of both Gwen and the bartender.

"You'd better have a drink," Greniston advised, "and a seat."

Feeling quite weak at the knees, Gwen joined him at his table.

"Now, before you judge me too harshly," Greniston said, "I want you to know that I only did it for the children."

"Did what?" Gwen asked faintly. "And what children?"

"Wrote all those awful books. *Seduced in Savannah, Desperate in Damascus, Rapture in Ravenna*, . . . need I continue?"

"You wrote those?" gasped Gwen, "You? You can't really mean that you, Greniston of Greniston Manor, are Henrietta Amberly!"

"Shhh," said Greniston, his finger to his lips, "you don't have to tell God and everybody."

"But . . . this is unbelievable," said Gwen, gratefully sipping the Brandy Alexander the waiter placed before her. "If this is true—and I can scarcely believe it is—why?"

"I needed the money. You see, a few years ago, I became involved in some charities— charities for children and things. I was able to contribute in a modest and steady way by managing the family securities well. But then there was an earthquake in Sri Lanka that devastated a hospital I had helped to fund. A great deal of money was needed, more than I could lay my hands on in a lump sum. I was desperate to try to find a way to help. One day, I was buying cigarettes at a kiosk in Charring Cross Road. I looked over at the paperback books and saw row after row of the most mindless drivel . . . "

"You mean, romance novels," Gwen corrected.

"As I said, mindless drivel. I picked one up, and read the first page. Then I promptly tossed it away, thinking in disgust, 'Any fool could write better than this,' . . . and that was when inspiration struck."

"You went home and wrote one yourself?"

"Exactly. I didn't really think anything would come of it. Everyone says it's so hard to get published. I just felt honor bound to try anyway, to raise funds. I dashed the thing off in less than a month, sent it off to a publisher, and forgot about it. Imagine my surprise when a few weeks later, the publisher called me, offering me a very nice sum, and an advance on a second novel. Apparently, that almost never happens with unknown authors." Greniston sighed. "I almost refused to write the second one, but then I thought of all the medical supplies and food another check could buy. . . ."

"And so you wrote another book," Gwen said, "and another, and another."

Greniston nodded. "Henrietta lives. I am her prisoner." Slowly, Gwen finished her drink and tried to digest this information. "You're Henrietta Amberly," she kept murmuring, as if in shock. At last, she rallied, and said, "Well, thank God you are. If you hadn't written *Clandestine at Camelot* and described the countryside of Somerset so lovingly and so well, Mrs. Gordon might never have booked her trip, and I might never have met you."

"That makes it all worthwhile," Greniston acknowledged.

"I always told you Henrietta was a cut above the rest," Gwen said mischievously. "And it makes sense, actually. . . . You couldn't resist putting the best of yourself into a book about this area. It's true, the plot was corny . . ."

Greniston winced a little at this.

" . . . but the descriptions of the woods and castles were magnificent. I remember saying to Filipo, 'I'm in love with the England this woman describes.' Of course I was, I was already falling in love with you. That book was part of what drew me here."

Gwen shook her head, marveling at the facts. Then she began to laugh. "No wonder you hated Mrs. Gordon's wedding present," she exclaimed.

Then she realized something was amiss. "I received a note to meet Leo Hawker here. So what is Henrietta doing here?"

"I'm getting out of this cursed outfit," Greniston growled, clearly wanting to avoid her question. "Only wore it for the book photo. Can't stand it any longer."

"That's just as well, dear," said Gwen sweetly, "your bosoms are slipping."

***

Nearly ten minutes later, Greniston reappeared, looking, Gwen was relieved to see, very much his old self. He placed a slim package, wrapped in dark blue paper, on the table before her.

"What is this?" Gwen asked, wonderingly.

"A wedding present. Open it."

Intrigued, Gwen tore off the paper and found herself holding what seemed to be a manuscript.

"'Pendragon,'" she read, "'a new play by . . . Leo Hawker?'" She looked at Greniston questioningly.

"Turn the page," he said.

"'Dedicated . . . to my beloved Gwen.' What does this mean?" Greniston sat back in his chair and smiled.

"I—I don't understand," said Gwen. "Does this mean that you are Leo Hawker?"

"It would seem so."

For a few minutes, Gwen scarcely knew what to say. "Have another drink," Greniston suggested, ordering one for her.

"You are both Leo Hawker *and* Henrietta Amberly," Gwen finally said, struggling to come to grips with these facts.

"Mild-mannered playwright by day, flamboyant *Dame de lettres* by necessity, something like that," Greniston agreed. He looked at Gwen with some concern. "I say," he said, "you look more shocked than I intended. I never could resist a good joke, but perhaps this has gone too far. I really am both these authors, though. Will you forgive me for springing the facts on you so suddenly, and do me the honor of dining with me in style, at the restaurant of your choice?"

Gwen shook her head. "No?" said Greniston, in some surprise.

"I have a date already," Gwen explained.

"A date? With whom?"

Gwen smiled and held up the manuscript. "With Leo Hawker, a man after my own heart."

CHAPTER TWENTY-SIX

The day before her wedding, Gwen felt a strong desire to run away, not from the prospect of marrying Greniston but from the mounting excitement that surrounded every detail of their "small, quiet ceremony."

If one more person asks me one more question about corsages or hymns or ring pillows, I shall go mad, she decided.

She wished that she could be with Greniston, but he had gone to Cambridge to fetch his sister Julia. Julia was five years older than Greniston and pursuing a seemingly endless graduate degree in religious studies.

"If I don't go get her in person, she'll forget what day the wedding is and miss everything," Greniston explained.

Gwen was very curious to meet this sister, but had nonetheless nobly volunteered to stay home and help with the last-minute preparations. Besides, Filipo and her brother Sean were both due to arrive that afternoon, and she wanted to be there to greet them.

"You'll meet Julia tonight," Greniston had said. "I guarantee you, she'll be wearing a navy blue silk dress with a cameo brooch. That's what she always wears for important occasions. And she'll present us with a copy of the O.E.D."

"How do you know?"

"She always gives people the *Oxford English Dictionary*. That, or the *Oxford Book of Carols*, are the only two presents she ever gives. But this being a big event, rather than just a birthday, I opt for the O.E.D. I've got four of 'em already. We can give this one to the Walmsley children."

"They might like it," Gwen had agreed.

"Like it? They'll love it. They can use the little magnifying glass to set things on fire. That'll give them endless hours of pleasure, and so educational, too."

With that, Greniston had been off, leaving the lady of his heart to braid several yards of cream, silver, and pink ribbon that were to decorate the church.

Gwen knew that it would be a lovely wedding. She was very grateful for all the help her new friends had provided to make it so. Mrs. Walmsley had done wonders with her dress, and Mrs. Hodges had outdone her own genius, preparing food for the reception. As for the Pennington sisters, they and the Vicar's wife were busy transforming the church into a fairy tale dream with ribbons and candles and garlands. Mr. and Mrs. Steadworthy had heroically offered to take the Walmsley children to Tweeverton for the day, a suggestion eagerly accepted by all.

Having at last finished braiding the seemingly endless yards of ribbon, Gwen headed toward the kitchen, hoping for a quiet cup of tea. When she was still far down the corridor, she heard the sound of feminine voices raised in a shrill twitter of excitement. Something about napkin rings for the reception, which had engaged the full attention of Mrs. Hodges, Mrs. Walmsley, and Sarah, from the inn. Gwen heard not a single male voice. Robert, Bosley, Logan, and Bob Walmsley all seemed to have gone to ground.

A wise choice, Gwen thought. Turning around, she headed not for the kitchen but for the nearest door. Once outside, she felt a delicious sense of escape, like a schoolgirl who has managed to skip algebra class. She headed for the woods.

Soon enough, she reached the mounds. Most of the dead leaves had been blown quite away, and the clearing was covered with a carpet of rich, green grass. She sat down on its emerald softness. The encircling daffodils had been replaced by wild roses, and the oaks, which only a few weeks before had carried but a froth of new green, were now covered in rustling leaves. Gwen leaned back and listened to the sound of the wind moving through those leaves.

"Gotta light, luv?"

Gwen looked up and found an old, old man in faded workman's clothes gazing down at her.

Where did he come from? she wondered. She saw the unlit cigarette in his hand and fumbled in her pocket for a lighter. She certainly didn't smoke herself, but so many people in England did that she had taken to carrying a lighter as a reluctant courtesy to them.

"Here you go," she said, rather awkwardly lighting the flame, "but I'd rather you didn't— for your sake, you know."

The old man leaned forward and puffed on his cigarette. He smiled, as if amused by her comment, then said, "Ta, ducks."

Gwen liked the look of him. His clothes, though old and worn, were very clean. So were his pale, wrinkled skin and what was left of his snow-white hair. He wore a red rose in his buttonhole.

After taking a couple of drags on his cigarette, he sat down beside her, as if taking it for granted that she would enjoy his company.

"Lovely place, this," he remarked. Gwen nodded her agreement.

"I've always needed to return to this place," the old man continued.

"You've been here before?" Gwen asked, surprised.

The old man laughed. "A thousand times."

"You're not from Far Tauverly, are you?"

"Not exactly, luv."

What a mysterious person, Gwen thought. She glanced at him out of the corner of her eye, trying to measure who and what he was. A hobo? Too clean and tidy. A retired professor, interested in local lore? Too tattered, and wild, somehow. *Wild*—that was an odd word to put to the gentle old man beside her, and yet it fit him, somehow. She couldn't place what he was; she couldn't even decide how old he was. On the one hand, he could have easily been eighty. There was something so sad and wise about his wrinkled face, as if he had seen enough experience to fill a thousand lifetimes. Yet the light that looked out of his blue eyes was young and seemed to grow brighter every time she glanced at him, as if his tired, old body was wearing away, like a piece of a tattered silk lantern, so that someday soon the candle inside would be free to blaze forth, as young and shining as sunrise, as if he was growing younger and freer with every passing century. . . .

What a strange thing to think, Gwen realized. *No one lives for centuries.* Yet the old man certainly did look ancient enough to know some local folklore.

"They say these are Merlin's Woods," Gwen ventured.

"Ah," her companion replied, noncommittally.

"They say these woods are haunted by Merlin's cry . . . "

"Merlin's cry? Merlin's cry? What would you be wondering about Merlin's cry?"

The change in the old man was electric. Suddenly he was all attention, gazing at her with luminous blue eyes. Come to think of it, were they blue? Or gray? Or gold? Whatever color they were, they seemed suddenly to scan her very mind, heart, and soul, probing. . . .

"Well, I've heard it," Gwen blurted out. Then, to her surprise, she found herself telling the old man the whole story, starting from her first glimpse of the lion's gate in the guidebook to the night on the mound, right up to that present moment.

"It's come out happily for you, hasn't it?" the old man asked.

"Yes," said Gwen. "But happiness isn't everything. I mean, I suppose that sounds ungrateful, but, you see, I've learned something about Arthur's quest: 'wherever there is darkness, to grow a greater good.' I shall remember, and try to live up to that for the rest of my life. And God knows, I've learned some things about myself. But Merlin and that cry, they are still a mystery. Yet it all started with Merlin, and so . . . "

"You think it should end with Merlin," the old man finished for her. "But don't you see, luv, Merlin's story is never finished."

So he does know something, Gwen thought. The next instant, she found herself gazing deep into the old man's eyes, spellbound.

"Merlin, Merlin, Merlin," he said, in a strange, lilting voice. "Well, when you're trying to understand Merlin, you need to know, he's not so much a person as something that works *through* a person. People come, people go, like shadows in a lantern show, but life itself goes on, you see. People always get so fastened on to the part that passes by. They cling to their memories like madmen, trying to glue last year's leaves back onto this year's spring branches. When will they cling to the part that doesn't pass away: the thing that *makes* the leaves, the seasons, and them?

"Merlin. Merlin is something, a power, a force, that gets into some people throughout the ages. A person here, a person there, why, you might meet Merlin anywhere. Merlin is like the wind of the sea. You don't say the wind is the same as the sails of the boat it fills, yet it can speed the little boat along. Merlin is like the wind in the trees. You don't say the wind is the same as the rustling of the leaves, yet they make a lovely music together."

"But what is this Merlin, then, and where does it come from like a wind over the sea, and what does it want with people?" Gwen asked in a whisper.

"Ah, well, I suppose you could say that Merlin is a helper, a servant of life. As to where it comes from, well, that's hard to explain in your terms, but it's very far. As to why, well, think on this: Suppose life has a purpose; all of it, from the pebbles to the stars, is part of a great plan, and human beings have a part to play in that plan, a vital part. But you see, it's very rough down here in this place called Earth; it's very hard, and people keep forgetting what they are here for. So, from time to time, helpers appear to help people remember what they are here for. Merlin's a part of that scheme, you might say, the crash-course in humanity, and Merlin's got a great longing to touch people with his help, but no one believes anymore, that's why his cry seems so sad. But sometimes, someone, somewhere, hears that cry, and a bit of Merlin's understanding gets inside them like a seed, and grows. A bit of it got into your friend, Lord Peter, and that's why he knew so much. Perhaps a bit of it has gotten into you as well. We'll see, time will tell. . . ."

"But what is this purpose humans are meant to fulfill?" Gwen asked earnestly.

The old man laughed. "People never value treasure unless they have to find it for themselves," he said, "It's part of the plan, luv, it's part of the plan. But I can tell you this, if you want to go treasure hunting, there's a map in this place. I wouldn't go nosing around libraries for clues to life, I'd start in these woods. That mystery you seek, 'tis in the rowan and the oak, 'tis in the force that made the stars, 'tis in the sparkle in your true love's eyes, and in your own wonder at what you are, . . . 'tis in the willow, and in the wind, 'tis in the marvel of your own skin, and in the fact that all creatures are kin."

Abruptly, the old man stopped speaking in his strange, singsong voice. He took out another cigarette, while Gwen fumbled for her lighter again, rather shakily this time. Then he said crisply, "Fond of nature, are you?"

"Why—yes," Gwen said.

"Hmmm . . . would you like to see what this place *really* looks like?"

Not sure what he meant, Gwen nodded all the same.

Very lightly, the old man tapped her right shoulder. For an instant, just an instant, Gwen saw the woods within the woods. She saw the fairy folk, dancing as tiny sparks of colored light among the roses and the lilies of the valley. She saw globes of colored light, hanging like living Christmas balls upon the trees, gently turning. She saw threads of silver, which, finer than a spider's web, seemed to connect all things, from the earth beneath her feet to the unseen stars. Faintly, very faintly, she heard music unlike any she had ever known. The slow turning of the galaxies was part of that music, and the waves of the sea; the wind in the trees was part of it, and the delicate fanning of butterflies' wings. Her own breath was part of it, too, and the sound of the old man's voice, saying, "There's no magic like the facts, luv, there's no magic like the facts."

Then, the old man snapped his fingers. Gwen looked around. The woods looked as they had always looked, and in the distance, she heard a lawnmower—Robert, no doubt, making sure the grounds were ready for the reception tomorrow. The old man was no longer sitting beside her but standing on the far side of the clearing, watching her.

"You might not always see the woods the way you just saw them, but believe me, the magic will always be there. It's real." He smiled and added, "Don't get too caught up about Arthur and the others, will you? Their *quest*, yes, but don't go trying to figure out who's the great-great reincarnation of whom. It doesn't work like that, you know. They were themselves once and once only, but their quest, their courage, their purpose, that can be reincarnated in a thousand lives at once! That's a reincarnation worth having: Arthur's nobility, Lancelot's courage, Guinevere's love. They can live on in a thousand hearts at once. The Gods aren't miserly. There's no limit on real treasure, if only you can find it, luv, if only you can find it."

The old man paused, scratched his head, and said abruptly, "Well, thanks for the light. I must be on my way."

He turned to go, moving already into the dappled light and shadow of the encircling woods.

"Wait!" cried Gwen. "There's someone I think is looking for you."

The old man turned back. "Looking for me, luv?"

"Well, looking for what's looking out of your eyes."

"Ah. And who might that be?"

"His name is Davey Lee."

"Davey Lee, Davey Lee," the old man mused. "Cheeky sod? Romani lad? Dark eyes and a good heart? Light-fingered? Sweet talker? Friend of a horse named Chieftain?"

"That's the one," Gwen said.

"He's on my list," the old man said. He laughed, and for an instant, his face looked young, as young as Lord Peter's in the portrait at the museum, and his laughter was as young as a young man's laughter.

Yet, that laughter must be very old, Gwen thought. *It has welled up in different people for thousands of years, but it sounds so young. Where does it come from, the laughter itself?*

The old man waved good-bye, just an old man again, a hobo, perhaps. He stepped into the woods and disappeared, not as if he had walked away but as if he had been instantly absorbed into the forest itself.

***

521

The distant bells of St. Aethelrood's tolled three p.m. Soon, Gwen realized, she needed to go meet Filipo's train. Yet she lingered for a moment, listening to the wind and the birds, all the humming activity of the woods. She heard very clearly the gurgling of the little spring on the farther mound, an old, old spring, whose water gushed forth ever fresh and new. Merlin's spring.

"Hello," a gentle voice called out. "You must be the bride!"

Gwen spun around and found herself face to face with a slender woman in her late forties. She couldn't remember ever having seen her before.

"Julia Greniston," the woman explained, offering Gwen her hand. "I just arrived on the two-thirty train, but I guess Gren forgot to meet me, so I thought I'd walk."

"You're Julia?" Gwen asked, surprised. This sister did not look at all as Greniston had described her. Gwen had been led to expect a typical spinster-scholar, and she realized that her imagination had supplied spectacles and a dumpy figure, with long dark, silver-streaked hair in a severe bun. The person who stood before her, though, was slim and fine-boned. Her chestnut hair was streaked with silver, but it was cut in short, feathery curls that surrounded her delicate face with a playful softness. There was intelligence in her light brown eyes, with a touch of Amelia Earhart, a touch of Peter Pan; it was a face that would always seem young. She was not wearing the predicted navy blue silk but rather a white blouse with a russet scarf knotted at the neck, a beige skirt, and a very chic pair of leather boots. Gwen searched her appearance for a resemblance to Greniston then realized that Julia reminded her of Lord Peter, in the young, museum portrait.

"I'm very glad to meet you," Gwen said, shaking Julia's hand warmly. Then she added, "Oh dear!"

"Is something wrong?"

"Greniston—your brother—he drove to Cambridge, to pick you up! He's probably there by now."

"Oh dear," sighed Julia. "Gren is so forgetful!" Fondly, she added, "That's just like him. I told him just yesterday that he didn't need to bother; I could manage quite well on my own! But you see, he gets his own plans, and he forgets what anyone else says. Unless," she added, with a sparkle in her eye, "he forgot on purpose, so he could have a restful drive in the country, escape the last minute fuss. . . ."

"He might well do something like that," Gwen agreed with a smile. "Accidentally, of course. In any case, I'm glad you're here. Let's get your bags to the manor, and . . ."

"Oh damn," interrupted Julia, in tones very like Greniston's, "the daffodils are gone! The roses are lovely, of course, but I always like the daffodils best. Like in Lord Peter's prophecy."

"Lord Peter's prophecy?" Gwen asked.

"You know, the part about 'encircled by gold?' I always thought that meant the mound, encircled by daffodils."

The image of Claire's drawings of a golden yellow necklace came to Gwen's mind.

"And what do you think the treasure is?" Gwen asked.

Julia smiled in a way that showed two dimples. "Ah, the treasure. Well, I suppose there is some gold and silver lying about somewhere. But I always liked the description Lord Peter gave in his second volume of poetry."

"Second volume?" Gwen asked, remembering only one.

"Yes, the green-bound one, . . . the one I borrowed three years ago," Julia realized, "and forgot to return. Well, you must see it some time, if you are interested."

"Very," replied Gwen.

"Fortunately, I pretty well remember the one poem about the treasure. It goes something like this:

> 'Treasures of the deep earth,
>   Treasures of the sea,
>   Greatest of all treasures
>   Is human mystery.
>   To glimpse a glimpse of God's deep plan
>   And our own possibility;
>   Richness of true lives gathered round,
>   Greater than jewels in any mound.'"

Of course, Gwen realized, *that is what Claire was trying to show me: all of us, sitting like jewels around the mound. That is the real treasure Arthur wanted the Grenistons to keep safe—the treasure of true human lives. Of course! And it begins to be fulfilled as we make a home together at the manor. Of course, why didn't I see it before? Filipo did, I'm sure of it.*

"Make sense to you?" Julia asked.

"Oh yes," said Gwen, as she bent to pick up one of the other woman's astonishingly heavy, perhaps O.E.D.-laden bags. "There's no magic like the facts."

"I quite agree," said Julia with a gentle smile. "I quite agree."

CHAPTER TWENTY-SEVEN

Wyatt Walmsley bustled importantly toward the altar. "The bwide is almost weady," he whispered to the Vicar, so loudly that the entire church full of people heard and chuckled.

"Thank you, my boy," the Vicar said.

Proudly, Wyatt took his place next to his brothers and sister along the altar rail. He was very glad that Gwen and Lord Greniston had chosen them to be their wedding party.

"It's a little unconventional," the Vicar had said at first. "Usually two adults are asked to be best man and maid of honor."

"Yes," Greniston had replied, "but these are unconventional children. And we are an unconventional couple."

"True," Rev. Sterling had acknowledged.

And so it was that the High Council of the Independent Kingdom of Greenstone, True Knights of Arthur's Quest, Guardians of the Sacred Treasure stood beside Lord Greniston at the altar. The children were arrayed in the full regalia of their Kingdom, which had been considerably spruced up by their mother's skill with a needle and thread. Claire wore a long, fairy-princess dress of blue silk, with a garland of lilies of the valley on her red hair and blue and green ribbons streaming down her back. She carried a wand with a cardboard star at the end. The star was covered with blue glitter, which kept coming off and, as the Vicar's wife put it, "oh, dear, getting into everything." Wyatt thought this was a lovely touch.

Osborne and Charles were resplendent in matching white tunics and red capes, Osborne had a sash of midnight blue, and Charles, of forest green. As for Osgood, he looked every inch the king in a longer tunic of gold lame with a purple leather belt. He had insisted, though, on wearing his old crown of cardboard and aluminum foil, saying that if it was good enough to meet King Arthur in, it was good enough for everyone else.

Wyatt had a tunic of green with a yellow scalloped collar and a cape of silver cloth. He felt this had a Robin Hood flavor that he quite enjoyed. To complete the outfit, he had rose-colored tights and turquoise slippers.

"It's rather bright," his Mum had said doubtfully.

"But I like colors," Wyatt had replied, a sentiment Davey Lee would have appreciated.

Wyatt thought that Lord Greniston looked pretty good, too, for a grown-up. He had on something called "formal dress." It was pale gray, like the breast of a mourning dove. In his lapel was one pale, pink rose. Lord Greniston seemed happy, but nervous, too. Wyatt couldn't understand why he kept asking Osgood if he was sure he had the rings.

As for Filipo, he looked more like a pirate than a grown-up. He had on a white silk shirt with full sleeves, burgundy velvet pants, and a vest embroidered in burgundy and gold. He was sitting in the pulpit with his guitar. The Vicar said that was unconventional, too, for him to be sitting up there, but that it was okay. The pulpit was trimmed with garlands of pink roses and white baby's breath and many colored ribbons. Filipo looked down from it like a strange angel on a Christmas tree, Wyatt thought.

Yes, Wyatt thought, surveying the congregation, *everyone looks fine*. The ladies all had on pretty dresses and flowered hats like ladies wear, and the men all looked scrubbed and smelled better than usual. Everyone was there, including several people Wyatt had never met before, like Gwen's brother Sean, who seemed to be having a jolly time with Sarah from the inn. The presence of new people caused Wyatt's flaxen hair to quiver with interest. At first, Gwen had said they were going to have something called a "small ceremony," whatever that was, but then Lord Greniston had said, "Who the devil can choose, let's have 'em all!" Now the pews were packed full, and people were standing along the sides, too. Even Bill Saxton was there, although whether he had come for goodwill or for a good feed at the reception, no one was certain. He had at least dressed up for the occasion, though, and Wyatt smiled beneficently at him, wanting no one to feel unwelcome on this happy day.

The church looked as beautiful as the people did, he thought. Its old stone walls were softened with garlands of pink roses and festoons of pink ribbons, and everything smelled like ladies perfume and soap and beeswax and flowers. The day had dawned misty and still, so all the candles had been lit. The feeling of the gray outside and the candlelight inside was wonderful to Wyatt. It was like winter mornings when it was still dark out, and you sat in the kitchen and ate your toast, and the lamplight in the kitchen and the darkness outside made each other all the nicer by being side by side like that. It was cozy and exciting at the same time, somehow. Yes, the candlelit church with the mist outside felt just like those special mornings, somehow; everyone gathered in together. Wyatt felt a great tenderness, looking out at them all sitting there. He wished they could always be like this, friends together, nobody angry, nobody sad, nobody left out. *This is good*, he thought. *This is how it should be.*

From the pulpit, Filipo began to play "Lady Carey's Dompe." It was the song Gwen had played for Lord Greniston on her first visit to the manor. A stillness came over the church as people listened to the ancient melody. Lord Greniston smiled.

In the guest room of the vicarage, where many another bride had prepared before her, Gwen put the finishing touches to her appearance. Then she called to Logan, who was waiting outside in the hall, "You can come in now."

Logan had known she would look beautiful, but even so, he was not prepared for the purity that greeted him. For a moment he did not quite recognize Gwen; she looked like a bride from long ago, from Arthur's time, perhaps.

Her long dress was as simple as a medieval robe. Of silver-white silk, it fell to the floor in gleaming folds. Gwen's auburn hair streamed in loose curls about her shoulders; upon her head, she wore a garland of cream-colored roses and dark green leaves. She wore no veil over her face, but a long veil of silver-white chiffon trailed behind her, almost transparent and as delicate as mist. She carried a bouquet of roses mixed with wildflowers, and it seemed right to Logan that she should bring that bit of wildness with her, for she looked like a princess from the fairy realms, a sprite of the wildwood. She wore no makeup, and a silver locket was her only jewelry; it was as if she wanted to greet her beloved exactly as she was. Logan felt that she looked all the more beautiful for the slight pallor of her excitement; her face was as pure as a candle's white flame.

"My Lady," he said with a bow, "it's nearly time."

"Yes."

As Gwen took his arm, Logan had the sense that he was escorting not only this bride but all brides. The dignity of the ceremony itself sat upon Gwen like a crown. A phrase he had read somewhere came to Logan's mind: "That peculiar fleeing forward men call courage." Ladies had it too, he realized. For what was a marriage but just such a leap into the unknown, a gesture of faith, beyond all normal reason, in the continuing of love, the going-on of life? An old, old gesture, yet in each true bride's shining eyes, ever new.

He led her gently out of the vicarage and across the misty lawn toward the church.

"Look! There's a bird circling above the church spire," Gwen said, stopping for a moment to look.

"It's a hawk," Logan said. "Perhaps it's a Merlin."

Gwen smiled. She lingered a moment longer on the misty lawn.

"You know," she said, "after this hour, I shall never again be quite my old, free self again. I suppose real life is always like this, a thread of sorrow mixed in with all the threads of joy."

"That is true," agreed Logan.

"After this hour, I shall be different, forever. I shall be more woven into things. I shall be Lady Greniston. Greniston—he won't be an easy man to be married to. . . ."

Logan smiled. "No, I don't suppose he will be. But worth it?"

"Oh, yes," said Gwen firmly, her face shining with love. "Definitely worth it!" She gazed at Logan with a sudden radiance that made his heart ache at the sheer beauty of it.

The church bells tolled nine o'clock. They heard Althea Pennington strike up the "Wedding March" on the organ.

Taking Logan's arm once more, Gwen went gladly forth, to meet her struggle and her joy.

***

"Yes, it was a grand wedding and a grand reception," said Logan Knowelles to Mark Avery a few days later. "Now, mind, lad," he interjected, "that you take old Mrs. Primby's mail right up to her door. Don't leave it at the box out here by the road. Too far for her to walk, with her bunions and all. Take it right up to the door and knock."

"Rather nasty looking pug over there," the younger man commented, as they opened Mrs. Primby's gate.

"Ah," said Logan, "that's where these come in." Out of his pocket, he pulled a box of Doggie Delights. As the pug came snarling toward them, Logan tossed it a generous handful of the nuggets, muttering, "Choke on 'em, you little Cerberus." Happily diverted, the pug let them pass.

"Well," said Logan, after they reemerged onto the main street of Far Tauverly, "that's the lot. My last day is complete, and the route is yours, lad." With some ceremony, Logan handed the leather mail pouch, now empty, to his successor.

"Sure you feel ready for it, lad?"

"Oh yes," replied Mark Avery.

The two men gave a mutual sigh of relief. Logan Knowelles liked his replacement. Mark was a local man, an honest young fellow, whose wife had unexpectedly just had triplets—on the day of the wedding, in fact. In honor of this, she had named the babies Grenville, Grenly, and Grendon. With all these mouths to feed, Mark Avery certainly appreciated the job. But over the years, Logan had developed a system of sorting mail that approached the hieroglyphic. Mark Avery looked forward to establishing his own kind of order in the little office, although he would never have dreamed of saying so.

As for Logan, he, too, was ready to move on. Everything except his bedroll had already been moved to Shalimar House, which was painted and cleaned and ready to receive him, with his books on the shelves, his rocking chair by the fireplace. He would spend his first night there tonight, and tomorrow, begin restoring the manor's south rose garden, with Bob Walmsley's help.

"I'll tell you what, lad," Logan said to Avery, "let's have a pint to celebrate. My treat. And I'll finish telling you about the wedding." Avery had missed the ceremony, being at the hospital with his wife.

"A pint? But it's only noon. There's still the afternoon mail." The young man looked doubtful.

"Come on, lad," Logan said indulgently, "I can see you've still got a lot to learn."

Once they had settled into the welcome shade of the Greenstone Arms, Logan resumed his tale of the wedding.

"The day started misty," he said, "but after the ceremony, the sun came out, and the lawns of Greniston Manor never looked finer. There were tents pitched here and there with food and drink, and bright banners on the tents, it looked as grand as Camelot must have! And the music! Gwen's friend Filipo played guitar, and there was also a string quartet from Bath, and Morris dancers and folk musicians, too. So grand a party it was that it went on for hours, long after the bride and groom had slipped away to their honeymoon."

"And where did they go?" asked Mark Avery with interest.

"No one knows," Logan replied mysteriously. "Lord Greniston said he was whisking her away to the ends of the earth on a magic carpet to have her to himself for a while." Actually, in his capacity as Lord Greniston's

Steward, Logan happened to know exactly where they went, but he was not about to breathe a word of it to anybody.

"Yes," he continued, "the festivities went on far into the night, and when twilight came, there were thousands of fairy lights that came on in the trees and paper lanterns hanging here and there, like a rainbow of full moons. Every guest was given a garland of flowers, and they all wore them, even the Vicar. As the stars came out, it was like a 'Midsummer Night's Dream.' Generous it was, in food, and spirits, and joy."

"Ah, Logan," said Mark Avery, "you're generous yourself, generous with words. You make me feel like I was right there myself, like I didn't miss a thing." And then he added, as people so often did, "You should have been a bard, Logan."

"I am," Logan replied.

But Avery did not hear; he had turned to order another drink.

Logan smiled. He knew what he was, and that was all that mattered.

***

Some hours later, as St. Aethelrood's bells tolled midnight, the new tenant of Shalimar House at last put down his book and turned out the light.

Night settled in around the little house and around the gardens and the woods beyond.

No one now disturbed the quiet of Greniston Manor or of the Greniston land. And yet, out in the darkness, the wind sighed through the full-leafed branches of summer; the mouse rustled in its nest; the owl called, gliding through the soft air on silent wings. The starlight gleamed upon the lion's faces on the ancient gate, and on the mounds, the long summer grass stirred. Slowly, earnestly, like partners in some perfect dance, Aquarius appeared over the edge of the eastern treetops, and Leo began to slip, heart first, behind the western horizon.

And at the little spring that some call Merlin's Spring, the water trickled forth in the darkness. Its sound was like the echo of a great music that often goes unheard and yet is always there, as close as breath, as real as life itself.

JJ Shefa and Patricia O'Donovan have been great friends and co-writers for many years. They are delighted to share their love of all things Arthurian with others, through this book. They hope everyone enjoys reading it as much as they have enjoyed writing it.